ReSCued

RESCUED

JERRY B. JENKINS
TIM LAHAYE
with CHRIS FABRY

TYNDALE HOUSE PUBLISHERS, INC.
WHEATON, ILLINOIS

Visit Tyndale's exciting Web site at www.tyndale.com

Discover the latest Left Behind news at www.leftbehind.com

Rescued is a special edition compilation of the following Left Behind: The Kids titles:

#13: The Showdown copyright © 2001 by Jerry B. Jenkins and Tim LaHaye. All rights reserved.

#14: Judgment Day copyright © 2001 by Jerry B. Jenkins and Tim LaHaye. All rights reserved.

#15: Battling the Commander copyright © 2001 by Jerry B. Jenkins and Tim LaHaye. All rights reserved.

#16: Fire from Heaven copyright © 2001 by Jerry B. Jenkins and Tim LaHaye. All rights reserved.

Cover photo copyright © by Digital Vision. All rights reserved.

Published in association with the literary agency of Alive Communications, Inc., 7680 Goddard Street, Suite 200, Colorado Springs, CO 80920.

Scripture quotations are taken from the *Holy Bible,* New Living Translation, copyright © 1996. Used by permission of Tyndale House Publishers, Inc., Wheaton, Illinois 60189. All rights reserved.

Some Scripture taken from the New King James Version. Copyright © 1979, 1980, 1982 by Thomas Nelson, Inc. Used by permission. All rights reserved.

Designed by Jenny Swanson

Library of Congress Cataloging-in-Publication Data

Jenkins, Jerry B.
    Rescued / Jerry B. Jenkins ; Tim LaHaye.
        p. cm — (Left behind—the kids) #4 Vol. 13-16
Special ed. compilation of four works, previously published separately in 2001.
    ISBN 0-8423-8354-9 (hc)
    1. Christian life—Juvenile fiction. [1. Christian life—Fiction.] I. LaHaye, Tim F. II. Title.
PZ7.J4138 Re 2004
[Fic]—dc22   2003016696

Printed in the United States of America

08   07   06   05   04
9   8   7   6   5   4   3   2   1

1

JUDD clung to a steel railing as the motorcycle disappeared into the river. He tried to climb the side but knocked more concrete from the edge. If Judd didn't hang on, it meant certain death. He cried for help.

The shaking stopped. Then came a splattering in the woods. *Tick, tick, tick.* He wondered if this was another judgment of God. Then something hit his head. Raindrops, slowly, then pouring.

Judd slipped and nearly let go. The rain beat fiercely. A steel support lay between him and the river. He didn't want to hit that on the way down.

His strength was giving out.

Judd tried once more and found something firm with his feet. He was almost to safety when the slab gave way and tumbled into the water. He fell back, his hands barely grasping the railing. Judd closed his eyes and gritted his teeth, but he couldn't hold on.

As he let go, someone grabbed his arm.

The room felt ice-cold. Everywhere Vicki saw sheet-draped bodies on tables. A hand stuck out from the body in front of her. She willed herself to pull the sheet back. The face was chalky white.

Ryan.

Dead.

Vicki screamed as she awoke. Darrion and Vicki sat up in the small tent.

"What's wrong?" Darrion said.

Through the flap Vicki watched men carrying bodies. The earthquake was over. Fires dotted the campsite, casting an eerie glow.

"Nightmare," Vicki said. "Where's Shelly?"

"Somebody came and asked for volunteers," Darrion said. "Shelly said to let you sleep."

Vicki scurried out of the tent, still wearing the same tattered clothes from the morning.

"Where are you going?"

"I have to find Ryan."

Shelly raced toward them. "Good news," she said. "A lady says they've opened a shelter a few blocks from here. It's the closest one to your house, so Ryan might be there."

"Let's go," Vicki said.

"We have to wait till dawn," Shelly said. "They're shooting looters."

"I don't care," Vicki said. "I have to find him."

"We don't need another death," Shelly said. "Get some sleep and we'll find him in the morning."

Vicki dragged herself back to the tent and tried to sleep, but she kept seeing the white, chalky face in her dream.

Lionel turned the gun over beside him on the bed. The GC insignia was engraved on the barrel of the pistol. He had signed papers that made him a Global Community Morale Monitor. He felt proud, but at the same time, things didn't seem right.

"I thought you'd be asleep by now," Conrad said, sitting next to Lionel's bed.

"Looks like you're going to be my partner," Lionel said.

"Guess so."

"You don't seem too excited," Lionel said.

"I don't know what I'm supposed to feel," Conrad said. "Everything's changing so fast. And that stuff in your luggage has me spooked."

"What stuff?" Lionel said.

"The Bible and your journal," Conrad said. "I can't wait to get on the Internet and see if this rabbi guy will answer me."

"Maybe when we get to Chicago, we'll figure it out," Lionel said.

The man Judd had talked with on the mountain pulled him to safety. His forearm was huge, and he easily lifted Judd over the side.

"Let's get out of here before another aftershock," he yelled over the rain.

Back in the cave the man handed Judd a blanket and sat him near a fire. "We watched you from up here. You almost made it over."

"I should have waited," Judd said.

Judd was exhausted. The frightened-looking people in the cave were lucky the rocks hadn't fallen on them.

The man introduced himself as Tim Vetter. His wife was a small woman named Marlene. Tim introduced Judd then asked, "Why were you out here? Trying to get to Chicago?"

Judd wasn't sure what he should tell them. If they were somehow linked with the Global Community, he should keep quiet.

"I was traveling with a friend," Judd stammered. "He didn't make it."

"That wasn't your bike, was it?" Tim said.

"I borrowed it," Judd said.

The other men laughed. "There's not much difference between stealing and borrowing during an earthquake," one man said.

"Tell the truth," Tim said.

"I helped a guy out, and he told me to take it," Judd said.

Was God preparing Vicki to face the death of one of the Young Trib Force? She tried to shake the idea but couldn't.

The birds were out again the next morning, singing in

the few trees left standing. It seemed strange that all the sounds were perfect when the sights were so awful. She and her friends passed smoldering craters and collapsed buildings. Car taillights stuck out of the ground. Moaning and crying still came from the rubble.

The shelter was an apartment complex where workers had cleared plants and furniture from the atrium. Vicki told a guard holding a clipboard that she was looking for her brother. The guard showed them a list of names. On another sheet was a list of numbers for those who had not yet been identified. Some numbers were crossed out and had the word "deceased" written beside them.

Shelly pointed to a description. "This could be him."

A nurse led them to a storage room filled with beds. In the corner lay someone staring at the wall, a white bandage covering his head.

Vicki looked at Darrion and Shelly.

"You can do it, Vick," Shelly said.

"He can't talk," the nurse said.

Vicki approached warily. The face was covered except for holes for his eyes, nose, and mouth. His left arm was bandaged as well, and Vicki realized he had been badly burned.

"Ryan?" Vicki said.

The kid stared at the wall.

Vicki knelt beside him. "Ryan, it's Vicki," she said.

The boy shook his head. He motioned for pen and paper. "Not Ryan," he wrote.

Vicki sat staring at him.

"Go away," the boy wrote.

Vicki wiped away a tear. "I'm sorry you were hurt," she said.

Vicki asked the nurse if there was anywhere else Ryan could have been taken.

"A furniture store somehow made it through," the woman said. "A couple hundred survivors are there. More than we can handle."

People stirred in the cave as Judd awoke. The men huddled around the fire. Tim motioned for Judd to come and eat.

Judd was sore and had scratches from skidding on the bridge. He ate hungrily.

"Some of us are going back to look for food," Tim said. "There might be a relief site set up by the Global Community."

Judd flinched. "I wouldn't be surprised."

"Will you come with us?" Tim said.

"Think I'll try to keep going," Judd said.

Tim scratched at the embers with a stick. "There's something you're not telling us," he said. "It may be none of our business. But when you share our food and shelter, I think we deserve to know what's up."

"You've been very kind," Judd said. "I owe you my life."

Judd wondered if this was why he hadn't been able to complete the jump. Maybe God wanted him to tell his story, despite the risk.

"My name is Judd Thompson," he began.

Lionel took tests and signed more papers in the morning. Though the earthquake had knocked out communication and travel, the Global Community rolled on. A GC doctor declared Lionel fit and ready to continue his classes. Conrad stopped by as the doctor left.

"I don't understand," he said. "Thousands are dead or dying, but the GC has everything set up and ready to go. It's like they expected this."

"That's not possible," Lionel said.

"What if it is? Maybe they were waiting for some kind of disaster to put their next plan in motion. That would explain why they're so hot to get us out of here and on the job."

Conrad showed Lionel his gun, standard issue for Morale Monitors. "Why do they trust kids our age with guns?"

"Maybe when they see how you shoot this afternoon at the range, they won't," Lionel said, smiling.

The girls wound through neighborhoods, taking shortcuts through what had been backyards. They climbed over huge mounds of dirt and rocks, then went around craters. Smoke from the still-burning meteors made them choke.

The furniture store was on the way to the Edens Expressway, a few minutes' drive away. But with downed utility poles, flattened buildings, pavement that had disappeared, and the girls on foot, it took much longer.

Shelly pointed to a neon sign on the ground. "My mom and I used to eat at that place," she said.

Vicki knew the furniture store. She had been there with her family. The sales staff had eyed them suspiciously, as if they knew she lived in a trailer and had neither the money nor the room for the bedroom set she wanted.

Only the roof of the building was visible. The rest had been swallowed whole. Rescue crews filed in and out, but there was no hurry. Everyone taken from the building was in a body bag.

"This could be a wild-goose chase," Shelly said. "What if he's not there?"

"We're gonna find him and take him home with us," Vicki said.

"How?" Shelly said. "What if he can't walk? We gonna carry him?"

"I'll find a way," Vicki said.

The furniture store was still standing, but there were no roads around it. Emergency vehicles pulled as close to the front as they could, then unloaded more injured.

"Most look pretty healthy," Vicki said. "Maybe Ryan's not that bad."

"We've got another problem," Darrion said.

Vicki gasped when she saw Global Community guards at the entrance. Only the injured and those with clearance cards were getting through.

The girls split up, then met again a few minutes later.

"The back is guarded too," Shelly said.

"The side doors are locked," Darrion said. "There's a

lot of smashed windows, but they're too high to crawl through."

"We'll have to get in another way," Vicki said, smearing mud on her forehead. She tore off a piece of her shirt.

"What are you doing?" Shelly said.

Vicki lay on the ground. "Carry me," she said. "And I expect some tears from you two!"

Shelly smiled. She grabbed Vicki's arms, and Darrion took her legs.

Vicki moaned. Shelly and Darrion began crying as they neared the store.

A Global Community guard stopped them at the entrance. "You can't bring her here."

"You have to help," Shelly said. "We have to get her to a doctor."

Darrion kept her back to the guard so he wouldn't recognize her. Shelly wept bitterly. "Please help us," she cried.

"All right," the guard said. "Put her down."

Vicki rolled her eyes and winked at them.

2

VICKI closed her eyes when the men carried her inside. She wailed when they sat her in a line of injured people. A Global Community staff worker took information. When she turned her back, Vicki quickly slipped out of line and down the hall. She ran up a flight of stairs.

What had been a showroom now held cots. People were sleeping, some badly wounded.

Vicki didn't want to risk talking with anyone, so she stayed out of the way. The doctors and nurses were so busy, no one seemed to notice her.

She looked at faces, read names on charts, and darted into a bathroom when a GC guard passed.

A woman in one of the stalls was crying. Vicki found a clipboard on a sink. At the top of the chart were numbers. Under "T-1" she spotted "Ryan Daley."

What's T-1?

The woman came out of the stall. Vicki washed her face, then quickly walked out.

As she hurried down a narrow corridor, she heard someone behind her, then felt a hand just above her elbow.

"You are under arrest."

Judd watched the group as he told his story. They didn't react strongly but seemed interested in what he thought of the disappearances. He told them what had happened to his family, about meeting Bruce Barnes, and about watching the videotape the former pastor had made.

"Before, I thought church was a stuffy place that didn't want you to have fun. They told you everything you weren't supposed to do. Now I see it as a place of life. God wanted me to know him. If anyone wants what I found, I can help you."

Tim looked at the other men and nodded. "We know what we have to do," he said.

The men dragged Judd to a corner of the cave. He struggled but couldn't overcome them. They tied his hands behind him.

"We were warned about people like you," one man said. "People like you are against Nicolae Carpathia. You're against the Enigma Babylon Faith."

"I didn't say anything about Carpathia," Judd said.

"You didn't have to," the man said.

Judd shook his head. His gut reaction about the people had been right.

"We're taking you back to town," Tim said. "We'll turn you over to the GC."

"For telling you about God?" Judd said.

"You must be running from something," Tim said, "or you wouldn't have taken such a chance. If you're innocent, the GC will let you go."

The group walked Judd down the hillside with his hands tied. He would soon be back in the hands of the enemy of his soul.

The men left Judd near the Enigma Babylon church building under the watch of Tim's wife, Marlene.

"We'll be back with food and water and the GC," Tim said.

A chill ran down Vicki's spine and she turned, thinking she would see a Global Community guard. But a wild-eyed young man with stringy hair, eyes darting, said, "Scared you, didn't I? You thought I was the police. Not supposed to be in here, are you?"

Vicki took a breath. "Do you always ask that many questions?"

The young man smiled, still looking away.

"What's your name?" Vicki said.

"Charlie, Charles, Chuck, Charlie." He spoke quickly, and his body seemed out of control.

"You scared me, all right," Vicki said. "You like scaring people?"

Charlie giggled. His teeth were crooked and discolored. "I like when they jump. I used to make my sister jump. Real high. She don't jump no more. Big shake got her."

"The earthquake?" Vicki said.

"Yeah, yeah," Charlie said. "Earthshake. Lotsa things got broken at our house. Big crash. Boom!"

Charlie screamed and laughed, and Vicki jumped.

"Be quiet," Vicki said.

Charlie put a finger to his lips. "Shh. Quiet."

"Are you a patient here?" Vicki said.

"No, my sister worked here. They had big TVs downstairs. Used to let me watch them. All busted now. Want to see 'em?"

Vicki shook her head. "I'm looking for a friend who might be here."

"Friend. I had a friend. His mom said I was strange, and he couldn't come over anymore."

"I'll be your friend," Vicki said. "I just need your help."

"I can help," Charlie said. "I can lift and carry stuff and hold doors open and SCARE PEOPLE!"

"Stop screaming," Vicki said. "There are sick people in here. Now I'm trying to find room T-1, or something like that."

Charlie squinted and squeezed his chin. "Is a *T* the letter that looks like a snake?"

"That's an *S*," Vicki said. She drew a *T* in the dust on a window.

"I know what a *T* looks like," Charlie giggled. "Come on."

He hopped along, taking big leaps with his right leg and dragging his left behind him. When Vicki finally caught him, he was out of breath and excited.

"Right here," Charlie said.

The sign above the door said Trauma 1.

Charlie opened the door slowly. "There's really sick people here. Better not be too loud."

Bright children's furniture lined the wall. Vicki passed cribs and strollers.

"Stay close," Vicki said.

Judd sat in the rubble of the Enigma Babylon church, now both hands and feet tied. He could tell the church had once been beautiful, but its stained glass windows lay in pieces. After all his work to escape, Judd was almost back in the hands of the Global Community. He had hoped the GC would find the van destroyed and assume he was dead.

Marlene Vetter paced, looking at Judd, then glancing away.

Judd rubbed his ankles together, trying to loosen the rope. The rope around his wrists was already loosening.

"How long have you lived here?" Judd said.

The woman looked like she had a secret. "I'm not supposed to talk to you."

"Why?" Judd said. "I'm dangerous?"

"What you say is dangerous," Marlene said. "Look where it got you."

"The things I say are true. I don't care where it gets me."

The more Judd talked, the more Marlene looked away. That gave Judd a chance to work free of the ropes. Finally Marlene said, "You really believe all those things?"

Judd spoke carefully. "The vanishings, the earthquake, the meteors, all that was predicted in the Bible."

15

Marlene shook her head. "I'm talking about God forgiving you without you doing anything but admitting what you did. I always thought if your good outweighed your bad that God, whoever he was, would eventually accept you."

"Is that what Enigma Babylon teaches?" Judd said.

Marlene sat and pulled her knees to her chest. "They say God is within us. We don't need to be 'saved' from anything but our own low self-esteem."

"What do you think?" Judd said. "Does that make sense?"

"I'm not sure anymore."

Judd kept working at the ropes.

Someone yelled for Charlie.

"Oh," he said, "I'll stay with you."

"No," Vicki said. "Go so they don't suspect anything. Promise you won't tell them about me."

"I promise," he said, scampering off giggling.

Vicki strained to see the patients in the darkened room. Several had died, and sheets covered them.

Vicki heard the familiar beeps of monitors scattered throughout the room. Finally, toward the end of one row, she saw Ryan. She rushed to him and ran a hand through his hair. It was caked with mud. His eyes were closed, and a bruise showed on his forehead.

Vicki's tears fell on Ryan's face. She hugged him, but he felt cold. She stepped back in horror. Vicki felt for a pulse.

16

Someone took Vicki by the shoulder. "What are you doing in here?" a woman said.

———————————————————

Marlene looked at Judd. "I've tried to believe like I should, but it doesn't work."

"You want me to go through it again?" Judd said.

Marlene nodded.

Judd explained that even though people are sinners, Jesus had died for them. "The only way to God is through Jesus, not through doing good things or believing in yourself. He created us. Sin separates us from God. To become his child, we have to be adopted into his family."

"But only if you're perfect?"

"I'm not perfect by a long shot," Judd said. "Ask my friends. But when God forgives you, Jesus lives in you. God doesn't see me and my faults. He sees Jesus."

"So I don't have to do anything?"

"You accept what God gives," Judd said.

Marlene stared off and shook her head. "Tim would kill me if he knew I talked to you."

Judd finally freed his hands from the rope.

"What you say sounds good," Marlene said, "but I don't know if I can trust you."

"Trust me," Judd said, showing her his hands. "I could free my legs and be out of here in seconds."

"Why don't you?"

"God's working on you," Judd said. "I can't leave you now."

17

Judd heard footsteps and hid his hands behind his back.

Vicki jumped back, turning to face the woman dressed in white.

"Charlie told me you were looking for a friend," the woman said sternly. "Is that true?"

"His name's Ryan Daley," Vicki said.

"Are you Vicki?"

"How did you know that?"

The woman pulled a piece of paper from her pocket. "He wrote this for you."

Vicki couldn't open the letter. "I have to know if he's alive," Vicki said.

"Not for long, I'm afraid," the nurse said. "He's in a coma."

Vicki bit her lip and wiped her eyes.

"Stay a while," the nurse said.

Vicki thanked her and sat on the floor. She unfolded the letter.

I'm writing this to you, Vicki, but I'm hoping you'll be in touch with Judd and Lionel as well.

First, I shouldn't have been surprised at what happened because this was everything Bruce said. The wrath of the Lamb and all. We can be glad God keeps his promises, I guess. The nurse said I should write to you. I never was a letter writer, but she thought it was a good idea.

You've been like a big sister to me. I never had one. Judd was a big brother, and Lionel was a good friend. I hope I wasn't too much of a pain to have around.

I guess there's a chance I could get up and walk out of here, but it doesn't look good. So I want to tell you all to hang in there. God didn't let us survive this long without there being a reason. No matter where you go or what happens, I want you to remember how much you mean to me. I can't thank you enough.

Maybe somebody else will come and take my place at your house or in the Young Trib Force. I hope they do. If you care for them half as much as you cared for me, they'll be really happy.

Promise me you'll take care of Phoenix. Tell Chaya and Shelly and Mark and John that I was thinking of them. I hope you all made it through the earthquake. I'll never forget you.

Love,

Ryan

Vicki lay her head on the floor and wept.

God, please don't let him die.

3

VICKI sat up, clutching Ryan's note. The nurse helped her stand and took her by the shoulders to a chair in the next room.

"It's my fault," Vicki said. "I told him to stay inside! He would have been OK if I hadn't insisted—"

"Ryan was smart," the nurse said.

"Was?"

"Is," the nurse said. "You're right. There's still a chance. But either way, this is not your fault. Last night Ryan tried to tell me something but couldn't find the words."

Vicki squinted. "What did he say?"

"Something about God, but he was out of his head by then. He really got to me. He's about the same age as my son."

"Charlie?"

"No, my son disappeared in the vanishings," the nurse said.

Vicki straightened. "I know what Ryan was trying to tell you."

———————————

Tim Vetter and the other men carried bags of supplies and blankets. Judd kept his hands behind him.

"Enough provisions for a few days," Tim said. "No GC yet."

"Just leave the stuff here and I'll keep an eye on it," Marlene said.

Tim pursed his lips. "The GC has a station on the south side. We'll take him with us. You stay with the supplies."

Tim untied Judd's feet and helped him stand. Judd kept his hands tight against his back. The other men were big and burly. Tim was the only one who could catch him if Judd ran.

Judd saw his chance at the corner. With the others behind him, he took off toward a mound of earth in the center of town. Tim was a few yards behind when Judd hit the embankment.

Judd scrambled up but slipped. Tim grabbed Judd's pant leg, and the others came lumbering. Judd kicked free and struggled to the top. Tim was close behind but slipping. The other men split into two groups, working their way around the pile.

Judd slid down the other side and raced toward a road by the river. He looked for a place to hide, but the quake had flattened houses and trees. He kept running.

"My son was a good boy," the nurse told Vicki as they walked the hallway between wards. "Never got into much trouble. Loved his video games. I was working the late shift the night it happened. It was crazy. We had pregnant women lose their unborn babies just before they were delivered. A friend of mine vanished from an operating room. It was awful.

"Then I came home to check on Chad. All that was left were his clothes. I blamed my husband at first. I guess that was wrong."

"What do you think happened?" Vicki said.

"I've read all the explanations," the nurse said. "An energy force, alien abduction, some kind of social cleansing. Whatever it was doesn't really matter. Chad's gone. When I saw Ryan, it made me think of him again."

"Did your son ever go to church?"

"As a matter of fact, he did. We went as a family only at Christmas and Easter. But Chad got involved in a youth group with one of his friends. They met during the week for some kind of study."

Vicki took a breath. "This is going to sound weird, but I know what really happened to your son," she said. Vicki told the nurse about meeting Ryan and how Pastor Bruce Barnes had shown them a videotape that explained the vanishings. Vicki knew then that what her parents had tried to tell her had come true.

"My mom and dad tried to get me to listen," Vicki said. "They told me Jesus Christ was going to come back

23

for his true followers. When I found their clothes, I knew I had been left behind.

"Your son was a Christian," Vicki said. "A true believer."

The nurse turned away as Charlie entered the room.

"I'm sorry that boy in there made you sad," Charlie said to Vicki.

"It's OK; he's a friend of mine," Vicki said.

The nurse gave a wary glance to Vicki and said, "I'll get in trouble if you're found in here. You need to go."

"But I want to tell you more about this," Vicki said. "And I don't want to leave Ryan."

"Come back late tonight," the nurse said. "I'm back here around ten. I'll meet you at the back door and let you in."

"I'll bring a friend," Vicki said.

Judd doubled back on his pursuers. He crouched behind the rubble of a house while the men passed. Several others had joined the search.

"I know where some GC guards are," one of them said.

"Go find them!" Tim yelled.

When the men were a safe distance past, Judd took off. He climbed the huge mound of earth, then stopped and peered around the corner to see if Marlene was alone.

"What are you doing here?" Marlene said as Judd rushed to her.

"They'll never think of looking for me here," Judd said, out of breath.

Marlene motioned Judd to the end of the street so they could watch for the others. "You should get out of here," she said. "I don't know what they'll do to you if they catch you. But now they know something's up."

"I'm OK," Judd said. "I couldn't leave and not finish our discussion."

Marlene took a breath. "I'm interested in what you're talking about," she said, "but I can't believe like you. It's too easy. If you're right, I basically don't have to do anything."

"You got it," Judd said. "You just accept what God's done."

"I'd feel a lot better if you told me I had to do something," Marlene said.

"That's the point," Judd said. "We're helpless. That's why Jesus lived a perfect life and died for us."

Marlene stared off. "Why would God . . . ?"

"In the Bible it says God is love," Judd said. "God doesn't want anyone to die without knowing him. But it's up to you."

Marlene got a wild look on her face. "If what you're saying is true, that changes everything," she said. "The Enigma Babylon Faith is a big lie."

"Exactly," Judd said. "That's why I want you to—"

Marlene jumped back from the corner. "Here they come!"

"I'm not leaving until you—"

"You have to," she said.

"All right, but ask God to forgive you," Judd said. "Tell him you're sorry. Tell him you accept his gift."

"Go!"

"Will you do it?" Judd said.

"I'll think about it."

Judd peeked around the corner. Tim and the others moved slowly toward them, no doubt dejected that Judd had escaped. Beside them was a GC guard.

Judd picked up the ropes he had been tied with and tied Marlene's hands and feet. He tied a rag tightly over her mouth.

"I overpowered you," Judd said. "I stole food, and you couldn't scream because I put this in your mouth. Got it?"

Marlene nodded and jerked her head, telling him to leave.

"God, thank you for letting me talk with Marlene," Judd prayed out loud. "I pray she will become your child. Keep her safe, and may she be able to tell others about you in the days ahead."

Judd heard footsteps. He ran the other way and grabbed some bread from the stash of provisions. He waited until the group turned the corner, then ducked into a brick-strewn alley.

Judd figured they had told the GC his identity, but with communication lines down, he doubted they would know he was supposed to be in a reeducation camp. They would expect him to cross the river and head toward Chicago. Instead, Judd ran the other way. Away from his home. Away from his friends.

The nurse showed Vicki the rear entrance that wasn't guarded by the GC. Vicki promised she would return late that night. "I want to talk to you more about what Ryan said," Vicki said.

"Just go," the nurse said.

Vicki circled the building and found Darrion and Shelly still waiting.

"What happened?" Shelly said.

Vicki tried to be strong, but she broke down as she told them about Ryan. Darrion took the news hard.

"What are we going to do now?" Darrion said.

"I'm coming back tonight to check on him," Vicki said.

"I'm in," Shelly said.

Darrion shook her head. "My mom. I've waited too long. I have to find her, and—"

"Don't do this," Shelly said. "The GC will be all over you. Your face has been plastered all over the news."

"I can wear a disguise," Darrion said.

"They'll lock you up like they did your mother," Shelly said.

"I don't care! She'd do the same for me. I have to find her."

Vicki led the girls back the way they came.

Shelly tried to talk Darrion out of leaving. "We need to stick together," she said. "If you leave, that's just another person we'll have to find. And if the GC gets you, you'll wind up like Judd."

Vicki looked hard at Shelly.

"Sorry," Shelly said. "I just don't want to lose anyone else."

"This is my mother," Darrion said. She looked away. "I can't expect you to understand."

"Why? Because my mom was trailer trash? Because I know she's dead?"

"I didn't mean it that way," Darrion said.

"Enough," Vicki said. "Shel, you're right, we ought to stick together. But Darrion needs to find her mom too."

"I'm really sorry about Ryan," Darrion said. "I wish I could do something to help."

Vicki said she understood. "You and Shelly should leave this afternoon and go—"

"No way," Shelly said.

"I can do this myself," Darrion said.

"I know you can," Vicki said. "That's not the point. I'll go back tonight and monitor Ryan. You've got a few hours of daylight left to find your mom. If you get into trouble, Shelly can help."

Darrion frowned and looked at Shelly. "I didn't mean to knock your mom."

Shelly looked away.

"Would you come with me?"

"I think it's the best idea, Shel," Vicki said.

Shelly sighed. "I guess if that's what Vick thinks I should do."

"We're almost to the end of the expressway," Darrion said. "The GC holding place was a few miles from here."

"I know where it is," Shelly said. "There's no way we can make it there and back before nightfall."

"Find a shelter nearby and stay till morning," Vicki said. "I'll meet you back at the tent tomorrow after-noon."

"Wait," Shelly said. "How are you going to get to Ryan after curfew? If you're out, you'll get shot."

"I've got a plan," Vicki said.

Judd ran south along the interstate, backtracking until he came to the bridge where he had helped the motorcycle rider, Pete. He hopped on the back of a four-wheel drive pickup that was transporting more bodies to the morgue.

When they arrived, Judd was surprised to see the injured lying outside on the ground. "Did they spend the night out here?" Judd asked a volunteer.

"The nearest hospital's flat," the man said. "Other buildings aren't safe. You got a better idea?"

Judd located a list of injured and looked for Pete's name. He was afraid the man had died but was relieved when he flipped the page over. Pete's name was on the back.

Judd didn't want to upset the man, but he knew he had to tell him the bad news about Pete's girlfriend. Judd found him sitting up and groggy.

"Didn't expect to see you for a long time," Pete said. "Couldn't make it to Chicago?"

"Ran into a little problem and had to leave your bike at the bottom of the river; sorry, man. How are you?"

"Doc says I have some temporary nerve damage," Pete said. "I feel pretty tingly right now, but I'm OK. It'll take more than that to do me in. You find my place?"

"Yeah," Judd said. "You left your bike outside the shed. It was a good thing, because everything else was destroyed."

Pete grimaced. "Same for the house?"

"I'm afraid so," Judd said.

Judd knelt beside the big man. The day before Judd had explained the forgiveness offered in Christ, and Pete had prayed. Pete's one concern was that his girlfriend hear what Judd had said.

"I managed to get inside the house," Judd said. "I couldn't find your friend for a long time and thought she might have gotten out. Then . . ."

"Oh, no," Pete said.

"She was in the laundry room when the quake hit. She didn't suffer."

Pete shook his head and wept. Judd felt embarrassed seeing such a big man cry. Judd put his hand on Pete's shoulder.

"What you said yesterday changed me," Pete said. "It really did. All I could think about was telling Rosie. Now she's gone."

Night fell. Pete cried. Judd slept on the ground beside him.

VICKI waited until dark, then made her way back to the hospital. She encountered Global Community guards and police several times. She dropped to the ground and waited until they passed.

Vicki crouched low when she came near the furniture store. Huge spotlights lit the receiving area. Vicki stole to the back and waited for the nurse. There was no way she was getting inside the front of the building with what she had planned. Finally, the back door opened.

"You have to come quickly," the nurse said.

"Is Ryan still alive?"

"Yes. Barely."

"You go ahead," Vicki said. "I don't want to get you in trouble."

The nurse left the door ajar. Vicki moved into the shadows, grabbed Phoenix's collar, and walked him inside. The dog panted and followed obediently.

"You have to be really quiet," Vicki said, hoping Phoenix would understand.

Vicki led Phoenix up the back stairs to the third floor. She reached for the door but heard footsteps and scampered back down the steps. A GC guard opened the door. The beam of the flashlight narrowly missed her. After a few moments, the man closed the door and walked away. Vicki headed for Ryan's room.

Phoenix shook, as if he were scared of the makeshift hospital. The strong medicine smell and all the bodies seemed to spook him. When he reached Ryan's side, the dog sniffed at the boy and licked his hand.

"I brought your best friend," Vicki whispered in Ryan's ear.

Phoenix put his paws on the bed and licked Ryan's face.

"What in the world?" the nurse said as she walked into the room. "Get that animal out of here! I could lose my job!"

"You don't understand," Vicki pleaded. "This is his best friend. They've been together—"

Vicki stopped when she saw the look on the nurse's face. The nurse pointed to the bed.

Ryan's hand twitched, and his eyes fluttered. Vicki's heart raced as she watched.

"Ryan, it's me, Vicki!"

Ryan tried to open his eyes but couldn't.

"It's OK," Vicki said. "I'll do the talking."

Vicki told Ryan where he was and that he had been hurt in the earthquake. Ryan nodded, and with each sentence he seemed to stir a little more.

Phoenix wagged his tail and whimpered.

"Lamb," Ryan finally said.

"That's right," Vicki said, "the wrath of the Lamb!"

"Water," Ryan said with a raspy voice.

Vicki grabbed a plastic pitcher and poured him a glass. Ryan's lips were chapped. She put the cup to his lips and helped him drink slowly.

"How did you find me?" Ryan said.

Vicki wiped away a tear. She was so overjoyed to talk with Ryan she choked as she spoke. "I had some help," was all she could say.

"What about the others?"

"Darrion and Shelly are OK. Judd was still in GC custody when the quake hit."

"Lionel?"

"Haven't heard," Vicki said.

Ryan looked toward his nightstand. "The letter."

"I got it," Vicki said. "Now listen to me. You're going to be OK. You'll pull out of this."

"No," Ryan said. He reached out and weakly patted Phoenix on the head. The dog licked him. Ryan's hand fell to the bed. "I'm ready."

"I know you are," Vicki said. "You have to get better; then we'll get you out of here."

Ryan shook his head. "Going home."

Vicki took his hand. "I can't move you right now or I would, you know that," she said.

Ryan smiled. "You don't get it."

"What don't I get?"

Ryan tried to raise his arm. He pointed a finger to the ceiling. Vicki bent closer as he said, "Home in heaven."

Vicki felt a chill go through her. "No. You've been through a lot, but you're still here. There's a lot the doctors can do."

He tried to sit up but couldn't. "When I went to the hospital the day of the bombings, Bruce couldn't talk much," Ryan said. "I think he knew he was going to die."

"That was different. We've lost too much as it is. You can't go."

"Friends," Ryan said. "They're waiting. I want to see Bruce. Raymie. Mrs. Steele."

"You'll get to see them soon enough," Vicki said. "You have to hang on."

The nurse touched Vicki's shoulder. "Can I talk to you a minute?" she said.

"I'll be right back," Vicki said to Ryan.

"As a nurse, you see things," the woman whispered. "I think he hung on because he thought you'd come. He's doing this for you."

"Then why won't he fight it?" Vicki said. "He can't die. I won't let him."

"It's not your fight," the nurse said. "You talked about believing in God. You must think Ryan's going to a better place."

"Yes, but not now. Not yet."

The nurse took Vicki's face in her hands. "He needs you to be strong. He needs you to tell him you'll be OK."

Vicki wiped her tears and nodded. "I just don't know if I will be."

Vicki returned to Ryan. His eyes were closed, his face pale. His hair was a mess. White beads formed at the corner of his mouth. Suddenly, Ryan's eyes fluttered. His face flushed with color. He smiled.

"They're coming," Ryan said.

"Who's coming?" Vicki said. "Who is it?"

Ryan opened his eyes and stared at Vicki. "I have to go now," he said. "I'm sorry."

Vicki wanted to scream. She wanted to run from the room. But she knew God had allowed her to be with Ryan in the final moments of his life. She had to think of Ryan, not herself. But it was so hard. She couldn't imagine what life would be like without him.

"I'll be OK," Vicki said.

"You have to stay safe," Ryan said. "Who will take care of Phoenix?"

Vicki smiled. "Hey, I was the one who talked Judd into letting you keep him."

Ryan closed his eyes again. "Can you hear them?" he said.

"Who?" Vicki said, but Ryan didn't answer.

Vicki buried her head in her hands. She and Ryan had been through so many scrapes together.

The nurse touched her shoulder. "It's time," she said.

Vicki summoned all her strength and took her friend's hand. "Ryan," she whispered, "you've been like a little brother to me. And you've been so brave."

Ryan smiled. A tear escaped one eye and rolled the length of his cheek.

"You have to trust me on this, OK?"

Ryan squeezed her hand.

"I don't want you to go. I want you to live and see the

Glorious Appearing of Jesus like Bruce talked about. But if you have to go now, I understand. It won't be the same without you."

Vicki turned and wiped her eyes.

"I feel like I'm letting you down," Ryan said.

"No," Vicki said, "don't ever think that. You've never let me down."

"You'll be OK?" Ryan said.

"Yeah. But you have to do me a favor."

"Anything."

Vicki closed her eyes and put her head next to Ryan's. "When you get home, will you tell Bruce I said hello?"

Ryan raised his head a few inches and opened his eyes. He looked straight at Vicki. "I'll tell him you were the best big sister anybody ever had."

He smiled again, then rested his head on the pillow and closed his eyes.

"So don't worry, OK?" Vicki said. "I'll take care of Phoenix. He'll take care of me."

A few minutes passed. Vicki watched as Ryan faded. His breathing became erratic. Phoenix whimpered.

Vicki came close to Ryan and whispered in his ear, "I love you."

"Love you," Ryan whispered.

Then his chest fell with a final breath, and he was gone.

Judd heard someone scream and awoke. Pete thrashed about yelling his girlfriend's name. Judd subdued the big man.

"Too late," the man cried. "We were too late to save Rosie."

"Just hold still," Judd said. Then he realized the man was moving his lower body.

"Pete," Judd said, "your legs!"

Pete looked startled, then gingerly sat up. "Help me," he said.

Judd helped him stand, wobbly at first, then Pete stood straight. "Look at me," he said. "Bet you didn't know I was this tall."

In a few minutes, Pete was walking. A few patients roused and clapped softly.

"You've got a little limp," Judd said.

"I'll take it," Pete said. "Come on, let's get out of here."

"You can't just walk away," Judd said.

"Watch me," Pete said. "I have work to do."

Vicki sat with Ryan a few minutes longer. The nurse felt for his pulse, then said, "He's gone." She knelt in front of Vicki and put a hand on her shoulder.

"You did a good thing here today. You made his last moments easier. I'm glad you came."

Vicki cried. She felt an emptiness she'd never felt before. When she lost her parents and family, she hadn't been able to say good-bye. She woke up the next morning, and they were gone. But this was different. Ryan's body was right next to her. She knew he wasn't there any longer, and her heart ached.

"What happens now?" Vicki said.

"With so many bodies, they aren't doing many buri-
als. A lot of them are being burned."

"I don't want that for him."

"There's no way around it."

"Can you give me a few hours?" Vicki said. "I could
find someone to help me carry him."

"It's out of the question. As soon as I report him
deceased, they'll take him away."

"Can't you hold off till morning?" Vicki said.

"I don't know—"

"Please," Vicki said.

"I can try," the nurse said.

Phoenix jumped onto Ryan's bed and whimpered.

"Get down!" the nurse said.

Phoenix barked. A few patients stirred.

"You have to get him out of here!"

Phoenix barked again. Vicki grabbed him by the collar
and headed for the stairs. She heard someone running up
and looked through the window.

"GC guard!" Vicki said.

"In here!"

Vicki ducked into a closet with Phoenix as the door to
the stairwell opened. Phoenix panted. Vicki clamped his
mouth shut. She heard the muffled sounds of the guard
and the nurse.

"I heard a dog bark," the guard said.

"Up here?" the nurse said. "You've gotta be
kidding."

Another bark. Phoenix perked up his ears.

The guard shouted something. A door closed. A moment later, the nurse ushered Vicki and Phoenix out. Charlie was standing by the exit sign.

"I got chewed out, chewed out good," Charlie said with a grin. "I was watchin' you guys. Hope that was OK."

The nurse frowned. "I have to go on rounds. Get out fast before they find you."

"Yes, ma'am," Vicki said.

"I can do really good dog sounds," Charlie said. "I saw the guy come looking for your dog, so I made it sound like him, and the guy thought I was the dog. Pretty neat, huh?"

"Yeah," Vicki said, heading for the door.

"I can do a squirrel too. You wanna hear?"

"Not right now," Vicki said.

Charlie came close and whispered, "I can help you."

"You can help me do what?"

"Carry your friend," Charlie said. "I'm a real good carrier. One time I helped my sister carry a piano all the way from her apartment—"

"You want to help me carry Ryan?"

"Carry Ryan," Charlie repeated. "Carry him anywhere you want. Actually, I didn't carry the piano from her apartment, I dragged it—"

"OK," Vicki said, "I'd like your help, but we have to hurry."

———————————————

Pete led Judd out of the camp. They found a man asleep in his truck, and Pete convinced him to give them a ride.

A few minutes later, Judd and Pete were in front of Pete's demolished house.

"We should wait until morning," Judd said.

"I can't let her stay in there another minute," Pete said.

Pete found an old lantern, and the two tore wood from the house until they reached Rosie's body. The sun was nearly up when Pete carefully carried her from the rubble. He dug a grave by the creek that passed his property and gently placed her in the ground.

"I don't know what to say," Pete said. "Shouldn't we read something or pray?"

"Whatever's in your heart," Judd said.

Pete sighed and bowed his head. He looked like a mountain. "God, I don't think Rosie knew about you. I'd give anything to talk to her now.

"I know I don't deserve you forgiving me after all I've done, but I believe you have. Help me to live right and follow you and make you proud. Thank you for my new friend. Amen."

Pete looked at Judd. "How was that?"

"Straight from the heart," Judd said. "You can't get better than that."

Pete threw his shovel at the demolished shed. "Now we gotta get you back to Chicago."

Vicki led Phoenix out. Charlie carried Ryan's lifeless body. As they slipped into the night, Charlie huffed and puffed. Vicki could tell it wasn't going to be an easy trip.

They rested as often as Charlie needed. At times, Vicki helped, but mostly Charlie carried Ryan alone.

A flood of memories came over her as they walked. Ryan had grown taller since they first met. She remembered their trips searching for Bibles. She had been there when Ryan found Phoenix. She had seen Ryan stand at Bruce's memorial service and say he was willing to give his life for the sake of the gospel.

By morning, they were near Vicki's house. Construction crews were busy clearing rubble and collapsed roadways. Vicki took Charlie near the spot where New Hope Village Church once stood.

While Charlie scampered off to find a shovel, Vicki pawed through the loose stones that led to Ryan's secret chamber. There was no sign of life at the church. Vicki moved enough dirt and bricks to crawl through. She grabbed a Bible and crawled out.

When Charlie was finished digging the grave, Vicki helped him lift Ryan. She unfolded the sheet from around him and placed the Bible in his hands.

"Is that for luck?" Charlie said.

"No," Vicki said. "The Bible was really important to him. He studied it just about every day."

"I had a Bible once," Charlie said. "Somebody took it."

Vicki reached into the grave and took the book from Ryan's body.

"What are you doing?" Charlie said.

"He wouldn't have wanted to be buried with it," Vicki said. "He'd want you to have it."

As the sun rose, Vicki knelt on the cold ground. She

looked at Ryan, and the tears came. Charlie stood back, his head bowed.

Softly, Vicki sang the words to one of Ryan's favorite hymns.

Amazing grace! how sweet the sound—
That saved a wretch like me!
I once was lost but now am found,
Was blind but now I see.

She made a crude cross and stuck it in the ground at the head of the grave. She wondered how many more crosses she would have to make in the days ahead.

5

VICKI awoke near Ryan's grave. Phoenix was sprawled out on top. When Vicki moved, Phoenix whimpered and pawed at the loose dirt. Charlie was gone.

Vicki shivered from the cold. She wished she could see Judd and talk with him about Ryan. If this was what it would be like for the rest of the Tribulation, she didn't know if she could go on.

God, why did you have to take him? Vicki prayed.

Vicki returned to the shelter but couldn't find Shelly or Darrion. A man asked for volunteers. "We need help with the injured."

Vicki raised a hand and followed him.

Lionel took the gun instructions seriously. He watched carefully as the instructor taught them how to clean it and use it safely. At the shooting range Lionel scored the highest. The instructor patted him on the shoulder. "Watch this guy and you'll learn how to shoot," the man told a girl beside Lionel.

"I'm not that good," Lionel said when the instructor left.

"Better than me," the girl said. She held out a hand. "I'm Felicia."

Lionel introduced himself, then headed to the morning session. "Once you've blended in with the communities you'll be sent to," the instructor said, "you'll listen for specific things. No one in their right mind is going to come out and say they're against the Global Community."

A computer generated images and phrases on a screen in front of the class. The words *Antichrist* and *Tribulation* flashed before Lionel.

"Anyone who talks about there being an Antichrist is someone you want to watch closely. If the person believes we are experiencing what they call the 'Tribulation,' these may be enemies of the Global Community."

The instructor stopped and looked over his glasses. "There are actually people who believe Nicolae Carpathia is an evil man." The class responded with groans and laughter.

A Global Community chopper landed in a nearby field, interrupting the class. The sound of the rotor blades was deafening.

"You are witnessing the arrival of your new boss," the instructor said. "Terrel Blancka. Never—I repeat—never call him by his first name. You'll want to call him Commander Blancka or simply Commander."

Lionel watched as a man with a barrel chest and a graying mustache strode to the practice area. He wore a GC field uniform with a beret. He carried a clipboard and spoke gruffly to the instructor.

"What do you make of him?" Conrad asked Lionel.

"Looks like he means business," Lionel whispered.

The instructor formally introduced Commander Blancka, and the burly man stood ramrod straight, his hands behind his back.

"Boys and girls," Commander Blancka said, "and you are boys and girls until we get through with you." He scanned the group for any response. When there was none, he continued. "I've made it no secret that I didn't want this assignment. I don't have time to baby-sit. But when the most powerful man in the world calls and gives an order, I follow it.

"Now listen carefully. You are part of an elite group, chosen for a specific purpose. You are the first of the Global Community's Morale Monitors.

"There's no question you're young. But that doesn't have to be a drawback. We think it's an asset. We'll send you into hot spots, places where we feel there may be resistance to the purposes of the Global Community. I can't emphasize enough the importance of this job. Let me tell you about my conversation with the potentate."

Lionel caught a glance from Conrad. Commander Blancka's message made Lionel feel important.

"Nicolae Carpathia came to me and asked that I put this program together," the commander continued. "The success or failure of it depends on you. And that means my success or failure depends on you. So I'll be watching."

Commander Blancka looked steely eyed at the crowd. "That means you will succeed. The potentate made it clear. The secret to the success of the Global Community is UNITY!" The kids jumped as the commander shouted.

"Those who want to divide us will be exposed. People who want to live in peace and harmony will enjoy exactly that. But those who want to cause trouble will be dealt with. Swiftly."

A boy near Conrad timidly raised a hand.

"What!" Commander Blancka barked.

"Is the potentate safe, sir?" the boy said.

"Good question," Commander Blancka said. "Nicolae Carpathia was prepared for this. He's in a safe place, getting ready to have his ten international ambassadors join him. Any more questions?"

Felicia raised a hand. "Sir, from what you've said, we're in kind of a war, aren't we?"

"You bet we are," Commander Blancka said. "But not with bombs and artillery. We're in a war of thought. We can enforce laws on people's actions, but we want to go beyond that. The potentate said he wanted a group of elite enforcers of pure thought. Healthy young men and women like yourselves. Strong people who are devoted to the cause of the Global Community. So devoted that they would be willing to train and build themselves. We want people eager to make sure everyone is in line with the potentate."

The commander scanned the crowd. It seemed to

Lionel that the man looked in each person's eyes. "Are you that group?" he said.

"Yes, sir," the kids said.

"You call that eager?" Commander Blancka barked.

"Yes, sir!" the kids said louder.

"That's better," Commander Blancka said. "You will not wear uniforms. We want you to blend in with the rest of society. You will, at all times, carry your weapon and a communication device. If you find yourself in mortal danger, or if you discover a situation to report, contact the base immediately. The communicator also works as a homing device so we can find you if we need to.

"One of the hallmarks of the society you've grown up in is free speech." Commander Blancka bowed his head and shook it. "Sadly, we can't afford that luxury. That's why we've trained you. You will root out those who by word or action oppose the purposes of our cause.

"A good soldier knows his or her enemy," the commander said, pacing now. "Who is the enemy? If you're smart, you're asking that question. I'll tell you. The enemy is anyone who seeks to divide. Anyone who says *they* know what's right and not the potentate. One of our main targets will be those fundamentalists who say their religion is the only true religion."

Lionel raised a hand. "What power are we given, sir?" he said.

"A Global Community Morale Monitor has no limit to his or her powers," the commander said. "We find the enemy. We subdue the enemy. By any means necessary."

"That means using a gun?" Lionel said.

"That means using whatever we must. If you do your job well, we'll have no need for you within a few years. The enemy will vanish."

After a few hours of sleep, Judd and Pete set out to locate another motorcycle. They found a large one at Pete's friend's house. The man had also been killed by the earthquake. Before they left, Judd located an old laptop computer in an office near the front of the house.

"I could use this to make contact with some friends," Judd said. "You think we can take it?"

"My friend's not gonna use it anymore," Pete said.

Pete showed Judd another route home. "You'll want to avoid the place you just came from."

"Actually, I'd like to go back the other way."

"You've gotta be outta your mind!" Pete said.

Judd explained the situation with Marlene. "I have to know if she accepted Christ."

"Don't you think that's too dangerous?" Pete said. "People have to make their own decisions."

"True. But I have to know."

"Then you won't go alone," Pete said.

"What do you mean?"

"We'll get close enough; then you point her out to me. I'll see if I can talk to her."

Judd smiled and nodded. He noticed a bruise on Pete's forehead. "I didn't see this the other day," Judd said.

"Must have smacked my head when they were trans-

porting me," Pete said. "Besides, you've got a smudge of
your own."

Judd looked in the mirror but didn't see anything.

Lionel paid attention as Commander Blancka warned the
kids. "We don't know about radiation with the meteors,"
he said. "Best to stay away from them. Avoid looking like
an authority. Blend in. Make friends. But always remember you have the power to enforce the Global Community's rules."

"Do we go back to school?" a girl asked.

"School as you knew it, no. The Global Community
has an education plan for the future. Central learning
stations are being built as we speak. GC-approved instruc-
tors will teach via satellite links from New Babylon. You'll
uplink for tests and research. Everyone will be required to
participate."

When Commander Blancka completed his speech, he
told the kids to be ready to leave the following morning.
"You Monitors will be airlifted by helicopter."

"Why do they have someone that high up in charge of
us?" Conrad asked after the meeting was over.

"You heard him," Lionel said. "What we're doing's
important."

"But we're kids," Conrad said.

"We're GCMM now," Lionel said. "Get used to it."

Conrad pulled out his gun and twirled it on his
finger. Lionel grabbed it angrily. "You know that's
dangerous!"

Conrad took his gun and holstered it. "It's not loaded," he said. "Besides, who died and left you in charge?"

Lionel stared at Conrad. "If you don't think this is serious, why don't you quit?" he said.

"So, your first job is to monitor the Morale Monitors?"

"If I have to," Lionel said.

Conrad walked away.

Vicki helped in the main tent. The suffering was unbelievable. Finally she spotted Darrion and Shelly. She excused herself and caught up with them. Shelly looked exhausted. Darrion sat with elbows on knees. She didn't look up when Vicki ran to them.

"What happened?" Vicki said.

Shelly shook her head. "Long story. Bad ending."

"Mom's gone," Darrion said. "They had her locked in a cell. After all this time they were still questioning her."

"They wouldn't show us the facility," Shelly said. "It was roped off and patrolled. We stayed till dark to get a look."

"There's no way she could have survived," Darrion said. "The place was knocked flat. The whole thing must have come down on her."

"I'm sorry," Vicki said.

"We did get a look at the logbook," Shelly said. "Judd and Taylor Graham were taken away on the morning of the quake."

"So there's a chance they're still alive," Vicki said.

Shelly nodded. Vicki noticed something strange on Shelly's forehead. Shelly rubbed at the smudge, but it didn't come off. "What's it look like?" Shelly said.

"Like what they do in Catholic churches around Ash Wednesday," Vicki said.

"Maybe I tripped or something," Shelly said. "It was a long night. What about Ryan?"

Vicki told them. Darrion hung her head. Shelly lay back on the ground. "I can't even cry anymore," she said.

Vicki took them to the grave. Phoenix hadn't moved. The three girls stood in silence. Vicki wondered about Lionel. And Judd.

Judd described Marlene and told Pete where he might find the group. Pete dropped Judd off at a gas station that was still standing.

"I'll wait for you here," Judd said, taking the laptop with him.

The service station owner sat in a lawn chair near the gas pumps and held a large dog by the collar. The dog lunged at Judd. Judd saw the butt of a gun sticking out of the man's belt.

"You best move on," the man said, spitting in the dirt. "All the food's gone."

"Can I use your rest room? My friend will be back for me soon."

The man nodded to the corner of the building.

Judd noticed a telephone behind the counter when he returned. A light blinked on one of its lines.

"Is that phone working?" Judd asked.

"They're tryin'," the man said. "Comes and goes."

"Would you mind if I tried to hook up my computer?" Judd said.

"It'll cost you."

Judd had no wallet. No identification. The Global Community had taken all he had. He had scrounged for food since the earthquake. He wondered how he would live without money.

The man rolled his eyes when he saw Judd pat his pockets. "Local call?" the man said.

"Yeah," Judd said, "I just need to get the access number."

"I don't understand those things. Go ahead and use it if you have to."

Judd tried several times to dial out but got a busy signal each time. On the fifth try he got a ring and located the number for a dial-up line.

The computer was old and slow, but Judd felt like he was holding a gold mine. It was his first cyber contact with the outside world since he'd been arrested.

Judd first downloaded his messages but saw none from Vicki, Lionel, or Ryan. Next, he located a Web site with a people search. The Global Community was already tracking the number of deaths. He entered Vicki Byrne's name and held his breath. The computer ground slowly, then showed Vicki in the "no known whereabouts" listing.

At least she's not confirmed dead, Judd thought.

Judd entered Lionel Washington's name. "Injured." Judd typed in Ryan's name. "Confirmed dead."

Judd gasped. Could it be true? Could Ryan really be dead?

He typed in his own name. "No known whereabouts."

He checked the adult Tribulation Force. Rayford Steele was "confirmed alive." Chloe and Buck Williams were not accounted for. The same for Loretta and Donny Moore.

When Judd typed in Amanda Steele's name, he again gasped as he read, "Subject confirmed on Boston to New Babylon nonstop, reported crashed and submerged in Tigris River, no survivors."

Judd figured Amanda had been flying to see Rayford in New Babylon. The report said she hadn't made it. Judd hung his head. When would the death toll stop?

Judd called up his E-mail again and looked at the multiple lines of messages. He heard a click of the modem and realized the phone was dead. One message interested him. It was from Pavel, the boy from New Babylon he had met online. He tried to dial up again, but the line was dead. Judd wondered if Pavel had made it through the earthquake. If it was the worldwide quake the Bible talked about, being outside when it hit was probably the boy's only chance.

Judd tried to dial up again but couldn't get through. He heard a loud rumbling and saw at least ten motorcycles pull into the gas station. The dog barked, and the owner reached for his gun.

"No!" Judd shouted.

6

JUDD'S shout startled the owner and the riders. The group turned and stared at Judd as he ran toward them.

"Don't do this," Judd said.

"Stay out of it, kid," the biker nearest the owner said. He was huge and had long red hair.

"They think they're comin' in here and stealin' my gas," the owner said. "Over my dead body."

"Whatever it takes," the biker snorted.

The dog barked wildly as the hairy man got off his bike and approached the owner.

"I'm warnin' you," the owner said.

Judd heard another cycle. A trail of dust lifted in the distance. A moment later, Judd saw Pete flying along the path he had taken toward town.

"Is that who I think it is?" a girl on the back of one bike said.

"Sure looks like him," the hairy man said.

Pete took his time climbing off the cycle. Even the dog stopped barking. Pete pulled off his helmet and ambled toward the others.

"Pete?" the hairy man said.

"What's up, Red?"

"Just looking for a little gas, that's all."

Pete stopped in front of the owner and pawed at the ground with his boot. "This looks like an honest businessman," Pete said.

"Cash only," the owner said.

"Don't do this," Red said to Pete. "You get in our way, and there'll be trouble."

Pete stepped nose to nose with Red. Their combined weight was surely more than 600 pounds.

"I'm trying to keep you from doing something you'll regret," Pete said. "Now pay the man or leave."

Red clenched his teeth and his fists. Finally he turned and waved a hand. "Come on. We'll fuel up later."

As the dust settled from Red's gang's departure, the owner turned to Pete. "Sure am glad you two came along," he said, giving a toothless smile. "Fill your tank. It's on me."

"It was nothing," Pete said. "But get ready. I don't think you've seen the last of them."

"Did you find her?" Judd said.

Pete nodded, then asked the owner, "Mind if we use your office to talk?"

"Go right ahead," the owner said.

"I found the people," Pete said when they were a safe distance away. "Told them I was looking for a skinny kid who stole my motorcycle."

"Thanks a lot!" Judd said.

"They're still looking for you. Said you took some stuff and ran from the GC."

"I was hungry," Judd said. "I took a few pieces of bread. Give me a break."

"I saw the little lady you talked about."

"Talk with her?"

"Couldn't," Pete said, moving closer. Pete was only a few inches away. "But I saw the weirdest thing."

Judd stepped back. "What's the matter with you?"

"She's got the same kind of smudge on her forehead that you do."

Judd found a broken mirror in the bathroom but couldn't see the smudge. "Let me see your head again."

Pete leaned forward in the light and pulled back his long hair. Judd studied the mark closely. "This isn't a bruise like I thought," he said. "It's some kind of stamp or a mark. Maybe they put it on you at the shelter to keep track of patients."

"I don't remember it if they did," Pete said.

"It's almost like one of those 3-D images."

"You're right," Pete said, looking at Judd. "Holy cow, it looks like a cross."

"You see that on my forehead?" Judd said, looking in the mirror again.

"Yeah. I can see yours and you can see mine, but not in a mirror. What do you think it is?"

Judd's mind raced. "The pastor I told you about, Bruce Barnes, taught about a mark people would have, but that was supposed to be given by the Antichrist.

People will have to take it in order to buy and sell stuff."

Pete threw up his hands. "Hey, don't look at me. I'm new to this."

Judd ran to the computer and tried the dial-up. This time he got through and went straight to Tsion Ben-Judah's Web site.

"And Marlene had this same thing on her head?" Judd asked.

"Plain as day," Pete said.

Judd did a search of Tsion's Web site. "Bingo," Judd said. Pete looked over his shoulder as Judd read, " 'Many of you have noticed a mysterious mark the size of a thumbprint on the forehead of other believers. Do not be alarmed. This is the seal, visible only to other believers.' "

"A seal?"

"Yeah, like a stamp of approval," Judd said.

"And other people don't see it?"

"Go try it out," Judd said.

Pete walked outside to the owner. Pete pulled back his hair and said, "You see anything on my forehead?"

"Some lines and hair is all I see," the owner said. "Is there supposed to be something up there?"

"I guess not," Pete said. He came back to Judd, shaking his head. "This Bible stuff is gettin' weird."

"Listen to this," Judd said. " 'The seventh chapter of Revelation tells of "the servants of our God" being sealed on their foreheads.' "

"Why would God do that?"

"I don't know. I'm just glad he did. Now we know

58

Marlene is a true believer. She has the mark. She must have prayed after I left."

"I wonder if it'll help us in the future," Pete said.

"How?"

"I assume it'll be good to know who's on our side and who's not," Pete said.

Vicki collapsed in her tent. She had been working nonstop for hours. The number of injured and dead was staggering. Men and women walked in a daze looking for friends and family. Grown men thrashed about, saying they wanted to die.

Vicki was almost asleep when Shelly opened the tent. "There's a man out here to see you."

"Who is it?" Vicki said.

"I don't know, but I told him you were taking a rest. He said I should come wake you."

Vicki gasped when she saw the man. Chaya's father, Mr. Stein, stood a few yards from the tent.

"Vicki," Mr. Stein said.

Vicki rushed to him. "I haven't seen Chaya. She went to your house to—"

Mr. Stein held up a hand. "I was with her at the house. I made a solemn vow to find her friends. I'm here to keep that promise."

"What happened?"

"Chaya is dead," Mr. Stein said.

Vicki fell to her knees. "No," she choked.

Mr. Stein knelt beside Vicki. "We were in the house

59

together when the earthquake hit," he said. "We were trapped many hours. If they had found us earlier, she might still be alive."

Vicki closed her eyes. "I'm so sorry."

"I have lost everything. My wife. My daughter. My home and all my possessions." Mr. Stein looked away. "But what good are possessions when the people you love are gone?"

"Were you able to talk with her before. . . ."

"You know I did not want to speak with her again," Mr. Stein said. "We had great differences. But in those hours, I understood how wrong I was."

"Wrong about what?"

"For shutting her out. She was my flesh and blood."

"Did you talk?"

Mr. Stein nodded. "She tried to convince me that her belief in God was right and mine was wrong. Until the very end she was talking about her belief in Jesus as Messiah."

"She prayed for you constantly," Vicki said.

"She was misguided."

"A funeral. Would it be all right with you if—"

"There is no need," Mr. Stein said. "I buried her yesterday."

Vicki felt crushed. Ryan. Mrs. Stahley. Donny Moore. All dead. And now Chaya, the person who had the best grasp of the Bible of any in the Young Tribulation Force.

"Why, God?" Vicki whispered.

"I thought you had it figured out. Your God was supposed to have a plan. He wants good things to happen, right?"

Vicki shook her head. "Mr. Stein, whether you believe it or not, your daughter loved you. And God loves you. He wants you to know him not just by rules and laws, but—"

Mr. Stein put up a hand. "I did not come for another sermon. I made a promise to find you, and I kept my word."

Mr. Stein turned to leave.

"The Bible doesn't say God will only cause good things to happen," Vicki said. "It says he takes everything that happens and works it for good to those who love him."

Mr. Stein frowned. "I am through arguing."

Vicki put her face in her hands.

"Do you have need of anything?" Mr. Stein said.

"We're like everyone else now. No house. No food. We'll make it somehow."

Mr. Stein handed her a card. "I don't know when the phone lines will return, but if you have need, call me or come see me. My office escaped serious damage. I may be able to help you in some way."

Lionel and Conrad packed for their trip north. The group waited near two choppers where Commander Blancka and his staff would transport them. Lionel knew he and Conrad would be in the Chicago area, along with Felicia and another girl, Melinda.

"How do they expect us to cover an area that big with four people?" Conrad said.

"Remember," Lionel said, "they're testing the program. If it works, they'll expand it."

"I've heard there's a lot of looting in Chicago," Conrad said. "Think we'll get mixed up in that?"

"I talked with the instructor after the commander left. He said we aren't peace officers, but in an emergency, you never know."

Conrad pulled a sheet of paper from his pocket. "I found that rabbi guy's Web site on the Internet."

"So?"

Conrad pointed to a paragraph at the bottom of the page. "This caught my eye. It says the good people are supposed to have some kind of a mark on their forehead."

Lionel smirked. "Why are you wasting your time on this? I don't see any mark on your forehead; do you see one on mine?"

"Guess not," Conrad said.

Lionel crumpled the paper and threw it away. "Get some sleep tonight. We've got a long flight tomorrow."

Conrad left. Lionel tried to sleep but couldn't. He went into the bathroom and looked in the mirror. There was no mark.

Judd finally opened his E-mail and checked the message from Pavel. The boy had miraculously survived the wrath of the Lamb earthquake along with a nurse who was attending him.

"The nurse insisted we go outside," Pavel wrote.

"Animals were going crazy. Then the earth started shaking. We were near the main building where Nicolae has his office. After a few moments, it crashed to the ground."

Pavel asked Judd to write if he had survived. Judd logged on and sent a message to see if Pavel might be online. In a moment, Judd heard a ding and saw Pavel's response.

"I'm so glad to know you're OK," Pavel wrote. "Shall we put on the video link?"

"Stay with text, I'm on an old machine," Judd wrote. Judd briefly explained what had happened to him and how he was trying to get back to Chicago. "What about Carpathia?" Judd wrote.

"Alive and well," Pavel wrote.

"Any news on his pilot? His name is Rayford Steele."

"Haven't heard, but if the rabbi is right, your friend should be safe. Tsion Ben-Judah believes the Scriptures say the Antichrist will stay alive until a little over a year from now. If the pilot is close to Carpathia, it may be the safest place."

"What about your father?"

"He's OK. And he tells the strangest story about Nicolae. Carpathia escaped certain death when he took a helicopter from the roof of his office. But his right-hand man didn't make it."

"Leon Fortunato?"

"Exactly. How did you know?"

"I met him once," Judd typed, smiling.

"My father said Fortunato is telling the story everywhere that Nicolae raised him from the dead!"

"That can't be!"

"My father was in Nicolae's shelter. It's a huge underground facility big enough for Nicolae's airplanes. Suddenly, the potentate walks in with Fortunato. Leon was covered with dirt."

"That doesn't prove anything."

"Fortunato tells it like it is fact," Pavel wrote. "He told the staff he fell to the bottom of the building, struck his head, and died. The next thing he remembers, he hears Nicolae's voice saying, 'Leonardo, come forth.' "

A chill went down Judd's spine. "Those are the same words Jesus used to call Lazarus from the grave. Sounds like a counterfeit to me."

"I know from reading different passages that a person dies once," Pavel wrote. "There are no second chances. But still, Fortunato lives."

"There has to be an explanation."

"I'm afraid people will be fooled," Pavel said. "The potentate will soon broadcast live to the world."

"I'm not in a place where I can see or hear anything from the media."

"I'll send you the text of his message once it is complete. My greatest fear is that people will proclaim Nicolae divine."

"Let's pray it doesn't happen," Judd said.

Judd heard the rumble of motorcycles and signed off. "Hopefully, I'll write you from Chicago."

Pete moved to the front window. "They're back."

"Maybe we should get out of here," Judd said.

"And let that old man fend for himself? I know how these people operate. They're like wolves. The old guy'll be so scared he won't be able to shoot anything. I'm not leaving him alone."

"How do you know so much about these people?"

"I used to be one of them."

7

THE OWNER of the gas station darted inside and shut off the gas pumps. Pete brought his bike inside and closed the garage doors. "Put your laptop away," Pete said as he went out the door. "We might have to get out fast."

"What's he gonna do?" the owner asked Judd.

"You got me," Judd said.

The gang pulled in and circled around Pete. The group had grown to twenty bikes. Judd couldn't hear what they were saying, but Red shouted, and Pete stood his ground.

The owner pulled his gun, and Judd put out his hand. "A little fuel isn't worth getting killed."

"This is all I got left," the owner said. "I'm not lettin' a bunch of cycle goons take it away."

Judd watched Red get off his bike and grab Pete by the hair. He jerked it back from his face and pointed. The others laughed.

"I'm not lettin' him die out there," the owner said, heading for the door.

"Wait!" Judd shouted. "Let it play out."

Red let go and stepped back. Pete seemed animated, gesturing and talking loudly. A few bikers stared at him. Others shook their heads and laughed.

Judd froze. He knew the danger outside, but he couldn't let Pete get killed.

"I'm going out there," Judd finally said. "If we need you, I'll signal you like this." Judd scratched the back of his neck.

"Got it," the owner said. "Now be careful."

Judd opened the door slowly. Pete still talked. The bikers sat with arms folded. When Judd got close to the pumps, he heard Red say, "Since when did you become perfect? Have you forgotten what you used to do?"

"I'm not perfect," Pete said.

A woman in the group spoke up. "How 'bout you and Rosie? You two were livin' together."

"I know what Rosie and I did was wrong," Pete said. "Believe me, I'd give anything to be able to talk with her like this."

Judd couldn't figure out what Pete was doing.

Pete turned and saw Judd. He smiled and said softly, "Bet you didn't know if this Christian thing would stick with me, huh?"

"I liked the old Pete better," someone said.

"Yeah, the boozin', cussin', fightin' Pete," another said.

"Look, I don't know all the verses and everything,"

Pete said. "This guy does. His name's Judd. He's the one who helped me."

Red got back on his motorcycle and kicked it to a start. "Don't want your religion," he said. "And next time you get in our way, you'll pay."

The other cycles rumbled to a start and followed Red. Pete watched the trail of dust and shook his head.

"You told them about God?" Judd said.

"They need to hear it as much as I did. They don't want to hear it, though."

"You didn't want it for a lot of years," Judd said.

"Maybe someday they'll listen."

Vicki awoke to bright sunshine. A man was speaking through a bullhorn. Darrion and Shelly followed her out of the tent. Vicki felt grungy and wished she could take a shower.

"All able-bodied people should move to the media tent for a special announcement," the GC guard was saying. "Potentate Nicolae Carpathia will make a statement via satellite shortly."

"You think he can use an earthquake for his own good?" Shelly said sarcastically.

"He'll use anything and everything," Vicki said.

The three girls reached the tent and watched a Global Community newscaster give the latest. "The number of dead and injured worldwide is staggering," the man said. "These pictures show the extent of the damage."

Video clips of major cities flashed on the screen. A

shot of Paris showed the Eiffel Tower in ruins. The Leaning Tower of Pisa was no longer leaning but flat on the ground. Shots of New York, Los Angeles, and Chicago made Vicki shudder.

"Other natural phenomena occurred during the earthquake," the newscaster said. "This amateur video was shot in New Babylon during the earthquake."

Vicki gasped. The camera was shaky, but there was no mistaking the fire in the sky. The moon had turned blood red.

"No matter how much they try to explain that away," Darrion said, "we all know that the moon turning that color is not a natural phenomenon."

Nicolae Carpathia's face flashed on the screen. He looked grim but composed. "Brothers and sisters in the Global Community, I address you from New Babylon. Like you, I lost many loved ones, dear friends, and loyal associates in the tragedy. Please accept my deepest and most sincere sympathy for your losses on behalf of the administration of the Global Community.

"No one could have predicted this random act of nature, the worst in history to strike the globe. We were in the final stages of our rebuilding effort following the war against a resistant minority. Now, as I trust you are able to witness wherever you are, rebuilding has already begun again."

Nicolae told viewers that New Babylon would become the center of the world for banking, government, and even Enigma Babylon One World Faith.

"Told you he'd use the earthquake to his own advantage," Vicki smirked.

"It will be my joy to welcome you to this beautiful place," Nicolae continued. "Give us a few months to finish, and then plan your pilgrimage. Every citizen should make it his or her life's goal to experience this new utopia and see the prototype for every city."

The screen switched from Nicolae to a virtual reality tour of the new city. It gleamed, as if already completed. The tour was dizzying and impressive. Carpathia pointed out every high-tech, state-of-the-art convenience.

"Looks pretty impressive," Shelly said.

"It's a fake," Vicki said. "The guy can only attempt to copy what God does."

The potentate continued with a stirring pep talk. "Because you are survivors, I have unwavering confidence in your drive and determination and commitment to work together, to never give up, to stand shoulder to shoulder and rebuild our world.

"I am humbled to serve you and pledge that I will give my all for as long as you allow me the privilege. Now let me just add that I am aware that, due to speculative reporting in one of our own Global Community publications, many have been confused by recent events."

"What's he talking about?" Shelly said.

"Must be Buck Williams's magazine article," Vicki said.

"While it may appear that the global earthquake coincided with the so-called wrath of the Lamb, let me clarify," Nicolae said. "Those who believe this disaster was God's doing are also those who believe that the disappearances nearly two years ago were people being swept away to heaven.

"Of course, every citizen of the Global Community is free to believe as he or she wants and to exercise that faith in any way that does not infringe upon the same freedom for others. The point of Enigma Babylon One World Faith is religious freedom and tolerance.

"For that reason, I am loath to criticize the beliefs of others. However, I plead for common sense. I do not begrudge anyone the right to believe in a personal god."

"Gee, thanks," Darrion muttered.

"However, I do not understand how a god they describe as just and loving would capriciously decide who is or is not worthy of heaven and effect that decision in what they refer to as 'the twinkling of an eye.'

"Has this same loving god come back two years later to rub it in? He expresses his anger to those unfortunates left behind by laying waste their world and killing off a huge percentage of them?"

"Look at that smile," Vicki said. "Makes me sick."

"I humbly ask devout believers in such a Supreme Being to forgive me if I have mischaracterized your god," Carpathia continued. "But any thinking citizen realizes that this picture simply does not add up.

"So, my brothers and sisters, do not blame God for what we are enduring. See it simply as one of life's cruci-bles, a test of our spirit and will, an opportunity to look within ourselves and draw on that deep wellspring of goodness we were born with. Let us work together to make our world a global phoenix, rising from the ashes of trag-edy to become the greatest society ever known. I bid you good-bye and goodwill until next I speak with you."

People around the tent stood and clapped. Vicki shook her head and remained seated. When the others sat, Vicki recognized a familiar face.

"Isn't that the guy who was at Judd's graduation?" Shelly said.

"Leon Fortunato," Vicki said.

Fortunato seemed friendly and looked straight into the camera. "I want to tell you an incredible story," he said. "So incredible that I would not believe it if it had not happened to me.

"I was in the top floor offices of the Global Community when the earthquake hit. Unlike the potentate, I was unable to escape. But I am glad he did, because if it were not for him, I would be dead.

"The building collapsed around us," Leon continued. "I wish I could say I was brave during this time, but like the rest, I went screaming into the rubble. I fell headfirst, and when I hit the bottom, it felt and sounded like I'd cracked my skull. The weight of the whole building came down on me, breaking my bones. My lungs burst. Everything went black."

Fortunato stopped. Vicki watched the crowd in the tent. They were leaning forward, listening to every word.

"I believe I died," Fortunato said. "It was as if someone pulled the plug on my life."

Another pause. "And yet, here I am. Alive. You ask me how? I say it was my friend Nicolae. I was not conscious of anything, like the deepest sleep a person could ever have. And then I heard a voice calling my name. I thought it was

73

a dream. I thought I was a boy again and my mother was softly calling my name, trying to wake me from sleep.

"Then I heard the loud, strong voice of your potentate. He cried out, 'Leonardo, come forth!'"

"I don't believe it," Vicki said.

"What?" Darrion said.

"Those are the same words Jesus used with Lazarus to bring him back from the dead," Vicki said.

A woman turned in front of the girls and shushed them.

Leon Fortunato wiped his brow and composed himself. "I'm sorry for being emotional," he said. "My only regret was that there were no witnesses. But I know what I experienced and believe with all my heart that this gift our Supreme Potentate possesses will be used in public in the future. A man bestowed with this power is worthy of a new title. I am suggesting that he hereafter be referred to as His Excellency Nicolae Carpathia. I have already instituted this policy within the Global Community government and urge all citizens who respect and love our leader to follow suit.

"As you may know, His Excellency would never require or even request such a title. Though reluctantly thrust into leadership, he has expressed a willingness to give his life for his fellow citizens. Though he will never insist upon appropriate deference, I urge it on your part."

"That's all I can take," Vicki said. "Come on."

Outside the tent, Shelly asked Vicki what she thought of Leon Fortunato's statement.

"Look," Vicki said, "God does miracles; there's no

question. All the enemy of God can do is copy the miracles. He fakes it. With the mind control Carpathia has, I wouldn't be surprised if he planted those thoughts about Fortunato being raised from the dead."

"But you heard him yourself," Shelly said. "He climbed out from the bottom of that building."

"Right," Vicki said, "and he claimed to have broken all kinds of bones and burst his lungs. Did those just heal over?"

Darrion spoke up. "The point isn't whether it's true or not," she said. "People are going to believe it. They're going to think Carpathia is some kind of Messiah himself."

Lionel and the others watched the speeches by Carpathia and Fortunato. Several outbursts of clapping and cheering were stopped by Commander Blancka. When it was over, the group rose to its feet. Everyone but Conrad.

"What's the matter with you?" Lionel said.

Conrad shook his head. "I'm just not in the rah-rah mood," he said.

"Didn't you hear?" Lionel said. "Carpathia actually raised somebody from the dead. Don't you know what that means?"

"Yeah, a new GC health care plan. Somebody dies, and Nicolae brings them to life again."

"You don't get it," Lionel said.

"I do get it," Conrad said. "I just have a hard time believing it. Let me ask you this. There were other dead people in that building who worked with Carpathia. If he's the wonderful leader everybody thinks he is, why did he only raise one person from the dead? Why not the whole bunch?"

Lionel stammered. He hadn't thought of that angle. Finally, he said, "You have to decide whether you're in or out."

Conrad shook his head. "I'm in. But only until I can find my brother."

———————————

It was evening when Judd and Pete neared New Hope Village Church. As Pete drove his motorcycle over chunks of asphalt and concrete, Judd looked at what once was a beautiful place of worship. Now, half the building was underground. The entire sanctuary appeared to have turned and was sitting at a weird angle.

The last time Judd had been in the church was at Bruce's funeral. How his life had changed since then. Now he was on the run from the Global Community.

"This is where my new life really started," Judd said. "After the disappearances, I met Bruce here."

"It's a shame. Looks like it was quite a church."

Judd got off the cycle and looked around the parking lot. Loretta's place was not far. He wondered if she was alive. And Vicki. Where could she be?

Pete broke Judd's silence. "I'm glad you made it back, and I hope you find what you're looking for."

"You're leaving?" Judd said.

"I want to check on that old guy at the gas station. We never got to tell him what you told me."

"You need to study and get grounded," Judd said. "Stay here."

"Can't. I have a few loose ends to tie and lots of people who need to hear what I know."

Judd put out his hand. "I hope this won't be the last time we see each other."

"It won't be," Pete said. "You can count on it."

8

AFTER an overnight stay in Indianapolis, Lionel and Conrad continued their flight to Chicago with Felicia and Melinda. Commander Blancka talked with his staff as they neared Glenview Naval Air Station.

Conrad tapped Lionel on the shoulder and motioned toward the commander. "Looks like something's up."

When they landed, the four kids hopped out, grabbed their belongings, and moved away from the chopper. A few minutes later Commander Blancka rushed up to them.

"We have a situation. I know you're prepared to work behind the scenes, but we need your help."

"What's up?" Lionel said.

"Looters. They're goin' wild. The GC needs all the help they can get. Are you up for it?"

"You bet, sir," Lionel said.

The others agreed. Commander Blancka told them to stay in radio contact and passed them to another GC officer. The man scoffed when he saw the kids. Commander Blancka bristled, and the guard escorted the four to a helipad. The chopper flew over a crumpled tollway and a river.

Conrad pointed to their left. "O'Hare's over there," he said. "Not much of it left."

They passed a forest preserve, then landed in a crumpled parking lot. A crooked sign said Woodfield Mall. The upper level of the huge building had collapsed. Several stores on the lower levels were intact. Lionel and the others walked over broken glass to get inside. Empty shelves and overturned tables littered store floors. The looters had done a job.

The guard stepped through water from a broken fountain and met another GC patrol. "I didn't know we were getting a bunch of kids," he muttered.

"You heard the commander," Lionel said. "We know what we're doing."

"If you four can contain this area," the patrol said, "it'll give the rest of us a chance to work some other problem spots."

"What happens if we see somebody stealing something?" Melinda said.

The guard rolled his eyes. "You could try to talk them out of it," the guard said, "but our orders are to shoot. I suggest you do the same."

Judd slept near New Hope Village Church. He awoke stiff and cold. The nearest house was Loretta's. He could tell someone had dug through the roof to get inside. A few garden tools lay at the back of the house. He shouted but no one answered.

He was amazed to find an empty crater where his own house had been. A meteor had struck it, and nothing was left but debris and the huge hole. In an open field he found the swing set he and his father had put together for his little brother and sister. Concrete was still attached to the foot of each post.

Judd bent to inspect the swings and found what he was looking for. He had written his initials in the concrete. On another leg of the swings he saw his little brother's handprint. Over it he had written "Marc." He saw the same on the next leg where Marcie had written her name and pushed her hand deep into the cement.

Judd knelt and inspected the last post. It was chipped, but he could still make out the letters "Da—." Judd put his hand in the imprint of his father's hand and closed his eyes. Judd's hand almost fit perfectly.

"I wish you were here now, Dad," Judd said. He thought of his father, brother, and sister. It seemed so long ago, like another world. It *was* another world.

Judd thought of his other family. Lionel, Ryan, Vicki, and Bruce. Judd guessed Ryan and Lionel would have stayed at his house. That would explain why Ryan was listed as dead. But how would Lionel have gotten away? Judd still held out hope for Ryan as he traced his way back to the church. After several wrong turns, he found the rubble of Vicki's place.

"Halt!" someone behind him shouted.

Judd turned to see a Global Community squad in a covered vehicle. "What are you doing?"

Judd knew the GC would shoot if he ran. He played it cool. "Looking for some friends of mine," Judd shouted.

"This area's been evacuated," a man said. "Check the shelters."

Judd gave a sigh of relief when the GC squad drove past him.

———————————

After the men flew away in the chopper, Lionel and the others paced in front of the darkened windows. One jewelry shop was completely gutted. Another that sold fine luggage had nothing left but some boxes high on the wall. Escalators tilted, and the silence was eerie.

"I hear they wasted Chicago at the start of the war," Conrad said. "Now this."

"What war?" Lionel said.

Conrad told Lionel the details of the war between the Global Community and the militia. "My brother said the GC was just waiting for a militia uprising. They wanted to blow them away and make it look like the Global Community was just defending themselves."

"Who's your brother?" Felicia said.

"His name is Taylor Graham," Conrad said. "Works for Maxwell Stahley in GC security."

"Stahley's dead," Felicia said. "You haven't heard?"

Conrad looked upset. "He was alive when they took me down South," Conrad said. "Was it a plane crash?"

"They found him in a building in some suburb," Felicia said.

Lionel held up a hand. The four stood in front of an upscale dress shop. "Somebody's in there," Lionel said.

"I see some things I wouldn't mind wearing," Melinda said. "But I don't see any looters."

Lionel climbed through the broken window. Glass crunched under his feet. He heard shuffling inside.

"Come on!" Lionel shouted to his friends. Lionel cupped his hands and yelled, "Halt! In the name of the Global Community, or we'll shoot."

"I'll cut through the next store and meet you in the back," Conrad whispered.

Melinda and Felicia were right behind Lionel, hurtling past the racks of expensive clothes. Lionel hit the ground and saw two people running for the rear exit.

"Stop right there or we'll shoot!" Lionel repeated.

The two kept running. Lionel pointed the gun to the ceiling and shot. Melinda screamed and lost her balance, sending Lionel headlong into a display.

"Are you OK?" Felicia said, helping Lionel up.

"Yeah," Lionel said, but he wasn't. He had a welt under his ear, and something was going on in his head. Things were coming back. About Chicago. About his life before the Global Community.

Vicki, Shelly, and Darrion were busy at the shelter. Vicki could tell the nurses appreciated the help. Hundreds of people poured in each day. Some were looking for a meal. Others were injured and needed medical help.

Vicki didn't want to think about the future. Each question made her stomach tie in knots. Where would they live? What would they do for money? She tried to concentrate and push the questions out of her mind, but they kept coming back.

Vicki heard Shelly shout first. Then Darrion called her name. Vicki asked the woman she was helping to stay where she was. She stepped out of the medical tent and spotted Darrion and Shelly. Both were smiling. Behind them was a man in dirty jeans with a few days' growth of beard.

"Vick," the man said.

"Judd?"

Judd ran to her. Vicki hugged him tightly.

"I've been looking all over," Judd said. "I'm so glad I found you."

"The GC wouldn't tell us anything. How'd you get away?"

"Long story," Judd said. "Is there someplace we can talk?"

Shelly winked at Vicki and said she would take over in the medical tent. Vicki and Judd walked toward the church.

Lionel ran out the back door, his head pounding. Felicia and Melinda were behind him. Lionel went from the darkened back room to bright sunlight. When his eyes adjusted, he saw two men struggling with Conrad. Lionel pointed the gun but couldn't get a clear shot. Before he could reach his friend, one of the men had wrestled the gun from Conrad.

"Stay right there if you want to live," the man said.

"Put the gun down," Lionel said.

"Yeah, right," the man said. "Who do you kids think you are anyway, the cops?"

"We're with the Global Community," Lionel said, keying the microphone on his shoulder. He gave their position and requested help.

"That was a mistake," the man with the gun said. He leveled the gun at Lionel.

Lionel fired at the knee of the gunman. The man stared at him, then shook his head. To Lionel's surprise, the man dropped the gun and walked toward the parking lot. Lionel knew he couldn't have missed, but the man kept walking.

Conrad scampered to retrieve the gun.

"Stay where you are!" Lionel yelled.

The men kept walking. Lionel heard a chopper. Above the building he saw Commander Blancka give him a thumbs-up. Lionel motioned toward the men, but the commander ignored him. The chopper landed nearby, and the commander jumped out.

"They're getting away, sir," Lionel said.

"No, they're not," Commander Blancka said. "They're being debriefed."

"What's going on?" Conrad said.

"It's one thing to know how to fire a gun and hit a

target," the commander said. "It's another to use it against a person."

"You mean that whole thing was staged?" Melinda said.

"Our guns were loaded with blanks," Lionel said.

"It was your last test, and you passed," the commander said.

Conrad looked depressed. "I don't think I did very well."

"We put you in a situation you weren't prepared for," Commander Blancka said. "Hopefully you learned something."

The commander ushered them to the chopper. "Here's where we have you set up," he said, pointing to a map. "Mount Prospect is just east of us. We're putting all four of you there. We've heard reports of some resistance in the high school.

"As I told you, school as you've known it won't exist in the coming months. What we hope you'll do is get situated and blend in with the community."

"Where will we stay?" Lionel said.

"Just like everybody else who lives there," the commander said. "You'll stay in a shelter until homes and apartments can be rebuilt."

Judd told Vicki about the earthquake and watching Taylor Graham fall to his death. It felt like Judd could tell her anything. He explained about the mark of true believers, and Vicki gasped when she saw the mark on Judd's forehead.

"You're right," Vicki said. "We all have the mark."

Vicki listened and asked questions about Pete and how Judd made it home. "You're lucky to be alive," she said.

"I feel like God's been watching out for me the whole time. What happened with you?"

Vicki explained about the *Underground* and how Mrs. Jenness had caught her. Judd couldn't believe Vicki's ordeal on the bridge.

"And I thought I had it tough," Judd said. "What about Lionel and Ryan?"

Vicki looked away.

Judd took her by the shoulders and looked into her eyes. "I read something on a Web site, but I want to hear it from you. Is Ryan dead?"

Vicki pursed her lips. "I feel like it's my fault. I told him to stay in the house. If he'd have been outside maybe he'd still be alive."

"Then he is dead?"

"They found him in the basement of my house. His back was hurt, and he had some kind of infection."

Vicki's voice broke. She put her head on Judd's shoulder. "I found him at a makeshift hospital. He'd written me a note the night before."

"Do you still have it?" Judd said.

Vicki pulled the crumpled piece of paper from her back pocket. "I got to talk with him before he died."

Judd opened the paper. He wiped away a tear as he read it, then sat on a fallen tree. "It doesn't seem real," he said.

"I had to get help bringing his body here." She pointed to the church. Judd saw a fresh mound of earth. Phoenix was perched on top.

Judd walked slowly toward the grave, then knelt beside it and stroked the dog's back. Phoenix whimpered and put his head on Judd's knee.

"It's not your fault," Judd said to Vicki. "You were just trying to protect him from the GC."

"But he died! And he's never coming back!"

Judd sat with the feeling. First his family. Then Bruce. Now it was Ryan. Judd kept seeing Ryan's face. He had called him a little guy for so long. He thought of Ryan's fights with Lionel, his love for Phoenix, and their trip to Israel together. That trip had shown Judd what Ryan was made of.

"You haven't told me about Lionel."

"Somebody from his family came and took him down South," Vicki said.

"I thought his family was gone," Judd said.

"Apparently a few of them were living and wanted him home. We haven't heard anything since he left."

"Weird," Judd said.

"At least you're back," Vicki said.

"But I don't know how long I can stay," Judd said. "The GC network will be up and running soon. The first place they'll look will be here. I think we need a permanent place to hide."

"You must be starving," Vicki said. "Let's go back to the shelter."

"Gimme a minute with him, OK?" Judd said.

Vicki walked to the edge of the parking lot while Judd put a hand on Ryan's grave.

"I feel real stupid," Judd said. "I mean, I know you can't hear me. So this is probably more for me than it is you.

"I'm sorry. Sorry I treated you like a kid. You were the best of us. You loved God with everything you had. You went out and found those Bibles. You saved me and Vicki that time under the L tracks.

"I'm gonna miss you. And it hurts like everything to let you go. But I know I have to say good-bye. I just wish I could see you one more time and tell you. . . .

"You were like . . . no, you *were* my brother. You are my brother. And I'm gonna see you again."

Vicki patted Judd on the back when he walked back to her. "I've done that a couple of times myself."

They moved toward the shelter. Judd said he would sleep outside near a fire. When they reached camp, Vicki relieved Shelly in the medical tent. As Vicki helped an elderly patient roll over, someone in the corner shouted, "That's her!"

Vicki finished with the patient and hurried to see what the problem was. Vicki finally realized the girl was talking about her.

"Nurse, get a guard," the girl said. "She's the one. That's the girl who killed Mrs. Jenness!"

VICKI was stunned. It wasn't true, but there was no way to prove her innocence. Anyone who might have seen her trying to rescue Mrs. Jenness could easily have thought she was trying to get rid of the woman.

A nurse came and quieted the shouting girl.

"I'm telling you, she's the one who offed Mrs. Jenness."

The nurse looked at Vicki. "Do you mind telling me what this is about?"

Shelly whispered to Vicki, "That's Joyce from Nicolae High. Let me see what I can do."

Vicki finally recognized her. Shelly tried to calm her, but Joyce kept shouting and calling Vicki a murderer.

"Were you in a car with Mrs. Jenness?" the nurse said.

"Yes. The earthquake hit as we were crossing a bridge. But I tried to save her, not kill her."

Joyce spoke up. "I was there when Mrs. Jenness drove away with you. I know you were in that car. This morning

91

I met a lady who was near the bridge when it collapsed. She described Mrs. Jenness's car perfectly and said when it went in the water there was a girl on top trying to push Mrs. Jenness back inside."

"That's not true!" Vicki said.

"She killed her!"

"I was trying to save her life."

"Calm down," the nurse said.

"I want a GC guard notified right now," Joyce said. "She's a murderer!"

Vicki saw Judd talking to a woman in the corner. A moment later the woman walked up and demanded silence. Vicki saw a smudge on her forehead. "There will be no more fighting about this." The woman looked at Vicki. "You go back to your tent."

"If you won't do anything about it," Joyce shouted, "I'm going to the authorities!"

"Give her something to calm her," the woman said.

"No!" Joyce shouted as the nurse grabbed a needle. "I'll get you for this, Byrne!"

Lionel and the others were flown to Mount Prospect by helicopter. They checked in at a shelter but were turned away.

"Head over to Nicolae High," a worker said. "They have more room there."

"That's where we're supposed to wind up anyway," Conrad said.

While walking, Lionel looked for anything familiar.

The streets and buildings were a mess. But the incident at the mall had stirred him. He now recalled the GC attack on Chicago. He remembered the day it happened and the sound of the bombers overhead. The explosions. The fear he had as he listened. But he couldn't remember the people, and he knew the people were the most important part of the puzzle.

"Do you still have those diaries?" Lionel asked Conrad.

"Didn't have room to pack them," Conrad said. "I brought your Bible, though. Been reading it."

Lionel looked at the inscription in the Bible as he walked. *Who is Ryan?* Lionel thought. *And what does he have to do with all this?*

"You think you're gonna find your friends?" Conrad said.

"The thought's crossed my mind," Lionel said.

When they neared Nicolae High, Lionel stopped the others. "We have to be careful not to come on too strong. We don't want to try and impress people with how important we are."

"Is that what you think we want to do?" Felicia said.

"I'm not saying—"

"You're not the boss of everybody," Melinda interrupted. She rolled her eyes.

"Like it or not, the commander put me in charge," Lionel said. "And I want it understood. We might not have anything to report for months. It's like going undercover."

"Give us some credit," Felicia said. "We went through the training too."

They walked in silence to Nicolae High. Lionel talked with a staff worker. "This place has been turned into a morgue," the man said. "We've had a hard time keeping track of all the bodies."

"Where are people staying?" Conrad said.

"We have four shelters in the area," the man said, pointing them out on a crudely drawn map. "Get to any of these and you'll find food and a place to stay warm."

"Are any teachers or administrators of the school still around?" Lionel asked.

"Plenty of them. They're under all those sheets."

Judd called a meeting of the Young Trib Force that evening. He commended Vicki, Shelly, and Darrion for the way they had handled themselves during the past few days.

"It's clear we need a place to hide," Judd said. "The GC will be looking for me, and this thing with Joyce could blow up in Vicki's face."

"What's the deal with her anyway?" Darrion said.

"I knew her from school," Shelly said. "After the disappearances, we hung out together. When I became a Christian, she turned on me."

"I remember talking with her," Vicki said. "Joyce said she believed Jesus came back. She thought it was the only explanation."

"So she's a believer?" Darrion said.

"No," Vicki said. "She said if the disappearances were God's idea of how to do things, she wanted no part of it.

Then she told me not to waste my breath trying to convince her."

"So she's chosen not to believe," Darrion said.

"Exactly," Vicki said.

"That may be why she's trying to pin murder on you," Judd said. "She must hate anything that reminds her of the truth."

Judd put together a list of people they knew who were missing or dead. They were all concerned about John and Mark. Vicki asked Judd to explain what he knew about the mark on their foreheads.

Judd noticed a strange young man walking toward them.

"Vicki!" Charlie shouted. "They kicked me out. Boom, just like that, out the door, on the street, no more Charlie in the store, or hospital, or whatever it is. Said I had to find my own place to stay."

"What about the nurse?" Vicki said.

"She got in trouble," Charlie said. "Lost a patient. I think it was that kid I carried for you."

"Oh, no," Vicki said.

"Oh yeah," Charlie said. "They kicked me out and told me not to come back."

Vicki introduced Charlie to the rest of the group. Charlie shook hands with Judd, but his hand was limp.

"What're you guys looking at each other's heads for?" Charlie said.

Judd looked at Vicki. Vicki shrugged.

"We're talking about . . . something that we all have in common," Judd said.

"You're in a club?" Charlie said. "Can I be in too?"

"Well," Judd said, "it's not really a club. It's more like—"

"You guys look like friends," Charlie said. "Happy. I want to join. Now what's with your head?"

"We all have a mark," Vicki said. "It means we're for real."

Charlie squinted at Vicki and looked her over. "You guys are crazy. There's nothin' on your head."

"You can't see it," Vicki said. "Only those who believe can see it."

"This is really weird," Charlie said.

Judd wondered if they were telling Charlie too much. He took Vicki aside.

"He's the one who helped me carry Ryan," Vicki said.

"I just don't want to take a chance and tell him stuff that might get us in trouble."

"How can we keep it from him? Isn't that why we're here?"

"Of course it is, but we have to make sure we can trust the people we tell."

"Oh yeah," Vicki said. "I haven't seen that in the Bible lately. Besides, you were talking about this stuff to a woman who's with Enigma Babylon One World Faith."

"She was asking questions," Judd said. "I had no choice."

"Charlie's asking questions too."

Charlie interrupted and pointed to Shelly. "That girl says if I believe like you guys, I get something on my head too. Can I get it now, or do I have to pay something?"

Lionel and Conrad unpacked two tents the Global Community had given them while Melinda and Felicia checked out the shelter for food.

"Recognize anything around here?" Conrad said.

Lionel was cautious. "Some stuff came back about the war when we were at the mall, but none of this looks familiar."

"How about the high school?" Conrad said.

Lionel shook his head.

"It was pretty messed up. Maybe we'll find somebody who knew you."

Felicia and Melinda were out of breath when they returned.

"Where's the food?" Lionel said.

"Just got a lead on something," Felicia said. "I met a girl in the medical tent who says somebody committed a murder during the earthquake."

"That's out of our league," Conrad said.

"The girl says the person who killed this lady is one of those religious nuts we're supposed to be looking for," Felicia said. "And get this. The girl was accused of trying to push her beliefs on people at Nicolae High."

"Sounds like it'd be worth checking out," Conrad said.

"How'd you find this girl?" Lionel said. "She just walked up to you and spilled her guts?"

"She said nobody's listening to her," Melinda said. "I told her we were with the Global Community."

"You what?!" Lionel said.

"I didn't say we were officially with them or

anything," Melinda said. "I just said we could look into it if she wanted."

Lionel shook his head. "Let's go back over there and get the story."

———————————————

Judd thought Charlie seemed a little odd. Slow. He looked away when he talked to Judd, and he had a funny walk. But Vicki was right. Those things didn't disqualify him from knowing about God.

"First thing I need you to know," Judd said, "is that this isn't a club you join. Do you get that?"

"Not a club, got it. What do I have to do to get one of those things on my head?"

Judd rubbed his neck. "You can't do this just because you want a thing on your head, Charlie."

"Come on, tell me. I want to see everybody else's."

"Then we have to talk seriously about what we believe."

"Believe about what?"

"About God. About what happened to the people who disappeared."

"My sister got killed in the big shake," Charlie said.

"That's what Vicki said. I'm sorry."

"They kicked me out of the store where she worked. Told me not to come back."

"You can stay with us for a while."

"Right. So what am I supposed to believe?"

Judd sighed. "Did your sister ever take you to church?"

Lionel told the others to wait outside while he talked with Joyce. "I don't want it looking like we're here on some kind of official business."

Joyce was still groggy from the medication, but she was able to talk. She repeated her story, then added, "The girl's name is Vicki Byrne."

Lionel thought about the name. It sounded familiar.

"I was near the office when Mrs. Jenness took Vicki out to the car," Joyce said. "I know she killed her. She's probably bolted by now."

"Why would she kill your principal?" Lionel said. He wrote the name *Mrs. Jenness* on a piece of paper.

Joyce cocked her head. "Do I know you? You don't go to Nicolae High, do you?"

"Not anymore," Lionel said. "Finish your story."

"Mrs. Jenness had the goods on her. She found something and was taking Vicki away."

Lionel noticed someone on the other side of the tent. A girl with red hair was looking at him. She smiled when Lionel spotted her and waved. Then she rushed toward him.

Joyce sat up in bed and screamed, "That's her!"

The girl with red hair stopped, then turned and ran out of the tent.

Vicki was out of breath when she found Judd. She interrupted his conversation with Charlie. "I saw him. He's here!"

"Who?" Judd said.

"Lionel! He was in the tent talking with Joyce."

Judd stood. "I'll be back," he said to Charlie.

"That's good," Charlie said. "I can wait. Go find your friend. I'm cool with that."

Judd wondered if it really was Lionel. His heart raced as he neared the medical tent.

"Go get her!" Joyce shouted.

"She won't get far," Lionel said.

"Your friend said you're with the Global Community. You can do something about her, can't you?"

Lionel frowned. "Sometimes my friends get carried away."

"But she told me if this really was a murder, the GC would look into it. She promised."

Lionel studied Joyce. It was possible they had been in the same hallway together only a few weeks ago at Nicolae High. Her locker could have been a few feet from his own.

"Don't you believe me?" Joyce said. "She's a murderer!"

10

JUDD recognized Lionel right away. Lionel wore different clothes and seemed surprised when Judd approached.

"Good to see you again," Judd said, smiling.

Lionel backed away. "Do I know you?"

"Of course you do."

Lionel paused. "Are you Ryan?"

Judd laughed. "This is a joke, right? It's Judd, remember?"

"That guy was in on it too," Joyce said. "Judd Thompson. Last year at graduation he gave this speech, and the GC—"

"I'll handle this," Lionel said. He turned to Judd. "How do I know you?"

Judd shook his head. "You stayed in my house. I drove you to school. We ate meals together. Went to church. Don't you remember any of that?"

Lionel looked down. "I remember reading something about you in my diary."

Vicki couldn't stand it any longer. She didn't care about Joyce, she was going to see her friend. She rushed up and gave Lionel a hug.

"That's her," Joyce shouted. "Somebody arrest her!"

"Enough," Lionel said.

Lionel bristled and Vicki pulled away.

"What's wrong?" Vicki said.

"He doesn't remember us," Judd said.

"That's crazy," Vicki said.

"I had an accident during the earthquake. I could remember stuff about the camp, but not anything before that."

"What camp?" Vicki said. "You went down South to be with your family, didn't you?"

Lionel frowned.

"A man from your family came to our school," Vicki said. "You had a hard time deciding, but you finally went. We didn't hear any more from you."

"I demand you do something," Joyce said.

Lionel held up a hand. "Give me a minute to think, OK?"

Lionel walked away. Images and thoughts swirled in his head. The school. A man taking him to a seedy hotel in Chicago. A van ride. Getting chased through a swamp. It was all coming back slowly and in pieces.

But Lionel also saw Commander Blancka's stern face. Lionel had pledged to serve the Global Community. If Joyce was telling the truth, he should report Judd and Vicki. If they were really his friends, he should help them. He felt trapped.

———————————

Judd and Vicki moved away from Joyce.

"What's going on with Lionel?" Vicki said.

"We can't worry about him. We have to figure out what's best for us. Maybe we should get out of here before something bad happens."

"And leave Lionel?" Vicki said. "No way."

Another boy joined Lionel, and the two returned. "This is Conrad," Lionel said.

Judd stared at the boy. He recalled Taylor Graham talking about a brother named Conrad.

"What's your last name?" Judd said.

"Why do you want to know?"

"Is it Graham?"

Conrad looked startled, then composed himself. "How'd you know that?"

"I knew your brother," Judd said.

Conrad's eyes widened. "You knew Taylor? How is he?"

Lionel held up a hand. "You can talk later. Right now I want to get to the bottom of the murder question."

"You don't actually believe her, do you?" Vicki said.

"I don't know what to believe," Lionel said. "Step outside the tent. I want to get more information."

103

Vicki walked away with Lionel. Joyce shouted behind them. "Why are you taking information? Are you some kind of police officer?"

"I'm a citizen of the Global Community like you," Lionel said.

Vicki took Lionel by the shoulders. "Look at me. You're talking crazy. Don't you remember? Your mother worked for *Global Weekly.* Then your whole family disappeared. I knew your sister, Clarice. We rode the bus together."

Lionel put away his notebook and pen.

"You and I met Bruce on the same day," Vicki said.

"Go back," Lionel said. "Tell me more about my family."

Judd walked outside with Conrad.

"You really knew my brother?" Conrad said.

"I'll tell you about your brother if you'll tell me about Lionel," Judd said.

Conrad nodded. "We've spent the last few weeks in a Global Community camp down South. They trained us to become GC Morale Monitors."

"Morale Monitors?" Judd said.

"We're supposed to blend in and report anyone suspicious to the GC command."

"Suspicious?"

"Yeah, like religious fanatics who talk about Jesus coming back," Conrad said.

Judd scowled. "Why doesn't he remember us?"

"Probably a combination of the mind control the GC used and the fact that he got conked on the head. Pretty much wiped out his hard drive, if you know what I mean. Before the accident, he was talking about going along with the GC program until he could get back up here to his friends. Now he's pretty much following them lockstep."

"Why are you telling me this? You're one of them, right?"

Conrad glanced about. "I've been reading Lionel's Bible and some of the materials he brought with him. I even got on the Internet and found that rabbi's Web site. I want to know more."

The more Lionel listened, the more sense Vicki made. His family had disappeared and left him behind.

"Didn't I have a relative?" Lionel said. "A guy?"

"Uncle André."

"Yeah," Lionel said. He closed his eyes as Vicki continued.

"He's dead. He had a run-in with some bad guys. That's when Judd took us all into his house. We had meetings just about every day with our pastor, Bruce Barnes."

Lionel shook his head, his eyes still shut. "I'm not remembering any of that."

"You and Ryan used to fight like cats and do—"

"Who did you say?"

"Ryan. You and Ryan used to fight over the stupidest things."

"Where is he?" Lionel said.

"Come with me," Vicki said.

Judd told Conrad the story of meeting Taylor Graham and flying to Israel. "We didn't know it at the time, but your brother was trying to protect you."

"He knew I was being held."

"Yes, but he protected us too. He was a good man."

"Was?"

"I can't be sure, but I think your brother didn't make it through the earthquake."

Conrad frowned. Judd described Taylor's fall into the gorge. It was the last Judd saw of him.

"If anybody could survive that, it's my brother," Conrad said. "Where'd Lionel and the girl go?"

Lionel sensed Vicki and Judd were telling the truth. In the back of his mind he saw Commander Blancka. The man would want to know everything. If Lionel contacted them, it would only be minutes before the GC converged on them.

"Do you know those two following us?" Vicki said.

Lionel turned and saw Melinda and Felicia. "They're in our group."

When they reached the church, Vicki led Lionel to Ryan's grave. Phoenix still stood watch, jumping up and growling when the group drew closer.

"Ryan's name was in my Bible," Lionel said.

"He found a bunch of them and gave you one. This is his dog, Phoenix. He named him that because—"

"—because he found him in the ashes," Lionel said.

"You remember?"

"No, just the story about the bird rising." Lionel kicked at the dirt around the grave. "Maybe if I saw his face. Do you have a picture?"

Vicki took Lionel by the shoulders again. "Look at my forehead. Do you see that mark?"

Lionel shook his head. "I've already looked. I don't have that on my head."

"You do," Vicki said. "I can see it. Look at my fore-head."

Lionel squinted, leaned closer, and said, "Yeah, it looks like a bruise or a smudge."

"When you asked God to come into your life, he sealed you. This is the sign of that seal. He's not gonna let you go because you bumped your head."

Lionel put his head in his hands and sat on the grave. "This is too much."

"Do you believe me?" Vicki said.

"It doesn't matter whether I do or don't. I have to file a report."

"You don't have to. Think about it. If we're really enemies of the GC and you're our friend, you're an enemy of the GC."

"What if you're lying?"

"Why would I?"

"To get out of the murder rap."

"It's Joyce's word against mine," Vicki said. "You can't believe her."

"Not true," Felicia said, coming up behind them. "We found the other witness."

"Where?" Lionel said.

"At the next shelter," Felicia said. "She told us she saw Vicki on top of Mrs. Jenness's car, trying to push her under the water. And it worked. The woman's dead. They just found her car this morning. Her body's still in it."

"What are you going to do, Lionel?" Melinda said.

"Just leave us alone a minute, OK?"

Melinda and Felicia walked away. Lionel rammed his fist into the grave. Phoenix barked and jumped up. His ears stood straight.

Lionel pulled Vicki close. "If I turn you in and you really are my friends, I'll have betrayed you. And I'll have betrayed the memory of my friend."

Lionel grabbed a fistful of dirt and held it in his hand. Judd and Conrad came close.

"You have to believe them," Conrad whispered to Lionel.

Lionel rubbed his eyes. Images flashed through his brain. A boy on a bike riding next to him. Running through a school hallway at night.

Lionel looked up. "We fought about something, didn't we?"

"You and Ryan fought about everything," Judd said.

"We were putting something in the back of a car," Lionel said, his eyes darting back and forth. "The other kid grabbed me around the neck and wrestled me to the ground."

"You were loading Bibles," Judd said. "I had to separate you."

"He had a stash somewhere. . . ." Lionel said, his voice quickening. "He'd go off and wouldn't come back for hours."

"We found it in the church," Vicki said. "Hundreds of them were stacked up in there."

". . . and the man showed us a tape . . . Bruce . . . it was right in there that I finally understood about God. . . ."

Lionel felt the emotion rising. Things were getting clearer, like a blindfold suddenly lifting. The closeness of his friends had brought everything back.

Lionel looked at Judd. "The rabbi?"

"We don't know where he is," Judd said, "but we assume he survived the quake."

Vicki handed Lionel the note Ryan had written. Lionel scanned it, then fell beside the grave of his friend. "I wasn't here for him."

Melinda and Felicia returned. "Excuse us, but we've got a situation here," Melinda said, pointing to Vicki and Judd. "She's accused of murder, and there's evidence he's against the Global Community."

"There's no way Vicki would have killed Mrs. Jenness," Lionel said.

"Are you taking their side?" Felicia said.

"I just want to sort this thing out," Lionel said.

"Let them explain their case to Commander Blancka," Melinda said.

"I'm not reporting anything until—"

Lionel was interrupted by the *thwock-thwock-thwock* of rotor blades. He could hear the chopper but couldn't see it yet.

"We filed a report a few minutes ago," Melinda said.

Lionel looked at Vicki and Judd. The memories were flooding back now. He was finally home, finally back with the people he loved. And they were in more danger than they had ever been in before.

11

LIONEL saw the chopper and had to do something. Judd and Vicki looked scared. *They should be*, Lionel thought. *I have to get rid of Melinda and Felicia.*

The two Morale Monitors started toward the chopper, then turned.

"You two go and get Blancka," Lionel said. "We'll let him sort out this mess."

"They could run," Melinda said, nodding toward Judd and Vicki.

"I'm staying," Felicia said.

Lionel grabbed his gun. "If they run, I'll shoot 'em."

The girls hesitated.

"Conrad and I can handle these two," Lionel said. "Go! The commander will be waiting."

Melinda and Felicia ran toward the chopper, and Lionel put away his gun. "We have to hurry. Conrad, I'm assuming you're with us."

"I don't know about this God stuff," Conrad said, "but I'm with you."

"Vick and I need to get out of here," Judd said. "Question is whether you guys go with us."

"We should work behind the scenes for now," Lionel said.

"You're crazy," Conrad said. "I don't want to stay here."
Lionel shook his head.

"It's almost dark," Judd said. "They won't be able to see us soon."

"We could hide or find what's left of my house," Vicki said.

"No way," Conrad said. "The chopper's high-tech. Lights, night vision, even heat sensors. They'll spot you in two minutes."

"Time's running out," Vicki said. "If we stay here, that commander guy—"

Judd cut her off. "Ryan's place. Under the church."

"You think we can get in there?" Vicki said.

"It's worth a shot," Judd said. "Could the chopper find us under all that concrete?"

"Yeah," Conrad said. "It wouldn't be easy, but they'd still spot you."

"Not if they think we ran," Judd said. "You two cover for us and send them the wrong way."

"If they'll believe us," Conrad said.

Judd took Lionel's flashlight. It was pitch black inside the church basement.

"You sure this is where Ryan's hideout was?" Vicki said.

"We're close," Judd said.

"Look stable?" Lionel said.

"Can't tell," Judd said, pulling at loose stones and dirt.

"Another tremor and you guys will be smashed," Conrad said.

Judd held the light while Vicki climbed through the opening. A block fell near Vicki with a sickening thud and she froze. Gathering herself, she continued.

When she reached the bottom she called out, "There's an old steel desk down here that should protect us."

Judd followed her inside. When he heard chopper blades, he turned. "What about you guys?"

Lionel pushed him. "We're OK."

"No," Judd said. "If those girls find us gone, they'll know you helped." Judd climbed out of the hole.

Lionel looked over his shoulder. "Get back inside!"

Conrad held out his gun to Judd.

"What?"

"Take it and smack me underneath the eye," Conrad said. "I'll tell them you overpowered me."

"I can't hit you."

"You're saving us both," Conrad said.

Judd took the gun and carefully hit Conrad just under his eye.

Conrad frowned. "My grandmother can hit harder than that." But his eyes watered and a red mark rose on his cheek.

"Get in there!" Lionel said, ripping the radio from

Conrad's shoulder and tossing it into the hole. "Sit tight and keep an ear on that. We'll be in touch."

Judd climbed into the darkness and followed Vicki's voice to the steel desk.

A shot rang out. Then two more.

"What was that?" Vicki said.

"Lionel," Judd guessed. "Hope he knows what he's doing."

Lionel had keyed his microphone when he fired. He wanted the commander to believe he and Conrad were hot after Judd and Vicki. But he also wanted to scare Phoenix away. It worked. Phoenix darted into the rubble of the neighborhood and disappeared.

Lionel keyed his mike. "This is Washington! The suspects are getting away! Graham got knocked down!"

Commander Blancka sounded enraged. "What's going on down there?"

"The guy hit him, sir," Lionel said, waving for Conrad to run with him. Lionel was out of breath. "He grabbed Conrad's gun! I got a couple of shots off!"

Lionel heard Melinda protest in the background. Commander Blancka said, "Where are they now?"

"We're in pursuit," Lionel said. "East of the ruined church. Send the chopper!"

Silence.

Come on, Lionel thought, *believe me!*

A few moments later the commander barked, "Washington and Graham, bring it in."

114

"They're getting away!"

"That's an order!"

Judd squeezed under the desk with Vicki. He turned the radio down. The dust made him cough. It felt good to be close to Vicki again.

There was a long silence. Vicki finally spoke. "I can't believe Ryan's not coming back. Why would God let that happen?"

Judd shook his head. "I remember how hard it was for Ryan when Bruce died. It was hard on all of us, but him especially. Now I know how the little guy felt."

"He hated you calling him that," Vicki said.

Judd nodded. "He had a lot of heart. He never gave up."

Vicki sniffed, and Judd could tell she was wiping her eyes. "Sometimes it feels like God doesn't care," she said. "Like he's a million miles away."

Judd's leg cramped and he scooted lower under the desk. He braced himself on the bottom of the desk drawer and felt paper taped to the underside. Carefully, he loosened a thick packet.

"What is it?" Vicki said.

Judd put the envelope on the floor and cupped his hands around the end of the flashlight. In the dim light Judd saw Ryan's name on the front of the envelope. Judd tore it open and looked inside.

"Verses," Judd said as Vicki held the light. "Bruce's handwriting."

Judd read aloud, "Ryan, if you ever lose hope, this will help you. Isaiah 40:30-31."

Even youths will become exhausted, and young men will give up. But those who wait on the Lord will find new strength. They will fly high on wings like eagles. They will run and not grow weary. They will walk and not faint.

Judd stuffed the envelope in his pocket. "There's a whole stack of those. And stuff Ryan wrote about talking to people about Christ."

"We'll read it later, right?" Vicki said.

"For sure."

It was dark when Lionel and Conrad reached the commander. Melinda and Felicia stood near him with arms folded.

Before the commander spoke Lionel said, "Start east of the church."

"We'll handle it," the commander said, inspecting Conrad's eye. "How'd you get this?"

"Guy hit me with my own gun," Conrad said. "Made Lionel put his down too."

"Lucky he didn't kill you," the commander said. "Where's your radio, Conrad?"

"Must have lost it in the struggle."

Felicia smirked. "Or maybe you two gave it to them."

Lionel turned on her. "We almost get killed, and you—"

"Enough!" Commander Blancka said. He radioed the

chopper pilot. "Search the area. Let us know when you have something."

"I'm telling you, sir," Felicia said, "these two were like big pals with Lionel. Why wouldn't they take his gun?"

"How should I know?" Lionel shot back.

"He's helping them," Felicia said.

"Enough," the commander said.

"Sir, request permission to help in the search," Lionel said.

The commander said, "You're here at base until this gets straightened out."

"But, sir—"

"You're staying. Is that clear?"

The radio squawked. "Got something, sir."

Vicki held her breath as the chopper flew overhead. Judd whispered, "Sorry to get this close, but the smaller we are the better."

"It's OK."

Vicki was glad Judd was back and safe, but their troubles were starting again. She had told God she would do anything to help others come to know him, but she wanted just one day where everyone she loved was safe. Every time she thought of Ryan she felt a pain in her chest.

The chopper hovered, then turned south and away from them.

"What happens if they catch us?" Vicki said.

Judd put his head against the desk and sighed. "Lionel's smart. He'll lead them the other way."

"Then where do we go?" Vicki said. "Every place we know is flattened. The GC are crawling all over the shelters. They're sure to spot us there."

"How about Darrion's house?" Judd said. "That bunker Mr. Stahley built under the hill was like a steel fortress. If the hill hasn't collapsed around it, we might be able to get inside."

"That's pretty far away," Vicki said. "I don't see how we can get there on foot."

"We'll have to find a vehicle," Judd said. "What do you think?"

"I'm willing to give it a shot. We just need to—"

Judd put a finger to Vicki's lips. "Someone's outside."

12

JUDD'S heart beat furiously. Someone was trying to get in. Dirt and rocks fell.

Judd picked up a stone. He wouldn't be taken prisoner by the GC again. Judd thought about running. If the chopper pinpointed their position, they were easy targets.

Vicki grabbed Judd's arm and whispered, "What if it's Lionel?"

Judd shook his head. "He would have said something."

Judd eased out for a better look. The ghostly moon glowed through the hole. Suddenly, a figure appeared in the entrance. Judd braced himself and tried not to breathe. The figure stepped toward the hideout, then backed away.

A high-pitched whine, then breathing. Judd stood. "Be right back," he said.

"Don't," Vicki said.

But Judd crawled away. He returned and plopped Phoenix down between them.

"Hello, boy!" she said. Phoenix licked Vicki's face.

Judd placed Phoenix on top of the desk and said, "Stay!" Phoenix put his head down and whimpered.

"Maybe they'll see him and not us," Judd said.

"I wish he'd brought us something to eat," Vicki said.

Lionel stayed with Commander Blancka's aide while the others followed the chopper. He and the aide set up a tent for the commander.

A few minutes later the group trudged in. Conrad winked at Lionel. The commander held Vicki's friend Charlie by the shirt and dragged him inside.

When he first met the boy, Lionel thought Charlie was strange. Charlie wouldn't look him in the eye. His hands and feet were always moving.

"I told you I don't know where they are," Charlie said nervously.

"Let's start over," the commander said. "How do you know them?"

"I met the girl at the store, or the hospital, whatever you want to call it," Charlie said. "My sister was killed in the big earthshake. So I went over—"

"Focus!" the commander shouted. "How did you know this guy and girl?"

"I helped the girl," Charlie said, shaking. "We carried the kid over here and buried him one night. Real spooky."

"You buried a body?" the commander said.

"She asked me to help, so I did."

The commander looked to Melinda and Felicia. "Is that the girl accused of murder?"

"Yes, sir," Melinda said. "Sounds like more than one."

Lionel knew Vicki hadn't killed Mrs. Jenness, and to think she had harmed Ryan was crazy. But he couldn't say anything.

Conrad tugged Lionel's sleeve and nodded toward the door. "Back in a few," he whispered. "Cover for me."

Lionel nodded. Conrad slipped into the night as the commander continued with Charlie. "What did you do after you helped them bury the body?"

"I talked with that guy about his head," Charlie said.

"His head?"

"They had a club and I wanted to join. If you made it, they put something on your head that people outside the club couldn't see. If I believed like they do I'd get a thing on my head. Something about God and how all the people disappeared."

Lionel was sweating. Charlie knew Vicki and Judd were his friends. Would he tell the commander? Lionel tried to stay out of Charlie's sight.

"I got kicked out of the store where my sister worked," Charlie continued, "so I came here. They told me to wait, and I did till that big helichopper came. Didn't like all the noise. I ran away."

"And you have no idea where they are now?" the commander said.

"Last I saw they were down by that kid's grave. The

121

girl cried. She gave me this." Charlie held up a Bible. "I think she was real sorry about him dying."

"Sorry for killing him," Melinda said, "or sorry she might get caught."

Lionel fumed.

The commander threw the Bible in the corner. "We'll go to the church." He looked for Conrad.

"He went to get his eye checked, sir," Lionel said.

"Keep an eye on that guy," the commander told Lionel. "Send Graham our way when he gets back."

Judd told Vicki more about his escape from the GC. "I told the people in the cave my name. I figure they passed it on to the GC."

"But the quake knocked out most of the communication lines," Vicki said.

"They're going up all over," Judd said. "It's like Carpathia was ready for this. The information will get back that I'm not dead. If they catch me now, who knows where they'll send me?"

Phoenix growled and the hair on his back stood straight. "Easy, boy," Judd said. "We need you right where you are."

Someone fell into the room with a thud. Phoenix barked, and Judd and Vicki stared into the beam of a flashlight.

"Good," Conrad said. "I thought you might have run." He brought them up-to-date.

"That Charlie is bad news," Judd said.

122

"He's sweet," Vicki said. "He deserved to hear the truth."

Judd said, "Conrad, you'd better get back before they miss you."

"Not yet," Conrad said. He sat cross-legged in front of the desk. "By daylight we might be able to move you."

"You think it'll be safe then?" Judd said.

"Lionel will have a plan." Conrad scooted closer. "I also came down here because I want to know more."

"About what?" Vicki said.

"About God. You know, the forehead stuff."

Phoenix sat up again and bristled.

"Guess we can't talk now," Conrad said. "Later?"

"I don't think we'll be getting much sleep," Judd said.

"If we have to run," Vicki said, "tell Lionel we'll try to make it to the Stahley house. He should tell Darrion and Shelly to meet us there."

"I don't know where that is, but Lionel will, right?" Conrad said.

"Right. Darrion can lead you there if she needs to."

"Sit tight as long as you can," Conrad said as he crawled through the entrance. He looked back at Phoenix. "And keep him quiet."

Lionel sat Charlie down and looked at him sternly. "You know Vicki didn't kill Ryan."

"I know, but the big man talks mean, and I'm scared he's going to yell at me."

"You have to tell the truth."

"You're one of them, aren't you?" Charlie said.

Lionel nodded. "But don't tell the commander, OK?"

"I won't if you tell me how I can get a thing on my head."

Lionel pulled up a chair. "Charlie, this isn't a club. And you can't be part of the group if all you want is something on your head."

"Then how can I join?"

Lionel struggled to remember his own story. His past with the other kids had flooded back quickly. Now, as he talked with Charlie, he relived the moment when he finally understood the truth.

"I treated church like a club when I was a kid," Lionel said. "It was just a place to hang while my parents sang and did their Bible study."

"So you didn't have the thing on your forehead back then?"

"Charlie, stop talking about the mark and start listening."

"Right, got it. Start listening."

"The thing I missed was that God is real. He made you and me for a purpose. And he wants us to know him."

"I believe that," Charlie said. "I don't think we got evolved or came from monkeys or whatever they say we came from."

"Good," Lionel said. "But it's not enough just to believe God exists. He offers each of us a gift."

"You mean the thing on—"

"Stop with that!" Lionel shouted. Charlie shrank in his chair. "God offers everybody forgiveness. When I first met Judd and Vicki, I didn't even know I needed it. I was so scared because all my family had disappeared. Deep down I knew I'd missed the most important thing. I had never asked Jesus to forgive me. That's the gift. If you ask God to come into your heart and forgive you—"

Commander Blancka's aide returned.

Vicki held Phoenix and tried to keep him quiet. She strained to hear voices outside.

"This is where they were standing," a girl said.

"And this is the grave?" a deep-voiced man said. "Dig it up."

Vicki looked at Judd in horror. Judd put a finger to his lips.

Vicki heard Conrad, out of breath. "Sir, I saw movement near a house about a hundred yards back."

Commander Blancka radioed the pilot the information, and Vicki heard chopper blades.

"Located your radio?" Commander Blancka said.

"Not yet, sir," Conrad said.

"That's easy enough," the commander said. He keyed his microphone. "Commander Blancka requesting a radio locate."

"What's that, sir?" Conrad said.

"The radio has a homing device. Lets us find you."

The radio squawked. "Commander Blancka, we need the ID number for the radio."

Vicki quickly turned off the radio. They had to get rid of it.

13

LIONEL heard the commander's call and knew Judd and Vicki still had Conrad's radio.

"Where you going?" the aide said as Lionel stood to leave.

"I'm done baby-sitting. I'm going to catch these two."

"But the commander—"

"When I turn them in, he'll be glad," Lionel said as he rushed through the door of the tent. "Keep an eye on Charlie."

As he ran toward the church, Lionel formed a plan. He would tell the commander he had helped Judd and Vicki escape. They were long gone. The GC would court-martial him or worse, but Lionel didn't care.

Lionel felt guilty. If he had only said no to the man who had taken him south. If he had resisted the GC training after his accident. He shook his head. He couldn't think about that now. He had to get to the commander before anyone found Judd and Vicki.

Lionel's radio squawked. "We've got that locate you wanted on the radio, sir."

"Give me the coordinates," Commander Blancka said.

"Sir, the unit is moving."

"That means they're on the run!" the commander said. "Where are they?"

"From the description of your own location, I'd say they're only a few yards away."

Lionel's heart sank. The underground shelter had become Judd and Vicki's prison. Lionel had given them Conrad's radio. *How could I be so dumb!* he thought.

Lionel swore.

So, he thought, *there's some of that still in me.* He picked up his pace and neared the group. The helicopter was in position over the church with its lights trained on the commander and the others.

"Somebody's running!" Melinda shouted, drawing her gun.

Lionel shouted and held up his hands.

"What are you doing here?" the commander shouted. "I told you—"

"Sir, I have something I need to tell you," Lionel said.

The pilot said, "They're a few yards to your right."

"Sir," Lionel said.

"Hang on to it!" the commander shouted.

"This is important, sir," Lionel said.

"Commander, look!" Conrad shouted, pointing to a figure in the shadows.

Melinda and Felicia pointed their guns toward the figure. Lionel fumbled with his own gun, then turned,

128

hoping he wouldn't see Judd and Vicki with their hands up. He gasped when he saw Phoenix bounce out of the shadows and into the beam of the searchlight. Conrad's radio was neatly tied around the dog's neck. Phoenix sat and put his paw in the air.

"It's a dog!" the commander shouted into his radio. "They're not here! Keep looking!"

The chopper flew away. Melinda and Felicia moved toward Phoenix, their guns still up. Phoenix growled. "He might be booby-trapped," Felicia said.

"Booby-trapped, my eye," the commander said. He strode past them and unhooked the radio from the dog's back. "They're taunting us with this dog, trying to make us look like fools. They're probably miles from here at one of the shelters by now. Probably gettin' a good night's sleep while we're out here hunting them down."

"What should we do, sir?" Conrad said.

"We're gonna find 'em," the commander said. "Not one of us is going to stop until we find those two."

Felicia objected when the commander told each of them to go in a different direction. "I don't trust Lionel," she said.

"Fine," the commander said. "He goes with you."

"But—"

"No buts!" the commander barked. "Graham, strap your radio on and follow this dog. See if he leads you anywhere. And Washington, what was it you were going to say a minute ago?"

"It's not important now, sir," Lionel said.

Vicki trembled. "Do you think it worked?"

"The chopper moved away," Judd said. "That's a good sign."

They sat still a few minutes, waiting for someone to burst into their hiding place, but no one came.

They had outfitted Phoenix with the radio and pushed him out the entrance. In the noise and confusion they had gone unnoticed, and Phoenix had done exactly what they wanted. He had gone away from the church.

"What now?" Vicki said.

"We wait," Judd said.

"But they'll see us through the chopper's heat sensor," Vicki said. "I think we ought to bolt while we have the chance."

"That's what they want us to do," Judd said, "lose our cool and run."

Vicki frowned. "I'm not losing my cool; I'm looking for our best options."

"I didn't mean it like that," Judd said. "They think we're on the run. We'll hide here until Lionel tells us to move."

"What if we split up?" Vicki said. "Wouldn't that give us a better chance?"

"Not with that chopper," Judd said. "I think we should stick together and wait to hear from Lionel."

Vicki felt cramped under the desk. "Let me outta here," she said. "My legs are going to sleep."

Vicki shoved her way out and knocked over a pile of rocks.

"Watch it!" Judd said.

"Just because you're a year older doesn't mean you can boss me around," she said. "You're doing the same thing you did with Ryan! You bossed him and made him feel like a jerk!"

Judd hung his head. "I want to talk, but if you don't whisper, you'll lead them right to us."

"You're doing it again," Vicki whispered. "You don't think I know we need to be quiet?"

"We have a different opinion about our next move," Judd said, "but we're on the same team. We both want to get out of here alive and stay away from the GC."

"We do have that in common," Vicki said.

Judd sighed and turned his head.

"What is it?" Vicki said.

"The truth is, I feel a sense of responsibility for you."

Vicki bristled.

"Not like you're my child," he continued, "but my friend who I wouldn't want anything bad to happen to." Judd's voice cracked. "Vicki, I really care about you. And believe me, I've kicked myself a thousand times for the way I treated Ryan."

"I know you care," Vicki said.

"It's your call," Judd said. "If you want to run, I'll go with you."

"We'll stay," Vicki said as she crawled under the desk. "I'm sorry for saying that about Ryan."

Judd nodded and sat beside her. She put a hand on his shoulder. He seemed so tired.

131

Judd awoke twenty minutes later as Conrad slipped into their hiding place.

"I could only talk to Lionel for a minute, but he agreed with me," Conrad said. "We'll create a diversion after I leave and get you two out of here. This place is going to be crawling with GC by morning."

"Are we that important?" Vicki said.

"The commander's taking it personally. He wants you two bad."

Conrad went over the plan and made sure their watches were in sync. He also said they would find Shelly and Darrion and get them to the Stahley mansion as soon as possible.

"Something else," Conrad said. "If the GC get close, remember, they have guns. We have orders to shoot to kill."

Judd looked at Vicki.

"And if they catch you, don't do anything stupid. Lionel and I will figure out something."

"What if the Stahley place is destroyed?" Vicki said.

"There's a picnic area in the forest preserve behind it," Judd said. "We can meet there."

The commander's voice blasted over the radio. "Graham, where are you?"

"Still following the dog, sir. No sign of them yet."

"Roger. Keep an eye on him. Out."

Conrad rolled his eyes. "I have a few minutes before

we put the plan in motion. Would you mind telling me more about the God thing?"

"How much do you know?" Judd said.

"I've checked out the rabbi a couple of times on the Web. I know all the stuff that's happening was predicted in the Bible."

"It took us a while to figure it out," Judd said. "A pastor who got left behind helped us. He's gone now, but the message is the same."

"Which is what?" Conrad said.

"God came back for his true followers, and a lot of people who thought they were religious didn't make it."

"Why not?"

"Because it's not about being religious," Judd said. "It's about a relationship with God through Jesus Christ."

"What does that mean?" Conrad said.

Vicki jumped in. "I had the same question. My parents changed big-time and wanted me to. They kept saying I should accept Jesus. It wasn't until they disappeared that I figured it out. Accepting him means you admit you can't get to God on your own. You ask him to forgive you for the bad stuff you've done. And with me there was plenty of bad stuff."

"Me too," Conrad said.

While Vicki told more of her story, Judd turned on a flashlight and grabbed a small Bible from Ryan's stash. He showed Conrad verses in Romans that said everyone had sinned.

"I read that on the Web site," Conrad said, "but it didn't make sense until now."

"You can pray anywhere," Judd said. "Even here."

"Yeah," Conrad said. "How do I do it?"

Judd led Conrad in a short prayer. "God, I know I've sinned. I'm sorry. Please forgive me. I believe Jesus died for me and came back from the dead. I accept your forgiveness right now. Come into my life and change me. Amen."

Judd handed Conrad a Bible. "Did you get to talk to my brother about any of this?" Conrad said.

"Ryan and I got to talk about God with him," Judd said. "He heard the truth."

"But he didn't believe, did he?"

Judd turned his head. "He didn't tell me he believed, but only God knows his heart."

Conrad nodded and pointed to Vicki's forehead. "I can see it," he said. "No matter what happens now, at least I know I'll see you guys again."

———————————

Lionel glanced at his watch. The plan would go into effect in two minutes. He hoped Conrad had made it to the hiding place.

Felicia and Melinda continued to eye him as they walked through the rubble. They had searched two shelters and were heading to a third when Conrad's call came in.

"This is Graham," Conrad said. Phoenix was barking wildly in the background. "I think I just spotted them. Their dog's goin' crazy over here."

"Location!" Commander Blancka shouted.

Conrad gave his position. Conrad was leading them away from the area Judd and Vicki would need to travel.

"We got 'em now!" the commander shouted.

The chopper flew overhead, its lights filling the sky. Lionel wondered how Conrad had gotten Phoenix to bark like that.

Judd counted down the minutes. Vicki nervously paced in front of the opening.

"It's time," Judd said.

"You go first," Vicki said, helping Judd up to the ledge that led to the opening.

As he reached back to help Vicki up, the earth trembled. The concrete wall he was standing on swayed. A large beam fell, and with it came bricks and mortar.

Vicki let go of Judd's hand and fell back. Judd was thrown forward, outside the church. As quickly as the aftershock had started, it was over, but the hole Judd had crawled through was blocked by debris.

Judd whispered Vicki's name, but she didn't respond. He grabbed handfuls of dirt and rocks and pulled bricks from the opening. He felt like he was clawing for his life.

When the hole was big enough, he stuck his head through. He whispered again, and this time he heard a faint coughing coming from the floor.

"Vick, can you hear me?"

"There's something on my leg," Vicki choked.

"Hang on. I'll get you out!"

"No," Vicki said. "This is your chance. Go!"

"If you think I'm leaving you now, you're crazy," Judd said, frantically moving debris from the entrance.

"Even if you could get me out—"

"Save your breath," Judd said. "I'm almost through." He carefully squeezed through the hole. "I can't see you, Vick. Talk to me."

"I can't move my right leg at all," Vicki said.

Judd felt along the mound of dirt until he touched Vicki's hand.

"I got you now," Judd said, pulling at the dirt and rocks. A few minutes later only the beam trapped her.

"I have to get some leverage to get you out," Judd said. He found a stick outside and brought it in, but it broke in half when he tried to move the beam.

"Time's running out," Vicki said.

"Hang in there. I've almost got it."

The tree branch lifted the beam, and Vicki managed to slide backward before it fell. Vicki got up and hobbled toward the entrance. "I can't put any weight on my leg," she said.

Judd climbed outside and pulled Vicki through. Judd felt her ankle.

Vicki winced. "That's it."

"It doesn't feel broken," Judd said. "But it's bad."

"Let me see if I can walk on it again."

Vicki stood but crumpled to the ground in pain. "It's no use. I can't go."

"I'll carry you," Judd said.

"I'll slow you down."

136

"I'm telling you, I'm not leaving you."

As Judd lifted Vicki into his arms, he heard the sound of the chopper, then footsteps nearby. He reached for his rear pocket and felt for Conrad's gun. It was still there.

14

LIONEL ran with Melinda and Felicia toward the chopper. The earth tremor answered his question about Phoenix. The dog was going wild because of the shudder of the earth. Lionel hoped Judd and Vicki had gotten out of the church.

The radio was busy with reports about the quake. Commander Blancka said, "Keep going and find them. I'll join the chopper." He gave his location and asked the pilot to pick him up.

Melinda led the group with a flashlight and a global positioning device the commander had given her.

"Where are you going?" Lionel said.

"Conrad should be due north if my GPS is right," Melinda said.

Lionel looked in horror. Melinda was taking a short-cut toward Conrad's position. She was leading them straight through the demolished parking lot of New Hope Village Church.

Judd had carried Vicki only a few yards when he saw the beam of the flashlight and heard voices. It sounded like Lionel, but someone was with him. Judd ran to a fallen tree and placed Vicki on the other side. He tried not to breathe.

"How much farther?" a girl said.

"About half a mile," another girl said.

The three Morale Monitors passed a few feet on the other side of the downed tree. Judd heard Lionel say, "I hope that aftershock didn't damage the shelters."

When the three passed, Vicki tried to walk but stumbled in pain. "I don't want you to have to carry me all the way to the Stahley place."

"You're light," Judd said. "It's not a problem."

But Judd knew Vicki was right. No matter how light she was, he couldn't carry her that distance. As he ducked in and out of crumpled subdivisions, he frantically looked for a bike, a motorcycle, or anything that would help them get away. After ten minutes, Judd put Vicki down and fell to his knees, exhausted.

"You can't do this," Vicki said. "Leave me here and come back later."

"No way," Judd said. "Just let me catch my breath."

Lionel knew they needed to give Judd and Vicki as much time as possible. As they topped a hill, the helicopter's searchlight scanned a row of houses.

"There he is!" Melinda shouted, pointing at Conrad.

Conrad held Phoenix by the collar. Commander

Blancka had just arrived. Phoenix growled and barked at the man when he came close.

"All right, where'd you see them?" the commander said.

"I saw two people in there," Conrad said, pointing to a small, white house a few yards away. "The dog was going crazy."

"Did you see them run in or come out?" the commander said.

"No, sir, they were moving around inside."

"Then we've got 'em!" The commander barked orders to the chopper. It trained its searchlight on the house as the others took position.

Suddenly, the door opened and a man in his night-clothes walked out. A woman in a robe held a baby. The man put his hands up and squinted.

"On the ground!" the commander shouted through a bullhorn.

The man fell to the ground and put his hands behind his head. The woman came outside and sat beside him with the crying baby. The commander waved the chopper away.

"We didn't do anything," the man said.

"Is that them?" the commander shouted.

"No!" Melinda shouted.

"Maybe they're inside," Lionel said.

The woman cried and shook her head. "Someone flashed a light in our bedroom window, then we felt the earthquake."

"Search it," Commander Blancka yelled.

Lionel followed the others inside. He knew Judd and Vicki hadn't been there.

"I thought I saw them, sir," Conrad said. "The dog went wild, and—"

"Don't think anymore!" the commander said. "Let the dog loose."

Conrad let go of Phoenix's collar. Phoenix sat. The commander kicked at him and yelled, "Go find your friends!"

Phoenix dodged the commander's boot, and the man lost his balance and fell. Phoenix ran into the night. The chopper followed with its searchlight. Phoenix sniffed at the ground and headed back toward the church.

Judd found that carrying Vicki over his shoulder made running easier. She said she didn't mind, but Judd knew the jostling couldn't be comfortable.

Judd passed a house with a four-wheel-drive vehicle parked in front. A light was on in the living room, and Judd spotted someone sitting in a chair.

"Just act like you've passed out," Judd told Vicki.

"A few more minutes and I won't have to act," Vicki said.

Judd kicked at the door. "Hello? I need help!"

Judd peered through a broken windowpane. A man walked into the front hallway.

"Hi. My friend was hurt in the aftershock, and I was wondering—"

"Go away," the man said.

"I need to get her some help!"

The living room light went out. Judd reached inside the broken window.

"What are you doing?" Vicki whispered.

"Looking for a key to that car," Judd said.

When he couldn't find the key, he carried Vicki down the street. Two blocks later he spotted a crumpled bicycle with something attached behind it.

"It's one of those kid carriers," Vicki said.

"It might work," Judd said.

Judd quickly unhooked the carrier. Vicki fit in the stroller, but she had to keep her feet in the air. Judd pushed her a few yards but noticed the front wheel was bent. The ground was so uneven that Judd abandoned the idea and picked Vicki up again.

"Do you know where we are?" Vicki said.

A dog came at them. Judd kicked at it and kept moving. "About a third of the way there. If we can make it by daylight, we've got a chance."

Lionel had to make a tough decision. If he let Phoenix continue, the dog would lead them straight to Judd and Vicki. He thought of shooting Phoenix. It would keep his friends safe a little while longer.

What am I thinking? Lionel thought. I can't shoot Phoenix, no matter what.

Lionel caught up with Conrad. "Nice try."

"I thought that might hold them off longer," Conrad said. "It was murder trying to find a house with somebody in it and hold that dog back at the same time. What do we do now?"

"Hang back and see how this plays out. Judd and Vicki might get away. If the worst happens and they get caught, we can pull our guns on the GC."

"You forgot," Conrad said. "I don't have a gun. Judd got mine."

"If you have to, disarm Melinda or Felicia. Take them by surprise."

"Do you really want to take on Blancka like that?" Conrad said. "I'm through with the GC myself, but there's no way you can work from the inside if you pull a gun."

The chopper followed Phoenix through the twisted wreckage. Phoenix kept his nose to the ground and darted through the rubble. Without the chopper it would have been impossible to keep up with him.

A call from headquarters came over the radio. Someone had just reported two prowlers running through the neighborhood west of New Hope Village Church. Commander Blancka asked for the exact location and got it. He instructed the chopper pilot to abandon the dog and go for the prowlers.

———————————

Judd kept moving. He jogged through backyards and parking lots. He looked for grass. The roads were terrible. Huge chunks of asphalt heaved up.

Dogs were not an enemy, but they seemed so spooked at the aftershock that every one of them barked. More than once Judd stumbled and nearly fell. He hit his head on a low-hanging tree limb, and Vicki's clothes got caught in the branches.

Then the sound Judd feared most. The chopper.

Judd saw light a short distance away and ran toward it. He knelt in the grass a few yards from a series of tents.

"It's another shelter," Vicki said, as Judd gasped for breath.

"The chopper's right behind us. If we don't figure out a better way to get around than this, we're sunk."

"Maybe we can buy some time if we hide in there," Vicki said.

Judd felt the beating of chopper blades, and the wind picked up.

Lionel met with Conrad while they waited for orders from Commander Blancka. Conrad took Lionel's flashlight and turned it on his own face.

"See anything new?" Conrad said.

Lionel shook his head. "What?"

"Don't you see anything right here?" Conrad said, pointing to his forehead.

Lionel smiled. "All right, brother! Good to have you on board."

Vicki hopped to the rear of the tent and fell to the ground. She scooted under the edge and held the flap for Judd. There was little light inside.

145

"Feels creepy in here," Vicki whispered.

Judd put a finger to his lips.

When her eyes got accustomed to the darkness of the room, Vicki gasped. "Nobody's going to hear us in here. They're all dead."

Sheets draped the bodies around the room. By the size of the bodies Vicki could tell some were young, others older.

"I bet we're near the high school," Vicki said. "This has to be the morgue."

Judd shuddered. "Sorry."

"It's perfect," Vicki said. "Nobody to rat on us."

The chopper hovered over the shelter. People ran from tents and scrambled out of sleeping bags. A car drove up a few yards away.

"I want all of these tents searched," a man yelled. "Washington, you two check here. You two, that tent."

An older woman shouted, "What's going on here?"

"Commander Blancka, Global Community. We're looking for two suspects."

"Everyone in camp is registered," the woman said. "Would you like to see the records?"

"No, ma'am," Commander Blancka said. "We're gonna eyeball every person here to make sure."

Vicki looked at Judd. The tent flap opened.

"That's the morgue," the woman said.

"Ick," a girl said. "I'm not goin' in there."

"Washington," Commander Blancka said, "you check the morgue."

146

Lionel lifted a few sheets and looked at the faces of the dead. He shook his head and was about to leave when he heard hissing.

"Psst, over here!"

"You guys are in deep," Lionel whispered as he grabbed two sheets at the front of the tent and handed them to Judd and Vicki. Judd explained the situation.

"You can't stay here," Lionel said. "They'll be taking the bodies out of here in the morning."

"Think we can get the commander's jeep?" Judd said.

Lionel smirked. "Oh, that would be too cool. But there's no way."

"If you could create one more diversion, I might be able to get it."

"But the chopper'd be on you in a second," Lionel said.

"It's worth a shot, don't you think?" Judd said.

The tent flap opened and two men came in carrying a body. Lionel covered Judd and Vicki and stood.

"Another stiff to check out?" Lionel said.

The men didn't answer. They put the body down, covered it, and left.

"OK," Lionel said. "Here's what I'll do."

The helicopter circled the camp with its light still on. Lionel approached the commander slowly. Melinda and Felicia were searching tents nearby.

"Sir, I found something kind of strange in the

147

morgue," Lionel said loudly enough for everyone to hear. "I wonder if you'd take a look."

Lionel led the group into the tent and took them to the side where Judd and Vicki had entered.

"I found one of the tent pegs out and these two sheets."

"I'll bet they crawled in here and pretended to be dead," Melinda said.

"Good call," the commander said.

"Sir, I wasn't able to search all these bodies. I think we ought to do that now."

Commander Blancka lifted the two sheets. He pulled the edge of the tent up and cursed.

"My jeep! They're in my jeep!"

15

WHEN Judd got the jeep rolling, he handed the microphone to Vicki and said, "Push this and hold it. It'll jam the frequency of the pilot. Then keep quiet."

Vicki keyed the microphone just in time. The jeep was barely past the morgue when Vicki saw Commander Blancka and the others rush out.

Vicki tapped Judd on the shoulder and pointed behind them. Judd nodded, pointed to the microphone, and gave Vicki a thumbs-up.

Judd drove onto roads he would never have thought were passable. The jeep rolled up embankments and over downed power lines. He kept the car going toward the Stahley mansion, zigging and zagging past collapsed buildings and burned-out cars. The helicopter remained over the shelter. Judd looked at the gas gauge. The tank was almost empty.

Lionel watched a frantic Commander Blancka try to con-tact the pilot. Blancka called several times but got no response. The man ripped the radio from his shoulder in disgust. "They're jamming us! Somebody get his attention!"

The man waved his arms. Melinda and Felicia joined in, shouting and yelling.

Conrad rolled his eyes and pulled Lionel aside. "You know where I stand with you guys. Now that I'm one of you, there's no way I can stay inside the GC."

"Why not?"

"It's clear what's ahead. We're coming down to the end. Just a little more than five years and the game's up, right?"

"Sure, but what's that got to do—"

"We're looking at one huge countdown clock," Conrad said. "I'm choosing sides now, and it's not with the GC."

"But choosing sides doesn't mean you leave your friends when they're in trouble," Lionel said.

"I don't want to leave them, but—"

"If it were just you and me," Lionel said, "I'd be out of here in a second. But I'm thinking about Judd and Vicki."

"All right. But when we know they're safe, I'm gone."

The girls waved wildly at the chopper. Melinda finally made it to the searchlight and pointed toward the camp. The chopper turned.

"It won't be long now," Lionel said. "I hope Judd's far enough away to ditch the jeep and make it on foot."

Judd drove fast, twisting and winding through the churned-up roads. A few spots had already been repaired by GC crews, and on those Judd was able to make good time. But most roads were like a giant jigsaw puzzle that had been shaken apart.

Vicki tightly wrapped a rag around the microphone and put it under the seat.

"How much gas do we have left?" she said.

"Not much," Judd said. "They've probably made contact with the chopper by now."

"Do you know where you're going?" Vicki said.

"I know the right direction," Judd said. "Don't recognize these roads, though."

They came to an intersection littered with debris. Judd drove around it until he came to a house in the middle of the street. "Cover your head," he said.

"You're not actually going through there, are you?" Vicki said.

Judd floored it and broke through the brittle wall and out the other side.

Vicki threw pieces of wood from the jeep. "I know where we are now," she said. "This is how I came back after leaving Mrs. Jenness."

Judd rolled over two yellow bumps, and Vicki told him it was all that was left of a fast-food restaurant.

"The river's that way," Vicki said.

When Judd crested the hill he couldn't believe his eyes. Twisted pieces of metal were all that was left of the bridge. The road ended at the edge of the river.

151

"How did you ever survive that?" Judd said.

Vicki shook her head. The memory of her ordeal with Mrs. Jenness was fresh.

"If I'm right, the river runs through the forest preserve," Judd said. "That means we're not far. That's the good news."

"And the bad news?"

"The Stahley place is on the other side of the river. We're going to have to find a way across."

"There's probably not a bridge within miles that survived the quake," Vicki said.

"Then we'll have to swim. Or get a boat."

Vicki turned in horror. "Look!"

The chopper hovered in the distance, its searchlight darting across the road. Judd stopped the jeep. "Quick," he said, "get under what's left of the bridge!"

"I'll try," Vicki said. She hobbled out and headed for the riverbank.

Judd turned the jeep around, unwrapped the rag from the microphone, and pushed in the cigarette lighter. He unscrewed the gas cap and stuffed the rag into the hole. He looked for a stick or a piece of wood long enough and finally found a tire iron behind the backseat.

Judd checked the sky. The chopper was closing ground. He looked back and saw that Vicki was almost hidden.

I hope there's enough gas in there! he thought.

When the lighter was red-hot, Judd lit the rag. He wedged the tire iron against the accelerator and put the jeep in gear. He hoped the car would travel a good distance from the river before it overturned, but it only went a few hundred feet before the front wheels turned and the jeep ran straight into a demolished house. Seconds later an explosion rocked the street. The jeep burst into flames.

Judd ran from the wreck as the chopper flew near.

Lionel stayed close to the commander and listened for news from the pilot. The commander had gone to a different radio frequency, and the chopper immediately pursued the jeep.

"We've got something here, Commander," the pilot said a few minutes later.

"Go ahead."

"An explosion. I'm just getting to the site now. Yeah, it looks like it's your vehicle. It crashed into a house. It's on fire, sir."

"Put down as close as you can and see if those two are in there," the commander said.

"If they are, they're toast," the pilot said. "I don't see any bodies outside the building."

Lionel glanced at Conrad. Conrad shook his head. Melinda and Felicia looked excited.

Vicki couldn't see the chopper, but she heard it and tasted dust. The pain in her leg was so great she had to concentrate on putting one foot in front of the other as Judd helped her move along the side of the river.

"Why'd you blow it up?"

"Thought about sending it into the river," Judd said, "but I figured it was better they find it burning. Might give us a few more minutes to run."

"This is not running," Vicki said.

"You're doing fine," Judd said.

"Any chance they might think we're dead?"

"I hope so," Judd said. "It'll take a while to sift through the wreckage. How's the ankle?"

"Hurts," Vicki said, "but you were right about the sprain. If it was broken, I wouldn't be able to walk at all."

The river had changed since Vicki had last seen it. The bank was much steeper. The river was wider and swollen. In places, the earth had shifted, creating small waterfalls. The water looked much too swift to swim.

"How much farther?" Vicki said.

"Maybe a mile or two."

Judd moved to the edge of the water, then returned. "Too deep to cross. Keep moving."

Vicki saw whitecaps in the moonlight as the river rushed past. Pieces of the bank were still crumbling into the water.

"Look at that," Judd said, pointing to the middle of the river.

Vicki saw a front porch sticking out of the water, being swept downstream. The white picket fence on the porch was still attached, but the rest of the house was underwater and rolling. When it reached the first waterfall, the house hung on the edge, then with a sickening crunch, crashed over the side and broke apart.

It was difficult to walk along the churned-up ground.

154

Vicki slipped several times and had to be helped to her feet. "Let's move to the top of the bank," she said.

"We'll be too easy to spot up there," Judd said.

"If he's got night vision, it won't matter," Vicki said. She took another step and her ankle gave way. She plunged down the hill, grabbing at dirt and grass as she tumbled. But she couldn't hang on. With fistfuls of dirt, she splashed into the chilly water.

Lionel heard the call from the pilot and rushed to the commander's side.

"Go ahead," the commander said.

"Heat's pretty intense here, sir. I don't see any bodies inside or out. Looks staged."

"Those vehicles don't just burst into flames," the commander said. "Continue the search. We've got a second chopper on the way to help you."

Judd heard Vicki cry out. He turned as she flipped and rolled down the embankment. A splash. Vicki was in the churning water.

Judd scampered down the hill. His foot caught on a tree root and he, too, tumbled headfirst into the water. The current was swift and took him under. He surfaced and yelled for Vicki, but she didn't answer. Then a strange sound mixed with the gurgling water in Judd's ears. It was the *thwock, thwock, thwock* of the helicopter.

155

For a moment, Judd felt a sense of relief. The GC chopper could rescue them. But Judd knew once he was in the hands of the GC, he and Vicki would be separated and probably punished.

The chopper darted over the water, the blades whipping up waves and making the swimming harder. It flew from bank to bank. Judd went under and stayed as long as his lungs could stand it.

Vicki was underwater for what seemed an eternity. She didn't have time to take a breath when she fell in. The current pushed her downstream into the roots of a tree. The water was black and icy. She struggled to get free, breaking a branch that snagged her clothes, but soon she was caught on another. Finally, the current took her away from the tree, and she rose to the surface.

Vicki gasped for air. She grabbed for the bank, but it was too far away. The swirling water took her under again. When she surfaced, she called out for Judd.

Vicki's cry was close. Judd turned and saw her shadow against the searchlight. This was their chance.

Judd swam with all his might, and the current pushed Vicki toward him. He screamed and reached out for her.

Judd touched her hand once, then took two more strokes to get closer. *Just a little more*, he thought.

As he strained toward Vicki, a piece of the splintered

house hit him and forced him underwater. When he surfaced, he barely heard Vicki's cry above the noise.

Vicki screamed for Judd, then lost sight of him. A bright light blinded her as the water kicked up around her.

"Stay where you are," a voice boomed overhead.

Like I can control where I'm going, Vicki thought.

Out of control, Judd twisted and turned in the river. He tried to swim to shore, but just as he felt he was making progress, the current pulled him under.

When he surfaced, a section of roof hurtled toward him. He couldn't dodge it, and it was too big to swim under, so Judd grabbed the edge and tried to crawl on. As he did, he sent shingles plopping into the water. Finally, Judd made it to the center of the spinning roof.

Where's Vicki? he thought. He didn't know which was worse—being found by the GC or being at the mercy of the river.

He spotted the chopper hovering near the spot where they had fallen in. Judd kicked himself for not being more careful. If only they had walked farther up the bank. If only he had held on to Vicki.

The roof spun completely around, and water washed over him. When Judd could see again, he noticed a rescue line dangling from the chopper. The pilot was shouting something through his loudspeaker. "Don't get on, Vick!" Judd screamed.

Vicki went under and swam toward the shore, but the current was too swift. The chopper hovered closer and dropped a lifeline.

"This is the Global Community!" the pilot shouted. "You are under arrest. Grab the harness and put it around you."

Vicki went under again and kicked as hard as she could. Swimming was easier than walking, but her ankle felt like it was on fire. When she surfaced, the pilot moved into position.

"Grab the harness," the pilot said. "This is your only chance. There's a huge waterfall around the next corner. You don't want to go over that. Grab on and I'll pull you up."

What about Judd? Vicki thought.

"No!" Judd shouted as he watched the chopper pull Vicki from the water. He slammed his fist on the roof of the house and rolled off. When Vicki was in, the chopper flew slowly toward Judd. Before he was spotted, Judd dove underneath the floating roof. He found a pocket of air and stayed there until the chopper passed.

The roof picked up speed. When Judd surfaced, he thought the chopper was back. But this wasn't the sound of rotor blades. This was a roar. He swam against the current and watched in horror as the roof of the house disappeared over the edge of a chasm.

16

LIONEL stiffened when he heard the pilot's voice.

"We've apprehended one of them," the pilot said. "We have a female in custody. Search for the male is negative. I think he might have drowned."

"Bring the girl back and keep going," Commander Blancka said from the other chopper. "Morale Monitors on the ground, the GC has taken over police headquarters on Maple Street. I want the two girls to head this up. Get everything you can out of her."

Lionel clicked his microphone. "What do you want Graham and me to do, sir?"

"Stay where you are. We'll pick you up."

"This changes everything," Lionel said to Conrad. "Vicki will have no hope unless we help her."

"I'm no chicken, but I'm not a hero either," Conrad said. "And if Vicki's at this police station halfway across town, what are we supposed to do?"

"I don't know yet," Lionel said. "But there's no way I'm letting Blancka decide her fate."

"What about Judd?" Conrad said. "You think he's still alive?"

Lionel hesitated. "Judd'll be all right. He can take care of himself."

Judd tried to swim against the current but couldn't. With nothing to hold on to he took a deep breath, held out his arms, and plunged over the fall into the darkness.

He hit the surface with his feet, and water surrounded him. He sank deeper and deeper. He was afraid he would black out and drown from the fall. With his lungs nearly bursting, he reached the soft bottom and tried to push up. His feet stuck in the muck. Judd struggled and finally kicked free. He rose to the surface and gasped for air.

The water was calm now. The current carried him slowly downriver. Judd found a piece of wood and clung to it with his remaining strength.

Judd watched the riverbank for anything familiar. After a half hour of drifting, he let go of the wood and swam to shore. He climbed through the mud to the top of the bank. Something slick passed him.

Snake.

A chill went through him, and he clawed his way to the top. Judd tried to get his bearings. He knew he had to go west to get to the Stahley place, but which way was west? The stars were brilliant in the sky. Since the earthquake, they seemed brighter. Without the haze from the city, Judd found the North Star easily.

Once again Judd heard the helicopter. He ran. This time it would be looking for his body.

They're not going to find it, Judd thought as he took off into the forest.

Vicki shook from the cold as she hobbled into the police station. Commander Blancka led the way into the interrogation room. Melinda and Felicia followed.

"Young lady, I'm going to give you a chance," the commander began. "If you cooperate, that'll be taken into consideration when it comes time to sentence you."

Vicki said nothing.

"If you refuse to cooperate, refuse to give us information, I'll have no choice but to be severe with my punishment." The commander looked at Vicki without emotion. "And I can be severe."

After the commander left, Melinda said, "We know your name is Vicki Byrne. Why did you kill Mrs. Jenness?"

"I didn't kill her," Vicki said. "I told you that."

"We have witnesses."

"You have one person who says she thinks she saw something. It won't stand up."

Melinda smiled. "You don't understand. This isn't a court. There won't be a trial. Whatever Commander Blancka decides is final."

"I have a right to a fair—"

"You lost your rights when you disobeyed the Global Community," Felicia said. "They could have left you in the water to die. Or shot you for stealing GC property. If the commander decides you murdered that lady, he's told us what will happen."

"And what's that?" Vicki said.

Melinda leaned close. "Death."

Judd huddled in a thicket of bushes. The chopper stayed near the river.

The forest had felt the effects of the earthquake just as the city had. Trees were uprooted. Whole sections of the forest had been swallowed. Judd recognized what was left of the access road and ran toward a meadow. He found the small grove of trees where he had knelt with Ryan and Taylor Graham. Judd found the remote entry box and pushed the button. He glanced at the hill. Nothing happened. He pushed the button again. Still, nothing happened.

Judd looked around for any sign of the GC. He couldn't see the house, but he assumed it was deserted. Both Mr. and Mrs. Stahley were dead. There was no reason to guard it unless they were still looking for Darrion.

Judd ran to the door built into the hill. He tried to find an opening, but the shifting ground had sealed the entrance. Digging would take hours.

He walked around the meadow and onto the Stahley property. The huge fence that surrounded the property was on the ground. The security gate at the front of the property was also in shambles. Judd hoped the earth-quake had scared off the dogs.

Judd climbed through broken glass on the patio area. The swimming pool was empty. Judd leaned over and saw a huge crack in the bottom of the pool. The roof had collapsed over the kitchen, but the house hadn't been damaged like many Judd had seen.

Looters had been there. The refrigerator was open, food strewn around the kitchen. The high-tech television and stereo equipment were gone from the living room.

With the sun coming up, Judd felt exhausted. He wanted to see the hideout downstairs. If the equipment was still there, and if the phone lines were up, he might be able to contact others in the Trib Force. Someone had to help Vicki.

Judd put his head down on the couch. *I'll just lie down for a moment*, he thought.

As soon as he put his head down, he was asleep.

Though the commander ordered him to stay, Lionel left to find Darrion and Shelly. He found them sleeping at a nearby shelter. He woke them and explained what had happened to Vicki.

"What about Judd?" Shelly said.

"We don't know," Lionel said. "We hope he got away. There's a chance he could have drowned."

Shelly shook her head.

"We have to help Vicki," Darrion said. "Is there any way to hire a lawyer or have someone negotiate for her?"

"It's worth a shot," Lionel said. "Commander Blancka has full power from the Global Community. He's the judge and jury."

"Who could we get?" Shelly said. "I don't know any lawyers."

"What about Mr. Stein?" Darrion said. "Vicki said he offered to help any way he could."

Lionel told Shelly and Darrion to get Mr. Stein. If they couldn't find him, they were to go to Darrion's house. As soon as Vicki's case was settled, the remaining members of the Young Tribulation Force would meet there.

Judd awoke at noon, hungry and aching. He stumbled to the kitchen and found an unopened box of crackers. That eased his hunger for a while. He hoped the earthquake hadn't damaged the secret entrance to the underground hangar.

He found a picture of the Stahleys hanging at a weird angle. He pried the secret entrance open and crawled onto the landing behind the wall. The ladder that led to the secret room had fallen, so Judd scampered back to the kitchen and found a piece of rope. He climbed into darkness and activated the entrance.

Inside the chamber Judd found the safe still open. He had taken the secret documents but left gold coins and a stack of bills. The door to the safe was still open, and the money and gold were gone. He pulled Ryan's packet from his pocket, still damp, and placed it inside the safe.

Judd checked the hangar for the stash of food Taylor

Graham had shown him. It was still there. He went back to the computer room and picked up the phone. Dial tone. That meant he could access the Internet.

A few minutes later he was viewing Rabbi Tsion Ben-Judah's Web site. Judd sent an urgent message to the man, hoping he would be able to help with Vicki. While he waited, Judd read the rabbi's latest posting. Thousands of messages had poured in since the earthquake. Many identified themselves as members of the 144,000 Jewish witnesses. An on-screen meter showed the number of responses as they were added to the central bulletin board. The numbers whizzed past.

Judd only wanted to spend a few minutes on the Net, but he couldn't stop reading Dr. Ben-Judah's message. The main posting was based on Revelation 8 and 9. Tsion believed the wrath of the Lamb earthquake began the second period of the Tribulation. Tsion wrote:

> There are seven years, or eighty-four months, in all. You can see we are now one quarter of the way through. As bad as things have been, they get worse.
>
> What is next? In Revelation 8:5 an angel takes a censer, fills it with fire from the altar of God, and throws it to the earth. That results in noise, thunder, lightning, and an earthquake.
>
> That same chapter goes on to say that seven angels with seven trumpets prepared themselves to sound. That is where we are now. Sometime over the next twenty-one months, the first angel will sound,

and hail and fire will follow, mingled with blood, thrown down to the earth. This will burn a third of the trees and all the green grass.

Judd knew he needed to make contact with someone about helping Vicki, but he couldn't stop reading. He was looking at what he would have to experience if he survived.

Later a second angel will sound the second trumpet, and the Bible says a great mountain burning with fire will be thrown into the sea. This will turn a third of the water to blood, kill a third of the living creatures in the sea, and sink a third of the ships.

Judd was stunned. He shook his head and tried to imagine all those things taking place. The world would be in even greater turmoil than it was now, after the worldwide earthquake. He read on.

The third angel's trumpet sound will result in a great star falling from heaven, burning like a torch. It will somehow fall over a wide area and land in a third of the rivers and springs. This star is even named in Scripture. The book of Revelation calls it Wormwood. Where it falls, the water becomes bitter and people die from drinking it.

Judd heard a ding and a window popped up saying he had an E-mail. It was Dr. Ben-Judah.

"Judd, I have been praying for you and your friends. Is everyone all right?"

Judd brought Tsion up-to-date and gave him the bad news about Ryan. There was a long pause.

"I am sorry you have to go through such a painful experience. Losing a friend like Ryan is very difficult. His love for God's Word was an encouragement to me. I will miss him greatly."

"What about the adult Trib Force?" Judd wrote.

"Buck is searching for Chloe even now," Tsion wrote. "Please pray. Rayford is alive in New Babylon. Unfortunately, his wife, Amanda, was on a flight that is reported missing. Rayford still holds out hope that she is alive, but the reports are not encouraging."

"What about Loretta and Donny at the church?"

"They are both in the presence of Jesus," Tsion wrote. "Donny's wife as well."

Judd shook his head. Loretta had been like a second mom to him. He told Tsion about Vicki, and the rabbi said he would stop everything and pray for her.

"O God," Tsion wrote, "you have delivered your servants from the lions, from the furnace, and from the hands of evil authorities. I pray you would deliver our dear sister from any harm now. May your peace wash over her and may she remain faithful to you in every word and action."

———————————

Vicki wondered when Melinda and Felicia would tire. She was barely able to keep her eyes open as they asked question after question. Finally, they escorted her to a cell.

Vicki put her head down on a cot. Her ankle was

swollen and turning blue, but it didn't hurt as much. Her clothes had dried so she wasn't cold anymore.

She knew she should feel afraid, but she didn't. When she had asked God to forgive her, she didn't know how dangerous that decision would be. Now, if she had to give her life for the cause, she felt OK. Ryan had done it. Bruce had given his life as well.

If God wants me to go through the same thing as them, then so be it, she thought. She closed her eyes and for the first time in days slept soundly.

17

JUDD was thrilled to talk with Dr. Ben-Judah. When Judd asked where Tsion was staying, the rabbi replied, "I think it is safer if neither of us knows where the other is."

Tsion signed off. Judd e-mailed Pavel, his friend in New Babylon. Pavel had read Tsion's Web site and talked with Judd about receiving Christ. Judd was grateful this new believer had survived the earthquake. While he waited to make contact, Judd revisited Tsion's Web site. The rabbi wrote:

> How can a thinking person see all that has happened and not fear what is to come? If there are still unbelievers after the third Trumpet Judgment, the fourth should convince everyone. Anyone who resists the warnings of God at that time will likely have already decided to serve the enemy. The fourth Trumpet Judgment is a striking of the sun, the moon, and the

stars so that a third of the sun, a third of the moon, and a third of the stars are darkened. We will never again see sunshine as bright as we have before. The brightest summer day with the sun high in the sky will be only two-thirds as bright as it ever was. How will this be explained away?

Judd shook his head. "People explained away the fact that Jesus came back from the dead, too," he muttered. He read on with chills. What Tsion was writing would one day come true.

In the middle of this, the writer of the Revelation says he looked and heard an angel "flying through the midst of heaven." It was saying with a loud voice, "Woe, woe, woe to the inhabitants of the earth, because of the remaining blasts of the trumpet of the three angels who are about to sound!"

Tsion said he would cover more in his next lesson and ended with an encouraging message. The rabbi said he believed there was a time coming when many would believe in Christ. Tsion called it a "great soul harvest." He wrote:

Consider these promises. In the Old Testament book of Joel 2:28-32, God is speaking. He says, "And it shall come to pass afterward that I will pour out My Spirit on all flesh; your sons and your daughters shall prophesy, your old men shall dream dreams, your young men shall see visions. And also on My

menservants and on my maidservants I will pour out
My Spirit in those days."

I wonder if that means me? Judd thought. He continued.

> "And I will show wonders in the heavens and in the
> earth: blood and fire and pillars of smoke. The sun
> shall be turned into darkness, and the moon into
> blood, before the coming of the great and awesome
> day of the Lord.
>
> "And it shall come to pass that whoever calls on
> the name of the Lord shall be saved. For in Mount
> Zion and in Jerusalem there shall be deliverance, as
> the Lord has said, among the remnant whom the
> Lord calls."

Judd read on. Tsion wrote that Revelation makes it
clear that the judgments he mentioned would not come
until the servants of God had been sealed on their foreheads.

"That's just happened," Judd said, putting a hand to
his forehead.

> We are called by God to be servants. The function of
> a servant of Christ is to communicate the gospel of
> the grace of God. Although we will go through great
> persecution, we can comfort ourselves that during
> the Tribulation we look forward to astounding
> events outlined in Revelation.
>
> Revelation 7:9 quotes John saying, "After these

things I looked, and behold, a great multitude which no one could number, of all nations, tribes, peoples, and tongues, standing before the throne and before the Lamb, clothed with white robes, with palm branches in their hands. . . ."

These are the tribulation saints. Now follow me carefully. In a later verse, Revelation 9:16, the writer numbers the army of horsemen in a battle at two hundred million. If such a vast army can be numbered, what might the Scriptures mean when they refer to the tribulation saints, those who come to Christ during this period, as "a great multitude which no one could number"?

Judd sat back. He saw the logic. God was about to do something incredible on the earth and if he lived, Judd would get to see it.

Do you see why I believe we are justified in trusting God for more than a billion souls during this period? Let us pray for that great harvest. All who name Christ as their Redeemer can have a part in this, the greatest task ever assigned to mankind.

Vicki awoke. She couldn't tell whether it was morning or evening. The only window was toward the back of the jail area, out of her sight. She had slept soundly and awoke refreshed and hungry. Her ankle was tender, but she could at least stand on it without falling over.

An hour later a GC guard brought her some bread and soup. "Can you tell me what time it is?" Vicki said.

"Almost six," the man said.

"A.M. or P.M.?" Vicki said.

"P.M., miss," the guard said. "And you have a visitor waiting. They're getting him cleared right now."

Vicki couldn't imagine who it was. It couldn't be Judd, unless he was wearing some kind of disguise. A few minutes later Vicki heard the clicking heels of a well-dressed man. The guard opened the door, and the man stood in the shadows. He took off his hat and stepped forward.

Vicki gasped. "Mr. Stein!"

———

Pavel contacted Judd a few minutes later. Judd brought him up-to-date with all he had been through.

"I'm glad you're safe for now," Pavel wrote. "Many things are happening here as well."

"Like what?" Judd wrote.

"The rebuilding effort is going strong. Thousands are working with Cellular-Solar to get the communications network up. Some are being forced to help rebuild airports."

"Carpathia cares more about people traveling and talking with each other than he does about the sick and dying," Judd wrote. "The people at the shelters are doing the best they can. That's where the relief effort should be going."

"You are right," Pavel wrote, "though everyone here has been glowing about how Nicolae is handling the disaster. They talk of him as if he were a god. In fact, that may be what he thinks he is."

Judd sat forward. "What do you mean?"

"My father survived the quake. He said strange things about Nicolae. There are people who believe he is more than human."

Mr. Stein smiled. The guard would not allow him inside the cell. Instead, he sat on a stool outside.

"How are you?"

"Considering I almost drowned, I'm OK," Vicki said. "How did you know I was here?"

"A little bird," Mr. Stein said. "No, make that two. They told me what happened and that you were in trouble."

"That's an understatement," Vicki said. "Are you a lawyer?"

"No, but I know enough about the legal process to help. I would contact one of my lawyer friends, but I'm not sure there is time."

"Why?"

"This commander who will make the decision about you seems to have made up his mind. I told him I wanted to represent you, and he asked why I would bother. He seems very anxious to move ahead."

"Which means what?" Vicki said.

"If there is any arguing or convincing that will be done, it has to be done now."

"And you're going to try?"

"Unless you have another idea."

Vicki shook her head.

"First, you must tell me if you are guilty of the charge of murder."

Vicki explained what had happened with Mrs. Jenness. Mr. Stein listened intently and took a few notes. He scratched his chin when Vicki told about trying to pull Mrs. Jenness from the sinking car.

"This woman was your enemy," Mr. Stein said. "She was against you and those you were working with."

"I didn't really see her as an enemy," Vicki said. "She didn't know the truth. I always hoped we would some-day be able to break through to her. That's what I was trying to do when the earthquake hit. I was telling her that Jesus is—"

"Enough," Mr. Stein said. "I know your position by heart. Now tell me this: Why would you go back to help her? If you had saved her, she would have handed you over to the Global Community."

"A person's life is worth a lot more than my comfort or safety," Vicki said. "I tried to help her because she needed it. Sure, she could have turned me in, but if I hadn't tried, I couldn't live with myself."

Mr. Stein frowned. "I'm asking these questions because this is what the commander will ask. You're saying you helped Mrs. Jenness because . . . "

"There's a verse in the Bible that says there's no greater love than for a person to lay down his life for a friend," Vicki said.

"But she wasn't your friend," Mr. Stein said.

"Exactly," Vicki said. "And I wasn't a friend of Jesus when he gave his life for me. I was sinful and against him, and he still died for me."

"So you used that example to give you the strength to help Mrs. Jenness."

Vicki hung her head. "I only wish it would have worked."

Mr. Stein leaned forward. "I can't lie to you. When I talked to the commander and the young ladies he employs, they were rounding up the witnesses who say you actually murdered this woman."

"They have a girl who hates me and would say anything to get me in trouble, and they have another lady who saw me on the bridge in Mrs. Jenness's car."

"I admit the evidence is slim, but it is your word against the two of them. And Mrs. Jenness is dead. Is there anyone you can think of who could testify on your behalf?"

"Anyone I'd ask would be in bigger trouble because of it," Vicki said, leaning forward. "I want you to know, if I had it to do over again, I'd take the same chance. I don't care what happens. They can lock me up if they want."

"It will be much worse than that," Mr. Stein said.

Someone knocked on the door and motioned for the guard.

"Let me do the talking," Mr. Stein said.

———————————

Judd shuddered. "Are you sure no one can trace this?"

"I'm sure," Pavel said. "I'm using a line my father had

installed that cannot be accessed. When I am done, I take my computer back to my room."

"All right," Judd said. "What are the people in the inner circle saying about Nicolae?"

"Leon Fortunato, Carpathia's right-hand man, says he thinks the potentate could be the Messiah."

Judd blinked at the screen. "What does he base that on?"

"Fortunato thinks that because he was raised from the dead, Carpathia has to be some sort of deity."

"And what does Nicolae say about it?"

"He doesn't confirm it or deny it," Pavel said. "My father overheard one of Nicolae's conversations. The potentate said it was not time to make the claim that he is the Messiah, but he wasn't sure it was untrue."

"He thinks he's the Messiah, the savior of the world?"

"He said he knows there are people who say he is *the* Antichrist. He would love to prove them wrong."

"What does your father think?" Judd said.

"He looks at what Nicolae Carpathia has accomplished and says he wouldn't be surprised if Nicolae was sent by God."

Judd shook his head. "And what do you think?"

"I believe there is the one true Messiah and Savior," Pavel wrote, "and that man is Jesus Christ. Nicolae Carpathia is our enemy."

The guard opened the cell door. Melinda led Vicki and Mr. Stein into a conference room.

"When will we be able—," Mr. Stein said, but Melinda waved a hand.

"You can talk with the commander when he gets here," she said.

Vicki waited nervously, then closed her eyes.

"Are you tired?" Mr. Stein asked.

"I'm praying."

Mr. Stein sighed. "I think you had better do more than that."

"There's nothing more powerful I can do," Vicki said. "For some reason God wants me to go through this. I don't know why."

"Why would God want you to be jailed or killed for something you did not do?"

Vicki thought for a moment. *Maybe that's it.*

"In the New Testament there were many people who were killed or sent before authorities," Vicki said. "God said he would give them the right words to say. Maybe the commander or those two girls need to hear the message. Maybe one of them will be used by God to do something great for him."

"You need to be thinking of yourself," Mr. Stein said.

"I thought of myself my whole life," Vicki said. "That got me left behind."

Commander Blancka came in and glared at Vicki.

18

VICKI watched the commander carefully. He didn't look capable of kindness. His voice was low and gravelly.

"I'll review the charges, then you'll have a chance to respond," the commander muttered. "But this is not a trial. Under the Global Community statute during states of emergency, I'm the judge, the jury, and the one who will pass sentence."

Vicki nodded. Mr. Stein put a hand on her shoulder.

"Vicki Byrne, you're charged with the murder of Mrs. Laverne Jenness. You're also charged with stealing and then destroying Global Community property. You won't give us information on an escapee of a GC reeducation camp, a person whose name is Judd Thompson. That means you're harboring a criminal and subject to the same penalty as the accused.

"You're also charged with crimes against the Global Community and a number of smaller charges—"

179

"What crimes?" Mr. Stein interrupted.

Commander Blancka looked up. "You will not interrupt me!" he said. "Who are you anyway?"

"My name is Mitchell Stein. Vicki is a friend of the family. I am here to help in her defense."

"As I said, this is not a trial."

"Call it what you will, sir, but your decision will greatly affect my friend's life. She deserves representation."

"We'll find out what she deserves," the commander said. "I have statements from three people. One says Vicki was the last person seen with Mrs. Jenness before her body was found. Another woman says Vicki was seen on the roof pushing Mrs. Jenness inside the car."

Vicki shook her head.

"And the third witness says he helped Vicki dispose of a dead body."

"Commander," Mr. Stein said, "I think it would be helpful to hear Vicki's side of the story."

"I've read her statement," the commander said. "It's her word against the others. The fact that she ran from us, stole our vehicle, then destroyed it, and that she's been charged with speech against the Global Community in the past is pretty strong evidence, don't you think?"

Mr. Stein cleared his throat. "I am concerned that you do not have the entire story. Surely, if you are going to decide whether such serious charges are true, you should hear from the accused rather than what someone else said."

Vicki looked at Melinda and Felicia. Both girls scowled.

"Vicki is a young woman of faith," Mr. Stein continued. "This is something the Global Community has
encouraged."

"The GC hasn't encouraged anyone to commit
murder," the commander fumed.

"And if you will hear Vicki out, I think you'll conclude
that murder was the last thing on her mind that day. She
has a heart of compassion, not murder."

"All right," the commander said. "She can speak."

———————————

Judd heard a noise upstairs and muted his computer
speakers. Someone was inside the house. *Could be GC,
could be burglars,* Judd thought.

Moments later someone climbed down the rope
to the secret entrance. Judd looked for a weapon to
defend himself, then hit the light switch. The ceiling
moved. Judd flipped on the light. It was Darrion and
Shelly.

Judd welcomed them.

"We've got a surprise," Darrion said, pointing to the
opening. "Look who we found."

Mark stuck his head into the room and grinned. "You
were going to attack us with a computer keyboard?" He
smirked.

"It was the only thing I could find," Judd said, putting
the keyboard down. "Thought you might be the GC."

Mark crawled through and gave Judd a hug.

"Have you heard from John?"

"Who's John?" Darrion said.

Judd told Darrion about meeting John and Mark at Nicolae High.

"He was away at school when the quake hit," Mark said. "I've looked on every list of dead and injured I can find but I don't know anything for sure yet." Mark paused. "I heard about Ryan. I'm sorry."

Judd nodded and bit his lip. "What happened to you?"

"Long story," Mark said, pulling up a chair. "I was at my aunt's house when it hit. She has a dog that doesn't bark at anything. Too lazy. Well, this thing had him running back and forth in the front room, whining and barking. I figured it out before it hit, but I had a hard time convincing my aunt to follow me outside.

"When the roof in the kitchen started cracking, she believed me. I pulled her out just as the wall buckled. We got down the stairs before they collapsed. Then the whole neighborhood went. It was like trying to walk on concrete water."

"Was your aunt hurt?" Judd said.

"She ran back for the dog in the backyard," Mark said. "Glass from next door hit her in the face and neck. Lots of blood. I grabbed the dog in one arm and held her up with the other."

"Between the attack on the militia base and the earthquake, you've had some pretty close calls," Judd said.

Judd brought them up-to-date on what he knew about the Trib Force. They still hadn't heard if Chloe was alive, or whether Rayford's wife, Amanda, had been on the plane that had crashed during the earthquake.

"I just hope the next people we see coming through that opening are Lionel and Vicki," Judd said.

———————————————

Lionel listened outside the conference room. He didn't want to go in unless Commander Blancka called him.

"We need to plan for the worst," Lionel said. "If she's convicted, we have to be ready."

"For what?" said Conrad.

"To spring her."

———————————————

Vicki felt nervous, but Mr. Stein's smile calmed her.

"Vicki, why don't you tell the commander about the morning of the earthquake?"

Vicki nodded. "Mrs. Jenness caught me before school with some papers," she said. "I was trying to warn people about the earthquake."

"Wait," the commander said. "You knew there was going to be an earthquake?"

"It's predicted in the Bible," Vicki said. "I didn't know it was going to hit that morning, but it was the next event that was supposed to happen. I can show you if—"

The commander waved a hand. "No, just go ahead."

"Mrs. Jenness was angry. She destroyed the papers, and we headed toward a GC facility."

"Is it true you spent some time away from school because of a behavior problem?" the commander said, glancing toward Melinda.

"Yes," Vicki admitted. "The school thought I was behind the *Underground* newspaper so I was sent away."

"So you were guilty and trying to hide it?"

"Yes," Vicki said.

"Tell us about what happened on the bridge," Mr. Stein said.

Vicki told them the truth about trying to save Mrs. Jenness's life. When she was through, the commander leaned forward. "You must think I'm crazy," he said. "You actually think I'll believe you tried to save a woman who was trying to put you away?"

Mr. Stein stood. "Commander, I had a hard time believing it myself. Then I took a look at this girl's background. She stayed in our home for a brief time.

"Vicki lost her father, her mother, and her younger sister in the vanishings. The family had gone through some sort of religious awakening. Everyone but Vicki. The disappearances upset her. She couldn't think straight. So she came up with this idea of God taking her family away."

"Wait a minute," Vicki said.

"Quiet, I want to hear this," the commander said.

"To strengthen her belief she began to tell others about it. The more people she told, the more convinced she became it was true. This student newspaper is a good example. She knew it would be a disaster if she were ever caught. But she wanted to spread her message."

"How does this fit with Mrs. Jenness?" the commander said.

"You have to understand her belief," Mr. Stein said.

"She thinks Jesus was the Messiah. She bases everything in her life on the notion that Jesus came to take away true believers—and will come again. She lives by his teachings, prays to him, even memorizes the words of the Bible."

Mr. Stein smiled and rummaged through his briefcase. "When I asked her the same question about saving Mrs. Jenness's life, she quoted a verse to me." He flipped open a Bible. Vicki saw it was Chaya's.

"Here it is," he said. " 'The greatest love is shown when people lay down their lives for their friends.' "

"And that convinced you she tried to save Mrs. Jenness?" the commander said.

Mr. Stein took off his glasses and walked toward the commander. "Sir, you may call this young lady misguided. You can say she is confused, that her beliefs are wacky, or that she's sick. But her life is controlled by the notion that Mrs. Jenness needed to believe the same way Vicki does to have any hope of heaven."

"And that kind of belief is dangerous to the unity of the Global Community," the commander said.

"You must be the judge of that, sir," Mr. Stein said.

"And I will be."

Vicki stood. "I want to say something."

The commander put his hand to his forehead and squeezed. "Sit!"

"I know what Mr. Stein's trying to do," Vicki said. "He's trying to make it look like I'm mental. I'm not. Take a look around you. People have disappeared. Treaties have been signed. There's been a worldwide earthquake,

185

something the experts said would never happen. All of it was predicted in the Bible. If you ignore this and go on like it hasn't happened, then I say *that's* crazy."

"Do you see what I mean?" Mr. Stein said.

"Stop trying to make me out to be insane!" Vicki shouted.

"Can I have a moment with her, sir?" Mr. Stein said.

Judd grilled Mark about what he had seen.

"Buck Williams is the only person I've seen from the Trib Force," Mark said. "And I only saw him as he passed in his Range Rover."

"So you stayed at shelters?" Judd said.

"I helped my aunt get to one, then a bunch of GC guys came through and loaded anybody healthy onto the back of a truck."

"You must have been scared out of your mind," Shelly said.

"They had no idea who I was," Mark said. "They were just looking for anybody who had the strength to work."

"Let me guess," Judd said. "Cellular-Solar."

"You got it," Mark said. "They worked us all that day and into the night clearing the way for the new communication towers. We cut down old ones and dug holes for new ones. They've got cell towers and satellite receivers just about everywhere."

"How did you get here?" Judd said.

"Saw my chance to run and took off," Mark said.

"I came back to check on my aunt and found Shelly and Darrion."

"How's your aunt?" Judd said.

"She'll live, but it'll be a while before I can move her," Mark said.

Lionel stood as Vicki and Mr. Stein walked into the hall-way. He had heard most of the conversation and thought the commander might be changing his mind about Vicki.

"You're trying to make me look like a fool," Vicki whispered to Mr. Stein.

"I'm trying to save your life," Mr. Stein said. "Which do you care more about, your reputation or your survival?"

"I don't care what people think about me," Vicki said, "but you're trying to make what I believe look sick."

"If he lets you go, what does it matter?"

"It's not the truth!" Vicki shouted.

Lionel approached. "Vick, it may be a way out for you," he whispered.

"I can't believe you'd go along with this," Vicki said.

"I just want you to get out of here alive."

"And so do I," Mr. Stein said.

The door opened. Melinda and Felicia scowled.

"All right, time for you to get back inside," Lionel barked. He followed them inside.

Melinda whispered something to the commander, then turned and glared at Lionel.

"You have something to say?" the commander said to Mr. Stein.

"Yes," Mr. Stein said with a sheepish look. "Vicki wants to make sure I do not represent her in any way as being sick or crazy."

"Right," the commander said. "Washington!"

Lionel jumped to his feet. "Yes, sir!"

"I'm told you know this girl and her friend who took the jeep."

Sweat rolled down Lionel's forehead. He wiped it away. "Before I went south to the camp I did."

"Have any idea where this Judd Thompson might be?"

"Believe me, sir," Lionel said, "if I knew where Judd was, I'd be there right now."

"Have any comment about this Byrne girl before I decide what to do with her?"

Lionel hesitated. He looked at Vicki. "I don't have any comment, sir, except to say that I know she'll get what she deserves in the end."

Lionel turned and saw a look of surprise on Melinda's face.

The commander shuffled papers and cleared his throat. Before he spoke, a guard entered the room and approached him. The two talked quietly, then the commander hurried to the back door.

"Take her back to her cell," the commander said. "I'll give my decision tomorrow morning. Meet here at 0800 hours."

19

VICKI was taken to her cell. Mr. Stein followed and was allowed inside.

"What happens now?" Vicki said.

"Your guess is as good as mine," Mr. Stein said. "Sounds like the commander will decide between now and tomorrow morning."

"Do you think there's a chance—?"

"If he believes you are a little off in the head," Mr. Stein said, "he might just send you to a reeducation camp."

"And if not?"

"I don't want to think about it."

"I'm not afraid to die for the gospel," Vicki said.

Mr. Stein shook his head. "I'll never understand why fanatics say things like that. You think it impresses me. It doesn't. There are many people who would give their lives for something foolish."

"The point isn't whether I would die for my faith," Vicki said. "The main thing is whether what I put my faith in is true."

"You sound like my daughter."

"If they said it was illegal to talk about God," Vicki said, "I would die giving you that message. But I'd rather live to see you accept your Messiah. That's what Chaya was praying for all along."

"They're coming for you tomorrow morning," Mr. Stein said, "and the best you can hope for is to go to a reeducation camp. Why would you be concerned about me when you're facing that?"

"Lionel said it best."

"He was against you."

"No, I understood. He said he knew I'd get what I deserved. Because of Jesus, I have the hope of heaven. The Global Community can't take that away."

"I wish I were as confident as you about the future," Mr. Stein said.

Vicki scribbled the address for Tsion Ben-Judah's Web site on a scrap of paper. "Please, when you get home tonight, look this up. I don't know if the rabbi survived the earthquake, but I'm sure his postings from the past few months are there."

"This is the man who was on television," Mr. Stein said. He rose and called for the guard. "I'll be back in the morning."

"You saved Chaya's Bible," Vicki said. "Why?"

Mr. Stein bowed his head. "Losing Chaya so soon after her mother's death was difficult. So I kept it. I can't tell you why."

"Have you read it?" Vicki said.

"I looked up the verse you talked about, but only for the purpose of helping you."

"You're a man of your word," Vicki said. "You promised Chaya you would find me, and you did. Now promise me something. No matter what happens to me, promise you'll look at that Web site and then read the Gospel of Matthew. It was written to Jewish people."

"I can't promise—"

"It would mean a lot to me," Vicki said.

The guard opened the cell door. Mr. Stein flipped to the first book of the New Testament and smiled. "I am a klutz when it comes to computers. But I will try to read this Matthew passage."

"I have your word?"

"You have my word."

Vicki smiled.

———————————————

Judd tried to find out about Vicki through the Internet, but there was nothing. He e-mailed Tsion and asked the rabbi to pray. Judd suggested contacting Buck Williams, but Tsion said Buck wasn't available. He was still frantically looking for Chloe.

The kids talked about Ryan and traded stories. There were laughter and tears. Finally, Darrion said, "I think Shelly and I should go back to get Vicki."

"No way," Judd said.

Shelly said, "Darrion's right. It's dark. No one would see us. If they do, we'll say we're just looking for shelter."

"The GC have orders to shoot anyone moving around at night," Mark said. "We'd have to wait till morning."

"Vicki may not have that long," Darrion said.

"They'll probably send her to a reeducation camp like they did me," Judd said. "We can work on getting her out after she's sent there."

"Probably doesn't cut it," Darrion said. "That girl Joyce and the other two Morale Monitors have it in for her. If they believe she murdered her principal, they might give her the death penalty."

The four kids were silent. Judd thought of Vicki waiting in a cell. Or maybe they had already passed the sentence.

"We only have two options," Judd said. "We can try to find her and get her out, or we can wait and let Lionel and Conrad try. They're inside the GC machine."

"He's right," Mark said. "We have to trust Lionel and Conrad."

Lionel and Conrad secretly met outside the Global Community station.

"What happens if we get her out and then get caught?" Conrad said.

"We'd probably be shot for deserting," Lionel said.

Conrad sighed. "I don't see how we can let her go in there tomorrow morning. But I don't want the commander to pull the trigger on me either."

"He won't have the chance," Lionel said. "If my plan works, we'll be out of here by midnight. We can make it to the hideout before sunup."

"What if somebody sees us?"

"We're Morale Monitors," Lionel said. "We're searching for the other kid."

Conrad nodded. "All right, what's the plan?"

Judd and the others searched for blankets and pillows. Darrion said she was going upstairs to find a change of clothes. Mark surfed the Web for any information about Vicki. A few minutes later he called for Judd.

"Take a look at this on the Enigma Babylon page," Mark said.

Judd watched as an image of a smiling Pontifex Maximus Peter Mathews appeared on the screen. The man wore a huge hat and a funny outfit. Underneath was a message to "every soul on earth."

"Wherever you are in the world, whatever you're going through, know that Enigma Babylon One World Faith will be there. When disaster strikes, when governments fail, when your life crumbles before you, trust in Enigma Babylon."

"Looks like a commercial, doesn't it?" Mark said.

"The sad thing is, people will buy into it," Judd said.

Judd read on. "Don't be fooled by those who would cause you to fear for your future. Do not be led away from the hope of a new world order. Be part of a new breed of global citizenship."

"From reading that you'd think this Pontifex guy was competing with Carpathia," Mark said.

Judd sighed. "We've got bigger problems than Enigma Babylon right now."

Mark turned his chair toward Judd and spoke softly. "You're worried about her, aren't you?"

"I'm going out of my skin because there's nothing I can do. I want to march down there, grab Vicki, and run. But I know I can't."

Shelly burst into the room. "Have you guys seen Darrion?"

"I thought she went upstairs," Judd said.

"I've looked," Shelly said. "She's not upstairs or in the hangar."

_____

Lionel found Melinda alone in a snack room at the station. He bought a drink and sat at a nearby table.

"Where's Felicia?" Lionel said.

Melinda didn't look up. "Went back to the shelter to get our stuff. We're staying here tonight."

"It'll be more comfortable than sleeping on the ground," Lionel said.

Melinda looked up. "What's with you? Why the small talk?"

"I'm really sorry about everything," Lionel said. "You guys were right. If I'd have listened to you, we'd have both of them in custody and the commander wouldn't be out a jeep."

"He told us he was going to have a talk with you tomorrow after the sentencing."

"I deserve it," Lionel said. "I just don't want this to break up the team."

Melinda eyed him warily. "You mean it?"

Lionel nodded. "Let me buy you some hot chocolate or something."

194

"Sure," Melinda said.

Lionel put money in the machine and turned his back to Melinda. "So why'd the commander rush out of here?"

"Didn't tell us," Melinda said, "but you know it has to be important. I think he wanted to finish with this girl tonight."

Lionel stirred the drink and handed it to her. "Know what I think? I say Vicki's in that cell thinking this is the last night of her life."

"It probably is."

"But what if it isn't?" Lionel said, dragging his chair close. "What if the commander buys into what that Stein guy says, that she's crazy or something."

"The commander's too smart for that—"

"Even in situations like this, you can't execute crazy people," Lionel said. "There's a chance he could send her to a reeducation site."

Melinda sipped her hot chocolate and shook her head. "He wouldn't do that. He can't. The girl murdered that principal."

"Melinda, there's a chance the commander might let her go. If he was going to give her a harsh sentence, why wouldn't he have done it before he ran out of here?"

Melinda took another sip.

"Now if I'm that girl," Lionel said, "and I'm thinking this is the last night of my life, I'd do or say anything to get out of it."

"What are you suggesting?"

"The commander wants the guy, Judd, right?"

"He'll find him."

195

"Eventually. But what if we get the information ourselves?"

"We don't have the commander's OK," Melinda said. "They won't even let us in to talk with her."

Conrad walked into the snack room. "What's up?" Lionel filled him in.

"No way," Conrad said. "I'm in enough trouble with the commander as it is."

"This could get us all some points," Melinda said. "If we get the information, we can deliver this Judd guy by the time the commander passes sentence."

"Exactly," Lionel said.

Conrad crumpled his can of soda. "Call me chicken or whatever you want, I'm not going down there."

Melinda drank the last of her hot chocolate. "I'm in. Let's go."

Judd led Shelly and Mark through the darkened house. Judd found the staircase that led upstairs. It was pitched at an angle and didn't look safe.

The three called for Darrion, but there was no answer.

"She told me her room was upstairs," Shelly said.

"Let me go first and see if it's safe," Judd said.

When he got to the middle, the staircase cracked and collapsed. Judd grabbed the railing overhead and pulled himself up. "You guys OK?" he said.

"Didn't hit us," Mark said. "See if you can find her room."

196

Judd knew where Mr. Stahley's office was. He went in and looked through the drawers. On the other side of the house he found Darrion's room. He tried a light, but the bulb was broken. The moonlight shone through the window. Judd saw clothes on the floor. He rushed to the stairs and used the railing to let himself down.

"She changed clothes upstairs," Judd said.

"The front door was open a bit," Mark said. "You think she's gone?"

"I think it's worse than that," Judd said. "Mr. Stahley's revolver is gone."

"You think Darrion has a gun?" Shelly said.

"Unless the looters got it."

An engine revved outside. Judd flew out the door in time to see a motorcycle bouncing through the grass near the entrance to the estate.

"Is that Darrion?" Shelly said.

"Has to be," Mark said, "but where'd she get the bike? Everything in the garage was gone."

"Stahley had all kinds of hiding places," Judd said. "Probably had the bike stashed for an emergency."

"Where do you think she's going?" Shelly said.

"She's trying to rescue Vick," Judd said.

Lionel knew he had to get Melinda into the cell quickly. Getting past the guard would be their major problem. But which tactic? Make the guard sympathize with them or play hardball?

"I don't have authorization to let you in," the guard said.

"The reason you don't have authorization is Commander Blancka had to leave on important business," Lionel said. "He expects us to get the information from the girl tonight."

"Why do you think he delayed the sentencing?" Melinda said, scowling at the guard.

"I'd let you in if I had—"

"That's fine," Lionel said. "When the commander comes back here in the morning and finds out you wouldn't let us in, it's your problem, not ours."

Lionel pulled at Melinda's arm. "Let's get out of here."

"Wait," the guard said. "So, you just want to go talk with her, right?"

Melinda turned. "This guy who blew up the commander's jeep—she knows where he is. Now's our chance to get it from her."

"OK," the guard said. "I'll let you in. But you have to leave your weapons here and sign in."

———————

Mitchell Stein opened his laptop. He took the scrap of paper and typed in the address. Reading the words of a traitor to his faith turned his stomach, but a promise was a promise.

Mr. Stein read through some of the E-mails that had poured in since the earthquake. "These people are like sheep," he muttered.

He clicked on an icon that took him to a separate section written by Rabbi Ben-Judah.

> For those of you who still doubt our message, or who need the information to make an informed decision, I have written the following. The texts are found in the book of Romans, a logical layout of what we believe, written by the apostle Paul. Scholars have long been amazed at the sound reasoning and unity of thought contained in this book.

Mr. Stein wanted to stop, but something drew him to the words on the screen.

> Early in the book, Paul writes, "From the time the world was created, people have seen the earth and sky and all that God made. They can clearly see his invisible qualities—his eternal power and divine nature. So they have no excuse whatsoever for not knowing God."
>
> If it is true that God has put the knowledge of himself on our hearts, what would keep a person from understanding the true and living God? The answer is found two chapters away. "For all have sinned; all fall short of God's glorious standard." A little further in the book Paul writes, "For the wages of sin is death, but the free gift of God is eternal life through Christ Jesus our Lord."

Mr. Stein read on about God's Law and how people had tried to make a way to God themselves. The rabbi wrote:

It will not work. God's Law is holy and perfect and can accept nothing but perfection. You and I are imperfect. The more you read about God's Law, the more you understand how imperfect we are.

That is true, Mr. Stein thought.

The only way to God is through accepting the gift he has given in Jesus. He lived a perfect life. He died in our place. He took the penalty for our sin. "Salvation that comes from trusting Christ . . . is already within easy reach," Paul wrote. "For if you confess with your mouth that Jesus is Lord and believe in your heart that God raised him from the dead, you will be saved. For it is by believing in your heart that you are made right with God, and it is by confessing with your mouth that you are saved."

There were more verses and a prayer the rabbi included at the end, but Mr. Stein couldn't read any further. He sat back in his chair and stared at the ceiling. He had believed his wife and daughter were mistaken. He had thought they were confused about their faith. Now he was confused.

20

VICKI was glad to see Lionel, then she noticed Melinda behind him. Lionel unlocked the cell door, and the two walked in. Vicki sat up on her cot and looked them over. Lionel and Melinda stared at her.

"What's up?" Vicki said. "Has the commander decided?"

"What do *you* think?" Melinda said. "You counting on him letting you out of here?"

"I don't know what he'll do," Vicki said. "All I know is that I'm innocent."

Lionel laughed. "That's a good one. You're as innocent as those militia people."

Vicki couldn't believe Lionel would turn on her like this. Had he lost his memory again?

"You've only got one hope now, Byrne," Melinda said. "You tell us what you know about this Judd Thompson, and we'll have a talk with the commander before he sentences you."

"I don't know where—"

"Think hard before you answer," Lionel said, getting down in Vicki's face. Lionel winked. "Tell us where you and Judd were going before we caught you."

Vicki felt relieved. Lionel was up to something. She wanted to play along but didn't know what to say. Finally, she said, "If I tell you, what happens to Judd?"

"What is he, your boyfriend?" Melinda said. "Do yourself a favor and give him up."

"All right," Vicki said. "If you promise to talk to the commander."

Judd and the others looked in the garage, but there were no vehicles left. The Stahleys' cars had either been stolen or taken by the GC.

"What do you think she'll do?" Mark said.

"Who knows," Judd said. "She's lost her mother and father, and now Ryan's dead. She'll probably risk it and go into the GC camp and wave that gun around."

"She doesn't even know where they're holding Vicki, if she's still alive," Shelly said.

"Vick's alive," Judd said. "She has to be."

Lionel shouted at Vicki. He glanced away and saw Melinda put her hand to her head and wince. Just a few more minutes and his plan would work.

"Judd and I were headed back to the church," Vicki said. "There's an underground hideout there. And we would have made it if that stupid chopper hadn't shown up."

"You were miles from the church when they found you," Melinda said.

"We tried to throw the GC off by driving away," Vicki said.

Melinda sat on the floor. "I don't feel so good." She rubbed her head and moaned.

Lionel knelt beside her. "What's the matter?"

"It's my head," she said, running a hand through her hair. "Everything's spinning. I want to go back to the other room."

"Should I call for the guard?" Vicki said.

"No," Lionel snapped. "Just lie down. You'll be OK in a minute."

Melinda's eyes widened. "You! You put something in my drink!" She reached for a cell bar to pull herself up, but Lionel grabbed her and put a hand over her mouth. Melinda tried to shout, but she was helpless.

"Help me get her to the bed," Lionel said to Vicki.

Vicki grabbed Melinda's arm, and the two dragged the girl to Vicki's cot. By the time her head hit the pillow, Melinda had passed out.

"Listen close," Lionel said. "We're not out of this yet. I'm going down the hall to signal Conrad. You change clothes with Melinda. When Conrad comes, you have to be ready."

"What about the guard?" Vicki said. "He'll know!"

"That's where Conrad comes in," Lionel said. "You have three minutes to make the change."

With tears streaming down her face, Darrion flew into the night. She hated going against Judd and the others, but she couldn't sit still and watch another person she loved die without a fight. Vicki had taken her in and helped her when it seemed the whole world was against her. Darrion couldn't bear the thought of Vicki's execution or even imprisonment.

She felt the gun on her hip and wondered if she would have to use it. She wished she had tried to rescue her mother before the earthquake. She wouldn't make the same mistake again. Still, Darrion had no idea how she would find Vicki or get her out. But she knew she had to try.

Darrion had believed in Christ long enough to know she needed God's help to do anything. But she couldn't think of that now. She didn't even want to pray. God didn't seem to be doing anything to help her friends, so she would take over.

Darrion's father had taught her a lot about motorcycles. But nothing had prepared her for this ride. The road was jagged, and she nearly lost control several times. She slowed when the beam of her headlight shone on water.

I have to cross the river.

She backtracked along the bank until she saw work crews with huge lights working on a bridge. The top of the bridge was intact, but the pavement had crumbled. The GC workers pounded nails in boards.

The workers looked up as Darrion gunned the engine and shot past them across the rickety boards.

"She'll never make it to the end," someone shouted.

But Darrion had been trained well. She picked her way through the shaky maze of boards and steel girders. The lights showed a huge gap between the end of the bridge and the riverbank. She gunned the engine again, shot past the last row of men, and soared into the air.

Lionel ran to the back of the jail and signaled Conrad with his flashlight. A moment later Conrad sent an identical message back.

"Good," Lionel said. "Everything's working."

Lionel quickly moved to the front door and listened for the guard. A cell phone rang. The guard said, "Hello? Hello?"

Lionel ran back to Vicki. Melinda lay limp on the cot in Vicki's dirty clothes.

"What did you give her?" Vicki said. "She's totally out."

"I saved a couple of sleeping pills they gave me after the earthquake," Lionel said. "One pill helped me sleep. I figured two would knock her out."

"What happens—?" Vicki said.

"I don't have time to explain. When I give the word, you hustle past Conrad and me and head for the front door. Don't stop for anybody, got it?"

"Got it," Vicki said. "But—"

Lionel held up a hand. A door opened outside. Conrad shouted something.

"She's in there," the guard said.

On cue, Conrad burst into the cell area and shouted,

"Where's Melinda? Commander Blancka wants her right away!"

"Commander Blancka!" Lionel shouted. "Come on, let's get you out of here."

Vicki ran past Lionel. Conrad blocked the view of the guard.

"Hey, you have to sign out," the guard shouted as Vicki ran out the door.

"I'll sign for her," Lionel said.

"I wonder what the commander wants," Conrad said.

"Must be pretty important," Lionel said as he signed his name and Melinda's.

"Did you get that girl to talk?" the guard said.

"She clammed up," Lionel said. "Went to sleep. We gotta get outta here and see what the commander wants. Thanks for your help."

Lionel and Conrad followed Vicki a few blocks away. They ducked into a darkened alley. All three were out of breath.

"I'm staying," Conrad said.

"No way," Lionel said. "We agreed as soon as Vicki was free, you'd get out of here."

"We need somebody inside," Conrad said.

"They'll pin this on you," Lionel said.

"I'll tell them I got a call from someone who said they were an aide to Commander Blancka. What was I supposed to do—ignore it?"

Lionel bit his lip. The plan made sense, but he knew Conrad was scared of staying with the GC. "Are you sure?"

206

Conrad nodded. The three put their hands together.

"God go with you," Conrad said.

"You too," Vicki said. She hugged him.

"Let's go," Lionel said.

Vicki's ankle felt much better. She and Lionel ran side by side. Vicki got her bearings and noticed some of the same neighborhoods she and Judd had gone through.

"Someday you're going to have to tell me how you got mixed up with these morale people," Vicki whispered.

"Just get me to the Stahley place and I'll tell you anything you want to know," Lionel said.

As they came over a hill, a light hit them from below. Vicki ducked, then started back. Lionel grabbed her arm.

"Stop or we'll shoot!" a man shouted from below.

Lionel whispered to Vicki, "You're a Morale Monitor, remember that." He put his hands over his head and led Vicki down the hill. When they came close to the GC guards, Lionel said, "We're working with Commander Blancka on finding a missing kid."

"Where's your side arm?" the guard said suspiciously.

Lionel winced. "It's a long story. Commander Blancka said we had to find this guy or we'd get the same punishment. We let him get away."

"Him?" the guard said. "Too bad. I thought I might be able to help you."

"What do you mean?" Lionel said.

"We picked up a girl on a motorcycle about ten

minutes ago," the guard said. "She had a GC-registered side arm. Wouldn't give us her name."

"Doesn't sound like who we're looking for," Lionel said. "We're looking for a Judd Thompson."

"I'll send a report to the other patrols," the guard said. "Give me your names."

Lionel gave him his name and Melinda's. When the guard was gone he said, "That was close."

"What happened to your gun?" Vicki said.

"Left it when we got you out," Lionel said.

"It's a good thing we didn't run away from them," Vicki said. "I just don't want to be out here when they find Sleeping Beauty in that cell."

Judd didn't sleep all night. He paced the floor of the computer room, then moved upstairs when he saw he was keeping the others awake. His body wasn't on the same schedule as everyone else's.

It was nearly sunup when he finally sat on the couch and grew tired. A noise startled him. He heard footsteps in the kitchen, and voices.

GC, Judd thought. *They've caught Darrion, and she led them back here.* Judd scooted down on the couch and reached for his gun. These guys wouldn't take him without a fight.

The voices came nearer. "It's gotta be around here somewhere," one said.

"I thought they said it was near a hallway that led to the kitchen," another said.

Judd peeked over the top of the couch. He clicked the safety off and yelled, "Hold it right there!"

The two scrambled backward and put up their hands. "Don't shoot!" one of them said.

Judd stood and walked closer.

"Judd, is that you?" a girl said.

"Vicki?" Judd said.

Judd finally saw their faces. *Vicki and Lionel.* A wave of relief swept over him. He put the gun away. Vicki ran to him and they embraced. Judd put an arm around Lionel.

"I didn't know if I'd ever see you guys again," Judd said.

"It wasn't easy," Lionel said. He told Judd the story of their escape and meeting the GC patrol. "We had to talk our way across a bridge. I'm glad we're finally safe. All except Conrad."

"And Darrion," Judd said. "She took off last night on her dad's motorcycle."

Vicki gasped. "The patrol said they'd taken a girl on a motorcycle into custody."

Judd sat down hard on the sofa. "Once the GC figure out who she is, she's in big trouble."

"We're all in trouble," Vicki said.

"You think she'd lead them back here?" Lionel said.

"Not on purpose," Vicki said, "but they'd be able to trace that bike."

Conrad and Felicia were waiting at the door the next morning when Commander Blancka walked in. "Why did you want to see Melinda last night, sir?"

"What are you talking about?" the commander said.

"I got a call last night that said you wanted to see Melinda. The man said it was urgent and she should meet you at the helipad."

"I never gave that order," the commander said. He looked at Felicia. "Go check on her."

"I was there all night, sir," Felicia said. "Melinda never returned."

The commander glared at Conrad.

"I went down to the cell to give her the message—"

"What cell?" the commander said.

"Where you were keeping that girl, Vicki. That's where Lionel and Melinda were."

The commander barked into his radio as Conrad continued. "I saw them in the snack room. They were planning on getting information out of that girl. They wanted to find the guy by this morning and impress you."

The guard at the cell block said Melinda and Lionel had signed out late the previous night.

"Bring the Byrne girl here immediately," the commander said.

Mr. Stein came in. Conrad thought he looked upset.

"Have you reached a decision, sir?" Mr. Stein said.

"You'll find out soon enough," the commander said.

"Sir, if you intend to execute this young lady, I must know now."

The commander stiffened. "Sit down and wait."

The guard hustled into the room. Behind him was the groggy prisoner. "She's out of her head. Says she was tricked."

Felicia gasped. "Melinda!"

The commander slammed his fist on the table. He looked at Mr. Stein. "You tricked my guard!"

"I did nothing of the sort," Mr. Stein said.

The commander fumed. "You're all under arrest until I find the person responsible for this!"

21

THE NEWEST member of the Young Tribulation Force shook his head as Morale Monitor Melinda accused him of working against the Global Community.

They don't know where Vicki and Lionel are, Conrad Graham thought as Commander Blancka fumed.

"You helped Vicki escape," Melinda said, still groggy from sleeping pills Lionel had given her the night before.

"You're crazy," Conrad said. "You and Lionel blew that. I told you questioning her was a bad idea!"

"That was part of your plan," Melinda said.

The commander interrupted. "Graham, tell me about the call."

"Some guy said you wanted to see Melinda," Conrad said. "I just delivered the message."

"You didn't verify it?"

"There was no reason," Conrad said. "Besides, everything's been crazy around here."

"He knows something and he's not telling," Felicia said.

Conrad turned on her. "How do we know Melinda didn't set this up with Lionel? Ask her what she was doing in that cell—"

"Lionel drugged her!" Felicia said.

"Enough," Commander Blancka said, glaring at Conrad. "Until I sort this out, you'll stay locked up like Stein."

"But, sir—"

"Take him away!"

Judd and the others inspected the underground hangar and found scattered rocks and dirt. Airplane equipment lay strewn about.

Mark pointed out the steel girders. "That's why we're safe here," he said.

Judd found the wall the GC had cut through to get to him and Ryan. Plaster and flooring from above covered the hole.

"We have only one way in or out," Judd said, showing Mark the collapsed secret door in the hillside.

"We can dig a new opening," Mark said. "Won't be fancy, but we'll have another exit."

The kids grabbed tools. After a few minutes, Vicki threw down her shovel. "Have you guys forgotten Darrion and Conrad?" she said. "They're facing Blancka!"

"Darrion said the same thing about you," Judd said, "and look where she is now."

"At least she cared enough to do something," Vicki said.

"Don't give me that!" Judd shouted. "I risked my life to get back here."

"To do what?" Vicki said. "Save us?"

Mark and Shelly stopped digging.

"Settle down," Lionel said. "We're on the same side, remember?"

"Yeah, but Judd always has to show us who's boss," Vicki said.

Judd shook his head.

"The GC are going to figure out who Darrion is," Vicki said. "We have to get her out."

"They'll probably trace the cycle back here," Judd said. "That's why we're digging."

Vicki rolled her eyes. "My point exactly," she said. "You care more about yourself—"

"If Darrion had listened, she wouldn't be where she is."

"Like you've never made a mistake," Vicki said.

"Judd's right," Lionel said. "Conrad's our best bet to get her out."

"He might not even know they have her," Vicki said.

Judd reached for Vicki's shoulder, but she jerked away.

Lionel stared at them. "Is something going on here?"

Judd scratched his head. "Give us a minute."

Lionel returned to help Mark and Shelly.

"You're upset about Darrion," Judd said.

"That's not all," Vicki said. "We got out of there so fast there wasn't time to bring Phoenix."

"You're worried about a dog?"

"I promised Ryan. Maybe promises don't mean that much to you—"

"Stop it!" Judd said. "I know you promised, but risking your life for Phoenix doesn't make sense."

"You get mixed up with a biker gang and try to jump a motorcycle over a river, and *I* don't make sense?"

Judd took Vicki by the shoulders. "This is partly because of us."

Vicki squinted. "Don't flatter yourself!"

"I care for you, Vicki, but—"

"Get this," she interrupted. "I don't go for arrogant types who think they're always right. If you want to be friends, fine. Other than that, no."

———————————

Conrad sat back against the cell door.

"Know anything about Vicki?" Mr. Stein said from the next cell. When Conrad hesitated, Mr. Stein added, "I only want to know that she is safe."

"If the GC don't know where she is, she's OK," Conrad said.

Mr. Stein sighed. "You are one of them, are you not?"

"What do you mean?"

Mr. Stein told his story. His wife and daughter Chaya had believed Jesus was the Messiah before Chaya was killed in the earthquake. Mr. Stein had laughed at them. "Now I'm not so sure they were wrong. I read a part of the New Testament last night, plus some of Tsion Ben-Judah's Web site."

"The Web site got me too," Conrad said. "Then Judd and Vicki explained it, and it all came together."

"I do not know what to believe," Mr. Stein said. "I have so many questions."

Conrad inched closer to the bars. "I don't know that much, but like what?"

"All right," Mr. Stein said, "if Jesus really is the Messiah, how could he forgive someone who has been against him all his life?"

"That's me too," Conrad said.

"But—," Mr. Stein said. "I am a Jew who rejected his Messiah. And the way I treated Chaya! Surely God could not forgive such an offense."

"There are stories in the Bible about people who turned around," Conrad said.

"That is not my only problem," Mr. Stein said. "If this is all true, God has caused millions to die or suffer."

"I don't think he's mean," Conrad said. "I think he's trying to get our attention."

"But there's another problem. If my wife and daughter were right, Nicolae Carpathia is the Antichrist. With all the good he has done, how can I believe that?"

A guard came and took Mr. Stein away. A few minutes later another prisoner was led in. Conrad peered through the dim light to see who it was.

Vicki retreated to a corner. She was crushed but didn't want anyone to know. She had hoped Judd had feelings for her, and several times he had started to say something but never finished. Under the desk in the rubble of New Hope Village Church, she felt close to him. But now he had changed, and Vicki felt foolish.

Shelly came and sat next to Vicki. "Mark punched through the dirt wall about half an hour ago, no thanks to you."

"Sorry."

"What's up?"

Vicki shook her head.

Judd sat by what was left of the Stahley's pool, throwing in clods of dirt and watching them break apart. He wanted to tell Vicki how he felt, but it was clear her feelings weren't as strong as his.

Evening shadows stretched across the Stahley property.

Vicki is too young anyway, Judd thought. But her angry words had hurt him. They had been through so much together. And now this.

Something caught Judd's eye at the edge of the woods. Branches moved and leaves rustled. He sat still. The sounds stopped. Judd relaxed. Then came the squawk of a radio. He dropped and crawled toward the house. Inside, he moved to the window. Nothing.

He quietly called Lionel and told him to watch the other side of the house. Suddenly, Judd spotted two uniformed GC officers heading toward them and more scattered in the woods. A helicopter flew overhead.

Lionel ran to Judd. "How could I have been so stupid!"

"What?" Judd said.

"My radio! It has a homing device. I led them right to us!"

Conrad motioned to Darrion. She seemed to recognize him but looked cautious. Conrad pulled back his hair and showed the mark on his forehead. "Do they know who you are?" he said.

Darrion shook her head. "The commander kept saying he couldn't place me. I said I was Laura Grover and that I'd found the motorcycle in a big house. I have to figure a way out of here," Darrion said.

"Hang tight," Conrad said. "They might turn you loose in a few days."

"And if they figure out who I am?"

"Then I'll have to get us both out."

Vicki and Shelly ran to the others when they heard the commotion.

Mark said, "The GC is tracking Lionel's radio. Be ready to run."

Vicki frowned. "Give me the radio."

Lionel handed it to her. "I hope you know what you're doing."

22

JUDD and Lionel helped Mark brace the new exit so it wouldn't cave in. The opening was the size of a window.

Mark stuck his head through the opening. "GC is almost to the house. And they're armed to the teeth."

Judd ran to the computer room. *I gotta get Vicki and Shelly out of there!*

"Are you up for this?" Vicki said.

"This is my acting debut," Shelly said. "Get that picture over the entrance so they don't find you guys."

Judd hurried in. "We have to get out of here now," he said.

"Help me get this picture in place," Vicki said.

Judd pulled out Conrad's gun. "You don't understand—they're almost inside!"

"Help me!" she said.

Judd grabbed the picture, and something cracked. The picture fell.

"Someone's in there," came a voice.

"Hold it in place," Vicki whispered.

"Let's go now," Lionel said.

"What about Judd?" Mark said.

"Do what you want," Lionel said. "I'm heading for the woods."

Mark moved through the opening, but before Lionel could follow, Mark scampered back inside. Lionel heard chopper blades. When the helicopter flew toward the river, Lionel followed Mark outside. They crawled to a small hill. They tucked their arms close to their bodies and rolled to the bottom, then crouched and hurried into a wooded area.

When they stopped to catch their breath, Mark said, "No way Judd can hold them off."

Lionel backtracked and found a drainpipe in a clump of bushes. He pulled out his flashlight and peered inside.

"Judd said there was a landing strip somewhere near here."

The helicopter grew louder.

Vicki heard crunching glass coming from the kitchen. The helicopter hovered, then flew away. Vicki gasped at the click of a rifle.

"Oh, hi there," Shelly said.

"Hands in the air now!" a man shouted.

"What do you want with me?"

"On the floor!"

"You don't have to be so mean," Shelly said. "I just took some crackers."

"Where are the others?"

"Others?"

"The radio!" a man shouted. "It gave you away."

Shelly said, "You can have that thing. I don't want it."

"Where did you get it?"

Shelly filled her mouth with crackers. "This black kid comes up and asks if I'm hungry," she said. "He could tell I was. So he says he'll tell me where to get some food if I do him a favor."

"Washington, sir?" a man said.

"Yeah, let her keep going."

"There's not much more," Shelly said. "He said if I'd take his radio and keep it until somebody found me, he'd tell me where I could get something to eat. Crackers is all I found."

"Was there anyone with him?" a man said.

"A girl," Shelly said. "Redhead. Scrawny."

"Exactly where?" a man said.

"Across the river," Shelly said. "They headed south or west, whatever's away from the river."

Someone radioed the chopper.

"What do we do with the girl?" another said.

"I'll see what Blancka says," the leader said.

Vicki's arms were tired from holding the picture in place.

_____

The chopper blew sticks and leaves into the drainpipe.
Lionel and Mark crept deeper into the pipe, a trickle of
water rushing past their feet.

"Hope there's no snakes," Mark said.

"Better snakes than the GC," Lionel said.

The boys moved deeper until they could barely hear
the chopper. In several places, the earthquake had crinkled the pipe.

"We'd better turn back," Mark said. "We're not gonna
find anything."

Lionel heard fluttering wings. "Get down!" he yelled
as bats flew past. Lionel shuddered, but he was curious
about what might be ahead. They came to a break where
dirt blocked their way. The earthquake had opened a hole
in the pipe. "Look at this!" Lionel said.

A natural cave stretched several hundred feet.

_____

Judd struggled to hold the picture. He wished Vicki
would rest so she could return the favor.

The GC leader sent others searching throughout the
house. Judd heard the man talking on his radio in the
next room.

Judd told Vicki, "I don't think I can hold this
anymore."

Vicki closed her eyes. "We have to."

The painting slipped and banged against the floor.
Judd massaged his arms and bent double from exhaustion.

"Did you hear that?" the leader said.

224

Shelly said, "Stuff's been falling since I got here. The earthquake, you know."

Someone knocked on the wall, and a knife sliced through the picture of the Stahleys. Judd and Vicki squeezed to the side as a flashlight came through.

"Anything?" the leader said.

"Lotsa dust."

The flashlight scanned back and forth as Judd leaned out of its beam.

Shelly screamed. The light went away.

"I saw someone out there!"

The leader took several men and bolted out the front door toward the driveway. Judd propped the picture up as best he could.

"You guys better leave now," Shelly whispered.

"Not without you," Vicki said.

"They'll know something's up. Go!"

Judd and Vicki slipped into the underground computer room. They looked for Lionel and Mark in the hangar.

Lionel and Mark took ten minutes to break through the dirt and rock. When they finally pulled themselves inside the cave, Lionel gave a low whistle. "It's huge."

The cave was twenty feet high. The floor was rocky but fairly level and dry.

"This would make a great hideout," Lionel said.

"Sure," Mark said. "No food, no heat. Just like home."

Lionel noticed a small beam of light coming from the

back of the cave. Mark helped him reach a ledge, and Lionel pulled himself up.

Lionel said, "This could be another entrance."

"No tree roots," Mark said. "We may be right under that landing strip. One good jolt and the whole thing could come down on us."

Judd was alone when Lionel and Mark returned that evening. "The GC bought Shelly's story," he said. "Took the radio and told her to get to a shelter before she gets shot for looting. They headed for the river, but we'd better not risk staying here long."

Lionel told Judd about the cave.

"Let's check it out after dark," Judd said.

Conrad was fascinated by Darrion's story. She had gone from having everything she wanted to having nothing.

"I shouldn't have tried to rescue Vicki," Darrion said. She put her head against the bars. "God didn't seem interested in us, so I tried something on my own."

The door opened and Mr. Stein was led back to his cell.

"They still suspect me," Mr. Stein whispered after the guard left. He rubbed his forehead. "I wish I could talk to Vicki."

"If they suspect you, they might let me go," Conrad said. "Then I could help you both escape."

"They will not let the girl go," Mr. Stein said. "They know who she is."

"Vicki?" Darrion said.

"No, *you,* my dear. They suspect the others are at your house. One group has already been there and gone. They are sending another group tonight."

23

WHILE he ate, Lionel walked through the hangar and gathered supplies. He found a long piece of rope and a metal hook strong enough to hold his weight. He nailed together five other pieces of wood, then screwed the hook in the middle.

"What's that?" Shelly said.

"You'll see tonight," Lionel said.

Lionel looked over Judd's shoulder and read the computer screen. Judd had pulled up Tsion Ben-Judah's Web site. A fast-moving number on the edge of the screen showed how many people were logging on.

"That can't be right," Lionel said. "The numbers are going by too fast."

"I've never seen anything like it either," Judd said.

Judd had logged on to download a Bible, but he found himself distracted by the Web site. He felt guilty for how little he was studying. He knew devotions weren't possible when you were running from the Global Community. Still, he wanted to stay "in the Word" like Bruce had taught them.

From the moment Judd had prayed to receive Christ, he felt hungry for the Bible. He wanted to know all the things he had missed the first time. He wrote verses on scraps of paper and tucked them inside his pockets.

But after Bruce had died, no one checked on him or asked him how things were going. Slowly, with all he had to do, he found it easy to let it slide.

As Judd looked over the message on Tsion's Web site, he wondered who else might be reading it. Perhaps members of the 144,000 witnesses. Perhaps Nicolae Carpathia himself. His friend in New Babylon, Pavel, had told him Nicolae checked Tsion's Web site frequently.

If he's reading this, Judd thought, he has to be seething. Judd read:

> Good day to you, my dear brother or sister in the Lord. I come to you with a heart both heavy with sorrow and yet full of joy. I sorrow personally over the loss of my wife and teenagers. I mourn for so many who have died since the coming of Christ to rapture his church. I mourn for mothers all over the globe who lost their children. And I weep for a world that has lost an entire generation.

How strange to not see the smiling faces or hear the laughter of children. As much as we enjoyed them, we could not have known how much they taught us and how much they added to our lives until they were gone.

I am also sad because the great earthquake appears to have snuffed out 25 percent of the remaining population. For generations people have called natural disasters "acts of God." This is not so. Ages ago, God the Father gave Satan, the prince and power of the air, control of Earth's weather. God allowed destruction and death by natural causes, yes, because of the fall of man. And no doubt God at times intervened against such actions by the evil one because of the prayers of his people.

Tsion went on to say the recent earthquake was an act of God necessary to fulfill prophecy and get the attention of those who don't believe in Jesus. He said he was amazed at the work of the Global Community in setting up communications so quickly. But Tsion said he was shocked at what he saw in the media.

"Do they still have a television around here?" Lionel said.

"Maybe in one of the bedrooms upstairs," Judd said.

Judd continued reading. Tsion grieved the way society had forgotten God at a time when they needed him most.

If you believe in Jesus Christ as the only Son of God the Father, you are against everything taught by Enigma Babylon.

There are those who ask, why not cooperate? Why not be loving and accepting? Loving we are. Accepting we cannot be.

Enigma Babylon does not believe in the one true God. It believes in any god, or no god, or god as a concept. There is no right or wrong. The self is the center of this man-made religion.

My challenge to you today is to choose up sides. Join a team. If one side is right, the other is wrong. We cannot both be right.

But I do not call you to a life of ease. During the next five years before the glorious return of Christ to set up his kingdom on earth, three-fourths of the population that was left after the Rapture will die. In the meantime, we should invest our lives in the cause. A great missionary martyr of the twentieth century named Jim Elliot is credited with saying this: "He is no fool who gives up what he cannot keep [this temporal life] to gain what he cannot lose [eternal life with Christ]."

And now a word to my fellow converted Jews from each of the twelve tribes: Plan on rallying in Jerusalem a month from today as we seek the great soul harvest that is ours to gather.

And now unto him who is able to keep you from falling, to Christ, that great shepherd of the sheep, be power and dominion and glory now and forevermore, world without end, Amen. Your servant, Tsion Ben-Judah.

Lionel returned with a small television. Judd watched him flick through channels. Before the Rapture Judd had seen things he knew his parents wouldn't have liked, but nothing compared to this.

One game show allowed the winner to kill the other contestant. The next channel showed the torture and murder of innocent people. On another, a séance was performed as people tried to communicate with the dead. Enigma Babylon approved of an educational program that taught viewers how to cast spells on enemies. As Lionel flicked the stations, things got worse.

"Turn it off," Judd said.

"Dr. Ben-Judah was right," Lionel said. "This is the bottom."

Conrad explained his plan. Darrion and Mr. Stein agreed to help.

"I just wish I could talk to Vicki again," Mr. Stein said. "I keep thinking about what she and Chaya said to me. I can believe that Jesus was a great man. A good teacher. Even a prophet. But I am still not sure about him actually being God."

Darrion said, "Why would you call him a good teacher if he told a lie?"

"I don't understand," Mr. Stein said.

"Jesus said a lot of good things," Darrion continued.

"Be kind to your neighbor. Do to others what you would have them do to you. But he also said he *was* God. So if you think he was just a good man, you call him a liar."

"I did not say that."

"Saying you're God is crazy, unless it's true," Darrion said. "If he was insane, he's nobody you'd want to follow."

Mr. Stein sighed.

"What she's saying is right," Conrad said. "Jesus taught great things and claimed to be the Son of God. Then he backed that up by doing miracles. Even coming back from the dead. If that doesn't prove he was who he said he was, nothing will convince you."

Mr. Stein put his face in his hands. "The weight I feel is immense. If you are right, I have rejected the Holy One, and I haven't believed my own flesh and blood."

Darrion came close to the bars. "Vicki told me Chaya prayed for you every day. You don't have to feel guilty. She only wanted you to believe."

As night approached, Lionel gathered his materials and went to meet with the others. He found Vicki alone. "You want to talk about it?" he said.

Vicki shook her head.

Judd called them together and went over the plan.

"If we have to move, why don't we take all our stuff now?" Shelly said.

"We want to be sure this cave won't collapse," Judd said. "We don't want to lose any of our supplies."

As they left, Mark backtracked and tied a string across the patio doorway to the mansion. He ran it outside to a pane of glass perched above the concrete.

Lionel led the way. Mark helped him carry the equipment that would lower them into the cave. The ground was spongy and filled with crickets.

Judd held the flashlight and searched for the opening as they walked. After several minutes, Mark suggested they go through the drainpipe.

Judd held up a hand. "Hold on," he said.

Looking closely, Lionel spied a hole about the size of a fist surrounded by grass and rocks. Judd and Mark dug out the hole to about three feet in diameter.

Lionel wedged the boards between two rocks and let the rope down. Judd went first and shinnied into the cavern. His voice echoed as he called out, "You guys were right. This is perfect."

Lionel covered the door he had made with mud and grass. He dug out a landing where the kids could climb and then push the door open. When he had finished, he covered the area with extra dirt and a few small rocks.

"How's it look?" Lionel said.

"You'd never know it was there," Vicki said.

A crash behind Lionel sent him to the ground. "What was that?"

"What I was afraid of," Mark said. "Company. Somebody tripped the wire."

Lionel heard a sound that gave him chills.

Dogs.

Conrad watched Mr. Stein. He seemed to be in pain. A guard unlocked Darrion's cell.

"What's going on?" she said.

"We know who you are," the guard said. "Commander wants to see you. They're gonna catch those other two tonight."

"I don't know what you're talking about," Darrion said.

"Sir, tell Commander Blancka it worked," Conrad said.

The guard turned and eyed Conrad.

"Tell him I did what he wanted," Conrad said. "I got the information."

"Of all the dirty tricks!" Mr. Stein screamed.

"You said you were one of us," Darrion said.

"And you were foolish enough to believe me," Conrad said.

The guard looked confused. Mr. Stein grabbed Conrad's shirt and banged him against the cell bars.

"Let him go, now!" the guard shouted.

"Don't trust this little weasel!" Mr. Stein shouted.

"I said, let him go!" The guard pulled his nightstick. Mr. Stein turned Conrad loose.

"I'll report this to the commander," the guard said.

"Just hurry up," Conrad gasped.

Darrion winced when the guard pulled her through the door.

"I did not hurt you badly, did I?" Mr. Stein whispered after they were gone.

Conrad smiled. "Don't worry about it. I'm just a weasel. Where'd you come up with that?"

"Probably the movies I watched when I was younger," Mr. Stein said. "We must pray your plan works."

"Pray?" Conrad said.

"Pray to the God of my fathers, Abraham, Isaac, and Jacob. And pray to the Son of God himself, Jesus Christ."

"Then you believe?" Conrad said.

"My daughter was right. I believe Jesus is the only way and that I cannot come to God except through him."

Conrad smiled.

"I am ashamed to have been so blind," Mr. Stein said. "Chaya's last moments were spent trying to tell me the truth, but I would not listen."

"I can help you with the prayer, if you'd like," Conrad said.

Mr. Stein nodded.

"Just ask God to forgive you for the wrong stuff you've done. Tell him you're sorry for not believing sooner."

Mr. Stein prayed.

"Now tell him you believe that Jesus died for you and rose again. Tell God you don't trust in anything you've done, but only what Jesus has done. Ask him to be your Savior and Lord."

Tearfully, Mr. Stein completed his prayer. "Oh God, please forgive me," he cried. "Come into my life."

———

Vicki broke into a sweat when she heard the dogs.

"What's going on?" Judd shouted from below.

"Quiet!" Vicki said.

"Everybody in," Lionel said. "We don't have time to figure out who it is."

"What if it's Conrad and Darrion?" Vicki said.

"With dogs?" Lionel said. "No way."

"Get in the cave," Shelly said as she took off for the house.

"What is she doing?" Lionel said.

Lionel helped Vicki onto the rope. She was nervous about climbing that far. When she got to the bottom, she put a hand on Judd's shoulder. "Shelly will be all right. She can do it."

24

THE NEXT morning a different guard returned for Conrad. Darrion had been gone all night.

"Don't believe anything he says," Mr. Stein yelled as the man led Conrad away.

Melinda and Felicia waited outside the interview room and scowled when Conrad sat beside them.

"I wanted to tell you guys what was up, but I didn't want to blow my cover," Conrad said.

"What are you talking about?" Melinda said.

"The commander put me down there so I could listen to those two talk," he said. "I got what he wanted."

"I don't believe you," Felicia said. "You're one of them."

"I was just as surprised as you when Lionel turned up dirty."

The girls turned away.

"I need your help," Conrad said, moving where he

could see them. "I'm going to catch Lionel, the girl, and that other guy."

The door opened. Commander Blancka came outside. "What is this, Graham?"

"Commander, sir, I figured since I was innocent, you put me in with the others to spy. It worked."

The commander cleared his throat. "I didn't. I mean . . . what did you find out?"

"Darrion's definitely one of them, sir," Conrad said.

"We've had someone talking to her all night," the commander said. "She says she doesn't know them."

"If it's all right with you, I'd like to see the look on her face when I tell you the whole story," Conrad said.

The commander motioned the three inside. Darrion looked exhausted. Her eyes were puffy and red. *The commander probably talked about her parents*, Conrad thought.

Conrad knew this would be the tough part. If he could convince the commander he wasn't partners with the others, he had a chance to get Darrion and Mr. Stein out.

Vicki was worried when she awoke and Shelly hadn't returned. She felt stiff and sore from sleeping on the cave floor. In the light of the embers from Judd's fire, she crept to the other side to inspect the drainpipe. Vicki hadn't told anyone, but she was scared she wouldn't be able to climb the rope that led out of the cave. Coming down wasn't so bad, but she had never been very good at climbing in gym class. She couldn't let anyone know. Especially Judd.

Vicki watched the trickling water go through the pipe

and wondered how long they would have to be on the run. Staying in the cave wouldn't be bad if they had food and sleeping bags, but they had none.

Vicki looked at Judd. He was asleep. Part of her just wanted to get out and not have to deal with him anymore. He had yelled at Lionel for letting Shelly go. Vicki couldn't imagine being cooped up with him for a few days, but she couldn't imagine not having him around either.

Lionel stirred and saw Vicki. "She's not back yet?" he said.

Vicki shook her head. "I hope the GC didn't take her away."

"Judd was right. I should've stopped her."

"He was not right," Vicki said. "Shelly can take care of herself as well as anyone."

"What's going on between you and Judd?"

Vicki frowned. "Nothing. That's the problem. I thought he really cared for me but we're too far apart."

"You mean, you're from a trailer park and he's a rich kid?" Lionel said. "I'd say that's not much of an issue at the moment. You're both sleeping in a cave."

Vicki smiled. "It's not the time to let these feelings take over."

"I know one thing," Lionel said. "Judd cares a lot more than you think."

Vicki was startled by a *tick, tick* sound from the pipe behind her. Lionel craned his neck.

"You think we should wake Judd and Mark?" Vicki said.

Lionel shook his head. "I'll check it out."

Lionel returned a few minutes later carrying a blanket. Shelly was right behind him. Vicki gave her a hug and watched as Lionel opened the blanket on the floor. Inside were food, a few bottles of water, and the laptop computer from the hideout.

When Shelly caught her breath, she said, "I went to the front of the house. I figured if these were GC, they'd recognize me from before. They were GC all right, but a different group.

"I ran in the front and screamed. The guys about shot me! I told them you guys came back and held a gun on me."

"We're gettin' to be as mean as snakes," Lionel said.

"Don't say that," Shelly said. "I think I saw one as I came up the drainpipe."

Vicki shivered. "What happened next?"

"They asked which way you went, and I pointed toward the woods. They took their dogs down there but came back a few minutes later. Said they were going to stay all night and watch.

"I told them I wasn't going to let you two come back and get me, that I was going to stay with them. They searched the whole house but didn't find the hideout."

"How'd you get out?" Lionel said.

"I thought they'd leave, but they kept looking through their binoculars. I told 'em I was going to sleep and then head for a shelter at sunup."

"They bought it?" Lionel said.

"I guess," Shelly said. "They kept searching in the

garage and near the patio. That's where the dogs kept going."

Judd awakened and welcomed Shelly.

"When they took the dogs upstairs, I slipped behind the picture and into the hideout. I figured Judd could use the computer. I hope it's charged up."

Judd picked up the laptop and inspected it. "Good thinking."

"I came back upstairs and pretended to sleep," Shelly said. "I remembered Mark talking about another entrance to the pipe."

"Are you sure nobody saw you?" Judd said.

"Don't think so," Shelly said.

"You could have led them right to us," Judd said.

"She just saved us!" Vicki screamed, waking Mark. "If she hadn't gone back there, the GC would have tracked us down for sure."

Vicki's voice echoed through the cave. Then came barking.

"Come on," Lionel said. "We have to block the drain!"

"I heard everything," Conrad said, looking straight at Darrion. "She tried to get Stein to be a part of their group."

"What group is that?" the commander said.

"Some religious order," Conrad said. "They go around with stuff on their foreheads."

The commander looked at Darrion. "I don't see anything," he said.

Conrad laughed. "They claim it's invisible."

Melinda and Felicia chuckled.

"Darrion tried to convince the guy, but he wouldn't budge. She told him Judd and Vicki had gone to her house, then went back to the basement of their church."

The commander scribbled notes on a pad.

"You lying double-crosser!" Darrion shouted.

"You're the liar," Conrad said as a guard subdued Darrion.

"What about Washington?" the commander said.

"I'm afraid he's one of them too," Conrad said. "Lionel planned to get Vicki out all along. I should have seen it."

"And Stein?"

"From what I picked up, Vicki was a friend of his family. He's misguided but not guilty of anything."

The commander nodded and whispered to a guard.

"Commander, I don't like this," Felicia said. "From the time Lionel and Conrad met those other two—"

"I appreciate your concern," Commander Blancka said, "but this is valuable information. Go back to the church and search every inch. I want Washington back here to stand—"

The commander's radio squawked. He excused himself, then called Conrad, Felicia, and Melinda into another room.

"Looks like they were at this Stahley girl's house last night," the commander said. "We've got a team waiting in case they come back. I'll assign backup. My guess is you'll find them at this church."

Judd and the others dug furiously. They filled the pipe with dirt and rocks. The dogs barked at the end of the tunnel. When the entrance was blocked, Judd stayed close. The others prepared to leave.

The dogs pawed at the earth on the other side. Two men caught up to them. One cursed. "They must have stayed right here last night."

"Probably took off with the other girl," another said.

The dogs were back at the dirt again, and Judd heard one yelp. The two men left.

"Looks like we're safe for a while," Judd told the others.

Judd asked Lionel to carefully look from the top entrance. Lionel climbed the rope with ease and lifted the opening a few inches. He slid back down and sat by Vicki.

"They're headed back to the house," Lionel said.

Judd opened the laptop while the others ate breakfast. The battery was almost dead.

"We'll only have one shot to see our messages," Judd said.

"You don't have a phone line," Vicki said.

"This works on a regular line and it also has a sat-phone built in," Judd said. He dialed up and logged onto his E-mail. There were hundreds of messages forwarded from Tsion Ben-Judah's Web site. Judd scrolled down the list. A small screen popped up, saying the battery was running out.

Judd scanned the messages and recognized one with a Global Community address. It was from Conrad.

As he opened the message, the laptop went blank.

Judd pounded the floor of the cave.

"What did it say?" Vicki said.

Judd shook his head. "Couldn't read it. Maybe Conrad got Darrion out. Maybe he's in trouble and needs our help."

"We could sneak back up to the house and try to recharge it," Mark said.

"Too risky," Judd said. "But at some point we'll need to communicate with the outside."

"There's gotta be someone who can help us," Mark said.

"There's always your friend with the motorcycle," Vicki smirked.

Judd stared off but didn't say a word.

25

TWO days later, Judd knew the kids were desperate. The GC hadn't discovered them, but they had no food and only the water from the dripping drain. They had tried to keep the fire going, but they were running out of fuel.

"Somebody's going to have to get some wood," Lionel said.

"Won't do any good," Judd said. "No matches."

Shelly put her head on a rock and held her stomach.

"We have to get supplies and recharge this battery," Judd said.

"Maybe they've pulled out," Mark said.

"Wouldn't bet on it," Lionel said. "Probably at least one guard will stay behind for a few days."

"How about digging into the back entrance at night?" Shelly said.

"They'd spot us," Judd said.

"Then we have to create a diversion," Lionel said. He drew a plan in the dirt. One of them would go in for supplies.

"There won't be time to recharge the computer," Judd said.

"Then whoever goes in stays all night. We come back the next night to get him."

"Him?" Vicki said.

"Or her," Lionel said.

"We could just make a run for it," Mark said.

"I know how these guys operate," Lionel said. "They've got a net out for us. They'll be waiting."

The kids agreed to chance the nighttime break-in.

"Who goes?" Lionel said.

"I'm the one who knows the place the best," Judd said.

"We'll draw straws," Vicki said.

Mark held up five splinters of wood. When they had drawn, Lionel held the shortest.

Conrad showed a picture of Lionel and Vicki to a worker at a shelter. The worker shook his head. "Haven't seen them," he said.

Melinda and Felicia joined Conrad. "Any luck?" he said.

The girls shook their heads. "I don't want to go back to the commander and say we've spent two days and have nothing to show for it," Melinda said.

"We could try the high school again," Conrad said.

Felicia frowned. "Like it or not, we'd better head back. Our meeting's in a half hour."

Conrad had tried not to be too friendly with the girls. He wanted them to believe he was on their side, but he didn't want to act like fast pals. Conrad could sense that the girls still distrusted him. At times they whispered to each other. He had read somewhere in the Bible that he was supposed to do good to his enemies, but he didn't know what that meant to people like Felicia and Melinda.

Conrad wanted to talk with Mr. Stein. The commander had released him two days earlier, but a guard was secretly watching the man's house. Conrad feared Mr. Stein might still have questions or doubts. Or he might have changed his mind about Jesus. Conrad had seen the mark on the man's forehead, but he wasn't sure if a person could un-pray a prayer. He couldn't wait to see Judd again. He had a million questions.

Conrad hoped to slip past the guard and visit Mr. Stein late that night, assuming he could get away without Melinda or Felicia seeing him.

Conrad was also concerned about Darrion. He knew the commander had withheld food and water from her. The GC's efforts hadn't worked. But how long could she hold out? Conrad tried to slip her a bottle of water before they met with the commander, but Melinda and Felicia stayed close.

"We've been to fourteen shelters in the area, sir," Conrad told the commander. "Some of them twice. The hospitals haven't treated anyone fitting their description. We found the location of the Washington and Thompson homes and checked there. The Byrne girl was staying with a pastor. The church is empty."

The commander grunted.

"He was killed at the start of the war," Conrad continued, "and it looks like this Byrne took in a bunch of kids. There's nothing left of that house."

"People don't just disappear," Commander Blancka said.

"Heard anything from the Stahley girl's house?" Melinda said.

The commander shook his head. "We've still got guards there, but I don't think they'll come back. My guess is they've found a place they think is safe, and they hope we'll forget about them." The commander looked out the window. "Well, I'm not going to forget. These kids have caused a lot of trouble. The top brass is watching. The whole Morale Monitor program could hinge on what happens here."

"We'll do all we can, sir," Felicia said.

The commander stared at the kids. "We'll break this Stahley girl soon. She has to talk. We'll find the others and make an example of them."

At dinner, Conrad excused himself. He had written a note to Darrion earlier in the day. It read, *You and the others are alive as long as you hold out. Don't give up. I'll try to get you some water tonight.* He put a rubber band around the note and attached it to a candy bar.

He darted behind the former police station. Darrion was in the farthest cell down the hall, and she was the only prisoner. He put his hand through the window and rattled the wrapper. Darrion looked up. Conrad put a finger to his lips. He threw the candy bar as hard as he could and watched it skid to a stop a few feet from Darrion's cell.

Darrion used her blanket to pull the candy closer until she reached it. She ate it hungrily as she read the note. When she was finished, she mouthed, "Thank you," then licked the wrapper.

As Conrad raced back to the tent to finish his dinner, a light rain began to fall.

"What took you so long?" Felicia said suspiciously.

"If you have to know, I got some bad water," Conrad said, taking two bottles from the table. "I've been—"

"That's enough," Melinda said. "Not at dinner."

Conrad shrugged. "You asked."

Melinda leaned close. "You feel up to a little night-time investigating?"

"Sure, where you going?"

"We're gonna hit that Stein guy," Felicia said. "We've got a hunch he has those kids hidden somewhere."

Conrad's eyes widened. "They could have gone there before we put the guard on him. Where's he live, anyway?"

"His house is demolished," Melinda said. "And his daughter died in the earthquake. He's living at his office in Barrington. We leave at midnight."

Lionel asked Judd for his E-mail password, and Judd scribbled it on a scrap of paper. "Look at all you want," Judd said, "but you'll have to go through a lot of forwarded messages from Tsion."

Judd explained how to recharge the laptop, then said, "If you'd rather I go—"

"Oh no, you don't," Vicki said. "Besides, Lionel knows as much about computers as you do."

Judd shook his head as Vicki walked away. "She hates me," he said.

"I don't think so," Lionel said. "You guys can work out whatever's come between you."

Judd changed the subject. "I can't remember, but there might be a battery backup in the desk. If you find one, make sure you—"

"I'll charge it up," Lionel said. "Are you looking for any special E-mails other than Conrad's?"

"His is most important," Judd said. "Write Tsion and tell him to pray."

Lionel climbed the rope and peeked through the entrance. It was raining harder, and water was leaking through the hatch.

"The rain's good for us," Judd said when Lionel returned. "I don't think the dogs can follow as well."

"How much food and water do you want?" Lionel said.

"As much as you can carry," Judd said.

Conrad met Melinda and Felicia near the jail. The girls had signed out a jeep from the commander. The rain was coming down hard as they started toward Barrington.

"Got an idea," Conrad said. "I brought a disk with me to do a data dump from the guy's computer. He might have some information stored."

"Good," Felicia said.

Melinda drove cautiously. Some of the main roads had been bulldozed and were easy to pass. Others were still in rough shape.

The kids were stopped twice at GC checkpoints. When the guards saw they were Morale Monitors, they waved them through.

A light was on upstairs at Mr. Stein's office. Melinda and Felicia walked across the street and found a man watching the building.

"What did he say?" Conrad said when the two returned.

"We're cool," Melinda said. "The guy radioed his buddy around back to watch for anyone trying to sneak out."

Conrad thought it odd that there were two guards and that the one in front hadn't questioned the girls further. Melinda tried the door. To Conrad's surprise, it was unlocked. The girls pulled out their guns.

"Maybe he's expecting us," Conrad whispered.

The office was dark. Conrad shone his flashlight around the room. There were several desks with computers. Some were on the floor. The walls of the building looked stable, though other buildings on the street had collapsed. They found Mr. Stein sleeping upstairs on a couch, an open Bible on the man's stomach.

That's a good sign, Conrad thought.

Melinda nodded toward the computer. Conrad waved them back outside.

"If we wake him up, he might alert the others,"

Conrad said. "I'll get on the computer while you guys check downstairs. Maybe there's some kind of basement where they're hiding."

Conrad pulled a disk from his pocket. When he was sure the girls were gone, he crept to the couch and gently shook Mr. Stein awake.

Conrad put a hand over the man's mouth and whispered, "You have to be quiet. Two Morale Monitors are downstairs."

Mr. Stein nodded. Conrad took his hand away. Conrad was glad to see the mark of the true believer on Mr. Stein's forehead.

"Is anyone hiding here?"

"No," Mr. Stein said. "How is Darrion?"

"Hungry," Conrad said, "but there's no time to talk. I'm loading a message on your computer. It has Judd's E-mail address. Follow the instructions I give and we might be able to get Darrion out alive."

Mr. Stein nodded.

"It's embedded in a file called *Chaya*," Conrad said. "I thought that would be easy for you to remember."

Mr. Stein smiled.

"Now go back to sleep and don't wake up until those two come back," Conrad said.

Conrad put the file onto Mr. Stein's hard drive, then erased the file from his own disk. He began copying files from the computer, but soon realized many of them were from Tsion Ben-Judah's Web site.

I can't let them see this! Conrad thought.

Melinda and Felicia returned.

"Almost finished," Conrad whispered.

"Has he been awake?" Felicia said.

Conrad shook his head.

Felicia kicked the couch, and Mr. Stein jumped like he had just been awakened. "Where are you hiding them?" Felicia screamed.

"What?" Mr. Stein said.

Felicia put her gun to the man's head. "I said, where are you hiding them?"

"Go ahead and pull the trigger," Melinda said.

Lionel crouched by the bushes near the back patio. The rain was blinding. It was difficult to see even a few feet ahead. Lionel pushed the light on his watch. Three more minutes. He edged closer to the house. He kept the laptop under his shirt and hoped the rain wouldn't damage it. Lionel saw two glowing objects in the house.

As planned, at exactly midnight, Lionel heard the scream and the gunshot. Two dogs barked. Cigarettes fell to the floor. The front door opened. A man shouted orders into his radio.

Lionel ran into the kitchen and nearly lost his balance as his wet shoes hit the floor. He rounded the corner and made it to the slashed picture of the Stahley family.

Lionel moved the picture and climbed through the opening. He prayed Judd and Vicki would be able to get back to the cave in time.

26

JUDD preferred to have Mark join him, but Vicki insisted. The rain matted her hair. It had been Vicki's idea to scream. Judd thought her piercing wail would not only alert the GC but also scare them.

Once Judd made sure the GC guards were after them, they bolted toward the clearing. The rain fell hard. Judd held up a hand to block it. He saw Mark's signal in the distance, a blinking flashlight.

Judd was right about the dogs. They couldn't track as well in the rain. He heard their yelping and turned. Two flashlights scanned the bottom of the hill.

A few yards from the entrance to the cave, Judd picked up the signal again. A flashlight beam crossed their path. Judd's heart sank.

"There they are!" a man yelled.

Judd grabbed Vicki's arm and pulled her away from the hideout.

"To the woods," Judd yelled over the noise of the rain.

Conrad's first instinct was to reach out and grab Felicia's gun, but something made him hold back. The two girls seemed icy cold.

Mr. Stein turned pale. "I don't know what you're talking about," he said.

Felicia gritted her teeth and pushed the gun harder against the man's scalp. "Where are you hiding them?"

"I told you, I haven't seen Vicki or any of the others since—"

"Just get it over with," Melinda said. She glanced at Conrad. "Or maybe he wants to do it."

Conrad understood. In the split second when Melinda caught his eye, he knew the two were trying to trap him. Perhaps they had the commander's approval. That was probably why the guard at the front hadn't put up a fight about them searching the place. The whole evening had been a test.

Conrad shrugged. "You know this isn't gonna look good," he said.

Felicia pulled the gun away slightly, and Mr. Stein took a breath.

"I don't care what you do to the guy," Conrad continued, "but it's clear the commander wants him watched. If you two off him, I don't think the commander will be happy. Like it or not, this guy might be our best shot at finding Lionel and the others." Conrad put the computer disk in his pocket. "It's up to you. I don't mind a little blood."

Felicia looked at Melinda and put the gun away. She pushed Mr. Stein back on the couch.

"The authorities will hear about this!" Mr. Stein yelled.

Conrad jumped on the man, pushing him hard into the wall. "We are the authorities!" he yelled.

Vicki ran after Judd through the pouring rain. They hit the edge of the woods, and both went tumbling into the wet leaves and mud. Lightning flashed, and Vicki saw they were on the edge of a drop-off.

"They'll think we're headed for the drainpipe," Judd yelled. "We have to find a place to hide."

Vicki's heart pounded. She had been upset with Judd for being so bossy. Now she didn't mind. "How about up there?" she said, pointing to a gnarled pile of wood and leaves.

"Good," Judd said. "We can get out as soon as we see them go toward the drain."

Vicki and Judd scampered back up the hillside and covered themselves with wet leaves. The rain pelted them. Vicki was glad to see the dogs enter the woods fifty yards from them. Judd and Vicki lay perfectly still. Lightning flashed again.

When it was clear the men were going toward the drain, Judd whispered, "If they see us, don't stop. Keep running for the cave as fast as you can."

Vicki nodded. Judd ran through the trees ahead of her. She didn't dare look back.

Lionel plugged in the laptop when he reached the computer room. The battery would need an hour or two to recharge. Rummaging through the scattered contents of the desk, he was surprised to find two batteries. He put them next to the laptop and ran to the hangar.

Lionel found the supplies but left them there. Something bothered him. If the GC came back and found his wet tracks leading to the hideout, he was sunk. While the GC were looking for Judd and Vicki there was time.

Lionel looked for some rags and found a stack of blankets near the food stash. He took off his shoes and socks, still dripping from the rain, and climbed through the opening. On his hands and knees, he dried the wet spots. Something in the entryway caught his eye. It had a greenish glow. He inched his way over on top of the blanket.

On the floor next to one of the chairs was a cell phone. The display glowed with the last number the man had dialed.

Suddenly the room lit up with the searchlight of the passing helicopter. Lionel scrambled into the shadows. He stuck the phone in his pocket and crawled toward the hideout.

Back in the computer room he inspected the phone closely. He found the ringer and turned it off. He looked through the list of numbers. One of them said *Comm. B.*

Lionel clipped the phone to his belt and moved to the hangar. He spread three blankets on the floor. In the first he loaded bottles of water. In the second and third he placed the dried and canned food. He tied each blanket and lugged all three to the landing near the picture. He would be ready when the kids returned the following night.

With the physical work complete, Lionel sat at the computer. The battery was 50 percent charged. He pulled out Judd's instructions and opened Conrad's message.

Don't reply to this, Conrad wrote. *Wherever you are, stay there. The GC are still looking, but don't have a clue. I'm trying to get Darrion out, but it might take some time. I'll be in touch as soon as I can. Conrad.*

Lionel smiled and deleted the message.

_____

Conrad got out of the jeep first. "I'm gonna get some sleep."

"Give us the disk," Melinda said.

"No problem," Conrad said. He pulled the disk from his pocket and gave it to Felicia.

"It's broken!" Felicia said.

Conrad grabbed the disk and shook his head. "It must have cracked when I jumped on the guy," he said.

Conrad went toward his room, then ducked behind a building. Melinda and Felicia turned and headed toward the commander's tent.

_____

When they hit the clearing, Judd looked toward the Stahley house. A helicopter hovered with its searchlight trained on the mansion. He hoped Lionel hadn't been caught.

"Keep going," Judd said as he and Vicki stayed close to the ground. The rain came down at an angle, stinging Judd's face.

Judd couldn't find the opening or Mark's signal. The dogs bellowed from inside the drainpipe. Vicki tripped over something in the grass.

Mark stuck his head out of the hole. "Thought you guys were goners," he said. "Get in here."

Judd and Vicki crawled onto the ledge with Mark. Shelly made room for them and started down the rope.

"Flashlight's batteries are almost out," Mark said. "I stopped signaling you a while ago."

Before the hatch closed, a flash of lightning lit up the cave. Judd squinted at the floor. He grabbed the light from Mark and turned it on.

"You're gonna run it totally—"

"Shelly, stop!" Judd screamed. "Stay right where you are."

"I can't hang on," Shelly said.

"What is it?" Vicki said.

The dim light barely showed the horror of what lay a few feet beneath Shelly.

"Snakes," Judd said. "The cave floor is full of them!"

Lionel found a message from Mr. Stein. He opened it and read the information about Conrad.

They were just here, Mr. Stein wrote. Conrad left a message. Please write as soon as possible. I have wonderful news.

Lionel pulled out the phone and dialed the number Mr. Stein included at the bottom of his E-mail.

"How did you get a phone?" Mr. Stein said.

"Long story," Lionel said. "Are you sure this line isn't tapped?"

"I don't believe it is."

"Good," Lionel said. "What's the news?"

"My daughter's prayers have been answered," Mr. Stein said. "I have become a believer in Jesus Christ."

Lionel nearly dropped the phone. "That's great," he said.

"I have been reading Dr. Ben-Judah's Web site," Mr. Stein continued. "I tried to contact him."

"Judging from the amount of mail he's getting, that's a long shot," Lionel said.

"I believe God has chosen me to be one of his witnesses," Mr. Stein said. "I want to go to Israel and attend the meeting. It is only a few weeks away."

"Sir, we're in deep trouble here," Lionel said.

"Of course," Mr. Stein said. "How can I help?"

"The message you received from Conrad," Lionel said. "Read it to me." When Mr. Stein finished, Lionel said, "I don't know about letting Darrion go much longer with the commander."

"It sounds as if Conrad has the situation under control," Mr. Stein said. He described the threat on his life by Felicia and Melinda. "If Conrad can get the GC to trust him, he'll have a better chance to get her out. But, as he says here, it may take up to two weeks."

"What about Israel?" Lionel said.

"You are my friends," Mr. Stein said. "I'm sure God will work something out."

"If the GC get your phone records, they'll find out about this call. It won't look good."

"I'm willing to risk anything," Mr. Stein said. "Tell me where you are. I will come get you."

"No," Lionel said. "We've found a safe place."

"Once Conrad sets the plan in motion, do you have anyone to help you surprise the GC while you get away?"

"I'll talk with Judd," Lionel said.

Lionel heard movement above him and whispered, "I'll call you tomorrow night." He turned off the phone and listened as the GC entered the house.

———————————

"Don't look down!" Judd shouted to Shelly as she swayed above the cave floor.

"I can't hang on much longer," Shelly said.

"The water must have made them go for higher ground," Mark said.

"Are they poisonous?" Vicki said.

"I don't want to take the chance," Judd said, grabbing the rope and climbing down as quickly as he could. He didn't want to knock Shelly off, but he knew she wouldn't be able to climb up by herself.

Mark held the flashlight. Judd saw Vicki cover her eyes.

"I don't feel well," Shelly said.

"Hang in there, Shel," Judd said. "You've gotta help me climb back to the top."

When Judd got near, he let go with his legs and slid close to Shelly. "Put your arms around me and hold tight," he said.

Shelly grabbed Judd's belt with one hand and tried to

pull herself up. She slipped, but Judd caught her with a hand. Shelly put her arms around Judd's neck.

Judd hung on while Mark and Vicki pulled the rope up an inch at a time. When they made it to the ledge, Judd collapsed. Shelly fell into Vicki's arms, crying.

"Maybe we should have made a run for it," Mark said.

Judd tried to catch his breath. The rain was coming harder, and the chopper wasn't going away.

27

JUDD was drained. The kids couldn't go through another night like this. But Lionel needed them. *What if Lionel was caught?* Judd pushed the thought from his mind.

Shelly, Vicki, and Mark braced themselves at the top of the cave. Judd knew they couldn't stay in that position all night.

"My leg's cramping," Vicki said.

Judd turned on the dim flashlight and scanned the floor. The cave was dry. The snakes weren't leaving. Judd noticed an area under them that the snakes avoided.

"I'm not going down there," Shelly said.

"If you go to sleep, you'll fall," Judd said.

"I'm not going down," Shelly said.

Judd climbed down the rope. He didn't know much about snakes, but he could tell many of them weren't poisonous. He knew that wouldn't make the others feel much better.

Judd noticed a ledge to his left. The rock wasn't wet and there were no snakes. He threw a rock, which hit with a thud. The snakes hissed and moved back. Judd described the ledge, but Vicki and Shelly shook their heads.

"There's room for all of us to stretch out and sleep," Judd said. "We're going to need the rest."

"We need food," Shelly said.

"We'll get it tomorrow when Lionel gets back," Judd said.

"Why don't we sleep in the meadow tonight?" Vicki said.

The helicopter passed again, slivers of light shining through cracks in the opening above them.

"Any more questions?" Judd said.

"So if we go down there, what's to keep our squirmy little friends off us?" Mark said.

"I'll take the first watch," Judd said. "They're just as afraid of us as we are of them."

"Right," Shelly said. "They don't look scared to me."

Judd led the way down and helped Vicki, Shelly, and Mark onto the ledge. The girls were wary of the snakes, but Judd assured them he would keep watch.

Judd turned the flashlight on every minute or so. He threw rocks and sand at the snakes that came near.

A few minutes later, Judd heard the soft breathing of the others as they slept. Judd stretched his legs and yawned. The rainfall overhead and the occasional clap of thunder brought back memories. When a storm would come in the night, he would run into his parents' room and sleep by their bed.

He threw a few more rocks toward the snakes and stretched out by the ledge. The flashlight was almost use-less now. With its dim light he could see only a few feet away.

Judd felt his eyes getting heavier. He shook himself awake. He had to stay awake.

———————————

Lionel heard the Global Community guards return. The helicopter widened its search and finally gave up. The GC radios squawked upstairs, but Lionel couldn't make out the conversation from his hideout.

Lionel finished preparing the supplies and checked the computer. He pulled out a blanket and curled up in the computer room. He knew he would need the rest for the night ahead.

He awoke refreshed a few hours later and plugged in another battery. He turned the computer speakers off and logged on to Judd's E-mail. A message from Dr. Ben-Judah caught his eye.

Judd, I know you have been concerned about Chloe, and our prayers have been answered. Buck has returned with her. She has many injuries from the earthquake, but if she hadn't run from her home, she would have died. Thank God she and the baby are all right.

"The baby?" Lionel said out loud. He smiled. So Buck and Chloe were going to have a baby. Cool. Lionel wanted to see Vicki's face when she found out.

Buck is nervous about my plans to travel to Israel, Tsion continued, but I know this is of God. I will go there if it is his will.

269

*Please pray for this and another matter. Buck and Chloe
have a friend who is in terrible trouble. I won't
go into the details, but this woman needs God in her life.*

Let me know how I can help. I pray for you daily.

Tsion closed with a verse of encouragement. Lionel
put his head on the desk. It had been so long since he
had experienced a normal day. He longed to sit in a
church service with other believers, or in a small group
and talk about the Bible. Lionel couldn't imagine when
that would happen, or if it would ever happen again.

Vicki awoke stiff and cold. She noticed a bit of morning
light coming through the top of the cave. The rain had
stopped. She looked at Judd and gasped. He was asleep,
and several snakes were lying next to him.

Something heavy was on her legs. She lifted her head.
Two huge snakes stretched out beside her. Another had
crawled on top of her legs.

Vicki trembled and tried not to scream. She looked at
Shelly and Mark. The snakes hadn't gotten to them.

"Help," she whispered. She said it three more times
before Mark awoke.

"OK," Mark said, wiping the sleep from his eyes.
"They've just found a warm place. Don't make any
sudden movements."

"Get them off me," Vicki said.

Mark looked behind him and grabbed a long stick.
"Lie back and don't watch," he said.

Vicki closed her eyes. Mark lifted the snake with the

stick. Vicki opened her eyes and saw the snake's head inches from her face. Mark threw the snake to the other side of the cave and it landed with a thud. He pushed the two other snakes away from Vicki, and she scooted closer to Shelly.

Mark climbed off the ledge and put his hand over Judd's mouth. He whispered something to him. Mark picked the snakes off one by one and threw them in the corner. Shelly watched in horror. When the snakes were gone, Judd stood and leaned against the ledge.

Judd shook his head. "I'm sorry," he said. "Couldn't keep my eyes open."

Shelly stood and said, "I'm not staying here another night."

"We have to get Lionel out," Judd said.

"I don't care if I get caught by the GC," Shelly said. "I don't care if they throw me in jail or put me in a reeducation camp. Anything's better than living like this."

"Look!" Mark said, pointing to the other side of the cave.

Vicki squinted and noticed the room full of snakes had disappeared. Only the ones Mark had thrown on the other side remained.

"We have to keep our heads," Judd said.

Shelly jumped down, watching each step closely. "I'm telling you, I'm climbing out of here now."

Judd nodded to Mark. Mark grabbed Shelly and held her by the arm.

"If you don't let go, I'll scream!"

"If you climb out of here now, it could endanger the rest of us," Judd said.

Shelly cried. "You don't understand."

Vicki climbed from the ledge and put an arm around Shelly. The girl was falling apart. Vicki didn't want to stay in the cave any more than Shelly did, but Judd was right.

Vicki tried to calm her, but Shelly began to shake and sob. "I have to get out!" she screamed.

Vicki put an arm around Shelly. "What's going on?" she said.

It took Shelly a few minutes to calm down. "I feel so bad," she cried. "I'm trying to hold together, but I can't."

"It's OK that you lost it," Vicki said. "I'm scared of the snakes, too."

"Not like me," Shelly said. "When I was little, my mom left me and went to a bar. I was playing in the back-yard. We had a rusty, old slide and a swing. There was this snake sunning itself on the end, but I didn't see it."

"How awful," Vicki said.

"I tried to stop, but I couldn't. I knocked it onto the ground. It probably wasn't poisonous, but it scared me. I cried and cried, but my mom was out drinking. Every time I see snakes, it comes back to me. I'm so sorry."

Shelly put her head on Vicki's shoulder. "It's OK," Vicki said.

After a fitful night's sleep, Conrad reported to the commander's office with Melinda and Felicia. The commander had circles under his eyes, and his jaw was tight.

"The Stahley girl still hasn't talked," the commander said. "Without food or water she should be starving by now."

Conrad knew why Darrion hadn't starved. In addition to the candy bar, he had gotten two bottles of water and some sandwiches to her.

"We're putting a ring around the Stahley place," the commander continued. "There must be something inside that house the kids want."

"Sir, could we have another go at her?" Melinda said.

The commander nodded and looked at his computer. The screen saver was a flying insignia of the Global Community that morphed into the smiling face of Nicolae Carpathia.

"The top brass is asking questions," the commander said. "They've heard there's been trouble. I've been able to cover so far, but they want to know if we can supply Morale Monitors in the new schools."

"When will they need them?" Conrad said.

"Next month," the commander said.

Melinda stood. "Give us another chance," she said. "We'll get something out of her."

While he was on-line, Lionel saw a window pop up. It was Pavel, Judd's friend from New Babylon. Lionel turned on the speakers and looked at the boy.

"You are not Judd," Pavel said.

"I'm his friend Lionel."

"Your face is in shadows," Pavel said. "Lean closer to the camera so I can see your forehead."

When Lionel did, the boy smiled. "It is good to talk with you, my brother," Pavel said. "Where is Judd?"

Lionel explained their situation. Pavel gasped. "I was afraid things would get worse for Judd."

"What's going on over there?" Lionel said.

"Nicolae Carpathia is angered by the response to Tsion Ben-Judah's Web site," Pavel said. "It is being read by millions around the world. The potentate himself has been reading it."

"What for?" Lionel said.

"My father says the Global Community wants to sponsor the rabbi's return to Israel. It's supposed to show how loving the potentate is. I believe he has sinister plans."

"The rabbi's smart," Lionel said. "He won't walk into an ambush. Besides, the GC should look at what Tsion is saying about the one-world faith."

"That is another interesting story," Pavel said. "The potentate is at odds with Enigma Babylon's top man."

"You mean Mathews?"

"Correct. Mathews thinks he and the one-world religion are bigger than the Global Community."

"So Carpathia has competition and he doesn't like it," Lionel said.

"He doesn't like Mathews or Ben-Judah, and he hates the preachers at the Wailing Wall. He's convinced they're speaking to him."

"Wouldn't be surprised if they are," Lionel said.

"My father heard him scream, 'I want them dead! And soon!' "

Lionel shook his head. It had been a long time since

he had seen the prophets Moishe and Eli. They would tell the truth about Nicolae and wouldn't hold back. Lionel couldn't wait to tell the others what he had learned.

"One more thing," Pavel said. "My father had a talk with a man in Carpathia's communications department yesterday. He told him there are missiles pointing into outer space."

"Missiles?" Lionel said.

"The potentate is afraid of meteors sent by God."

———————

Conrad winced when Melinda slapped Darrion across the face. Darrion didn't answer her questions. She only looked at the girls and said, "Water. I need water."

Felicia took her turn hitting Darrion and yelling at her. Conrad knew they expected the same from him.

He kicked Darrion's chair out from under her and shoved her under the table. Out of sight he winked. "You're doing great," he whispered. "Keep it up."

———————

Judd knew if anyone could calm Shelly, it was Vicki. Shelly kept saying she had to get out. Judd and Mark stayed back.

"She's losing it," Mark whispered.

"I can't blame her," Judd said. "I should have stayed awake."

"We'll get Lionel back in a few hours," Mark said. "A fire and some food will change things."

Judd nodded. He wanted to believe Mark was right, but he wasn't sure.

Lionel heard more movement upstairs and crept near the GC officers. One was talking on the radio.

"Go ahead, Commander," the man said.

Lionel felt a chill when he heard his boss's voice.

"Ferguson, you and Wilcox stay there until nightfall," the commander said. "We'll send a chopper for you."

"What if they come back, sir?" the man said.

"I think they've moved on," the commander said. "No use wasting manpower."

When the commander was through, Ferguson said to Wilcox, "Awful lot of trouble to go through for a bunch of kids."

"He wants to make a lesson of this one," Wilcox said as he rattled a piece of paper. "Washington. Kid made him look bad."

"He's not gonna exactly throw a party for the other two, Byrne and Thompson."

"Cute girl," Wilcox said. "Wonder what they did?"

"Get your stuff together," Ferguson said. "We'll catch 'em. And when we do, the commander will make sure none of these little Morale Monitors ever cross him again."

28

THE COMMANDER'S conversation had left Lionel uneasy. He should have been happy the GC were pulling out. That would make things easier. They wouldn't have to stay in the cave. But the way the commander talked troubled Lionel. Something didn't seem right.

Lionel took the three packs of provisions and put the most important stuff into one blanket. Food, water, matches, and the laptop. All the batteries were charged, so the kids would have enough power for hours of computer use.

Lionel dug his way through the mound of dirt that covered the secret entrance. When he was nearly through, he pulled out the GC officer's phone and scrolled through the list of names and landed on *Comm. B*. Lionel punched the Send button and listened.

"Ferguson?" an aide to the commander said.

"Yeah," Lionel said, trying to sound like Ferguson.

"Glad you called. Commander wanted me to give you a message. You found your cell phone?"

"Yeah, it was under the chair," Lionel said.

"Too bad," the aide said.

"What do you mean?"

"You know, we hoped whoever was in the house had taken it."

"Right," Lionel said. *They know I'm in the house!*

"Here's the plan," the aide said. "You and Wilcox make a big deal about getting out of there. Slam the door, whatever you have to do. Flank the house on both sides until your backup comes. They'll be there within the hour."

"How many are you sending?" Lionel said.

"We went over this," the aide barked. "We'll have a chopper and ten men. Now the kids may try to come back in, or the one inside will go to the others. It's important we get them all."

"I got it," Lionel said. He hung up the phone and gave a low whistle. He only had one chance, and he had to act fast.

Vicki stayed with Shelly the whole day. Staying at the top of the cave had calmed Shelly. Vicki left her only once to get her a drink of water, but Judd stopped her.

"This stuff needs to be boiled before we drink it," Judd said.

"She needs something," Vicki pleaded. "Let me just give her a little."

278

"It'll make her sick," Judd said.

Vicki stomped off and climbed the rope again. She put her feet on the side of the cave to balance herself. The more she did it, the better she got at climbing.

"Just a few more hours," Vicki said. "We'll get a fire going, get some food and water—"

"I don't have the strength to help tonight," Shelly said.

"It's OK," Vicki said. "You rest, and we'll take care of getting Lionel."

Vicki watched Mark and Judd gather the remaining sticks and wood from the cave. She was so hungry. Her mouth was dry and her lips cracked. The only good news was that the snakes were gone. But Vicki wondered if they would return if it started raining again.

Lionel shoved the blanket filled with provisions through the hole until it almost fell out the other side. He didn't hear a chopper or any GC troops. He crawled on hands and knees to the middle of the opening and pulled the cell phone from his pocket. He found the number listed for Larry Wilcox and pushed Send.

The guard with the deep voice answered. "Wilcox."

"Ferguson still hasn't found his phone?" Lionel said angrily.

"No, sir," Wilcox said. "We think—"

"Never mind what you think," Lionel interrupted. "The commander wants you inside until the chopper gets there with the others."

279

"All right," Wilcox said.

"Where are the dogs?" Lionel said.

"Outside, on either side of the house, like we were told," Wilcox said.

"Bring them in," Lionel said.

"But, sir—"

"Do you want me to get the commander on the line?" Lionel said.

"No, sir," Wilcox said. "We'll bring them in right away."

Lionel waited a few minutes, then pushed the pack of provisions the rest of the way out with his feet. He wiped the dirt from his face and looked around. Light was fading. No one was in sight. He grabbed the heavy pack, slung it onto his back, and took off for the meadow.

He heard a faint rumbling in the distance. On the horizon he spotted a helicopter. It was still at least a mile away. Lionel ran as fast as he could toward the cave.

———————————————

Judd went over the plan once again. He and Mark would go for Lionel while Vicki and Shelly stayed behind. Vicki seemed miffed that she didn't get to go, but Judd wasn't going to worry about that now.

"Somebody's coming!" Shelly said from the top of the cave.

"Quick," Judd said, "get down!"

Judd pulled out his gun and aimed it at the opening. Dirt fell as someone tried to get in.

"Lionel!" Vicki shouted.

"Somebody give me a hand with this stuff," Lionel said as he replaced the door. Judd climbed up to help. Shelly and Vicki tore into the blanket and found the water.

"Why didn't you wait for us?" Judd said.

Lionel told him what he'd discovered. In the middle of his story he stopped. "Chopper's landing," he said. "If I'd have stayed, they'd have caught you guys for sure."

Judd lit a match, but Lionel blew it out. "The GC might see the smoke," he said.

The five ate and drank until they were full. Lionel spread the supplies out and showed them the phone and laptop. "We'll have to conserve the food," he said.

"How long are we gonna be here?" Shelly said.

"The GC won't give up looking for us," Lionel said. "I think we have to wait here until we find a better place."

"No way," Shelly said.

"What about Conrad and Darrion?" Vicki said.

"Conrad's message said for us to stay where we are," Lionel said. "Until we run out of supplies, I think that's exactly what we should do."

"Anything has to be better than this," Shelly said. She told Lionel about the snakes.

"I don't like snakes any more than you," Lionel said, "but—"

"I'm telling you, I can't stand another night in here," Shelly said.

Lionel nodded. "I know you're scared, but there are a dozen GC troops out there right now looking for us. If they find one of us, they'll find the rest. You might get off with a reeducation camp. But they'll court-martial me, and who knows what they'll do to Judd and Vicki."

Shelly looked away.

"We'll keep you safe," Judd said.

Shelly stood. "That's what you said last night. I just can't handle another night in here, OK?"

Shelly walked away.

Lionel told the others about his conversations with Pavel and Mr. Stein. When Vicki heard the news about Mr. Stein and his belief in Christ, tears welled up in her eyes. "I wish Chaya were here," she said.

"There's something else," Lionel said. "Chloe's going to have a baby."

Vicki's mouth dropped open and she cried harder.

Judd grabbed the cell phone. Lionel showed him the number. Mr. Stein answered.

"Are you all right?" Mr. Stein said. "I was so worried after talking with Lionel this morning."

"We're OK," Judd said. "Lionel told us about you."

Mr. Stein chuckled. "Do you know that I am probably one of the 144,000 witnesses?"

"I imagine so," Judd said.

"There is so much to learn. I need to meet with you and Vicki. I want to become strong and tell others about God. Just like the apostle Paul."

"Keep reading Tsion's Web site," Judd said.

"I am. But I've also written Nicolae Carpathia."

"You what?" Judd said.

"There were so many messages pleading with the potentate to provide safety for the rabbi. I wrote Nicolae himself and said surely a lover of peace, who helped the rabbi escape his homeland, has the power to return him safely to Israel."

"Carpathia took the credit for getting Ben-Judah out of Israel?" Judd said. "Buck said—"

"Of course he took credit," Mr. Stein said. "He wanted to look good in the eyes of the world."

"Did you get a reply?"

"Not with words," Mr. Stein said. "This afternoon, Global Community officers appeared and took my computer away. I have others, of course. They asked again about my involvement with Vicki."

"What did you say?" Judd said.

"I told them the truth. I don't know where she is."

Judd heard a click on the line.

"I have withdrawn all my money from—"

"Mr. Stein," Judd said, "hang up and get to a safe place."

"What's wrong?"

"I think someone's listening."

"But Dr. Ben-Judah believes each of the witnesses is protected by God. Not everyone who has the mark on their forehead is protected. Only the 144,000 evangelists."

"Then be safe and get out of there."

"All right," Mr. Stein said. "But how will I reach you?"

"Use my E-mail address and tell me where to call you," Judd said. "Hurry."

Lionel and the others prayed that Mr. Stein would get to a safe place. Though their gathering wasn't the church setting Lionel had longed for, just being with other believers made him feel better. He prayed for Shelly and asked that her fear of the cave be taken away.

When they were through, Lionel hooked up the laptop. Just like the food, they would need to ration the use of the computer.

"If the batteries last as long as they say," Lionel said, "we could go forty minutes a day for more than three weeks."

"You think we could be in here that long?" Vicki said.

"I think we have to prepare for the worst," Lionel said.

Lionel logged on to the site where Eli and Moishe were shown live each day. The camera at the Wailing Wall carried live audio as well. Lionel knew these were the two preachers predicted in the book of Revelation. Judd pointed out their smoky burlap robes. They wore no shoes and had dark, bony feet and knuckled hands.

"They look like they're a thousand years old," Vicki said.

Their beards and hair were long, and they had dark, piercing eyes. They screamed out warnings to those who continued to reject Jesus as Messiah. As some in the crowd protested, Eli said, "Do not mock the Holy One of Israel! He came that you might have life, and have it to the full.

"Woe to you who reject the Son of God," he said. The camera showed a close-up of Eli's face. It was leathery and sunbaked. "And woe to those who fall prey to the one who sits on the throne of this earth."

"Who's he talking about?" Vicki said.

"The only person I can think of is Nicolae Carpathia," Lionel said.

———————————

Conrad rushed to the commander's tent with Melinda and Felicia. The commander smiled and came out to meet them.

"We've just heard a conversation between Stein and Thompson," the commander said. "This guy fooled us. He is in contact with them, and he's one of the fanatics. Told Thompson he was part of their elite group of 144,000, whatever that means."

The commander answered a phone call. When he was finished, he slammed the phone to the ground.

"The computer they took from his home came up empty," the commander said. "But we have enough on him now."

"What will you do, sir?" Conrad said.

"Question him and see if he'll talk now that we have him on tape," the commander said. "If he doesn't tell us what we want, we'll execute him."

"And if he does tell you?" Conrad said.

The commander smiled. "We'll execute him anyway."

29

FOR the next three weeks, Judd tried to make contact with his friend Pete. Pete had access to motorcycles, but he hadn't returned Judd's calls. The kids all agreed they would be safer away from the Mount Prospect area, but none of them wanted to leave without Conrad or Darrion.

Judd and the others coaxed Shelly into staying. She slept in the highest spot in the cave each night and kept an eye out for snakes. Vicki still talked about finding Phoenix. Judd tried not to discourage her, but he didn't hold out much hope.

"Maybe that biker group got Pete," Vicki said. "After what happened at that gas station, they sounded pretty upset."

"That's it," Judd said. He phoned the gas station and left a message.

Their food was running low, but Judd knew if they

were careful, they could last a few more days. Judd and Mark had made two midnight attempts to retrieve more supplies. Each time, they had to turn back. The GC still had guards posted at the house.

Though there was enough room in the cave, the kids quickly got restless. Each time they accessed the Internet, Mark searched for his cousin John. After two weeks he still had no word.

Judd and the others limited their computer time to twenty minutes each morning and twenty minutes each night. It was their only contact with the outside world.

One evening they gathered around the computer, and Judd read aloud an E-mail from Tsion Ben-Judah.

If you see media reports about a shooting in Denver, it is true that Buck was there, Tsion wrote. *Don't believe anything else about the reports.*

Judd clicked on a news flash and saw a video of the shooting in Colorado. The reporter said, "Two men, one claiming to be Nicolae Carpathia's pilot, broke into this clinic and killed a receptionist and a guard."

Footage from security cameras showed blurry video footage of three men.

"Isn't that Buck in the middle?" Vicki said.

Judd nodded. "Tsion said something about a friend of Chloe's being in trouble," he said.

The video showed a picture of a woman embracing Nicolae Carpathia. "That's Hattie Durham!" Vicki said.

"The two killers reportedly abducted the fiancée of Potentate Nicolae Carpathia," the reporter said. "The public is asked to provide any information about the identities of these men, or the whereabouts of Ms. Hattie Durham."

The news channel showed an enhanced photo of Buck and another man, along with Hattie Durham. Judd shook his head. "I want to hear Buck's version of what happened," he said.

With their water running low and no word from Pete, Judd had to make a decision. They hadn't heard from Mr. Stein, and Judd feared the man had been caught. His fears were confirmed the next morning when Conrad sent an urgent message.

We brought Mr. Stein in late last night, Conrad wrote. He stayed hidden as long as he could, but we got a call from one of the shelters. He went for food, and someone recognized him from a photo the GC had passed around.

I was with Melinda and Felicia when we found him. He's lost a lot of weight. He saw me and almost said something. I felt so bad taking him in. The commander's questioning him now. He's threatening to execute him if he doesn't give you guys up. Behind closed doors the commander says he'll execute him by noon, no matter what.

"That's in a few hours!" Vicki said.

Judd kept reading the message. *I don't know what to do. The commander is talking about shipping Darrion away by the end of the week. If we're going to do anything, now's the time.*

Judd turned off the computer and hung his head. "We're going to get him out of there," he said. "Darrion too."

"How?" Mark said.

Judd's phone rang.

"Hey, pal, what's up?" Pete said.

Judd told Pete their situation.

"I want to help," Pete said, "but there's no way I can make it by noon. Need time to get other riders together."

"What about tomorrow?" Judd said. "If we can stall them long enough, we have a chance of getting our people out."

"Sounds good," Pete said. "I can meet you at eight tonight, then have my other people there in the morning."

Judd gave Pete directions and thanked him.

"Hey, you saved my life," Pete said. "Plus, I've been wanting to see you. I have a surprise."

Every day Conrad felt more confident about his standing with Commander Blancka, Melinda, and Felicia. The girls no longer whispered when he was around. Together, Conrad and the girls followed leads and looked for Lionel and the others.

Commander Blancka was astounded that Darrion could last so long without food or water. Conrad knew he was taking a great risk slipping Darrion her provisions. He had now come up with a different plan. During one of their meetings he spied a letter in Commander Blancka's trash sent by an upper-level GC officer. He stuffed it in his pocket while no one was looking, then photocopied the insignia onto another sheet. He wrote a brief note that said, *A starving girl in a GC prison would not reflect well on the potentate or his friends.*

Conrad found a plain brown envelope and scribbled

T. B., the commander's initials, on the outside. When
Melinda and Felicia were on an assignment, Conrad
rushed to the commander's tent.

"I was told to give this to you, sir," Conrad said.

Conrad turned to leave as the commander opened the
envelope.

"Hold on," the commander said. "Who gave you
this?"

"I'm not sure, sir," Conrad said. "I've never seen him
before. He headed back toward the airfield."

"Did you read this?"

"Should I have, sir?" Conrad said.

The commander scratched his chin. "No, I just wish I
knew who was behind it."

The next day Darrion received three meals.

Conrad had very little contact with Darrion after that.
Only a wink or a nod in the interview room when no one
was looking. Conrad listened closely and tried to pick up
information.

A chill ran through Conrad as he heard the
commander talk about Mr. Stein. "After tomorrow there'll
be one less fanatic in the world," the commander said.

Judd talked over the plan with the others, and they agreed
it was their best shot to save Mr. Stein's life. Judd dialed
the number. Commander Blancka's aide answered
gruffly.

"This is Judd Thompson. I want to speak with the
commander."

Conrad watched as the aide rushed in and handed the commander the phone. "It's Thompson," the aide said.

"Are Washington and Byrne with you?" the commander said.

Conrad's plan to save Mr. Stein was to try and whisk the man from the back of the jail. But Conrad knew that would endanger his rescue of Darrion, who was now being held in a different area.

"What do you propose?" the commander said.

"First of all, if you harm Mr. Stein in any way, or if the girl is harmed, the deal's off."

"You're making a deal with *me*?" the commander said. "You're not in that kind of position."

"I'm one of three people you want in custody," Judd said. "From the way you guarded that house, you want us bad."

"And I'm still going to get you."

"I'm offering an even trade," Judd said. "I'll come in if you let them go."

The commander laughed. "No deal. I want Washington and that Byrne girl too."

"Three for two?" Judd said. "Doesn't sound fair to me."

The commander lowered his voice. "Thompson, I can make it easy for you. Are the other two right there?"

"I can talk."

"We have to make you pay for what you did to GC property," the commander said. "Honestly, you'll be in and out in a couple months max. I'll put in a good word for you."

292

"I thought you were the one making the decisions," Judd said. "If I need to talk with someone else—"

"You're right," the commander interrupted. "I do make the decisions, but those are always reviewed. Now, I'm willing to work with you, and I assume that by your call you're willing to work with me."

"What about Vicki and Lionel?"

"Now's not the time to concern yourself with them. Byrne has a murder rap and an escape on her head. Washington . . . we have to make an example of him. But I'll do what I can. You just come in—"

"You have to assure me that Mr. Stein and Darrion won't be hurt," Judd said.

"We can hold off on our plans for him if you come in today," the commander said.

"Tomorrow," Judd said. "Five o'clock at New Hope Village Church."

Judd hung up.

Conrad studied the commander's face as he told them what Judd had said.

"Couldn't we trace the call?" Melinda said.

"Not with a GC phone," the commander said. "Unfortunately, they have one."

"What are you going to do?" Felicia said.

"We're going to give them the girl and Stein," the commander said. Conrad began to protest. The commander held up a hand. "They're going to walk to a trap, and you three are going to be there to watch it."

Judd volunteered to meet Pete at the bridge. The others had questions about how they were going to overpower the commander and get away.

"You know they'll be waiting for us," Mark said.

"That's where Conrad comes in," Judd said. "He'll be working from the inside."

Vicki shook her head. "If Mr. Stein is right and he's one of the 144,000 witnesses, he's going to come through this. But we don't have that kind of guarantee."

"You're not actually planning on having us all there, are you?" Shelly said.

"That's the plan right now," Judd said. "We'll talk with Pete—"

"I don't need to talk with anybody," Shelly said. "You've kept me cooped up here for weeks and for what? You want me to surrender to this commander guy? No way."

Judd held up a hand. "We want to get Darrion and Mr. Stein out of the GC hands, right? If somebody has a better plan than this, I'm open to it. Let me go get Pete, and we'll see how he can help us."

Judd plastered mud on his face and tunneled through the wall of mud and rocks in the drainpipe. He listened carefully when he came to the mouth of the pipe and didn't hear anything.

The sky was cloudy and made traveling difficult. He didn't want to use Lionel's flashlight until he had to. It had been weeks since Judd was outside. The smell of the earth and the fresh air made Judd feel alive.

He climbed over fallen trees and up steep hillsides along the riverbank. Judd saw the lights of the bridge in the distance. He moved cautiously toward it.

The bridge was complete, though it looked nothing like it once did. Pieces of plywood covered the holes. At the other side sat two GC guards.

Judd crawled beneath the bridge and waited. With his back against a pylon, he nearly fell asleep. In the distance he heard a rumbling and saw two headlights approach.

The guards looked over some papers and waved the two ahead. When the cycles neared the end, Judd signaled the lead driver with Lionel's flashlight.

Pete parked his cycle and ran down the embankment toward Judd. The two embraced. Judd had to catch his breath after Pete's hug. He was as big and burly as ever.

"Good to see you," Pete whispered. "Been praying for you."

"We've got a big job ahead of us tomorrow," Judd said. "I'm not sure we're up to it."

"God is," Pete said. "I've seen him do some amazing things the past few weeks."

The other rider parked his motorcycle and walked with a limp toward Judd and Pete. He was tall and thin.

"I almost forgot," Pete said. "You're gonna love this."

Judd stared at the man. Bruises and scratches covered his face.

"Don't you recognize him?" Pete said.

Judd fell back against the bridge and gasped. "It can't be," he said.

30

JUDD blinked. "Is it really you?" he said.

Taylor Graham dropped his helmet and goggles and put out his hand. Judd noticed a huge bruise on the side of his head.

"Didn't think you'd ever see me again, huh?" Taylor said.

"I saw you go over the cliff," Judd said. "I looked for your body."

"The log hit me in the head," Taylor said. "I stayed conscious until I went over. When I woke up, I was on a ledge next to the water. Bodies were floating everywhere."

"I hate to break up this reunion," Pete said, "but those guards are gonna get suspicious."

Judd helped Pete and Taylor hide their motorcycles under the bridge. The three ran toward the meadow. Taylor asked about the Stahley hangar, and Judd briefly told him their story.

"How's Ryan?" Taylor said.

Judd took a deep breath and told him about Ryan's death.

Taylor shook his head. "He was a good kid," he said.

The three slipped through the top of the cave. Judd introduced Pete and Taylor to the others.

"Finish your story," Judd said. "How'd you get out of that lake and hook up with Pete?"

"Hank and Judy," Taylor said. "I couldn't climb out myself, so I just waited to die. I don't know how long it was, but this farmer and his wife spotted me and got a rope long enough to reach."

"The same couple who helped me," Judd said.

"After I told them about the quake and the van, they said you had been there and left. I wasn't in any shape to travel, so they let me have their son's room."

Judd explained that the couple were also tribulation saints and had a son who had died in the earthquake.

"A couple of days later GC guards came by," Taylor continued. "A few people from the reeducation camp had escaped. Hank and Judy covered for me. They told me their story. Tried to get me to believe like them."

Judd looked closely at Taylor's forehead. There was no mark. "They're really good people," Judd said.

"They *were* good people," Pete said. "I went to see 'em a few days after I met this guy. The GC had come back and found out they'd been hiding people."

"What happened to them?" Vicki said.

"They were executed on the spot," Pete said.

Vicki gasped.

"This guy almost got himself killed too," Taylor said, pointing to Pete.

Pete shook his head. "Wasn't like that," he said. "I was just giving some friends the gospel."

"Your former biker group?" Judd said.

"We had a score to settle at that gas station," Pete said. "I found the owner and told him about Jesus. Said he wasn't into religion, but he was impressed with the way I'd helped a stranger. So he prayed with me like I did with you.

"Next thing I know, the gang is back. That's when Taylor comes walking into the middle of our fight. Only it turns out not to be a fight."

Taylor laughed. "This big monster was preaching to the rest of them. Couldn't believe it."

"It was the second time I'd told them," Pete said. "Not everybody responded the way I wanted, but most of them believed. They're coming to help tomorrow."

Lionel listened to the stories and held back as long as he could. He could see the resemblance of Conrad in Taylor's face.

When there was a lull, Lionel said, "I know your brother. He's been worried about you."

"Conrad?" Taylor said. "How do you know him?"

Lionel explained how the two had met. "Conrad's working on the inside trying to get our friends out," he said.

"Sounds like something Conny would do."

"He's changed since you last saw him," Lionel said. "He believes in God. He has the mark."

Taylor shook his head. "Not that again."

"God's after you, man," Pete said. "Your brother's no dummy. Why can't you see—"

"I don't argue that you people have something," Taylor interrupted. "I just don't think it's for me. At least not yet."

"None of us knows how long we have left," Pete said.

"Before I turn to religion, I've got a few scores to settle," Taylor said. "And the first thing I want to do is get Conrad away from the GC."

Judd told Pete and Taylor what they would do the next day.

"Doesn't sound like much of a plan," Taylor said.

"Exactly," Mark said. "We need guns, grenades, and a few snipers in position."

Judd looked at Mark. "I thought you learned your lesson with the militia," he said.

"We're not going to kill anybody. We just want to get our own people out."

Pete yawned. "We're all tired," he said. "Let's get some sleep and talk in the morning."

Judd made sure everyone had a place to sleep. As he lay down he noticed Taylor and Mark whispering.

Conrad couldn't sleep. He kept going over the plan in his head. There were things Judd didn't know, things Conrad didn't have time to explain.

Melinda and Felicia were almost bursting with glee

about the prospect of getting Lionel, Vicki, and Judd. They had talked about it on the way to their tent that night.

"The commander told me they're all gonna get it tomorrow," Felicia had said. "There's no way they're going to let that Stahley girl go. And Stein is toast."

Conrad had also overheard the commander talking with another officer about the operation. The GC would have men in position overnight with the latest high-powered rifles. The commander didn't want any surprises.

Conrad needed to talk with Darrion and Mr. Stein about the plan, but he couldn't get to them. He would have to wait and hope they followed his lead the next day.

Conrad sat up and checked his gun again. He could think of only one way to get Darrion and Mr. Stein out. And he knew his plan could get him killed.

Judd awoke from a deep sleep. Pete was shaking his shoulders.

"Do you know where Taylor is?" Pete said.

Judd saw the empty spot on the ground. "Could he have gone for some firewood?"

"Not likely," Pete said. "He was pretty fired up last night once he found out where his little brother was."

Judd woke Mark up. "What were you guys talking about last night?" Judd said.

Mark looked sheepish. "How wimpy your plan is," he said. "Taylor said there's no chance of any of us getting out of there the way things stand."

"Do you know where he went?" Judd said.

Mark shook his head. "He said he might leave early. I asked to go with him. He said he'd think about it."

Judd checked both entrances but found no sign of Taylor. He pulled out the computer and figured there was only enough battery power for one more session.

Conrad's last message gave Judd the location of the GC snipers. *I'll be right next to the commander, he wrote. Be warned. They're not taking prisoners.*

"We're walking into a trap," Mark said.

"We have to chance it," Judd said.

Vicki spoke up. "Maybe God wants us to stop running. Maybe he wants us in one of those reeducation camps."

"Don't you understand?" Mark said. "Conrad said they're not taking prisoners. They're going to make an example of you." He turned to Judd. "If I can get a rifle, I could pick off—"

"No!" Judd said.

Mark walked away. Judd looked at Shelly and Vicki. "You guys don't have to go," he said. "I could have Pete take you somewhere."

"I don't know what'll happen," Vicki said, "but I'm not leaving Darrion and Mr. Stein alone. I'm in."

Shelly hesitated. "I can't take it anymore," she said. "I'll take a ride."

Before they left the cave, Judd pulled a piece of paper from Ryan's packet he had found. "I found this last night," he said. "It's in Ryan's handwriting."

Judd spread the verse out on a rock. It said: *Zechariah*

4:6, *"It is not by force nor by strength, but by my Spirit, says the Lord Almighty."*

Mark said, "I want to do things in God's strength too, but this is like putting David in front of Goliath without a slingshot."

"You don't have to go," Judd said.

"You know I don't mean that," Mark said.

Pete stood, and the kids grew silent. "I haven't been at this long, but I know if somebody's in trouble and I can do something, I'm going. I think we should pray."

Vicki's hand was dwarfed by Pete's. One by one the others joined hands.

"God, you showed me the truth about you, and I thank you," Pete prayed. "I thank you for these brave kids who want to help their friends. Show us what to do and when to do it. Amen."

Conrad stayed close to Commander Blancka throughout the morning. Melinda and Felicia went to the church to view the progress. Reports from the site didn't sound good for the kids.

"The snipers have been in place since early this morning," Melinda radioed back. "They're hidden so well I had to have them pointed out."

A few minutes later Felicia made contact with the commander. "We've found that weird kid, Charlie," she said. "He was staying down here with a dog. What do you want us to do?"

"Get him to one of the shelters," the commander said, "and keep everyone else away from the area."

The commander rubbed his hands together and talked to his aide. "We'll let them come to us," he said. "I want no choppers, no observation of any kind. We want them to think everything's just like I said."

Vicki squinted at the sky as she climbed out of the metal pipe. Her skin had grown pale inside the cave, and it felt good to be out. The sun was blocked by dark clouds, but the natural light felt good. The kids followed Pete to the bridge and found only one motorcycle.

"Where do you think Taylor went?" Judd said.

Pete shook his head. "Can't worry about it now," he said. "Duck under here."

The kids watched the patrols on the other side. "How are we gonna get across?" Vicki said.

"Watch," Pete said.

Vicki saw a cloud of dust about a mile away. When the cloud moved closer, the roar of motorcycles echoed across the water.

"We go now," Pete said, starting his motorcycle and heading for the other side.

"Stay close to me," Judd said as he trotted across the bridge.

The patrols stopped the gang. The motorcycles revved their engines and drowned out the noise made by Pete. As he rode past, he snatched the gun out of one guard's hands and knocked the other to the ground. One bearded man picked up the gun and motioned for both guards to get on the ground.

"What are they doing?" Vicki said.

"They won't hurt them," Judd said. "They'll lock them in the guard building and take their radios until this is over."

Vicki and the others walked past the guards. Vicki counted fifteen motorcycles, each with a single rider. Most were men, but there were also three women. They were dressed in leather and wore helmets or bandannas.

"I was hoping Red would be here," Judd said.

Pete shook his head. "Still workin' on Red," he said.

Shelly climbed on a motorcycle.

"Take her to the place," Pete said.

The female rider nodded. As the two sped off, a woman stretched a gloved hand out to Vicki. "Sally," she said.

"Pleased to meet you," Vicki said.

The group roared off. Vicki felt queasy.

_____

Conrad looked at his watch. It was a few minutes before 5:00 P.M. His hands were sweating. Thick blue-and-black clouds rolled into the area.

The commander sat on his jeep, looking through binoculars. A cloud of dust appeared on the horizon. Conrad noticed a faint rumbling.

"What in the world?" the commander said. He looked to his aide. "Find out what that is."

"Sir," the aide said, "you said no one was to—"

305

"Just get somebody up there!"

"Yes, sir," the aide said.

Conrad unsnapped his holster and waited. A lone figure appeared on a small hill above the church. Conrad looked at the snipers hidden behind trees and in the church rubble. They were poised to fire.

Two other figures appeared on the hill.

"There they are," Commander Blancka said. He clicked his radio. "They look unarmed, but be careful. No one fires unless I give the order. We've got them now."

31

CONRAD watched the scene closely, wondering when to make his move. The commander lowered his binoculars and said, "Bring those two up here."

Two guards kept watch over Darrion and Mr. Stein. Conrad hurried to them and gruffly led them away by handcuffs. When they had gone a few steps, Conrad slipped a key to Mr. Stein. "Unlock them, but keep them on," Conrad whispered.

"Are we going now?" Darrion whispered.

"Not yet," Conrad said. "If you try to run, they'll be all over you."

"I don't believe they'll let us out of here alive," Mr. Stein said.

"Don't worry," Conrad said. "I still have to get you to the Meeting of the Witnesses in a couple of days."

Mr. Stein sighed. Darrion shook with fear.

"We're gonna make it, I promise," Conrad said.

The three were nearly back to the commander's position when Conrad whispered, "When I make my move, you two stay as close to me as you possibly can. Right next to me, OK?"

Darrion and Mr. Stein nodded.

Judd pointed toward the jeep. "That has to be the commander," he said.

"Where're Darrion and Mr. Stein?" Vicki said.

"There," Lionel said, as Conrad led the two into view.

The kids stood on a knoll that overlooked the church property. A black cloud hovered over them.

"If I'm right," Lionel said, "they'll have snipers around the church and—look there, behind the tree."

"Let's just hope Conrad can come through for us," Judd said.

A squeal from a loudspeaker split the air. The commander blew into the microphone and said, "Put your hands in the air and come down the hill! Nothing will happen to you."

Conrad watched Judd turn to confer with Lionel and Vicki. *Don't do it,* Conrad thought.

"Send Darrion and Mr. Stein halfway, then we'll come down," Judd said.

The commander cursed, then clicked the microphone and spoke calmly. "Now, Judd, I gave you my word nothing would happen. We're here waiting, like we said. We didn't try to find you or follow you."

"What are the snipers doing at the church and along the tree line?" Judd yelled.

The commander radioed the snipers and told them to get ready. "Fire on my command," he said.

Conrad reached for his gun. Suddenly, the sound of engines roared in the distance. Motorcycle riders encircled the three on the hill.

"I count ten cycles," someone said on the radio.

"They're not armed, sir," another said.

Conrad saw a huge man get off his cycle and say something to Judd. The engines revved, then shut off.

Judd yelled, "You said no one would try to stop us! What are your troops doing moving around behind us?"

Commander Blancka fumed. He meant to key his microphone but spoke over the loudspeaker instead. "I told you people to stay out of sight—" When he heard his voice echo, he clicked on the microphone. "Pull back! Pull back!"

"Commander, we have clear shots on all of them," a sniper said.

Conrad studied the commander's face. If the snipers started shooting it would be all over in seconds.

———

Lionel heard movement behind them. Mark crawled up the hill. "Cycles are ready," Mark said. "Enough for us and the three of them."

"Start them now," Judd said.

A wind kicked up and blew dirt and sand in their faces.

"Assuming we get all three," Vicki said, "where are we going?"

"Leave that to me," Pete said. "I got it covered."

Conrad reached for his gun again. The commander bit his lip. "I wanted to bring them in without this," the commander said.

"Targets are clear, sir," a sniper radioed.

"This is probably as good a time as any," the commander said. He keyed his microphone.

"No!" Conrad yelled, pulling his gun and holding it against the commander. The man was so stunned he kept the microphone on and shouted, "Graham, what is this?"

Darrion and Mr. Stein closed in on them.

"I've got a gun on the commander," Conrad said. The commander looked down and let go of the microphone. Mr. Stein slipped his handcuffs on the man.

"Hold your fire," Conrad heard a sniper say. "One of the Morale Monitors has a gun on the commander."

Vicki shielded her eyes from the wind. "What's he doing?" she said.

"It's part of the plan," Judd said. "He doesn't want to hurt him—his gun's not even loaded—but the GC don't know that."

"Bring 'em out, Conrad," Lionel coaxed.

"Everybody down," Judd said.

310

From the ground, Vicki saw a comical sight. Mr. Stein and Darrion held hands around Conrad and the commander. The group turned in circles as they moved toward the hill.

"Why's he doing that?" Vicki said.

"The snipers," Lionel said. "They won't want to hurt the commander, and it's harder to hit a moving target."

Conrad ripped the radio from the commander's shoulder. It was just after 5:00 P.M. but it looked like night.

"You'll pay for this, Graham," the commander said.

"We don't want to hurt you," Conrad said. "Keep moving."

Conrad heard someone running. Darrion screamed. Melinda ran at them with her gun outstretched. When she saw Conrad she yelled, "You traitor!"

A deafening roar split the sky as a helicopter rose up behind Melinda. The pilot trained his spotlight on her. The wind blew the chopper. The pilot couldn't keep it steady. Melinda fell to the ground in terror.

"We got you now!" the commander shouted. "You might get to your group, but you'll never escape the Global Community!"

The chopper, only a few feet off the ground, turned and faced the rubble of New Hope Village Church. "Stand clear of the building," the pilot said on a loudspeaker. A missile shot from the side of the helicopter. Snipers scattered from the building as the bomb exploded, sending a plume of smoke and debris into the air.

"What in the world—?" the commander said.

The pilot turned the chopper and faced the small group. The blades beat the air above their heads. Conrad peered into the cockpit and saw the pilot give a thumbs-up and smile.

"Taylor?" Conrad said. "It's my brother!"

Taylor motioned for them to get in. With the commander still in the middle of the group, Darrion, Mr. Stein, and Conrad stepped onto the struts.

Conrad was inches from the commander's face. "You'll never get away," the commander said.

Conrad opened his gun to show it had no bullets. "We might not, but you can't say we didn't give it a good try," he said. He handed the gun to the man as the helicopter lifted off.

"Fire, fire!" the commander shouted as the door closed.

Bullets pinged off the bulletproof glass.

Judd and the others rolled away from the hilltop as bullets aimed at the helicopter whizzed past them.

"What's happening?" Vicki said.

"New plan," Judd said. "Just get ready!"

The helicopter landed just over the hill. Darrion, Mr. Stein, and Conrad scampered out.

"I'll hold them off," Taylor yelled. "Get out of here!"

Taylor lifted straight up. The wind swirled and lightning flashed above the kids.

"Here they come!" Vicki yelled.

Judd peeked over the hill and saw a wave of GC soldiers. Commander Blancka ran with handcuffs still on.

Another helicopter appeared from behind the GC troops. Taylor shot a missile into the ground before the oncoming soldiers, and they fell back. The other helicopter bore down on Taylor with its guns blazing.

Lionel tugged on Judd's arm. The two ran down the hill as an explosion rocked the earth. One of the helicopters had crashed. Judd hopped on the back of Pete's motorcycle, and they sped away.

Judd turned and saw a group of snipers topping the hill. They knelt and aimed their rifles at the kids.

Judd gulped. *And we were almost out of here*, he thought.

But the snipers didn't fire. Instead, they ducked, put hands in the air, and fell to the ground. Judd felt something on his head, like someone was throwing gravel. Pete and the others stopped and tried to cover themselves with their motorcycles. Judd felt sharp stings on his arms, his neck, his back.

"It's hail!" Pete said.

Then the sky opened up. The hailstones grew bigger and pelted the motorcycles. They were almost the size of golf balls, falling around them and piling up like snow. Judd watched from ground level, protected by the motorcycle. The hail clanged off the gas tank and cracked the speedometer.

An orange glow encircled them. Judd thought it was lightning at first, flashing across the sky, but it wasn't. The hailstones, at least half of them, were in flames!

"What's happening?" Pete yelled.

"One of God's judgments!" Judd screamed. "I read something by Dr. Ben-Judah about an angel throwing hail and fire to the earth."

Judd saw Vicki a few yards away, huddled under a motorcycle. Mr. Stein had pulled his shirt over his head for protection. When the flaming hail hit the ice, it sizzled, and smoke curled from the ground.

Some of the fiery hail hit trees. They burst into flames, their branches sending fire and smoke into the air. Grass caught on fire and scorched the hillside. Judd was mixed with fear and wonder. God had promised this thousands of years ago. Now it was coming true before his eyes.

Judd saw more ice fall on the blackened ground. It piled up white, then in sections began to turn red. The drops looked like paint balls exploding on the ground and spreading in all directions.

"Blood!" Judd said.

It poured from the sky. The melted hail mixed with the blood, sending rivers of red around them. Judd put a hand into the stream of red. It was thick, oozing through his fingers. He held it to his face. It even smelled like blood.

Lightning flashed and thunder shook the ground. The hail started again, this time bigger. Some were as big as softballs. The trees that had burst into flames now sizzled as the hail put out the fire.

Judd could only cover his head and pray. It was like being in a video game with thousands of fireworks falling around him. Only this wasn't a game.

The black cloud rolled on. As the last of the hail fell, the sun peeked out. Judd saw the results of the angel's judgment. The trees had turned black as ash. Bushes and shrubs were burned to a crisp. The blood and water seeped into the ground. Charred grass broke through the white and red.

Pete pushed the bike upright. Red blotches marked his face where he had driven into the first volley of hail. Judd jumped on the back of the cycle, and Pete kicked the machine to life.

They slid through the slush and blood. Mr. Stein's motorcycle wiped out. The man came up with blood dripping from his shirt.

Judd had heard the screams of the Global Community soldiers who lay unprotected as the hailstorm began. He didn't want to think about what the softball-sized hail could do to a person without any protection. He wondered if Taylor Graham had been in the helicopter that crashed.

Judd counted heads as they made their way over the wet earth. The Young Trib Force was alive, at least for the moment.

Judd glanced back to see if Commander Blancka and the others would give chase. The motorcycles topped a hill and looked down on the scene. Several soldiers lay lifeless in the red earth. The charred remains of a GC copter lay smoldering nearby.

Pete gunned the engine and raced away. Moments later Judd heard the roar of rotor blades. He held on to the motorcycle and prayed.

32

JUDD held on as Pete drove recklessly through the blood and slush. A few minutes after the sun came out, most of the hail and blood had dissolved into the ground. A helicopter passed nearby. Judd guessed the pilot had lost the bikers in the woods. He glanced at Conrad. The boy looked grim.

Pete found a main road and picked up speed. They passed abandoned cars with broken windshields. A crater had opened in the middle of the road. The remains of an exploded fuel truck lay in the bottom of the hole.

They drove through the crater and on the other side saw a helicopter coming right for them. Pete stopped. The aircraft was pocked with dents from the hail.

To Judd's surprise, the helicopter landed and Taylor Graham stepped out. He gave a thumbs-up to the group. "Almost out of fuel," he said. "Think you could give me a ride?"

Pete motioned for one of the single riders to come forward. As he did, Taylor fired up the chopper and perched it on the side of an embankment by the road. Taylor left the rotors going and stepped out. The rotors slowed, and then the black craft tipped forward and fell into the ravine. A fiery explosion shook the earth.

"Better leave before they see that smoke," Taylor said.

Vicki was glad Conrad's brother was safe. She didn't like it that he had tried to kill the commander and the others, but he had gotten Darrion, Mr. Stein, and Conrad out alive.

Vicki held tight to the motorcycle driver. She kept looking over her shoulder, thinking the GC would be right behind them.

They drove without resting, the wind in their faces. When night fell, the motorcycles looked eerie with their headlights piercing the darkness. Vicki was exhausted when they finally reached a gas station. The manager came outside with a gun, then grinned at Pete.

"Don't park out here, bring them on in," the man said.

The kids and Mr. Stein went inside while the others pulled their motorcycles into the garage. Shelly had prepared hot chocolate and sandwiches. The kids ate hungrily.

"Boyd Walker," the man said, extending a hand to each of the kids. He pointed at Judd. "This young fellow and Pete helped me out in more ways than one."

Along with grease stains, Vicki saw that the man had the mark of a true believer on his forehead.

Boyd told the story again of how Pete had saved his station from the motorcycle gang. Then Pete had returned and told him the truth about Christ's return. "I been readin' that rabbi on the Internet," Boyd said. "Got a computer in the back."

Vicki noticed that Conrad and Taylor Graham were in a heated discussion outside.

"That's not how we do things," Conrad said. "How many did you kill to get that bird from the GC?"

"I saved your tail back there," Taylor said. "A simple thank-you would be nice. Besides, I gave those guys warning before I shot."

Conrad shook his head. "I'm glad you're alive. But you have to stop trying to get revenge against the GC and start listening to what I'm saying."

"Like I told the others, I don't have time for religion right now."

Boyd had given Mr. Stein a T-shirt to replace the bloodstained one. Mr. Stein embraced Vicki. "I didn't think I would ever see you again," he said. "I still have so many questions, but Rabbi Ben-Judah is answering them now."

"Chaya would be so happy," Vicki said.

Mr. Stein blinked tears away. "I can only tell you how sorry I am," he said. "God has forgiven me for my hard heart. I know one day I will see Chaya and Judith again."

"Conrad said you're pretty set on going to Israel," Vicki said.

"The meeting is this weekend," Mr. Stein said. "I'm

afraid I'll have to watch it on the Net like the rest of the world."

Vicki thought about Phoenix. It would have been impossible to bring him with them, even if she had found him. But she still felt guilty not keeping her promise to Ryan.

Lionel found Boyd's tiny black-and-white television and tuned in a station. Darrion sat beside him with a cold drink. "I can't wait to see what kind of spin Carpathia's newsmen put on what's happened!" she said.

The news anchor looked flustered, as if he had witnessed the hail and didn't believe what he was reading. The anchor gave staggering statistics about the amount of hail the area received in the few minutes the storm raged. "But Illinois was not the only area hit. In fact, this seems to have happened worldwide at the exact same time."

"So how do you explain it?" Lionel said to the TV.

The anchor introduced an expert who said the event was a "one-time occurrence" and was easily explained as an "atmospheric disturbance."

Darrion shook her head. "Yeah, and it definitely did not have anything to do with God or with his judgment of the earth."

"As many of you saw earlier, Potentate Nicolae Carpathia responded to this world crisis with decisive action," the news anchor said. "He held a news conference less than an hour ago in which he outlined the Global Community response."

Nicolae was dressed casually, as if he had strolled in from a dinner party to answer questions. But Lionel could tell the man was concerned. If he had been reading Dr. Ben-Judah's Web site as Pavel said he had, he knew this was no fluke. This was God speaking in a forceful way.

"Because of the momentary disruption in communications, I have called a halt to all travel. This means the meeting scheduled in Israel that I had approved will have to be rescheduled."

"How convenient," Darrion said.

"Citizens of the Global Community should not be alarmed," Carpathia continued. "We have everything under control, and the effects of this storm should not hinder us as we move forward in our quest for a better world."

"So if it's no problem," Lionel said, "why does he have to postpone the Meeting of the Witnesses?"

The news shifted to local effects of the storm. Video showed traffic snarls and streets filled with hail. The anchor referred to the "sticky red substance" but never called it blood. He said a few fires were also reported.

"Look!" Darrion shouted. Bikers gathered from around the station.

A shot of a downed GC helicopter flashed on the screen. Several GC soldiers lay facedown in a field near New Hope Village Church.

"At the time of the storm," the anchor continued, "the Global Community was conducting a training exercise in Mount Prospect."

"Training exercise!" Lionel yelled.

"Seven soldiers were killed by the hailstorm, and a dozen others were treated for fractures and burns at a local shelter. The leader of the exercise, Commander Terrel Blancka, has reportedly been reprimanded and will be given another assignment."

"You know the real reason they're upset with him," Darrion said.

"Yeah," Lionel said. "He let us get away."

Judd found the laptop in the saddlebag of Pete's motorcycle. It had taken a beating from the hail but still worked. He hooked it up beside Boyd's ancient machine and logged on to the Net.

"That thing's got some speed," Boyd said, admiring the laptop.

The list of forwarded E-mails from Tsion was growing. Now that they were away from the GC, Judd thought he might have a chance to answer some of them.

Judd let out a whoop and yelled for Mark.

"What's up?" Mark said.

"It's from John," Judd said.

John's message was short. It read, *If you get this E-mail, please respond. If you've seen any of my friends or family, please report.*

Judd quickly wrote and gave Boyd's phone number. He sent a second E-mail detailing their flight from the Global Community. He sent the second message and logged off. The phone rang a few seconds later.

"Yeah, he's right here," Boyd said, handing the phone to Judd.

It was John. "I've been trying to call since I saw your first E-mail," he said. "Did everybody make it OK?"

"Ryan's gone," Judd said.

John didn't speak.

"And you knew Chaya Stein. She was killed in the quake too."

"What about Mark?" John said.

Judd handed the phone to Mark. The two talked a few minutes and then Judd got back on the line. "Give us the update," he said.

"You won't believe it," John said. "The quake hit in the middle of classes at college. I saw the lights shake and remembered what Tsion said. I made it out the window before the whole building came down.

"Then everything went crazy. I helped pull bodies out of buildings and get help to the injured. The GC showed up a couple days later looking for anyone who could walk. There's a naval base on the coast, and some of their guys didn't make it."

"You volunteered?" Judd said.

"You don't volunteer with the GC," John said. "I said I was a first-year engineering student, and they told me to get in the truck. I didn't have a choice."

"Where are you now?" Judd said.

"I'm finishing up training," John said. "They put me in communications. We're pulling out tomorrow for the Atlantic."

"You're right," Judd said. "I don't believe it."

"The good news is I have access to everything," John said. "We get orders and reports from New Babylon just about every day. Plus, I saw your picture, which was sent from Chicago yesterday."

"A picture?" Judd said.

"More like a wanted poster," John said. "They had mug shots of you, Vicki, and Lionel."

"Have you heard the reports about what happened?" Judd said.

"You mean the training exercise?" John laughed. "The report I get is that the head guy, Blancka, has been demoted from his Morale Monitor position. They don't even know whether they'll continue the program or not."

When he was finished with John, Judd called a meeting of the Young Trib Force. Pete and a few of the other bikers sat in, along with Boyd.

"I have a message from Tsion I want to read," Judd said, "but first, I have to say something. We're wanted by the GC. They know about Darrion, Vicki, Lionel, Mr. Stein, and me. We have to make a choice. Do we stay together? And when the GC school starts, should we attend? Where do we go?"

Mark raised a hand.

"If it's OK," Judd said, "I'd like you all to sleep on it, make some notes, and be ready to talk tomorrow."

Judd opened Tsion's E-mail and read it.

> We serve a great God who delivers his children. I have been praying for you since I heard of your difficulty, and will continue to pray.

I am going to Israel as soon as possible. Eli and Moishe confirmed that the time is right. The other day Eli said, "Woe unto him who sits on the throne of this earth. Should he dare stand in the way of God's sealed and anointed witnesses, twelve thousand from each of the twelve tribes making a pilgrimage here for the purpose of preparation, he shall surely suffer for it."

Then Moishe said, "Yea, any attempt to impede the moving of God among the sealed will cause your plants to wither and die, rain to remain in the clouds, and your water—all of it—to turn to blood! The Lord of hosts hath sworn, saying, 'Surely, as I have thought, so it shall come to pass, and as I have purposed, so it shall stand!' "

This lets me know the time is close. The first of the seven angels have sounded their judgments with fiery hail and blood which burned a third of the trees and all green grass.

Next to come is the second angel, which brings with it a great mountain burning with fire. This will turn a third of the earth's water to blood, kill a third of the living creatures in the sea, and sink a third of the ships.

The third angel's trumpet sound will result in a great star falling from heaven, burning like a torch. It will bring disaster with it, and many will die.

I tell you this not to scare you, but to prepare you for what is ahead. Be bold. You may be asked to give your life. Ryan and Chaya already have.

Judd paused. Mr. Stein wept. Judd felt the emotion well up. He turned to the screen to keep from crying himself, and he read:

> Wherever you are, I encourage you to think of the great soul harvest before us. I wish I had believed before the Rapture, but I rejoice in the opportunity before us. Many will become believers in Jesus in the next few months.
>
> Be careful. The next judgments may come soon. May God help you make right decisions as you seek to lead others to the truth.

33

JOHN Preston sat at the communications center of the United North American States ship *Peacekeeper 1*, wondering if he would ever see his friends again. Less than two years earlier, he and his cousin Mark Eisman had met Judd Thompson Jr. on their first day back at Nicolae High. The kids had seen their share of trouble, and even death. Several times John had begun typing a message but erased it when someone came near. He had to wait for the right moment.

John had hoped the kids could be together at the Meeting of the Witnesses in Jerusalem. Now that seemed out of the question. John had set up a computer in his quarters to record each session and couldn't wait to hear Tsion Ben-Judah teach live.

An alarm sent people scurrying. Officers barked orders. John studied a blip on a radar screen and pointed it out to his friend, Carl.

Carl nodded. "Finally gonna see some action."

After the Wrath of the Lamb earthquake, John had been taken from college and put to work with the Global Community Navy. Carl had taken John under his wing. There didn't seem to be anything about computers or technical equipment Carl didn't understand.

Carl smiled. "Only ships allowed out here now are GC approved," he said.

"Who else would want to be?"

"Drug pushers, weapons dealers, you name it," Carl said. "We consider them modern-day pirates."

"Three miles and closing, sir," an officer shouted.

"Should we be worried, Carl?"

Carl smiled. "Not even God could sink *Peacekeeper 1*. Best communications, most precise weaponry, and amazing speed."

John stared through a scope at what looked like a cargo ship.

"No registry evident, sir," an officer reported.

Carl raised his eyebrows. "Guys on deck," he said.

John saw patrols with high-powered rifles walking back and forth.

"Attention," the captain said over the loudspeaker. "The ship we're intersecting is in violation of Global Community maritime law. We could destroy it from here, but we suspect illegal weapons and hostages."

Carl shook his head. "I don't like their chances."

"We're sending a team into the water before the ship spots us," the captain continued. "We'll give the hostages every chance."

John watched the undersea monitor. *Peacekeeper 1*'s small sub approached the cargo ship, and men in wet suits floated through the hatch. Another monitor displayed a few climbing the side of the ship.

The captain rushed to the communications center and pushed the talk button in front of John. "Stay down! Stay down! Unfriendlies coming your way."

But they had been spotted. The men in wet suits dropped back into the water as men onboard opened fire. John saw blood in the water. One diver made it back to the sub.

The captain ordered pursuit, and the sudden acceleration threw John back in his chair. The cargo ship turned to flee, but it was no match for *Peacekeeper 1*.

"They don't stand a chance," Carl said.

"What about the hostages?" John said.

Carl shook his head.

As they closed in, bullets pinged off the hull, and John saw the frightened faces of the enemy patrols.

"Warning," the captain said over the loudspeaker. "Release your hostages now or we sink your ship."

The patrols fled below deck. John thought they might release hostages, but two masked men returned with bazookas. John felt the explosion, and the captain rattled off a series of orders. The *Peacekeeper 1* turned its guns on the scared crew.

Carl shook his head. "Idiots," he said.

Peacekeeper 1's cannon opened a huge hole in the cargo ship. It tipped one way, then the other. As water filled the hole, the crew leaped overboard. John saw one of the divers from the *Peacekeeper 1* scramble onto the deck of the other ship and disappear into a smoke-filled stairwell.

"Pelton, no!" the captain shouted. "Get him out of there!"

Carl clicked a button and spoke to the diver, but there was no response.

John's heart raced as five civilians appeared through the smoke. As soon as they hit the sloping deck, they slipped and fell over the railing. Within seconds the submarine surfaced and picked two civilians from the water. John watched for any sign of the diver who had performed the rescue. Just as the stairwell sank below the waterline, the diver emerged. The submarine surfaced. John moved closer to the monitors.

Seconds seemed like an eternity. A whoop went up in the ship as the lone diver shot out of the water with the three remaining civilians clinging to him.

Since the judgment of fire, hail, and blood, the kids had hidden at the gas station. Judd was surprised by the anger of the Young Trib Force.

Shelly began, "We've been—"

"I don't want to hear her," Mark said. "She turned and ran."

"What are you talking about?" Shelly said.

"You took the easy way out and got a ride without facing Blancka," Mark said.

Vicki's face flushed. "You have no right to judge," she said. "You don't know what she's been through."

"We've all been through a lot," Mark said. "Let's not decide stuff on emotion."

Shelly's lip trembled. Judd cut in. "Everybody is equal," he said. "We'll listen to everybody."

Vicki crossed her arms. "He probably wants to go blow people up, like Taylor Graham."

"If it weren't for Taylor," Mark said, "we'd have never gotten out of there. Judd's plan was wimpy."

"Everybody be quiet!" Judd yelled. Judd saw Taylor storm out the front of the gas station.

Conrad put his face in his hands. "I didn't know it was gonna be like this."

Judd closed the office door. Boyd Walker, manager of the gas station, and Judd's friend Pete stood nearby.

Shelly stood up. "That's it. Either Mark goes or I do."

Mr. Stein stepped forward. "I am new to this," he said. "We have been through a lot. We could have died yesterday."

"Not her," Mark said.

"From what I understand," Mr. Stein said, "this young woman intervened on your behalf at the Stahley mansion."

"Yeah," Vicki said.

Mr. Stein put up a hand and stared at Mark. "Is it not true she put her life on the line and could have been arrested by the Global Community guards, not once, but twice?"

"I'm not saying she can't be part of the group," Mark stammered, "I just—"

"I have read only a little of the Scriptures, but aren't we supposed to love each other?" Mr. Stein sat. Everyone seemed a little calmer. Judd nodded at Lionel.

"Tsion's E-mail got to me," Lionel said. "With all the judgments coming, we don't know how much longer we have left. We have to be smart but bold."

"What does that mean?" Vicki said.

"People need to know the truth," Lionel said. "If we hide, we're wasting a chance to be part of the soul harvest."

Judd said, "The Global Community knows our faces. We're spending our energy running from them."

"Shelly, Mark, and John are the only ones they're not onto," Lionel said.

Darrion spoke up. "My family has a place in Wisconsin," she said. "If it survived the earthquake, we could go there."

"I'm tired of running," Vicki said.

The meeting ended. The kids argued every day. Mr. Stein pestered Judd for Tsion Ben-Judah's private E-mail address, but Judd was reluctant. Tsion was busy and Judd didn't want to bother him. But Judd had finally relented, and Tsion had written to Mr. Stein. The rabbi encouraged him to get to Israel, but recommended against a face-to-face meeting in the States.

Mr. Stein said he had hidden a stash of money before he was arrested by the Global Community. In the wee hours of the morning, Mr. Stein, Taylor Graham, and Judd's friend Pete prepared to retrieve the money. Judd awoke and heard the rumble of motor-cycles.

Pete stuck his head in the door. "Looks like we've got company. Hide."

Judd recognized the voice of Red, the big, long-haired biker with an attitude. "Guess you're pretty proud of yourself for breaking up the gang," Red said.

"We didn't have to split," Pete said. "You decided to leave."

Red cursed. "The holy rollers in there?" he said.

"If you mean the rest of the gang, no," Pete said. "They moved on. You want to come inside?"

"Done talkin'," Red said.

Judd saw a light in the window of the gas station. He ducked but it was too late. A bearded man with two gold teeth looked at him. "Gotcha," Gold Tooth said. "Hey, Red," the man shouted as he ran to the front. "Think we got something back there!"

Before his shift began, John stood on deck and watched the sun rise over the ocean. He had grown up singing about God's love being as wide as the sea, but he had never seen anything so impressive.

Carl approached, clutching a piece of paper.

"I was thinking about those kidnappers," John said. "You think the sharks—"

"Look," Carl interrupted. He handed John a fax. It looked like a drawing of something in space.

John shook his head. "I don't get it."

"You will," Carl said. "It's a new meteor."

John rolled his eyes. "Big deal."

"It *is* a big deal," Carl said. "This thing's headed straight for Earth."

John remembered Tsion Ben-Judah's warning about an object falling from the sky. A judgment from God. He studied the picture closely.

"When's it supposed to hit?" John said.

34

JUDD hurried to the front of the gas station. The guy with the gold teeth ran to Red.

"I thought you were smarter than that," Judd heard Red say. "I know who's back there."

"God's trying to get your attention," Pete said.

Red pulled a crumpled piece of paper from his back pocket. "And the Global Community's gonna get yours," he said. "There's a GC post about a half hour from here."

Pete looked toward the station and frowned. Judd knew what was on the paper.

"Don't do this," Pete said.

"Watch me," Red said as he kicked his motorcycle to a start and sped off. The gold-toothed man followed.

Pete ran a hand through his hair and walked into the station. He handed Judd the paper. Mug shots of Vicki, Lionel, Conrad, Darrion, and Judd. Also a description of

Mr. Stein. "Reward for information leading to an arrest and conviction."

The others slowly filed into the room.

"Think he'll turn us in?" Vicki said.

Pete shook his head. "Can't take the chance," he said. He put on his helmet and started his motorcycle. "If I'm not back in an hour, get out of here."

"You can't go up against all of them," Lionel protested.

"I won't let Red do this to you," Pete said. He throttled and roared off.

Boyd Walker leaned quietly against an old soda machine. "I have an idea if you're interested," he said. "A fellow in Des Plaines owns a gas station a lot like this one. His son has a little business on the side—tattoos. He might help you."

"I don't understand," Judd said.

"Kid's a genius," the man said. "Phony IDs and disguises."

"New identities?" Lionel said.

"I can't see us going anywhere near there," Vicki said.

"Zeke and Zeke Jr.," the manager said, writing it down.

Shelly stepped forward. "We need to do something now." She found a pair of scissors and some hair coloring for sale on a dusty shelf. Vicki's hair went from strawberry red to jet black and shorter than ever. Judd was almost bald when Shelly was through with him. The kids stood in a line.

"Not bad," Mark said. "Now all you guys need are some fake IDs."

The phone rang. The manager handed it to Mark.

"John?" Mark said.

Judd and Vicki gathered around. Mark said a few words, then put the phone down.

"What did he say?" Judd said.

"Told me there wasn't time to talk," Mark said. "Didn't want them catching him making the call. He said to turn on the television and watch. Then he said it was going to be some ride."

Judd flicked on the television. News bulletins interrupted every station.

Newscasters reported that only a few hours ago astronomers had discovered a brand-new comet on a collision course with Earth. The Global Community Aeronautics and Space Administration (GCASA) had probes circling the object. The data they sent back was startling.

"Under normal conditions," a spokesman for GCASA said, "we would have seen this a few months or even a few years ago. But these aren't normal conditions. I can't explain why we just located it today."

"Doctor, this meteor is how far from us right now?" the male anchor said.

"*Meteor* is the wrong term," the scientist said. "You were correct when you called it a comet. The data shows the comet to have a consistency of sandstone. Very brittle. When it enters Earth's atmosphere, it should disintegrate."

"Should?"

"It's impossible that it will miss us, unless it can be destroyed before it enters the atmosphere."

"And when will that happen?" the anchor said.

The scientist squirmed. "I'd rather let our director address that when he gives an update."

Judd moved closer to the television as a picture from the probe flashed on the screen. "Look at the size of that thing."

"What else have you learned?" the anchor said.

"The comet is irregularly shaped, but it's immense. Global Community astronomers estimate it is no less than the mass of the entire Appalachian Mountain range."

"Wow!" Lionel said. "How could they not see that until this morning?"

The anchor furrowed his brow. "And what kind of damage could something that big actually do?"

"The potential is enormous," the scientist said. "On a scale of one to ten, ten being the worst, I'd say this is a . . . ten and a half."

"We're all gonna die!" Shelly said.

Judd turned.

"W-w-we studied this in school," she stammered.

Vicki hugged Shelly. "It's gonna be okay."

"That's not gonna happen," Judd said.

"Let's say it is as hard as granite," the anchor said. "What then?"

"Once the object comes into Earth's gravitational pull, it will accelerate to thirty-two feet per second squared. No matter what it is made of, it will burst into flames. Pieces will fall to Earth."

"Worst case, what could happen?"

The scientist stared at the camera. "Worst case? Earth would be split in two."

The news anchor sat speechless.

The scientist added, "Or our orbit could be altered. Either would be disastrous for the planet."

"We're gonna die," a biker said.

Someone handed the anchor a piece of paper from off camera. "This message from GCASA," he said, stunned. "The . . . uh . . . collision will occur at approximately 6 P.M. New Babylon time, which is midnight in Tokyo, 3 P.M. in London, and 10 A.M. New York time."

"Nine our time," Vicki said.

"It's seven now," Lionel said.

In his quarters, John pulled out his Bible and turned to Revelation. He remembered something Tsion Ben-Judah had said about a meteor.

John found the passage that talked about the hail they had just come through. The next verse said, "Then the second angel blew his trumpet, and a great mountain of fire was thrown into the sea. And one-third of the water in the sea became blood. And one-third of all things living in the sea died. And one-third of all the ships on the sea were destroyed."

The verses sent a chill through him. The comet is coming from God. It will fall somewhere over the water. But where?

John pulled up the rabbi's Web site and found a message concerning the disaster.

This is the second Trumpet Judgment foretold in Revelation 8:8-9. Will we look like experts when the results are in? Will it shock the powers-that-be to discover that, just as the Bible says, one-third of the fish will die and one-third of the ships at sea will sink, and tidal waves will wreak havoc on the entire world? Or will officials reinterpret the event to make it appear the Bible was wrong? Do not be fooled! Do not delay! Now is the accepted time. Now is the day of salvation. Come to Christ before it is too late. Things will only get worse. We were all left behind the first time. Do not be left wanting when you breathe your last.

John put his head in his hands. He thought of Carl. He hadn't talked with him about God. *Maybe it isn't too late.*

He quickly typed a message to the rest of the Young Trib Force and sent it. He ran to the command center and found Carl amid a whirl of activity.

"I have to talk to you," John said.

"Things are nuts right now," Carl said. "They're talking about shooting the thing down before it hits." Carl handed John a printout. "It's going to hit here in the Atlantic. They say it's the best possible scenario."

"Best for who?" John said. The Global Community predicted tidal waves would engulf coasts on both sides of the Atlantic for up to fifty miles inland. Coastal areas had already begun evacuating.

"If they don't shoot the thing down there's no way we'll survive," Carl said.

John looked at a monitor and saw a simulation of the impact. An incredible wall of water stretched to the sky. Carl was right. No way anyone could survive.

Vicki was relieved when the news anchor reported the comet was heading for the Atlantic. She drew close to the screen. The earthquake had killed so many people, but it came without warning. This was worse.

"Those military personnel and passengers and crew members on other oceangoing vessels that can be reached in time are being airlifted to safety."

"John!" Vicki said. "He was headed to the Atlantic, wasn't he?"

Judd nodded and looked around the room for Mark.

"I'll get him," Vicki said.

Vicki found Mark outside, staring at the sky. She explained the situation, and Mark's shoulders slumped.

"We've been through so much," Mark said.

Vicki left Mark. She found Judd intently watching the coverage. An anchorman put a hand to his ear and nodded. "We're being told now that His Excellency, Potentate Nicolae Carpathia, is prepared to address this crisis. We go now to the Global Community Headquarters in New Babylon."

Nicolae spoke from his plush office. "My brothers and sisters in the Global Community, we have weathered many storms together, and it appears there is another on the horizon. Let me first answer a question that has come up, and that is, How could we not have known?

"I assure you, our personnel alerted us to this potential disaster as quickly as possible. We could not have known about this phenomenon any earlier.

"I am also confident, having taken precautions with my military advisors some time ago, that we have the firepower to destroy this object. However, we have been advised that an attempt to destroy the comet would be too great a risk to life on our planet. We cannot predict where the fragments might fall. The risk is simply unacceptable, especially considering that this falling mountain is on course to land in the ocean.

"We will keep you informed of any developments as we know them. Please cooperate with the officials in your area. We will get through this difficult time together, as we build a stronger world."

The crew of the *Peacekeeper 1* assembled on deck. They stood at attention as the captain explained the situation. The men looked shell-shocked.

"I had hoped to have better news," the captain said. "Potentate Carpathia has decided not to try and shoot the comet down."

The crew groaned in unison.

The captain held up a hand. "We're heading away from the impact point as fast as we can, but if the scientists are correct, there's no way we'll outrun the thing.

"There is one chance," the captain continued. "We've recovered the submarine. If we get far enough away from impact and the sub goes down far enough, some may be able to survive."

"That thing can hold only a handful of people," John whispered to Carl.

"We'll draw names within the hour," the captain said.

35

JUDD watched for Pete while the kids searched for the latest about the comet. Finally, Pete rolled in. He did a double take at Judd and the others.

"What happened?" Judd said.

Pete shook his head. "Don't want to talk about it. Let's just say you're safe for the time being."

The group gathered around the television. Updated pictures from the probes showed the comet in more detail. It was light in color. The anchorman reported, "Ladies and gentlemen, I urge you to put this in perspective. This object is about to enter Earth's atmosphere. It should burst into flames any second."

Lionel called Judd to the laptop and showed him what Tsion Ben-Judah had written. Judd ran a hand over his head. "I sure hope John's not near that thing."

The coverage switched to a local reporter. The man's voice sounded urgent. "GCASA projects the collision at approximately 9:00 A.M. Chicago time. If the predictions are accurate, the collision will take place in the middle of the Atlantic Ocean. But keep in mind that if the comet splits, fragments could possibly fall in the Midwest."

"Splashdown is less than an hour away," Vicki said.

The reporter continued, "I'm told by one meteorologist that this kind of disruption could cause severe weather around the globe. We won't deal with tidal waves like the coastal areas, but we may see strong winds and possibly tornadoes."

The crew stood silently watching as the captain picked the remaining names to occupy the sub. The rescued hostages were given priority. That left only seven seats for the crew.

John looked at Carl. "I don't like these odds," Carl said.

The sixth name the captain called was John's. Carl patted him on the shoulder. John sighed heavily and nearly fell to his knees. But he couldn't shake the truth. He hadn't given the most important message to his friends.

"You're the lucky one," Carl said, shaking hands.

"I need to talk with you," John said. "Now."

When the last name was called, John took Carl to his room and opened his Bible. "I haven't talked to anybody on the ship about this. I was scared to."

John quickly explained the plan of salvation. He told Carl everyone has sinned. "Everyone is separated from God. Jesus died to bring us back to God. People who ask forgiveness in Jesus' name will spend eternity in heaven."

Carl shook his head. "Staring at death makes you think. I figure God will accept me for the good stuff I've done. If not, saying a prayer won't help."

"It's not like that," John said. "God can't accept anything that's less than perfect. That's why Jesus came. He lived a perfect life—"

"Preston!" the captain shouted. "If you want to get off this ship, you go now."

John looked at Carl. Carl shrugged. "Sorry, I can't buy it."

"Preston, now!" the captain said.

"Sir," John said, "I'd like to give my spot to Carl."

The captain furrowed his brow. "Don't be foolish, son. This is your chance to survive."

John opened his Bible. He scribbled something inside the cover. "Read this later. I want to do this. I have some friends who can help you. If you make it back, look them up and tell them what happened."

Carl staggered. "You can't do this, man. You hardly even know me."

"I know what I'm doing," John said. "Read this stuff. It'll change your life if you let it."

The captain scowled at John and took Carl away. John took a deep breath as Carl squeezed into the sub. The crew stood on deck and watched as the sub slipped beneath the surface and headed to the bottom of the ocean.

"I don't know why you did that," the captain said when he returned to John.

"I'd like to speak with the others," John said, "before splashdown."

The captain shook his head. "I'd like to let you, Preston," he said. "After what you did today, you deserve it. But it's against policy."

"Sir, with all due respect, we're gonna die in less than an hour. I have something to say that could change everything. For you and the others."

"Sorry, Preston," the captain said. He walked away.

———

Vicki felt nervous about the comet. Even though it was supposed to land in the ocean, part of her felt they were still in danger. The way Pete acted when he returned spooked her as well.

As the moments ticked down, the kids watched the updates. A disabled cruise ship was stranded in the Atlantic.

Shelly put a hand to her mouth. "Those poor people," she said.

"Other Global Community vessels are at sea," the reporter continued, "but rescue operations are impossible with the splashdown so close. Efforts to move boats to safety along the Atlantic shoreline have stopped."

There were reports of some who refused to evacuate their homes. "Stayin' right here," a grizzled old man said. "Lived through the disappearances and the earthquake. Don't see any reason why I can't live through a big wave."

Vicki looked at Judd. She had been so angry and hurt by him. But the possibility of losing their lives put things in perspective. Their fights seemed petty compared to the fact that a comet could split the earth in two and send them hurtling into space. She believed that wouldn't happen because of what the Bible said, but the prospect made her shudder.

Vicki thought about Phoenix and her promise to Ryan. She longed to find the dog, not only to keep her word, but also because the dog reminded her of Ryan. Phoenix had helped Ryan move through the pain of losing his parents. Vicki thought the dog could do the same for her.

After the launch of the sub, John and the rest of the crew were in a daze. They were trapped. Moving to any part of the ship was pointless. They were about to see a wave unlike any in the history of the world.

John knew his decision to let Carl have his spot would be considered heroic by some and foolish by others. He didn't feel like a hero. He was sorry that he hadn't told the others about Christ.

John looked at the empty command center and thought, *What have I got to lose?*

He hurried to the command center and punched the controls that sealed both entrances. He flipped the switch that let him speak to the entire ship and pecked on the microphone.

"Test . . . can you hear me?" John said.

The captain and a few officers came running. When they tried to open the door, John put up a hand. He prayed silently, his hands shaking. Then he keyed the microphone.

"My name is John Preston. The captain wouldn't let me talk to you, so I've had to sorta take over. I don't mean any harm by this, and I promise to open the doors in just a minute. First, I want you to hear me out."

The captain beat on the door. John couldn't hear the man's voice, but he could read his lips. "This is mutiny," he said. John turned his back and knelt under a desk.

"My name was chosen to go in the sub, but I let a friend take my place. I couldn't go and not tell you guys about living forever."

John peered through the transparent but bulletproof glass and saw the entire crew standing on deck. Some looked toward the command center. Others turned and walked away. John heard pounding behind him and kept talking.

"When I was a kid, my parents used to take me to church. I sang and did my time in Sunday school. But it didn't sink in. I never really thought what I was singing about was true.

"Then came the disappearances, and most of my family was taken away. I wished I'd listened closer. Maybe some of you lost friends and family too.

"When the captain called my name, I was relieved to have a chance to survive. But the more I thought, the more I knew I had to stay. I want to tell you about the person who can save you."

John didn't hear pounding and wondered whether the captain was listening or figuring out a way to get in.

"The comet is a judgment from God. It's meant to get

your attention. It's predicted in the Bible. Everything the Bible says has come true.

"Unless a miracle happens, we're gonna die. Each one of us will stand before a holy God. If you've done anything wrong, *anything*, God will have to turn you away."

John looked out over the crew. Several stood with their arms crossed, listening intently. Others milled about and laughed nervously. John turned. The captain had a gun. Someone was talking with him. *The diver who had saved the hostages!*

"Everybody's done wrong things," John said. "Everybody deserves to be turned away. But God loved us enough to put himself on the line and give his life. Jesus was God. He lived a perfect life and died in your place, in my place."

A burst of light flashed. John heard a boom that shook the window. The crew hit the deck.

"We don't have much time," John screamed. "If you ask Jesus to forgive you, he will. And when you're in front of God, he won't see the bad things you've done. He'll see the perfect life of Jesus."

Some of the men talked to each other. Several cried and looked toward the sky. The captain stared at John, his hands against the glass.

An eerie silence fell over the gas station as Judd and the others watched. As the news anchor talked, he picked up a pen, then repeatedly pulled off its cap and put it back on.

"The Global Community military has positioned aircraft so we can see the first glimpse of this more than one-thousand-mile-square mountain as it enters our atmosphere," the anchor said.

A spokesman for the Global Community Aeronautics and Space Administration revealed a final report. The object consisted largely of sulfur. When the mountain broke through the atmosphere, Judd and the others heard a terrific boom. Windows in the station shattered.

"The comet has now entered our atmosphere and has burst into flames," the spokesman said. "The trajectory will take it into the Atlantic as expected." He paused. "The next few minutes should be spectacular."

The sky turned black as the comet eclipsed the sun. The burning ball of death was heading straight for them.

John turned on the outside microphone and listened as men cried out, "No! God help us!"

"You can be sure of heaven," John continued, trembling. "Pray with me. God, I'm sorry for the bad things I've done. I believe Jesus died for me. Come into my heart right now and forgive me."

Most of the men were still lying on the deck. A few knelt. John saw several with marks on their foreheads. "I'll meet those who want to talk more at the front of the ship," John said as he opened the doors.

The captain burst through with two guards. "Arrest him!"

The captain grabbed the microphone and yelled, "We're going to die like men! We don't need religion."

The crew panicked. A group rushed John and the guards who were holding him.

"Get him to the brig, now!" the captain yelled.

"What's going to happen to us?" a young man screamed.

Officers whisked John down the stairs before he could answer. They left him in a dank cell.

A few minutes passed. John wondered if he would die in this room. Then keys jangled and John saw the face of the diver who had rescued the hostages. The man turned slightly. In the dim light John saw the outline of the tell-tale mark on his forehead.

"You're being released into my custody," the man said.

"Why?" John said. "How?"

"Come on. There's not much time." He put out his hand. "I talked with the captain after you were taken away. I convinced him you could calm the crew down."

John followed the man on deck and walked to the front of the ship. The man held up a hand and asked for quiet. Clouds above them scrolled back. The wind picked up and the water became choppy. John held on as the ship bobbed on the surface like a child's toy. The man turned to John and nodded. "Go ahead. Say what you want."

John shouted over the noise, "Those of you who prayed, look at me. This mark on my forehead means I've been sealed by God. I'm his."

"I can see it," one man said.

"What mark are you talking about?" another said.

"If you can't see the mark," John said, "it means you don't believe." John went over the message again. A few prayed. Others had questions.

The sky took on a ghostly appearance. Black clouds rushed over the crew. The force of the comet was creating a weather phenomenon never experienced by anyone. Hurricane-force winds blew between the comet and the surface of the sea.

John looked at the men scurrying across the ship. He called together all who had the mark. "Go to everyone you can and tell them what happened to you. These guys need God. It's their last chance."

The men, shaking, spread out on the deck. Many of the crew ran to their quarters when they saw the darkening sky. One man wrestled a gun from a guard. He ran to the edge and raised the pistol. A shot rang out. His body fell into the surging water.

John bit his lip. *Just a few more minutes before it hits. It's hard to believe this is really happening.*

36

MAYHEM. Confusion.

John had never seen anything like it. The sea churned. Men screamed and grabbed anything to keep from going over the edge.

The wind was furious. It nearly ripped John's clothes from his body. He fell to his hands and knees and crawled to the stairs leading to the command center.

"What are you doing?" the diver yelled behind him.

"I have to get a message to my cousin and his friends," John screamed.

"They'll throw you in the brig!" the diver said.

John turned. Huge waves washed over the bow. "I have to try."

Judd watched as experts paraded through the Global Community broadcasts. "What we're seeing may be a repeat of what happened millions of years ago with the dinosaurs," one scientist said.

"I still don't understand how this could sneak up on us," the anchor said.

"Funding for research has been small until the last few months," the scientist said. "Our best guess is that the comet was somehow thrown off course and came directly toward Earth."

The anchor took a deep breath. "I'm told we're about to see our first glimpse of the comet," he said.

Even on the small screen the sight made the kids gasp. The shot from the airplane showed a huge glowing mass heading for Earth. Gray and black clouds encircled the plane and the cameras lost sight of the comet for a moment.

Judd watched Mark fumble with the computer through tear-drenched eyes. "I just sent John a message," Mark said.

Judd put an arm around Mark.

"Five minutes until impact," the scientist said.

The captain threatened to throw John in the brig again, but the diver was able to talk him out of it. Several officers had been sick in the room. The smell turned John's stomach. As the crew in the command center grew frantic, John strapped himself in behind a computer and began typing.

One man urged the captain to turn the boat around. The captain shook his head. "No way we can outrun this.

They're predicting tidal waves on both sides of the Atlantic. Where do we go?"

"We have to do something," the man said.

The captain looked at John and lowered his voice. "What you said before seemed to calm them. Can you do anything?"

John swiveled his chair toward the frightened men. Again he explained the gospel. The men listened. "God, you give a peace that passes our human understanding," John prayed. "I ask that you would help each of these men to know you now and that you would give them that peace."

"I've got a wife and a baby back at the base," a man interrupted. "What about them?"

John led the man in a prayer and told him to quickly e-mail his wife and give her Tsion Ben-Judah's Web site. "She'll find out what to do by reading that."

Others left the room, but John was glad he had been given another chance. He opened an E-mail from Mark and read the hastily written message.

If you're where we think you are, Mark wrote, *you probably don't have time to read this. We all want you to know we're praying for you. You'll see Bruce and Ryan and Chaya before we will, so tell them we said hello.*

John finished reading through blurry eyes.

I know we've had our disagreements, and I haven't been the best cousin, Mark continued, *but I'm proud of you. I'll miss you.*

John put his head on the console and wept. He would never see Mark in this life again. Never talk with Judd or

Vicki. If he'd gone in the submarine . . . but he couldn't think that way now. He recalled what Jesus said to his disciples: "The greatest love is shown when people lay down their lives for their friends."

"There it comes!" an officer shouted.

The others moved toward the window. John looked up.

Blinding light.

Clouds whirled.

Wave after wave tossed the ship.

John shielded his eyes. His skin, though exposed only a few seconds, turned red. John saw one man on deck put his hands over his eyes. The ship pitched and the man lost his balance, flipped, and tumbled into the railing. Like a rag doll, he went limp and fell over the edge.

John shook his head. The diver who had helped him came close. "Guess this is it," the man said.

"I can't remember your name," John said, extending a hand.

The man shook it firmly. "Jim Pelton."

"We'll have a lotta time to talk once this is over," John said, "when we're finally home."

"I don't like the thought of dying," Jim said. "I wanted to live until the glorious appearing of Christ. But I just realized, today I'll see members of my family who disappeared."

The comet streaked behind a dark cloud. The sky looked golden. The wind blew harder and the ship rocked violently.

"It's funny, the things that go through your mind,"

Jim said. "I remember a preacher at our church talking about the *Titanic*. He said there were only two types of people on that boat: those who were saved and those who were lost at sea."

John nodded.

"The guy asked what we'd do if we only had an hour to live. I went out in the parking lot with my friends. We made fun of him. Now I wish I'd have listened."

The comet appeared again, a huge, burning ball of smoke and flame. Men on deck shuddered and cried out.

"Let's go down there," John said. He looked at the captain and nodded, but the man didn't return his gaze.

John led the way to the deck, shielding his face and trying to keep his balance. Others who had the mark followed. At the center of the ship, the men joined hands and knelt. The crashing of waves didn't drown out John's voice.

"God, I thank you that you're true to your word, that what you say happens. I pray right now you would give us the strength to go through this and that you would bring others to yourself."

Men prayed. Some yelled, "Help us!"

As the comet neared the surface of the water, the sky peeled back, revealing a smoking trail miles long. The heat from the object singed hair and melted John's watch-band. He peeled it off and threw it over the edge.

The wind died. The comet reached the horizon and fell out of sight. Then the most terrifying sound. An explosion on the surface of the water.

Vicki covered her mouth with a hand as the GC plane transmitted images of the impact. The water boiled from the intense heat and steam rose, along with water spouts and typhoons. The plane broadcasting the event was knocked out of the sky by the force of the impact.

"They're gonna be showing this video for a long time," Lionel said.

John grabbed a metal post and hung on. The sky surged in turmoil. The captain shouted over the loudspeaker for the men to remain calm. Some grabbed extra life preservers and jumped overboard.

John calculated that the ship's position was two hundred miles east of the comet. A few minutes after he lost sight of the comet, the ship was drawn backward toward the splashdown site. Water surged around them. It felt like he was a kid standing at the edge of the beach, the tide rushing around his feet.

Part of him wanted to go below deck and hide, but John couldn't stop watching God's mighty judgment. The ship gathered speed and surged along, powered only by the turbulent ocean. Men were swept overboard as they stood and felt the awesome wind. There was no sound but the howling of the wind and the thundering of water.

Then John saw it. It started on the horizon and slowly rose as the ship rushed toward it. A wave so huge it seemed to scrape the clouds. Blue water rose skyward. John had seen pictures of waves that looked like canyons, with boats nothing but specks. But he had never seen anything like this. The blue turned to red. The bloody water churned all around the ship. It splashed on board. John felt it ooze down his back. He rubbed the liquid between his fingers. It was thick and sticky.

The thought of drowning had terrified John as a child. Now, he felt a sense of peace. *I'm ready for home, God*, he prayed.

The ship sped on, men screaming when they caught sight of the wave. John looked at Jim and nodded. Nothing to say and no one to hear it if you did.

The wave blotted out the sky. The ship rose against it, then turned slightly and rolled. John held on to the metal pipe as the ship plunged into the water. Submerged, the blood stung his eyes. He was in what felt like an underwater typhoon. Bodies and ship and equipment became one with the wave.

In the sea of red, John held his breath. The pressure of the water was unbearable. Seconds later he tried to breathe.

No air. John reached for the surface, but he felt miles away. Panic. Blackness.

Then light. Blessed light.

Judd gasped as newscasters described the devastation. Hovering aircraft showed America's Atlantic coast. Billions of tons of water crashed onto homes and businesses up to fifty miles inland. The remains of shrimp boats were scattered over roadways. An oil freighter, whose crew had been plucked from the deck by a helicopter just in time, lay on a mountainside in Virginia. A plane flew over the area where the old man had refused to leave his house. It was completely underwater.

Judd tried to think of something to say to Mark, but couldn't. Vicki shouted for Mark to come to the computer. "It's from John!"

Judd read over Mark's shoulder.

Incredible opportunity to give the message, John had written. Nothing like a killer comet to wake you to reality.

Some day I hope you meet Carl. He can tell you what happened here. No time now. Just enough to say I love you all. Keep fighting the good fight. We'll be cheering you on. Never give up. John.

Judd put his face in his hands.

"He probably died within minutes after sending that," Mark said.

Vicki and Shelly held each other and cried. Lionel put a hand on Mark's shoulder.

"You had a great cousin," Lionel said.

Mark nodded. "I know."

Nicolae Carpathia responded to the crisis with a grim face. In another address to the world he revealed that all travel would be affected by the damage. The meeting of the Jewish witnesses would be postponed another ten weeks.

"The loss of any human life is tragic," Carpathia said. "We grieve with the families whose loved ones perished in this latest catastrophe. However, our experts were correct. Had we attempted to explode the object, many more lives would have been lost.

"But we can do something in memory of those who died. We can rebuild. Travel routes and cities that have been wiped out will be restored. Let this hardship draw us together to create a new world that loves peace."

In response to the potentate, the two witnesses at the Wailing Wall went on the offensive. Judd and the others watched on the Internet as Moishe and Eli boiled in anger.

"Behold, the land of Israel will continue to be dry, as it has been since the signing of the unholy treaty!" Moishe said.

Eli picked up the message. "Any threat to the evangelists who are sealed will be met with rivers of blood!" he said.

To prove their power was from the Almighty, Moishe and Eli called upon God to let it rain only on the Temple Mount for seven minutes. From a clear, blue sky came a sheet of rain. The dust turned to mud. Televised reports showed families running from their homes, laughing and dancing. They believed their crops were saved. But seven minutes later the rain stopped. The mud returned to dust. The people were speechless.

"Woe unto you, mockers of the one true God!" Eli and Moishe shouted. "Until the due time, when God allows us to be felled and later returns us to his side, you shall have no power over us or over those God has called to proclaim his name throughout the earth!"

37

THE COMET affected weather around the globe. Vicki watched thick clouds roll into the Midwest. The news reported a tornado warning.

Vicki knew Mark was grieving John, but she didn't know what to do when he went off by himself. She offered to get him food, but he waved her away.

Judd and Mr. Stein were at the computer.

"People are begging to know God," Judd said. "I don't think Tsion has time to—"

"If he does not have time, he does not have to talk," Mr. Stein said.

"He's already talked to you," Judd said.

"Judd, if I am one of the 144,000 evangelists described in the Bible, I want to know," Mr. Stein said. "And I think Rabbi Ben-Judah will welcome a conversation."

Judd logged on and tried to contact Tsion. Vicki saw hundreds of messages. "Are those all questions for the rabbi?" Vicki said.

"They're waiting to be answered," Judd said. "I did as many as I could last night—"

A beep interrupted Judd. Vicki was excited to see the face of Tsion Ben-Judah on the screen. Judd gave Tsion an update about the kids. Tsion was saddened to hear about John. "He is another of the tribulation martyrs," Tsion said.

Judd introduced Mr. Stein, who leaned toward the camera and waved. Mr. Stein was shaking with excitement.

"I am glad to see you," Tsion said.

"My brother," Mr. Stein said, "I had to get in touch once more. I want to know if I am a Witness and what my assignment will be."

"I'm afraid only God can reveal that," the rabbi said. "I urge you to come to the meeting."

"Perhaps I could go with you," Mr. Stein said.

Judd flinched.

"I'm afraid that would be impossible," Tsion said. "Thousands of people are pleading with me to come to their countries and train them face-to-face. The Meeting of the Witnesses is designed to accomplish this.

"God is working out the details. The first twenty-five thousand to arrive will gather in Teddy Kollek Stadium. The rest will watch on closed-circuit television at sites all over the Holy Land. I will invite Moishe and Eli to join us. It will be a great time of teaching and learning."

Mr. Stein looked dejected. "I had hoped you could help me personally," he said.

"You have me now," Tsion said. "What are you concerned about?"

Mr. Stein glanced at Vicki and Judd. "I have doubts," he said. "I believe that Jesus is God, that he died for me. But I feel so unworthy. At times I think I will somehow go back to my old life. I fear God could not possibly use me."

"You struggle with sin," Tsion said. "You think you should be perfect and you are not."

"Exactly."

Tsion smiled. "The apostle Paul struggled with the same thing. Read Romans, chapter 7. You are not perfect and never will be until you are with God."

"But at times I do not even feel like I am a follower of Christ."

"Your enemy is at work. He does not want you to follow Christ. This struggle shows you are not falling away. Just the opposite. As you grow in your faith, you will see more of your sin. How much you care about yourself. It is happening to me every day.

"But this fight is not a sign of defeat. God is working in you."

Mr. Stein nodded. "But what if I don't feel like—?"

"Feelings are always difficult," Tsion said. "Do not base your faith on your feelings. Instead, read what God says in his Word about you. If you have asked God to forgive you and come into your life, he has.

"Second Corinthians 5:17 says you are a new person. God has begun a new life in you. Romans 15:7 says you have been accepted by Christ. When God looks at you, he no longer sees your sin. He sees the perfection of Jesus.

"In Romans, chapter 8, Paul asks, 'Can anything ever

separate us from Christ's love?' " Tsion paused. "Do you have trouble? Are you in danger from the Global Community? Paul says, 'Despite all these things, overwhelming victory is ours through Christ, who loved us.' "

Mr. Stein rubbed his forehead. "But how could God love that way? I have done terrible things."

Tsion smiled. "We judge people by *our* standard. When you believe in your heart that Jesus died for you and was raised from the dead, God views you no longer as an enemy, but as a son.

"The Scriptures are clear. God is working in you to do the good things he planned for you. You are kept not by your own power to do good things, but by his love and mercy."

Mr. Stein nodded. "I have many more questions."

"I'm sure," Tsion said. "Continue studying. See if what I say is true. It is clear now. The world is taking sides. Many people will follow the Antichrist. But many will believe in God's only Son. It is our job to take that message to everyone."

Vicki felt encouraged by Tsion's talk with Mr. Stein. Before he signed off she asked about Chloe.

"She is making great improvement," Tsion said. "Wait right there."

Vicki watched Chloe hobble to Tsion's computer. She smiled when she saw Vicki. "I want you to know how saddened I was about Ryan," Chloe said.

"What happened to you?" Vicki said.

"Long story," Chloe said. "When the earthquake hit, I ran from Loretta's house. Someone found me and transported me to a Wisconsin hospital. Buck caught up to me in Minneapolis. The GC had some kind of plan, but we were able to escape."

"Is it true about you having a baby?" Vicki said.

Chloe beamed. "It's true," she said. "Buck's acting like a mother hen, but we're both really excited."

Vicki asked about Chloe's father, Captain Rayford Steele.

"Pray for him," Chloe said. "Amanda's body was found in the plane wreckage. He had to dive into the Tigris River. Her death really shook him up."

Chloe said hello to Judd and the others. Judd asked about Buck and what happened in Denver. "Is he really being charged with murder?"

Chloe whispered something to Tsion. The rabbi nodded. Chloe said, "Buck went there to get Hattie Durham. She's pregnant with Nicolae Carpathia's child."

Vicki gasped.

"The Global Community is after Hattie," Chloe said. "Buck went to rescue her. He hit a guard in self-defense after the guard killed a staff worker. The guard died. They blame Buck, but it's not true."

"Is Hattie okay?" Vicki said.

"As well as can be expected," Chloe said. "We've got a new member of the Trib Force. A doctor. He's been helping both of us as we try to recover."

"Is Buck still working for Carpathia?" Judd said.

"He's putting the magazine together on the Internet," Chloe said. "He doesn't know how much longer he can work for such an evil man."

Vicki wanted to talk with Chloe about Judd. Vicki had remained cordial to him, but she felt something brewing under the surface. Chloe asked about the kids' escape from the GC and heard the story of Mr. Stein.

"We really need your help with E-mail," Chloe said. "Some of the messages are people saying they're praying. But many need replies."

"As soon as we figure out our next move," Judd said, "we'll get two or three people on it."

Chloe thanked them. "I miss having you guys around. I wish we could keep you here."

"We understand," Vicki said. "I hope we can talk more sometime."

Chloe gave them her cell phone number for an emergency. Tsion prayed for the kids and closed the connection.

Vicki heard a rumble of engines. Pete, who had been sleeping in the back of the service station, ran to the front. He cursed, then looked at the kids. "Sorry. You guys are going to have to hide again."

"What's going—," Judd said.

"No time to explain," Pete interrupted. "Hide."

Judd and the others climbed into the oil-changing bay while Boyd parked a car overhead. The room was dark and smelled like gasoline.

"I wish we could see what's happening," Lionel said. "You think it's Red back with the GC?"

"Pete said Red wouldn't bother us," Judd said. "I don't know who it could be."

Judd whispered to Boyd, but the man said, "Keep quiet. There's a GC guy out front."

A few minutes later someone came inside. Judd heard angry voices. Finally, motorcycles started and drove away. Boyd moved the car, and the kids climbed out.

"What?" Judd said.

The manager bit his lip. "I don't know what to tell you," he said. "Pete said he had to go with the GC."

"I heard what happened," another biker said. It was Sally, who had given Vicki a ride to escape the commander. "I talked with Pete this morning. Had to drag it out of him, but he finally told me.

"Red was going to report you guys. Pete wanted to catch up to him and talk him out of it. When he did, Red freaked. He drove wild and tried to force Pete off the road. Pete yelled at him, but Red wouldn't stop.

"Red and Clyde, the guy with the gold teeth, both forced Pete onto a road that leads to a rock quarry," Sally continued. "Red tried to cut Pete off, but Red lost control of his bike. He hit Clyde, and they both went over the edge. I guess it was hundreds of feet to the bottom and nothing but rock."

"How awful," Vicki said.

"But the GC think Pete killed them?" Judd said.

Sally shrugged. "Pete said he'd show the GC where Red and Clyde fell. I hope they believe his story."

Judd frowned. If the GC suspected Pete, they would return.

"Everybody get ready to move," Judd said. He dialed the number Boyd had given him.

"This is Zeke," an older man said.

"I'm looking for your son," Judd said.

"What for?"

"We were told he could help us," Judd said. "We're in some trouble."

The man yelled, "Z!" and a moment later Zeke Jr. was on the phone. He seemed cautious and asked who had recommended him. Judd told him and Zeke Jr. laughed. "Boyd? That old coot?"

"Can you help us?" Judd said.

"I don't know you from Adam," Zeke Jr. said.

"The Global Community is on our tail," Judd said. "It's only a matter of time until they find us."

Zeke Jr. paused. "I think I can scrounge up some papers for you," he said. "As far as changing your faces, we'll have to see. When?"

"Tonight," Judd said.

"Whoa," Zeke Jr. said. "That's a little fast. There's bad weather between you and me. Tornadoes."

"Any way you can come to us?" Judd said.

"Not a chance," Zeke Jr. said. "You come to me or I pass."

Judd gave him the name and descriptions of each of the members. "When will you be ready for us?" he said.

"Make it before sunup," he said.

38

JUDD gathered what the kids would need for their trip. He asked Taylor Graham to help Mr. Stein locate his hidden money, but Taylor refused.

"I'll go," Mark said.

"If Pete doesn't come back, I'm going for him," Taylor said.

Conrad frowned. "You're gonna get the Global Community any way you can."

"That's right."

"You're gonna get yourself killed," Conrad said. "Pete can take care of himself."

Taylor smirked. "You don't get it. I'm not just going to get the GC back for what they've done; I'm gonna stop them."

"If you really want to do damage," Conrad said sarcastically, "why don't you kill Nicolae Carpathia?" Taylor stared at Conrad. "You wouldn't try anything that stupid, would you?"

Judd couldn't believe what he was hearing. "You don't need revenge."

Taylor rolled his eyes. "I know, I need God. Well he's never done anything for me. If you guys want to play your Bible games and try to figure out what's happening next, fine."

Darrion Stahley stepped forward. "I've known you since I was a kid. You're smart. Hasn't any of this sunk in? The disappearances? The earthquake?"

"I know your mom and dad are dead, little lady," Taylor said. "And the Global Community's responsible. I'll stop them if it's the last thing I do."

"God saved your neck for a reason," Conrad said. "Don't waste an opportunity—"

"I saved my own neck," Taylor snapped. "I don't believe you people. If you want to get something done, you do it yourself. You don't wait for some god to do it for you."

"That's enough," Judd said, looking at Conrad and Darrion. "He's free to make his choice." Judd turned to Taylor. "We could use a pilot."

Taylor looked away. "If I can help you, I will. But I don't promise anything."

"Fair enough," Judd said.

The wind howled. Tree branches scraped the windows of the gas station. "We leave at midnight," Judd said. "Hopefully we'll be at Zeke's place by sunup."

Vicki heard voices. Crying. Kids ran through the woods in front of her. Someone waved her forward. A boy. She could only see the back of his head. It looked like Ryan.

Breathing hard, Vicki tried to catch up. The woods

were dense. She could see her breath in the crisp air. She wanted to turn back, find safety, but she couldn't let the kids down. She kept going.

Someone was after the kids, after her. She turned around but no one was there.

Clouds hid the stars. Hard to see. One foot in front of the other. A branch. A fallen tree. She fell and scraped a knee.

Then flickering light in the distance. She stood and limped toward it.

She reached the clearing and saw a few kids bounding across a meadow toward a building. Others gathered on a second-floor balcony.

Vicki heard movement to her left and saw the boy running toward her. Behind him were soldiers. Vicki screamed.

Vicki followed the boy, scared. Kids lined the balcony, waving to her. "Run," they shouted. "Come on!"

The light was coming from the house. Beams shone through windows. "I don't understand!" she shouted at the boy.

"What's to understand?" he said.

It sounded like Ryan. She ran faster.

"What is that place?" Vicki said.

The boy didn't answer but kept running. Vicki glanced behind her. When she turned, the boy was gone.

"Hurry!" someone said from above.

Vicki reached the steps. The soldiers stopped, turned around, and went back into the woods.

"Why did they leave?" Vicki said.

"Why did who leave?" Shelly said, shaking Vicki awake. "Come on, time to go."

Vicki rubbed her eyes and followed Shelly outside. Members of Pete's group had loaned their bikes. Darrion rode with Judd. *Good*, Vicki thought. She put on a helmet and sat behind Conrad. Lionel rode alone on the third bike.

"Good luck," Shelly said. "I hope I don't recognize you when you get back."

Conrad followed Judd. Vicki relaxed and thought about the boy in her dream. Did she miss Ryan that badly? Could it be some kind of message?

"Did Mark and Mr. Stein leave?" Vicki yelled to Conrad.

"Half hour ago," Conrad said. "Pete's still not back."

The wind had blown down makeshift power lines. Judd held up a hand, and the kids carefully drove around the dangerous wires.

"What happens if we run into GC?" Vicki said.

"Judd said we'll try to outrun them," Conrad said. "I hope we don't have to."

The kids stayed away from main roads, even going across fields. By early morning Vicki was tired of all the ruts and ridges. She was glad to find paved roads again, even though they still had huge cracks from the earthquake. Dogs barked as they rode through neighborhoods.

Vicki told Conrad her dream. "What do you think it means?" she said.

"Could mean you haven't been getting enough sleep," Conrad said. "Then again, it might be God trying to tell you something."

376

"What?" Vicki said.

Conrad shrugged.

Judd stopped and turned off his motor. They were on the edge of what had once been downtown Des Plaines. The streets were deserted. A light was on in a broken-down one-pump gas station.

"Let me check it out," Conrad said. "I'll signal if it's okay."

Judd nodded. Conrad crept toward the filling station. A few minutes later Vicki saw a light flash inside.

Zeke Jr. opened the creaky garage door and the kids pushed their cycles inside. Zeke Jr. was in his mid-twenties, had long hair, and was covered with tattoos. He wore black cowboy boots, black jeans, and a black leather vest over bare arms and flabby chest.

"People call me Z," Zeke Jr. said as he looked at each of their foreheads. "I guess 'cause it's easier."

Judd said, "Where's all your equipment for—"

"I know it didn't look like much," Z said. "By the time I'm through, this place'll be a shopping center for believers."

Vicki looked around the station. Dirty rags lay on black oil drums. There were out-of-date calendars with pictures of cars. An oily phone book lay on a counter. Everything looked grimy. Vicki wondered how they could trust someone who kept such a dingy business.

Z seemed to read her mind. He grinned. "Follow me," he said. Z led them to a tiny washroom. The sign said Danger. High Voltage. Do Not Touch.

"Anybody puts a hand on here and they get a little

buzz," Z said. "Not enough to hurt, just make 'em think twice. Come on."

Z knew where to push. The panel opened and Z slid it out of the way. He led the five kids down a wooden staircase to his shelter. It was fashioned out of the earth beneath and behind the station. Deep in the back Vicki saw boxes of food, medicine, bottled water, and assorted supplies.

"If you guys need anything back there, let me know," Z said.

The room had no windows and was cool. *Perfect,* Vicki thought, *to keep the food and medicine fresh.* A TV news broadcast was on low in the background. Beside the TV was a dog-eared spiral notebook and a laptop.

"When I'm done, we'll need to get a picture," Z said. As he set up his camera he told the kids his story.

"Before all this I did a few tattoos, pinstriped cars and trucks, airbrushed some T-shirts, and even painted murals on some 18-wheelers. That business dried up a long time ago."

"What happened to the rest of your family?" Vicki said.

"My dad, Zeke, runs the station," Z said, fiddling with the camera. "My mom and two sisters died in a fire the night of the disappearances. We were tryin' to get over that when this friend of my dad's, a long-haul trucker, comes through. Starts talkin' 'bout God and his plan. I didn't buy it at first. The more he talked, the more it made sense. He gave us a Bible, and we started reading in Revelation, of all places.

"I don't mind tellin' ya, I've done a lot of drugs. When I wasn't smokin' or shootin' up, I was drinkin'. I'd stay high until I needed some more money; then I'd go back to work a few days.

"God got hold of both of us. My dad and I go to an underground church in Arlington Heights now. I want to be a major supplier to Christians. Hopefully, with my contacts with truckers, we'll turn this place into a warehouse for believers."

"You mean you'll ship stuff from here?" Judd said.

"With what's ahead, somebody's gotta do it," Z said. He pointed to the computer. "Rabbi says it's gonna get worse and worse. We have to prepare."

Z tacked a sheet on the wall. "Before I take your pictures," he said, "we gotta figure out what to do with you." He looked at Vicki. "That's not your natural color, is it?"

Vicki shook her head. "Red."

"The hair's okay, then," Z said. He put on plastic gloves and opened a desk drawer. Inside were dental materials. He fitted a device over Vicki's front teeth. They stuck out a little and seemed to change the shape of her face.

"You should be able to leave this on all the time, once you get used to it," Z said.

"Incredible," Lionel said. "What can you do for me?"

"You're a challenge," Z said. "We'll shave your head to start. Then a scar on your face might draw some attention. Sunglasses, maybe."

Z worked on the kids' appearances. He changed hair

color, cut hair, and added scars and tattoos that amazed the kids. When he was finished he took their pictures.

A bell rang above. "Dad's probably still asleep," Z said. "Let me get that and I'll be right back."

Z unlocked the station and helped a customer with fuel. When he returned he squatted behind an old couch and swung open a rickety filing cabinet. He grabbed a cardboard box filled with different types of identification. Some were driver's licenses. Some were student IDs.

"Sorry I'm not too organized yet," Z said.

"Where did you get those?" Vicki said.

Z slammed the filing cabinet shut with his boot. "The earthquake claimed a lotta lives. These weren't doing the dead any good, and they could sure help out our cause in the future."

Vicki looked at the faces and names scattered throughout the box. "All of these people are dead?" she said.

Z nodded. "I get the wallets before the GC gets the body." He dumped the contents onto a table. "Don't go by the faces," he said. "Try to find somebody who's close to your age."

Vicki rummaged through the cards and found a girl a year older than she and about the same height.

"Jackie Browne," Z said. "Looks good. She's an organ donor, too. Good citizen of the Global Community."

"How much can we change on this?" Judd said.

"If you want me to get this done today, you have to take it the way you find it," Z said. "Give me a couple of days and I can make you a member of Enigma Babylon, or even a GC soldier."

"We don't have that kind of time," Judd said.

Lionel found a smaller box on the filing cabinet. "What's this?" he said.

"Those are from this week," Z said. "I don't use ones that fresh."

Lionel rummaged through the box and gave a low whistle. "Look at this."

The kids crowded around. The military ID card showed a stocky man with medals and decorations. Beside his picture it read *Commander Terrell Blancka*.

"I remember that one," Z said. "Strange. Found him in a culvert near a church, or what was left of it. Looked like an execution. Gunshot wound."

"I thought he was being reassigned," Vicki said.

"He was," Lionel said. "Permanently."

Vicki glanced at the stack of cards and gasped. Among them was Joyce's, the girl who had accused Vicki of murdering Mrs. Jenness. "Do you know how she died?" Vicki said.

Z shook his head. "I've got a friend at one of the GC morgues," he said. "A believer. I got that one from him."

Vicki felt a sudden sense of relief. If her accuser was dead, she was off the hook for the murder rap. Then Vicki felt a wave of guilt. Joyce had heard about God but rejected him.

Z gave the kids blankets and showed them an area where they could rest. Vicki was exhausted. She watched Z through the doorway as he turned on his magnifying light and began cutting the pictures. From this day on she would be Jackie Browne.

39

MARK thought about John as he drove beside Mr. Stein. The video of the comet's crash kept flashing in Mark's mind. It was so spectacular that the networks would run the footage for weeks. Reports of lost boats had filled the news. Mark had logged on to the list of crew members on the *Peacekeeper 1* and found John's name.

He was so engrossed in his thoughts that he didn't realize he had lost Mr. Stein. Mark turned the motorcycle around and backtracked. He found the man and his cycle in a ditch.

"I must have hit the accelerator instead of the brake," Mr. Stein said, limping away from the bike.

"Climb on," Mark said.

Mr. Stein hobbled onto the back of Mark's motorcycle.

"Is the money in cash?" Mark said.

"Large bills," Mr. Stein said. "I hope we can take it in one load. . . . Are you thinking about your cousin?"

Mark nodded.

"I am sorry for your pain," Mr. Stein said. "I was just reading the passage where Jesus said those who mourn are blessed."

"If that's so, you've had a double helping," Mark said.

"Tsion teaches about this," Mr. Stein said. "He points those who are struggling with the death of loved ones to the end of Revelation. God says he will remove all sorrows, and there will be no more death or crying or pain."

"Can't wait for that," Mark said. "But I gotta be honest. I don't understand why God would let all this happen."

"You have been a believer longer than I have," Mr. Stein said. "I should be asking you these questions."

The two rode in silence. Mr. Stein pointed the way. When they got close he said, "My office is on the next street. Stop here."

Mark pulled to the curb. Businesses were in shambles. A construction crew had cleared the road of debris, but the sidewalk was twisted.

"The GC might still be guarding your place," Mark said.

Mr. Stein nodded and gestured for Mark to follow him. They squeezed between two buildings and checked for cars near Mr. Stein's office.

"I don't see why we're risking this," Mark said. "If your money's hidden somewhere else, let's go there."

Mr. Stein pointed to a broken window in the bottom floor of his office. "We'll crawl through there," he said.

"But—"

"My money is here," Mr. Stein said, "if the Global Community didn't take it."

Mark followed Mr. Stein and kept watch. They passed a wall safe, its door lying broken on the floor.

"Just as I suspected," Mr. Stein said.

They moved upstairs. Mr. Stein pointed to desks with missing computers. "Either vandals or the GC," he said.

They reached a second-floor office with a couch and desk. The computer tower was gone, but the old monitor was still on the desk.

"Good," Mr. Stein said.

Mark watched in amazement as Mr. Stein unscrewed the back of the monitor.

"I was on the phone with Judd when he alerted me there was a bug," Mr. Stein said. "I had already hidden the money, but I wanted whoever was listening to think otherwise."

Mr. Stein took out the last screw and opened the back of the monitor. The contents of the monitor had been removed, and the space was crammed with bills. The man pulled out wads of hundreds. Mark had never seen so much money in his life.

Glass broke downstairs. Someone cursed. Two voices. One of them said, "Got almost everything last night. There's still some computer stuff upstairs."

Mr. Stein looked wildly at Mark.

Footsteps banged on the stairs.

"Quick, help me put the money in the drawer," Mr. Stein whispered.

They dumped the cash in the drawer and fumbled

with the back of the computer. At the top of the stairs the footsteps stopped. Another man, this one with a squeaky voice, said, "I thought you said this place was deserted."

"Come on," the other said.

Mr. Stein motioned for Mark to get behind the door. When the two came into view, Mark was safely out of sight. Mr. Stein sat in a chair, his feet on the desk.

"Welcome, gentlemen," Mr. Stein said cheerily. "I'm glad to see you're back."

Squeaky Voice was short and walked with a slight limp. The other man was tall and thin. He looked like the picture of Ichabod Crane Mark had seen in his reading book as a kid.

"Who are you?" Squeaky said.

"I'm the proprietor of this establishment," Mr. Stein said. The two stared at him. "The owner," Mr. Stein explained. "This is my office."

Mark noticed Ichabod had a gun. Mr. Stein pointed to it and said, "There's no need for violence. You're welcome to whatever you'd like."

Squeaky squinted and jerked his head sideways. "You *want* us to take stuff?"

Mr. Stein smiled. "When I found the office standing, with all the other buildings on this block in ruins, I was shocked. The insurance won't pay unless there was real damage. But now that you boys have 'cleaned up' for me, I should be paid quite a bit."

Squeaky still didn't understand.

"He's in it for the insurance money," Ichabod explained.

386

"Did you find the safe downstairs?" Mr. Stein said.

"Oh yeah, that was a piece o' cake," Squeaky said.

"How about the telephone equipment in the basement?" Mr. Stein said.

"Didn't know there was a basement," Ichabod said.

Mr. Stein pointed them toward the correct door, and the thieves left. Mr. Stein followed them. Mark opened the drawer and stuffed the money into a black satchel. When Mr. Stein returned he said, "We must hurry. There is no telephone equipment down there."

Mark cleaned out the drawer. The satchel was full and very heavy. Mr. Stein grabbed the satchel and raced down the stairs, Mark right behind him. Mark was almost out the window when he heard Ichabod shout, "Hey, there's two of them!"

The sun was coming up as Mark raced toward the alley. A shot rang out. A bullet pinged against a brick wall nearby. Mark took the satchel from Mr. Stein, who was lagging behind, and ran for the bike. By the time Mr. Stein made it, Mark had the motorcycle roaring. Mr. Stein clutched the satchel tightly to his chest as Mark sped away.

Vicki awoke first and, peeking through the doorway, found Z still at work on the IDs. Judd was now Leland Brayfield. Conrad found the driver's license of James Lindley, two years older. Darrion had become Rosemary Bishop. But it was more difficult for Lionel. Z admitted his stash of African-American IDs was lacking. The closest Lionel could come was a twenty-five-year-old who was at least fifty pounds heavier. Z said making too many changes to "Greg Butler" could tip off whoever scanned Lionel's new ID, but he would do it anyway.

Z was laminating Lionel's card when Vicki shuffled into the room. She yawned and sat by his desk. It was nearly noon.

"You've been at it quite a while," Vicki said.

"Not so bad," Z said, pulling the magnifying light down to inspect the card. He handed "Jackie Browne's" card to her.

Vicki gasped. "This is amazing," she said.

Z blushed. "Where are you guys headed from here?"

Vicki laughed. "Who knows? We've been fighting about our next move since we escaped the GC."

"What kinda choices you got?"

"Darrion's folks have a place in Wisconsin," Vicki said. "It'd be good for us to get away from Chicago, but . . ."

Z nodded and opened a packet of beef jerky. He leaned back in his chair as he chewed. Rolls of fat jiggled under his black vest. "Who says you guys have to stay together?"

Vicki paused. The Young Trib Force had been separated before, but it had never been their choice.

"If you guys are fighting about what to do," Z said, "split up. You may be able to do more good apart."

"What do you mean?" Vicki said.

"I'm helping people get supplies and fuel," Z said, "and keepin' the Global Community out of your hair. If the rabbi's right, pretty soon more and more people are going to need supplies, which means more people will have to help. I could use somebody right here in the office."

Vicki admired Z and his dad, but she couldn't imagine working for them. But something stirred in her as he spoke.

Z picked up a notebook by his laptop and turned to the back. Vicki couldn't read a word of the scratching. "I'll tell you another thing that's gonna happen," he said. "With parents raptured or dead, a lot more young people like you are gonna be on the run. Especially believers."

Vicki looked straight at Z and said, "The dream."

"What's that?" Z said.

"I had this dream," Vicki said. "I was running through woods, following a boy. The GC was chasing us. We ran down by a river and came into a clearing and saw a huge house. There were kids on the balcony, waving and calling. When I made it to the front door, the GC stopped. It was like I disappeared. Then—"

"This is spooky," Z said, sitting forward, the chair legs slamming on the floor. He opened a desk drawer and rummaged through some papers.

"Tell me what the house looked like," Z said.

"I don't remember except that it had a balcony and was really long," Vicki said. "I think there was some kind of pole in front. Like a flagpole."

Z stared at her. "I don't believe it."

He rummaged through another drawer and moved to the filing cabinet.

"What is it?" Vicki said.

Z snapped a piece of paper from a file. "Got it!" he said.

He handed Vicki a ten-year-old real estate listing. Statistics covered the bottom half of the page. Fifty acres, zoned residential, well water, etc. On the top half was a picture that took Vicki's breath away. The photo was fuzzy, but it looked exactly like the house Vicki had seen in her dream, even though the house was blocked by trees.

"It even has the flagpole," Z said, pointing to the right side of the picture.

"What is it?" Vicki said when she caught her breath.

"An old boarding school," Z said. "About forty miles south of here. My grandpa bought it from the state. Hadn't been used in years. He didn't do much with it. Then he died and left it to my dad. Nearly sold it a few times, but the buyers always backed out."

Z pointed to a brown streak behind the house. "And it's in a flood plain," he said. "Right next to a river."

"What are you going to do with it?" Vicki said.

"It's not that far from a major trucking route. Plan is to store supplies there. We already have some meds, food, water—that kind of thing."

"Won't it attract attention?" Vicki said.

Z pulled out another sheet of paper. Along the top was written *Condemned*.

"This document says the place is a hazard and people should stay away. Some of the neighbors think the place is haunted. They don't come around."

Vicki scratched her head. "You're going to think this is stupid," she said.

"Go ahead; I'm listening."

"For a long time I've had this idea of a place where kids can go," Vicki said. She stood. Thoughts swirled in her mind. Ideas came fast. "What if we use this as a training center for the Young Trib Force? What if kids who want to know the truth come there to study? We could make it a distribution center for all your food and medicine, too."

Vicki could see it, a fulfillment of her dream. Z put his hands behind his head and listened.

"It's far enough away that the Global Community wouldn't find us," Vicki continued, "but close enough to help believers who need supplies."

"What would that mean for the rest of the group?" Z said. "If some want to go to Wisconsin or they don't like the school idea, what happens then?"

Vicki turned and saw Judd in the doorway. He looked funny with all his changes. But Vicki didn't smile.

"I guess we'll each have to make our own decision," Vicki said.

40

JUDD didn't like Vicki's idea. Something about taking over the school bothered him. The others awoke and joined them.

"You're taking for granted that Z is offering," Judd said.

Z handed him some beef jerky. Judd declined.

"This place has been in the family for years," Z said. "I'd have to ask my dad, but I see it as a win-win. You guys get a place to stay, and we get someone to watch the supplies."

"What about Wisconsin?" Darrion said.

"Everybody has to choose," Vicki said. "We can't force people to join us."

"You're talking about splitting up the group," Judd said.

"You don't like it because it wasn't your idea," Vicki said.

"That's not true!" Judd shouted.

Lionel held up a hand. "Hold it! What's important isn't whose idea it is; it's that we respect each other."

Vicki explained the school option to the whole group. Darrion held up a hand. "Wisconsin reminds me of my parents, but Vicki's idea sounds good. If God gave her that dream, maybe we should do it."

Judd looked at Vicki. "I'm not trying to shoot this down. I don't think we can base an important decision like this on a dream."

Vicki squinted. "Remember when you went to Israel to check on Nina and Dan? Wasn't that partly because you'd had a dream about them?"

"That was different," Judd said.

"Forget the dream," Lionel said. "We need a place that's safe, and it sounds like we can help Z and his dad with supplies."

Z nodded. "I can't say when we'll start running. Let me go talk with my dad." Z left.

Lionel looked at Conrad. "What do you think about all this?"

Conrad pursed his lips. "I don't know. I'm mixed up. Makes you wonder if God's really helping us, or if we're trying to do this on our own."

"What do you mean?" Vicki said.

Conrad swatted at a fly. "If we're all on the same team, why do we argue so much?"

"Just because we disagree doesn't mean we're not on the same team," Lionel said.

Vicki scooted closer to Conrad. "Is it deeper than that?"

"What Mr. Stein said to Tsion," Conrad said. "I just don't know if this is real."

"You heard what Tsion said to Mr. Stein, right?" Judd said.

"What if I turn away?" Conrad said. "What if I go with Taylor and try to kill Nicolae, or just turn my back on the whole thing?"

Z came back in the room. "Good news—"

Judd held up a hand and pulled out his pocket Bible. "Let's go over this again. John, chapter 1. Everyone who believes in Jesus and accepts him becomes a child of God. They are reborn."

Conrad nodded.

"John, chapter 3 says everyone who believes in Jesus has eternal life, and chapter 5 says those who believe will never be condemned for their sins, but they have already passed from death to life.

"Romans 10 says if you confess with your mouth that Jesus is Lord and believe in your heart that God raised him from the dead, you will be saved."

Conrad read the verses with Judd.

Vicki spoke up. "I've been reading Revelation to see what's ahead. I love the verses that talk about the Book of Life. When you believed, Conrad, your name was written there. God knows you."

"So I can't un-save myself?" Conrad said.

Judd smiled. "When you asked God into your life, he saved you by his power. And he'll keep you by his power. It doesn't mean you won't have doubts or you won't sin." Judd looked at Vicki. "And it doesn't mean you'll always treat your brothers and sisters the way you should."

Conrad was silent. Finally, Z said, "My dad thinks your idea about the school's great."

Vicki took the key and the directions to the old schoolhouse. "One more thing," she said. "I want to look for Phoenix."

Judd shut his eyes and held his tongue.

"You mean the dog that was with you?" Conrad said. "I might know where he is."

"Can I talk with you for a minute?" Judd said to Vicki. "Alone?"

Vicki climbed up the narrow staircase and entered the gas station in front of Judd. Z's father was with a customer.

"If you kids only wanted to use the rest room, you have to buy something," Zeke said.

"Yes, sir," Judd said. He picked up a couple of candy bars from a cardboard bin on the counter and left two bills by the cash register.

"Teenagers," the customer said in disgust.

Vicki knew Zeke was covering for them. The customer didn't have the mark of the believer. This is what it would be like. To stay alive, they would have to be careful with everyone without the mark.

Judd handed Vicki the candy bar and they walked outside. Vicki blew dust from the wrapper. Clouds blocked the sun and a hazy gloom hung over the area.

"I didn't want to talk about it in front of the others," Judd said.

"You don't want me going for Phoenix," Vicki said.

"What I want or don't want isn't the point. You saw what Conrad's going through."

"Which is exactly why this school would be such a good idea," Vicki said. "Kids need to understand what the Bible really teaches."

"There's nothing wrong with the idea, but why can't kids get the same thing from Tsion's Web site?"

"They can get information there, but I think they need a person to show them. Flesh and blood." Vicki stopped walking. "Try to picture it. Believers coming together to study, soaking up the teaching, asking questions, figuring out what to do. At the same time, we help set up a supply line so people can survive."

"Would you let anyone in who wasn't a believer?"

Vicki started to answer, but Judd cut her off. "What if some say they really want to know more, but their real intent is to expose us to the Global Community? What if they want to lead them right to us?"

"We have to use caution," Vicki said. "We'd have to discern—"

"Use your power of discernment like you did with that guy Charlie?" Judd said.

Vicki threw the stale candy bar on the ground. "I cared about Charlie. He helped me carry Ryan's body."

Judd walked a few more steps. Vicki stood her ground. "Maybe it's time we split up," she said.

"That's exactly what I'm talking about," Judd said. "You're driving a wedge into the group."

"And you're the only one who can have an idea? You want women to remain silent and be good little girls. If God gives me an idea, I'm not gonna keep quiet."

"You know I've valued your input," Judd said.

Vicki scoffed. "As long as I agreed with you."

Vicki clutched the key and directions in her hand. "I'm going back for Phoenix right now!"

"Vick, that's crazy! In broad daylight?"

"Conrad said they caught Charlie with Phoenix and sent him to a shelter. I'm gonna keep my promise to Ryan, no matter what you say."

"Vick, wait!"

When Vicki reached the station she looked back and saw Judd kneeling on the ground.

———————————

Judd and Lionel waited until evening to leave Z's place. Lionel didn't ask about Vicki. Z scribbled another set of directions to the old schoolhouse and gave them to Judd.

"Sounds like you guys have been through a lot," Z said.

Judd nodded. "More than I can tell you."

Z scratched at a few scraggly hairs on his chin. He tipped his chair back. "I ain't an expert on anything but tattoos, but I do know one thing. When you got people you care about, no matter how much you fight, you got somethin'."

Z looked away. His eyes pooled with tears. "I'd give

anything to spend one hour with my mom and sisters. I'd give anything to tell them about God."

When they left, Z shook Judd's hand and put an arm around Lionel. "You need anything, you holler. We could use a couple guys like you to drive for us, if you decide to help out with the supplies."

"We'll let you know," Judd said.

Lionel started his motorcycle. "I hope Pete's back when we get there."

Vicki, Darrion, and Conrad drove near the remains of New Hope Village Church. They parked their bikes behind the rubble and looked at the damage. The downed helicopter had been removed. The grass and trees were black from the scorching hail.

Vicki found shell casings from rifle fire. The bullets had been intended for her and her friends.

"From what I remember," Conrad said, "Charlie and that dog were taken to a shelter near here."

"Should we split up?" Darrion said.

"Let's stay together until we get close," Vicki said.

The three hiked to the nearest shelter. The smell of campfires and outdoor cooking made Vicki hungry. They passed tents and people in sleeping bags. Vicki motioned to Conrad and Darrion to stay back as she entered the medical tent.

A stout woman with black hair rushed about. Vicki caught her eye. "I'm looking for a friend. He has a dog with him."

"This isn't an animal hospital," the woman said.

A younger girl heard Vicki's question. She said she had seen a boy with a dog and described Phoenix perfectly. "Saw them two days ago," the girl said. "The boy seemed a little strange."

"Where'd they go?"

The girl shook her head. "A couple guys took them away in a jeep. Haven't seen them since."

Vicki thanked the girl.

"Doesn't sound good," Conrad said when Vicki returned. "The GC might have taken him in for questioning."

"Where?" Vicki said.

Conrad held up his hands. "No way, you can't—"

"They won't recognize me with the changes Z made," Vicki said. "I have to find Phoenix."

Darrion darted behind a tree. "Get down," she whispered.

Vicki and Conrad crouched low. Melinda and Felicia, the Morale Monitors, crept into the medical tent. "What could they be doing?" Vicki said.

"I don't know," Conrad said, "but if you're gonna look for Phoenix at the GC headquarters, now's the time to do it."

As Judd and Lionel reached Boyd's gas station, Shelly met them. She was frantic. "I thought you guys had left me. Pete still hasn't come back, but Taylor said he was going to find the GC and get him out."

Judd winced. First Vicki and now this. Boyd opened the garage door and let them in.

Judd heard a rumble and saw a motorcycle coming.

"Maybe that's Pete," Shelly said.

"No, it's two people," Judd said.

Mark and Mr. Stein brought the cycle in. Mr. Stein had a satchel with him.

"Did you get the money?" Judd said.

Mr. Stein nodded. Mark briefly told them about their adventure. Judd explained where Vicki and the others had gone. He looked at Boyd. "Can you point me toward the GC headquarters?"

"You can't!" Shelly said.

"I have to try," Judd said.

"Perhaps money would help," Mr. Stein said.

Judd shook his head. "Whatever's happened to Pete, I don't think any amount of money will help him now."

41

VICKI rode with Darrion. They followed Conrad to the GC headquarters in Des Plaines. Vicki was glad Commander Blancka was out of the picture, but Melinda and Felicia were not far away.

The kids parked their motorcycles two blocks from headquarters. Conrad led them to the side window. Someone was sleeping in a cell, but there was no sign of Phoenix.

Vicki walked around the corner and tripped on something metal. It clanged against the back wall. A dog barked. A door opened and a shaft of light hit the yard. Vicki gasped. Phoenix stood in a pen behind the station.

"Shut your yap!" the man yelled at Phoenix, but the dog kept barking. "This'll shut you up." The man picked up a stone. The rock bounced off the cage and Phoenix cowered.

When the door closed, Vicki rushed to Phoenix. The dog barked, then whimpered when he saw Vicki. A wave of relief spread over her. She had thought about Phoenix every day since the earthquake.

"Hey, boy, how are you?" she said gently.

Phoenix looked like he hadn't eaten in days. He wagged his tail. Vicki tried to get her hand through the fence, but the opening was too small. Phoenix tried to lick Vicki's face but couldn't.

"I'm glad to see you, too."

Conrad inspected the lock on the pen. "No way we're gonna get him out without the key."

"Why would they lock him up here?" Vicki said.

Conrad shrugged. "Maybe they're still using him to look for us."

"Wish we had some wire cutters," Darrion said.

"Let's dig him out," Vicki whispered.

The kids got on their hands and knees and scraped at the dirt. Darrion found the piece of metal Vicki had tripped over and used it to dig faster. When they had dug a few inches, Conrad sat back.

"The fence is deep," Conrad said. "We're never gonna get him out this way."

Vicki pulled at the top of the cage, but it was welded tight. Phoenix whimpered and paced, keeping his eyes on Vicki.

"We're gonna get you out of here, boy," Vicki said.

Suddenly the back door opened. Light shone in the kids' faces.

Judd and Lionel rode nearly past the small, two-story building the Global Community had seized. Lionel stayed with the bike while Judd moved closer. Judd ran toward a lighted window, peeked over the edge, and ducked when he saw someone walking toward him. He looked again. Pete sat patiently in a chair near the window.

Judd ran back to Lionel. "Pete's in there. No hand-cuffs, and it doesn't look like the guy is threatening him."

"Probably only a matter of time," Lionel said.

Lionel touched Judd's arm and nodded toward the building. Someone was inching up the side.

"That's Taylor!" Judd said.

Judd and Lionel rushed to him. Taylor's face was painted black.

Taylor climbed down, and the three moved away from the building.

"What are you doing?" Judd said.

Taylor took a knife from his mouth and put it in its sheath. "Jump a guard and get Pete out of there."

"You were going to kill somebody?" Lionel said.

"If I have to, yeah," Taylor said.

Judd shook his head. "No need to kill anyone. Let me try."

"I'll give you five minutes," Taylor said. "If they take him to a cell, I'm coming after him."

Judd took Lionel aside. "If Taylor leaves, alert the GC. Nobody gets killed over this."

"But—"

"Do it," Judd said.

Judd ran to the window, which was open a few inches.

The GC officer shuffled papers on his desk. "I've already told you, we believe you. The marks on the road are consistent with your story."

"Let me explain it another way," Pete said.

"I have things to do."

"Please," Pete said.

The officer's chair squeaked. "What you're saying could get you in bigger trouble than if you would have killed those guys."

"I think you're ready to hear it. If you weren't, you'd have thrown me out of here a long time ago."

"Maybe I should have," the officer said.

Judd looked through the window. Pete was leaning forward, his hands on the officer's desk.

"I don't care who you work for or what you've done in the past, God loved you enough to die for you. If you ask him to forgive you for the bad things you've done, he'll make you a new person and you can live with him forever."

The officer spoke in a low voice Judd could hardly hear. "Do you realize what my superiors would do? We're talking life and death—"

"Exactly," Pete interrupted. "What I'm talking about is life and death, too. If you reject God's way, it means you're separated from him forever."

Judd knelt. He knew Pete was bold, but he didn't know he would be this bold. He looked for Taylor but didn't see him. Lionel sat with his back to a tree.

"If I believe what you say," the officer said, "and I'm not saying I do, how would I do it?"

As Pete explained what the man should pray, Judd looked closer at Lionel. He was struggling. Judd ran and found Lionel tied and gagged.

"Taylor must have heard us," Lionel said as he gasped for air. "He grabbed me from behind." Lionel pointed to the building. "Look!"

To Judd's horror, Taylor Graham had already climbed to the second floor of the building.

"We've got to stop him!" Judd said.

———

Vicki rolled to her right and out of the light. Darrion and Conrad went the other way. A thin man closed the door and walked toward Phoenix. She thought they had been seen. Finally, she lifted her head.

The man held something in his hand. He opened the narrow slot and dropped it on the ground inside Phoenix's kennel. Phoenix approached warily and sniffed.

"There you go, boy," he said. "They wouldn't let me feed you. I found some scraps. Hope you like 'em."

The voice sounded familiar but Vicki couldn't place it. When he turned, Vicki whispered, "Charlie!"

Vicki rushed to him. Charlie jumped back. "What do you want? I was just feedin' the dog. I won't do it again."

"It's okay," Vicki said. "I'm not going to hurt you."

Charlie held his arms close to his chest. *He doesn't recognize me*, Vicki thought. *Good.*

Vicki signaled for Conrad and Darrion to stay where they were. "Why do they have the dog in the cage?"

"Those guys in there are using him," Charlie said. "They're trying to find some people."

"Really?" Vicki said. "I've been looking for a dog like this. He seems nice."

"He is," Charlie said. "He's kept me company ever since my friends got killed."

"What friends?" Vicki said.

"A girl and a guy and some others," Charlie said. "They got killed by the commander before he died."

Vicki stepped closer. She wanted to talk with Charlie and tell him the truth, but she was afraid the GC officers would find them any moment.

"I have some good news," Vicki said. "Your friends aren't dead."

Charlie scrunched his face. "What?"

"Your friends are alive, and I know where they are," Vicki said. "I can take you there if you'll help me get the key to this cage."

"The guys in there'll be really mad if I do that," Charlie said. "They're looking for these two girls, and if I run off—"

"What two girls?" Vicki said.

"I can't remember their names," Charlie said. "They were with that commander guy a lot."

"Melinda and Felicia?" Vicki said.

"Yeah, yeah, that's them. They got away."

Vicki thought a moment. Why would the GC want Melinda and Felicia?

And then she knew.

"This is really important," Vicki said. "If you go in and get the key, I'll take you to your friends."

"How do I know you're telling the truth?" Charlie said.

Vicki took him by the shoulders. "Because your name's Charlie. I'm here to help you."

Charlie smiled. "How'd you know my name?"

"Will you get the key?" Vicki said.

Someone yelled for Charlie. His eyes darted to the door. "Okay."

"Don't tell anyone I'm out here," Vicki said.

"I won't," Charlie said. "You just stay here, and I'll see if I can find the key. Stay right here."

Conrad and Darrion approached as Charlie scampered off. Vicki took them to the side of the building.

"I've got a bad feeling," Vicki said. "I think the GC is trying to wipe out all the people who were involved with us."

"You think the GC killed Blancka?" Conrad said.

Vicki nodded. "And now they're after Felicia and Melinda."

"Good," Darrion said. "I hate those two."

"When they find them," Vicki said, "they'll get rid of Charlie, too."

Conrad bit his lip. "Blancka is dead. Joyce, the girl who accused you of murder, is, too. They're looking for Melinda and Felicia, and they have Charlie and Phoenix in custody. Everybody who was connected with us is winding up dead."

409

"Why?" Darrion said.

"Who knows," Conrad said. "Image and control are everything to the GC. If Blancka messed up, it was easier to get rid of him than give him a second chance."

"And that means they have to get rid of everybody who knew that wasn't a training exercise in that field," Vicki said, "including us."

"Just when you thought it was safe," Darrion said.

Vicki thought about the schoolhouse. They had to get Charlie away from the GC fast.

Judd watched as Taylor Graham disappeared into the second floor of the GC building. Lionel followed Judd to the front door.

"Get by the window," Judd said. "If the officer goes out, tell Pete what's up."

"Got it," Lionel said.

Judd rushed up the steps and looked inside. A man in a uniform sat at the front desk, talking on the phone. A female officer drank coffee at a desk in the rear.

Judd opened the door and calmly walked in. The man behind the front desk raised his head. Judd didn't make eye contact.

"Can I help you?" the officer said.

Judd didn't answer. He walked straight to the back hallway and closed the door.

"Hey, you can't go in there!" the man shouted. The woman put her coffee down and drew her gun.

Judd shut the door and flipped on the light. He breathed a sigh of relief when he saw the fire alarm. He pulled it. A piercing buzz filled the headquarters. Judd found a back door and rushed outside. He darted to the front and found Lionel, and the two raced to their motorcycle.

"I figured the alarm would clear the building," Judd said. "Did you talk with Pete?"

"Yeah," Lionel said. "He wants us to go on without him. I told him about Taylor. He said he'd handle it. Pete seemed to think the guy he was talking with was really close to making a decision about God."

"Let's just pray they both get out of there alive," Judd said.

42

VICKI waited outside GC headquarters, peeking in the window every few seconds. Conrad and Darrion walked the motorcycles closer. Charlie finally returned with a key.

"Gotta get to my friends," Charlie said, handing the key to Vicki. "Gotta get that thing on my head. They promised me."

Conrad rolled his eyes. Vicki tried the key. It didn't work. Phoenix whined.

"I'll go back and get another one," Charlie said.

Conrad put up a hand. "We can't let him go back in there," he said.

"How are we going to get Phoenix out?" Vicki said.

Conrad ran around the building and disappeared into the darkness. A few minutes later he returned with a tire iron. "Found it in the jeep out front."

Conrad placed the tire iron at the top of the kennel door and pushed until the door bent slightly outward.

"Gonna take more than that," Darrion said.

Charlie helped. Their combined weight opened the door a few more inches. "See if you can get him," Conrad said to Vicki.

Phoenix whimpered and backed away.

"Come on," Vicki coaxed. Finally she grabbed his front paws.

Footsteps behind them.

Vicki let go of Phoenix. "You have to cover for us," she said to Charlie. Vicki and the kids scattered. Charlie stood by the door of the cage. "Cover for you," he said.

"What are you doing out here?" a man shouted.

Charlie stuttered, "Just feedin' the dog, sir."

"I thought I told you to stay inside!"

"Yes, sir," Charlie said, "but the dog was whining and hungry and I didn't think—"

"Do me a favor," the man said. "Don't think. Just do what I tell you. Come inside."

The man left. Vicki heard a voice inside the building say, "He's more trouble than he's worth. We oughta get rid of him tonight."

Vicki hurried to the cage. She took Phoenix by the paws and tried to lift him out.

"Hurry," Conrad said.

Phoenix yelped in pain as Vicki pulled his head through the small opening. Darrion tried to calm him.

"Get Charlie out of here," Vicki said.

"We're not leaving without you," Conrad said.

"They're gonna off him," Vicki said. "At least get him on a cycle so we can bolt when I get Phoenix."

Conrad led Charlie to a motorcycle, and they both climbed on.

Darrion put her arms through the cage opening and pulled at the dog's body. Phoenix yelped.

"Hey!" a man shouted. "They're stealing the dog!"

Conrad started the motorcycle. Phoenix slipped through the opening, sending Vicki and Darrion to the ground. Phoenix growled and ran toward the building. The man retreated.

Darrion and Vicki ran to the motorcycle. She tried to start it, but the engine sputtered.

Phoenix stood at the open doorway and barked.

"Go!" Vicki yelled at Conrad.

Conrad shook his head. A shot rang out.

"Phoenix!" Vicki yelled.

The motorcycle roared to life. Conrad sped off.

"Wait!" Vicki shouted. She called for Phoenix. Two men exited the doorway with guns drawn. Phoenix jumped, grabbing one man by the arm. The other man turned to get a shot at the dog, but couldn't. Phoenix bit hard and the man dropped his gun. Vicki screamed again, and this time Phoenix bounded away from the man on the ground and jumped into Vicki's lap.

Darrion gunned the engine. Vicki held on tight to Phoenix and kept her head down. When they turned into an alley, Phoenix yelped in pain and squirmed in her arms.

"It's okay, boy," she said. "You're safe now."

415

Darrion caught up to Conrad and Charlie. They rode without headlights through the moonlit streets. Vicki knew they had to get to the schoolhouse.

Judd and Lionel raced to Boyd's gas station. Some of Pete's gang waited for news. Judd explained what happened. Shelly said she would keep watch so Judd and Lionel could get some sleep.

Early the next morning, Judd was awakened from a deep sleep. Taylor Graham stood over him. He grabbed Judd by the collar and picked him up.

"Why did you do that?" Taylor screamed.

"Let go," Judd said.

Taylor did and Judd fell hard to the floor.

"That's enough," Pete said, grabbing Taylor by the arm.

"The GC almost caught me because of him," Taylor said.

"I told you to wait," Judd said. "Pete wasn't in any danger."

"He's right," Pete said. "Pulling that alarm kept you from doing something stupid."

"Killing people isn't the answer," Judd said.

"And talking about God is?" Taylor said. "I'm through with you people."

Taylor knocked shoulders with Pete and stalked outside. A moment later, an engine revved.

"He's got your bike!" someone said.

Pete waved a hand. "Let him go."

Mr. Stein looked at the floor as Taylor roared off. "How will I get to the Meeting of the Witnesses?"

"You'll find a way," Lionel said.

The kids moved to the office. "Where's Vicki?" Shelly said.

Judd told them about Vicki's decision to try to find Phoenix and the idea about the old schoolhouse. "She might not be coming back."

Shelly stared at him. "You're not breaking up the group, are you?"

Judd thought a moment. "We all have to make our choices," he said. "I can't stop Vicki any more than I can stop Taylor."

"But it's such a good idea," Shelly said. "We should be at the school right now."

Lionel spoke up. "Did Z give you directions?"

Judd nodded. He pulled a scrap of paper from his pocket and looked at Lionel. Something was happening. Judd felt he was losing control. Would the kids leave him behind to follow Vicki?

He handed the paper to Lionel and turned to Pete. "What about the Global Community officer?"

"Talked with him more after the fire alarm," Pete said. "He didn't pray with me, but I could tell he was close. He knows how to do it if he wants to."

Judd bit his lip. "It was pretty risky talking with him that way."

Pete sat and put his feet on Boyd's desk. "I'm not into risk. I didn't tell that guy the truth because I want to get in trouble. I could tell he was lookin'."

Judd stared at the floor.

"We've been left here for a reason," Pete said. "If people are interested, I tell them. It's as simple as that. If I read it right, the GC police have just the same chance as the rest of us."

"I'm just saying it might not be smart—"

"This isn't about smart," Pete said. "If I didn't tell that guy about God, who was going to?"

Judd looked away.

"Havin' said that," Pete continued, "I can't be sure he won't come after us. And it's a possibility Red's gang will come for revenge."

"I'm going to find Vicki," Shelly said.

"Me, too," Lionel said.

Vicki hung on tight to Phoenix as Darrion and Conrad zigzagged through the torn-up streets of Des Plaines and headed south. When they made it to what used to be I-55, she felt safer. Several times she had the feeling someone was following, but when she looked back there was no one.

Vicki gave Darrion directions as she strained to see the map Z had given. The kids rode past farmhouses and sloping fields.

"Turn here," Vicki said, seeing a dirt road leading up a hill.

Conrad and Darrion rode back and forth along the road an hour before they gave up and pulled to the side.

"Let's get some sleep," Conrad said. "We'll find it in the morning."

The kids found a grassy area a few yards off the dirt road and went to sleep. Phoenix curled up next to Vicki. When Vicki awoke, Conrad was studying the map.

"If the map is right, we gotta be really close," Conrad said.

"When do I get to see my friends?" Charlie said.

"Soon," Vicki said. "Real soon."

"What's that?" Charlie said, pointing to a brown spot on Vicki's shirt.

"It almost looks like blood."

"Phoenix!" Conrad yelled.

The dog lay still on the ground. His fur was matted with dried blood along one side. Vicki held her breath. Conrad leaned over Phoenix and inspected the wound.

Vicki couldn't look. "Is he dead?" she said.

Phoenix whimpered.

"Looks like a bullet grazed his back," Conrad said.

Vicki cradled the dog's head in her lap. Phoenix licked her hand as she petted him.

"He didn't lose that much blood," Conrad said, "but we'd better find something to disinfect the wound."

"Z said they have medicine stored at the schoolhouse," Vicki said.

While Charlie stayed with Phoenix, the kids searched for the road. A few minutes later, Darrion shouted. Vicki found her near some downed trees.

"This is why we couldn't find it last night," Darrion said, pointing to the logs. "It's blocked."

"If this is the right road, it's perfect," Conrad said. "Nobody'll find us unless they know what to look for."

Charlie carried Phoenix, and the kids walked the motorcycles around the logs. The road had shifted and would need some repair if they expected to bring truckloads of supplies to the hideout. Around a bend they found a small pond; then the road opened to a meadow. On the hillside stood the old schoolhouse. Shutters dangled, a screen door hung at a crazy angle, and the paint was peeling.

"Incredible," Vicki said.

Vicki opened the door with the key Z had given her. A long staircase leading to the second floor was just inside the door. Straight ahead was the kitchen area with a table and a few chairs. To the left and right on the first floor were classrooms.

"This is almost as big as my house!" Darrion said.

"It'd take a year just to find all the rooms," Conrad said. "There's even a bell tower upstairs." He opened a door under the stairs. His voice echoed. "There's a huge basement, too."

"Z said the bedrooms are upstairs," Vicki said.

Charlie carried Phoenix inside and put him on the floor in the kitchen. Vicki and the others searched for the supply room and found it at the north end of the house.

"What do you put on a dog who's been injured?" Vicki said, looking at the boxes of medicine. "Their skin is different from ours, isn't it?"

Vicki found a bottle of antiseptic used in hospitals. She blotted the brown liquid on Phoenix's back. The dog yelped and scampered away.

"Maybe that stuff doesn't work on an open wound," Darrion said. "Maybe some soap and water?"

Conrad held Phoenix as Vicki and Darrion washed the wound. Vicki tried putting on a bandage, but Phoenix chewed it off.

"You told me I could see my friends," Charlie said.

Vicki pulled out a chair and asked Charlie to sit down. "Do you notice anything familiar about me?" Vicki said.

"Your voice," Charlie said.

"Who do I sound like?"

Charlie shrugged.

Vicki took the dental device off her front teeth. Charlie's eyes opened wide. "How about now?"

Charlie squinted. "I still don't know what—"

"Picture me with red hair."

Charlie screamed, "Vicki!"

43

JUDD walked Lionel and Shelly outside. "If I don't hear anything from you, I'll assume you made it."

Lionel shook hands with Judd. Shelly had tears in her eyes. "Why don't you come with us?"

Judd looked at the ground. "Maybe later. I'll stay with Mr. Stein. Get in touch if you need me."

When they were gone, Judd logged onto the Internet and found several messages from Pavel, his friend from New Babylon. A few minutes later he was talking with Pavel live.

"The satellite schools were set to open," Pavel said, "but the comet set them back. I'm amazed at the rebuilding, though. Carpathia has troops opening roads, airstrips, cities, trade routes, everything. And he's using each disaster for his own good."

"What do you mean?" Judd said.

"New Babylon is the capital of the world!" Pavel said. "The worse things get, the more people feel like they have to depend on the Global Community."

Judd nodded. "And you can bet Carpathia will use the next judgment for his own good if he can."

Pavel rolled his wheelchair closer to the monitor. "My father has been able to observe the potentate through his position with the Global Community. Carpathia is furious with Tsion Ben-Judah, the two witnesses, and the upcoming conference."

"From the loads of E-mails Tsion has sent me," Judd said, "Carpathia can't be too happy about the people who want to know more about Christ."

"Have you seen the exchange between Carpathia and the rabbi?"

"What exchange?"

Pavel took out a disk and sent the data to Judd. While Judd opened it, Pavel said, "My father says Nicolae has always been an intense man. Very disciplined. But now he works like a madman. He gets up early, before everyone else, and he works late into the night."

Judd read the document. It was Nicolae Carpathia's attempt to compete with Tsion Ben-Judah. His messages were short. One read, *Today I give honor to those involved in the rebuilding effort around the world. The Global Community owes a debt of gratitude for the sacrifices and tireless efforts of those who are making our world a better place.*

Another brief message encouraged readers to give their devotion to the Enigma Babylon faith. Carpathia also repeated his pledge to protect Rabbi Ben-Judah. *Those who are sincere in their beliefs should know they have the full protection of the Global Community,* Carpathia wrote. *Should Dr. Ben-Judah choose to return to his home-*

land, I pledge protection from the religious fanatics or others who wish to harm him.

"Now look at how Ben-Judah responded," Pavel said.

Judd scrolled down and read the rabbi's words aloud. "Potentate Carpathia: I gratefully accept your offer of personal protection and congratulate you that this makes you an instrument of the one true, living God. He has promised to seal and protect his own during this season when we are commissioned to preach his gospel to the world. We are grateful that he has apparently chosen you as our protector and wonder how you feel about it. In the name of Jesus Christ, the Messiah and our Lord and Savior, Rabbi Tsion Ben-Judah, in exile."

"Did your dad say anything about how Carpathia reacted?" Judd said.

Pavel smiled. "The Potentate went into a frenzy. He didn't even respond to Ben-Judah's message."

Judd signed off and asked Mr. Stein to join him. "Boyd said we could fix up a little hideout in the oil bay. One of the best ways to learn about the Bible is to help me answer people's questions."

Mr. Stein put his hands in his pockets. "My heart is in Israel with the upcoming conference," he said, "but I suppose I should learn as much as I can."

Vicki heard the sound of the engine first. She was working on a railing of the balcony when she saw two people on a motorcycle coming through the trees. She whistled the danger signal and everyone met in the kitchen. The kids had planned a strategy in case they had visitors.

When Vicki realized it was Lionel and Shelly, she let out a whoop. She ran and embraced the two.

Lionel said they had arrived late the previous night, but couldn't find the road to the school.

"Same thing happened to us," Vicki said. She gave them a tour. Lionel looked shocked when he saw the supply room. The kids had reorganized it since moving in.

"We've got a lot of ideas," Darrion said. "I want to dig an underground tunnel in case the GC ever find us." She pointed to the hillside. "It'd come out somewhere near the river."

Lionel nodded. "We need to hide a boat down there."

"The big drawback is that we don't have electricity or phone," Vicki said. "There's a fuel tank buried in the back and Conrad found a gas-powered generator, but we haven't been able to get it to work."

"Give me a shot at it," Lionel said.

When they were alone, Vicki asked Shelly about Judd.

Shelly shook her head. "He's so stubborn. I begged him to come with us, but he wouldn't."

Judd and Mr. Stein answered E-mails that poured in. People begged to know God. Mr. Stein observed how Judd answered questions and gave advice to young people who didn't know how to begin a relationship with God.

Mr. Stein learned quickly. He kept a list of verses and passages of Scripture they used frequently. Judd checked his answers to make sure they were accurate. Soon, Mr. Stein and Judd took shifts. While one person answered E-mail, the other slept or got exercise.

Several weeks later, Pete returned. Judd and Mr. Stein were thrilled. Pete told them about finding his former gang and their reaction to Red's death.

"Some of them wanted to kill me," Pete said, "but most of them knew how quick-tempered Red was. I tried to talk with them about God again, but they wouldn't listen."

Pete turned on the television and switched to a news channel. "You see this?"

The reporter talked about a Global Community base that had been bombed. "I saw something about it on the Internet," Judd said. "You think there are still militia members alive?"

"The base had planes," Pete said. "They were all destroyed. All except one. It was a fancy six-seater the commanding officer used to get back and forth to New Babylon."

Judd gasped. "Taylor Graham."

Pete nodded. "They're not telling everything in the report. Gotta be Graham's work."

"Can you stay with us?" Judd said.

Pete smiled. "Wish I could. Truth is, I'm not the sit-still type. A few of us are headed down south. There are a lot of people who need to know the truth."

Pete said he would leave one motorcycle for Judd and Mr. Stein to use. Judd told Pete about the boarding school and the possibility of transporting supplies to believers. Pete scribbled something on a piece of paper. "This is a truck stop where I'm headed. I know some long-haul truckers who might be interested."

"They're believers?" Judd said.

Pete smiled. "Not yet. But then, I haven't talked to 'em yet, have I?"

Pete hugged Judd and Mr. Stein. Boyd smiled at Pete. "Don't know what I'd have done if you hadn't come along."

"I can't guarantee the gang won't be back," Pete said. "I'll have a couple people check on you."

The manager thanked him. "Next time you get back here, I hope this place'll look like Zeke's station, complete with a shelter underground."

Pete had been gone an hour when the phone rang. It was Lionel.

"This is the first call we've made since we've been here," Lionel said. "Took me an hour to find a pay phone."

"How's the school?" Judd said.

"You gotta see it," Lionel said. "Z's got enough supplies for an army. It's hidden, and there are a bunch of logs across the road that leads here, so we don't have to worry about the GC. And we could sure use a computer. There's no electricity or phone, but we've been trying to fix up an old generator. No luck yet."

"How's Vick doing?" Judd said.

"Okay," Lionel said. "Darrion too. We get up in the morning and start fixing the place up. We work till sundown. Vick's started a Bible study. We take turns leading it. Wish you were here."

"Yeah," Judd said.

"How about Stein?"

Judd cupped his hand around the phone. "He's learned a lot in the past few weeks, but he's driving me crazy about going to Israel."

"Bring him here."

"I'll talk to him," Judd said. "I don't think he'll settle for less than being at Teddy Kollek Stadium. And if you guys don't have electricity, I know he won't come. He'll miss watching the meeting."

Vicki couldn't believe the feeling of freedom. In the time since she had become a follower of Christ, she seemed to always be looking over her shoulder. At Nicolae High it had been Mrs. Jenness. At the detention center, she had watched her back constantly. Since the earthquake, the Global Community was her main threat.

Now, in the peaceful setting of the boarding school, she looked forward to getting up and going to work. The jobs were ordinary. The kids had to take turns preparing food. Everyone worked cleaning up the place. Darrion's tunnel idea was put on hold. There was simply too much essential work to be done first.

Other than Judd, Vicki's biggest frustration was Charlie. He pestered the kids constantly about getting the mark on his forehead. Vicki would explain the gospel again, but something was holding Charlie back from understanding or accepting the message.

Phoenix improved. His wound healed into a scab, and

a few weeks later Vicki could hardly tell he had been hurt. She wondered if Phoenix missed Ryan as much as she did.

Each night Phoenix would make his rounds. He would visit each room where the kids were sleeping. Finally, he would push the door of Vicki's room open and nuzzle against her.

If only Judd were here, Vicki thought.

————————————————

Judd was working on E-mails late one night, a few days before the start of the rescheduled Meeting of the Witnesses. Mr. Stein had gone to bed dejected.

Boyd burst into their downstairs hideout. "You gotta come see this!"

Judd ran to the office and saw a frantic-looking spokesman for the Global Community Aeronautics and Space Administration trying to explain yet another threat in the heavens. The news anchor asked how another comet could get by the watchful eyes of the Global Community scientists.

"I do not have an answer for that," the spokesman said, "except to say we have been on constant alert."

"Can you give us an estimate on the size and potential damage?" the spokesman said.

As the man talked, the network ran footage of the splashdown of the previous comet.

"This object is similar in size to the previous burning mountain," the spokesman said, "but it has a different makeup. This one seems to have the consistency of rotting wood."

"Wormwood!" Judd shouted.

"What?" Boyd said.

Judd grabbed a Bible and flipped to the book of Revelation. He found the reference in chapter 8.

"What does *wormwood* mean?" Boyd said.

"It's Greek," Judd said. "Tsion says it means 'bitterness.' "

The news anchor asked the GCASA spokesman, "Sir, we know now that the last comet killed a tremendous amount of fish and devastated ships on the Atlantic. What damage would this do?"

"I am told that Potentate Carpathia, along with his military and science advisors, have come up with a plan," the spokesman said. He held up an enlarged photo of a ground-to-air missile.

"They're gonna blast it from the sky," Judd said.

"If it's made of rotting wood," Boyd said, "it'll go into a million pieces."

"That's what I'm afraid of. The Bible says Wormwood will fall on a third of the rivers and on the springs of water. It'll basically poison the water supply. A lot of people are going to die because of it."

"When is the missile set to launch?" the news anchor said.

"The comet will be in range about midmorning tomorrow," the spokesman said.

"Vicki!" Judd shouted.

"What about her?" Boyd said.

"She and the others don't know about this," Judd said.

"Does this water affect believers too?" Boyd said.

"I don't know," Judd said, "but I can't take that chance. They might be drinking from a well. They have to be warned."

Mr. Stein agreed to go with Judd. After he was packed, Judd realized he didn't have directions to the boarding school. He dialed Z's place, but a message said there was trouble with the phone lines.

"We have to find Z," Judd said.

44

JUDD raced toward Chicago. He was mad at himself for not making a copy of the map. The sky was black. Mr. Stein pointed to an orange glow overhead. "There it is," he said. Throughout the drive the glow got gradually brighter.

Judd found a phone and called Z, but still couldn't get through. Near daybreak he and Mr. Stein pulled up to the station. The place looked deserted. Judd banged on doors and went to the back. Finally, Z's father, Zeke, let them in.

"Where's Z?"

"Couple suspicious people been hangin' around the last few days," Zeke said. "He's lyin' low."

Zeke scribbled directions on a scrap of paper. "I can't say what kind of shape the access road will be in."

"How long will it take us?" Judd said.

"A few hours."

Judd thanked him and told him about Wormwood. "I

been watchin' it on TV," Zeke said, pointing to an ancient black-and-white set.

Nicolae Carpathia's face flashed on the screen, and Zeke turned up the volume.

"And I commend the members of the scientific community for coming up with this brilliant plan," Nicolae said. "Ever since the last threat from the skies, our team has been working around the clock. Their hard work has paid off.

"In less than an hour, we will launch this marvel of technology. I assure you, this burning mass of solar driftwood will be vaporized as soon as our missile reaches it. We should see little or no effect on the earth's surface."

Judd shook his head. "Don't bet on it."

Zeke handed Judd and Mr. Stein a few bottles of water. "Be prepared."

Judd and Mr. Stein roared off, going as fast as they could toward the boarding school. Judd wished he could see the launch of the missile. He was sure Carpathia would try to make as much out of it as possible. Not only could he use this to impress the world and gain followers, but the launch would also take attention away from Tsion Ben-Judah.

Judd had pulled onto I-55 when he saw a flash of light. He pulled to the side of the road and unsnapped his laptop. "I have to see this!" he said.

Moments later, Judd and Mr. Stein watched live Internet coverage of the missile's launch. As Carpathia beamed, a team of scientists showed charts and simulations of what would happen when the missile hit its target.

To everyone's amazement, the missile didn't strike Wormwood. Instead, the flaming meteor split itself into billions of pieces. The missile passed through the dust without exploding, as pieces of Wormwood wafted toward the atmosphere.

Judd shut his computer and drove on. By late morning they were dodging bits of fiery wood that landed everywhere, including waterways and reservoirs.

"Surely they will see this and know not to drink from contaminated waters," Mr. Stein said.

"I hope so."

Judd followed Zeke's directions until he came to a road blocked by logs. "This has to be it."

When he and Mr. Stein drove up, the members of the Young Trib Force welcomed them.

Vicki was the last to emerge, her hands dirty from working on the generator. Mr. Stein hugged her. She put out a hand to Judd, then realized it was black with grease.

"It's okay," Judd said, taking her hand. "We were worried since you guys didn't have—"

"Wormwood," Vicki said. "We've been studying. Didn't you think we could handle it?"

"It's not that," Judd said.

Vicki walked away.

Judd put his computer on the kitchen table and pulled up the coverage. Video reports showed fragments of burning wood falling on Paris, London, New Babylon, Seattle, and Bangkok. Reports filtered in about those who drank the contaminated water. A reporter in South America stood near a small village. The camera panned away from him, showing scattered bodies of men and women in the road.

A panic for clean water sent people scurrying to stores. Shocked owners were dazed as hundreds of people emptied the shelves in minutes.

A grim Nicolae Carpathia faced the camera once again. This time he did not praise the work of his scientists, but called the Global Community to order.

"We must work together to overcome this terrible tragedy," Carpathia said. "I am asking the cooperation of individuals and groups. I once again must ask those who have been waiting for the conference in Israel to postpone your meeting."

"What?" Mr. Stein said.

"For the safety of attendees," Carpathia continued, "I believe it is best for all concerned to delay this important conference."

"I'd like to know what Tsion thinks about that," Vicki said.

The kids didn't have to wait long. Judd accessed the rabbi's bulletin board and within minutes saw a message. The first half spoke to Jewish believers. The other half was aimed at Carpathia himself.

The time has come, Ben-Judah wrote. *We must not waste another moment. I urge as many of the 144,000 witnesses as possible to come together in Israel next week. This will be a time of teaching, training, and encouragement we will never forget.*

Tsion then referred to Nicolae as simply *Mr. Carpathia*.

"With all the titles that guy keeps getting," Lionel said, "that has to get to him."

We will be in Jerusalem as scheduled, with or without your approval, permission, or promised protection, Tsion wrote. *The glory of the Lord will be our rear guard.*

Before dinner, Vicki approached what the kids called the reading room. Lionel had asked her to meet him there. She walked in and was surprised to see Judd.

"What are you—?" Judd said.

"Lionel asked me to come here," Vicki said.

"He asked me the same thing," Judd said.

Lionel came up behind Vicki and closed the doors. "Okay," he said, "now that I finally have you two together I wanna get a few things straight."

Vicki folded her arms. Judd leaned against a window that overlooked the balcony.

"I've taken an informal poll," Lionel said.

Judd scowled. "About what?"

"About you and Vicki," Lionel said.

Vicki said, "What happens between us—"

"Is my business," Lionel interrupted. "And it's the business of every member of this group. We're supposed to be part of the same body. We're supposed to support each other. We look to you two as our leaders."

There was a long silence. Finally, Judd said, "What did you ask the group?"

"If there was one thing you could change about the group, what would it be?"

"And?" Vicki said.

Lionel looked at the ground. "Other than getting Ryan back, we all agreed. It was to have you two working together instead of apart."

Vicki scratched her nose. Judd looked out the window.

Vicki started to speak but Judd interrupted. "That Charlie kid is on the ground out there."

"Haven't you been listening to anything Lionel said?"

"No, I mean, I think something's wrong with him," Judd said.

Phoenix barked. "What's Phoenix doing outside?" Vicki said. "We locked him up so he wouldn't drink any of the bad water."

"Well, he's out there on the ground with Charlie," Judd said.

Vicki rushed downstairs with Judd and Lionel right behind her. Charlie coughed and sputtered as he lay on the ground. He grabbed his neck.

"What happened?" Vicki said. "Did you drink from the well?"

"Only a little," Charlie said.

"I told you to leave it alone," Vicki said.

"I know," Charlie said, "I saw those girls and they asked for a drink."

"What girls?" Judd said, out of breath.

"I don't know their names," Charlie said. "I just remember 'em from back home."

"What'd they look like?" Lionel said.

"I don't know," Charlie said, coughing and sputtering harder.

"He's hallucinating," Judd said. "Get him a drink of good water."

Vicki rushed to find a bottle. Phoenix followed. Vicki locked the dog safely away. When she returned, Judd and Lionel had Charlie sitting up on the porch. Charlie drank deeply, but still seemed queasy from the well water.

"It was so sour," Charlie said. "I can't get the taste out of my mouth."

"It's lucky you didn't drink more," Judd said.

"One of the girls did," Charlie said.

Judd rolled his eyes.

Vicki kept a close eye on Charlie as they ate dinner. His face was drained of color and he said he was tired. Vicki made a bed for Charlie downstairs and Darrion volunteered to watch him.

Judd got Vicki's attention, and the two went to the balcony.

"I think Lionel's right," Judd said.

"About what?" Vicki said.

Judd sighed. "I know I've come across too strong at times. I admit that. And I've made you feel like your ideas aren't as good as mine."

"Right," Vicki said.

"I want to be mature about this and stop fighting," Judd said. "Maybe if we got back to being friends . . . "

Vicki put her hands in her hip pockets. "I can work on that. But you can't ask me to stop coming up with ideas. God worked it out. There's somebody out there right now who needs our help. I want to be here when he or she walks through our door."

Judd nodded. "I was wrong. This place is just what we're looking for."

Vicki closed her eyes. *If he'd only said that a couple months ago we wouldn't have had to go through this.*

When she opened them again, Judd was standing over the railing, peering into the woods. "What is it?" Vicki said.

"I thought I saw somebody at the side of the house."

Judd called a meeting of the Young Trib Force that evening. Charlie wasn't much better, but at least he wasn't getting worse. Judd wondered if it had been a good idea to bring Charlie to their new safe house, but he didn't dare bring that up with Vicki and the others now. The ice was just beginning to thaw.

Judd wondered whether he could lead the kids. Would they listen to him without thinking he would boss them around?

Mr. Stein asked to say something before the meeting began. "I appreciate all you've done for me. I have been insistent on going to Israel. It has been my main goal since becoming a follower of Jesus. But it looks as if the meeting will begin next week, and I still have no way to get there."

"What about a commercial flight?" Lionel said.

"If I were able to change my identity like you have," Mr. Stein said, "I would do it. But I'm afraid it's too risky.

I have enough money to buy my own plane, but I have no access to a pilot. I can only assume it is not God's will that I should go."

The kids groaned. Mr. Stein stood with his head down.

The door burst open. Judd whirled. Two girls. One had her arm over the other one's shoulder and looked pale. The other held a gun.

"Stay where you are, Stein!" the girl with the gun yelled.

Lionel glanced at Judd.

"Nobody moves," the girl screamed.

Vicki whispered something to Darrion.

The girls' clothes were in tatters, their hair out of place. They looked hungry and exhausted. But there was no mistake. These were the two surviving Morale Monitors of the Global Community, Melinda and Felicia.

"Everybody on the ground!" Melinda shouted.

ABOUT THE AUTHORS

Jerry B. Jenkins (www.jerryjenkins.com) is the writer of the Left Behind series. He owns the Jerry B. Jenkins Christian Writers Guild, an organization dedicated to mentoring aspiring authors. Former vice president for publishing for the Moody Bible Institute of Chicago, he also served many years as editor of *Moody* magazine and is now Moody's writer-at-large.

His writing has appeared in publications as varied as *Reader's Digest, Parade, Guideposts*, in-flight magazines, and dozens of other periodicals. Jenkins's biographies include books with Billy Graham, Hank Aaron, Bill Gaither, Luis Palau, Walter Payton, Orel Hershiser, and Nolan Ryan, among many others. His books appear regularly on the *New York Times, USA Today, Wall Street Journal,* and *Publishers Weekly* best-seller lists.

Jerry is also the writer of the nationally syndicated sports story comic strip *Gil Thorp*, distributed to newspapers across the United States by Tribune Media Services.

Jerry and his wife, Dianna, live in Colorado and have three grown sons.

Dr. Tim LaHaye (www.timlahaye.com), who conceived the idea of fictionalizing an account of the Rapture and the Tribulation, is a noted author, minister, and nationally recognized speaker on Bible prophecy. He is the founder of both Tim LaHaye Ministries and The PreTrib Research Center. He also recently cofounded the Tim LaHaye School of Prophecy at Liberty University. Presently Dr. LaHaye speaks at many of the major Bible prophecy conferences in the U.S. and Canada, where his current prophecy books are very popular.

Dr. LaHaye holds a doctor of ministry degree from Western Theological Seminary and a doctor of literature degree from Liberty University. For twenty-five years he pastored one of the nation's outstanding churches in San Diego, which grew to three locations. It was during that time that he founded two accredited Christian high schools, a Christian school system of ten schools, and Christian Heritage College.

Dr. LaHaye has written over forty books that have been published in more than thirty languages. He has written books on a wide variety of subjects, such as family life, temperaments, and Bible prophecy. His current fiction works, the Left Behind series, written with Jerry B. Jenkins, continue to appear on the best-seller lists of the Christian Booksellers Association, *Publishers Weekly, Wall Street Journal, USA Today*, and the *New York Times*.

He is the father of four grown children and grandfather of nine. Snow skiing, waterskiing, motorcycling, golfing, vacationing with family, and jogging are among his leisure activities.

COMING SOON!

Look for the next two books in the Young Trib Force Series!

www.areUthirsty.com

well . . . are you?

Undercover PRINCESS

Undercover
PRINCESS

CONNIE GLYNN

HARPER

An Imprint of HarperCollinsPublishers

Library of Congress Control Number: 2018941364
ISBN 978-0-06-284780-5

Typography by Jessie Gang
18 19 20 21 22   PC/LSCH   10 9 8 7 6 5 4 3 2 1
❖
Originally published in the UK in 2017 by Penguin Random House Children's
First US Edition, 2018

For my wonderful family and all the gorgeous witches who've charmed my life.

Special thanks to Richard and Mark, who have supported me ferociously in every step I've taken, Holly and Ruth for pushing me and helping me achieve my vision, and Evan for the much-appreciated math help. And one last thank you to my beautiful and kind audience— thank you, thank you, thank you.

Undercover
PRINCESS

PART ONE
Welcome to Rosewood Hall

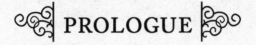

PROLOGUE

THERE ARE PLACES IN OUR world in which wondrous and whimsical things seem more capable of happening than anywhere else. You can recognize them because they are thick with an atmosphere that seems out of time and place with the rest of reality. Sometimes they exist naturally, with hidden waterfalls or secret meadows filled with flourishing wild flowers. Sometimes they are man-made, like empty playgrounds at twilight or dusty antique shops rich with history. But occasionally, although it is rare, these spaces exist in a certain type of person. You may have met such a person yourself. They may not, at first glance, seem particularly charismatic or especially intellectual, but as you spend more time with them, it seems they may possess the power to change everything . . .

Princess Eleanor Prudence Wolfson, sole heir of King Alexander Wolfson and next in line for the throne of Maradova, did not live in one of these spaces, nor was she one of these people, but she was in desperate need of both.

"I am going to this school!" Eleanor slammed the brochure on the table with a loud *thwack*, causing the cups of

breakfast tea to wobble on top of their saucers.

Alexander Wolfson didn't even look up from his newspaper to reply.

"No," he said blankly.

"I am next in line for the Maravish throne. I think the teeny-tiny decision of which school I attend is something I am capable of managing myself."

Alexander looked up at his wife, Queen Matilde, who was sitting across the table from him.

She shrugged. "She does have a point, Alex," she said amiably, delicately dropping a lump of sugar into her teacup and stifling a smile.

This was not the parental solidarity King Alexander had been hoping for.

"See?" said Eleanor. "Even Mom agrees with me."

Alexander remained firmly fixated on his newspaper, feigning an image of complete composure. He took a sip of tea.

"Edwina"—he gestured to their maid—"would you kindly take the empty plates to the kitchen, please?"

"Of course, Your Majesty." Edwina expertly stacked the crumb-covered trays and exited the dining hall with a skilled smoothness, her feet barely making a sound on the oak flooring. The large double doors closed behind her, creaking softly as she eased them shut.

Once Alexander was sure she was a reasonable distance

down the hall, and safely away from any domestic out-bursts, he looked back down at his newspaper and said, "My answer is no."

Eleanor let out an exasperated screech and stamped her foot. "You could at least *look* at the brochure!" she snapped, snatching the newspaper from her father's fingertips.

Alexander was forced to look up at his daughter.

Eleanor had always been a challenging child. She was anything but a typical princess; she would choose fiery political arguments and sneaking out to loud, rowdy con-certs over mild polite conversation any day, and more than anything she *despised* elaborate formal functions—or at least she assumed she did, having refused to ever attend one. But she was smart, she was confident, and she was passionate—and for Alexander, that was all far more important than any of the traditional values expected of her. Although occasionally he did wish she'd watch her language around her grandparents.

As much as he wanted Eleanor to be happy and live a life free of the commitments of royalty, the fact remained that she would be queen one day and would eventually need to accept that responsibility. He was determined to find a way to make his daughter realize she could enjoy her royal obligations; something he'd had to learn himself when he was younger.

"You are going to Aston Court, as have all the rulers of

Maradova for the last hundred years, and you're going to like it . . . whether you like it or not."

Matilde chuckled softly across the table as she sipped her tea.

"No." Eleanor echoed her father's stern tone. "I'm going to Rosewood Hall in England."

Eleanor's voice didn't waver. She was determined. She would be kicking and screaming long before she was caught entering the gates of Aston Court.

Alexander sighed deeply.

For Eleanor, attending Aston Court wasn't about simply "not getting her way" as it would be for most teenagers. It would be the end of her freedom as an undeclared royal altogether. She would officially have to come out to the public as the heir to the Maravish throne; she would no longer be able to sneak out or refuse to attend royal functions, and she'd have to stop dyeing her hair and start dressing more appropriately. Her responsibilities would begin and she could never lead any semblance of a normal life again.

Alexander picked up his newspaper and folded it neatly. He prepared himself for the ensuing heated shouting match, a regular occurrence since Eleanor had hit her teenage years.

"Please, Dad."

This caught Alexander completely off-guard, so rarely did his daughter plead; she was far too stubborn. He

looked up, expecting to see her usual indomitable pout, but instead was confronted with a look of real desperation. He found himself struggling to remember why he was so determined to say no, before quickly reminding himself that Aston Court was the only school that could guarantee her safety once she was officially announced to the public as their princess. There she would be under expert surveillance; she'd be safe and she'd be perfectly prepared for her future. It was Aston Court or nothing. Yet for all his certainty he found himself gingerly reaching out his hand as Eleanor placed the Rosewood brochure in his palm.

She wrapped her hands around his and squeezed lightly. "All you have to do is read it. That's all I ask."

Across the table Queen Matilde took another discreet sip of her tea before delicately placing the cup on her saucer. "You know, it may be the tea talking, but I've always been fond of England, haven't you, Alexander?" She looked up at her husband, her carefree expression dropping momentarily as her eyes locked with his. The Maravish king held his wife's gaze for what felt like the longest few seconds of his life. She had that effect on him.

He let out a long sigh before finally giving up.

"Fine, I will read the brochure, but that's it."

Eleanor let out a squeal of delight and relief. "Yes! Thank you, thank you, thank you! I know you'll be happy with it, Dad, I promise." And with that, she stuffed a croissant in

her mouth and ran out before he had time to fully register what had just happened.

The door slammed behind her, leaving Alexander and Matilde to sit in the wake of its echo. He looked up at his wife again as the sound slowly faded to silence. She smiled sweetly back at him.

"She can't go," he said. "It's too dangerous to have the sole heir to the Maravish throne traipsing around some British boarding school when she should be learning how to rule one day."

Matilde turned serious again, delicately repositioning her cutlery in front of her so that each fork, knife and spoon was perfectly in line.

As she looked up, Alexander was acutely aware of the fire twinkling behind her eyes.

"You know as well as I do that Rosewood is no ordinary school, and, secondly—" she stopped for a moment, forcing him to look her directly in the eye—"as you've stated before, she has not yet been formally announced. No one knows she's the princess, so this may very well be a way for her to live her last few years as a carefree teenager before taking on her royal duties. I *know* you wish you'd had that chance."

Alexander was momentarily taken aback. Was his wife really suggesting what he thought she was?

"You want her to go to this school undercover?" he asked.

Matilde instantly smiled again, dropping her intensity like it was as simple as putting on and taking off a hat.

"Right now all you have to do is read the brochure." She lifted her teacup to her mouth, then paused and added, "Besides, if things turn sour, we can always send in Jamie."

Alexander stared at his wife in bewilderment and adoration. He chuckled softly to himself. Something told him that reading the Rosewood brochure was not going to be the end of the matter.

1

THERE IS A SMALL BLUE bakery in St. Ives with bushy
clumps of wisteria growing on the pebbledashed walls.
Through the front windows there lies a visible thick coat
of dust over the sheet-covered surfaces that glitters in the
air when the sun shines. A faded candy-striped canopy
covers the doors with a sign above reading MS. PUMPKIN'S
PASTRIES, although no baking has taken place for many
years. Above the bakery you will find a previously humble home, now crammed with gaudy items and kitsch
displays, a futile attempt by the new owner to enhance
the homely setting. Yet one room remains untouched by
the new inhabitant, a soft haven filled with the house's
happy memories.

Lottie Pumpkin lives in the attic of 12 Bethesda Hill, St.
Ives, with her stepmother, Beady. There she has made herself a sanctuary, hidden away in the cozy loft overlooking
the sea. It is a room of creaky floorboards, walls lined with
photos from her childhood, and books bursting with fairy
tales. But today she would be leaving her bedroom and her

house, and Cornwall. Today she would be moving away to live at Rosewood Hall.

"Lottie!" Beady's piercing tone rang in Lottie's ears, making her freeze as she lowered the last item of clothing into a suitcase.

"Yes?" Lottie replied, her eyes involuntarily squeezing shut. She heard movement and Lottie's stepmother appeared in the doorway. A creamy green mask covered her face, and her red hair was hidden away in a neat towel bun. Beady was an incredibly beautiful woman who took her appearance very seriously. She was also *far too young to be burdened with the responsibility of taking care of Lottie* and it was *extremely generous of her to sacrifice her life for someone else's kid*, which she regularly reminded Lottie about.

"I completely forgot you were leaving today!" She said this as if it were extremely amusing.

Lottie gave her a pleasing smile that she'd performed a million times. "That's okay, I'm—"

Before she could finish, Beady let out a loud cackle.

"Just kidding, how could I forget? You never shut up about the place—" she laughed again—"although if they're letting you in it can't be *that* prestigious." Lottie flinched a little and Beady paused in her laughter. "I'm only kidding, Lottie. Don't take things so seriously."

Lottie held her smile tightly and attempted a laugh, but

Beady's eyes had moved to the two pink suitcases on the floor.

"Those are big. I hope you're not expecting a ride. That's a lot to ask of someone." Beady gave her an injured look, as if she were being very patient.

"No, it's fine," Lottie replied, trying to be as pleasant as she could. She absolutely did not want to upset Beady: she knew how difficult it had been for her having to look after Lottie when her mother passed away. All she wanted was to make life easy for her. "Ollie and his mom are giving me a ride."

Beady's eyebrows shot up in a disapproving way.

"That's very generous of them. I hope you make sure his mom knows how grateful you are she has to do that for you."

"Of course." Lottie nodded and that appeared to satisfy Beady.

"Good, well . . ." Beady paused, looking around the room as if taking it in for the first time. She chewed the side of her mouth, turning her gaze to give Lottie a once-over, then she took in a long breath as if preparing herself for what she was about to say. "You worked hard . . . I hope it doesn't disappoint you."

Lottie gulped. She knew Beady was happy she'd gotten into Rosewood; it meant she could have the house to herself at last. Getting into Rosewood not only fulfilled a

promise Lottie had made to her mom, but it was the greatest gift she could give her stepmother.

"Thank you," Lottie replied.

Beady waved her hand as if dismissing the conversation.

"Anyway, I need to go and wash off this face mask. Have a safe trip."

As soon as she was gone, Lottie quickly got back to packing, but it wasn't long before she was interrupted again.

"What on earth are you wearing?" Ollie's sarcastic tone drifted into Lottie's bedroom. He stood leaning against the door frame, his arms crossed as he watched Lottie pack up the last items in her room.

"Ollie!" Lottie's hand rushed to her chest in shock at the sudden appearance of her best friend. "How did you get up here? And how many times do I have to tell you to knock?" Lottie was huffing slightly from trying to squish down her suitcases. Ollie was thirteen, the same age as Lottie, but even though he was taller than her, he'd retained his baby face, which reminded her of soft-serve ice cream on the beach and other happy childhood memories.

"I had to sneak past the wicked witch. Did you know her skin's turned green finally?" Ollie said with a devilish smile.

Lottie giggled, but she couldn't ignore his comment from before. She looked down at her outfit, brushing down her dress self-consciously. "And what exactly is wrong with

my outfit?" she said indignantly.

Ollie laughed, grinning at her with his signature cheeky smile. Clumps of dog hair dotted his jeans, a permanent feature that he never seemed to care about.

"Isn't it a little too fancy for the first day of school?"

"*Too fancy?!*" Lottie couldn't believe he'd suggest something so ridiculous. "Nothing is *too fancy* for Rosewood Hall. I need to fit in. I can't have my clothes making me an outcast on the first day."

Lottie began picking at a nonexistent spot on the collar of her dress. "Most of the students probably have their clothes tailor-made out of gold or something."

Ollie casually strolled into the room, taking a seat on Lottie's bed. He pursed his lips as he glanced around the bedroom. Usually so alive with Lottie's special brand of handmade quirkiness, it was now stripped bare, everything she owned crammed into two pink suitcases.

"Well," Ollie began, reaching into his pocket, "if you can take a moment off from worrying about what other people think of you . . ." He pulled out a crumpled envelope and a worn-out Polaroid that Lottie recognized from his bedroom wall. "These are for you."

Lottie reached out for them, but Ollie whipped his hand back.

"You can't open the letter until you're on the train."

Lottie nodded with an exasperated smile and he slowly

placed both gifts in her hand. It was a photograph she'd seen thousands of times: the two of them at the beach, their noses covered in ice cream and beaming grins on both their greedy faces. Even though the colors had begun to fade to sepia, you could still see the tiara on Lottie's head and the horns on Ollie's. As children, the two had demanded to wear these dress-up items every day and everywhere. Ollie had declared he was the fairy Puck from Shakespeare's *A Midsummer Night's Dream* after they'd watched an open-air performance at the beach one evening. He'd been completely infatuated with all the mischief the character got away with and assumed he too could get away with being naughty so long as he was wearing his horns. Lottie's tiara, on the other hand, had a less happy-go-lucky origin. Her thumb lingered over the accessory in the photo, a little pang striking her heart as she remembered the day she'd received it.

"I'll give you some time to say goodbye," he said, before effortlessly picking up both her suitcases and carrying them down the stairs to the car. When he was gone she carefully placed Ollie's gifts with the rest of her most important belongings, which she'd laid out on the now-bare bed so as not to forget them. She put each item into her handbag: first the weathered Polaroid and letter from Ollie, followed by her favorite sketchbook, her most loyal stuffed companion, Mr. Truffles, a framed photo of her mother, Marguerite,

in her graduation gown, and, finally—looking very out of place among the other objects—a crescent-moon tiara, her most valued possession. It had taken Lottie all of sixty minutes to pack her entire life into two pink suitcases, one denim backpack, and a small over-shoulder handbag with a sturdy white strap. She looked over the empty room.

I did it, Mom, she thought. *I got into Rosewood just like I promised.*

To Lottie (the Honorary Princess of St. Ives),

Feels like I barely saw you this past year you were studying so much, and now you're off to live on the other side of the country. It won't be the same without you, but I'm sure you'll have enough adventures for the both of us.

I wanted to get you a fairy-tale book as a goodbye present as I know how much you love them, but I fear you own them all already, so I figured I'd give you this Polaroid to remind you of my existence every day.

Can't wait to hear about all the crazy things you get up to at Rosewood. I'm so proud of you for getting in, but I'll miss you a lot *pauses to shed a tear.* AND HOW DARE YOU LEAVE ME ALONE IN THIS TOURIST TRAP!!! TRAI-TOR!! (See how I turn my difficult emotions into anger as a defense mechanism??)

Your friend, Ollie

PS Bring me back a gold crown or something—I assume you get one upon arrival 😉

✳

Lottie smiled as she reread the note from her best friend and allowed herself a moment to feel a little sentimental about leaving her humble life in Cornwall. She gazed out of the train window at the lush countryside thundering past and thought back to the day last year when she had submitted her application to Rosewood Hall. Five years ago she'd promised her mother that she would find a way to go there. There had been a storm the night before and the world outside was soggy and wet. Her mother lay wrapped in four different blankets, her body skinny and weak from the sickness that had consumed her, but an unyielding strength persisted in her eyes. She'd looked at Lottie and smiled her familiar warm smile.

"You can do anything you put your mind to, little princess."

The submission process had been arduous and intimidating. Rosewood rarely accepted applicants on a scholarship unless they showed outstanding potential; it was a school that prided itself on excellence. Rosewood was not the type of school one just *decided* to go to; you couldn't simply pick up a brochure and say you wanted to attend. And, as Lottie lived alone with her stepmother in her late mother's bakery, there was no way she could pull together the funds to pay the school fees. But Lottie had persisted. She'd worked tirelessly, forgone social activities and hobbies, waking up early to do the chores before locking herself away in her

room to study relentlessly. All the while she dreamed of the day she would walk through the gates of Rosewood and take her place among the children of the elite. Ready, of course, to make a positive impact on the world.

"We are now approaching Rosewood Central. Please ensure you take all your belongings with you as you leave the train."

As she grabbed her two suitcases, Lottie wondered momentarily if she would be the only Rosewood student traveling to the boarding school on public transportation. She assumed most of the students would have private cars, but on the school map she and Ollie had spent hours studying, they'd seen what could only be a landing pad— did students really travel by helicopter? Should she have made the effort to also travel by helicopter? She knew it was a silly thought, but it succeeded in reminding her how different she was from the other students.

Suddenly very anxious, she felt around in her bag for her crescent-moon tiara. Her mother had been a fantastic storyteller and had read to Lottie every night before bed. *The Glass Slipper* was Lottie's favorite tale and she had asked her mom to read her every version of the story they could find, fascinated by how different they all were. Her mother had explained how fairy tales, like most things in the world, had evolved and adapted, but what Lottie was

most drawn to was the prevailing sense of putting good-ness out into the world. No matter which version of the story she read, the kindness of the princess remained, and more than anything that was what Lottie wanted to emu-late. And so, for her seventh birthday, Lottie's mother had given her a silver tiara with a crescent moon on top—a family heirloom. It had been handed down through gen-erations of Pumpkins, along with the legacy of Rosewood Hall.

Lottie watched as the scenery outside the train window blurred into the memory of her seventh birthday party.

"This was gifted to one of our ancestors, who had the privilege of attending Rosewood hundreds of years ago. He passed it down, and eventually my grandfather bestowed it to me. One day, if you have children of your own, you can pass it on to them."

Lottie barely took in her mother's words, unable to pull her eyes away from the object in the box.

She delicately placed the tiara upon her head. But, alas, her tiny seven-year-old head had been simply . . . too tiny. The tiara had fallen almost immediately, landing on the hard wood of her living-room floor and looking very out of place among the sea of birthday cake crumbs scattered about. Being the sensitive girl that she was, Lottie had proceeded to burst into tears. It was not necessarily the

fact the tiara didn't fit that had the young Lottie feeling so overwhelmed, but that the tiara—this pristine object of magnificence, so incongruous in her humble home—made everything surrounding it seem so painfully ordinary. It appeared to glow with a glittering grandeur, yet its light only succeeded in illuminating quite how plain the world around it was.

"Lottie's crying *again*," grumbled one of the party attendees.

"Shut up, Kate," Ollie said. "Don't be mean just because you didn't win musical chairs."

"THE SONG STOPPED ON ME!"

This sharp exchange had only served to make Lottie more upset—now her party guests were unhappy too. Just as Lottie had been ready to escalate into true floods of tears, her mother appeared at her side to save the day.

"Okay, settle down, everyone. Kate, there's a special treat for you, if you let Thomas keep his musical chairs prize, and, Lottie darling, you can clip the tiara on with these." Marguerite reached into her apron pocket and presented her with two crocodile hair clips.

"Now, everyone—this tiara is actually very special." She picked it up and Lottie noticed how natural it looked in her hand. "You see, this tiara has magic powers."

All the children calmed down instantly, eagerly awaiting

one of Marguerite's enchanting stories.

"Whoever wears this tiara can achieve anything they put their mind to, and touching it grants the wearer all the good qualities of a princess."

As she spoke, Marguerite Pumpkin carefully clipped the tiara on to Lottie's head, delicately sweeping her hair back to cover the clips.

"Now, what are three good qualities princesses have that we can think of?" She looked at the children, but they went shy, as children often do when put on the spot. "How about brave? Do you think princesses are brave?" They nodded their heads. "Now what else?"

"Oh, oh, they're pretty!" Ollie blurted.

Marguerite chuckled softly.

"Well, yes, they are often pretty, but that prettiness comes from within because they are . . ." She put out her hand, inviting someone to fill in the blank.

"They're kind!" said Kate, smiling at Lottie.

"Yes, good, Kate, what else?"

Lottie, feeling encouraged by Kate's smile, spoke up. "They never give up on their dreams."

"Excellent, Lottie. What's a word we could use to describe that?"

"DELUSIONAL!" Ollie shouted. Everyone laughed, except Lottie, who simply rolled her eyes.

"Er . . . hardworking?" offered Charlie. There was a moment of silence as the children continued to hum and haw, all trying to think of an appropriate word. Until it came to Lottie like a lightning bolt. It was so clear; this word suddenly seemed the most powerful and important word in the world.

"*Unstoppable.*"

Lottie knew as soon as she'd spoken it that this was the power she wanted the tiara to grant her: the power to never, ever give up, to be an unstoppable force of good whether the world liked it or not.

To think it was now six years since she'd received it seemed so odd. Her life had become vastly different after her mother passed away, and sometimes she still struggled to believe it wasn't all just a terrible, sad dream. She shook her head, forcing the bad feelings away, and put the Polaroid back in her purse before her fingers found the tiara in her bag. She took a moment to squeeze it, lightly caressing the little gems along the front. She would have preferred to put the tiara on, but touching it would have to do while she was on the train.

She then recited to herself her personal mantra. "I will be kind, I will be brave, I will be unstoppable."

She could do this. She would fit in. She would succeed at Rosewood, just like she'd promised her mother.

"This station is Rosewood Central. Disembark here for Rosewood Hall."

Lottie picked up her suitcases with a surge of determination. She was ready to start the next magical chapter of her life—and she would prove she belonged in this world.

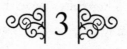

LOTTIE TOOK ONE OF THE shuttle cars from the station. It dropped her off at the school entrance, a grand set of cast-iron gates, ornately embellished with the letters R and H, set in the massive wall that enclosed the front grounds of Rosewood Hall. The open gates led to a large canopied structure, under which all the incoming students were gathering. The roof was supported by stone pillars that were decorated with carved thorns and roses. The wind through the pillars made an odd siren call, the noise sending an excited shudder down her spine.

She gazed around and felt a pang of nerves as she took in the other students and their incredible array of luxury cars. Lottie recognized a few of the vehicles from spending so much time with Ollie; she was sure he would be drooling if he could see them. None of the other students seemed to be carrying their own luggage and most of them were intently tapping away at their phones before they would have to hand them over for the start of term.

Rosewood was open to students from the age of eleven, so many of these children would know each other already,

making Lottie feel even more like an outsider. Lottie turned to thank her driver but an unexpectedly strong breeze blew through the pillars, drowning out her voice. That's when she saw her.

A mysterious figure on the periphery.

Behind the car that had brought her here was a girl— tall and lean with cropped, jet-black hair and clad in a beaten-up black leather jacket, a guitar case casually slung over her shoulder. She was not like the other students; something about the girl screamed of danger—she was like a dark brooding storm cloud. She was pulling suitcases out of the back of a private car with ease; the chauffeur tried to help but was met with dismissive hand gestures, so he stood to the side looking distressed. Lottie couldn't see the girl's face properly as it was covered by a large pair of sunglasses. She felt a sudden instinctive need to get a closer look at the girl. It felt as if there were an energy between them—something was drawing her toward her. But before she could come to terms with this strange sensation of familiarity, her view was cut off by a pile of books with legs.

"Excuse me, sorry, coming through!"

Lottie hurriedly pulled her pink suitcases out of the way. She'd never seen such a small person carry so much stuff. It looked as if she should topple over at any moment, but somehow she managed to appear balanced and composed.

Clearly this girl was much stronger than her size suggested. Even though her face was hidden behind piles of books and cases, Lottie could see masses of tight dark ringlets. How on earth she knew where she was going was a mystery. She stepped around Lottie just as a group of older students raced past, as if she'd timed it perfectly.

"*Greetings!*"

Lottie jumped as the girl's face popped out from the side of the books with a beaming grin, revealing two large brown eyes magnified by a thick pair of round spectacles. Lottie's brain immediately conjured up the image of an owl.

The tiny owl girl glanced down at Lottie's cases. "You must be a Rosewood fledgling—how exciting!" She looked up at Lottie, considering her curiously before her grin burst back on to her face and she laughed. "I appreciate your commitment to the color pink," she said, nodding at Lottie's outfit, cases, and accessories.

Lottie felt her cheeks going hot, a reflex she'd been cursed with since she was little.

"Thank you, I . . ."

"That's quite a prominent idiopathic craniofacial erythema you suffer from."

The owl girl leaned forward to scrutinize Lottie's face, causing her to involuntarily lean back and blink. She considered herself to have a pretty good vocabulary, but this was beyond her.

"Blushing, that is. It's quite charming really; although it can be an early symptom of erythematotelangiectatic rosacea . . ."

As the owl girl continued on like this, Lottie followed her along the path toward the school entrance, nodding dumbly.

Already Lottie felt like she had entered another world as she looked around. The pathway was framed by three stone arches. As they walked through them, Lottie could make out an intricately engraved copper portrait mounted at the top of each arch. She recognized the figures as the patrons of the three legacies to Rosewood: Florence Ivy in the middle, Balthazar Conch to the left, and the twins, Shray and Sana Stratus, occupying the last one on the right. They glared down at the students, the weight of their expectant gaze making Lottie gulp involuntarily.

Be brave! she repeated to herself.

"I personally think it's cute, but if you were also prone to erythrophobia that could be a problem."

The owl girl giggled to herself and turned to Lottie, smiling. It took her a moment to realize the other girl had finished talking and that she needed to respond.

"Erythrophobia?" she asked. Should she know this word? Had she just exposed herself as stupid?

The owl girl stared at her before unexpectedly bursting into laughter again. The sound of her giggling was so

adorable that Lottie felt as if she were being licked by a puppy.

"Sorry, I was definitely rambling. Here . . ." The girl did a strange shimmy, transferring her cargo to one hand.

Lottie was sure everything would topple this time, but to her amazement it stayed upright, like some kind of bizarre circus performance. The owl girl reached into her pocket with her newly freed hand and pulled out a small piece of paper. "I'm Binah."

Lottie took the offering and quickly realized it was a business card. A BUSINESS CARD? They were thirteen; what could any thirteen-year-old possibly need a business card for?

BINAH FAE

VOLUNTEER LIBRARY ASSISTANT

FOR STUDY ADVICE AND TUTORING PLEASE

SEND ALL REQUESTS BY MAIL TO:

Binah Fae, Stratus 304B,
Rosewood Hall, Oxfordshire

Lottie was momentarily overcome with dread; did she need a business card too? Was that the done thing for children of the "elite?"

She struggled to speak for a moment before replying.

"Hi, Binah. I'm Charlotte . . . but please call me Lottie." She prayed that her first name alone would be sufficient and, to her relief, Binah smiled with total sincerity.

"It's a pleasure to meet you, Lottie."

The two girls stepped out through the final archway and Lottie followed suit as Binah left her luggage with a woman in a golf cart, giving her name and year and watching her luggage disappear up the huge hill toward the main school buildings. Lottie slowly turned a full circle, taking in the school grounds. Behind her was the massive wall; to her right and left, disappearing around the back of the distant buildings, were the ancient rosewood trees that gave the school its name. The path was lined with roses of all different colors and species. They didn't simply flourish; they appeared to glow with hidden magic.

The uphill path took them to a stone archway that gave entry to a courtyard in front of the reception hall. The entrance to the reception was a vast pair of oak doors, framed by a stone arch carved with a thorny pattern. The delicate thorns escalated upward to reveal the name of each Rosewood house—Ivy, Conch, and Stratus, their order reflecting what they symbolized in the school motto: "*Righteous, resolute, resourceful.*" Above this was a huge gold engraving that read ROSEWOOD HALL: ACADEMY OF REMARKABLE ACHIEVEMENT.

She stopped a moment, her stepmother's words echoing in her head.

"I hope it doesn't disappoint you."

Lottie only faltered for a second, but it caught Binah's attention.

"Are you okay?" Binah asked, cocking her head to the side inquisitively.

"I'm just . . ." Lottie trailed off, not wanting to admit how nervous she was to see the school for the first time. "Tired from traveling so far."

If she'd only known in that moment the domino effect those words would have.

"You're from another country?" Binah asked, her enthusiasm bubbling back.

"Yes." *Wait, what? Did she say county or country?*

"That's *wonderful*. We have so many international students; you'll fit in no problem!"

"Wait, I think—" Lottie tried to interject, to explain she was just from Cornwall, but Binah continued on in excitement.

"No, no, don't worry at all." Binah beamed up at her with a brilliant smile that showed all her pearly teeth and left Lottie feeling a little dazzled. "You're a Rosewood novice and I take it upon myself to know everything so I can help everyone."

Lottie blinked a few times, amazed at how much Binah's

words reminded her of her own desire to put good into the world. She quickly remembered herself and opened her mouth to correct the misunderstanding, but Binah's eyes had moved behind her, squinting at whatever she was seeing.

"And, speaking of things you should know, here come three of them right now."

Lottie followed Binah's gaze as three impeccably well-dressed students walked toward them.

One of the girls had an iced coffee in one hand and a phone in the other that she was furiously talking into. She was clad in an oversized fur coat and Lottie could see designer logos peeking from her ensemble. This girl could have easily been a brunette Barbie doll come to life. The other students were a boy and girl who seemed to move in unison; they were so identical in build and appearance that they must have been twins. From a distance, they looked like doves, dressed almost entirely in white.

"*Binah!*" called the girl twin in a high-pitched squeal, leaping forward to give her a big squeeze.

Binah hugged her in return, then they all seemed to notice Lottie at the same time.

"Anastacia, Lola, Micky—meet Lottie. She's international."

Lottie groaned internally, praying no one asked to see her passport. The Barbie girl said a curt goodbye into her

phone then turned to Lottie.

"Pleasure," said Barbie flatly, holding out her hand, a slight French accent dripping through her words. Lottie shook her hand slowly, noticing how cold it was. "I love your dress," she added.

Lottie blushed, realizing that this girl probably had no idea how reassuring and kind that little compliment had been for her.

"Oh, thank y—"

But before Lottie could finish, the Barbie girl interjected, saying, "Okay, enough chit-chat. I'm sick of standing around and I want to make sure my luggage isn't being mistreated."

The twins giggled to themselves.

Binah leaned over to Lottie and whispered in her ear. "That one's Anastacia, daughter of the French ambassador. She's very dramatic."

Lottie nodded, watching as Anastacia and the others sauntered through the archway. Yet Lottie found she couldn't follow. She was overcome by a thick fragrance that seemed to flood the air around them—a mixture of lavender and roses that gave the air a deep, dreamy feel, like being plunged into another world. She looked up at the building looming over her. Lottie felt as though the school was calling to her, pulling her in with an atmosphere all its own. She was meant to be here; she knew it deep in her

bones. The tiara that lay hidden away in her bag burned at her side. She'd really done it. She'd made it to Rosewood. She realized then that it wasn't that she was scared the school would disappoint *her*; she was scared that she would disappoint the *school*.

"*Allez!* Some of us would like to get to Rosewood before they die of old age, thank you."

Anastacia's voice pierced Lottie's ear, pulling her out of her daze and forcing her legs back into action. "What are you doing?" she asked.

"I have absolutely no idea," Lottie replied as she took her first steps into Rosewood Hall.

4

THE HEAVY DOORS OF THE magnificent oak-walled reception were wide open to welcome the students, new and old, who were pouring in, all of them buzzing with enthusiasm like well-dressed bees in a hive. The way the light hit the archway behind Lottie in strange dappled sections gave the impression that the courtyard was a painting, as if crossing the threshold had plummeted her into a fantasy world.

"The welcome speech and fireworks aren't until later tonight," Binah explained, "so you'll want to get settled in to your dorm and relax, maybe try on your uniform. We can meet up before all that."

The five of them were standing in line for registration and Binah had pulled out a large beautifully bound document that Lottie recognized from her own Rosewood Hall welcome pack. Where Lottie's was purple, Binah's was yellow.

"Which house were you assigned after your aptitude test?"

Micky, Lola, and even Anastacia perked up at this question, each turning around to hear Lottie's response.

Along with the application, Lottie had had to take an aptitude test filled with "what if" and multiple-choice questions to evaluate which house would be the best fit for her.

"I'm in Florence Ivy."

The other students shared a look and Lottie wondered if she'd said something stupid.

Binah laughed and patted Lottie's shoulder, which would have felt condescending coming from anyone else, but her sincere smile made it impossible to take it as an insult. "Sorry, sorry! We never call them by their full names. It's just Ivy, Conch, and Stratus."

Lottie couldn't stop herself from blushing yet again.

"I see you're in Stratus—" Lottie said, pointing to Binah's yellow notebooks.

"*C'est n'importe quoi*," Anastacia interrupted, her expression inscrutable behind her sunglasses.

Lottie had a limited understanding of French, but she could still grasp that Anastacia had said something along the lines of *nonsense*.

"Binah was one of the only students ever to be offered all three houses—and for some reason she chose Stratus over Conch," explained Anastacia.

"Hey!" exclaimed Lola, looking genuinely hurt.

"Nothing personal, Lola. It's just Conch is clearly the superior house and red is a superior color."

Lola and Micky rolled their eyes in unison, obviously used to this kind of statement from Anastacia.

Binah shrugged at Lottie, trying to act as if it were no big deal to be invited to all three of the Rosewood houses, but her bashful smile suggested she knew exactly how impressive it was.

At the front of the line an Ivy prefect, whose purple badge said FREDDIE BUTTERFIELD, took her phone for the term and handed her another welcome pack. Lottie had known this was coming—phones were strictly prohibited during the school year—but it felt as if she were handing over a part of herself. Since her mother had passed away she'd spent so long studying as hard as she could that she hadn't had time for friends, so Ollie was the only one she ever really messaged. She couldn't even email him because internet usage was strictly monitored. The idea of him not being easily contactable made her a little nervous, but she quickly gulped it back down.

"Welcome to Rosewood, Miss . . . Pumpkin." Lottie felt a twinge of embarrassment over her last name, but quickly quashed it. "This bag contains some gifts from the school to you; it also contains the keys to your room and your fob for entry to the Ivy dorm. All other necessary equipment will be found in your room. You will get your phone back at the end of the quarter. Thank you. Have a lovely day."

His tone suggested that he may have been enthusiastic earlier in the day but was now struggling to stay chipper, having repeated the same script to every other Rosewood student.

They stepped out of the reception hall and parted ways with Anastacia, who went off toward a bridge in the direction of Conch House, accompanied by a frizzy-haired blond girl who appeared to have been waiting for her. Lottie watched curiously as Anastacia wrapped the blond girl in a tight embrace. She almost wondered if she was imagining the scene; it seemed so out of character for the girl she'd just met to display so much emotion.

Binah took her on a scenic route through the school. They passed the main quarters of Stratus Side, the Stratus House dormitory, which, as the name suggested, was in the topmost tower of the school. Very fittingly, Stratus House was represented by the merlin falcon, a symbol for resourcefulness, which was carved on a plaque above the tower's entrance. The twins stopped there, giving Lottie a synchronized wave before ascending the tower.

As soon as they were into the main school grounds, Binah began an impromptu lesson on the buildings they passed. Her lips moved faster than Lottie could keep up with and she spoke with such an intense vocabulary that it bordered on being another language altogether.

"The intricate fenestration on the assembly hall's walls is an intentional pastiche of eighteenth-century gothic styles . . ."

Lottie nodded. Were all Rosewood students this articulate?

Anastacia had said that Binah was the only student to ever be invited to all three houses and Lottie felt a sudden intense determination.

I want to be this smart.

She was going to use her time at Rosewood to work as hard as possible and make her mother proud.

Once they were out of the main school cluster (which was not a short walk at all, and made Lottie very happy that she didn't have to carry her luggage), the path became cobbled, which meant they were getting close to the Ivy dorms. A quarter of the way down the hill, nestled among dense rhododendron trees that backed onto Rose Wood, was a grand-looking stone building. Through its cast-iron gate was Ivy Wood, her new dormitory. It was beautiful and looked like a hotel, such was its size—and indeed it was almost like one. Lottie had read that Ivy Wood had its own reception area, kitchen, dining hall, library, and study rooms. Ivy clung to the gray stone walls in tangled heaps, climbing up the sides of the buildings. The path to the front door was lined with thick bushels of wisteria covering trellised alcoves . . .

and there it was: her home for the next four years.

"What kind of architecture is popular in your country?"

Lottie was jolted out of her daydreaming by the unexpected question. She looked at Binah and her voice caught in her throat; it would be completely humiliating to admit to the misunderstanding, but she had to do it. Now was her chance.

"I . . ."

But that's as far as she could get.

"Oh, look, isn't he wonderful?" Binah clapped her hands together in excitement.

Lottie looked up and found her gaze drawn to the pond at the center of the Ivy garden. There was a bronze statue of a stag, its horns outstretched like a crown above its head, eyes piercing her own with an odd familiarity.

Binah sighed wistfully as she led Lottie toward it.

"He's called Ryley—he's the guardian of Rosewood, and your house symbol."

Lottie found she was struggling to pull her eyes away. She once again forgot to set Binah straight on the mix-up, almost as if the deer were intentionally distracting her.

"Come on." Binah gently reached out and stroked Lottie's palm with her thumb, as she escorted her away from Ryley to the entrance of the dorm. "Let's get you checked in to your dorm; you must be tired from your travels."

Lottie groaned internally. Being at Rosewood was already completely exhausting and she hadn't even started classes yet.

Binah marched her up to the door for the Ivy dorm and left her with a clear set of instructions for meeting later.

"I'll pick you up by the Ivy Wood gate at seven p.m. and take you to the Miracle Marquee to meet the others. If you need any help after I go, your house mother is Professor Devine . . ." Binah paused for a moment, bringing her finger to her lips in thought. "Although she won't be around now as she's giving the orientation speech, but I'm sure one of the prefects will be happy to assist you."

Lottie had religiously memorized the names of all her teachers and heads of faculty, but out of all of them she was most excited to meet deputy headmistress and Ivy house mother Professor Adina Devine.

Ollie had made numerous "jokes" about how that sounded like a witch's name. Lottie had reminded him that she was sensitive to jokes at the expense of people's names and pointed out that *"It sounds more like the name of a fairy godmother, thank you very much."*

"You're lucky; Professor Devine is an amazing woman," said Binah, a wide smile spread across her face. "Just be sure not to get on her bad side. She can shout loud enough to shatter glass."

Lottie gulped at this thought; she did not deal well with being shouted at.

Binah swiftly hugged her and Lottie found herself wrapping her arms around her and squeezing tightly, realizing that she didn't want her to go. Binah had helped her so much already. Lottie worried she'd be completely lost without her.

"Thank you so much, Binah." She gave her another little squeeze before pulling away.

Binah smiled at her again, her teeth glittering in a wide, comforting grin.

"You'll fit in just fine here, Lottie. I think you're exactly what this school needs." And off she went, skipping away toward the Stratus dormitory.

Lottie felt odd not having Binah at her side anymore. Everything seemed much bigger than it had a few minutes ago and she felt that same anxious loneliness creeping back.

Be brave.

Upon entering the dorm, she was greeted by an ornately decorated reception room with a large oak-framed painting of a tiny but stern black-haired woman in purple with a deer by her side. It was, of course, Florence Ivy. She scowled out at the world from inside the frame, demanding to be taken seriously and inspiring resolve in all who gazed upon her.

I won't let you down, Miss Ivy.

A chubby red-haired prefect with a badge that said ELIZA LOOPER was sitting at a desk at the entrance. She smiled at Lottie and checked her in. There was a distinct smell of gingerbread around her, and her heavily freckled face was like a little constellation map. Unlike Freddie from earlier, she seemed genuinely enthusiastic to be helping.

"Lovely to meet you, Lottie!" She handed Lottie a small booklet with SCHEDULE printed in gorgeous calligraphy on the front.

"This is your finalized schedule. You'll find out who you'll be in a company with, that is, who you'll be sharing most classes with—"

Lottie nodded. She'd already researched how the Rosewood Hall classes were structured. Each year was split into companies of about twenty students all from the same house. Most classes were attended in these companies and she was praying she had a nice group.

"If you want to send and receive any letters, your personal PO box address is in your welcome pack and you can send and retrieve larger packages from the mail room next to the Stratus building."

Again Lottie nodded; she'd been through the mail system about a million times with Ollie, reassuring him that they'd find a way to keep in touch.

"You're in Room 221. Your roommate arrived about thirty minutes ago. She's new too, so if either of you have

any more questions let me know," she said, beaming.

Roommate! The word was like an alarm bell in Lottie's head. How could she have forgotten she was going to be meeting her *roommate*. The girl she'd be spending at least the next two years of her life sharing a room with. She headed up two flights of stairs and reached Room 221 at the end of the corridor. The door loomed in front of her, large and white with glittering gold numbers. She took a deep breath, mentally preparing herself.

The first thing Lottie noted as she opened the door was how huge the room was; it made her little attic room in Cornwall seem like a closet. It even had a balcony, one of the perks of being on the second floor. There were two white metal-framed double beds on opposite sides of the room; between them was a large purple Persian rug, perfectly centered on the lacquered wooden floorboards. As expected, her new plaid Ivy uniform, also purple, was lying on the empty bed waiting for her. The bare bed and walls actually excited her; there was so much decorating potential.

However, something seemed slightly off as she took in the side of the room that had already been occupied. It was almost completely bare apart from a framed poster for the film *Rebel Without a Cause* on the wall. Her roommate hadn't even bothered to put her bedding on yet. Instead she was lying sprawled on her mattress with a book covering her face.

Was she . . . asleep?

Lottie was still jittery with the excitement of the day, and yet here was this girl, napping. She felt an odd sense of impatience. She knew she should let her sleep but she couldn't help herself. Lottie grabbed the door handle and slammed the door shut.

The girl sat up abruptly, the book falling off her face to reveal a mop of short black hair and dark piercing eyes that felt like they looked directly into her soul.

Lottie couldn't believe it. It was her, the girl from the drop-off.

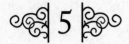

5

"It's you," Lottie breathed.

If she'd thought this mysterious girl was thrilling at first sight, up close she was like a whirlwind. She practically oozed teenage rebellion. Chaos and anarchy in human form. They could not have been more different. For everything Lottie was, this girl was the antithesis. Yet there was something eerily familiar about her that Lottie couldn't quite place.

She held herself with an enviable confidence and ease that made Lottie feel shy and awkward in comparison. Lottie suspected her cropped hair was dyed; it seemed too dark to be naturally black. Her makeup was bold and she wore a T-shirt for a band Lottie had never heard of and suddenly worried she should have.

"Excuse me?"

"Hi, sorry . . . Hi!" Lottie stumbled over her words, desperately trying to remedy any awkwardness from her moment of stunned silence. "Have we . . . have we met before?"

Something flashed across the girl's face, her eyes squinting before turning into an almost cocky smirk. "That's

highly unlikely," the girl replied, raising an eyebrow like some kind of eighties teen heartthrob.

Lottie immediately started blushing, but she couldn't quite figure out why.

The girl extended her hand for Lottie to shake. Even their hands were completely different. The other girl's tattered wristbands and the chipped black polish on her cracked nails made Lottie feel embarrassed about her own little gold bow ring and meticulously painted pink nails.

"I'm Ellie. Ellie Wolf."

Lottie grabbed her hand and there was a tiny static shock between them that almost made her jump. She shuddered at the sensation but didn't find it unpleasant.

"Lottie . . . Lottie Pumpkin," she replied.

"Pumpkin?"

Lottie mentally prepared herself for an onslaught of jokes at the expense of her odd last name that she'd have to pretend to find funny, but she was pleasantly surprised when Ellie smiled.

"Cute."

The light from the balcony window beamed in, illuminating her delicate collarbones and reflecting off a silver diamond-shaped locket around her neck, which had a wolf crest in the center.

Lottie blushed again and instinctively looked down. "Thank you."

An awkward silence crept its way into the room that Lottie felt she had to remedy.

"Do you know what company you're in?" she asked excitedly, and immediately told herself to calm down before she seemed too eager.

"I'm in Epsilon, I think," Ellie replied indifferently, emptying one of her bags out onto her bed.

"ME TOO!"

What did I just say about being too eager? Lottie mentally chastised herself, but Ellie turned and gave her a little side smile as if she found her enthusiasm endearing.

Lottie felt suddenly very uncool, but Ellie didn't even seem to notice. She turned back to her luggage and began rummaging through the objects on her bed.

It didn't take Lottie long to have her side of the room exactly how she wanted it. Back in Cornwall, in the oaky attic of the bakery, her bedroom walls were covered in art pieces, Polaroid pictures strung up with clothespins, an assortment of fairy lights and colorful bunting in pretty pastels. It was her cozy retreat, a little haven where she could hide away.

She smiled to herself, dusting off her hands and admiring her handiwork. It was perfect. The rosy bedsheets, the flowerpots filled with pink roses, the candles on the shelves in colorful crystal holders. Everything blended just as she'd planned with the white and purple furniture

of the Ivy dorm that she'd seen in the online brochure. She had also allowed herself to bring her most beautiful hardcover fairy-tale books, along with a collection of paperbacks, all her stationery, and Mr. Truffles, her stuffed pig, who looked very comfortable amid her lacy cushions. She'd done it. She'd officially moved in, and she'd made the place hers . . .

Lottie heard a clatter and turned around to find a war zone had broken out behind her. She gasped at the chaos on the other side of the room. If she hadn't known any better, she'd have thought a bomb had gone off. Piles of CDs and DVDs were spewed across the floor. *Who even owns CDs anymore?* Dark clothes lay in crumpled heaps next to mountains of dog-eared books and papers. It was the messiest room she'd ever seen and it hadn't even been lived in for a day. The only thing Ellie had bothered to place carefully was a framed photo of herself with her tongue out, an arm around a very irritated-looking boy in a black suit.

After all Lottie's careful planning for her perfect dorm room it hadn't even occurred to her that her roommate might be . . . a slob.

In the midst of the chaos was Ellie, sitting cross-legged on her bare bed with her big black boots, hunched over an unfinished sudoku with one earphone in, scruffy strands of hair obscuring her eyes.

"Interesting choice of decor!" Lottie tried to say this

lightheartedly, but an involuntary twinge of nervousness squeaked out.

Ellie looked up slowly, pulling her earphone out and letting it dangle over the bed.

"What . . .? Whoa." She pushed her hair back out of her eyes, letting out a long whistle of astonishment as she took in the room. "You just did all this?" The words came out less impressed than bewildered.

"Having a nice room is important to me," Lottie said quietly, the implication behind the words—she hoped—coming out very clear.

"Ha!" Ellie swung her legs over the bed. "Oh! I'm guessing my eclectic style is not so much to your liking?" Her voice was dripping with sarcasm, her earlier charm replaced with a cockiness Lottie wasn't sure she liked.

"Well . . ." Lottie began, not one hundred percent sure of the best way to approach the situation when what she really wanted to say was exactly what she'd say to Ollie in the same situation: *Clean your room, you animal*. "I'd be more than happy to help you sort it out, if you'd like?"

Ellie stood up and crossed her arms in front of Lottie, who had her hands firmly placed on her hips.

"And I suppose you want me to clean it all up then," Ellie said indignantly.

"It's not like the fairies are going to do it," Lottie said, surprising herself with her own sarcastic tone, something

that was very unlike her.

Ellie exhaled through her nose in an ironic laugh.

"Well, maybe I like it like this?" She was enjoying winding Lottie up. She sauntered over to Lottie's perfectly made bed and grabbed Mr. Truffles.

"Hey!" Lottie exclaimed. "Be careful with him!"

"It's fine, it's fine," Ellie replied, tossing him over her shoulder. "I'm just going to use him to even out the sides a bit . . . seeing as you clearly don't like my *aesthetic*." She said the word slowly, drawing out the syllables and making little quote marks with her fingers.

Lottie was terrified of any confrontation so watched as Ellie placed him on top of a messy heap of stuff by her bed.

"Ta-da!" She grinned. "Now you have your perfect room."

Lottie stared at her, mouth wide open. *She was being teased.* She felt tears sting the back of her eyes. She'd grown used to slights and jabs from living with Beady but had never imagined she'd have to deal with it at Rosewood. She took a deep breath and performed her mental ritual that had gotten her through so much before. Closing her eyes, she imagined wearing her mother's tiara.

I will be kind, I will be brave, I will be unstoppable.

She was determined not to crumble.

"Ellie, that's not funny." She tried to sound as firm as possible but she wasn't used to taking a tone of authority.

"Give him back," she said, holding her hand out.

Ellie turned back to her and cocked an eyebrow. "Just come get him," Ellie replied, sliding to the floor. "Better yet, why don't you come and join me in my trash pile?" She beckoned for Lottie to sit next to her. "Or do you not want to ruin your pretty little dress?"

Lottie found herself particularly upset by that statement. She'd been so happy after Anastacia had complimented the dress that she'd saved up so much money for, but now that joy had been dashed by Ellie's mocking words.

Ellie lay back in her pile of mess and began flapping her arms, making a junk angel on the floor, becoming at one with her piles of possessions.

"Ellie, stop, you're going to—"

But it was too late; Ellie's arm had caught the pile of stuff with Mr. Truffles on top. That, in turn, knocked over her can of Coke that was on the floor, spilling the whole thing and turning her mess into a puddle of sticky jumbled objects.

"Oops!" Ellie sat up and stared at the dark bubbling liquid as it spread across the wood toward Lottie, making no attempt to stop it. To Lottie's horror, a small splash had landed on Mr. Truffles's foot and she quickly swept him up.

"*Oops*? What do you mean, '*oops*'?" Lottie found herself overcome with frustration. She'd never met anyone who made her feel this way before. It was as if her whole body

was on fire and she realized for the first time since her mother had died that she was letting herself get angry. It felt like all the negative feelings she'd bottled up her whole life were ready to explode.

Ellie just shrugged in response.

"Urgh, fine!" Lottie stormed into the bathroom, gritting her teeth to stop from shouting, and grabbed a towel. "If you won't clean this up then I will."

She began soaking up the black liquid, decidedly ignoring Ellie's aloofness.

"Relax—jeez!" Ellie grabbed one of her books off the floor and sat cross-legged on her bed again, casually flicking a strand of loose black hair out of her eyes. "I'm sure you have a maid or something who can come and clean this up." She chuckled to herself and Lottie felt her stomach drop.

That is it!

It was clear Ellie had some chip on her shoulder, but Lottie would not let anyone make any prejudgments about her. Watching Ellie lounging on the bed, Lottie felt a storm building inside her.

"Look, I don't know what kind of assumptions you've made about me but I worked really hard to get into this school. I can't afford the school fees and I had to really prove myself, so the *least* you can do is keep your side of the room clean on the first day." She slammed the towel

down on Ellie's bed. "Oh, and you're right, I don't want to ruin this dress, because unlike some people I don't have the luxury of not caring about my things."

Ellie immediately stopped laughing.

There was an awkward long pause. Lottie couldn't remember the last time she'd been so honest. She glanced at Ellie, suddenly terrified of the repercussions, but to her shock she saw what seemed to be genuine regret.

"I . . . didn't realize . . ." Ellie looked away, pushing her hands through her hair in what was probably the closest she got to showing embarrassment.

Lottie unclenched her hands, which had unconsciously turned into nervous fists at her side. Then she noticed the clock on the wall that was ticking away. It was five to seven, just five minutes before she was meant to be meeting Binah.

Ellie's look of shame clicked with Lottie in a way she didn't quite understand and she felt like something important had just happened between them. *Be kind*, she reminded herself. She sucked in all her frustration and let it out in one long sigh.

"Are you coming to the fireworks?"

Ellie blinked in surprise, obviously not expecting the sudden change in tone.

"I'm going with some people I met earlier . . . I'm sure they wouldn't mind if you tagged along."

She looked thoughtfully at Lottie for a moment before turning away, her hair quickly falling back in front of her eyes.

"I'm gonna pass. I'm really tired from all the traveling and . . ." Ellie began fiddling with the locket around her neck. "I should probably tidy this up a bit anyway." She faced Lottie as she said the last words and gave her an apologetic smile.

For some reason Lottie couldn't quite figure out, the idea of leaving this girl now made her chest feel heavy; even after their awkward introduction. It had been years since anyone had upset her and she was still subconsciously waiting for her new acquaintance to punish her for her outburst. But she didn't. Instead she looked at Lottie in a way that made her feel as if she understood her, and it made her instinctively pull her hand to her chest.

"Thank you." Lottie surprised herself with the words, not entirely sure what she was thanking her for.

Ellie smiled—and Lottie felt like an unspoken truce had been made.

"No problem."

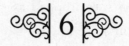

6

BINAH COLLECTED LOTTIE AT THE Ivy Wood gate as planned and they walked together across a bridge to the Miracle Marquee. Thoughts of her spat with Ellie melted away and Lottie focused on how she was going to clear up the misunderstanding with Binah.

Luckily seeing the school in the evening made a welcome distraction from her nerves. To her surprise, it was even more breathtaking at night, with soft flickering candles lining the pathways. When they reached the marquee Lottie immediately understood its nickname. Wooden beams were obscured by hundreds of roses, making the rooftop look as though it were floating. Inside, hanging out by the seating area, were Anastacia, who even in the dark was still wearing sunglasses, Lola and Micky, who were both eating lollipops, and a dark-skinned boy who Lottie didn't recognize.

As she walked toward them, she could hear the boy saying, "I still think they should extend curfew to ten p.m. for the older students. Someone should complain."

Anastacia scoffed. "Oh, please be our guest, Raphael,

and let us know how it works out for you the fiftieth time around."

The conversation was dropped as they spotted Binah and Lottie approaching.

"Yay, Lottie!" Lola ran over to her and gave her a big squeeze as if they had been best friends forever. There was a sweet smell like baby powder as she hugged her.

"Lottie, this is Raphael. Raphael, meet Lottie."

Raphael made a spectacle of bowing. "A pleasure to meet you, Miss . . .?"

"Pumpkin," said Binah.

Raphael chuckled softly. "Binah, it's too early in the year for your strange jokes," he said, straightening up. There was a very subtle American accent as he spoke that Lottie couldn't quite place.

"No . . . that's really my last name." Lottie could feel the blush creeping up her cheeks and prayed they didn't ask any more about it.

"Okay, people," Anastacia suddenly barked. "Professor Devine's speech starts in twenty minutes and Saskia's saved us a good place for the fireworks. Let's move!"

Everyone immediately started to walk to the viewing point. Lottie couldn't help but wonder if Anastacia had interrupted to get the attention away from her—but was Anastacia that considerate?

As they walked toward the field where the speeches

were being held, Micky pocketed his lollipop stick, only to start eating another lollipop immediately.

He noticed Lottie staring, and asked "Want one?" He pulled a bunch from his trouser pocket and held them out to her.

Lottie politely took one and put it in her bag for later.

"They're Tompkins branded." Lottie jumped as Binah whispered in her ear. "The lollipops . . . and Lola and Micky, they're Tompkins." It took Lottie a moment to register what Binah was saying to her. The twins were actual Tompkins? Tompkins was the most luxurious and delicious candy company in the world. No wonder Micky had such a sweet tooth. And suddenly Lottie realized what they reminded her of, with their striking white hair, soft blush, and dark lips. They were like human candy canes.

As Lottie processed this new information, they stopped walking and found themselves among a crowd of students, facing the frizzy-haired girl she'd seen Anastacia embracing earlier. Her mass of hair and lean body made her appear taller than everyone else, and she held herself in such a way that it made her simultaneously unthreatening and commanding. She wore a red sash with the bear symbol of Conch House—which meant that she was the head of her class.

She scrutinized Lottie for a moment before smiling.

"So this is the new Ivy student you mentioned, Anastacia."

This must be Saskia, Lottie thought to herself. She wondered what else Anastacia had said about her. She gave a polite smile in response and the girl returned it with a look of inquisitiveness. She held out a bag of books, asking, "Do you mind holding this for a moment?"

"Er, sure, no problem." Lottie took the bag and watched as Saskia rummaged around in her pocket before pulling out a business card.

Lottie groaned internally. *I really need to get some cards.*

"I'm Saskia," Saskia said, offering a tanned hand. "One of the heads of Conch House." She relayed the information as if it were no big deal, but Lottie knew it meant she had a lot of power in the school.

"I'm Lottie," she replied, suddenly feeling very shy.

"That's a nice name." Saskia gave Anastacia a sideways glance. "I hope Ani is being nice to you; we're childhood friends so—"

Before she could finish, Anastacia barged between the two of them, planting herself next to Saskia. Saskia gave Lottie a little knowing smile and giggled.

As they took their places, Lottie noticed adults in dark suits scattered around the perimeter, looking very serious. They made her inexplicably nervous. They seemed to radiate danger. What on earth were they doing in a school?

"Who are all those people in the black uniforms?" Lottie asked curiously.

"You don't know?" Raphael sounded so shocked you'd think Lottie had just told him she didn't know how to count to three. Binah quickly chimed in.

"They're bodyguards. There are a lot of children of very important people here, as you know—"

"I heard some of the bodyguards are Partizans," interrupted Raphael.

Lottie noted that Anastacia looked up over her sunglasses for a split second but quickly glanced back down.

Lottie, of course, had absolutely no idea what he was talking about.

"What's a Partizan?"

At this seemingly innocent question, they all looked at her, their heads snapping around in unison. Micky's jaw literally dropped, causing his lollipop to fall out of his mouth, which should have been funny, but right now just made Lottie feel extremely anxious. Saskia raised an eyebrow, an unfathomable look on her face. Lottie rattled her brain, trying to think of a way to get out of this but nothing was coming to her.

"Where did you say you were from again?" Anastacia said coolly.

Crap!

Lottie opened her mouth but couldn't seem to form any words. She could feel her palms going clammy. *This is it—now's the time to come clean and tell them about the*

misunderstanding. Do it! Quickly!

" . . . I'm not—"

"Students of Rosewood, welcome!" A melodic voice rang out across the field, immediately capturing everyone's attention. Lottie turned to see an Indonesian lady, possibly in her forties, wearing a white suit with a purple rose brooch on her chest. She stood at the center of the outdoor stage, arms outstretched, like she was beckoning to the world. Professor Adina Devine was every bit as mesmerizing in person as she had been in Lottie's mind. She exuded a powerful aura. As she smiled out at the gathered Rosewood students and faculty, there was such genuine warmth behind her eyes that Lottie felt the look was personally intended for her. Professor Devine's pristine white suit, lit by the stage lights, appeared to glow in the dark, and the long overlapping shadows behind her intersected like giant iridescent wings. Lottie looked over at the others and found they were all as captivated by the deputy headmistress as she was. To Professor Devine's left was a larger woman with long flowing hair, who was covered in jewels and wearing a yellow rose, and to her right was a tall bald ebony-skinned woman with fiery eyes, who was wearing a red rose: the Stratus and Conch house mothers, respectively. And behind them, barely noticeable in the shadows, was a stout-looking man, who resembled a baked bean thanks to his short stature and red face. Lottie

instantly recognized him as Professor Croak, headmaster of Rosewood and a fantastically underwhelming individual when placed next to these three forces of nature.

Professor Devine went on, now that she had her audience's attention. "Before we continue with the festivities I must inform you that the outdoor swimming pool by Conch House is undergoing renovation and is strictly out of bounds until after Christmas. I expect you all to respect these orders or there will be serious punishment." She paused to give the crowd a stern look, hinting at how terrifying she could be. Satisfied, she went back to her speech.

"Righteous, Resolute, and Resourceful! These are the three pillars of Rosewood Hall—each house is the keeper of one of these pillars and each pillar supports the other. At Rosewood Hall we believe that each student, teacher, house, and company must rely on one another to achieve greatness. Each house needs the other to truly reach its potential and it is through the unity of all these pillars of aspiration that we will prosper."

Kind, brave, unstoppable. Righteous, resolute, resourceful. Lottie couldn't help feeling like her own mantra fit well, and felt the fire of her determination to succeed at this school burn inside her.

"To those of you returning to us from your summer vacation, we are delighted to have you back. I encourage you all to strive to achieve even greater feats than last year. To

those of you who are new to us, I give you an extra-special welcome and ask that you take this moment to look around at your fellow students." Lottie complied, turning to Lola and Micky, who grinned back at her and made a peace sign. "Among your peers are countless fountains of potential. One of you is likely to be the next ruler of a country, an Olympic gold medalist, a Nobel Peace Prize winner." Raphael gave a little bow to Binah at the mention of this and she mimed an act of humble acceptance in response that made Lottie and the others stifle their laughter. "Do not fail the potential you have within you. This school aches to see you reach your most exceptional self: use your time here wisely; use your time here to become remarkable. Above all, never give up on yourself, or each other."

Unstoppable.

"Thank you, everyone, and enjoy this year at Rosewood."

Lottie stood for a moment in wonder as Professor Devine left the stage and walked off in a glowing pool of pristine white. Headmaster Croak nodded to the professor and slowly approached the podium with a happy little smile on his face, adding hastily, "Enjoy the fireworks!" before following the women off the stage.

Everyone looked up as the first firework went off in a magnificent burst of yellow. It was quickly followed by a succession of multicolored spurts, fizzling in the sky.

Lottie slowly let out a breath she hadn't realized she'd been holding.

"They're like trained assassins," Binah's voice whispered softly in Lottie's ear, once again making her jump in surprise. "Partizans, that is. They're trained from a young age in many fields from languages to martial arts and are assigned to a single member of an important family or group. And they will stop at *nothing* to protect them."

Lottie had almost forgotten about the whole Partizan thing; she'd been so engrossed in Professor Devine's speech. She turned again to look at the fireworks. In the distance she could see the reception building that she'd come through that morning, with its grand arched doorway that separated Rosewood from the rest of the world. Everything glowed with the lights of the fireworks, dazzling flashes highlighting the architecture. It truly was like she'd entered a magical realm. Were lethal undercover guards necessary here?

"There's not so much need for them in our modern society," Binah continued, "but some people still hire them as a status symbol."

Binah leaned back and glanced at one of the suited guards. She smiled wistfully. "I find the idea of them quite romantic, don't you?"

Lottie followed Binah's gaze. *Romantic?* It wasn't exactly

how she'd describe a potential personal killer, but she had to admit it was pretty exciting.

I wonder if I'll ever meet one . . .

After the fireworks, when Lottie got back to her dorm room, she almost tripped over a small white gift bag that had been left by her door. She picked it up curiously, wondering if maybe it was for Ellie, but the tag on the handle read: *For the Pumpkin princess.*

Lottie prepared herself for some kind of mean jab at her last name, but instead found something far more bizarre. She carefully pulled out a tattered book called *The Company of Wolves.* She scrutinized it for a moment in confusion then flicked through the pages. There, on the inside of the cover, in gold calligraphy, was written:

I know your secret.

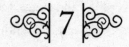

7

LOTTIE WOKE UP WITH A heavy feeling in her chest. She hadn't slept very well, trying to figure out what the "gift" had meant and who it was from. She'd wanted to ask Ellie if she'd seen anything, but her roommate had been asleep when she got back. Another, more worrying, thought had occurred to Lottie, that maybe Ellie had left it for her—had she even bothered to attend the speech and fireworks?—but she pushed that notion out of her mind . . .

She had this horrible sick feeling in her stomach that the gift might refer to that whole "from another country" mis-understanding. They probably all thought she was some awful liar. She decided that first thing that morning she was going to march straight to Stratus Side and tell Binah and the rest of them before her first class.

As they headed into the Ivy Wood dining hall together, Lottie grabbed a piece of toast and mumbled an excuse to Ellie, saying she had "some business to attend to." Ellie, aloof as always, simply nodded and offered to sign in Lottie if she wanted to skip their first class.

"What? Oh, gosh, no. I would never dream of doing something like that. I couldn't skip my first class!" Lottie was shocked at how easily Ellie suggested it.

Ellie smirked at her response but didn't press her.

"Well, I'm gonna make the most of this famous Rosewood breakfast. Come back and join me if you finish your 'business' early, but if not, I'll see you in class." Ellie grinned at her, chucking a blueberry into her mouth and winking.

Lottie gazed at Ellie's pile of food with envy. She would have given anything to stay for the magnificent breakfast buffet, laid out with every possible breakfast food you could imagine. Wooden tables lined the high-ceilinged hall, while huge windows looked out over the garden with a clear view of the pond and the statue of Ryley the deer. Lottie took one last lingering look before shoving her toast in her mouth and hurrying out of Ivy Wood and up the hill toward Stratus Side.

To Lottie's disappointment, when she reached Stratus Side she found she didn't have access. She was about to give up and head back to breakfast when a large blond woman came bustling down the corridor with an armful of art supplies.

"Oopsy!" The woman missed a step and proceeded to drop all her stuff over the floor, revealing her face. Lottie

instantly recognized her from last night's welcome party as Ms. Kuma, the Stratus house mother. Immediately Lottie bent down to pick up the fallen items. Ms. Kuma was a wonderfully poetic woman; as well as being the Stratus house mother, she was also head of the English department and would be teaching Lottie her favorite subject. She dressed in deep colors, unafraid of bold patterns and adorned herself in spellbinding jewels. Something about her seemed supernatural, like she might be capable of making the impossible happen.

"Oh, thank you . . . ?" She paused to allow Lottie to give her name.

"Lottie," she replied, grabbing the last item from the floor.

"Thank you, Lottie. That's very kind of you. I need to get this back to the art-supply cupboard before our staff meeting, but goodness knows how I'll get there in time."

"I can do it—just pass everything to me," offered Lottie with no hesitation.

"Oh, that would be marvelous," Ms. Kuma said, and clapped her hands together, a melodic trill in her voice. "It's the little wooden door if you follow the corridor to the end and go down the right set of stairs."

Lottie smiled up at her new teacher, careful to keep her balance. "No problem!"

It was tricky to get down the stairs with her arms full and she almost walked right past the art-supply cupboard door, which was tiny with a strange wooden knob that looked like a face. It looked like it belonged in Wonderland, not a school building.

She eased the door open to find that it wasn't quite a cupboard but rather a small cluttered room with shelves crammed with art supplies, and chests of drawers lining the back wall. She was carefully putting everything away when a huge pot of glitter fell off one of the shelves.

"Oh no!" Lottie groaned but then fell silent as she watched, mesmerized, as the cloud of glitter wafted through the air, settling behind one of the sets of drawers. Intrigued, Lottie heaved the drawers back with all her strength and gasped at what she found behind it. There was a hatch in the wall, hidden by the drawers. There was a small metal handle that sparkled, calling for her to open it. Curiosity got the better of her; she opened the hatch and began crawling through the tiny space. Inside was mostly wooden board and heaps of discarded fabrics. There was plenty of space for her to crawl but it was far too dark to not be a little bit creepy. In the distance she could hear the sound of rushing water and wondered how far out this tunnel went. She could see weak rays of light filtering into the tunnel, and began

hurriedly crawling toward them while keeping as quiet as possible.

After a few minutes, she heard a familiar giggle from an opening ahead of her. It was *Lola*. Lottie crept forward and discreetly peeked around the corner.

"She *looks* like she could be a princess, I guess . . . You know, with all that pink."

Lottie almost yelped as she came face-to-face with Lola and Anastacia. But they didn't seem to see her; in fact Lola continued fixing her hair as she spoke, and Lottie realized in shock: *I'm behind a mirror!*

"I *thought* Pumpkin was kind of an odd name." Lola snorted. "Do you think she transforms at the stroke of midnight?" She began inanely giggling at her own joke.

Lottie almost choked. They were talking about *her* . . . and they seemed to think she was a princess? Lottie willed her breath to be as quiet as possible as she listened on.

"It's true, she's the undercover princess—it's the only logical explanation," Anastacia replied.

This took Lottie completely by surprise. Had she misheard or was Anastacia, the most serious person she'd ever met, genuinely suggesting that Lottie was an undercover princess? Was this a joke? Or did that mean there was really a princess somewhere in the school?

The gift!

Was this what that creepy message in the book had been about? An unpleasant shiver ran up Lottie's spine for whoever the real princess was.

"Are you serious? How are you so sure?" said Lola.

Lottie leaned forward, listening intently to catch every word.

"Well"— Anastacia paused and moved closer to Lola— "you didn't hear it from me, but I heard a rumor that the unannounced princess of Maradova chose Rosewood over Aston Court and look . . ." She pulled a magazine out of her bag and flicked to a page that Lottie couldn't see. "That's the queen of Maradova. Doesn't she look familiar?"

"Holy chocolate biscuit!"

Lottie jumped and had to cover her mouth to stop from accidentally squeaking with laughter at this strange outcry from Lola.

"Shh, quiet," Anastacia snapped. "We cannot tell anyone. If this is true, then she obviously wants to keep her identity secret. Why else would she come up with a fake name like Lottie Pumpkin?"

Lottie felt a little wounded at this jab at her name. She'd spent a lifetime defending her unusual name and now it appeared to have got her caught in some strange princess theory.

"Besides," Anastacia added, "if she is the princess of Maradova, I definitely want to be on her good side."

Lottie almost burst out laughing at this. The scenario had become too surreal. She wondered momentarily if she'd ever even made it to Rosewood Hall at all. Maybe she'd fallen asleep on the train and this was all some elaborate dream. The idea that *anyone* could ever think someone as plain as her could be a princess made her feel like a terrible phoney. How could they not see how completely ridiculous that was?

"The rumor is that she wants to lead a normal life," said Anastacia.

"But surely people know what the princess looks like?" argued Lola. "Surely you've seen her at one of the international events?"

Lottie leaned in further, curious about this too.

"She never attends any; she refuses—part of the whole *I want to be a normal girl* thing."

Lottie felt her mind boggle at the idea of anyone wanting to be normal, especially a princess. What kind of person was this princess of Maradova?

"Micky and I definitely won't say anything, and Binah is always discreet, and . . . Raphael will do whatever you say—"

"Good," said Anastacia, quickly cutting her off. "Then

it's just between the five of us, okay?"

"Okay," replied Lola.

"*No way,*" Lottie breathed from behind the mirror.

She had to fix this rumor before it got out of control.

8

EVEN THOUGH IT WAS ON the other side of Rosewood, Lottie made it to her first class fifteen minutes early. She looked down at her new uniform regretfully. With all the running around she had been doing, her purple Ivy pinafore had become crinkled already, with a touch of glitter from her tumble in the supply cupboard.

Ellie arrived just before the bell rang and took a seat at the desk next to her. She had opted for a tight pair of purple plaid trousers and a set of suspenders over a shirt showcasing the Ivy emblem of a stag on the pocket.

Lottie sailed through her first two classes effortlessly. English was one of her best subjects, and having helped Ms. Kuma that morning she'd cemented herself as a favorite student. It wasn't until her lesson before lunch that she felt the weight of how intense the Rosewood classes could be. Math had never been Lottie's strong point—she'd had to work extra hard on the math part of her Rosewood application—and although she tried her best to concentrate she soon became distracted thinking about how she

could quell the rumor when she saw Anastacia and the others at lunch. How should she bring it up? Should she tell them she heard their conversation and that they had got it wrong?

"*Oh, hey, guys. I was spying on you earlier in the girls' bathroom after I followed a magical cloud of glitter to a secret passage and I thought you should know I'm not actually an undercover princess, but thanks for the compliment. Love ya.*"

Yeah . . . somehow she didn't see that going down well. To take her mind off it, she began doodling tiaras and gowns in her notebook, wondering what the princess of Maradova was really like.

"Miss Pumpkin, would you please remove your head from whatever cloud it is in and complete the equation?"

Lottie blinked at the sound of her name and looked up to find the whole class staring at her. She instinctively turned to Ellie, who had revealed herself to be a math prodigy. She'd raced through the textbook work and would probably be moved on to an advanced class pretty soon. It made Lottie feel completely inadequate sitting next to her. She gave Ellie a pleading look but was met with a side smile.

Mr. Trigwell was clearly not the type of teacher to let daydreaming slide, and she could not have planned a worse first interaction. He was tall and thin in an almost inhuman way, as if his limbs were a little too long for his body.

His nose was slightly hooked and his build paired with his attire reminded her of the Slender Man urban legend she'd read about online. She struggled with math on a good day, but, with her distracted mind and her instinctive fear of Mr. Slender-Man–Trigwell, her inability to think logically with numbers was amplified to an embarrassing level. She finished the class with "extra homework for Lottie Pumpkin" as her "distracted mind is craving something to fill up the empty space." She was mortified: she refused to fall behind in any subject and she had to prove herself, but she didn't know how she would get ahead in math without a supportive teacher.

"I can tutor you if you want?" Ellie said as they packed up their bags.

"Really?" Lottie felt a huge sense of relief fill her chest. "That would be amazing! If there's anything you need help with so I can thank you, let me know."

Ellie gave her a little side smile. "I can think of a few things . . ." she said slyly. "Hey, are you doing anything after classes?" she asked unexpectedly. Lottie was about to answer when she continued. "Actually it doesn't matter— just don't come back before five thirty. I have a surprise." Before Lottie could respond, Ellie swung her backpack over her shoulder and headed out the door, calling back, "Remember—not before five thirty!

Lottie blinked for a moment, wondering what on earth her roommate had planned.

Lottie had assumed she'd eat her first lunch at Rosewood in the main cafeteria with her new friends, using the time to properly get to know each other. Instead she found herself at a table on the patio, alone, eating artichoke soup and some kind of strange pickled vegetable that she didn't recognize. She'd considered looking for everyone she'd met the night before, but she still had no idea how to handle the ridiculous rumor, and an even more sinister thought had occurred to her. *What if one of them left that creepy gift?* She wished her mom was still around to give her advice— but Lottie was on her own. She didn't want to burden Ellie with her problem and Ollie would be of no help. She stirred her soup absentmindedly. As she stared out over the pond, a delicate red dragonfly landed on one of the lily pads, resting its wings, only to be swallowed whole by a large frog. Lottie winced as she watched the helpless creature being devoured.

"*Lottie!*" She jumped at the sound of a boy calling her name from behind her. "We've been looking *everywhere* for you." Before she had time to process the situation she found her previously empty table completely filled by Lola and Micky, Anastacia and Raphael.

"I was just . . . eating lunch," Lottie said stupidly,

wanting to kick herself for saying something so obvious. She couldn't exactly say she was avoiding them because she knew they thought she was a princess.

Lola leaned over, placing a slice of strawberry cake in front of Lottie.

"We got this for you. It took us *forever* to find you," she said dramatically.

Lunch had only started fifteen minutes ago and Lottie smiled at the exaggeration.

"You can't hide from us, though!" Raphael laughed as he said this, but Lottie froze at his words. Lola squirmed in her seat and Anastacia gave Raphael a quick scowl. "I mean, as in, in the school . . . you can't hide," he said, stumbling.

"Right," Lottie said, trying not to sound nervous. "What else could you have meant?"

A noise like a mouse squeaking escaped from Lola's mouth and Anastacia turned her scowl on her.

Lottie found it unexpectedly fun to mess with them.

"Thank you so much for the cake," she said, scooping a bit of whipped cream onto her finger. "Strawberries are my favorite. How did you know?" She licked the cream, trying to act as casual as possible.

"Oh, we know everything about you," Raphael said with a wink.

He is really not good at keeping secrets, is he?

He let out a little yelp as Anastacia obviously kicked him under the table.

Lola squeaked again and Anastacia gave her another look.

This was becoming very exhausting for her and Lottie realized what she had to do. She had to get one of them to crack and tell her that they knew so she could put them straight.

"All this food is so exciting," she began, putting as much wistfulness in her voice as possible. "I've never eaten anything so fancy in my life." That was actually not a lie.

Lola's eyes widened and once again she began squirming restlessly.

Anastacia tried to remain calm but her lip twitched. "Is that so?" she said through gritted teeth.

"Yes, and I love the uniform; it's so much nicer than anything I've ever worn before." This wasn't quite true, but Lottie couldn't help hamming it up.

Lola's face turned red and it looked like she was biting her tongue.

It's working!

Lottie only needed one more thing to push Lola over the edge. She let out a long sigh as she rested her chin on her hand. "I wish my life was always like this," she said, not having to fake any of the dreaminess in her voice. She

turned her eyes to Lola just as she exploded.

"I CAN'T TAKE IT ANYMORE!"

Bingo. Lottie had to stifle her smile.

"We-know-that-you're-the-undercover-princess-of-Maradova-and-we-know-you're-pretending-to-be-someone-else-and-we-promise-we-haven't-told-anyone-and-it's-only-us-and-Binah-and-Saskia-who-know-and-we-won't-tell-a-soul-we-PROMISE!"

"*Lola!*" Anastacia shouted out, but it was clearly too late.

A tense silence filled the air. It was obviously taking a lot of effort on Raphael's part not to start laughing and Lottie felt a similar sensation. Completely unaware of the tension, Micky leaned over and helped himself to the strawberry on Lottie's plate. It would have annoyed most people, but she just found it added to the comedy of the situation.

"Interesting . . ." Lottie said slowly, remaining calm when what she really wanted to do was burst out laughing and tell them all how completely silly this idea was. "But I think you have the wrong person." Anastacia turned her scowl to Lottie and it sent a cold feeling through her bones. "I'm flattered really, but I'm not sure why you all think this."

"Because—" Lola began indignantly, a pout forming on her lips.

"It's *obvious!*" Anastacia interrupted, looking annoyed. "You can't hide it from us! You look exactly like your mother . . . and your name is, quite frankly, ridiculous"— *Ouch!*—"and you already let it slip that you're from another country, but as soon as we pressed you about it you froze up."

It's time to come clean, Lottie thought. She couldn't have them thinking this, even if it meant they wouldn't want to be friends with her anymore.

"About that . . ." she began. "I'm not actually from another country; that was a misunderstanding." She smiled at them, hoping it might help. "I'm from Cornwall and my name . . . really *is* Lottie Pumpkin." They were all silent again, Anastacia's eyes squinting as they scrutinized her until finally Raphael cracked. A snort escaped his throat and he burst into laughter; Anastacia gave him another sour look, but he ignored it.

"Lottie, or whatever you want us to call you"—he paused to catch his breath between chuckles—"you are absolutely the worst liar I've ever met."

Huh?

He quickly continued. "If you want to keep your identity as a princess secret, you are seriously going to need our help."

Oh, come on! Lottie's mind was about ready to explode.

"But . . . I'm not lying. I really am Lottie Pumpkin."

This only caused Raphael to burst out into more laughter, and this time Lola and Micky started to giggle too.

"Stop, oh my God, I can't breathe!"

Lottie internally groaned. She'd tried to come clean, but it seemed that no matter what she said they wouldn't believe her. She groaned again, out loud this time, and buried her head under her arms on the table.

"We promise we won't tell anyone," Lola reiterated. "Your secret's safe with us."

Lottie kept her head planted on the table. "Thanks."

This was not how she'd planned her first day of school.

9

LOTTIE STOOD OUTSIDE HER DORMITORY door for what felt like a million years.

Her last two classes of the day had been electives, so they weren't with Ellie and the rest of their company, Epsilon. It appeared there would actually be a lot of classes they wouldn't have together, as Lottie had chosen mostly art subjects while Ellie had picked advanced science and math. Lottie had gone to the library until half past five as instructed and she had absolutely no idea what Ellie had planned. At least she felt better about the "princess" misunderstanding. As far as she was concerned, she'd tried to explain it and they hadn't believed her, so as long as they kept it between themselves then it wasn't her problem anymore. Right now, what she wanted to do more than anything was fix her less-than-fabulous first impression with Ellie.

So here she was, standing nervously outside Room 221 again, trying to think of a nice gesture while also worrying that some kind of terrible prank lay on the other side. She'd also made the decision to introduce Ellie to Binah and

the others at some point, though she wasn't exactly sure how that would go down. Lottie suddenly conjured the image of Anastacia and Ellie painting each other's nails at a sleepover and the whole scene was so completely unnatural that she found herself giggling involuntarily. Somehow she struggled to imagine they'd get along too well.

Lottie took a deep breath and slowly eased the door open. To her total shock, she found the room almost completely spotless . . . well, as spotless as it could be with all Lottie's books and Ellie's CDs. She must have come back and finished decorating her side of the room and, to Lottie's surprise, it looked kind of amazing. Their two sides were complete opposites of each other, split in the middle by the Persian rug. Ellie's collection of books, DVDs, CDs, and video games were stacked on the bookshelves, but she'd done an excellent job of shoving them all in as best she could. Posters for a bunch of cult films were hanging on her side of the room and her shelves were crammed with band merchandise. Everything had a pleasant motley vibe about it that fit Ellie's stormy aura perfectly.

"Ellie?" Lottie called cautiously, as she walked through her new and improved room. There was no response, but she could hear angry music drifting from the bathroom.

"ELLIE!" she called louder.

"In here! Erm . . . Can you come and give me a hand with something?" Ellie's voice echoed out from their

less-than-little bathroom.

"The room looks ama—OH MY GOD!" Lottie abruptly covered her eyes. Ellie was standing in her underwear, leaning over the bathtub with thick glops of black hair dye dripping down her neck. Lottie noticed that she was still wearing her wolf locket.

"I'm so sorry. I shouldn't have barged in." Lottie could feel her face going bright red with embarrassment.

Ellie's relaxed laughter floated through the room. "It's fine, Lottie," she chuckled. "We're both girls. I don't care." She heard splashes of water as Ellie turned on the hand-held showerhead. "Now get in here. I need help washing this dye out."

And so Lottie found herself leaning over their pristine white bathtub, gently washing thick black dye out of the hair of a girl she'd known for barely more than a day. She'd never, ever dyed someone's hair before and she found the whole process of massaging the shampoo in, pouring the water over each section of hair, and making sure the temperature was comfortable to be a very intimate experience.

"You're good at this," said Ellie cheerily as Lottie began applying the last part of the shampoo. "You sure you've never done it before?"

"Never. I didn't really have any girlfriends back home."

There was a short pause before Ellie added in a sad tone that implied she completely understood, "Me neither."

They continued in silence, watching the water trickle down the drain in a dark oily display. To Lottie's relief, Ellie had switched the music to the Velvet Underground, a less heavy alternative for her benefit.

"I'm really sorry about the mess in the room before," said Ellie suddenly, her voice very quiet but equally clear. "And your pig."

"Mr. Truffles," Lottie added quickly.

"Right, Mr. Truffles," Ellie said, smiling slightly.

Lottie didn't know what to say, and Ellie gently pushed the showerhead away to turn and face her. The dark dye was still dripping down her scalp, leaving lines of black across her white skin. She slicked her hair back out of her face. Like this, raw with no makeup on, hair pushed back, revealing her sinewy, flat-chested body, Ellie could easily have been mistaken for a boy. Yet there was nothing masculine about her; her frame was somehow soft and delicate, almost genderless.

"Most people here have their lives handed to them on a plate," she said, looking suddenly very serious. "They don't realize how lucky they are to get to come here . . . If I'd known you were here on a scholarship, I . . ." Her voice trailed off and she pushed back a loose strand of hair. "You're not like them."

Lottie hadn't really thought of it like that. She very much lived her life believing if you were an exceptional

person then you got to do exceptional things. All the time she'd been working hard to get into Rosewood, she hadn't spent much time thinking about how easy it had been for the other students. But even though the words were intended as a compliment—"you're not like them"—they still made her feel like a failure.

"You're different, because you had to work to get here. You can really appreciate it and actually do something good with your time here." Ellie grinned at her. "I'm really glad they put us in a room together."

Lottie felt totally lost. She'd spent the last year of her life desperately trying to prove she was as worthy as the other Rosewood students to attend the school; she'd wanted nothing more than to be just like them, but here was this storm of a girl suggesting the other students should have to match up to *her*. She didn't want to think like that; she couldn't get complacent and she couldn't let Ellie isolate herself from everyone in the school because she felt this way.

"Me too," said Lottie, and both girls smiled at each other, each perhaps thinking they would change the other's mind.

"Oh, and if anyone makes you feel like you don't belong here, I will gladly beat them up for you," Ellie added, flexing her arm muscles like a bodybuilder, revealing how delicate her frame actually was.

Lottie giggled. "Thank you, but please don't beat anyone up." Ellie faked an indignant pout. "I'm perfectly capable of beating up my own enemies," she said, mimicking Ellie's arm flex.

"Fine. I'll leave all the fancy, rich kids alone." Ellie sighed sarcastically, as if this was a huge ask for her, and leaned back over the tub. They went back to their routine of rinsing and scrubbing. Lottie watched in wonder as the water turned from black to clear as it washed down the drain, leaving no trace of the thick dark dye. As potions for friendship went, Ellie's hair dye was certainly a potent one.

The atmosphere felt completely different that night when they went to dinner. They decided to grab some food from the Ivy kitchen instead of eating in the main hall so they could spend the night alone and start on their homework. The kitchen was stocked with finger foods and snacks every morning, as well as the ingredients to make light meals like sandwiches and pasta, although Lottie doubted many of the students were familiar with cooking for themselves.

When they finally went to bed there was no more tension between them. Lottie realized she felt completely relaxed around Ellie, like she'd found a little home with her. With Ellie she didn't feel the need to prove herself, she didn't need to watch her words, she could just . . . be

herself. She drifted off happily, completely unprepared for what she would wake up to.

"Lottie! Wake up!"

Lottie jolted awake to find Ellie leaning over her, grinning wildly, the whites of her eyes glowing acid in the dark, looking manic.

"I've done something really bad." She was huffing slightly as if she'd just been running. "Quick, get up!"

Lottie sat up quickly, her mind coming up with numerous worst-case scenarios: she's started a fire, she's murdered the headmaster, she's messed up the room again.

"What's going on? What time is it?" Lottie whispered, sleep lingering in her voice. She could hear furious thuds echoing down the lit hallway, getting closer to their door.

"Ellie, what on earth have you done?" Ellie abruptly shoved something under Lottie's pillow and bolted over to her bed just as their door flew open.

Lottie covered her eyes from the harsh light streaming in from the corridor.

"Miss Wolf!" A voice came booming in from the doorway.

Lottie winced and to her shock saw deputy headmistress and Ivy house mother Professor Devine.

She was standing in a flowing white nightgown, the light

spilling in around her as if she were glowing, her hair in little tufts like she'd just rolled out of bed. "Would you please explain what you were doing in the Ivy House kitchen at three in the morning?"

Lottie had to bite her tongue to stop herself from screaming at Ellie. *Yes, Ellie, what WERE you doing, you big idiot?* she thought.

Ellie feigned a sleepy yawn as if she'd just been woken up. *Oh please! There's no way the professor will fall for that.*

"What . . . what's going on?"

Lottie was surprised by how convincingly Ellie's sleepy tone came out. Clearly this wasn't the first time she'd done something like this.

"Ha!" Professor Devine's cynical laugh came out more like a statement. "Do you take me for a fool, Miss Wolf?" Although her tone was sharp, Lottie spotted a glint of humor in her eyes.

Ellie stared her down for a moment. She had met her match.

"Come, both of you."

Both of us! That seemed very unfair.

"Oh, and, Ellie, you can bring those chocolate bars you stuffed under Lottie's pillow."

Ellie turned to Lottie with a look of total bewilderment. They were both baffled about how the professor could

possibly have known that.

They followed their house mother in reluctant silence down the corridor, Lottie in her pink Disney princess nightgown, and Ellie in her Star Wars two-piece, both looking very odd against the dimly lit baroque-style corridor. Lottie could only imagine the terrible punishment they were going to get. This all seemed completely unfair. She had been asleep; she was an innocent victim in all this.

As if hearing her mental frustration, Ellie leaned toward Lottie and whispered, "I was just trying to get us a midnight snack or something, you know, to cement our friendship or whatever . . ."

Lottie turned to Ellie and gave her the best *You've got to be kidding me* look she could muster, but it must have been pretty weak because they both snorted, using all their willpower not to burst out laughing at how ridiculous the situation was.

They came to an area of the Ivy dorm Lottie hadn't been to yet. The corridor was wider and it was even more ornate and luxurious than the regular dormitory. At the end, above the door to the house mother's rooms, there was a huge gold-framed painting of a small man with little square glasses smiling out at the world. Lottie recognized him as the founder of Rosewood, William Tufty.

Professor Devine opened the door and gestured for the

girls to go in. Lottie was expecting an imposing office, with dark grand furniture, a perfect scene for a mortifying reprimanding, but to her surprise they entered the quaintest little room she'd ever seen. The floor was a peachy marble, with a large plush rug in the center, on top of which was an intricately decorated cream coffee table, its glass topped with a sophisticated rose pattern. Two pink-trimmed love seats with gorgeous woodwork and golden linings sat on either side. Soft light from velvet lampshades gave the whole room a dreamy glow that seemed to mimic Professor Devine's own natural luminescence. Lottie felt completely out of place in her nightgown and half expected the room to come alive and refuse her and Ellie entry for being too scruffy.

"Take a seat, girls."

Ellie and Lottie sat next to each other, Lottie with her hands nervously in her lap, Ellie leaning back, getting instantly more comfortable than she should have been in the situation.

Professor Devine brought out a tray with a beautiful floral tea set and biscuits. This was not the punishment Lottie had been expecting. The deputy headmistress set them down upon the coffee table and sat on the love seat opposite them.

"Miss Wolf, this is your first warning," she said sternly.

"Do not let me catch you getting up to mischief again."

Lottie noted the odd choice of words. If she didn't know any better, she would have thought the professor was encouraging Ellie to be more cunning next time. They shared a look that Lottie couldn't quite understand. It was a tense stand-off, until finally Ellie sighed in defeat.

"How did you know I was there? I was so quiet."

Lottie held her breath for a moment, thinking Ellie had been tricked into confessing, but the professor simply laughed.

"I want you to know, Ellie, that I have eyes and ears all over this school." She tapped her nose twice. "Nothing gets past me." Ellie raised a disbelieving eyebrow in response. "Now, if you're going to wake me up, the least you can do is offer me some polite company for a while. That is your punishment." Her tone was light, a sharp smile spreading across her lips as she poured a cup of tea for each of them.

"To be fair, Professor, Lottie didn't actually do anything. She wasn't even awake," Ellie said honestly. "I wanted to surprise her with a big feast in the room for breakfast or something—"

Professor Devine held a finger up to silence her and turned to Lottie. "Miss Pumpkin, is it?"

Lottie nodded nervously. This whole night was just too strange; she was half convinced she was dreaming the whole thing.

"Pumpkin, what a charming name." The professor said the word melodically, seeming to truly delight in it. "I suppose you are a fan of Cinderella?" she added, gesturing to Lottie's nightgown.

"Oh yes," Lottie replied enthusiastically. "I love all the interpretations of old fairy tales."

Ellie smirked and Lottie instinctively stuck her tongue out at her.

The professor laughed good-humoredly and took a sip of tea. "I have met many girls like you, Miss Wolf. It seems I have quite the mischief-maker on my hands."

Ellie shrugged as if were no big deal.

"Now I know you did nothing wrong, Miss Pumpkin," she said, turning back to Lottie with a warm smile on her face, "but the fates have placed Miss Wolf in a room with you, so you must look out for her. The same goes for you, Ellie. This is a vital lesson for you both." Her face turned very serious all of a sudden. "I cannot express how important it is that you young girls do everything you can to support each other in a world that is so ready to belittle you and bring you down. We can achieve amazing things when we lift one another up."

Lottie and Ellie turned to face each other; it truly was amazing that two girls who were so vastly different would end up sharing a room—and getting along.

"Now off to bed, both of you. What on earth were you

thinking, getting me to serve you tea so late at night. Dreadful, completely unprofessional!" The professor winked at them before sending them off and heading back down the corridor in a floating vision of silky white fabric.

Lottie realized that neither she nor Ellie had even touched their tea.

What an odd night, thought Lottie.

"She's fun," said Ellie, grinning.

Lottie and Ellie clambered back into their beds, snuggling under the duvets. A warm feeling started to spread through Lottie as she looked around at their odd-couple decoration. Her place with Ellie had become their little sanctuary. She smiled to herself, feeling suddenly very at home. Maybe she'd be happy at Rosewood after all.

As the girls fell back asleep, something was stirring around Rosewood Hall, something that had all the students giddy and excited. A rumor like an unstoppable weed was spreading its way through the grounds, and it was going to have a life-changing effect.

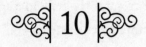

THE NEXT DAY WAS ONE of the most perplexing days of Lottie's life. Somehow everyone in Rosewood seemed to have discovered Lottie's royal secret, and they weren't very subtle about it. As she walked through the Ivy dining hall that morning, she could hear hushed voices gossiping at her expense and, worst of all, Lottie realized she was kind of enjoying it.

"Look, that's her!"

"She certainly looks the part."

"I thought Pumpkin was kind of a weird name."

Lottie purposefully ignored that last comment as she took her seat next to Ellie. *This Maravish princess must be a big deal*, she said to herself.

She'd already had little gifts left outside their door that morning, from bath bombs to perfume, all accompanied by business cards. *How are they so good at sucking up already?* she thought. Luckily she was able to hide them without Ellie noticing, one of the few perks of her terrible habit of "sleeping in." The idea of Ellie finding out about this ridiculous mess made her cringe. If Ellie was going to discover

the misunderstanding, she wanted to tell her herself.

"Good morning." A tall dark-haired boy with round glasses stood at the front of the hall on a speaker's podium, a short purple-trimmed cloak with a stag emblem around his shoulders.

"I'm George Ogawa, a head of Ivy House. I trust you are all settling in well," he continued, smiling at everyone with a charismatic expression that he'd probably practiced many times in the mirror. It fell a little flat as the dining hall continued to buzz with hushed whispers. "While those of you who are new here get settled into your classes over the next few weeks, I have been asked to remind you that you will soon be given the opportunity to join a club or team, an honor that should be thoroughly respected." He paused a moment to clear his throat and Ellie made a gagging motion. Lottie huffed at her, knowing how prestigious some of the extracurricular classes at Rosewood were. "So it will be in your best interests to consider carefully in which position you feel you will best represent Rosewood. Thank you and enjoy your breakfast."

George exited the stage and the hall immediately began chatting enthusiastically again. Lottie was acutely aware of the word "princess" being thrown about and was tempted to shove her face into a loaf of bread to hide.

"Here"— Ellie pushed a little apple tart on a rosy dish

across the table—"I had one of these yesterday. They're really good."

"Oh, I can't. I'm allergic to apples," replied Lottie, sliding it back.

"You're . . . ?" Ellie's voice trailed off and she looked around the hall, which had been so lively and loud the morning before, to find only hushed whispers and pointing fingers.

"Umm . . . why is everyone staring at you?" she asked, grabbing a *pain au chocolat* from the middle of the table and gnawing off a big chunk.

Lottie was amazed at how completely indifferent Ellie was to all the gossiping. She almost wondered if Ellie was teasing her again and actually knew about the whole thing.

"You haven't heard anything?" The words came out a little harsher than Lottie intended, but Ellie didn't seem to notice, instead taking another big bite of her pastry.

"We've only been here two days," she said, gulping down her food and immediately stuffing the rest in her mouth. "What could *you* possibly have done that's got everyone so worked up?" The words came out muffled through the food, but the "two days" was loud and clear. How on earth *had* she managed to cause such chaos in two days? Lottie felt like she should get a prize.

"Basically . . ." Lottie began. What difference would it

make if she told Ellie the truth? Better she tell her herself now, she'd probably just find it hilarious. "There's this ridiculous rumor—"

Lottie was abruptly cut off when Lola and Anastacia appeared at her side. Anastacia looked immaculate already. Her red Conch tartan dress was somehow more starched and pristine than anyone else's, and her hair was a perfect silky pool of chestnut brown cascading to her waist, a contrast to Lottie's sleepy bedhead. Looking at her made Lottie want to run upstairs and put a paper bag over her own head in shame. The only odd thing was that Anastacia was wearing sunglasses again. *What does she have to hide?*

"WE ARE SO SORRY!" Lola proceeded to get down on her knees and began making a big show of groveling.

Anastacia removed her sunglasses and rolled her eyes. *Did she seriously just take off her sunglasses for the sole purpose of rolling her eyes?*

"We promise we didn't tell ANYONE; we have no idea how this happened!" Lola remained firmly on her knees, looking up at Lottie like a little puppy. Everyone was staring now. She reached into her bag and pulled out a box. "These chocolates are for you. I'm so sorry, Lottie. I'm so, so sorry." Her bottom lip was quivering slightly and she looked like she might be about to cry.

Lottie stared at the box. TOMPKINS CONFECTIONERY

CHOCOLATE CARAMELS COLLECTION. Lottie mentally kicked herself for being excited by the chocolates. How could she have let this get so out of hand?

"Oh, get up, Lola, for God's sake—you're being ridiculous." Anastacia's French accent came out particularly strong as she pulled Lola off the floor.

"We didn't tell anyone," she said sternly. "I promise. None of us did. We really have no idea how this happened." Anastacia was deadly serious, so serious that she'd kept her sunglasses off and Lottie noticed her eyes were bloodshot, as if she hadn't slept well.

All of a sudden they both became aware of Ellie, who was sitting chewing her food like it was popcorn and watching them as if they were performing a play.

"Who's this?" Anastacia said, pointing at Ellie without actually looking at her.

"That's Ellie."

"I'm Ellie."

Their two voices came out in unison.

Anastacia seemed dissatisfied with this answer. "Okay, but WHO is she?"

Lottie decided to ignore how rude that sounded, as if everyone needed permission to be in Anastacia's presence.

"She's my roommate."

"I'm her roommate."

Again they spoke in unison. Lottie had to resist the temptation to shout "jinx," thinking this might not be the appropriate time.

"Can someone please explain what's going on here?" Ellie interjected. "You guys are kind of ruining breakfast, which, in my family, is actually punishable by death."

Lottie kicked Ellie under the table but had to stop herself from laughing.

"She doesn't know? Everyone in the school knows *except* your roommate?" Anastacia looked like she was about ready to explode.

"Hey! I know plenty of things," Ellie replied, as she forked some of the apple tart into her mouth. "Like . . . you know she's allergic to apples?"

"SHE'S WHAT?!" Lola screeched in disbelief. "Oh my God, it's perfect. A princess who's allergic to apples. It's like you're from a Disney movie!" Lola's burst of giggles was cut short by Ellie choking on her tart.

She quickly downed her orange juice trying to catch her breath. "*What?*"

Lottie had a sudden distinct feeling of déjà vu.

"Okay, this is getting tedious." Anastacia rolled her eyes again and turned to Ellie. "Your roommate Lottie Pumpkin is actually the undercover Maravish princess."

Ellie's eyes shot open so wide they looked like they might pop out of their sockets.

"Lottie?" She turned to her questioningly, and there was suddenly an intense and slightly terrifying energy radiating from Ellie that completely replaced her jokey mood from a few minutes ago.

The severity of this change made Lottie gasp and she found her words getting muddled in her throat. "I . . . couldn't stop it spreading."

Lottie wished she could kick herself in the face, she sounded like such an idiot.

"I thought you said you were attending on a scholarship?" There was a coldness now in the way Ellie was speaking.

"Yes . . . I didn't . . . this is . . ." Lottie tried to reply, but she was still stumbling over her words.

Ellie abruptly stood up, pushing her plates away. "I have to go," she said coolly, and just like that she stormed out of the dining hall.

Lottie's heart was thudding. That had gotten . . . unexpectedly serious.

Anastacia turned back to Lottie and shrugged.

Lola grinned and waved after Ellie as she left. "She seems nice!" she said.

Lottie tried to get through the rest of the day, praying that Ellie would show up to class. Lottie had looked everywhere: the library, the field—she'd even checked the little hidden spot she'd found by Stratus Side. Ellie had vanished. She went back to the Ivy dorm at lunch to look

for her, but Ellie clearly did not want to be found. Lottie hoped she'd show up at their room later, but she was also nervous about seeing her again. Ellie had made it very clear to Lottie what she thought of all the Rosewood students whose lives had been handed to them on a plate and as far as she was concerned now, Lottie was one of them. Not just one of them, but a big stupid liar as well. The worst part was this wasn't a lie; she really *was* attending on a scholarship and she really *had* worked her butt off to get in—but she didn't know how she'd even begin to explain the misunderstanding. But even still, Ellie's reaction seemed too intense. Why had she reacted like that? It didn't make any sense. She knew they had their differences but this was just . . . odd.

Lottie had one more look around campus after her last class but she knew deep down that she needed to head back to the dorm. She bumped into the prefect Eliza on her way through the gate and asked her if she'd seen Ellie at all.

"Oh, I think she came in about an hour ago. She said she wasn't feeling well."

Lottie said a quick thank-you, then hurried upstairs. She was just about to open the door to their room when she suddenly felt a wave of anxiety. *What if Ellie is really mad about this? Maybe she knows the Maravish princess?* All these possibilities started popping into Lottie's head

and she found herself not wanting to open the door. She reached into her bag and felt her tiara, finding comfort in always having it by her side. *You can do this*, she thought. *Face your fears*. Lottie gently pushed the door open and found . . .

Nothing. There was no one; the room was dimly lit and she couldn't see Ellie anywhere. She was just about to turn and leave to hunt for Ellie somewhere else when a voice came from behind her.

"You're a liar."

Lottie jumped as she turned to find Ellie waiting by their door. She looked furious. Her hair hung in front of her face, causing a dark shadow to mask her eyes, and her fists were clenched so hard Lottie feared she might draw blood from her palms.

Lottie quivered. "Excuse me?"

"I said"—Ellie shut the door firmly behind her before repeating more aggressively—"you're a liar."

Lottie was acutely aware that there was no way out of the room without going directly through Ellie.

"W-what are you talking about?" Lottie could feel herself begin to tremble but willed herself to stay composed.

"You're not the princess of Maradova," snapped Ellie.

Cold droplets of sweat began to build on Lottie's skin, her stomach knotted inside her, and her tongue felt like lead in her mouth. How could she get her to believe this

was all a big misunderstanding?

"Ellie, let me explain . . ." Lottie's words came out shaky and oddly pitched.

Ellie's face twisted into a humorless smirk. "I *know* that you lied because . . ." She paused to move to her bed and started to rummage through her bag, violently chucking various objects and pieces of paper to the side.

Lottie momentarily considered bolting for the door and running all the way back to Cornwall, but before she could finish that thought Ellie had located the item she was looking for and shoved it in Lottie's face. It was her diamond-shaped locket with the wolf crest expertly engraved on the surface. Ellie popped it open to reveal a small family photo: a king and a queen with a young girl at their side.

Lottie's face went deathly pale as she realized who the little girl in the photo was. Lottie turned her gaze back to Ellie, but she already knew how her sentence was going to end.

"Because . . ." she repeated, "*I'm* the princess of Mara-dova."

11

THE TENSION IN THE ROOM was so thick Lottie was sure she would suffocate under it. The awkward silence as the two stared each other down was only broken by the soft ticking of the clock above the door. Ellie's eyes were ablaze. She was truly furious and Lottie could feel the intense anger radiating toward her—that same storm she'd felt when she first saw Ellie at the school entrance. She willed herself to say something, anything to break the oppressive silence before it consumed them both.

"I tried to tell them it wasn't true."

Ellie laughed humorlessly. "You are so selfish—it's unbelievable."

Lottie flinched as if she'd been slapped. That stung. She prided herself on being kind, on being welcoming, helpful. Selfishness was the exact opposite of her nature. She hung her head in shame. "I'm so—"

"I bet it didn't even cross your mind once what this means for the real princess, did it?"

She couldn't argue with that; it hadn't. Not once had it occurred to her that the Maravish princess might actually

be at Rosewood. She'd thought it all sounded like a fairy tale. She suddenly felt exceptionally stupid that she ever thought that she could pass for an actual princess. A feeling she had never experienced had settled firmly in the bottom of her stomach, hard and cold, and wound its way up through her chest and caught in her throat. She was truly horrified. By not clearing up the misunderstanding as soon as it happened, she'd been partly responsible for the rumor spreading. She prayed that this wouldn't affect Ellie's attempt at a normal life.

Ellie stared at her, but Lottie couldn't think of any way to make it better.

"I'm sorry. I tried to tell people it wasn't true, but it got out of hand." Somehow the words felt empty and useless.

Ellie grunted in furious exasperation. She grabbed the photo of her and the mystery boy from her bedside table and sank into her bed, shoulders hunched over in a protective little shell. Her raggedy hair covered her face as she stared intently at the picture. Lottie wondered if the boy in the photo was her boyfriend.

Ellie sighed deeply, placing the picture frame back on the table. "I'm not going to tell anyone it's not you," she said firmly.

Lottie was incredibly confused. If Ellie was saying this to make her feel better, then she had to stop her—she couldn't face that much guilt.

"You can if you want to. I know I should have tried harder to correct everyone." Lottie sat opposite her on her own bed with a new feeling of resolution. "You can shame me as much as you want; I completely deserve it."

"No, you don't understand," replied Ellie. "I'm not even mad at you. I'm mad at the situation but . . ." She looked down at the photo again. "This might actually be a blessing."

Lottie blinked a few times, trying to understand how this could be a good thing for either of them.

"Maybe"—Ellie paused and took a deep breath—"maybe it'll be okay if we keep pretending it's you."

"*What?*" There was no way she'd heard that right.

Ellie responded with her usual little side smile.

Lottie quickly composed herself. "I mean, if that's really what you want?" The idea that she would actually get to pretend to be a princess sounded like a story she'd made up as a kid.

This caused Ellie to burst into fits of laughter. Lottie was starting to get the feeling she might be better suited for the title Princess of Mood Swings.

Ellie wiped the tears forming at the sides of her eyes as she snorted. "It's just so funny. I would do *anything* to be in your position, Lottie. All I've ever wanted is to not be a princess . . . And then I end up getting roomed with a girl who's obsessed with them." She let out a long breath.

"You know before I came to Rosewood I'd only met twenty people in my life? Twenty!"

Lottie's jaw literally dropped at this statement.

"Wow!" she said in amazement. "How is that possible?"

Ellie chewed her lip and began fiddling with her locket. "I'm the sole heir to the throne of Maradova, but I never wanted to be announced or play the part of the perfect princess so . . . the only option was to hide me away in the palace until one day I'd be ready to take on my role."

Lottie listened with fascination, her heart aching for the lonely little girl Ellie.

"Don't get me wrong. I'd sneak out sometimes, but that started some rumors and my parents had to put me on lockdown. So here I am, thirteen years old, and only the most trusted members of the royal Maravish household even know what I look like." Ellie didn't look up as she finished speaking.

Lottie had thought her life had been challenging, but at least she'd been free to make her own choices.

"I'm not obsessed . . . with princesses, that is." Lottie said the words before she had even processed them. "I know it probably seems really childish but"—Lottie paused, but she owed Ellie the truth considering she'd just shared so much with her—"it's my mom. See . . . I got this tiara from my mom before she passed away . . . and she taught me this silly phrase that I say to remind myself to be like a princess

when I'm anxious or frightened." She was sure Ellie was going to laugh at her, but she couldn't stop herself. "I say '*I will be kind, I will be brave, I will be unstoppable.*' And then everything seems clearer and I'm okay again . . ." Lottie looked away, scared to see the reaction on Ellie's face at her childish mantra.

"It's not silly," Ellie said sternly, surprising her. "You're not silly, Lottie—you're very smart."

Lottie looked up to see Ellie looking at her with complete and utter candor. She felt the sting of tears prick at the corners of her eyes. She hadn't realized how much she needed the validation until she got it.

"Thank you," she said softly.

Ellie gave her a little reassuring smile before lying back down again. She absentmindedly began tracing circles in the air until she abruptly stopped and turned to Lottie again.

"Eleanor Prudence Wolfson," she said quietly. "That's my real name. Not a lot of people know it."

Lottie looked at her properly then, as if they were meeting for the first time.

"It's lovely to meet you, Princess Wolfson."

Ellie grinned at her, clearly finding it funny to hear Lottie using her title, but her face slowly turned pensive again and Lottie waited calmly for her to unravel her thoughts.

"What I don't understand"—Ellie paused, rubbing her

forehead in consideration—"I don't understand how any-one figured out I was coming to Rosewood. We didn't even tell the headmaster who I really am."

Lottie didn't know what to say. She just assumed every-one knew everything here; they were all so inherently gossipy.

"Anastacia said she heard a rumor, but I don't know how the rest of the school knew or where the rumor started. She promised she didn't tell anyone."

"Do you trust her?"

Lottie took a moment to ask herself if she really did and found there was hesitation in her gut. "I would like to trust her, but I don't know who else could have told everyone." She hated playing the blame game but she couldn't think of any other logical explanation.

Ellie bit her lip before turning over to look up at the ceiling. "It's probably nothing to worry about."

Something told Lottie that she definitely didn't believe that.

12

IT WAS A TESTAMENT TO how occupied Lottie was with studying and fixing her less-than-perfect math grades that she
didn't remember the ominous book message until a week
later. She was sitting with Binah and Ellie in the small
oak-lined Stratus library that was open to Stratus students
and their guests. It was shortly before the 9:30 p.m. curfew and Lottie was writing her first letter to Ollie. Most
students were still thrilled by the idea of Lottie being the
secret Maravish princess so the cozy Stratus library was a
pleasant retreat from all the whispering.

Dear Ollie (the resident troublemaker of St. Ives),

*My personal PO Box is very easy to use so I'll be expecting
lots of letters from you and your mom, please. The address is:
Ivy 221A, Rosewood Hall, Oxfordshire.*

*You will truly laugh at me when you find out about the
pickle I've gotten myself into. I promise I'll tell you all about it
when I come home for Christmas. Give your dog a cuddle for
me and make sure your mom knows I'm doing really well here.*

Miss you so much,

Lottie

PS You can help yourself to the stash of chocolate hidden under the floorboard in my room, but only if you check up on what Beady's doing to the house.

"Big puffy rats make Dora always scared." Lottie looked up from her letter to see Binah leaning over Ellie's shoulder, the two of them staring intently down at the numbers on the paper. "That's how I always remembered it," explained Binah.

Ellie laughed in response to Binah's odd statement. "I suppose," Ellie said, rubbing her chin as she filled in another number on the paper. "I just always remembered the calculation order as BPRMDAS. I never bothered with cheats."

"It's not a *cheat!*" Binah protested. "It's mathematical mnemonics."

Ellie gave Binah a teasing smile that led to giggles from both of them. They had quickly bonded over a love of puzzles, particularly numerical ones. Although Lottie couldn't understand what they were talking about half the time, she loved watching them get enthusiastic about numbers.

Binah's face turned pouty and she reached into her bag. "Ellie, you're banned from teasing me until you crack my

code." She laid a piece of paper down on the table that was filled with complex equations. Lottie watched in fascination as Ellie's cockiness melted.

$$x1 = .92^* x12$$
$$x2 = (x1+4)/3$$
$$x3 = (x1+1)/2$$
$$x4 = x3$$
$$x5 = (3/4)x3$$
$$x6 = (x8-x9)^\wedge 2$$
$$x7 = (x1+x10)-x3^* x4/x5$$
$$x8 = x9-1$$
$$x9 = (x4+x5)$$
$$x10 = ROOT(x5)+ROOT(x12)+2i^\wedge 2$$
$$x11 = x1-x2+x3-x4+x5-x6-x7+x8-x9+2^* x10$$
$$x12 = ((x4-x3)-5)^\wedge 2$$

Lottie had never seen anything so confusing in her life. She could not even begin to imagine how to solve something so complicated.

"I made this puzzle especially for you, Ellie, and I have a little something for you both to go with it." Binah reached into her bag again and placed two blue leather-bound boxes on the table, a cool, iridescent sheen twinkling on their surface. Ellie immediately went to open hers.

"Uh-uh-uh!" Binah tutted, pulling the box out of her reach. "Neither of you is allowed to open these boxes until Ellie figures out this puzzle."

At this, Ellie pouted with indignation.

"Well, you *could*," Binah added, "but it would be a futile endeavor because they won't make sense until you've unlocked the message."

Lottie was relieved to see that Ellie seemed equally perplexed by this statement.

"Message?" asked Lottie in bewilderment.

Binah gave her a knowing smile.

"Yes, the coded message in the math problem."

Ellie and Lottie looked at each other again.

"How am I supposed to decode the message?" asked Ellie, frowning.

"You'll find a way," Binah replied with a little giggle, delighted at their baffled expressions. "Oh, and one more thing. I know how much you love fairy tales, Lottie, so . . ."

She pulled a beautiful red hardcover book out of her bag. A large wolf's head was engraved on the cover. Across the top in big gold letters it read LITTLE RED RIDING HOOD.

Lottie gasped, the memory of the "gift" from her first day flooding back: *The Company of Wolves.*

Binah looked confused at Lottie's expression. "Is something the matter?"

"No, no, not at all! It's gorgeous—thank you so much."

Lottie was suddenly desperate to get back to their room and show Ellie the creepy message. She took the book and gave Binah her best reassuring smile. "I just realized how close to curfew it is. We'd better get back before we get in trouble."

This wasn't exactly a lie. Lottie really was terrified of breaking any rules, especially after their little run-in with Professor Devine. She couldn't imagine her being so lenient a second time.

Binah nodded, but Ellie's expression remained skeptical so Lottie gave her a quick look that said she'd explain when they got back to their room. They said their goodbyes and as soon as Binah was out of sight Ellie turned to Lottie with an eyebrow raised.

"What's so urgent?" she asked, struggling to keep the excitement out of her tone.

Lottie took a deep breath before she spoke. "Ellie . . ." she began, nervous about how she'd react. "There's something I need to show you."

"You got this on the *first night*? And you didn't think to say anything! That was a whole week ago!" Ellie's voice came out a tight-lipped screech as she read the gold text inside the cover of the book.

Lottie looked away sheepishly. "Well . . . I was kind of worried you might have put it there yourself." Ellie choked

out a laugh and Lottie quickly corrected herself. "Just at first . . . because you seemed so grumpy . . . and . . . it was before I knew you were, you know . . . a princess."

The laughter stopped as Ellie stuck out her bottom lip in thoughtful agreement.

"Whoever did it was obviously trying to intimidate you . . . me . . . I mean, the princess, into reacting. It was an experiment. We need to find out who did this," she said abruptly, closing the book with a loud thud. "Whoever they are, they're probably also responsible for telling the whole school."

Lottie nodded; she'd been thinking the same thing. Together they sat on the floor and started thinking of potential suspects who could have left the book until they had fifteen names. All three Ivy heads and the six Ivy prefects, as they all had access to the dorms without looking suspicious. Then all the people Lottie had met on her first day, who thought she'd said she was from another country: Raphael, Saskia, Lola, Micky, Binah, and Anastacia.

"Well, it definitely can't be Lola or Micky because they didn't know until Anastacia told them," Lottie said defensively, "and Saskia didn't even meet me until before the fireworks."

Ellie nodded but was not really paying attention as she started flicking through *The Company of Wolves* again.

"Ellie?"

"It's a library book," she said flatly.

"It's . . . what?"

Ellie handed the book back to her and Lottie opened the back cover to see the little tear-away marks where a library-ticket holder had previously been.

"Ellie!" she exclaimed in excitement. "You're a genius! All we need to do is find out which students accessed the main library on the first day." She grabbed Ellie and hugged her.

Ellie returned it by softly patting her back, clearly not used to such sudden displays of affection.

Lottie quickly pulled away feeling embarrassed, a hot pink blush creeping onto her cheeks. "Right, anyway, we can do that first thing tomorrow."

"Tomorrow?" Ellie's face shifted into a mischievous smile. "There's no way I'm waiting that long."

"But it's past curfew," Lottie replied in confusion.

Ellie's face turned to a full-on grin, baring her teeth like a wild animal. "That's why they invented sneaking out."

13

LOTTIE COULD NOT BELIEVE SHE was doing this. She'd always prided herself on being a paragon of good behavior. She'd never had a single bad comment on a report card or anything close to a detention and yet here she was, dressed in a black shirt and jeans that she'd had to borrow from Ellie, climbing down the side of their balcony to break into the library. Lottie had protested, but Ellie declared she would be going whether Lottie came or not.

"And look at the vines on the wall," Ellie had said, "they're practically begging us to sneak out."

So once again Lottie found herself doing something completely out of character, overcome by a peculiar thrill that was becoming more familiar every day.

The lights outside the dorm room were dimmed after curfew, but the bright full moon lit up the grounds, leaving them feeling exposed on the path. They knew that the on-campus bodyguards would be watching the gate, so they would have to figure out another way around.

"We could walk back through the woods, under the bridge and back around to the front entrance?" Ellie

whispered. Lottie shook her head. There would definitely be surveillance at the front entrance too and, if they were going to do this, she was *not* letting them get caught. Professor Devine would definitely not forgive such a transgression.

"No, we'll go through the woods." She conjured up the map of the school in her head and the secret tunnel she'd found on the first day through the glitter cloud. She wondered if the tunnel might lead down toward the bridge. "I might know a secret way into the school."

Ellie looked at her with genuine shock, then gave her the little side smile that had Lottie feeling like a proud puppy.

"You sure do love to surprise me," she said with a hushed laugh.

Lottie blushed and quickly moved forward, signaling for Ellie to follow her while she explained about the tunnel she'd found. They ducked into the shrubbery and crawled to a clear spot before hightailing it into the woods. Lottie had not prepared for how intensely dense the woods would be at night and thoughts of werewolves and ghosts began invading her mind. The Rose Wood was mostly untouched with little in the way of a path for guidance, so they had to stay close enough to the school not to get lost—but far enough away to avoid getting caught. Ellie strode over the moss and roots of the oak trees fearlessly, as if this was

nothing more than a stroll in the park. Something barked in the distance, making Lottie jump and grab Ellie's arm for protection.

"It's just a deer," Ellie snickered, trying to contain her laughter.

Lottie did not find it so funny and had to muster up all her courage to let go.

It took a good ten minutes of walking until the soil turned soft as they reached the river and the bridge. The sound of the water gushing meant they were free to talk more, but it was far too dark to see where they were going without a flashlight and Lottie feared they might put a foot wrong and wind up in the water. They slid their hands along the riverbank, clinging to the dirt as they looked for any give that might be an opening. There was nothing there but sludge. She'd led them to a muddy ditch in the dark where they would most likely get caught and be in so much trouble that Ellie's undercover princess plan would be ruined.

Lottie's mind did a little hiccup. *Under!* she thought excitedly.

"Ellie, it's not on the side of the ditch—it might be beneath us," she hissed excitedly.

Ellie needed no persuading, walking directly to the river's edge and crawling around like a feral creature looking for an opening. Lottie froze, shocked by how much faith

Ellie had in her tunnel theory. Before Lottie could protest, Ellie disappeared under the water.

"Ellie!" Lottie tried to keep quiet but couldn't stop her voice coming out in a screech. Before she knew what she was doing she was running into the river to find Ellie, wading desperately into the cold to find her. Something grabbed her leg and her heart stopped. She opened her mouth to scream when Ellie popped up in front of her, quickly covering her mouth to stifle her yell.

"It's me!" Ellie was completely soaked, her hair dripping with river water. Lottie's heart was racing as she looked at her, her breath hot against Ellie's palm. Ellie grinned, her teeth glowing in the moonlight like a wolf baring its fangs. She slowly led Lottie through the water and signaled downward, still smiling. Lottie looked where Ellie was pointing. There it was, reflecting the starry light, a tiny metal latch glistening just above the water's surface. They looked at each other for a moment before leaning in together and pulling on the latch. It was much easier to open than Lottie had expected, but they had to be quick as the river water splashed into the opening.

"Wow!" Ellie exclaimed. "Good job, little princess."

Lottie felt her face glow but didn't have any time to dwell on the praise as Ellie immediately climbed into the tunnel.

"Ellie!" Lottie called. They had no idea how deep it was,

and it was impossible to see what was down there.

"Come down—I'll catch you," called the hushed voice from below her. Lottie stood shivering over the hatch, her heart still racing. She looked back at the woods once more, wondering how on earth she'd gotten here and realizing there was no going back.

Down the rabbit hole I go.

She lowered herself down into the tunnel, not caring that she was getting completely soaked. Two arms wrapped around her waist and helped her down. It wasn't as low as she'd expected and she could easily reach up and shut the latch with Ellie holding her. Lottie could barely see in the tunnel, the only light coming through a sliver of space at the top of the hatch in the riverbank. Ellie's hand grabbed hers; Lottie felt her face go hot and suddenly felt inexplicably nervous. Ellie leaned closer, her breath brushing against Lottie's cheek.

"Okay!" she whispered. "To the library office."

They took careful, deliberate steps through the tunnel, relieved to find it winding upward and, at last, they reached the art-supplies cupboard. Thankfully Lottie had forgotten to move the chest of drawers against the hatch and they were able to escape into the school. Quietly they crept through the school hallways, every tap on the stone floor ringing far too loud. Lottie had half expected to find teachers still hanging around as it was only midnight, but

there was no one in sight. There was something unmistakably creepy about the abandoned corridors at night, and she couldn't stop herself from imagining that the eyes in the huge paintings were watching her.

They had to go the long way around the hall to avoid the entrance of the Stratus quarters where there would be guards. Once safely out of the main building, they zipped through the courtyard and over a hedge to the back of the library building. It was locked. They couldn't enter with their student cards—it would be a dead giveaway that they had snuck out. Rosewood Hall kept a log of every student who entered and at what time.

Another thought occurred to Lottie. Did she even want to know who had taken the book out? Everyone was getting along; she was starting to feel like Rosewood was her home. Although people were still gossiping and whispering, she didn't feel like she was in any danger. So maybe whoever left the *gift* really hadn't meant any harm by it.

Before she could articulate these thoughts, Ellie jimmied open the glass panel of the door, reaching in to turn the handle from the inside. She clearly had experience with not just sneaking out, but breaking in as well. Next thing she knew Lottie would probably find out she had a personal trained assassin at her beck and call.

"I can't believe you persuaded me to do this," Lottie said as they walked in. Ellie just grinned at her. The office was

located on the second level of the library, a pristine crystal-decorated dome that overlooked the whole building. It was managed by a waif of a man named Clark. He kept the office so well organized that it was easy to find what they were looking for: a meticulous record of exactly who had checked out a book and when.

"Got it!" Ellie said, her tongue sticking out in concentration as she rifled through the folder.

Lottie felt her heart rate escalate again. She didn't want to know.

"You need to see this," Ellie said, failing to hide the satisfaction in her tone.

There were only a few names for the first day of school, and only three that they recognized. Written clearly on the paper in their own handwriting:

Binah Fae
Raphael Wilcox
Anastacia Alcroft

⚜ 14 ⚜

It took Lottie a whole night of begging to persuade Ellie not to confront anyone on the library sign-out list. They couldn't assume anything: it was not sufficient evidence and she didn't want to risk upsetting anyone over a hunch.

"It'd be better to file this information away and add it to anything new we discover," Lottie had pleaded. Ellie had agreed, but it was clear that she'd decided Anastacia was her enemy—and it was about to reach a breaking point.

The next day was oppressively hot. The air felt sticky, and there was a thick, stuffy tension as if the sky could explode at any moment. Although the majority of classes at Rosewood Hall were attended in companies, there were a few exceptions, and one of those was gym, which the whole year took together. This should have been great, a chance for everyone to get to know each other, but, as she soon discovered, Ivy House and Conch House did *not* play well together—especially when they had Ellie and Anastacia on opposing teams.

"Anastacia. Ellie," called Dame Bolter. "Would the two

of you please come forward as captains and pick your teams? Thank you."

Ellie and Anastacia glared at each other with such intensity that Lottie imagined sparks between them. They broke off their heated look and took their places at the edge of the field, ready to build their lacrosse teams. For Anastacia, gym class was very much about Conch House pride, but for Ellie it was personal. She was not only intensely competitive but had found a worthy opponent in Anastacia.

"Anastacia, you get first pick!" Dame Bolter shouted across the field. It was no coincidence that Conch always seemed to get first pick; Dame Bolter was the Conch house mother, and she was not like any gym teacher Lottie had ever had before. She was fiercely intimidating in a way that commanded respect. She was also the stable keeper and moved with just as much poise and elegance as if she were performing dressage. She was easily the most feared teacher in the school and Lottie couldn't imagine anyone in Dame Bolter's classes misbehaving.

"Raphael," Anastacia said matter-of-factly.

And here we go, thought Lottie. Anastacia would pick all Conch students and Ellie would pick all Ivy, and they'd both have a scattering of Stratus, who were quite frankly above all this competitive nonsense. Lottie almost envied them, sometimes wishing she could throw all her purple

Ivy stuff away and join the nice soft yellow world of Stratus, never having to worry about this silly rivalry.

Raphael sauntered over to stand by Anastacia, giving Ellie a little wink as he walked past, which earned him an eye roll.

"Binah," called Ellie. Lottie was not surprised by this choice. Ellie had been adamant that there was no way that Binah, one of the first friends she'd ever managed to make, could possibly have been the culprit. It also helped that Binah was an outstanding athlete.

Lottie reminded herself that Binah was the only student ever to be offered a place in all three houses so it made sense she was good at everything. Lottie was second to be called by Ellie, which was entirely undeserved as she was truly terrible at sports, and lacrosse in particular left her completely bewildered.

"Okay. This week we are going to *win!*" Ellie encouraged. Once she'd picked her team, she had them all huddled in a group to listen to her pep talk. "I believe in you, and, Lottie"—she looked over at her, her face turning surprisingly serious—"that means you too." Lottie groaned internally. She usually just stayed out of the way in team sports, tending to do more harm than good if she tried to help in any way. She'd never been at a school where they took physical exercise so seriously.

"Now, those Conch boys and girls might seem bigger and more intimidating and I know that four of them are on the school lacrosse team, but I believe with enough naive underdog spirit we can win this." As motivational speeches went, Ellie wasn't exactly the best—her sense of irony tended to get in the way. "Now let's do this."

"With the heart and stomach of a king," added Binah under her breath a little mockingly. At least it was a reference Lottie actually understood for once.

Dame Bolter blew the whistle and the first game began. Lottie stayed firmly out of the way as the lacrosse sticks violently smashed into each other.

How can anyone enjoy such a ferocious game?

Anastacia barely broke a sweat, expertly catching the ball in her stick and forcing it from the Ivy team. Raphael seemed to find extra joy in teasing Ellie, using every opportunity he could to intercept her. Watching his dubious tactics, it was becoming easier to imagine he may not be trustworthy.

Lottie sighed as she watched them, feeling completely ridiculous as she wandered up and down the field avoiding the action at all costs.

As they approached the end of the class, most people were panting and sweaty, except for Anastacia, who appeared completely unaffected. Binah and Ellie had

scored a majority of the goals but the score was an even 4–4, and with only five minutes left of game time it didn't seem likely that either team would be victorious.

Lottie was about to get back into position for the next whistle when Ellie grabbed her arm from behind.

"Lottie, listen to me a second." Ellie had a very rare look of sincerity on her face. "I know you think you're no help, but I really think if you try, you'll be amazed at what you can do." She squeezed her arm a little. "Be unstoppable." Before Lottie could respond, Ellie winked at her and ran back to her position.

The whistle blew and the game resumed. Binah managed to stick-check the ball off a Stratus boy on the other team and passed it to Ellie, who caught it effortlessly. She was instantly surrounded by the opposing team. She looked around for someone to pass it to but there was no one open. No one except . . . Lottie. She turned to her and got into position to pass the ball.

No, no, no! Don't do it, Ellie!

She could sense Ellie pulling her little side smile and then, sure enough, she pelted the ball in Lottie's direction.

It came flying toward her, whizzing as it split the air like a furious hornet intent on stinging her.

It's going to hit me on the head, she thought with reluctant acceptance.

It felt as if the world began to move in slow motion. The ball was getting closer and closer, and there was no way she could stop it. She held her stick up in a last-ditch attempt to stop it from whacking her and . . .

She caught it. Lottie stood in complete bewilderment for a moment staring at the ball that was very much in her stick. She'd really done it; she had really truly caught the ball.

"I DID IT!" she cried, doing an excited little jump.

"Look out!" came a boy's voice from down the field.

She looked up to see Anastacia bearing down on her, eyes cool and calculating, not even remotely flushed in the heat as she raised her stick ready to knock Lottie down and take the ball. Lottie gravely accepted her fate, her moment of pride bursting as she realized there was, of course, no way she could get to the net.

"*BRIKTAH!*" screamed Ellie as she smacked Anastacia's stick hard with her own, making a loud *thwack* that could be heard across the field.

Lottie had no idea what that meant but the intention behind it was clear.

Ellie's eyes blazed as she stared Anastacia down, blocking her way to Lottie. Anastacia moved her weight over to her left side and did a graceful little pivot, sliding her stick away ready to come back around, but Ellie was too quick. She spun back and caught Anastacia's stick again

mid-swing—the whole interaction like a strange furious dance.

"Lottie, *run*!" Ellie cried.

Lottie pulled herself out of her daze and mustered all her strength and determination, tearing off as fast as she could possibly go toward the net. Ellie had faith in her, Ellie believed she could do this and she didn't want to let her down. On the periphery she could see Raphael and a Stratus girl homing in on her from both sides.

Just keep running, just keep running!

There was no way she would make it all the way to the net, they were running too fast. She would have to risk throwing it from farther away, but the huge Conch boy in the goal would surely catch it if she didn't get close enough. Her heart was racing, but the net was just about close enough now to risk it. Raphael was only inches away from her, *a little farther* and . . . In a sudden moment of determination she mimicked the move she'd seen Anastacia pull earlier, veering left then pivoting back around to his other side. It was nowhere near as graceful as when Anastacia had done it but it worked, and Lottie found herself on the other side of Raphael with a perfect view of the net.

"GO, LOTTIE!" she could hear Ellie scream across the field.

She summoned all her willpower and let out a furious war cry as she catapulted the ball as hard as she could at

the net. It zipped out of the stick, burning through the air as it raced toward the goal like a comet. Everyone went silent, watching the ball in awe as it whizzed by. There was nothing the Conch boy at the net could do; it was moving too quickly and too powerfully.

It was unstoppable.

It hit the goal with such force it tore a hole through the netting and flew out of the back until finally it rolled to a stop.

Lottie took off her helmet and turned back to look at her team, her hair falling in sweaty clumps around her shoulders. "I DID IT!" she called, lifting her helmet up in the air in celebration and giving Ellie a big grin.

Both teams and Dame Bolter stared at her in shock for a moment before Ellie finally pumped her stick in the air and let out a victory cry, the sound tearing through the air like a wolf's howl. The rest of the team followed suit and began cheering along. Even some members of the other team were clapping in admiration.

Ellie pulled off her helmet, dropped her stick, and came tearing down the field. She grabbed Lottie around the waist and spun her around, still howling.

Lottie giggled uncontrollably as she turned, feeling completely elated. Ellie slowly put her down and said softly in her ear, "I knew you could do it, little princess." Lottie

found herself blushing and looked down at the ground, the heat nothing to do with the sun.

A whistle rang through the air, causing everyone to stop and turn to Dame Bolter.

"Congratulations, young lady—your team wins the game." Everyone started cheering again, except Anastacia, who was noticeably gritting her teeth, the least composed display she'd probably ever shown in her life.

Dame Bolter raised her hand to silence them.

"Miss Wolf, Miss Pumpkin, Miss Alcroft, please see me after class," she said sternly.

Lottie gulped. She wasn't sure exactly what they'd done but it couldn't be good.

Ellie, Anastacia, and Lottie stood in a line opposite Dame Bolter's desk. Her office was a beautiful eclectic mix of gorgeous traditional African ornaments as well as trophies and medals of all shapes and sizes. Her desk was large, made of dark mahogany and intricately patterned with winding vines. In this setting, her looming presence was amplified to a gargantuan level.

"I would prefer it in the future if you did not turn my gym classes into a sword fight, Miss Alcroft, Miss Wolf."

Ellie opened her mouth to protest, but Lottie quickly pinched her before she could, earning a scowl in her direction.

"But"—Dame Bolter turned from her desk and began admiring one of the trophies on the shelf, polishing a speck of nonexistent dirt—"you both displayed excellent stamina, agility, and poise. Now I know you will be allowed to pick your extracurriculars soon—"

"I'm sorry, Dame Bolter, but I have absolutely no desire to join the lacrosse team," Ellie said bluntly, cutting her off.

"Oh no, I don't want you two to join the lacrosse team." Dame Bolter smiled slightly, proffering a paper she'd lifted from her desk. "I want you to become sword fighters. I want you to join the fencing team."

Lottie was sure she saw Anastacia's fingers twitch, but other than that she displayed no sign of excitement.

"We very rarely offer places in the fencing team. Being a part of the Rosewood lancers is a tremendous honor, so consider the proposal seriously, girls. The tryouts are in the first week of December; you may practice with the current after-school classes but I advise you to make a hasty decision." She nodded at each of them. "Thank you, girls, you are dismissed."

Ellie shot Lottie a look of concern as they left her alone with Dame Bolter. Anastacia looked at Lottie, her eyes appearing to pass right through her before she too turned and left.

They stood for a moment in silence until the door was completely shut. Lottie wouldn't have been surprised if

Ellie was outside with her ear pressed up against it, ready to come and fight if she felt Lottie was being treated unfairly.

"Miss Pumpkin . . . may I call you Charlotte?"

This didn't surprise Lottie. A lot of adults she met had trouble with her last name, finding it a little too silly.

"Yes, of course, Dame Bolter," she said, pretending not to mind.

"Charlotte, I am a firm believer in the ethos of this school. It's why I love working here so much." She gestured for Lottie to sit in the seat opposite her and she happily complied. "I understand you are here under the Florence Ivy scholarship program."

It was not a question, but Lottie felt the need to nod.

"I take it upon myself each year to properly introduce myself to any scholarship winners. Charlotte, are you aware you are the first exceptional-circumstances scholarship winner in twelve years?"

"No, ma'am." Lottie could feel her hands trembling in her lap. She'd known it was a tremendous feat to get into Rosewood on a scholarship, but she hadn't realized how special her circumstances were.

"At the start of this class, I must admit, I thought maybe we'd made a mistake."

Lottie sat firmly, refusing to let the hurt show on her face. She couldn't deny that she had made little attempt before now to participate during gym classes.

"But today you surprised me. You pushed yourself and did something exceptional. You became exceptional."

Lottie's hands stopped trembling. "I . . . thank you," Lottie replied carefully.

"We will be monitoring your progress in the school carefully, Lottie. Do not disappoint us. We expect great things from you." She smiled at her then and it was such a wonderful sight that Lottie felt momentarily dazzled.

Lottie found herself leaving Dame Bolter's office feeling quite overwhelmed. She thought about her mother, about the tiara sitting on her bedside table, about Ellie and how she'd encouraged her so much already. She did not want to disappoint anyone. She was going to work her hardest to prove to everyone that she was worth having faith in. All she had to do was keep pushing herself and not get distracted by any silly princess rumors or gossip.

As long as she stayed focused and didn't let anything distract her, she could definitely make them proud.

I will be unstoppable!

❧ 15 ❧

AS THE UNSEASONABLY HOT SEPTEMBER drew to a close, the girls awoke one Friday morning to a particularly splendid thunderstorm. The lightning illuminated their room through the chiffon curtains. Ellie threw off her covers and ran to the glass doors, throwing them open and running out onto the balcony into the embrace of the torrential downpour.

Her *Star Wars* pajamas were quickly soaked through, hanging thick and sticky on her body, but she continued to dance around with her arms wide open, beckoning to the sky. She clamped her hands on the terrace wall and let out a howl in perfect unison with a burst of cracking thunder. Lottie stared, mesmerized by her affinity with the storm, and for a moment she was sure the thunder called out to Ellie in a deep growl through the dawn sky: *Let down your hair.*

The electricity in the air had the whole Ivy dorm giddy at breakfast that morning, and for the first time in weeks the buzz seemed not to be aimed at Lottie. Ellie and Lottie took their usual seats in the dining hall next to the window

overlooking the statue of Ryley. Having a space in the hall that was basically reserved for them was definitely a nice perk of pretending to be a princess.

The rain was still pelting down outside, clattering loudly as it hit the glass. The whole outside world was a watery blur through the giant two-story windows.

"This weather is insane!" exclaimed Ellie, stabbing a fork into a huge chunk of honey-roast ham and lifting the whole thing up in one. Lottie internally grimaced. She was already getting used to the extravagant Rosewood dining but, as a proud vegetarian from the age of five, the sight of meat made her queasy. Eating animals just didn't seem very princessy. How could she expect little woodland critters to assist her in her daily tasks if she was going to turn around and eat them?

"I'm more concerned about you catching a cold from running around in it," Lottie said seriously.

Ellie beamed at Lottie with a toothy grin. "I can't help it. Storms make people act strange." She gestured to the room. "Look."

Lottie followed her gaze around the hall. Ellie had picked up on a strange buzz that seemed to be spilling out of all the students. There was more giggling, whispering, and giddy mumbling than usual. Something was definitely causing a stir.

"It's probably due to the extreme changes in air pressure."

Lottie and Ellie both jumped and turned to find Binah at the side of their table, dripping wet with an excited grin on her face. *How did she even get in here?*

"Good morning, Ellie. Good morning, Lottie."

"Binah, oh my goodness, sit down—you must be freezing." Lottie quickly pulled off her purple Ivy blazer and wrapped it over Binah's shoulders. Her huge round glasses were almost completely steamed up and it was a mystery how she could even see anything. What was it with these girls and running around in thunderstorms?

"Looks like the air pressure may have gotten to you as well, Binah," Ellie teased, that familiar little side smile working its way onto her face.

Binah tutted in response, waving her hand as if batting the comment away. "Oh please. It takes more than a cumulonimbus cloud formation to affect my cognitive abilities . . . but you on the other hand . . ." She rested her chin on her hands, a wry smile crawling onto her lips. "How are you getting on with that puzzle?"

Ellie looked away in irritation and Binah laughed. She gently patted Ellie's hand. "Try to figure it out from the answers, not the equations."

Ellie was about to question Binah on this when she cut them off, a glimmer in her eye.

"I need you both to do me a favor."

Ellie and Lottie exchanged a look. Binah was usually

doing favors for people, not asking for them.

"There's a new student joining our year and your company."

Lottie looked out over the hall and realized this must be what had everyone so excited.

"No one knows anything about them and, as you know, I like to know everything so I can help everyone." Lottie smiled at this, remembering how helpful Binah had been on her first day.

"So what do you want us to do?"

"I want you to find out everything you can about them, of course."

Ellie hesitated for a moment, her eyebrows narrowing.

"Do you do this to every student?" she asked, a slight edge in her voice.

"Only the mysterious ones. Why do you ask?"

Lottie held her breath. *Could Binah have looked into Ellie?*

To her relief Ellie held her cool. "Just curious," she said, beaming.

"So what's her name?" Lottie asked, quickly changing the subject.

"Her? It's not a girl; it's a boy." Binah's eyes shot up to the clock at the front of the hall. "Oh my! I'd better be off or I'll be late to class." She picked up her soaking-wet backpack and threw it over her shoulder, her massive ringlets

flicking water across the room as she spun around. "See you later." She delicately skipped away before they had a chance to respond, indifferent to the trail of chaos she'd left in her wake.

Lottie breathed out slowly. "A new boy . . ." *That's what everyone is getting so excited about?* She had to wonder if there was something special about him to have everyone so giddy. Before she knew it her mind began asking a million questions. Why was he arriving over two weeks late? What was he like? Did he bring the storm with him? She wondered if he was some sort of Prince Charming. The last time everyone had been this excited was when they had decided she was a princess.

"Lottie?"

Lottie was pulled out of her daydreaming to find Ellie standing up, looking very distressed. "I've been saying your name for ages; what's wrong with you?"

Lottie couldn't help feeling embarrassed. She had the absurd thought that Ellie might be able to guess what she'd been fantasizing about.

"Sorry I was just . . ." *Being a cliché*, she thought to herself.

Ellie didn't even wait for her to finish, furiously grabbing her stuff and turning to leave.

"Let's go. I don't want to be in here anymore. Everyone's acting like idiots about a stupid new boy." She grabbed

another pastry and shoved it in her mouth. "What's so special about a boy anyway?" Ellie was being uncharacteristically moody, and the tension in her voice had Lottie feeling a little nervous.

"I'm sure . . ."

Lottie found her voice trailing off. She had no idea why this information was stressing Ellie out so she didn't know what to say to make her feel better. She followed her as she stormed out of the dining hall.

"I'm sure this new boy is just a boring kid who will have absolutely no impact on our lives whatsoever," Lottie said firmly.

She was not surprised when Ellie ignored these words of encouragement. Whatever was bothering her was clearly out of Lottie's hands.

16

LOTTIE FOUND HERSELF ALONE IN the English classroom twenty minutes before the class was due to start, nervously sharpening her pencils and wondering if Ellie would get in trouble for skipping a lesson. Their discussion after breakfast hadn't gone how Lottie had hoped. As soon as they had arrived back at their room, Ellie had proceeded to face-plant onto her bed with no intention of getting ready for class.

"Aren't you coming?"

"I'll see you there," came the pillow-muffled response.

"Will I, though? Skipping classes can become a very bad habit, Ellie."

"Well, we'll see if I'll see you there then."

"What does that even mean?"

"You'll see."

Lottie groaned and slammed her head down on the desk. She was starting to feel responsible for Ellie. If these really were her last few years of freedom before her royal duties began, then she wanted her to get as much out of them as possible.

"Excuse me."

Lottie jolted at the unfamiliar voice and shot upright. She proceeded to hit the owner of the voice hard on the chin with the back of her head, not realizing that the mystery person had been leaning over her.

She let out a little yelp.

"You scared me!" she cried, rubbing her head. She could feel tears springing to her eyes at the shock and had to will herself to calm down.

The boy behind her seemed completely unaffected by the collision. The only sign he showed of any pain was on the slow stroking of his chin as he sat down at a desk one space over from her.

Lottie felt her shock turn to a feeling she couldn't quite place. *This* was the new boy. He was dressed in the soft plum blazer of Ivy House. Although it fit him perfectly, he seemed too wild for such a tame uniform. An uncomfortable feeling began to creep through her and she felt the desire to both look away and stare at him forever all at once. But there was something more. As Lottie gazed at him, she felt like she knew him. He looked . . . familiar.

"Usually it's common practice to apologize when you hit someone," he said smoothly.

"I . . . excuse me?" Lottie blinked. "You can't be serious?"

"You hit me."

"You snuck up on me," she retorted, outraged by his

callous rudeness. "*You* should be apologizing to *me*."

"Well, good luck with that," he said curtly.

She rolled her eyes, all thoughts of Prince Charming vanishing with every irritating breath he took. It took all her willpower to be the bigger person and not say something she'd regret. Maybe it was the impulsive influence of Ellie, or maybe there was just something about this boy, but as it turned out "all her willpower" was not strong enough.

"You're going to regret being so rude to me, you know," she said sweetly, pretending to be looking at something in her book. Lottie was surprised with the words that came out of her mouth. This was so unlike her. *Be kind* was such a huge part of her mantra—but she couldn't stop herself.

His ears pricked up as he looked over at her.

Ha ha, thought Lottie. *Got you!*

A little half smile crept onto his face as a lock of shaggy dark hair flopped in front of his intense brown eyes. Lottie had a severe sense of déjà vu.

"And why is that then?" he purred.

Right into my trap. Lottie had to stop herself from squealing, the thought of embarrassing this pompous brat was too good to be true.

"You're forgiven, of course, as you're new. Let it never be said that the Maravish family aren't forgiving," she said, feigning a haughty tone.

"Maravish?" he said quizzically.

"Why, yes"—she closed the book and looked up at him with as much majestic posture as she could manage—"I'm the Maravish princess . . . but you can call me Lottie."

There was a pause in which the new boy simply stared at her blankly for a moment, making Lottie a little nervous.

"Amazing," he said with no emotion.

This had not been the response Lottie was expecting.

"Do you seriously not know who that is?" Lottie neglected to remind herself that *she* hadn't known who that was until a month ago.

"Oh I do." He smiled, the gesture not quite reaching his eyes. He looked her up and down. "I just didn't expect her to be . . . you."

Lottie found herself genuinely hurt by the insult, though she had to admit she wasn't acting particularly like a princess right now. She mentally recited her mantra to calm herself down.

I will be kind, I will be brave, I will be unstoppable.

No stupid boy would make her doubt herself. She realized she was sitting there opening and closing her mouth like a fish as she tried to come up with a clever reply, but before she could respond the door swung open and in walked Ms. Kuma followed by the rest of the class.

"Ah fantastic, you're already here, and making friends it would seem. Thank you, Lottie." She beamed over at her,

her long embroidered cloak swaying with her lyrical movements as she walked to the front of the class.

At least Lottie could count on English to be a pleasant distraction from her strange morning. She'd always loved English and she adored Ms. Kuma. It was no secret that her love of English stemmed from her childhood obsession with fairy tales. She was so fascinated by words and how they could be used to express abstract thoughts and feelings; it all seemed so beautiful and romantic to her.

"Jamie, please do stand up and introduce yourself," Ms. Kuma said grandly.

Some of the girls in the class blushed and giggled as he stood up.

"Good morning. My name is Jamie Volk and I'm not sure how long I will be at this school. My parents travel a lot so I doubt there's much point in me getting too comfortable here." With that, he sat back down. An awkward silence settled over the previously charmed students as the rest of the company tried and failed to figure out if he was joking.

As he finished his curt introduction, Lottie was distracted by the sight of Ellie. She was peering in through the circular glass window in the door, her mop of wet black hair suggesting she'd neglected to bring an umbrella with her. Lottie waved subtly at her, but Ellie's gaze seemed fixed on Jamie. She looked . . . uncharacteristically terrified. Jamie

glanced over at the door just as Ellie turned around and bolted away. Out of the corner of her eye Lottie was sure she could see Jamie's fists clench.

This is getting weird, she thought. Her whole body went rigid as a troubling thought came to her. *He could be a bad guy; maybe that's the weird feeling I felt earlier?* And she'd just told him she was the princess. She tried to steady her breathing.

"It says here that English is your best subject?" continued Ms. Kuma, unaware of any awkwardness. She gave a short humorous snort. "Looks like you have some competition, Lottie."

Jamie's eyes were still fixed on the door.

Who are you, Jamie Volk? And what do you want with my princess?

As if he'd heard his name spoken, he turned back and gave Lottie a vacant smile. To anyone else in the room it would have seemed like a harmless nod to their supposed joint love of English, but there was something more in his eyes that made Lottie shiver.

After what felt like the most tense and uncomfortable hour of Lottie's life, Ms. Kuma finally dismissed the class, pleasantly reminding everyone as they left their desks to bring in their *A Midsummer Night's Dream* homework for next week.

The second they were dismissed, Lottie made a beeline

for the door and bolted for the stairs.

Behind her she heard a boy's voice. "Wait."

She knew it was Jamie, but she wanted to get as far away from him as possible and find Ellie. Luckily Jamie was new so he wouldn't know the shortcuts back to the dorm. Something odd was going on and she wouldn't feel comfortable until she got some answers from Ellie.

She continued sprinting down the hill to Ivy Wood, determined to avoid him. The air was heavy with the smell of wet soil, and the flora was lush from the storm, brushing her uniform with thick strokes of rainwater as she ran past them. Panting heavily, she squeezed down a side trail, hidden by some ornamental bushes that Raphael and some of the other "rebellious" kids had commandeered as a secret place to skip class.

The hidden trail led directly to the pond outside the Ivy dining hall, if you crawled under the bush at the end. She would have to sacrifice her uniform to the mud, but that felt like the least of her troubles. She turned on to the last bit of pathway expecting to come face-to-face with the bush, but instead found herself confronted by . . . Jamie Volk.

They stood staring at each other.

Jamie was composed, serious and dry, his face partially masked by the shadows of the overgrown trees. He was the complete opposite of Lottie, who stood panting, her

uniform and hair wet, and she was sure she had little twigs stuck in her blond curls. The dappled light on her face through the leaves seemed only to accentuate her puffy red cheeks. Her mind was racing.

How did he know she'd come this way? How did he get here before her? What on earth did he want from her?

It hit her that she was in a secret area that no one knew about, trapped with a strange boy who thought she was the Maravish princess, and she felt hot red panic begin to prickle her skin. She had to run. She tried to turn around, but he grabbed her arm.

"I said wait," he commanded, pulling her back.

"Let go of me!" she screamed. She swiped at him with her free hand, but he caught it effortlessly.

"Lottie—"

"I will call the police," she continued, trying to pull away from him, but she seemed to only be mildly annoying him.

How is he so strong?

"Lottie, please, just listen for a—"

"LET GO OF ME!" She gave one final tug with all her energy and stamped down on his foot. He tried to pull his leg back but a strange static sensation shook him and the two tumbled quite ungracefully into the mud.

"Eek!" Lottie fell flat on her back, immediately thinking of her poor ruined uniform and hair. She had to remind herself that these were the least of her concerns right now

and that she needed to deal with the boy on top of her. She was ready to scream when a pendant around his neck fell against her chest; there was a familiar crest on it with an engraved wolf symbol.

The Wolfson family crest, the same one Ellie wore.

He glanced up and they were forced to look each other in the eyes. Their breath came out in steamy wisps as they slowly panted. Out of the shadows now she could see his cold, vacant mask had dropped momentarily and Lottie found herself suddenly mesmerized by the soft warm glow of his hazel eyes. There was something there, something vulnerable, something that made her feel both comforted and nervous. A clap of thunder filled the pregnant air around them and jolted Lottie out of her trance.

"You . . ." Lottie's eyes lit up with sudden, intense understanding. She looked into Jamie's eyes and felt all the pieces slot together. All at once she realized how she knew him, why he was so strangely familiar. She had seen him every day since she'd arrived at Rosewood.

He was the boy from Ellie's photo.

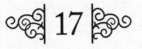

17

JAMIE AND LOTTIE STOOD AWKWARDLY outside her bedroom door. Their uniforms were both filthy but he wore it naturally, as if it made perfect sense for him to be covered in mud. Lottie felt like she was about to burst with worry. She was absolutely dreading Ellie's reaction to her bringing Jamie to their room. After their little tumble in the hidden trail they had talked, and Jamie's true purpose for transferring to Rosewood Hall had come to light.

He had been sent by Ellie's family to figure out what exactly was going on, and why their newspapers were reporting that the Maravish princess was at a school in England. He had known the whole time that Lottie wasn't the Maravish princess, which explained his attitude toward her. It left Lottie absolutely mortified.

"I'm the Maravish princess . . . but you can call me Lottie." If she could go back in time, that would be the moment she'd choose to kick herself in the face. She had stood blushing furiously and wondered if she could bury her head in the ground and maybe never, ever come out again. She would live there forever and never have the

chance to embarrass herself again.

"I'm not sorry for embarrassing you; I think you quite deserved it," Jamie had said sternly.

She couldn't disagree with him.

The west side of their dormitory was the girls' side, and boys were not supposed to be there. Jamie was quite clearly a boy and if anyone, particularly Professor Devine, caught them, they'd both be in tremendous trouble. Which led to her current predicament. She wanted nothing more than to be safe in the confines of her room where she could chuck Jamie out over the balcony should a teacher come by to check on them; he might break his leg or something but it was a small price to pay for her perfect school record. She could explain that she'd fallen in the mud and had to run back to change and everything would be fine. But she couldn't bring herself to open the door. She was just too mortified by this whole series of events. Their decision not to fix this princess mix-up may very well result in Ellie being flown back to Maradova, and Lottie felt like it was all her fault.

How many times will I find myself standing nervously outside 221? she wondered regretfully.

"And I suppose opening doors for yourself is against the rules of a princess, Miss Pumpkin?" The sarcasm came from Jamie, who was making a point of tapping his foot impatiently.

All thoughts of worry quickly changed to irritation again. There was something particularly annoying about how well spoken he was. It added about fifty percent more exasperation to the whole experience.

"You know what"—Lottie turned to him, clenching her fists in frustration—"I am getting a bit sick of your sarcastic tone."

Jamie did not miss a beat: "And I'm getting a bit sick of waiting for you to open this door."

"Well, I was just about to." Lottie puffed up her cheeks in a particularly childish display of stubbornness, causing Jamie to roll his eyes.

They heard the latch on the dormitory door click and the door began to creak open. They both turned their heads in unison to see Ellie, jaw wide open, looking very confused at the sight of the two of them covered in mud.

"Lottie?" Ellie suddenly blinked as if coming back down to earth and her expression changed from shock to aggravation. "WHAT THE . . . ?" she started yelling, but Lottie and Jamie both had the same reaction, to push Ellie back inside and cover her mouth to stop her shouting.

"*Shh!*" hushed Jamie as he pulled the door shut behind them. "Do you want us to get caught? You need to think about your school record."

Lottie snorted in annoyance.

He rolled his eyes again. She had a feeling she'd be

seeing him do that a lot.

Lottie felt a hand grab her arm and pull her backward. Ellie positioned herself in the middle of Lottie and Jamie, creating a block between them. There was a look on her face, the same fire she'd had when taking down Anastacia the other day on the field. Lottie moved to step out from behind her, but Ellie put her arm out protectively, pushing Lottie back. She looked up at her and Ellie gave her that trademark little side smile and affectionately pulled a twig out of a lock of her blond hair. "I see you've met my childhood friend, Jamie Volk."

She turned to Jamie and gave him a heated look, like some kind of angry warning. The atmosphere in the room had turned uncomfortably harsh. The whole exchange was very confusing. Jamie had said he'd known Ellie her whole life: surely she should be happy to see him?

"Jamie." She said the name curtly.

They stood staring at each other for a moment, really taking the other in for the first time since being reunited, the Wolfson crest lockets around their necks perfectly lining up.

"You haven't sent a single letter; your parents have been worried sick," Jamie said flatly. Ellie looked away and Lottie could see she was biting her lip anxiously. "Not to mention you've been skipping classes and breaking curfew and—"

"It doesn't even matter!" Ellie suddenly protested.

"Lottie has perfect attendance and, as far as anyone knows, *she's* the Maravish princess. So I can do whatever I want!" She tried to say the words with a sense of humor but it didn't have the desired effect.

"That is not how it works, Ellie," he said coldly, his tone the complete opposite of Ellie's.

"But what if it did?" There was the tiniest trace of desperation in Ellie's voice that made Lottie wince.

"You know we can't . . ."

"But she's basically a P—"

"*Briktah!*" Jamie barked.

Uh-oh, thought Lottie. That was definitely not a good word.

Ellie stamped her foot down hard, making Lottie jump. She barked something in another language, which Lottie guessed must be an old Maravish dialect, and started gesturing wildly with her hands. Lottie had never seen her like this and it was almost frightening. She was reminded just how intense Ellie's mood swings could be.

It was a strange sight, watching this mud-covered boy argue with a furious storm of a girl against the pretty rose-decorated background of Lottie's side of the room. There was something almost hilarious about it. Although she couldn't understand the language, the words "Lottie" and "Portman" kept popping up, and it was clear they were discussing something critical. Lottie wondered if

she should maybe leave them alone, but when she made a move to the side Ellie instinctively pushed her back without looking at her.

Finally, they seemed to reach an impasse. It was impossible to tell who'd won as they both still seemed frustrated. Jamie ran his hands through his hair in exasperation and sat on Lottie's bed. He picked up her stuffed pig Mr. Truffles and to Lottie's amazement he began absentmindedly rubbing its head before gesturing with his other hand as if giving Ellie permission to do something.

Ellie turned suddenly to Lottie, and the look on her face was so out of character—she appeared to be almost apprehensive—that Lottie felt very uncomfortable.

"Do you know what a Partizan is, Lottie?" Ellie asked uneasily.

Lottie instantly perked up at the use of a word she actually knew.

"Why, yes," she said proudly. "Binah told me on the first day actually. They're like fancy bodyguards . . ." The serious look on their faces had Lottie second-guessing herself. "I believe," she added more hesitantly.

"No, no . . . I mean, yes . . . you're right. They are." Ellie looked over at Jamie and something odd flashed across her face, something like regret. It was quickly replaced by her usual mask of confidence.

"Anyone willing to go through the arduous process

can train to be a Partizan nowadays, but a true Partizan is raised from birth for their role. Primed from childhood to be a lethal protector, loyal only to their master, they are very effective and very dangerous but, most importantly, they're discreet." Ellie looked up at Lottie again, a glint in her eyes.

Lottie found she was holding her breath. Binah had said Partizans seemed romantic, and she realized now what she'd meant. They were like something out of a story. Deadly, devoted assassins, trained from birth to protect their lord or lady.

I wonder how often they fall in love with each other? she thought to herself.

"Wow," she said aloud, then a thought struck her and she asked curiously, "Do you have one?"

Jamie and Ellie turned to each other then, and a look passed between them. They seemed to share some kind of telepathic conversation that Jamie responded to by giving a swift nod.

Ellie turned back to Lottie and started rubbing the back of her head sheepishly as if she were embarrassed to continue. "Jamie . . . Jamie's my Partizan." She bared her teeth in a little grin as if this information was no big deal. "The agreement was they'd send him here if anything went wrong and, well . . ."

A million questions began shooting around Lottie's head and she didn't know where to begin. *Who else had a Partizan in this school? Were Jamie's parents also Partizans? Had Jamie ever had to kill anyone?* She quickly crushed that last thought as she found it sent an unpleasant shiver down her spine.

"Lottie?" Ellie asked with concern.

Lottie sat down hard on Ellie's bed, feeling a little dizzy.

"Sorry, this is just a lot to take in," she replied, still in a daze. She looked over at Jamie apprehensively. If he looked odd against Lottie's pretty pink half of the room before, he now looked like a fish in the desert. No wonder he had been so cold and intense when they had first met.

This boy had been raised from birth to protect Princess Eleanor Wolfson of Maradova, and Lottie had unwittingly almost exposed her and put her in danger. To Jamie, Lottie must represent everything he'd spent his life guarding Ellie from.

No wonder he made her feel so nervous.

"Do you have your passport with you?" asked Jamie, who was avoiding eye contact on the other side of the room.

"I . . . yes, I do. It's in my bedside table." The words came out a little edgier than she expected and she knew there was no way she could hide her uneasy feelings from him.

"Good," he replied. "You'll be needing it."

He stood up finally and Lottie flinched. He was completely different to her now that she knew he was a lethal killing machine.

"What does that mean?" she asked as calmly as possible.

"It means, Lottie"—he walked over to the side of her bed and opened the drawer. His fingers traced along the rosy pink cover on her passport, a smirk on his lips—"you're coming to Maradova."

It was the last thing Lottie had expected to hear.

18

LOTTIE HAD HOPED THAT ATTENDING Rosewood would change her life dramatically, but she had never in her wildest dreams imagined that just a few weeks after she started she would be flying in a private jet with the riot-girl princess of Maradova and her deadly killing-machine-in-a-teen-boy sidekick. And she definitely wasn't dreaming. She'd checked.

"You don't need to be scared of Jamie." Ellie was distracting herself by trying to solve the puzzle Binah had given her, but was clearly having no luck. "He's harmless, honestly."

Somehow Lottie didn't believe that. No matter what Ellie said, she couldn't bring herself to trust him. She didn't like not being able to tell what he was thinking. He was sitting on the other side of the plane, apparently engrossed in a book, but she was sure he was discreetly surveying the area.

"Are you *sure*? How do you know he's not gone rogue and secretly informed someone at the school that you were coming to Rosewood?" It was a thought Lottie had been

mulling over during the flight. She was sure he was hiding something and it was driving her mad. She quickly cut herself off as she saw Jamie looking over at them. Lowering her voice, she added half seriously, "Does he have superhuman hearing as well?"

Ellie blinked at her for a moment, then burst out laughing. "Lottie, you are hilarious."

Ellie and Jamie would not tell Lottie why she had to come to Maradova. Ellie's irritatingly enigmatic response was: "If my plan works, then you'll find out why you needed to be there . . . and if it doesn't . . . well, let's not think about that." So that's exactly what Lottie was doing. Trying not to think about it.

The flight took five hours and they landed at around 7 p.m. Lottie had only ever flown twice in her life, and she had never been ushered straight through customs by an entourage of smartly dressed bodyguards in sunglasses. This was evidently a royalty perk. As soon as they were outside, Lottie was overcome by how very cold it was. There was ice on the ground and the air seemed frozen. They moved in relative silence once the entourage showed up. Ellie nervously chewed her bottom lip and distractedly rubbed the locket around her neck. Jamie remained completely composed and unreadable as always.

They all piled into a fancy black car, Jamie politely holding the door open for them. As Lottie was about to follow

Ellie into the vehicle, Jamie grabbed her arm and stopped her.

He looked at her with a fiery intensity. "You need to be on your absolute best behavior when we get to the palace, do you understand?" His voice came out as a low growl and made Lottie's whole body tremble, but she simply nodded in response. "And, no"—he leaned down and whispered in her ear—"I don't have superhuman hearing."

They drove in total silence and when they entered the palace grounds Lottie realized that the estate was so large she couldn't see the top of the building out of the tinted car window. They had to go through two elaborate gilded gates before they even reached the driveway of the palace, although "driveway" was a pathetically insufficient word to describe it.

Finally they pulled up by the door to the palace: magnificent in white oak with a gold, life-size snarling wolf's head in the middle, a knocker hanging from its bared jaws. The crunching gravel underneath the wheels seemed to echo as they came to a halt.

One of the mysterious bodyguards opened the car door, but Ellie scooted over and let herself out of the other side. Jamie tensed for a moment and gritted his teeth, but Ellie simply smirked at him before sauntering over to the front door. As they approached the looming figure of the wolf head, the door opened inward and they were greeted by

two women in pristine aprons and black dresses, hair neatly arranged. Lottie didn't get a chance to look directly at the wolf.

It was late and the palace was seeped in a milky-blue glow. Even the thick walls of the grounds couldn't keep the chill out of the hallways and Lottie stared nervously at the paintings of previous rulers that stared down at her, the eyes following them through the corridors in what seemed like a never-ending walk.

They were informed by a muscular woman, who introduced herself as Edwina, that the trial would take place the next morning, and that they should rest for the night. Lottie had no idea what she meant by that, but the word "trial" made her shudder.

Lottie was given her own room in the left wing of the palace with a view of the vast gardens.

Ellie quickly joined Lottie, but Jamie kept himself scarce once they were safely in the palace walls.

"I didn't know places like this really existed." Lottie couldn't conceal the wonder in her voice as she tiptoed around the guest room, absorbing every amazing detail of the lavish space. "I can't believe how beautiful everything is."

The vanity table had a collection of designer perfumes in gorgeous bottles that Lottie lined up to admire. Lottie had assumed that Rosewood Hall would be the height of

her luxury experience, but if Rosewood was magnificent then Maradova was otherworldly. It was a very welcome distraction from the trial, whatever that would be, the next day.

"I always found it too excessive," Ellie replied. As if on cue, the door swung open and in came a redheaded maid with a tray piled high with far too much food for two people.

"Please enjoy your dinner, Princess," said the maid, curt-sying respectfully.

"Thank you, Hanna, but please don't call me that."

"Of course, Princess." Ellie gave the maid a devilish smile and they both laughed before she exited the room, leaving them on their own. They sat on the bed to eat, but Lottie found herself too anxious to enjoy the food.

"It feels weird hearing you called princess," she said at last.

Ellie had been very quiet since they'd arrived at the palace, clearly lost in thought.

"It feels weird to me too," she said honestly.

Lottie watched Ellie as she absently piled bread and cheese into her mouth, her gaze distant and worried. She didn't like seeing Ellie like this; the palace obviously had a negative effect on her. Lottie wanted nothing more than to wrap her up and save her from her princess duties. *But how?*

Lottie was awoken in her soft bed the next morning by the same maid who'd brought them food the night before. She entered Lottie's room with a tray of tea and traditional Maravish pastries that reminded her of baklava and tasted heavenly. Without Lottie's knowledge, her clothes had been cleaned and pressed for her and laid out conveniently on the dresser. The same maid then offered to run her a bubble bath, which she enthusiastically accepted. She sat in the circular tub in her en suite for an extra-long time, wanting to prolong the luxurious experience as long as possible before coming back to reality and the looming trial. She sank her head under the warm water, squeezed her eyes shut and pretended for a moment that she really was a princess and this really was her home.

At 10 a.m. she was collected by an unassuming maid who took her into a plush living space in which Jamie and Ellie were waiting.

Jamie immediately began prepping her, and the enchantment she'd felt quickly crumbled as she came hurtling back to reality.

"When we are allowed entry into the throne room you will stand unless told otherwise. You will avoid eye contact unless told otherwise. And, above anything else, you will be silent unless told otherwise."

Lottie nodded at these instructions, feeling more out of place than she'd ever felt in her life and desperately trying to be as accommodating as possible.

Jamie was pacing slowly back and forth in front of a large gold-framed mirror on the wall as if addressing an army regiment. Ellie was slumped on a gold-embroidered sofa, her boots carelessly kicking the fabric.

"Jamie, you need to relax. You always act like the world is ending and it's always fine."

Jamie let out an exasperated breath from his nose and turned to face Ellie. "Ellie, this isn't about things being fine. This is the single most significant decision you've ever made regarding your future." Jamie's tone was somber, yet Ellie reacted by grinning.

"I know. This is the best plan I've ever had!" There was excitement in Ellie's voice that annoyed Lottie. She suddenly had the horrible feeling she was a chess piece in someone else's game.

"Umm," Lottie began, and Jamie swiftly turned his head toward her, making her jump, but she found the courage to continue. "If this is all so significant, can you please tell me what the trial is exactly?"

There was a short pause where they both looked at her as if seeing her for the first time.

"No!" was their simultaneous response.

"Well, can you at least tell me what to expect?"

Jamie raised an eyebrow, a strand of his slightly messy hair falling in front of his eyes.

"Expect the absolute worst," he said flatly.

Lottie gulped.

"Ha!" Ellie stood up and patted Lottie on the head. Lottie usually quite liked the gesture, but today she felt patronized. "You're going to meet my parents, and they're going to love you."

Jamie quite literally growled at this. "You . . ." he started, but quickly took a deep breath to calm himself. "You need to take this seriously, Ellie. This is not like before."

Her face distorted into a furious mask of indignation. "It's. Going. To. Be. Fine."

"Ellie, you don't understand. They're really serious." His tone was almost pleading and it made Lottie flinch. She wondered how many times Jamie found himself in situations like this, trying—and failing—to help Ellie.

"No, Jamie, *you* don't understand. Mom and Dad make *everything* seem like a huge deal but it's always fine in the end, and this time isn't going to be any different."

"Ellie, this *is* different, I promise. They've"—he faltered for a moment, then looked back into Ellie's eyes—"they've brought your *grandmother*."

Lottie almost snickered at this, but the horrified look on Ellie's face made her think better of it. Her eyes began

darting around very quickly as if she were thinking really fast.

"Lottie, listen to me. I need you to—"

Before Ellie could finish the door swung open.

The red-haired maid curtsied. "They will see you in the main hall now, Princess."

"Hanna, *please*, I told you not to call me that," Ellie said, jokingly rolling her eyes. She smiled at the girl and the maid giggled in response, still not looking up. Lottie could hardly believe that Ellie could behave so normally considering the tension in the room just seconds before.

"Thank you, Hanna." Jamie smiled charmingly at her, showing no sign of stress.

"Ellie, I need to *what*?" Lottie whispered, so Hanna wouldn't hear. "You can't start saying something, then walk out. Tell me what you need me to do!"

Ellie turned back to her with a big smile on her face that seemed painfully forced. "There's no time left."

19

THE LARGE OAK DOORS CREAKED open. Light flooded out of the throne room, bathing them in a bright white stream that made Lottie catch her breath and cover her eyes. When her eyes had adjusted to the strange lighting, she had to stop herself from gasping at the storybook scene in front of her.

The room seemed to glow from within. Intricate patterns were etched into the white walls and above them, peering down, was a scene of strange mythical monsters and beasts surrounding a crystal chandelier that sent light falling in little delicate dots like snow.

In the middle of the room sat Ellie's father, the king of Maradova. There was a distinct family resemblance in their dark eyes, but his hair was light and immaculately cut around his sharp features. The back of the throne on which he sat towered over his tall frame in a way that made it seem part of him. He gazed at the three teenagers in turn and gave a single terse nod to Jamie, which Jamie returned straight-faced.

A thin old woman sat to the right of him, mounds and mounds of long silver hair lavishly layered on top of her head. It did not take much deductive skill to figure out she was Ellie's grandmother. Her chair had a dark blue cushion with little gold tassels propped up to support her and in her right hand she held a magnificent cane topped with a solid gold wolf head. The way her hand gripped the cane suggested nothing of frailty but rather control, demanding respect and submission. Her eyes locked with Lottie's and for a split second Lottie felt a chill run through her. *The Evil Witch*, Lottie thought involuntarily; there was something undeniably terrifying about her.

On the king's left, standing with his hands clasped behind his back, was a tall man with what appeared to be a glass eye. He smiled at each of them, his eyes lingering on Lottie for a little longer than she felt comfortable with.

What am I doing here? Lottie thought to herself. *I don't belong here.*

"Her Highness Princess Eleanor Prudence Wolfson . . ." started the glass-eyed man.

"You have requested an official audience with the king to enact Act Six. Official enquiries into the suitability and benefit of this request have begun. The counterargument is . . ." He cleared his throat before continuing. "The counterargument," he repeated, "is that the princess has, to

quote the queen mother, 'continually disappointed on all previous arrangements without exception.'"

Lottie thought back to Ellie telling her how she'd snuck out before—and how naturally she could deceive.

Ellie's grandmother banged her cane on the marble floor once and let out a little laugh that sounded more like a cackle.

"Disappointed?" There was a sharpness in her voice that made Lottie flinch. "I think that is not quite the term I used. That would suggest we had any hope for you in the first place, dear Eleanor."

Neither Jamie nor Ellie reacted.

The king rubbed his forehead and sighed in frustration. "Duly noted, Mother." It became instantly apparent to Lottie that the king wanted to be there about as much as Lottie did. "Very well. Begin the enquiry."

The glass-eyed man cleared his throat again. "Miss Charlotte Edith Pumpkin . . ." he began.

"*Pumpkin?*" spat the old woman. "What a peculiar name." Her voice was taut as she said the word "peculiar," as if she were really saying "*what a completely ridiculous name.*"

Lottie looked down at the glowing floor, trying her hardest to hide her embarrassment and her growing sense of fear. The king cleared his throat before gesturing to the man to continue.

"Miss Charlotte Pumpkin, born Charlotte Edith Curran"—Lottie took in a sharp breath at having this information read aloud and turned to see Ellie chewing her bottom lip nervously; Jamie's face remained blank—"student at Rosewood Hall, rooming with Eleanor, of no notable nobility, lived in St. Ives, Cornwall, with her stepmother, Beady Curran, until September when she moved to permanent boarding at Rosewood. Mother passed away five years ago from leukemia, father works as a . . ."

The list seemed endless and, although she was fully clothed, she'd never felt more naked in her life. Why was this happening? Why was this necessary? She felt sick. She felt dizzy. These were all parts of herself she wanted to hide from, and now strangers were picking at her life as if she were a specimen in a biology class. She suddenly felt very angry with Ellie. She wished she'd been warned. She wished she knew why any of this was required. She wished she knew anything at all.

"Enough!"

"Okay, we get it."

Ellie and Jamie had simultaneously come to her rescue.

Maybe Jamie wasn't so bad . . .

The king looked surprisingly sympathetic.

"Skip to the end," he said bluntly. The glass-eyed man cleared his throat once again and Lottie slowly unclenched

her fists, which had balled up at her sides.

"In the top two percent of most of her classes, excluding gym and math, currently the second-highest achiever in English literature and history."

Jamie's blank mask slipped as he looked at Lottie.

"One of only twenty-two students in the history of Rosewood to be offered the exceptional-circumstances scholarship and it seems she was personally chosen by Professor Devine to join Ivy House."

Lottie felt her heart hammering wildly and was sure they must be able to see it under her shirt. They knew information about her that even she didn't know. She was a hard worker, everyone knew that; she prided herself on it, and she wanted to be great and do great things, but to have her past shoved in her face, followed by achievements she hadn't even known about—somehow it made her feel . . . humiliated.

Was Jamie questioning the legitimacy of these accomplishments? Why would it be funny that a girl so ordinary could push herself so hard?

"Quite the diligent little worker it would seem," the king said with a dry smile.

Lottie was about to burst into tears right then and there on the marble floor.

Be brave, be brave, be brave, she repeated to herself.

"Ellie, you shame us." The king's tone was cold. "If

even this girl, under her circumstances, can push herself to achieve such feats, then you, a future queen, have no reason to deny yourself similar accomplishments." His eyes drifted over Jamie and a look like regret flashed on his face but was gone too quickly for Lottie to register completely. "You forget how fortunate you are." Ellie looked as if she were about to speak but the king held up his hand. "You were allowed to attend Rosewood under the agreement that you would keep your identity secret with no exceptions. An agreement that you would acclimate to school rules without the pressure of your royal obligations. You have failed on both these counts."

The king's face seemed almost pained as he said these words. It was clear to Lottie that he truly must have hoped Rosewood would be the right choice for Ellie. Ellie's grandmother continued to sit stony-faced at his side.

Ellie's expression was still hard, determined not to let anything show, but Lottie could see the strain in her eyes: the misty look of someone desperately trying not to cry.

This is my fault, thought Lottie.

All at once her anxiety for her own fate dissipated as she realized what was really at stake here. Ellie opened her mouth to protest, but before she could get any words out something rang in the back of Lottie's mind. The voice of Professor Devine.

The fates have placed Miss Wolf in a room with you, so

you must look out for her.

Was this it? Was this her calling to Rosewood? Had her drive to become exceptional been entirely designed to bring her and Ellie together? That thought was comforting and suddenly she didn't feel so afraid.

"She's going to join the fencing team," Lottie stated matter-of-factly.

The whole hall turned to stare at her like a pack of wolves. Jamie looked completely horrified and mouthed the word *"Don't,"* but Lottie swallowed hard and continued.

"That is, with all due respect, you're wrong about her not acclimating to school life. She's been invited personally by Dame Bolter herself, an Olympic gold medalist, to join the fencing team. She also helps others excel: she helps me with my math homework, she's improved my grade in gym, she studies for fun with the smartest girl in school, and she even gives Anastacia Alcroft a run for her money in lacrosse. She belongs at Rosewood and I will do anything to keep her there."

Lottie paused and blinked, completely thrown by her own words.

"Anything, Miss Pumpkin?" The words came from a twinkling little voice behind her.

Lottie turned to see a petite blond woman with porcelain skin and eyes so icy blue they almost froze her on the

spot. She was smiling ever so slightly, but her eyes shone with sharp cunning. Although she was small in size, this woman gave off an edge that suggested she was most certainly not to be taken lightly.

Lottie hesitated for only a moment. "Yes," she said emphatically.

"Quite." The woman's smile widened and she took a small step from the edge of the room toward Lottie. "Would you even sign your life over to the Maravish royal family?"

Wait, what? And that was the moment everything went completely mad.

20

"ABSOLUTELY NOT!" CRIED ELLIE'S GRANDMOTHER, her face screwed up in a furious mask of indignation. "This is out of the question!"

The blond woman seemed entirely unaffected by this outburst and simply waved her hand, dismissing the statement.

Grandmother Wolfson did not appreciate this gesture and turned to the king. "Alexander, control your wife." The words came out more as a bark than a request.

That's Ellie's mother? Lottie turned back to stare at the wispy, ethereal blond woman and saw almost no physical resemblance between the two, and yet . . . she thought of the confident way she held herself, and her piercing eyes, the bold way she had dismissed the most terrifying woman Lottie had ever met. Maybe it wasn't so shocking after all.

The king turned to his mother then and, to Lottie's complete and utter surprise, he looked offended.

"Mother, may I remind you, this audience is requested for the sole purpose of an Act Six request? Or have you not been paying attention?"

Lottie almost laughed at this, even though she still had no idea what Act Six was.

"Oh lord," Ellie groaned under her breath, rubbing the bridge of her nose as if this were a regular occurrence. Jamie remained impassive, although his eyes seemed to be larger than usual.

The king turned then to Ellie's mother and his face softened; her presence seemed to dispel some of his tension.

So this is where she gets those mood swings from! Lottie thought to herself. These people made Ellie look normal in comparison.

"Umm, excuse me—" Lottie began, but was cut off as Ellie's mother gently ran a lock of Lottie's curly blond hair through her fingers, making her jump in surprise.

"Alexander, she could be one of ours—it's uncanny." She leaned into Lottie very closely, but it didn't feel like she was really looking at *her*. It made her feel as though she were a racehorse being inspected for purchase.

"Did you enjoy your night in the palace? We would love to have you again."

It took Lottie a moment to realize the queen was talking to her.

"Yes, I—".

"You cannot seriously be considering the idea that this"—the king's mother cut her off and gestured furiously to Lottie without looking at her directly—"common girl

could possibly take the role of a Portman?"

Portman! Lottie remembered the word from Ellie and Jamie's earlier argument. *Whatever could she mean?*

"Your daughter is merely looking for yet another excuse to avoid her responsibilities, and this time she's dragged an ordinary girl along with her."

"Ordinary?" Ellie's mother laughed. "In this instance I think we can all agree that her inconsequential background is most beneficial."

She began circling Lottie slowly as if she were her prey. "I, for one, think she's perfect. A blessing even."

"See, I told you; she's totally right." Ellie had regained the power of speech.

Jamie was clenching his jaw.

"I must agree," the king said. "It is a strangely fortunate situation we find ourselves in with this Miss Pumpkin."

Lottie found she was struggling to understand. "Excuse me, I—"

She was cut off by the glass-eyed man.

"She certainly meets the criteria, but the question is, Your Majesty"—he bent down so he was closer to the king's ear, the words coming out with a hiss—"will the princess truly uphold her end of the bargain? As has been said before, she tends to disappoint." He gave Ellie a sharp look as he finished speaking, a nasty grin creeping onto his lips. Ellie was noticeably gritting her teeth.

"That is, indeed, the question," the king agreed.

"Could I please . . ." Lottie tried to raise her hand this time.

The old woman cackled. "*Bah!* If that's the only question, then the answer is a blindingly obvious no. I suggest you pull her from the school, and send her to St. Agnes's Correctional Facility for Young Ladies where they will whip her into a woman worthy of the Maravish crown."

"If someone could just . . ."

"I think it's a splendid idea, and shows that our Eleanor is making active decisions in her role as princess, which we should be eagerly encouraging." Ellie's mother smiled at her husband and he nodded in response.

"If you can call the choice to be passive an *active decision*." The glass-eyed man chuckled softly.

The king and his mother openly laughed at this and Lottie found herself suddenly very angry.

"WOULD SOMEBODY EXPLAIN TO ME WHAT IS GOING ON?"

The hall went quiet again, the wolf pack turning to stare at her as if they had forgotten she was even there.

"Please," she added quickly.

The silence that filled the room was almost deafening. Jamie broke his mask for just a moment and looked at Lottie in astonishment before regaining his composure.

"Lottie . . ." Ellie's face softened. She clenched her fists

and turned back to the king with a hard look on her face. "Dad!" she said resolutely. "I don't care what the decision is. I'll accept whatever course of action you choose, but you need to make it now. I can't keep my friend in the dark anymore." She extended her hand to Lottie's and gave it a little squeeze. Lottie felt a pleasant sense of static between them.

The king eyed his daughter with fresh consideration, struck with the loyalty and severity in her stare. His dark eyes squinted as he contemplated a side of her he'd never seen before. His gaze moved to the girls' hands that were still clasped in solidarity.

"Very well." He turned to his wife, and she beamed at him with a knowing smile. "Based on the absurdly convenient suitability of the proposed Portman and what I, as the king, have deemed a clear sign of positive influence"—he paused for dramatic effect—"I sanction this request for Princess Eleanor Prudence Wolfson to enact Act Six with Charlotte Edith Pumpkin. Let it be written."

Grandmother Wolfson let out a furious cry, but the king held up his hand and she reluctantly quieted.

"I fear this is a grave mistake," she said darkly.

The king ignored this statement. "And, to put us all at ease, Jamie will continue his placement at Rosewood Hall. The school will be informed of the special arrangement."

Jamie tensed and the glass-eyed man seemed to be stifling a snicker.

"You are all excused."

Ellie let out an excited little squeal and grabbed Lottie's arm, leading her through the ornate doors with so much giddy energy she was almost skipping. Lottie followed, only dimly aware of her body moving, and still not entirely sure what had just been decided.

"Did you see that?" the king whispered to his wife when the door was firmly shut.

"Yes!" she replied excitedly. "Eleanor's made a friend!"

21

"Portman: one who is hired to officially act in the place of a member of royalty in order to protect their true identity. All public appearances and official duties are to be carried out with the utmost respect and *blah, blah, blah, blah*, so on and so forth . . ."

Lottie blinked in bewilderment as Ellie read aloud the passage from a dusty old book they'd been given by the glass-eyed man, who Ellie had informed her was the king's advisor, Simien Smirnov.

"So this is *my* job now?" Lottie said, her eyes bulging.

"Well, if you want it to be. You were basically doing it already," she said good-humoredly. "Now you'd just . . . be getting paid to do it."

"Okay, but . . . wait, paid?"

"Yes, you'll get a monthly payment, as well as travel, food, and clothing expenses."

Lottie almost choked; did they realize this was a dream come true? This hardly seemed like a job at all, getting all the benefits of being a princess *and* being paid for it.

"And this way, in the future when you inevitably have to

tell everyone that you're, in fact, *not* the princess of Maradova, you'll be able to say with complete truthfulness that it's because you were an official Portman. Perfect!" She gave Lottie a thumbs-up, which she responded to by blinking again.

The three teenagers had convened in Ellie's bedroom, which, although large, was surprisingly bare. Lacking Ellie's motley charm, it could be anyone's room. It was evidently not a place Ellie considered home. Ellie and Lottie sat on the vast four-poster bed while Jamie stood by the door with one foot propped up against the wood frame, resting his head back in silent thought. He'd informed her that as soon as they started back at school, he would begin training her to be a perfect Portman—something she was a little apprehensive about.

"How long have you been planning this?" Lottie asked, afraid to hear the truth.

Ellie looked sheepish. "Pretty much as soon as I confronted you in our first week."

Lottie balked at this. "You didn't ask me. You didn't . . ." She had to pause to stop herself from getting flustered; she was just so overwhelmed. "You should have told me what I was here for. You can trust me."

"You don't understand, Lottie. I couldn't! It would be breaking too many rules," Ellie pleaded.

"But you always break the rules!"

"Lottie, stop!" This came from Jamie, but his words weren't angry or cold; they were calm. "She really couldn't tell you. Portmans are a royal secret; barely anyone knows they exist and half the people who do know think they're just a fairy tale. We need to keep it that way to protect those who need them, do you understand?"

Lottie nodded. It did make sense, but it felt like they didn't have faith in her.

"I understand that, but *you* have to understand that I have Ellie's best interests at heart as much as you do." She turned to her friend, a fiery feeling in her belly. "If you trust me enough to be your Portman, then you should trust me enough to tell me about them."

Ellie chewed her lip for a moment, while Jamie straightened up and walked over to Lottie.

"You're right," he said.

"I am?" she asked in confusion. Had she just imagined that? Had Jamie just *agreed* with her?

"Yes. We should have told you. But Ellie truly had no choice in the matter," he said matter-of-factly.

"I'm really sorry, Lottie." Ellie pushed her hair out of her eyes as she spoke and Lottie knew she meant it.

"I forgive you, Ellie, and I really am happy to do this for you; it feels right. But we have to promise no more secrets going forward." She held her little finger out like she used

to as a kid, and Ellie laughed as she wrapped her own finger around it.

"I promise."

As Lottie sat on the airplane the next morning, preparing for takeoff, Jamie came and took the seat beside her. He was so quiet that she didn't even realize he was there until he said her name.

She turned abruptly and nearly banged her head into his, but this time he dodged it easily. His face was inscrutable as usual. She was starting to trust him more, but he still made her nervous.

"I really do agree with you," he said. "It was wrong of them not to tell you. In fact, you should not have been brought here at all. You should not have been told about Portmans, and you absolutely should not have been asked to take on the role of one."

Lottie was lost for words. She should've known Jamie felt this way, that he didn't think her capable or worthy to take on the role of an official Portman. She'd spent the majority of her life having people doubt her capabilities, yet hearing his words still hurt her deeply.

"I . . ." Her voice cracked and she took a breath to calm herself. She wanted them to believe in her, to see that she was capable of this role, even if she wasn't sure if she

believed it herself yet. "I'm going to impress you, Jamie."

He looked at her with a slightly sad expression that she couldn't quite understand, sighed, and took a little beaten-up book out of his jacket pocket. It was leather-bound with a silver floral pattern that reflected the light. He placed it on her lap and she flinched.

"I'm sure you will," he said, his smile returning. Then he stood up and left for his own seat without another word.

Lottie looked down at the book and carefully opened the first page to a beautiful cursive script:

> *I, Oscar Oddwood, Portman to the late Henric Wolfson, have collected the tales and advice of Portmans from around the world so that our collective wisdom may be passed down and augmented. May this book assist any of those that take on the ambiguous role of the Faithful Fake.*

Lottie gently flipped through it and saw illustrated pages full of different handwritings and languages. She felt as if there were magic radiating from the book; as if the item were sacred. She gently tucked the book away in her bag, too tired to appreciate it properly now. She leaned her head against the window to watch the takeoff.

The fluffy clouds parted below the plane, creating a peephole into the icy landscape of Maradova beneath

them. She looked over at Ellie who was asleep, her face covered by a book entitled *Well-Behaved Women Seldom Make History*. Jamie had his copy of *A Midsummer Night's Dream* out and was earnestly taking notes. They seemed entirely unaffected by the attentive staff and the luxury of the private jet. There was something effortless about the two of them: they were so sure of belonging, so confidently radiating their purpose into the world.

Lottie felt as though she was being allowed an insight into a realm in which she didn't truly belong. Rosewood Hall, royal Portmans, the Wolfsons—they were all so magnificent, and after her night in the palace she felt a deep desire to be part of it all. The clouds re-formed under the plane and Lottie lost her view of the land below, suddenly feeling very far from the ground and determined to find her place in the world.

PART TWO
How to Be a Princess

22

LOTTIE TOSSED AND TURNED IN her bed, but no matter what position she tried, she could not fall asleep. The covers were too hot and the air was too cold and no amount of counting sheep helped. This was the tenth sleepless night since her return from Maradova, and Lottie was starting to think she'd never dream again.

She looked over to see Ellie's sleeping face across the room and reluctantly sat up to start getting ready for the day. No matter what, she absolutely could not let Jamie or Ellie know she was having trouble sleeping or they'd think she wasn't cut out for her role as Portman. The strawberry-shaped alarm clock on her bedside table went off, signaling that it was time for her Saturday-morning class with Jamie, something she was calling her *princess lessons*. Ellie stretched in her bed and made a huge yawning sound, lethargically sitting up and swinging her legs over the side of the mattress.

"Ellie, you really don't have to come. You can go back to sleep if you want," Lottie said softly, worried that speaking too loud might disturb the early morning air.

Ellie yawned once more, her eyes not fully focusing. "Nope!" She rubbed her cheeks in an attempt to force herself awake. "If you have to get up early for these princess lessons, then I will suffer with you. It's only fair."

Lottie couldn't help feeling happy at Ellie's words.

They met Jamie in one of the Ivy study rooms overlooking the Rose Wood. The sun had not risen yet and it was difficult for Lottie to keep her eyes open in the warm room filled with dusty books. Jamie was pacing back and forth, asking her to translate ancient Maravish words while Ellie plugged away at homework. Since returning from Maradova, Lottie's days had become a strict schedule of school, homework, tutoring, and princess lessons. She was used to working overtime from when she'd studied to get into Rosewood, but with the addition of insomnia she was starting to feel run-down.

"*Sets?*"

"Prince."

"*Sessa?*"

"Princess."

"Good."

Jamie ticked something off in his little notebook that he kept for their lessons. His face remained unreadable and she had no idea if he was happy with her progress.

"Honestly, I don't see the point in her learning the

ancient Maravish dialect. It hasn't been used in nearly a hundred years."

Jamie scowled at Ellie, who'd been doing nothing but making digs at his lesson plan since they'd started.

"That's a good point, Ellie. Lottie, recite the history of the Maravish language."

Lottie groaned internally. It seemed like every time Ellie made a comment, she had to recite something. She squeezed her eyes shut for a second, willing away some of her tiredness.

"Maravish: of Latin origin; a dialect grown from mixing English and Russian. After the treaty of Serego, when Maradova gained independence from the British Empire, the people of Maradova kept English as their main language. The ancient Maravish dialect is now only used to—"

"Okay. Good." Jamie cut her off. "See how quickly Lottie's picked this all up, Ellie? You should be taking notes."

Lottie resented that the only real feedback she got from Jamie was in the form of a verbal jab at Ellie.

Ellie stuck her tongue out at him before turning back to her textbook.

Two Ivy girls on their way to tennis practice walked past the door and giggled to themselves as they saw Jamie before blushing and scampering off. Jamie was fitting in at Rosewood in his own way. The king had decided it was acceptable to make Jamie's role as a bodyguard public

knowledge—although everyone thought he was Lottie's bodyguard, not Ellie's. This had unsurprisingly established him as a heartthrob among the girls of Rosewood. Lottie wanted to gag at how predictable it was, forgetting that she herself had been swooning over the concept of a Partizan just last month.

Lottie took the opportunity to yawn while neither of them were looking, wondering how long she'd be able to keep them in the dark about her sleepless nights. She was pulled out of her thoughts when Jamie put a piece of paper down on her desk.

"I want you to name each of these members of the Maravish royal family." Lottie peered at the faces on the paper. She recognized Ellie's parents and the previous rulers, Ellie's grandmother and King Henric, but there was something not quite right about it. Someone was missing.

"In Oscar's diary he said the last king, Henric, had two sons. Doesn't that mean King Alexander should have a brother, Ellie's uncle?"

Both Ellie and Jamie stared at her as if she'd just cursed, their faces serious as they exchanged a look.

"Claude," Ellie said slowly, looking away. "He was meant to be king, but . . . he refused his royal duties . . ."

"He was banished from the kingdom," Jamie said bluntly. "The Maravish royal family is ruthless when it comes to

rules. It's important you understand that."

Lottie felt as if a piece of a puzzle had just slotted into place. This is what Ellie faced if she didn't want to rule. Banishment. Total denial of her existence. A shiver ran up her spine.

"How scary . . ." Lottie whispered under her breath.

"Quite, and speaking of scary things . . ." Jamie smiled as he retrieved a letter from his backpack.

He placed it in her hand and she marveled in wonder at the maroon wax seal that had already been broken. It was a strange symbol she'd never seen before: four triangles arranged in a square, overlapping to create two diamonds in the middle that made her think of wolf teeth.

"What is this?" she asked.

"This is our invitation to the Maravish Summer Ball," Ellie replied, "or rather, the Flower Festival." She said the name with an exaggerated eye roll. Lottie, on the other hand, had been lost at the word "ball." "It's completely ridiculous. They do it every year, but it's always thick with snow, and there's nothing summery about it."

But Lottie wasn't paying attention.

A royal ball! She was going to a real royal ball. She'd get to wear a gown, and there would probably be princes and princesses there! A REAL ROYAL BALL!

"Lottie!"

She blinked, crashing out of her daze to find Ellie waving her hand in front of her eyes, and Jamie's top lip twitching in annoyance.

"Royal ball, you say? Sounds great—where do I sign up?" She beamed at Ellie with her best *please let me go to the royal ball* look.

Ellie laughed, pushing her thick black hair out of her eyes. "You're in luck, Miss Pumpkin, the Flower Festival will be our . . . I mean, *your* debut as princess."

"*Really?*" Lottie stood up, pushing her seat back and smacking her hands on the table in excitement. Suddenly all the fatigue had evaporated from her body. This was like a fairy tale come true . . . until she saw Jamie's face. She coughed discreetly and slowly lowered herself back into her chair, blushing furiously. "I mean . . . that sounds perfectly enchanting."

Ellie snorted at Lottie's attempt at eloquence. Although Lottie knew that Jamie was trustworthy, she still felt odd around him and had a deep desire to prove herself.

Jamie sighed in a way that suggested he resented whatever he had to tell her next. "It's not that simple. Ellie will be attending formally as your guest, which makes her presence at events easy to explain, but all first-time principal attendees must partake in one full day at Lady Priscilla's Etiquette Assembly, which, fortunately for you, is being

hosted at Rosewood this year."

Lottie blinked in confusion, having absolutely no idea what any of this meant.

"That means you have to attend an etiquette class, Lottie!" Ellie said, stifling her laughter.

"An . . . etiquette class?" Were they making fun of her? Was this all some elaborate joke?

"This is not a joke, Lottie."

Lottie shivered, feeling like Jamie had just read her mind. "You will need to attend this class in two weeks and you need to make the absolute best impression you can. There will be other young royalty and children of important families and you need to fit in." He held her gaze, making sure she absorbed every word he said. She nodded.

"And if you can trip any of the snobby princes during the waltz you get extra points from me."

Jamie grumbled at Ellie's joke, making Lottie laugh.

Then he looked up at the clock and began packing up their stuff meticulously. "Here"—he held out a piece of paper filled with instructions—"this is everything we'll need to go over before the etiquette class. I'm meeting Raphael for a run. I'll see you both later."

Ellie made a retching motion with her finger. Jamie and Raphael had both been placed in the same language classes and had quickly bonded over their multilingual

backgrounds and love of long-distance running. It seemed like an odd pairing considering how humorless Jamie appeared. She wondered if, like Ellie, this was the first friend outside the Maravish family that Jamie had ever made.

Jamie paused by the door and turned back to them. "If you need anything, let me know"—he gave Ellie a sharp look—"and that does not mean coffee runs for fencing practice." Ellie grinned up at him, feigning innocence. "And, Lottie, you better be able to keep up."

Lottie held her breath as he exited the room. She thought she'd hid her tiredness well. As soon as he was out of sight, Lottie slowly exhaled. She needed to prove to Jamie she was cut out for this. She couldn't let any cracks show.

Thoughtfully watching Lottie, Ellie reached over across the table to grab her hand, gently stroking her palm with her thumb.

"I promise you'll be fine, little princess. You're a natural and this etiquette class will be easy-peasy."

Lottie blushed, realizing that Ellie thought she was worried about the etiquette class, and looked down at the instructions in her hand.

"Fine isn't good enough," she whispered to herself.

23

WITH THE WEATHER TURNING COLD, the students of Rosewood Hall were gifted with pleasant October evenings. Pretty little cutouts of bats and black cats lined the halls and all the dormitories were filled with carved pumpkins, giving the air an overripe smell.

Lottie stood in the line for the library cafe with Ellie and Binah, who were chatting about imaginary numbers, something Ellie had been teaching Lottie about in their tutoring sessions. Jamie had been given permission to use the school's phone to call the Maravish kingdom, to keep them updated on their well-being, and he'd be meeting them later. She looked out of the window at how dark it already was, even though school had ended less than an hour ago, and wondered if she'd be able to sleep that night.

"I'll have a slice of pumpkin bread and a white chocolate mocha"—Lottie checked to make sure Ellie wasn't paying attention—"with an extra espresso shot, please." She'd discovered a temporary remedy for her symptoms of sleeplessness: coffee and concealer, lots of both.

The library had quickly become Lottie's favorite place in Rosewood. She'd been apprehensive to return at first, after their little break-in adventure, but the unrivaled collection of books soon lured her back and, despite its size, it somehow felt cozy. Being surrounded by so much inspiring literature filled her with a happy, warm feeling.

As they went to take a seat in the study area, a few heads turned to Lottie. She'd become very good at pretending she didn't notice, but no matter how much time passed people couldn't get over the secret-Maravish-princess thing. Lottie couldn't blame them, though; she couldn't quite get over it either.

"Oh, over there!" Binah suddenly exclaimed, marching toward a table by the window.

Ellie and Lottie froze. Seated at the round table were Lola, Micky, Saskia, and Anastacia. Lottie was happy to sit with them, but she knew Ellie still felt weird about Anastacia, especially now that she was her fencing competition.

Before Lottie could say anything, Ellie's eyes narrowed and she took a determined step forward to join them at the table.

"Hey, guys! Is it okay if we sit here?" Lottie asked as Ellie sat down next to Binah.

Lola beamed. "Of course!" She immediately got out a bag of Tompkins Fizzy Toffees and held the packet out to

them. "Help yourself!" she said enthusiastically.

Lottie watched as both Ellie and Saskia leaned forward together, their hands catching as they went into the bag. She held her breath, not sure how Ellie would respond.

"Sorry, I— Have we met?" Ellie asked, a little smile creeping onto her face.

"Not formally!" Saskia pulled a toffee out and handed it to Ellie. "I'm Saskia."

"Ellie."

"I know," Saskia said coyly. Their eyes lingered on each other for a moment.

"She's the head of Conch House for the year above us," Lottie said quickly, feeling the need to distract them.

"I like being in charge!" Saskia grinned at Ellie, and the two laughed.

Lottie slowly sat down in the spare seat next to Anastacia, who was focused on her textbook. She looked over as Ellie laughed again at something that Saskia had said and was overcome with an odd feeling of being left out.

"I can see why you have so much trouble sleeping when you have such a raucous roommate." Anastacia's voice came out low and icy beside her.

"Excuse me?" Lottie asked in confusion. *How does she know?*

"Ellie, she's wild."

Before Lottie could process what she'd said, Anastacia turned to her, a serious look in her eyes as she considered Lottie's tired face. "I have something for you."

Lottie blinked in confusion as Anastacia reached into her bag, pulling out a small bottle and placing it purposefully on the table.

"What is it?" Lottie asked as Ellie leaned forward, grabbing the pink bottle and reading the label aloud.

"*Princess and the Pea Herbal Pillow Spray. For any princess who struggles to sleep at night . . .*"

Lottie gulped.

How did Anastacia know she wasn't sleeping? And why did she have to give her this in front of Ellie? Lottie wanted to bang her head against the table; the last thing she needed right now was for Ellie and Jamie to be worrying about this.

"Lottie, are you not sleeping?"

She jumped at the sound of Jamie's voice and turned to see him looming over her. *When on earth did he get here?* It was clear she couldn't evade his question, though.

Lottie became acutely aware that everyone in the library cafe was now staring at them. Jamie seemed to have that effect. She smiled at him as best she could and his eyes widened a bit.

"Your eyes . . ." he added, a hint of concern creeping into his voice.

"I thought you weren't going to get here until later?" It was a terrible attempt at sidestepping, but she absolutely could not have him thinking this was because she was stressed about her job as a Portman. Jamie was already convinced she wasn't cut out for it and she didn't want to prove him right.

"Lottie, why didn't you tell me?"

There was hurt in Ellie's voice, and Lottie suddenly found herself feeling very angry at Anastacia for getting her into this mess. She looked over at her, but everyone had their heads back in their books, pretending not to listen.

"It's fine. I'll explain later during math tutoring when everyone's calmed down," Lottie said, giving both Jamie and Ellie as firm a look as she could manage.

Ellie's face dropped and she looked a little sheepish. "Lottie, I thought I'd told you . . . I'm really sorry, but I don't know if I'll have time to tutor you anymore because of fencing practice." Lottie felt her heart sink. She loved Ellie's tutoring, and for the first time in her life she actually felt like she was getting good at math.

"That's fine." The words came out automatically. She couldn't ruin fencing for Ellie by making her feel guilty, especially when she was still getting up on Saturdays to keep her company during her princess lessons. "Everything's fine. I can manage." She wasn't one hundred percent sure who that last statement was aimed at.

"You need to keep your math grades up, Lottie," Jamie said unhelpfully.

"I can tutor you."

They turned to Saskia, who was leaning back on her chair casually. "If you want me to. I'm top of my class."

"Really?" Lottie couldn't hide the surprise in her voice. "That would be amazing. Thank you."

"No!" All eyes spun to Anastacia, who'd slammed her hand on the table. "*We* always hang out after school." Her voice came out uncharacteristically emotional, and Lottie almost thought she was joking.

Saskia didn't seem affected by the outburst, and simply smiled. "But aren't you gonna be in fencing practice too? The trials are only a few weeks away."

"Yes, but . . ."

"Then it's settled. I'll tutor Lottie."

The library intercom crackled overhead. "*Would the students at table eight please keep the noise down.*"

Lottie looked at everyone, sensing that there were a million more things they all wanted to say, but they silently turned back to their books.

What on earth just happened?

24

LOTTIE WAS PRACTICING BASIC ETIQUETTE with Jamie after school in the small gymnasium by Conch House, learning the fundamentals that the other students would most likely already know. They practiced everything from silverware placement to the correct way to eat an oyster, but the one thing he remained reserved about was the waltz, which he asked Ellie to teach her instead.

I didn't think he found me THAT annoying, Lottie had thought to herself.

There were only three days to go and Lottie had been working extra hard to hide her tiredness. The spray Anastacia had given her helped a little, but nowhere near enough to fix whatever was stopping her from sleeping. She stifled a yawn as they went over the appropriate greetings for different levels of nobility, earning a glare from Jamie. He was still angry at her for not telling them about her sleep problems. He looked as if he were about to comment on it when Ellie let out a low groan that sounded like a growl.

"THIS PUZZLE IS DRIVING ME MAD!" she shouted, throwing her workbook across the room. Lottie watched in amazement as Jamie effortlessly jumped up and caught it in midair. Ellie had taken to spending the "boring" parts of the lessons, as she called them, working on Binah's puzzle, which she was still having no luck with. Lottie had long given up on ever being allowed to open their gifts.

Jamie flipped through its pages indifferently before closing it with a loud smack.

"We'd appreciate if you could do your strange anagrams in silence," he said coldly, placing the book down on the bench that Ellie had commandeered.

She sat up like a jolt of lightning had gone through her body.

"Anagram?" she breathed, raising an eyebrow.

"Yes!" he replied, turning back to Lottie to adjust her arm to the correct position for her curtsy. "You haven't converted the numbers into letters yet, but it clearly spells out the founder of the school, William—"

"WILLIAM TUFTY!" the two girls shouted in unison.

Lottie broke her position as Ellie came running over. It all made sense now. Ellie had been so concerned with figuring out what the puzzle meant numerically that she hadn't bothered to look for words in it.

"Jamie, we're finishing early," Ellie called behind her as she pulled Lottie by the arm.

Jamie reached out to grab Lottie's hand but hesitated. "Fine, you're dismissed."

The two girls sat in the Ivy common room on a purple love seat underneath a large painting of Florence Ivy. Three other Ivy students were sitting by the TV, giggling as they stared at Jamie, who stood by the window doing an amazing job of appearing uninterested in everything. He'd demanded to inspect the gifts before they were allowed to open them, which had Ellie groaning impatiently. They'd bumped into a Stratus girl on their way back and asked her to tell Binah that they'd solved her puzzle if she saw her.

"I can't believe we've had these for weeks and not been able to open them," Lottie said as they held the lids of their boxes. They counted to three before pulling the lids and Lottie squeezed her eyes shut, terrified of an impending anticlimax. And that's exactly what she got.

Inside her box was a tiny fox brooch no bigger than her little fingernail. She looked over at Ellie who was equally puzzled, holding a small enamel mouse.

"I don't get it," Ellie said bluntly, looking up at Jamie as if he could give her another hint.

Lottie chewed the inside of her lip in thought.

"Well, it must have some significance." She grabbed Ellie's gift and held them both up in front of her. "A mouse and a fox, a mouse and a fox." She repeated the words to

herself in the hope it might unlock something. She saw Jamie's lip twitch out of the corner of her eye. "Am I doing something wrong?" she asked apprehensively.

"It just reminds me of something," Jamie replied, turning to stare out of the window again. His face showed an emotion Lottie hadn't seen before and she found she didn't want to look away. She forced herself to turn her attention back to their gifts.

Lottie felt her mind go cloudy, her eyes glossing over as a ghost from her childhood whispered in her ear. Somewhere in the back of her mind, she could hear her mother's voice reciting a verse from her distant past.

They found each other in the woods.
Together they did build a house.

A story her mother used to tell her, before she knew how brutal the world could be.

One was smart and the other was soft . . .

A rhyme about two very different creatures, coming together to help each other: "The Vixen and the Delicate Mouse."

"William Tufty wrote nursery rhymes!" Lottie exclaimed. The words jumped out of her before she'd fully

processed the thought. She looked over at Jamie, who was looking at her in surprise. "And you know it too—you remember the story!" For a moment she entirely forgot her nerves with Jamie. "The Vixen and—"

"—the Delicate Mouse," Jamie finished, and she felt her heart skip a beat unexpectedly. "I'd almost forgotten the name."

Lottie grinned at Ellie, returning her brooch. "I never would have remembered that the founder of Rosewood had written my favorite nursery rhyme as a kid. It was my mom's favorite rhyme too." She looked down affectionately at her gift, stroking the metal with her thumb. *Thank you, Binah*.

Ellie reached out and gently rubbed her hand, a soft look in her eyes. "So you think that's it? Binah wanted to tell us about his poems?"

Lottie felt a discomfort in her stomach, the kind that tells you when something isn't quite right. She racked her brain for more of the story and gradually fragments came back to her—of paintings and oak trees—but the memories were not enough to form a full picture.

"I think we need to find the whole rhyme . . ." she said, her eyes still lingering on the brooches. She turned to Jamie expectantly and he nodded. She wondered if he was excited about the poem too.

It did not take long to locate the William Tufty section

in the library. He had an entire area dedicated to not only his work, but also a section of books and poems he'd loved.

They found the rhyme in an anthology of children's stories, and Lottie sat down opposite the others as they waited for her to read it aloud. She cleared her throat, feeling nervous under Jamie's gaze.

"They found each other in the woods.
Together they did build a house.
One was smart and the other was soft,
The Vixen and the Delicate Mouse.
They were champions of hide-and-seek.
Every day they'd play a game.
The Vixen was so clever that
She hid inside the painting frames.
The oak trees grew and soon they held
A home for others to learn their tricks:
Wisdom, valour and righteousness.
They built their houses with stones and bricks.
And now within the master's office,
Where he looks down on his house,
His gaze on them with a gaze on him
Of the Vixen and the Delicate Mouse."

She looked up at Ellie when she was done, lightbulbs going off in her head.

"I think it's in the paintings." Ellie's eyes narrowed, and Lottie continued: "There're paintings of him all over the school . . . I think one of them might have the next clue in it."

Ellie stood, pulling Lottie up too and swinging her bag over her shoulders, ready to leave. Jamie didn't say a word.

"Well, what are you waiting for?" said Ellie. "Let's go and check them out."

Jamie seemed to remember himself and his face once again regained its moody composure. He stood up between them.

"You can save your painting appreciation for another day," he said drily. "It's nearly curfew and I'm sure you both have homework to finish and, Lottie"—he looked at her sharply and all the anxious feelings she associated with him came flooding back—"you need to get back to thinking about this etiquette class, which is in less than three days."

Lottie gulped. Jamie was right. Before she could get excited about any mysteries, she needed to survive this class.

❦ 25 ❧

THE MAIN HALL OF ROSEWOOD had been commandeered for the sake of the five-hour etiquette class run by a woman named Lady Priscilla. It was a rite of passage for the children of important families to attend one of these classes before their first public appearance at a significant function.

Although Lottie had walked through the main hall many times in her months at Rosewood and had become familiar with the grand space, it had never felt as cold and foreboding as it did then. Every step seemed to echo louder than usual; every breath seemed to be more visible in the air. There were children of her age from all over the world. They looked immaculate and natural in their attire, ranging from saris to embroidered jackets with tassels. Lottie had had to borrow a dress from Lola, who'd been more than delighted to dress her up, and they'd found an appropriate, mid-length white dress that she hoped met the dress code.

Jamie stood by her side. They had arrived early and watched the others slowly trickle in. Everyone had either a bodyguard or an assistant with them. Lottie wondered if

any of the bodyguards were Partizans, but they all seemed much older than their wards.

Jamie was running through the names of each attendee as they entered, which Lottie tried her best to remember: Veevee Indriani, royalty from Rajasthan living in the USA and set to be an Olympic figure skater; Lachlan Kidman-Dolman, son of Angus Dolman the painter and Ingrid Kidman the opera singer; Edmund Ashwick—

Lottie's attention was suddenly cut off by the entrants who followed Edmund Ashwick. To her complete amazement, Anastacia, Raphael, and Saskia walked through the door!

"Wh-what are you guys doing here?" Lottie spluttered. She hadn't spoken to Anastacia since the library incident the previous week, but she felt a little better about having people she knew in this class. Anastacia was wearing a demure, floor-length black-and-silver dress, stylishly complemented by Raphael's black-and-silver tuxedo. She was several inches taller than Lottie and her sharp heels accentuated the height difference. Behind her, Saskia was dressed sensibly in a dark shift dress, her golden mane tied up neatly.

"I assumed you knew," replied Anastacia smoothly. "This will be my first year attending your family's summer ball." Lottie blinked a few times and Jamie tensed at her side. Was this something she should have known?

But before Lottie could reply, Anastacia continued. "And Raphael is here because he"—she coughed—"he suddenly decided he simply must get this class out of the way upon hearing I was attending."

Raphael choked out a laugh. "Well, no one else is going to volunteer to practice the waltz with the wicked witch of the west dorm." He smirked at her but she ignored him. "I'm totally doing you a favor by being here."

Raphael winked at Jamie, and Lottie was pleased to see he didn't respond. She and Anastacia might not be the best of friends, but she didn't like the idea of her being spoken to like that.

"I'm . . ." Lottie faltered for a moment then decided to just say it. "I'm really glad you're here." And she was: she hadn't realized until they walked in how nervous she'd actually been, and even though Anastacia was a little cold, at least she was consistent. Anastacia was about to respond when suddenly Saskia interrupted.

"Lottie, I'm really looking forward to our first tutoring session." Her voice was level and calming, instantly making Lottie feel more relaxed. Saskia curtsied, then looked up and gave Lottie a clear smile. "I promise I'll get you a good grade; I'm a pro."

Lottie smiled back as best she could, wondering what Ellie would make of this whole situation.

"Saskia is attending as my plus one. Just like Miss Wolf is yours," Anastacia added, checking her nails for any non-existent scuffs.

At the mention of "Wolf," Lottie's mind flashed back to that first day and the mysterious book left at her door. A strange feeling fluttered in her stomach, as if there were something she ought to know but it was somehow out of her mind's reach.

"Thank you, Saskia," Lottie said, ignoring Anastacia and amazing herself with how calm she sounded. She couldn't explain why but she was suddenly very uneasy.

Jamie coughed loudly, pulling her out of her thoughts. "Okay—time's up. Remember the protocol."

In the distance Lottie could hear loud clicks of heels on marble coming down the corridor to the hall.

"Good luck," Lottie said quickly to her friends.

Raphael grinned, but Anastacia simply nodded before they all stood in a line.

The door burst open dramatically making Lottie jump. *Red.* That was the first thing Lottie thought when she saw her. Lady Priscilla wore a tight red skirt suit with elaborate ruffles and a white top. She looked older than Lottie expected and there was a tightness in her face that suggested she spent a lot of time scowling. Lady Priscilla entered the room with slow yet easy grace, gently tapping a

cane in the palm of her hand, taking in the room methodically. A thin smile appeared on her face, but it did not reach her eyes.

"There is little that pleases me more than when a child learns their place." Her voice was prickly like pins and needles in Lottie's ears, making her shiver. "Most of you are broken, tainted by a lack of discipline, and I delight in the opportunity to fix you. By the end of my class you will no longer be an embarrassment to high society. I will shape you until you fit in with the world into which you were all so undeservingly born."

Lottie felt queasy. Suddenly Jamie's rigorous preparation for the class made perfect sense. This woman was terrifying. She moved down the line purposefully, her rigid posture giving the impression of a cobra poised to attack. Her hair was coiled atop her head in a tight red bundle with a small jade ornament in the center like she had a little snake eye on the back of her head.

"You are all here because you were born into an important family, and it is my job to make sure that importance isn't wasted on you."

She stopped at Anastacia. "Miss Alcroft . . ." She tilted her head slightly, eyes slanted. "Good posture, modest choice of attire . . . Good."

She continued to move along the line, her heels making sharp clicking sounds. Lottie held her breath and chanced

a quick glance at Jamie, who stood with the other assistants and bodyguards against the left wall. His face was blank but his jaw was clenched. He did not return her glance.

"Master Singh." A thin smile spread across her lips that made Lottie shudder. "I had your brother in my class three years ago." She spat the words out like they were poison. "I sincerely hope you are more graceful than him."

The heels clicked closer and closer to Lottie.

Please don't stop at me! Please don't stop at me!

The bright red leather shoes stopped directly in front of Lottie.

"And this"—the woman loomed over Lottie, gesturing coldly at her with her cane—"must be the notorious Maravish princess." She lifted her nose up as if she were smelling something foul. "I must say, I for one was expecting someone a little more stimulating. From what I've heard of you I fear even my expertise will be lost on a calamity such as yourself." She slapped her cane into her hand, making a piercing thwack sound that echoed through the hall.

Lottie felt the dread sink into her stomach. After all her careful planning and preparation, it never occurred to her that she would have to remedy the reputation Ellie had already built for herself. She felt tears pricking the corners of her eyes and had to bite her cheek to stop herself from crying.

"I . . ."

"YOU WILL ONLY SPEAK WHEN SPOKEN TO!" Lady Priscilla's voice boomed, making Lottie nearly jump out of her skin in shock. The silence that followed was deafening. Lottie had never felt so humiliated in her life. She firmly believed there was no excuse *ever* to shout at someone like that, no matter what the circumstance.

Lottie bit her cheek even harder, desperately willing herself not to say anything more. She thought of Anastacia, Saskia, Raphael, and Jamie, who would all be watching her. She nodded slowly, looking straight ahead, thinking only of what it would mean for Ellie if she messed this up.

Lady Priscilla twitched her nose like a little rat and sniffed. "Good." She slapped her cane in her hand again. This time Lottie didn't even flinch. "Now let us begin our first lesson."

26

"Wrong!"

Lady Priscilla smacked her cane on the table next to Lottie. She had done this three times already but it never failed to make Lottie jump.

They were sitting at the large oak table that had been laid out with a full formal place setting for every student. There was a wide gap between Lottie and the two students on either side of her, as if they didn't want to catch the wrath of Lady Priscilla. They were practicing the order of cutlery and the correct way to hold each item, but apparently Lottie was doing everything wrong.

The worst part was that she wasn't doing it wrong. Lottie *knew* she was doing it right—she'd studied this over and over, but each time Lady Priscilla somehow managed to find one tiny detail that she was messing up, from moving slightly too fast to having her feet crossed improperly. Lottie quickly realized there was nothing she could do except drown her ego, nod along, and say, "Yes, ma'am."

Anastacia and Raphael were adamantly avoiding eye contact with her, while Jamie remained completely unreadable

with the rest of the left-wall ensemble. Lottie felt like a total outcast. It was all her worst nightmares come true: not only was she failing but she wasn't even blending in. Lady Priscilla was determined to make an example of her and there was nothing she could do about it.

Ellie, what did you do to get this reputation? You've only ever met twenty people!

Lottie fought on. She didn't think anything could get worse than the humiliating posture training, for which she was made to walk the hall twice in front of everyone while Lady Priscilla pointed out all her errors.

But she was wrong. It did get worse.

Lady Priscilla had them all stand in a line once more. Lottie was painfully aware of the large gap between her and the other students to her left and right.

"It's time for the most important lesson." Lady Priscilla tapped her fingernails along the side of her cane, her thin little smile creeping onto her lips. "You are going to practice the waltz."

Lottie's stomach sank. She'd been so excited about waltz practice but now all she felt was pure terror.

"Everyone pair up. Chop-chop!"

Oh my God! Pair up?

No one was going to want to pair with her after she'd been singled out by Lady Priscilla so many times. The only thing that could make this worse was if she looked down

and realized she was in her underwear. Lottie stood frozen in place as she watched all the other students find a dance partner.

"Oh dear." The voice came harsh and cold behind her, not a hint of regret. "It seems no one wants to dance with the sad little princess." Lady Priscilla tapped her cane sharply. "And if you can't do the waltz, then I'll have no choice but to fail you." Lottie imagined a cruel smile on Lady Priscilla's lips as she said this.

Lottie gulped. If she failed the class, she'd fail Ellie too—she had to do something. She looked over at Jamie but knew as well as he did that assistants and bodyguards could not partake in the class. What could she do? She would not let this woman stop her from going to the ball.

"I suppose you think dancing, along with all your other royal obligations, is completely asinine?" said Lady Priscilla, stepping around and aiming her steely glare on Lottie.

Maybe Ellie's right. Maybe these people are as awful as she says!

"No, please, I don't think—"

But Lady Priscilla cut her off. "No one wants to dance with you because you are a *shrew*."

Lottie mustered all her strength and discipline to stop herself from flinching—she would *not* give Lady Priscilla the satisfaction of seeing her react.

"Everyone knows about the untameable princess of

Maradova, and if you think for a second I will be fooled by your quiet act today, you are as senseless as I expected."

Lottie felt her fists clench at her sides. This woman didn't know anything about Ellie; she didn't know that she had taken time out of her day to help Lottie with her math homework, that she went to the gym every evening because she was so determined to make the fencing team, that she cared deeply about her friends and was trying her absolute best. Lottie's heart suddenly broke for Ellie. She'd spent all this time baffled that Ellie wanted to escape being a princess, but, standing there being victimized by this snake of a woman, Lottie found herself suppressing an overwhelming temptation to rip her dress and trash the room. Ellie didn't fit into the cookie-cutter image of a girl, let alone a princess. She was unapologetic and ferocious and this aristocratic world resented her for it. Lottie felt her fists tighten even more. Ellie didn't deserve this, Ellie wouldn't take this, Ellie was better than this.

"How dare—" Lottie was ready to tear this nasty woman down when she was cut off.

"May I interject, Lady Priscilla?" The smooth voice came from behind. She dared not turn around to put a face to the voice for fear of further irking Lady Priscilla. "I would be much obliged to have the honor of dancing with the princess myself." A gloved hand gently rested on

Lottie's back, causing her to inhale sharply. "I believe all she needs is a positive influence."

Lady Priscilla's entire demeanor shifted instantly. Her shoulders relaxed and her face turned from sour to saccharine, as if this mysterious boy had melted all the ice within her.

"Why, Prince Ashwick, I could not allow you to take on that burden."

Lottie felt a pang of irritation at "burden" but was distracted by the word "prince."

The boy purred a soft laugh. "Any shrew can be tamed with the right suitor, ma'am."

Lady Priscilla lifted her head slowly, scrutinizing the two of them. Lottie shoved the insulting Shakespeare reference to the back of her mind, telling herself that whoever this boy was he must know that the only way to persuade Lady Priscilla was to agree with her.

"Very well, Edmund." She gave her cane another thwack for good measure. "Let's see if some of your outstanding discipline can be absorbed." Lady Priscilla turned around abruptly and walked toward the record player. "Everyone assume a starting position."

At last, Lottie turned to face her partner and gasped out loud. *An angel!* He was beautiful. Prince Ashwick stood elegant and graceful before her, dressed in a princely white outfit with gilded shoulder pads. His blond hair reflected

the light and seemed to be made of gold. He turned to her and bowed low, but with complete sincerity. As he straightened up, Lottie was greeted with a soft smile and warm hazel eyes that contrasted with his sharp bone structure.

"May I have the honor of dancing with you, Princess?"

Lottie was speechless. *Prince Charming is real and he rescued me.*

"Y-yes," she said, breathlessly. The world seemed to melt around her as he took her hand into his own. His other hand rested delicately on her back, pulling her toward him. He smiled at her, a friendly glint in his eyes.

"Now, it is usually customary to bow or curtsy to your partner before the dance begins," said Lady Priscilla sternly, "but until I deem your dancing worthy enough, no one shall be bowing to anyone."

The music began to swell into the room, an elegant ensemble of strings and piano that sounded magical.

"We shall begin with the simple box step. Hear the rhythm: one, two, three; one, two, three; one, two, three . . ."

The prince eased into the dance effortlessly, and Lottie found she could match his steps flawlessly, as if they were a mirror image of each other. He led her gracefully across the floor. Both in white, they were snowflakes in the cold room, gliding smoothly around the hall as if they were floating. She felt weightless in his arms, the rest of

the world melting around her in a hazy cloud. She forgot Jamie; she forgot Anastacia and Raphael, her insomnia, the pressures of her role as Portman—it all dissolved with the music.

"You know you're far better at dancing than half the girls here."

Lottie blushed involuntarily, feeling silly for finding the compliment so pleasing. She didn't know how to respond. He was just so . . . charming.

"You're not so bad yourself, I suppose." Lottie shocked herself with how easily she spoke. *Where did that come from?*

He chuckled, the sound vibrating softly against her ear, then he abruptly swung her into a twirl that she somehow managed to step into gracefully, spinning out and then back into his arms. Her heart was racing, her feet moving naturally in time to the music.

"I hope I'll get the chance to show you how *not so bad* I can be," he added, smiling. She found herself giggling as they continued dancing in their dreamy cloud.

Then the music stopped, plummeting Lottie back to reality. She blinked, then looked around to discover that everyone was staring at them—silent, except for the occasional muffled whisper. Anastacia's expression was cold, her eyebrows furrowed, and she turned to Jamie. Lottie had never seen him look as terrifying as he did then. He

seemed to be radiating anger, and all her fears of him came flooding back like ice down her spine.

I must have really screwed up this time, she thought, feeling deflated.

She turned back to Edmund—and he was . . . smiling! He caught her eye, then took a flamboyant step back and bowed. Lottie put her hand over her chest and flushed at the gesture.

"It was an honor to dance with you, Princess."

Lottie felt weird being addressed in that way, but couldn't stop her whole face from going hot as her fellow students continued to stare.

"M-much obliged," she replied, trying not to let her nerves show.

Thwack!

The sharp crack of Lady Priscilla's cane tore through the silence in the hall with a deafening echo.

"That," she shrieked, all eyes turning to her abruptly, "was absolutely, outrageously, the most *wonderful* display I've seen in any of my classes for years."

Lottie had to stop herself from gasping. Had Lady Priscilla just *complimented* her?

"Elegant, precise—a gentleman and a lady blending into their roles effortlessly." Lottie found herself bristling at this statement. *What roles?* she thought, annoyed. "It was everything a waltz should be. Marvelous."

Then Lady Priscilla clapped her hands, applauding while the rest of the students stood awkward and confused. Her face had become almost comical, smiling so much that she looked as if she would burst into tears. Prince Ashwick winked at Lottie and she felt her whole body light up.

The class was breezy from then on. As long as Lottie was standing by the prince, Lady Priscilla was more than satisfied with her efforts, even though Lottie was painfully aware that she was doing everything exactly as she had been before.

Lottie occasionally caught Jamie's eye. He no longer wore his disinterested blank-faced expression. Instead his jaw seemed permanently clenched, as if she were doing something very wrong, though Lady Priscilla was clearly overjoyed with her. When the class came to an end, Lottie was feeling a little smug. She'd gone from Lady Priscilla's most despised student to a "shining example of how young girls can flourish when they step up to their responsibilities."

Raphael had to cover his mouth to stop laughing, while Anastacia looked intensely annoyed for no particular reason. She nodded to Lottie briskly as they all left the hall. Saskia smiled sweetly at her and wiggled her fingers in a little wave.

"We have to leave. Now." Jamie's voice came out low and cold behind Lottie, making her shiver.

Edmund narrowed his eyes at Jamie, then sighed dramatically.

"Well, it seems our time together is cut short, Princess Wolfson." He stroked a lock of Lottie's hair, letting the silky blond strand intertwine in his fingers. "I will find a way to contact you." He gently took Lottie's hand, before raising it to his lips and planting a soft kiss that sent sparks through her body. "I eagerly anticipate our next encounter." He winked at her before adding, "I'm sure you understand why," then he turned dramatically to the door as two terrifyingly large men materialized by his side to escort him out.

"Bye . . ." Lottie replied breathlessly after him.

Jamie marched her back to the Ivy dorm. He was obviously angry, but Lottie was too elated from her encounter with Prince Edmund Ashwick to take in his sour mood.

"I could've danced all day and never been bored. Did you see how impressed Lady Priscilla was?"

Jamie's eyebrows furrowed, but Lottie simply danced around him as they walked through the grounds, skipping happily and giggling to herself in the waning rose-tinted light.

"I was brave and kind and I was totally unstoppable—aren't you pleased with me?"

"Yes, Lottie, I'm very pleased. Now listen . . ."

"Wasn't it magical? Lady Priscilla's face was priceless. It was like something out of a story, and Edmund—"

"Lottie, listen, you can't—"

"He's like no boy I've ever met before. He's the real deal; he's a real-life Prince Charming!"

"Lottie, you can't—"

"I'm so happy I could just—"

"LOTTIE, YOU ARE ABSOLUTELY, UNDER NO CIRCUMSTANCES TO SPEAK TO PRINCE ASH-WICK AGAIN."

Lottie froze and took in the furious resolution on Jamie's face. That had not been what she was expecting at all.

27

"Edmund Ashwick?"

Ellie's voice shrieked through their room loud enough to make Lottie's princess mug shake on the table. "But he's a complete—"

"You're forbidden from interacting with him, Lottie," Jamie interrupted.

Ellie was pulling her fingers through her hair, filling the room with stress as she paced back and forth. Lottie sat firmly on her bed with her hands clasped in her lap, trying not to be annoyed that they were treating her like a stupid child.

"I think you're both failing to remember that he saved me in that class. Without him Lady Priscilla probably would have made me leave, and I wouldn't have been able to attend the Maravish Summer Ball." Lottie tried to keep her voice as calm as possible after Ellie's outburst.

"He's a total sleazeball."

"But Lady Priscilla—"

"Lady Priscilla is a backward traditionalist, and if she likes you because of your association with Edmund then

you definitely don't want anything to do with him."

Ellie was furious. Lottie could practically see bolts of static electrifying the air around her.

"It's sick, *sick*, I tell you, that that . . . slimy toad Ashwick . . . I bet he thinks . . ." Ellie shivered then looked up at Lottie with a new conviction on her face. "Lottie, I think we need to explain my reputation to you."

Lottie's brows furrowed. It was something she'd been curious about herself.

"Last year . . ." Ellie began, "gossip was spread about me, saying I did all these things I didn't do. It said I was caught sneaking around with a guy at a rock concert and that's why I was being hidden away from the public. It spiraled out of control and people started saying I was going to be just like my uncle. It's all completely stupid." Ellie looked away, her hands clenched in frustration.

Lottie's heart ached for Ellie—she understood her paranoia. *This is why she doesn't trust anyone.*

"Ellie, I think we need to start trusting people," said Lottie gently. "Maybe Edmund really wants to get to know the princess. Maybe there are people who want to know the real you. He was very kind and . . ."

Ellie's face softened as she saw the disappointment in Lottie's eyes.

"It's not just that, Lottie. If it did go sour with Edmund, think about all the gossip. It could ruin my reputation

even more." Ellie was trying to sound calm, but there was tension in her voice. Lottie didn't understand what Ellie meant. *What could go sour?*

"Well, shouldn't you know better than anyone what it feels like to have people make assumptions about you?"

Maybe Edmund was being misjudged.

Ellie sighed as if Lottie was being a petulant child instead of a girl who felt like she'd met the love of her life.

"You need to trust us, Lottie." Ellie's voice was quieter now, but she still wore her fiery expression.

"Maybe you have to trust *me*!" Lottie exclaimed, standing up to face Ellie head-on. "We can't judge a person based on rumors and hearsay. Surely you of all people can understand that."

"Lottie, for once in your life would you stop being so painfully naive?"

Lottie jolted at the severity of Jamie's tone. She turned to see his face twisted into a furious scowl, and a cold feeling spread through her body. "You're just a foolish little girl who's obsessed with fairy tales. You're being childish and you're going to put Ellie at risk."

Lottie found herself lost for words. She stood frozen, tears pricking her eyes as she tried to compose herself. She was used to being called naive—she was even used to people thinking her interests were childish—but it was a whole different thing when she was being told her attitude

could hurt someone else. She'd worked hard in that class and thought maybe she'd finally proved to Jamie she was capable. She'd failed; she'd failed to impress him, and she'd apparently failed Ellie. It took all of her willpower not to burst out sobbing in front of them.

"I'm . . . so . . ." Lottie whimpered.

Ellie let out a frustrated groan. "You," she said, pointing at Jamie, "shut up for a minute." She turned back to Lottie and grabbed her by the shoulders, forcing her to look directly into her eyes. That storm was there, thundering in the background, but Lottie felt calmed by it.

"Now listen to me, Lottie—*really* listen." She took a deep breath. "It's okay to daydream about boys"—the twitchiness in her voice suggested this was difficult for her to say—"and I love that you try to see the good in everyone. Who knows, maybe Edmund really doesn't have an ulterior motive. I love you and all your wonderful quirks and I will never, *ever* call you naive." She paused to scowl at Jamie. "But"—she took another breath as she mentally prepared herself—"I don't want you to be disappointed if things don't turn out the way you expect."

"Ellie." Lottie breathed her name softly. Guilt grew inside her as she looked at the pain on her friend's face. She didn't want them to worry about her; she needed to reassure them that she was capable of handling herself. She forced a smile, wondering what she'd actually do if

Edmund contacted her.

"I promise you guys can count on me," she said determinedly.

Ellie looked at her, her mouth breaking into her little side smile, though it didn't quite reach her eyes.

"Well, either way, Jamie's not allowed to shout at you anymore. I'm forbidding it." She paused before holding her index finger in the air. "That's a royal order."

Lottie turned to him, expecting to see him still furious and determined, ready to roll his eyes and lecture them both, but instead he looked . . . pained. He was looking away and one hand reached up and rubbed his forehead, clearly stressed. The guilty feeling in her stomach doubled. Once again she was overcome with sadness that Jamie had had to deal with far more responsibility than most other boys his age did. It was no wonder he reacted so harshly; Ellie and her reputation had to come first.

"Don't worry, Jamie." She waited until he looked at her. "I understand."

They held their gaze for a moment and he nodded. She knew he understood what she meant, but now she had to prove it. *Ellie has to come first*, she repeated to herself.

"Okay . . . are we all calm now?" Ellie quipped.

"I think so." Lottie turned back to Jamie and put on her best happy expression. "Now, Jamie, you've got to leave. Ellie has homework to finish and I think we could all do

with some downtime."

Jamie allowed a half smile to creep onto his lips as he turned to leave.

"Very well. I'll see you both tomorrow morning," he said as he reached for the door handle. "Oh, and, Lottie—" he caught her eye, the half smile still on his lips—"try to get some sleep tonight."

"Of course," she said cheerfully, but a thick feeling of dread filled her stomach.

The door clicked shut and she pulled out the sleeping remedy Anastacia had given her. Something told her things were not going to get any less exhausting any time soon.

 28

THE END OF THE FIRST term was fast approaching. Icicles lined the eaves of the school buildings and the pond outside the Ivy dorm had frozen over. Every day the sky threatened to snow, yet every day the air remained icy and still. It turned out it was easy not to speak to Edmund, as there was no easy way for them to stay in touch. Lottie had been working extra hard to be a "perfect princess" since Jamie had lost his temper with her, partly because she didn't want anyone to see how tired she was, but mostly because she realized how important it was to help fix Ellie's tarnished image.

Be kind, she reminded herself.

One quiet Thursday evening the girls took the opportunity to solve Binah's puzzle, before the rush of winter exams and the approaching fencing tryouts. Lottie reread the passage she thought contained the clue, hoping the answer would reveal itself.

> *And now within the master's office,*
> *Where he looks down on his house,*

His gaze on them with a gaze on him
Of the Vixen and the Delicate Mouse.

Ellie stared at Lottie as she recited the poem again. They stood at the foot of the stone stairs to the headmaster's office. The heart of the school.

"So 'he' must be William Tufty," Lottie deduced. "And surely this must be 'the master's office,' right? I don't think it's talking about the one in Ivy Wood. So there has to be a painting of Tufty in the headmaster's office," she added. "It's the only plausible interpretation."

"I'll have to take your word for it." Ellie raised her eyebrows. She was not the best at finding symbolism and hidden meaning in words—she preferred numbers over letters.

"You really should brush up on your riddle skills," Lottie cautioned. "What if you need to solve one to get out of a sticky situation someday?" The scenario seemed unlikely, but it was something she'd read in the Portman's diary. An old story of an eastern European royal's Partizan, who'd sent a coded message in a letter back to the kingdom by spelling the family dog's name wrong so they'd know she was being held captive. Lottie had decided that you could never be too ready.

Ellie smirked, clearly not taking her riddle advice seriously.

"How did your first tutoring session with Saskia go?" she asked unexpectedly. Something about the way she said Saskia's name irritated Lottie.

"It was fine." *I wish it was with you, though*, she added in her head.

"Just *fine*? I thought it was really cool of Saskia to offer to tutor you. I'd be thrilled."

Lottie couldn't figure out why she was being so guarded about it. Saskia *was* a great teacher; she just felt weird when Ellie talked about her.

"It was great—she's great and I'm learning tons. Is that better?" Lottie realized she sounded an awful lot like Anastacia and she looked away, embarrassed. "Sorry, I think I'm just . . . tired, and I don't want you thinking her tutoring is better than yours."

Ellie's face softened and she chuckled sympathetically. "Well, of course she's not better than me," she said, laughing. "I just want to make sure she's good enough to tutor you." Lottie couldn't help grinning at this. "Now come on. We have some mysteries to solve." Ellie grabbed her hand and they marched up the stone stairs together.

The plan was simple. They would knock on the door under the guise of wanting to ask about the history of the school for a class project. While they were inside, Lottie would examine the painting and look for any clues.

The large curved oak door to the headmaster's office

had two twisted metal handles in the middle. The carved thorns and roses on them had been worn away over four hundred years of use, and were barely visible. Lottie took a deep breath as she knocked. The headmaster was a mystery to her. She was becoming so familiar with Dame Bolter, Ms. Kuma, and Professor Devine, but Headmaster Croak kept to himself, an invisible force quietly working away in the background.

She knocked twice and waited. There was no answer. Ellie looked at the door in annoyance then knocked even louder. Still no response.

"Hellooo! Anyone in? Excuse meee!" Ellie bellowed as she banged on the door with her fists.

Lottie nudged her. "*Ellie!*" she whispered harshly.

Ellie laughed, giving her the side smile that made it impossible to stay mad at her.

"Well, I guess he's not in," she said, banging on the door again for good measure.

Lottie looked down in defeat. Their plan had seemed so simple and easy. She'd never considered that the headmaster wouldn't be in.

She sighed. "I guess we'll have to try again some other time."

Ellie let out a single sarcastic laugh as she leaned on the entrance. "Or we could just sneak in and take a look for ourselves. I'm sure that's what *the Vixen* would have

wanted," she said with a cocky grin.

"Ellie, we can't. That's too—"

But before she could finish, Ellie had turned the metal handle and pushed the heavy double door open like it was no big deal at all.

I can't believe I'm doing this.

This was definitely not "perfect princess" behavior, but she didn't stop herself from following Ellie.

The headmaster's office was not what Lottie had expected. When she imagined this central point of the school—the room that held the most power and authority—she'd pictured large looming furniture and opulent ornamentation. Instead she found a quaint hexagonal room with a modest mahogany desk in the center, and piles of papers and books covering every inch of floor space. It almost seemed as if the room contained every document and book ever accumulated in the four hundred years that Rosewood Hall had existed. But there was one thing in the room that stood out: a gargantuan, gold-framed painting that peered down over the room with all-seeing eyes.

William Tufty.

"He's almost as messy as me," Ellie said, giggling, side-stepping a pile of books in an attempt to get closer to the painting. Lottie would have laughed, but she found herself completely mesmerized by Tufty's gaze. He sat within the

painting, little half-moon glasses on the bridge of his nose, eyes staring down at her. There was a glimmer of thoughtfulness in his expression that the painter had perfectly captured in the soft way his lips turned up at the edges. His hands were clasped in his lap holding a small, circular mirror with a murky reflection of him. His delicate frame was a stark contrast to the vastness of the main hall in the background. Lottie narrowed her eyes at this depiction of William Tufty, at the way he looked out at them with a knowing smile.

The Vixen and the Delicate Mouse.

What did Binah want them to know? Lottie was about to speak when a gruff male voice behind them said, "He's quite fantastic, isn't he?"

Both girls almost jumped out of their skin. Headmaster Croak stood by the door, one hand planted firmly on a simple wooden cane.

"Headmaster Croak . . . we're so sorry . . . we . . ." Lottie trailed off, suddenly unable to speak. *You're going to get expelled*, a nasty voice inside her head whispered, a voice that for some reason sounded horribly like her stepmother. She looked at Ellie, who was also frozen. Lottie knew that getting in trouble would be far worse for her. She tried again. "We were just waiting for you to—"

The headmaster laughed, a throaty guffaw. "Oh hush!

You think you're the first students to ever be wooed by the siren call of Sir William Tufty?" He let out a soft chuckle as he took a shaky step into the office. "I had your friend Miss Binah Fae in here gazing up with that same look not more than a month into her first year at Rosewood." Lottie felt a strange sense of comfort in this, that Binah had been caught too—and that thought quashed the voice of her stepmother.

"Sorry," said the two girls in unison.

The headmaster smiled again. Then he turned to the painting, his face turning pensive as he gazed at the founder of the school. "He was a very wise and extremely reserved man."

Lottie regarded the patient face of William Tufty. There was something there, something she couldn't quite place.

"I've heard he was a kind man," the headmaster said, turning to Ellie and Lottie and smiling. His face was wrinkled, covered in lines of experience and emotion. He tapped his cane thoughtfully before continuing. "But his greatest attribute was his ability to be quiet." Croak laughed to himself and Ellie cocked an eyebrow at Lottie, wondering if she'd heard him correctly. "Sometimes the world can get very loud, and people can get caught up trying to get their own voice heard. They end up silencing those who really need the space to speak. William understood this, and he used his position in the world to give others the chance to

be heard." He turned his eyes to his weathered hands. "I try my best to emulate that about him."

Lottie wasn't sure why but this information resonated with her. She looked up at the painting again.

Hide-and-seek.

The frame around Tufty's image. She knew there was something there.

Every day they'd play a game . . . she hid inside the painting frames.

"And I hope I can be wise like he was, and give quiet to those who need it."

Wise and quiet.

Lottie stared into the eyes of the man in the painting, then at Ellie, the girl living a dual life, secretly hiding under the guise of Ellie Wolf.

The Vixen and the Delicate Mouse. All of a sudden, a thought like a distant memory crystallized in Lottie's mind, and she asked herself, *If William is the Delicate Mouse, then who is the Vixen?* Lottie looked up at the painting again and finally saw it.

"Thank you," she said calmly.

The headmaster smiled at her, giving the signal that they were dismissed.

She gave Ellie a meaningful look, letting her know she'd figured out something important.

They walked down the stairs and out of the main

building, pulling on their big coats and scarves. Ellie looked at Lottie but could see she was thinking very hard about something and, remembering the headmaster's words, gave her the silence she needed.

Once they were heading toward the Ivy dorm, Lottie paused—and Ellie paused too.

"I think . . ." Lottie lifted her fingers to her lips, not just in thought but as if conjuring a memory. "I think William Tufty might not have been born who he became." Ellie's head cocked to the side inquisitively. "I mean," Lottie continued, "I think he was born a woman."

"*What?*" Ellie asked in confusion. "How do you know?"

"Do you know *The Arnolfini Portrait?*" asked Lottie.

Ellie shook her head.

"Well, in it, the artist hid himself in the background, in a mirror. Mirrors in art can symbolize many things, but they're most often associated with women, truth, and, of course, reflection. I could tell there was something slightly off about Tufty's painting, and then I realized. The entire painting is reflected in the tiny mirror in Tufty's hand, all exactly the same, except one crucial detail. Tufty is painted as a fox." Ellie's eyes widened. It was such an easy detail to miss if you weren't actively looking for it. You might just think it was a blurry image. "The Vixen and the Delicate Mouse—they're both him; that's what the painting and the rhyme are saying." She looked at Ellie in

excitement. "Whoever or whatever they were born as, they hid themselves as William Tufty, and that's who they were happiest being."

"He's a little like me then," Ellie breathed, her gaze distant.

Lottie nodded. "I wonder who they were," she wondered out loud.

"I don't know if it matters," Ellie replied, a small melancholy smile on her lips. "They were who they were and we should respect that."

Lottie nodded again. If they were meant to find out Tufty's identity, she was sure they would one day.

Ellie's face went blank, and then a look of comprehension creeped into her eyes. Lottie suddenly knew what she was thinking.

Binah knows.

29

LOTTIE SAW LITTLE OF JAMIE and Ellie over the next few days. She used all her time to study for exams while Ellie focused on training for her fencing tryouts—both of which forced them to put Binah's puzzle and the revelation about Tufty out of their minds. For now there were more important things that they needed to think about.

The Rosewood Hall fencing team was one of the most highly regarded in the world, not simply because it had produced numerous Olympians but also because it was believed that joining the team would cast a spell on you. It was a centuries-old superstition that claimed you would be destined to be adored by all. Lottie had a feeling it was because the requirements of the team probably meant you were pretty cool already, but it was still a fun story.

One evening the tiered benches were packed with students of all three houses, yellow, red, and purple, elegantly dotted among the stalls. Today they would be picking five students from their class who would be allowed to choose fencing as their option for the rest of their school years. Lottie envied anyone who'd picked an extracurricular class

already. She'd only glanced at the list and found it horribly overwhelming.

Antiques; archaeology; astronomy; badminton; canoeing; cheese appreciation; choir; classical studies; clay pigeon shooting; coding; debating; engineering; equestrian training; events planning; fencing; figure skating; filmmaking and theory; fine art (introduction to); fine dining; French; garden design; German; high fashion and design; horticulture; Japanese; jewelry making; kickboxing; Latin (introduction to); law (introduction to); Mandarin; orchestra; patisserie craft; philosophy; photography; poetry; sculpture; swimming (lane); swimming (synchronized); tea appreciation; tennis; theater (drama); theater (light and sound); theater (set design); wrestling . . .

The list seemed to go on forever and Lottie still had no idea what she should do. She was feeling particularly run-down today. It seemed no matter how much coffee she drank, she couldn't push the dizziness from her head. She was trying her best to hide this from her friends, but found it difficult when they were all so close to her. Jamie and Raphael were sitting to her right, leaning close to each other, talking in their usual hushed tones. Saskia was sitting a few rows above with some girls from her class, but she quickly came to say hi when she spotted Lottie.

"I was hoping to find Ellie before the tryouts and wish her good luck." Saskia looked around as if hoping she might spot Ellie. *Of course you were*, Lottie thought begrudgingly,

then quickly reminded herself that that wasn't a very kind thought for someone who was taking time out of their week to tutor her.

"Thank you, Saskia. I'll let her know when I see her."

Saskia smiled at her before running back to join the girls in her year, and Lottie turned to take a seat with the others. Lola and Micky were scarfing a giant bag of candy on her left; it was truly a wonder how they remained so small with the amount of sweets they consumed. The only person missing was—

"I wonder if they'll spar with a foil, épée, or saber?"

"Hello, Binah," the group said in unison.

Lottie had become accustomed to her ability to appear out of nowhere, not even flinching when her voice miraculously sounded behind her. Lottie and Ellie both felt a little different around Binah now—they didn't know how much she actually knew about the princess and the Portman situation, and they knew that they couldn't really ask her.

"Good evening, my fellow spectators!" Binah took a seat between Lottie and Lola. Her hair was up in two massive puffs on each side of her head, which somehow gave the impression of puppy ears. Lola wordlessly held out a yellow candy that Binah popped in her mouth. She readjusted her glasses, causing the light to reflect off the lenses, obscuring her eyes. "Lottie!"

Please don't mention the princess thing, please don't mention the princess thing.

Jamie squinted at Lottie and she held her breath, worrying that he could read her mind.

Binah simply smiled at her and pulled out a wispy-patterned green box from her bag. "I got this for you; I thought you might need it."

Lottie read the words on the top of the lid:

Sleepy-time tea: to combat stress
and help you slumber

Lottie blinked at the box for a moment. *Oh, come on! Does everyone in the school know I'm not sleeping?* On second thought, Lottie realized that it was silly to think there was anything Binah didn't know.

"Thank you, Binah . . . I'll give it a go." She smiled back at her with as much positivity as she could, desperately trying not to let on how tired she really was. Binah gave her a soft look and gently rubbed her arm as if she could sense that Lottie was putting on a brave face.

"Sometimes the gifts people give us can help in more ways than we expect." She winked and Lottie was sure she saw a little twinkle in the air as she did so.

How could sleepy-time tea possibly help her in other ways?

She racked her brain, knowing now that Binah's riddles were not to be taken lightly, but was jolted back into the world when a horn blared out. It was time.

Dame Bolter stepped forward, effortlessly capturing the attention of the hall with her fierce authority. She was accompanied by a young man with fluffy brown ringlets, who stood a few steps back; Lottie instantly recognized him as the fencing captain and head of Conch House, Jacob Zee. He was a big name at Rosewood to say the least and he was definitely adored. Their personalities were comically different: Dame Bolter a scorching blaze and Jacob a soft, delicate brook. It was hard to believe they were from the same house.

"Good evening, students of Rosewood." Dame Bolter's voice boomed through the gymnasium, effortlessly intimidating as usual. "Tonight marks our three hundredth anniversary of the fencing trials. Today we will pick five students who will be honored with an invitation to join the Rosewood Hall fencing team next year." She paused for a moment to take in the room and Lottie was sure her eyes lingered for an extra second on her. "This is a grand turnout tonight and I expect the utmost respect from your spectatorship." She turned to Jacob. "Any words of encouragement for our young hopefuls?" He smiled brightly at her before bowing ever so slightly in respect, an act so subtle Lottie almost missed it. Lottie heard a few giggles as

Jacob stepped forward, the same reaction she was used to hearing whenever Jamie entered a room.

"Today is not about winning your fights; it's about showing the most potential. There's some wonderful promise here tonight and I'm only sad that I won't get to lead you next year after I graduate. Good luck, everyone." He directed his happy smile at the line of prospective fencing hopefuls.

It was impossible to tell which ones were Ellie and Anastacia. There was a line of twenty almost identical statues, their faces covered by mesh masks and bodies shielded by matching white uniforms. They were completely void of gender or personhood, transformed into a group of robotic dancers. One of them broke off from the group and flexed their muscles before turning to the others and shouting, "BRING IT ON, LOSERS!"

Yep, that's Ellie.

Lottie turned to see Jamie cover his face with his palm and she had to stifle a giggle. A loud boom of laughter rang out from the left side of the hall. It was Professor Devine, who leaned against the wall of the gymnasium, her presence somehow outshining the spectacular marble statues on either side of the giant door. Lottie gulped; she'd had no idea the professor would be attending. She suddenly felt a thousand times more nervous for Ellie, even though Ellie didn't appear to be nervous at all.

The first match began. Two of the white-clad androids walked up to what Lottie had decided to call the stage as the whole thing seemed so very theatrical. They bowed to each other before beginning and that was about all Lottie could keep up with. As soon as the match began, their swords were moving too fast for her to follow, a blur of white and silver elegantly parrying one another. It became clear that the person on the right was the one to watch; they moved with such lightning speed that their opponent could barely get a single strike against the barrage of unstoppable hits. She looked over to see Jamie and Raphael watching the match with squinted eyes, then back at Saskia, who winked.

Binah was grinning broadly. "I wonder who that could be . . ."

The next match began, then the next, and Lottie found that she was being lulled by the movements, mesmerized by each feint and attack. She'd lost track again of which one was Ellie. The only one Lottie was aware of was the unbeatable person from the first match. She wished she understood more about the sport so she could know for certain who was doing the best, but she was worried that if she asked anyone they'd think it was odd for her not to know, so she kept her mouth shut and allowed herself to be hypnotized by the strange dance.

Dame Bolter called for the final match and the

unbeatable person walked up to the stage to take on the other strongest competitor. The tension in the room was palpable as the two faced each other. This match felt different than the others. The two bowed and the atmosphere seemed to light up with prickly electricity. And then it began.

Their swords moved in furious flashes, the two fighters darting and lunging with such intricate precision that they seemed more like deadly ballet dancers than thirteen-year-old students. This time it was impossible to tell who was on top; when one forced the other to retreat, they effortlessly disengaged and brought the fight back to the center until the other took over again. They twirled and twisted, bodies taut, two relentless forces persistently attacking and feinting in a loop of complex tricks. Lottie tried to keep focused, but her mind kept slipping. It felt as though with each clash of their swords a strange dark feeling filled Lottie's head, making her thoughts turn cloudy and confused.

And then it was over. In her haze, Lottie couldn't tell who had won.

The two duellers walked up to each other and the whole audience collectively held their breath. The unbeatable fighter pulled her mask off and a cascade of luscious chestnut hair came loose. Lottie gasped at the sight of Anastacia, elegantly shaking out her hair. Standing there in her white gear, sword by her side, she looked ferocious enough to

take on a whole army. Those in the audience wearing red began cheering wildly.

Slowly the other contestant pulled off her own mask and a thick mop of black sweat-drenched hair appeared.

A prince!

Lottie felt a sudden rush of heat enter her cheeks as she took in her roommate. Ellie beamed at the audience as they cheered for her. Anastacia and Ellie held their hands out to each other and shook. As soon as their hands met, Lottie felt it—a swell of exhaustion like a wave crashing over her. She swayed involuntarily.

Focus, Lottie, this is Ellie's big moment.

The hopefuls moved to stand in a line at the back of the stage, all masks off now. Dame Bolter cleared her throat as she approached the podium to speak.

"I will now read the names of the five students we have chosen to join the team."

Lottie felt her breath catch in her throat; something was wrong. Her body felt as if it were suddenly moving in slow motion.

"Ellie Wolf."

The audience cheered. Lottie tried to join in, but the dizzy sensation was overpowering her.

I need to sleep, she thought desperately, but there was something else, something clawing at the back of her mind.

"Marzia Hart." The cheering began to get distant and Lottie helplessly bashed her hands against her ears, trying to will some clarity into her mind. What had Binah said about gifts again?

"Thomas Carter." She looked up at the duellers, but their white armor seemed to be fading in front of her. Everything started turning black and she desperately tried to blink it away.

"Lottie, are you okay?" The voice was coming from Binah, but Lottie pushed her aside to get to the stairs.

"Riyadh Murphy."

Lottie desperately waded through cheering people. The world seemed to be spinning around like she was stuck on a nightmare carousel. She frantically racked her brain to figure out what her mind was trying to tell her.

"And, finally, the last person joining the Rosewood Hall fencing team will be . . ." The world was fading around her fast and her footsteps began to swerve as she reached the bottom of the steps.

"Anastacia Alcroft."

The name smacked into her head, igniting a hidden thought until it burned so bright it blocked out all others . . .

Anastacia's gift . . . The Princess and the Pea!

She turned sharply in confusion just in time to catch a

glimpse of Jamie's concerned face in front of her. "There's something under my mattress," she cried out over the noise of the crowd.

And then the world around her blacked out.

I NEED TO GET OFF this carousel or I'm going to be sick!

Something was spinning her round and round and she wanted it to stop.

"Lottie?"

That's Jamie's voice.

The distant voice called her name, but she couldn't quite get hold of it.

"Lottie, can you hear me?"

Why is the room spinning so much?

"Lottie, you need to wake up now. Lottie, hello?"

Wait, it's not the room spinning. I'm spinning . . . I fainted . . . Where am I? Who did this?

"Princess and the Pea!" Lottie jerked awake suddenly to see a crowd of people around her. Her eyes focused and she looked up into the face of a very worried Professor Devine.

"Sounds like you were having an interesting dream there, Lottie." A concerned smile lingered on the professor's lips and Lottie instantly felt awful. She couldn't stand the thought of worrying anyone.

"Sorry, I . . . my bed." Lottie fought to get the words

out, desperately trying to form her thoughts into sentences through the haze in her head. "I need to get to bed."

She tried to sit up, pushing herself away from the professor's arms. Ellie and Jamie instantly appeared at her side to assist her, and the sinking feeling in her stomach returned as she took in Ellie in her pristine white fencing gear, hair slicked back.

I ruined the tournament, she thought despairingly.

"You've only been out for two minutes."

Lottie perked up at Jamie's words, feeling a creepy sense that he'd just read her mind again.

"Now what was that about your bed?" Jamie looked at her very seriously, even for him. Ellie too seemed uncharacteristically tense.

"Yes . . . I have to get to bed. I seem to have remembered how to sleep." She smiled at Jamie and held his gaze as she spoke, trying to convey that she wanted to tell him something—something important. He and Ellie exchanged a look.

"Absolutely not, Miss Charlotte," blared out Dame Bolter's voice. "You need to go straight to the infirmary to see Nurse Sani."

Lottie didn't have time for this; she needed to know if her hunch was true. She turned to Professor Devine and gave her a pleading look. "Please! I just need to get to bed!"

Her house mother raised an eyebrow and Lottie

wondered if she might say no. But then the professor smiled at Dame Bolter and said reassuringly, "Actually, Mercy, I think in this instance a good night's sleep is what's in order."

Dame Bolter looked at Lottie suspiciously. "Maybe so . . ." she said slowly.

The professor clapped her hands. "Chop-chop, then. Jamie, would you kindly help Ellie take Lottie back to her room so we can finish this ceremony?"

"Yes, Professor," they replied in unison.

The three walked out of the hall, both supporting Lottie, their arms around her waist. As they walked past Anastacia, Lottie thought she saw her clench her fists in fury.

"Princess and the Pea," Lottie said resolutely, her hands firmly on her hips.

"Yep, she's gone mad from no sleep. Told ya."

Lottie scowled at Ellie, who was giggling at her own joke. Jamie and Ellie sat on Ellie's bed as if they were in a class and Lottie was their teacher. It always amused Lottie how perfectly the two of them blended into Ellie's dark, edgy side of the room.

"No, that's my clue," Lottie said, rolling her eyes. "Don't you remember the fairy tale?"

Ellie shrugged, but Jamie nodded.

"They place a pea under twenty mattresses and they

know that the girl sleeping on them is a princess because she can feel the pea during the night and it stops her from sleeping."

"Ahh, yes," Ellie said with a grin on her face. "I can't sleep either when I need to pee." Lottie snorted and quickly covered her mouth, and even Jamie allowed a tight smile to crawl onto his face. "But seriously," Ellie continued, "you think there's a pea under your bed?"

"Honestly I don't know . . . I just feel there's something . . ." Lottie turned to stare at the bed. It didn't look inviting anymore; it felt as though something dark were nesting within it and she wanted it gone. The two nodded at Lottie in understanding and began wordlessly getting to work.

Lottie grabbed Mr. Truffles and they proceeded to throw all the bedding and pillows onto Ellie's bed. Jamie walked over when they were done and effortlessly lifted the mattress as if it weighed no more than a feather. Lottie held her breath . . . and there it was.

In the center of the mattress, taped down, was a piece of paper showing a wolf's head within a circle, crossed through with two thick red lines.

Ellie gasped and raised a hand to her mouth.

Jamie let out a furious curse. Lottie almost couldn't believe she'd heard him swear but this was not the time to protest.

"What is it?" she asked timidly. She almost didn't want to know; it had to be awful to get such a strong reaction from the two of them.

Jamie pulled the paper off the mattress and stormed over to the desk, slamming it down with such force it made Lottie jump. Ellie stared blank-faced at the desk, eerily calm.

"That's the Wolfson House sigil," Ellie said vacantly. "And it's got a death mark through it."

❦ 31 ❧

"WE'RE TELLING YOUR PARENTS."

"*BRIKTAH!*" Lottie cringed at the Maravish word as Ellie snapped out of her daze. "No, we're not."

Jamie was already flattening the paper, clearly intending to send a copy back to Maradova as fast as possible. Ellie grabbed at him wildly, scratching and pushing to try to get it, but Jamie held her off easily. Lottie stood, stupefied and useless. Someone had put that paper there, probably someone she knew.

Another thought pinged into her mind and she felt sick. *It must have been the person who left the gift at the beginning of term. It's a curse and that's why I couldn't sleep—and somehow Anastacia had known about it.*

Ellie and Jamie continued to battle it out, the piece of paper with the death mark radiating negative energy. Lottie imagined tendrils of wispy dark smoke oozing off it and filling the room with a toxic tension.

It was here to scare the princess; it was here to scare her out of Rosewood.

"Jamie, you can't." The words came out of Lottie's mouth before she even registered her own thoughts.

"But, Lottie, you might be in danger." His voice was strained and it caught her off guard.

"So?" Lottie replied, feigning calm. "Isn't that the point of my job as Portman?" Jamie eased slightly and turned to meet her eyes. "I deal with all the danger and problems so that Ellie doesn't have to," Lottie continued. "So that Ellie can *stay* at Rosewood."

Lottie faced them, determined that whoever had done this would not jeopardize Ellie's time at Rosewood—she would not let them win. They would find out who was doing this no matter what.

Jamie released a long breath, then turned to Ellie. His expression seemed almost disappointed.

"Is this what you wanted?" Jamie hissed at Ellie in a low voice, barely audible to Lottie.

Ellie looked at the floor, a shadow hiding the unmistakable look of shame on her face. She refused to look at him, continuing to stare at her feet.

"No, stop. You aren't listening to me," Lottie said, surprising herself with her own determination. "If Ellie gets taken away, then they win and the threat still remains. With me here we can lure them out. Whoever they are, they're getting bolder—we can catch them."

Ellie flinched and Lottie realized what she'd just said. She was about to speak again but Jamie stopped her. His face was cold.

"Has something happened before?"

Lottie felt her breath catch in her throat. *Oops.*

Jamie slowly put the paper down and turned back to her, but she was unable to form any words. "I asked you a question, Lottie." He gave her a look so forceful she could almost feel the blow.

"Yes," she replied, unable to hold eye contact.

He turned to Ellie and she didn't look away this time.

"On the first day of school," she said, straight-faced, "Lottie got a library book with a message saying they knew she had a secret, so we snuck out to find out which students had used the library that day."

Jamie's lip twitched, but he managed to remain calm. "And?" he asked, the chill in his voice more threatening than if he was shouting at them.

"And we found Anastacia's, Raphael's, and Binah's names," Ellie said. This time she did look away.

"And neither of you thought to tell me this?" His voice raised a little, making Lottie instinctively hold her breath. "Even though I'm here to protect you, you hid this from me?"

Ellie shook her head violently. Lottie could see a storm brewing inside her.

"Maybe I don't want you to protect me!" she roared, baring her teeth like fangs. As soon as she said the words, she grimaced, a look of regret on her face. The silence that followed was painful. Lottie had absolutely no idea what Jamie was thinking and it scared her. Ellie's chest heaved up and down.

"I'll always be here, Ellie," Jamie said, his voice quiet but cold, "whether you like it or not." There was a weight to his words—Lottie knew something had just happened between the two of them that she would never understand.

How did you become a Partizan? Lottie desperately wanted to ask.

Ellie slowly looked down. "I didn't mean . . . I know . . ." she said, running her hands through her hair.

Jamie took another deep breath and turned back to Lottie, once again stoic and composed. "Do you accept the danger of being bait, Lottie?" His dark eyes held hers, but she remained as poised as possible. She knew she had to remain calm if she was going to persuade Jamie that she wasn't affected by the messages.

Who are you really? she wondered, not for the first time.

She nodded once, not trusting her voice to keep up the facade.

He turned to Ellie once more and again they shared a look she couldn't quite understand. "I want you both to be wary of Anastacia and Raphael," he said coolly. Lottie

could feel Ellie relax, yet she couldn't do the same. "I don't trust them."

So that's why he's staying so close to Raphael.

"You cannot let them know we suspect them. We need to keep a close eye on them."

"Does this mean you're not going to report it?" Ellie asked, the eagerness in her voice pulling Lottie from her thoughts.

He frowned disapprovingly at his own decision and Ellie grinned. "But if I feel for even one second that you're in imminent danger I won't hesitate to report back to your parents."

Jamie was letting them keep it secret.

Ellie winked at Lottie. "We'll catch whoever it is before it gets to that."

Lottie found herself faking a determined smile, but a voice in her head whispered all the mysteries still left to be solved. *Who's leaving these messages? What do they want? Why is Ellie so uncomfortable with Jamie being her Partizan? How did Jamie become a Partizan?*

"Agreed," Lottie said flatly. "We'll uncover the truth."

She wasn't sure exactly which mystery she was referring to.

⚜ 32 ⚜

A FOCUSED CALM ENVELOPED ROSEWOOD Hall with the onset of the winter exams. The students gathered in the libraries and study halls, a collective hush as they concentrated on absorbing all that they'd learned so far.

Lottie was relieved that the years of hard work to get into Rosewood Hall had paid off. She found that the studying and the exams themselves were not as daunting as she thought they'd be, especially with the support of her friends—and the endless supply of Tompkins sweets from Lola and Micky.

As soon as the exams were over, most students prepared to travel back home for Christmas. Lottie, Jamie, and Ellie had temporarily halted their decoding of the message as they studied for the exams, but there was something else keeping Lottie's mind off the mystery. Ollie was upset with her.

Dear Lottie,

I'm not going to lie: I'm really sad you're not coming home for Christmas, but I'm sure whatever this crazy thing you've

got caught up in is very important.

If you do suddenly change your mind and want to spend Christmas at Casa de Moreno, there's always room for you at the table.

Don't forget about us in your new exciting school.

Merry Christmas.

Your first and most loyal friend,

Ollie

She'd never been the type of person to be obsessed with her phone, but she wished more than anything that she could just call Ollie and hear his reassuring voice. It was far too late now to hop on a train back to Cornwall and see Ollie, but, worst of all, it had been her idea to stay over Christmas.

Ellie had invited her to Maradova, but Lottie didn't know how she'd be able to cope with the strange setting. Ellie, however, was more than happy not to go home for Christmas as she was dreading seeing her grandmother, so here they were, spending the holidays at Rosewood Hall. But Lottie couldn't get in the Christmas mood.

She sighed deeply as she reread Ollie's letter before folding it up and putting it in her pocket. Even though Ollie's letter probably wouldn't have seemed too bad to most people, she knew that he was upset.

"I thought Saskia said this was a 'small gathering'!" Ellie

scoffed as she prodded a large ice sculpture of an angel that had been placed on the food table. Saskia had invited some of the other students staying over the holidays to a party in Conch House to exchange gifts, and the girls had arrived early to help set up.

Lottie was about to reply when the front door creaked open to reveal Anastacia and Raphael, who were effortlessly balancing trays of fancy foods on their arms like they were circus performers.

Maybe those etiquette classes really are good for something! thought Lottie.

She tensed as they placed their trays on the table. It had been easy to avoid Anastacia and Raphael since the winter exams started, but tonight would be Ellie and Lottie's first real test in pretending they didn't suspect them.

Anastacia dusted her hands off and, without looking up, she said, "Ellie, stop eating the party food or I'll poison it."

Ellie quite literally choked on the pig-in-a-blanket she was shoving into her mouth, making Lottie wince. That particular party snack was just too much for her animal-loving heart: a pig-in-a-blanket of its own flesh . . . The horror! Ellie gave Anastacia a little side smile before reaching for another one.

"Oh please, you don't need an excuse to poison anyone," Ellie teased, making Raphael snort and instantly earning him a dangerous look from Anastacia. This poison talk was

definitely not helping Anastacia's case.

Lottie was glad that Jamie was busy picking up a Christmas tree from the main hall. If he were here to witness this, he'd be furious with them for "fraternizing with the potential enemy."

"No one is poisoning anything," Lottie chided. "We've put far too much effort into arranging every—ELLIE, FOR THE LOVE OF GOD, STOP EATING ALL THE FOOD!"

Ellie paused with a chocolate roll halfway to her mouth, then slowly put it back down again.

"As you wish, Your Highness." She gave her an over-the-top bow before heading to the door. "I need to go and get my guitar anyway; Jamie and I are gonna sing you guys a little song." She fluttered her eyelashes with a mocking, sickly sweet smile on her face.

Lottie gasped in surprise. "Jamie sings?"

The thought of Jamie pouring his heart out in a song seemed totally unnatural for someone so serious. Once again, Lottie found herself painfully aware of how little she actually knew about the two of them.

Ellie instantly turned back to her and gave her a sharp look that said, *"He's supposed to be your bodyguard; you should know he sings."*

"You didn't know your own bodyguard sings?" The voice

came from behind her and she quickly turned to see Saskia by the entrance to the kitchen, carrying a small table, and a posse of Conch House students behind her, all holding big bags of miscellaneous party items. "Seems a bit strange," she added as she effortlessly set down the table.

"Well . . . no, I mean"—Lottie scrambled for the right words but somehow found it even harder to think in the presence of Saskia's questioning smile—"I didn't know he sang in public . . . He's usually so shy about it."

"Hmm." Saskia began placing things on the table, giving Lottie a little sideways glance.

Lottie's eyes flicked to Ellie, but she was staring at Saskia strangely, not dissimilar to how she'd been looking at all the party food.

"What are you staring at?" Saskia asked coyly, flicking her hair out of her face as if she were a mermaid emerging from the water.

"Who says I'm staring?" Ellie replied casually.

Saskia laughed a deep throaty laugh in response, a hand moving to her hip to smooth her dress over her thighs. Something inside Lottie bristled sharply at the exchange.

"Go and get your guitar and treat us to a song—then I might forgive you for pecking at my food, *pequeña pollo*." Ellie smiled at the pet name and Lottie felt the prickly feeling intensify.

With Ellie gone, Lottie suddenly felt self-conscious, surrounded as she was by mostly Conch students who seemed to know each other quite well, so she resigned herself to meticulously arranging the food and decor in elaborate Christmas displays. She might not be in a Christmassy mood, but she still liked decorating.

"You're surprisingly good at stuff like that."

Lottie looked up to see Anastacia eyeing the snowflake patterns she'd made out of some paper doilies. It was hard not to take offense at the word "surprisingly," but the fact she was getting any form of compliment from Anastacia made up for it. She wore a red dress and her chestnut hair was pristine as usual. She looked like something out of a Christmas ad, and it made Lottie feel childish in the little reindeer headband she'd thought would be "cute."

"Thanks, actually I . . ."

"You're nothing like I expected you to be."

Lottie blinked in surprise, not sure how to respond. *How exactly did Anastacia expect me to be? Does she think I'm a bad princess?*

Anastacia looked at Lottie seriously, her lips parted as if she were about to say something important, and Lottie was transported back to that time in the library when she'd felt the same determination radiating from her. "Lottie, I know—"

"LET US ENTERTAIN YOU!" Ellie burst through the

door dramatically, all eyes instantly turning to her as she raised a guitar in the air like a trophy. She was followed by a particularly irritated-looking Jamie. He too had a guitar in his hand but seemed less than thrilled about it. Ellie gave him a sharp kick in the shin and he reluctantly raised a party horn to his mouth and gave it a comically unenthusiastic blow.

And he plays guitar? Does he also do ballet and sing soprano? Lottie felt that wisp of curiosity about Jamie creep through her again.

How did you become a Partizan?

She turned back to Anastacia but she'd vanished, now suddenly at Saskia's side.

Lottie had to stifle a laugh as Ellie forced two Conch kids off the seats in the center of the room like it was her own personal stage. They grumbled indignantly and looked to Saskia, but she simply laughed her delicious laugh and gestured for them to move.

"Sometimes I'm surprised you weren't put in my house; you're certainly resolute."

Lottie instantly went cold at this. Ellie was in *her* house and no one could change that. Ellie winked at Saskia and gave her that trademark side smile, making Lottie's blood turn acidic. Why was this bothering her so much? She hated that she felt like this about Saskia, who was nothing but kind to her, but every time she was around Lottie just wanted to get away.

Everyone gathered around Jamie and Ellie as they prepared to play. They didn't seem even a little bit nervous and Lottie envied how relaxed they were.

"Play something Christmassy!" called out one of the Conch girls, who was wearing a Santa hat.

Ellie made a disgusted face, completely dismissing her. "No, we're playing something for Lottie," she said bluntly as she twiddled with the strings.

"For me?" Lottie felt simultaneously nervous and happy. That unpleasant feeling in her belly diminished for a moment as she reveled in Ellie's attention.

Ellie passed a pick to Jamie and he stuck it in his mouth as he began adjusting his own guitar strings. There was something strangely enchanting about the whole procedure, the shared concentration, the absolute assurance in what they were doing—two professionals engaging effortlessly with their craft.

"We're playing you a song from your country. Because you're not home this Christmas we thought we'd bring home to you." Jamie spoke with intensity, and she knew he wanted her to take this seriously.

"Thank you," she replied hesitantly.

The rest of the room exchanged tentative looks with each other, as unsure as Lottie of what was about to come.

The room hushed as they got into position. They shared a private look and began. The first note pierced the air and

the entire room seemed to shake. Lottie looked around but no one else appeared to have felt it. A collective chill ran through the listeners as Jamie's and Ellie's voices rang out in a haunting harmony. The song was sweet and painful at the same time, filling Lottie's chest with a dull ache. Jamie's voice was hypnotizing and Lottie found herself swaying, bewitched by the spell of the music. Everyone was silent and wide-eyed, captured by the unexpected intensity of the performance. Each chord on Ellie's guitar plunged Lottie further and further into the enchantment. Her body began to prickle with pins and needles, the world around her fading as she shut her eyes, giving herself over to the song, letting it consume her completely.

And then she could see it.

The ancient Maravish lyrics came alive, thanks to her princess lessons, and the story it told materialized in her mind.

Her name was Ester—she was both a Portman and a Partizan—and her princess was Liana. She was the most striking and devoted Portman the country had ever known, and she and her princess loved one another in deeper ways than just professional loyalty. Lottie could imagine them both, wispy ghosts of the past floating inside her head. They were a vision of red and black; they were fierce and forthright and adored by all who knew them. Princess Liana demanded that upon her emergence Ester would be

declared her royal hand so that they might rule together. But upon the night of the princess's coronation and emergence, Ester was stolen from her bed in an act of war by a neighboring country as a prop in negotiation. Instead of forcing her princess to choose between her people and herself, Ester took her own life. It was such a powerful act of loyalty that the gods took pity on her and allowed one last message to be delivered from her to her princess via a white dove. In a blinding rage and with the spirit of her fiery Portman inside her, the princess had the entire neighboring kingdom destroyed. Lottie could see the flames bursting from the castle, burning her skin as they blazed around her. And then the song ended.

The ghosts blinked out of her mind and her eyes blinked open, plummeting her back into the real world to find herself reaching out, tears streaming down her face as she tried desperately to grasp at the vision and bring it back.

Everyone was staring at her.

❧ 33 ❧

Lottie coughed awkwardly.

"That was . . . lovely," she said casually as she wiped her eyes, pretending nothing was out of the ordinary and she hadn't just burst out crying over an imaginary ghost princess and her Portman. Everyone was staring at her as if she were some kind of freak in a circus show.

Her mind raced, desperately trying to come up with anything to make the situation less awkward.

"I'm just . . . really homesick," she said, wiping her eyes again dramatically and sniffing before excusing herself to the balcony so no one could see how shaken she was.

"Right . . ." Anastacia's voice echoed sarcastically behind her and mocking laughter followed.

Lottie grabbed the side of the balcony and gulped down as much of the fresh, frosty air as her lungs could take. She exhaled, the puffs of breath a mirror of her internal fog of confusion and panic. The light outside was pale blue, the dwindling sun hidden behind thick masses of curling clouds that mirrored the frost over Rosewood Hall. Everything

around her was blue and white, as though they'd sunk into another world and were submerged in a strange muted version of her school. She looked down at her white knuckles, her hands gripping the balcony ledge.

What was that? What just happened?

The image of Liana and Ester burned in her mind as she squeezed her eyes shut. Suddenly "homesick" wasn't so far from the truth. In that moment she wished more than anything she could be back in Cornwall, cuddled up reading about other people's exciting lives, far away from any of the madness herself. Maybe she wasn't cut out for this world.

"Lottie?"

Lottie quickly wiped her eyes again at the sound of Ellie's voice. She turned to see her and Jamie standing by the double doors to the balcony.

Slowly Ellie stepped over the ledge and Jamie moved to follow.

"I'm fine, guys. You don't have to come out—" Jamie wrapped a large red blanket from the Conch dorm around her shoulders without saying anything. "Thank you." Lottie pulled the blanket around her, not realizing until then how cold she really was.

"Can we have a moment alone?" Ellie said softly. It wasn't a question, and Jamie nodded before returning to

the festivities and closing the glass doors. It was the first time Lottie had really seen Ellie take a tone of authority with him.

"Ellie, I really am fine—"

"What happened in there?" Ellie asked.

Lottie paused, then rubbed her forehead in thought. The truth was she didn't know what had happened and she didn't know how to explain it, but she knew it was important. Everything felt important since she'd started at Rosewood.

"Do you ever think . . ." Lottie shook her head and looked out over the school. "Do you ever think that there's something weird about Rosewood?"

Ellie followed her gaze, a soft smile creeping onto her lips while her eyes remained distant. "All the time. It's why I like it."

Lottie watched Ellie's face for a moment before taking a step nearer and resting her head against her shoulder. They stood like that, intertwined, until Ellie huffed and turned to face her. "Lottie, I'm really sorry."

Lottie blinked in surprise. It was so rare that Ellie ever said that word.

"This is probably the worst Christmas you've ever had. Stuck at school away from home. It's not the same." Ellie made a remorseful face and Lottie sniffled out a

giggle at how silly it sounded.

"I don't really care about Christmas," she said, "and it was my idea to stay here." Lottie pulled the blanket tighter around herself. "I stopped really caring about Christmas after my mom died anyway." Lottie hadn't known how true this was until she'd said it. It was why she was so scared to go to Maradova and see what Ellie's family Christmas was like. A Christmas with a full family. What if it wasn't like she'd imagined it?

Lottie was pulled out of her thoughts by Ellie making a frustrated sound.

"I'm supposed to be the one who doesn't care about stuff like that," she griped, rubbing Lottie's head affectionately. "You're supposed to love things like Christmas and carols and all the tacky stuff that goes with it." Lottie laughed and Ellie gifted her that little side smile. "Anyway, I was going to give this to you later, but . . ." Ellie pushed her hair back as she pulled something from her bag. "I want you to have this now; it feels like a good time."

She held out a poorly wrapped box with the word *Lottie* scrawled across it in black marker.

"Ellie, you shouldn't have. I really—"

"Just open it," Ellie said quickly, looking away.

Lottie considered the gift for a second, then pulled the paper back thoughtfully. Inside was a large rose-gold velvet

box with a dazzling embroidered sun on the lid. The little gems along the sides reflected the blue light in a milky moonlit glow.

"Ellie, this is beautiful." Lottie's voice came out a soft whisper as she took in the box.

"It's for the tiara your mom gave you. I noticed how you just keep it in your bag or your bedside table so I thought you could keep it in here." Ellie sounded shy as she said this, making Lottie smile even more.

"It's like us," Lottie said, grinning at Ellie excitedly. Ellie looked confused. "A crescent-moon tiara with a sunshine box. Total opposites that go together," she explained.

As she said it, all Lottie's worries disappeared. She looked down at the box again, taking in the beautiful image on the lid. She wasn't worried about the message, or her exams, or the ball. With Ellie by her side she was sure she could do anything.

"Come on—let's go back to the party," she said, grabbing Ellie's hand.

"Actually . . ." Ellie said, pulling her hand back. "Why don't we just spend the rest of Christmas together in the Ivy dorm?"

Lottie beamed at her, not wanting to say out loud how much she didn't feel like spending Christmas in Conch House.

"I'll even steal some mince pies for us," Ellie said, winking.

Lottie squeezed Ellie's hand. "That sounds like the best Christmas ever."

✥ 34 ✥

IT WAS 9:30 P.M. ON December 31, and Lottie, Ellie, and Jamie were making the most of the extended curfew for holiday-stay students by taking a late stroll around the rose garden by the main hall. It was freezing cold, the grass underneath them crunchy with its icy coat. Lottie pulled her heavy wool-lined Ivy cape tight around her shoulders.

"Look!" she cried, pointing up at a huge firework exploding in the distance over the walls of the school. It lit up the grounds in gorgeous pink light and she couldn't help moving toward it.

"Lottie, wait." Jamie reached out and grabbed her arm, pulling her back. "Do you hear that?"

He held a finger up to signal them to stay silent and Ellie took a small step toward Lottie. Lottie stayed as quiet as possible, trying to hear what Jamie was hearing and wondering if they were in danger. A muted rustling came from a tree nearby and Lottie held her breath, her heartbeat increasing.

This is it, she thought. *Whoever left that message is coming for us.*

Slowly, crouching low, Jamie took five purposeful steps in the direction of the noise. Before Lottie could register what was happening, his arm reached out behind the tree and roughly grabbed their would-be attacker. Jamie kicked his leg out from under him and within seconds he had the figure on the ground with their hands pinned behind their back.

"PLEASE DON'T HURT ME! I'm sorry, I'm sorry!"

"Raphael?" Lottie said in confusion. Jamie didn't let up on his grip.

"Jeez, Jamie! I was just coming to get you guys and then I thought it would be funny to scare you and—" Raphael yelped as Jamie pulled him up. Raphael rubbed his arm and chuckled to himself as he took in Jamie's serious face. "I realize now that wasn't my smartest idea . . ."

Jamie considered him for a moment, then looked over at Lottie and Ellie. Lottie shrugged, trying not to laugh, partly because she'd been so terrified, and partly at how ridiculous the whole thing was.

"You never were one for thinking things through," Jamie said sternly.

Raphael burst out laughing. There was something in his movements that seemed off, which Jamie picked up on.

"Are you feeling okay?" he asked, raising an eyebrow.

"I'm fine, I'm fine! We're doing something . . . fun. I didn't want you guys to get left out." He grinned at them, his charming smile slightly too bright.

Ellie chuckled, taking a step toward Raphael. "I've gotta see this. Lottie?" She turned to Lottie, grinning.

Another firework went off in the distance; this time it turned the ground red.

"Let me lead the way," Raphael replied as the crimson air fizzled around them.

They walked to the outskirts of Conch House. Night had fully enveloped the school and the fiery lanterns by the doors were blazing like little dancing figures on each side of the entranceway. There was a commotion at the gate, accompanied by wild fits of laughter and muted conversation.

Ellie beamed excitedly. "Sounds like a party."

Saskia, Anastacia, and a small group of other Conch students were standing against the wall of the dorm with towels on their arms, looking giddy.

"What are you guys doing?" Jamie asked Raphael matter-of-factly as they approached.

"We're going to break into the Conch House pool," he said, grinning wildly.

"But it's off limits!" Lottie immediately felt like an

idiot for stating the obvious.

"Well, duh! That's what makes it fun!" This came from a petite Conch girl with a red bow in her hair.

Lottie looked to Saskia, who was giggling. Why was she letting this happen?

Lottie thought about how incredibly uncool it would look for her to try to dissuade them. She wished Binah or Lola and Micky were there and she could just do fun, safe things with them like drink hot chocolate and watch Disney films.

"Yes! A break-in!"

Lottie jumped as Ellie dived forward, wrapping an arm around Saskia's shoulder, saying, "Y'know I always liked you, Saskia."

They both burst out in senseless laughter and Lottie found herself feeling that familiar prickly sensation in her chest. She wanted to pry the two apart and tell Saskia to go away.

Ellie caught her eye and smiled at her as if she knew what she was thinking.

"We're not going," Jamie's serious voice cut in.

Saskia squinted at him, her whole mood suddenly changing. "It'll be fun—"

"Quiet!" Jamie gave her a sharp and furious look, and Saskia instantly fell silent, a cold expression on her face.

She shook her head and put her smile back on. "Well,

you know where to find us if you change your minds."

Saskia made a signal and the group moved off down the path. Anastacia hesitated only for a moment, her eyes lingering on Lottie, before glancing at Ellie as she walked past. She didn't seem pleased, and it was clear that Anastacia was the only nongiddy member of the group.

Ellie turned sharply to Jamie and shoved him, a totally futile move as he didn't budge.

He blinked slowly at her like she was a child having a tantrum. "We are not going, Ellie," he repeated.

She stared at him for a moment, then looked down the path at the others. When she turned back she had that determined look on her face that could only result in trouble.

"We have to," Ellie replied. "We can't let them think we're afraid."

Jamie remained firm. "No."

"Well, *I'm* going. You guys can do whatever you want." She stuck her tongue out at him and quickly pivoted out of Jamie's reach.

"Ellie, come back *now!*"

"You'll have to catch me!" she called, running to meet up with the others.

Jamie grunted in annoyance and took off in a sprint after her.

"Ellie, if you and Jamie go, then I have to . . . GUYS!"

It was too late. She would either have to stand there on her own or follow them. Begrudgingly she began walking after them.

I'm definitely going to regret this, Lottie thought.

❧ 35 ❧

As soon as Lottie and Jamie walked in, Ellie pressed two plastic cups and a plate of snacks into their hands.

"Here, eat something, you two, and lighten up!" Ellie smiled down at them in an attempt to make them feel better.

Lottie and Jamie stood by the side of the pool under the gazebo, wrapped in blankets and looking very much like they had accepted that the world was about to end. Lottie resented that she agreed with Jamie about how stupid this was, but an off-limits pool and a cold night in December just seemed like a really terrible combination.

"It's freezing out," Jamie said firmly. "I have a respons—"

"Just drink your lemonade. Anastacia warmed it up," Ellie said, rolling her eyes.

Jamie took one of the cups begrudgingly and allowed himself a tentative sip. "Fine," he said.

Lottie took the other cup, grateful for its warmth.

They sat under the gazebo in awkward silence, Jamie occasionally taking furious gulps of the hot lemonade,

while Lottie warmed her hands round hers.

Ellie was dancing with Saskia on the other side of the pool, twirling and dipping her like she was some kind of Prince Charming and Saskia was her princess. An involuntary pout crept onto Lottie's face. She told herself it was only because she resented being there, and *not* because she was jealous of Saskia. That would be completely and absolutely ridiculous.

"I bet you ten pounds someone falls in the pool," Lottie said.

Jamie continued staring stony-faced across the water, gritting his teeth as hot air escaped from his nose into the cold. "Twenty pounds says I push one of them."

Lottie almost choked. Was that genuine humor? Her mind was thrust back to when they had first met, before she knew he was a Partizan, before she'd given her life over to being Ellie's Portman. It almost felt like there were two of him: the serious, mature mask he wore and the kid who was hidden underneath him. Again that voice whispered in her ear. *Who are you, Jamie Volk?*

"Don't you ever wish you could just be an ordinary boy?"

Lottie blurted out the question before she'd even processed it in her own head. Jamie didn't reply at first, and she wondered if she'd blown her chance of ever uncovering his mystery.

"I'll never be an ordinary boy."

She tensed at his response. There was something undeniably vulnerable in his voice. She felt as if she were luring a deer toward her, afraid to scare it away.

Jamie stood up slowly, knocking over the dregs of his drink as he shook off his blanket. She watched as he walked to the gazebo's edge, leaning on one of the stone pillars, and stared out almost wistfully into the water's sapphire surface.

Carefully, with the deer still in her mind, Lottie stood beside him.

The Conch House pool was hidden away behind thick rosehip bushes and crab apple trees, the red berries peeping out from the branches, stark against the dreamy blue atmosphere of the silky moonlit pool.

"But hypothetically," Lottie asked gingerly, "if you could be?"

He smirked and gave her a little sideways glance. "I almost wonder if you're insulting my skills as a Partizan."

Jamie laughed at her confused expression.

"What I mean is," he went on, "it's my job to try to blend in with the other students as much as possible. Do you not think I'm like other boys?" he asked, a glint of humor twinkling in his eyes.

Lottie pretended to think for a moment, tapping her finger on her chin as if trying to tap the thoughts out of

her head. "Hmm," she began, "I mean, for one you have about zero sense of humor, and you're so freakishly strong that you're basically a superhero. You're definitely not like other boys."

A soft smile spread over Jamie's lips and he laughed low. Then the twinkle vanished from his eyes and he was serious again. Lottie worried that she'd scared away the deer, but he turned back to the water, and she could sense he was still with her.

"When you live your life for someone else, you find strength you didn't know you were capable of." He spoke with a sense of certainty—and Lottie found the words made her heart ache.

"That sounds awfully sad," she said, involuntarily hugging herself as if trying to find comfort.

He looked at her earnestly, his head tilted slightly, his eyes glossy and intense. "Really?" he asked. "Are you not doing the same thing? Did you not sign your life over to the Maravish royal family?"

But I had a choice, Lottie thought, trying to stop the tears springing to her eyes.

And once again, as if he could read her mind, he leaned close to her and said gently, "This is our choice, Lottie."

His breath brushed her cheek, making her shudder. It had a strange sweet smell, like baby powder, which made

her nose tingle. She looked up and realized how close their faces were.

Something wasn't right. Jamie was not himself.

What was in his drink?

Jamie's eyes turned hazy and he leaned forward, forcing Lottie to step back toward the wall that separated the gazebo from the pool, one hand resting on the stone for support.

"Jamie . . ."

The moonlight twinkled between them and the look on his face made her catch her breath. His manic grin reminded her of a wolf. His eyes were dark under his messy hair; it was a distinctly predatory look that made Lottie's heart race.

He snickered as if reading her mind again.

"You're still afraid of me," he said with a smirk.

Lottie felt a blush creep onto her cheeks, but not because she was embarrassed. His words had made her suddenly very angry. "Afraid of you? Of course I'm afraid of you!"

This was obviously not the response he'd been expecting and his face showed it.

"Nothing I do will ever impress you," she added.

He shook his head in confusion. "You don't need to impress me—"

"But I *do*! I need to prove to you that I'm capable."

"I don't think you're not capable." His face twisted a bit as if he were struggling to summon the right words. "I think you shouldn't *have* to be capable."

"I . . . what?" Lottie blinked at him, perplexed.

"You're just a kid, Lottie." He said this softly, whispering in her ear.

"Well . . . so are you then." She tried to sound confident, but her words were uneven.

Jamie looked distant for a moment, the haze completely consuming him. "I never had that luxury"—he turned back to Lottie, a pained look taking hold of him—"and I can't stand seeing it taken away from you."

He leaned in so close Lottie could feel his heartbeat. She was leaning as far back as she could now without falling in the pool.

"Jamie, you're sick or something—something in your drink . . ."

His expression instantly changed, all the softness being replaced by confusion.

"No. I'm . . ." Then realization dawned on his face, confusion shifting to anger. He grabbed his head in his hands, trying to will some kind of stability into his thoughts.

"Lottie, I'm going to pass out. Listen . . ." He scrunched

his eyes shut, desperately forcing his mind and mouth to work together. "You can't trust Anastacia . . ."

And then he fainted into her arms, plummeting them both over the wall and into the freezing-cold water.

36

COLD WATER FLEW UP LOTTIE'S nose, and her blood felt like ice in her veins. She opened her eyes under the water to see Jamie, still unconscious, a muddled blur sinking with her.

I have to get him out.

She wrapped her arms under his shoulders.

Hold on, Jamie! Please don't drown! Please don't drown!

She'd swum against wild currents in the sea in Cornwall, and she'd dived to retrieve coins at the bottom of the local swimming pool, but pulling another human from the water, fully clothed, felt like a gargantuan task.

I will not let you drown.

But no matter how much she tried to push for the surface, they were just too heavy in their shoes and clothes. She was running out of time, every second felt crucial.

I need more momentum.

Slowly she allowed them to sink, then firmly planted her feet on the bottom of the pool and pushed up with all her strength.

They broke the surface and Lottie desperately gulped in as much air as she could as she struggled to the side.

She could see people at the pool's edge calling out but she couldn't hear them. Hands came down and lifted her and Jamie out of the water.

They were hauled onto the grassy bank and someone was saying her name, but she pushed them aside; she had to get back to Jamie. She leaned over him. He was still out cold, his tan-brown skin coated by a porcelain sheen of frailty.

It felt wrong: Jamie was supposed to be strong, unwavering, and unbreakable. She wanted him to wake up and shout at her, tell her it was a test, and chastise her for getting so worried—but, no matter how much she willed it, he remained still, not breathing.

What do I do? She felt tears pricking her eyes. *What do I do?*

Somewhere in her mind a soft voice replied: *Kiss the princess to wake her up.*

Her body moved on autopilot. She pushed down on his chest three times, covered his nose, and gently placed her mouth over his, filling his lungs with her air. Then she did it again, and again and . . .

Jamie coughed underneath her abruptly, making her jolt back.

He drew in a shaky breath before mumbling, "That's not how you do mouth-to-mouth."

Lottie gasped at his voice. He spluttered a few more

times, his eyes trying to focus, before he reached up and stroked her cheek. His hand was freezing against her face. "So warm," he muttered, before passing out again.

Lottie sat beside him, still holding his hand against her cheek.

He's okay. I did it. I saved him.

Tears began to fall down her cheeks and she finally looked up. Everyone was standing around them, their faces glum. Ellie, in particular, looked horrified.

"It's okay, guys . . ." She hiccuped a little sob. "He's okay."

Slowly she looked up. There stood Professor Adina Devine, her winter cloak billowing in the wind like a whirlwind of furious power.

"All of you. To my office. NOW!" She stormed over to where Lottie was kneeling on the ground by Jamie. "Raphael, Thomas, help me get Jamie to the infirmary."

Lottie watched as they hauled him up, desperately wanting to go with them. Everyone began walking off, but Lottie couldn't move.

A hand gently rested on her shoulder and she turned to see Ellie holding a blanket. "I'm sorry, Lottie, I shouldn't have made you guys come out here . . . I'm . . ."

Lottie took the blanket from Ellie, still looking off into the distance.

"Someone did something to his drink . . ."

Ellie stared at her, dumbfounded. "What? Who?"

"I don't know . . ."

You can't trust Anastacia.

It was the only logical conclusion. It had been her drink they'd been given; all signs were pointing to her. She looked at Anastacia as she walked off with the rest of the group, a blurry red figure slowly moving away. Lottie couldn't understand why she would do it. What could she have wanted to gain? It didn't make any sense.

"Lottie, you're shivering—we need to get you inside."

Lottie let Ellie wrap the blanket around her and slowly they walked to the Ivy dorm. She wasn't even nervous about going to Professor Devine's office. Something weird was going on at Rosewood. She needed to figure out what it was before it was too late.

37

As punishment for breaking into the pool, they were all given one month of leaf sweeping and litter collecting and had to write a five-page essay on the importance of respecting water. Saskia was grounded until term started again and Professor Devine stated, "She should count herself lucky she isn't having her title revoked."

Lottie had wanted to protest her punishment—she hadn't wanted to go to the pool in the first place—but she remembered what the professor had said about being responsible for each other, and held her tongue. The guilt was punishment enough for Ellie, judging from the somber look on her face.

Jamie was released from the school infirmary after only an hour. They couldn't find any evidence of anything suspicious—no toxins, no poisons, absolutely nothing—but Lottie couldn't shake the memory of that strange sweet smell that she'd noted on his breath. Something wasn't right.

They sent him to his room to rest and he insisted that he

was "fine," even though he could barely remember a thing. He gave Lottie a particularly stern look as he told them to "forget the whole thing ever happened."

Meanwhile Ellie and Lottie had been left alone with Professor Devine.

She eyed them coolly, before gesturing to the cushioned seats by her desk. "You may sit. I will keep this brief as I can see our young Miss Pumpkin is quite distressed."

Lottie was still wrapped in blankets, soaking up the warmth of the fireplace in the corner.

The professor's gaze fell upon Ellie, and Lottie had to bite her cheek to keep from crying again, as Professor Devine continued to speak.

"I can very well understand a desire to explore the many forbidden areas of the school"—even in Lottie's weary state her brain clung to the word "many," holding on to the information for later—"and, Lottie, it was quite tremendous indeed how you aided Jamie. It is not easy to think clearly in situations such as those, and we will remember your bravery. But," she said with a note of caution, "what disappoints me is that two such promising Ivy girls failed to bring out the best in each other tonight." She rubbed her forehead in thought for a moment and Lottie felt a wave of warmth from the flames beside her. "I shan't keep you here longer; I feel this is a lesson I cannot teach you in words.

It's best now that you go back to your room and consider what has happened." She gave them each a weighty look. "You're dismissed."

Lottie lay in her bed, staring vacantly at Mr. Truffles as she chewed her lip. She didn't even register Ellie's warm body climbing in next to her.

"I really am sorry about tonight," Ellie whispered, gently stroking Lottie's hair.

Lottie nodded, trying not to let any more tears escape.

"You really think someone did something to his drink?"

"It's the only explanation."

Ellie hesitated. "And you're sure you guys didn't just fall in the pool and he hit his head?"

There was skepticism in her voice, as if she were convinced Lottie wasn't telling her the whole story.

"No, Ellie, you didn't see him before we fell in the pool. He was . . . weird." Lottie buried her face in Mr. Truffles, feeling the blush creep onto her cheeks as she remembered just how odd he'd been. "He said . . ." She paused. All evidence was pointing to Anastacia, but Lottie still couldn't understand why she'd do it. "He said again that we can't trust Anastacia."

Ellie nodded somberly, then wrapped an arm around Lottie and nuzzled into her hair, making Lottie giggle as she felt her breath tickle her neck.

"At least I can trust you." She exhaled the words slowly into Lottie's ear. Lottie turned so they were face-to-face, tears streaming down her cheeks and her nose running. Ellie held her against her chest until she stopped crying.

"I'm sorry," Ellie repeated, though this time it was unclear what she was apologizing for.

They remained tangled together, sharing the warmth in their marshmallow cocoon, like two cubs in a den. Lottie's eyes and throat ached from crying, but gradually she began to relax in Ellie's arms, her friend's heartbeat pumping softly against her ear. Eventually Ellie climbed out of their den, switched off the lights, and went back to her own bed.

That night, as Ellie slept soundlessly in her bed, Lottie awoke in a cold sweat from a terrible nightmare of Anastacia drowning Jamie.

She tried to get back to sleep, but her mind was too drained and frantic to rest again. A shiver ran through her body that she couldn't get rid of. She sat up and checked her clock. It was an hour into the new year. The chill ran through her again and she shuddered; it was too cold to try to sleep again.

She eased the door open as quietly as possible, not wanting to wake Ellie, and turned the corner to the storage room where she could get more blankets. On her way back she passed the mailboxes and had to do a double take when she realized hers had something inside. It was a golden

envelope with a delicate black pattern around the edges, winding up from the corners like smoke. She opened it carefully and found herself struck by the scent of peppermint. She pulled the card out slowly. It was black, with gold writing. It read simply:

See you at the summer ball, Princess.

xx

Lottie clutched the card to her chest, then quickly tiptoed back to her room and hid it in her bedside table under the box Ellie had given her. Jamie and Ellie would be furious if they knew.

Edmund has finally sent me a message.

Her heart was beating uncontrollably. She was sure this one little secret would be okay. What's the worst that could happen?

PART THREE
Presenting the Princess

38

THE NEW TERM STARTED A week later, and with it came a soft sheet of snow over the school grounds. Everyone had switched to the thick, fluffy winter uniform, which made the whole school look as if it were filled with colorful sheep. The excitement of a fresh start buzzed through the corridors, but for Lottie, Jamie, and Ellie, it was time to get serious about the mysterious threat to their lives.

They sat in the main hall waiting for the opening speech to begin. It was far too cold to have the event on the field, but Lottie found that since the pool incident she felt a little claustrophobic in a crowd.

"I still think their plan must have gone wrong," Jamie said. "I think they intended to incapacitate both Lottie and me, but it's unclear why."

"I don't think they intended for anyone to get badly hurt." Lottie wasn't sure of this but whatever had been put in Jamie's drink had had no long-term side effects, and he'd pretty much recovered instantly. "Otherwise they would have used something worse." Lottie felt sick at that idea.

"Either way, we can't let Anastacia think we suspect

her. We need to keep her close," Ellie added, checking that no one else was listening.

Jamie chewed his lip in thought. "I just wish we had a sample of whatever it was so that I could get it analyzed."

"What exactly did it make you do other than pass out?" Ellie asked curiously.

Jamie and Lottie froze. They both turned to look at each other and a stern expression appeared on Jamie's face. He had claimed a million times that he didn't remember anything, and yet every time it came up he went rigid.

"I don't remember," he said again.

"Well, Lottie must remember," Ellie said helpfully. "Was he manic or mellow or confused? It could help us figure out what it was." Jamie gave her another sharp look and his words from that night pounded in her head.

"I can't stand seeing it taken away from you."

Lottie gulped at the memory. "He was straightforward," she said at last.

"Straightforward?" Ellie's eyes narrowed, but before she could say more a cheery voice came from behind them.

"Good morning!" Binah, Lola, and Micky took up the space next to Lottie, halting their conversation. Jamie let out a small breath as if he were actually relieved by their arrival.

"I heard about what happened over the holidays. Jamie,

I hope you're all okay," Binah said, real concern etched on her face.

"We're fine." Jamie's eyes remained on Lottie as he spoke.

"I can't believe you dived in and rescued him, Lottie," Lola said excitedly.

"You're like a superhero." The twins spoke in unison.

Lottie wasn't sure how this rumor had started, but she could see it was making Jamie's lip twitch.

They all turned as Ms. Kuma approached the podium, dressed in a fluffy yellow coat and matching hat that reminded Lottie of a daffodil. It seemed fitting with her bouncy and colorful attitude that she would be doing the opening speech for spring term.

"Good morning, everyone, and welcome back to a fresh term at Rosewood. I am pleased to see such enthusiasm among you even with this dreadfully cold weather." She shivered to accentuate her point. "I hope you have all had a pleasant break and are ready to take on this term with even more passion and determination. Many of you will have the added pressure of preparing for next term's exams. It can be tempting to lose momentum in the spring term with no immediate examinations looming, but I have the utmost faith that all of you will rise to these challenges and face them head-on." Then her cheerful smile turned rueful and

she cleared her throat before continuing. "On a less pleasant note, due to an incident over the holidays, the nine p.m.
curfew will be upheld to the strictest order. If any student
is not signed in to their dorm by this time, they will face
an appropriate punishment; we would rather you didn't
have to find out what that punishment is." She looked over
the students with pursed lips, making it clear that this was
not something to be taken lightly. Lottie could sense eyes
burning into the back of her head and she turned to see
Anastacia behind her with Saskia and Raphael. Anastacia
quickly looked away when Lottie caught her eye.

You can't trust Anastacia.

Lottie felt a shiver run up her spine. She couldn't get
Jamie's ominous message out of her head.

She leaned over to Ellie. "Anastacia is behind us. We
should make sure to say hi to her later so she doesn't think
we're avoiding her."

Ellie nodded, resisting the temptation to turn around.

"Now before we let you get on with your day we have
one final bit of news," Ms. Kuma continued. Lola and Micky
let out a little squeal, and Lottie wondered what could be
so exciting. "This year the Tompkins Confectionery Company will be sponsoring our Valentine's Day celebrations,
so you can thank them for the extra-special displays. If
any of you would like to get involved with the decorations,

please do come and find me in my office this week."

The twins turned to Lottie, Lola smiling giddily. Lottie attempted her best smile in return, but the truth was she really didn't like Valentine's Day and she certainly didn't want to have to explain why to anyone.

Another thing to worry about.

The speech ended and everyone made their way out of the main hall. Lottie could see Anastacia a little way in front of her and wondered if she should approach her. Ellie must have had a similar idea because as soon as they were outside, she ran past Lottie and grabbed Anastacia's arm to get her attention.

"Hey, Anastacia, we just—"

Anastacia turned abruptly, her bag falling off her shoulder, and the contents spilled over the floor. "*Mon dieu!*"

"Crap!" Ellie cursed.

Ellie and Lottie immediately kneeled down and began helping her pick up her stuff.

"Don't!" Anastacia cried, reaching to stop them.

"I'm really sorry, Anastacia—we just wanted to come and say hi. We didn't mean to—" Lottie's hand brushed over a photograph and she froze.

The photo was slightly fuzzy, but it was clearly Anastacia, grinning with a red bow in her hair. The Eiffel Tower was in the background and a huge ice-cream sundae was

on the table in front of her. Next to her stood a girl with a large mop of tight blond curls and caramel skin. It was Saskia. She was braiding Anastacia's hair and the two were grinning. Lottie had never seen Anastacia look so happy.

"Don't touch that!" Anastacia snapped, pulling the photo out of Lottie's hand. "You two do nothing but cause trouble." She grabbed her bag and pulled it close to her, marching off furiously to catch up with the other Conch students.

"Wow!" Jamie chimed in sarcastically. "That really could not have gone worse."

Lottie barely even took in the words. She couldn't stop thinking about the photo and Anastacia's reaction. *"You two do nothing but cause trouble."*

Anastacia was usually so composed. For her to react this way definitely wasn't a good sign. Lottie looked at Ellie, who gave her a shrug.

She couldn't help feeling like she was missing something important.

❧ 39 ❧

LOTTIE BURIED HERSELF IN HER studies over the next few weeks, all the while feeling like there was something she was not understanding, until finally the worst day of the . year came around: Valentine's Day. Or, as Lottie knew it, the anniversary of her mother's death.

Lottie awoke on the dreaded morning of February 14 and, as it was a Saturday, made her way to her early morning princess lesson with Jamie and Ellie. She was grateful, at least, that she was able to sleep again, and that getting more sleep was helping her to keep calm, which she desperately needed to do today of all days.

The whole school was thick with the oppressively strong smell of chocolate and red roses, while heart-patterned streamers forced their romantic agenda on everyone. Lottie was glad to have the lesson as a distraction. Jamie had picked the greenhouse in the rose garden by the main hall that morning, meaning they had a clear view of the Valentine's Day preparations. He had obviously picked it as a compromise for them missing out on the festivities, not realizing that Lottie wanted no part of it.

"Lottie?"

Jamie's voice jolted Lottie back to reality. "Sorry! Could you repeat the question?"

Both Jamie and Ellie scrutinized her for a moment, Jamie's eyebrow lifting in concern.

"I asked you what your favorite story from Oscar's diary was, and how you've found it useful." Jamie stood over her expectantly.

"Oh, that's easy," Lottie replied. "The story of Sun Dao and Shau Zu because— Have I said something wrong?" Lottie took in Jamie's face. His eyes had widened as if he'd heard something surprising.

"No, no. Not at all, it's just . . . That's my favorite too." Lottie was overcome by a sudden inner warmth—it was so rare that Jamie shared anything about himself, and she felt like she'd just won a prize. He cleared his throat, bringing her out of her thoughts. "Would you care to elaborate?"

Lottie nodded, happy to take her mind off Valentine's Day. She took a deep breath and prepared to plunge into the tale of Prince Shau Zu.

"It was 300 AD in China, a time when Portmans had become so accepted that you could assume most of the dynasty were not who you thought they were. Prince Shau Zu and his Portman Sun Dao were guests in the palace of Emperor Qin Shi Xiao, a powerful warlord and terrifying force. But their stay turned sour when it became clear

that the emperor had invited them to his home to capture the prince. But Sun Dao was too smart for the emperor. Knowing that it was a great dishonor to harm a Portman once you knew their role, he double-bluffed and persuaded Qin Shi Xiao that *he* was the prince. The emperor unwittingly kept the real prince, Shau Zu, as a 'special guest' within the palace, one who was not permitted to leave. Sun Dao, posing as the prince, endured eight whole days of deadly 'games'—from crossing a tightrope over boiling oil to dodging arrows in the garden—until finally the prince's army arrived to rescue them. Once they'd escaped from the evil Qin Shi Xiao, the prince asked Sun Dao, 'How do I reward such loyalty?' To which Sun replied, 'Allow me to do it all over again.'"

Lottie had been looking at the roses as she told her story, doing her best to recall the details. When she turned her gaze to Jamie and Ellie, she was taken aback to find them both staring intently at her. Pride filled Lottie as she took in their enthralled expressions. It reminded her of how she used to look at her mother when she read her fairy tales, and suddenly she felt a heavy ache in her chest.

Ellie blinked a few times before letting out a whistle. "I need to read this diary!" she exclaimed.

Jamie's lips curved slightly and he gave Lottie a sideways glance. "And why is this story useful?" he asked.

"Well . . ." Lottie looked down, feeling embarrassed

by her answer. "It shows that there's strength in loyalty. There's power in the duty of a Portman."

Ellie snickered at the response, earning her a harsh glare from Jamie. Lottie felt herself getting annoyed: she was just too sad to find any humor in anything today.

"Don't worry, Lottie, you're not going to have to walk over boiling oil!" Ellie cracked up as she said it, and Lottie felt her brows furrowing.

Jamie glared at her. "Ellie, that's—"

"You have no idea what we might end up having to do!" Lottie interrupted before Jamie could finish.

Ellie stopped laughing but the grin remained on her face. She didn't realize how distressed Lottie was getting.

"But that's *insane*! Don't get me wrong. I wish my life was that exciting but—"

"You *wish* your life was that exciting?"

Lottie couldn't believe Ellie had said something so ridiculous.

"Well, yeah! Being a princess for me has always meant I was just stuck inside all day and—"

"Ellie, you have no idea how exciting and amazing your life is. Most people will go their whole lives only dreaming of a world like the one you live in." Lottie could feel her hands clenching in frustration. She couldn't seem to stop herself getting upset.

"Well, *most people* don't know how horrible it is. Lottie,

what's wrong? You know how terrible my family can be—"

"At least you HAVE a family!" Lottie immediately covered her mouth as the words escaped but she couldn't stop the tears spilling from her eyes.

Now you've done it, she thought. *Now you're not going to be able to stop crying all day.*

"Lottie . . ." Ellie's voice came out strained.

Lottie knew she'd overreacted, but it was too difficult for her to get her thoughts straight. She rubbed at her eyes and stood up. She didn't want to cause any more damage.

"I'll see you both later." Her words came out in a little sob that she hated herself for, and she ran to the garden's exit. She didn't look at Jamie as she ran past; she couldn't stand to see what he was thinking.

"Lottie, wait!" Ellie called after her, but she kept running.

She ran until her lungs were aching and she thought she might be sick. She ran until she finally reached Ivy Wood, but she didn't stop there. Her feet wouldn't let her.

And she ran straight into the Rose Wood.

❦ 40 ❦

LOTTIE'S EYES AND CHEEKS STUNG with the salt from her tears, and her nose was bright red from the biting cold. She stopped to catch her breath and found that she couldn't see the school buildings at all—she'd run deep into Rose Wood. She was covered in a sheen of sweat, but she realized too late that she'd left her coat back in the rose garden.

She walked on a little farther until she found the biggest tree she'd ever seen. It was an ancient oak with a trunk large enough to build a home inside, its branches extending out in a huge circle. Lottie dropped down under the tree, letting her body absorb the cold to try to stave off some of the bad feelings. She felt embarrassed for being so melodramatic. She always got upset on this date, but usually she was alone in her room in Cornwall, able to deal with her sadness privately. Being at Rosewood somehow made her mother's passing seem even closer and more vivid than usual.

"Lottie." She could hear her mother's gentle voice in her mind. The image of her in the hospital bed, skinny and weak but still smiling, pierced her thoughts. *"I'll be proud*

of you whatever you do in life, as long as you promise me—"

"I will be kind, I will be brave, I will be unstoppable."

Her mother had laughed, the sound coming out in a pained wheeze. "Yes, Lottie, I know you will be. But promise me you will also be happy. I want you to say it."

Lottie had stared at her mother, knowing they didn't have much time left together. "I promise I will get into Rosewood Hall and then I'll be happy."

She couldn't do it. Lottie couldn't promise her mother she'd be happy because she wasn't sure she could be without her. But Lottie had been sure that getting into Rosewood would fix that. If she got into Rosewood, she would be happy and fulfill her promise to her mother. So why wasn't she happy?

Another shiver ran through her body and she hugged her knees close. She didn't know how she'd find her way out of the woods or what she'd say when she saw Jamie and Ellie. She didn't want to think about anything; she just wanted to curl up under the tree and be alone.

"Lottie!"

Her head jerked up at her name, not sure how much time had passed. Her whole body was shivering and she could feel the chill in her bones.

The voice called louder. "LOTTIE!"

She slowly got up, damp earth sticking to her clothes.

Someone was approaching on the other side of the tree,

and she looked around the trunk to see Jamie standing there—with her coat and a blanket.

She rubbed her eyes, feeling the embarrassment creep back over her. *How did he find me?*

"I can follow tracks."

Lottie blinked at him, her eyes sore and misty.

"Come on," he said, holding his hand out. She took it and he tenderly wrapped the coat and blanket around her. His arms lingered on her shoulders and she was surprised by how comforting it felt to be close to him after their awkwardness earlier.

"We're sorry. We should have remembered what today is for you. That was a significant oversight on my . . . I'm sorry."

Lottie sniffed. "I'm fine."

A soft rumble of laughter escaped Jamie's throat. "You always say that."

There was a hint of regret in his voice that forced Lottie to look into his eyes. The tree cast a huge blue shadow over them, as if they were in their own hazy world. His expression had a sweet ache to it, and she knew she was witnessing something rare.

"I really miss her. But I don't want her to worry about me," Lottie said. Somehow it didn't feel strange to be sharing this with Jamie.

Jamie nodded, his face solemn, and Lottie truly believed

that he did understand. But there was something about his empathy that struck her. Did he have a sad secret from his past too? What happened? And there was that question again: *How did you become a Partizan?*

"Come on! It's time to go back now—Ellie's got something for you."

Lottie let him lead her through the woods. He was so sure of where they were going, not troubled at all by the density of the trees.

She ran inside as soon as they reached Ivy Wood, eager to change out of her dirty clothes and wash her face. Clean at last, she paused by her bedside table and pulled out her tiara from the box Ellie had given her. She put it on her head and took a deep breath. *Be brave.*

"Do you want to go to the hall?" Jamie asked when she came back downstairs.

Lottie considered it for a moment: the other students in their pretty Valentine's Day outfits, everyone smiling and laughing. The promise she'd made to her mother echoed in her head, and a melancholy smile crept onto her lips. "I want to see Ellie."

Lottie followed Jamie to the main dining hall, where the Valentine's preparations were truly under way. Big bouquets of red and pink roses lined the tables against the walls, with strings of heart-shaped bunting strung across the ceiling. In the center of the hall, where there were

usually large tables, was an enormous white chocolate fountain surrounded by an array of fruits and sweets, all emblazoned with TOMPKINS CONFECTIONERY.

As if on cue, Lola's voice squeaked from behind her. The twins stood beside each other, dressed smartly for the occasion in matching white and red. They both held wicker baskets filled with heart-shaped cupcakes.

"We've been looking for you!" Micky held out a pink cupcake topped with a candy heart that said PRINCESS LOTTIE.

"Everyone gets a cupcake. Except *Jamie*." Lola said his name like it was poison. "He's banned from having cupcakes because he said he doesn't like sweet food."

"Which is sacrilege," the twins said in unison.

Lottie blinked at them, taking in their serious expressions, then laughed. She'd been so sure that all she wanted to do that day was hide away from everyone, but here with the sugary-sweet twins she found it impossible to feel sad.

"Well, that's fine anyway," Jamie said sarcastically, appearing at Lottie's side, "because cupcakes are disgusting."

Lola gasped as if she'd just received a blow and Lottie snorted.

"Blasphemy!" Micky replied. They both shielded their cupcakes as if protecting them from Jamie's harsh words.

"Thank you so much for mine," Lottie said cheerily. "It looks as sweet as you two."

Lola regained her composure and grinned at Lottie.

"You are most welcome."

The two then skipped off happily to hand out the rest. Lottie turned back to Jamie, but a sight in the doorway made her heart skip a beat.

Ellie.

She spotted Lottie and came racing over, nearly knocking over a Stratus girl, who was carrying a plate of sugar cookies.

"Ellie, I'm sorry about earlier . . ." Lottie blushed as she said the words.

Ellie shook her head. "No, Lottie, you have nothing to apologize for. *I'm* sorry." She gave Lottie a tender look. "I was so stupid. I know this is an important day for you . . ." Her voice trailed off and she ran a hand through her hair bashfully. "I know this won't fix anything, but I got these for you." From behind her back, she revealed a small bouquet of marguerite flowers, the flower Lottie's mother was named for. Lottie felt a wave of emotion hit her as she looked at them, and couldn't stop a tear from escaping.

"That's . . ." She had to pause to take a breath. "Thank you so much, Ellie, I love them."

Jamie coughed, reminding them he was there. "I'll catch up with you two later," he said, and left them on their own.

Ellie and Lottie sat on the veranda outside, overlooking the rose garden, with their cupcakes. Lottie still felt raw. She

realized she'd never opened up to anyone like that before, but Ellie and Jamie hadn't been mad at her or told her she needed to calm down. They'd both been so comforting. Thinking about it sent a warm feeling through her body.

"It's a blessing that Jamie doesn't like sweets really," Ellie mumbled, her mouth filled with frosting. "Because it means I always get to eat his dessert."

Lottie giggled as she watched Ellie shove half the cupcake in her mouth at once, leaving a trail of frosting around her nose and lips.

"Let me get that for you!" Lottie leaned forward and gently wiped a bit of frosting off Ellie's cheek then licked it from her finger. Ellie grinned at her, shoving the rest into her mouth before starting on the next one. Lottie was about to take a bite of hers when she noticed something odd in the icing. There was a small dent in the decoration where a piece of paper had been poked into the frosting. That feeling of dread that she'd become so familiar with lurched in her stomach. She pulled the paper out, making sure Ellie didn't notice, and carefully unfolded it, wondering if it was from a secret admirer. It was not.

Roses are red.
Violets are blue.
Watch your back, Princess.
I'm coming for you.

She quickly shoved the paper into her skirt pocket, trying to hide away from the words. She felt dizzy.

"Are you okay, Lottie?"

Ellie's voice startled her back to reality. Her friend's eyes were wide with worry, her concerned smile providing a small amount of comfort.

"It's nothing, I . . ." The message blinked in Lottie's mind and the writing blurred. She couldn't do it. She couldn't tell Ellie. She couldn't deal with another threat, not today. "I'm just a bit emotionally run-down, but this cupcake will help." She beamed her best reassuring smile.

She couldn't tell Ellie. If Jamie found out, and her family thought they were in danger, they might take Ellie away.

"Are you sure?" Ellie asked again, still looking concerned.

Lottie stared at her, face covered in frosting, strands of black hair falling around her features. She couldn't lose her.

"Just peachy," she lied.

EASTER BREAK WAS NOT MUCH of a break at all. Lottie once again threw herself into studying for her end-of-year exams as an escape from thinking about the threatening message she'd received in the cupcake. There were no more scary messages, and she was almost able to persuade herself there was no problem at all. As term wore on, everyone fell back into the routine of cram sessions and study groups. Rosewood Hall was not a place for students who weren't ready and willing to work hard.

Soon the trees around Rosewood were filled with colorful buds and the flowers and trellises bloomed, a flamboyant indicator of the approaching summer exams. Yet, a lavender-scented calm enveloped the school, accompanied by a twitchy anticipation that *something big* might happen. For most students this was the end-of-year exam results, but Lottie had another looming event: the summer ball.

Study leave began on the first day of May and Lottie's last exam was math on the twentieth. They would get

their grades on the final day of the month. Once Ellie and Lottie had their results, they would fly back to Maradova and begin preparing for the ball—so long as they did well on their exams.

Lottie shot out of bed on results day, pulling herself out of a nightmare in which her grades had been so bad that she was not only banned from being a Portman, but also she had to become a court jester and perform circus tricks for the Maravish royal family. She clutched her hand to her chest, panting heavily, and looked up to witness the most shocking thing she'd seen all year. Ellie was awake before her.

"I'm nervous about the exam results," Ellie said frankly as they left the Ivy dorm, chewing the cuticle on her thumb.

"Hypothetically, Ellie, if we had failed them . . . Couldn't you just, I don't know, pay someone to change your grades?"

"Ha!" Ellie cackled. "I wish. A wolf never cheats, Lottie."

They met Jamie by the gate and Lottie noticed that his eyes were more sunken than usual, like he hadn't slept well either.

Could he be nervous too? She couldn't imagine Jamie getting nervous about anything, but she felt too awkward to ask him about it. Ever since he had come to find her in the Rose Wood, she couldn't seem to look him in the eye, and she was sure he was avoiding her too.

They stood in the line with all the other anxious students who'd woken up extra early to check their grades.

This was the make-or-break moment. If she'd failed, she'd not only have her scholarship revoked, but she'd no longer be allowed to continue her role as Portman.

Ellie was fidgeting, rubbing her fingers together as she chewed her lip, all the while gazing into the distance. This was equally terrifying for her. If she didn't get adequate grades, her parents would consider the Rosewood Hall experiment a failure and pull her from the school.

Lottie took a deep breath and held it. They were in the grand oak-walled reception hall. She'd walked through it on her first day of school and had thought it so magnificent, but this time it felt overbearing and intimidating.

They took one final step forward in the line. Sitting in front of them was one of the Stratus heads of year, Angus Berkeley, the merlin symbol of his house visible on his yellow sash.

"Name— Oh! Lottie, we have your file here."

Princess perks!

Angus reached to the side and pulled up a green hardcover file with the three-rose symbol of the school on the front. "Also your phone can be returned now," he said as he handed everything to her.

"Thank you," Lottie said, taking the file with shaking hands.

*

They stood together in the courtyard by the entrance next to the large archway. Binah had come to join them and her enthusiastic energy only made Lottie more nervous.

"I'm so excited!" Binah trilled, opening her file with no hesitation. Her expression turned into one of disappointment, though, as she glanced at the grade summary on the first page. "Oh."

Lottie's heart sank. If Binah had done badly, then how terribly had Lottie and Ellie done? But her worries quickly turned to groans when Binah added, "Top marks in everything. How very boring."

Ellie had to stop herself from snorting. "You ready?" she asked Lottie, putting her fingers on the cover, ready to open it.

Lottie puffed up her chest and nodded resolutely. "Yep."

They opened their files together, and Lottie saw Jamie twitch out of the corner of her eye. She shuddered at the thought of what his reaction would be if she'd failed. She felt sick. She felt like she was going to pass out. She finally looked down at the page before her.

She'd done it.

She'd passed everything.

She was in the top five in her class for English! Her heart skipped a beat as she took in her most difficult subjects. Math, chemistry, and physics were all in the top

fifteen grades. She felt tears sting her eyes as she looked up at Jamie and nodded, then turned to Ellie, who was still staring at her grade summary, her face blank.

"Ellie?" she asked apprehensively.

Ellie shook her head. "I can't believe this," she said slowly. "I'm ranked seventeenth in the whole class. I made the top twenty."

Lottie felt a huge wave of relief. She'd seen Ellie's exam results from previous years. "Lacking effort" would have been an understatement.

"Of course you did!" Binah tutted, rolling her eyes. "If any of you weren't in the top twenty percent I would be furious." She smiled at them. "You're some of the smartest, most hardworking people I know."

Ellie was still stunned at her grades. She looked at Jamie, who was struggling to suppress a smile.

"See what you can achieve when you actually apply yourself?" he said sternly, but then his expression softened and he nodded to both of them. "I'm proud of you."

Lottie grabbed a chunk of the huge celebratory cookie that was on the main table in the Ivy common room, with CONGRATULATIONS in big purple frosting letters. She sidestepped out of the way as two older Ivy girls came dancing into the room, singing and shouting with excitement at passing their exams.

"But I wanted top marks in everything—a B is not good enough!" Another Ivy girl was crying on the phone to her parents about her one "bad" grade. Lottie gave her a comforting smile.

Ellie and Lottie sat back in the purple chairs of the common room, watching and laughing at everyone celebrating. They were having their luggage flown back to Maradova the next day and would have a short stop in Paris to collect their dresses for the ball, so they were happy to spend the evening enjoying themselves before their next adventure.

While everyone packed and said their teary goodbyes, Lottie had one more thing she needed to fix before going to Maradova for the summer.

She excused herself, went to her room, and turned on her phone for the first time since she had arrived at the school. It felt weird to have it in her hand again; she'd gotten so used to being disconnected from everything outside the Rosewood walls that it almost felt overwhelming to see it come to life in her hand.

Messages from Ollie appeared on the screen. The first was from the first day of school.

I know you can't use your phone until the end of the year, but I wanted you to get this message when you finish your exams. I know I tease you a lot, but Mom and I are really proud of you and I'm sure you've done amazingly.

The second was from three weeks ago.

I don't know what's going on with you but I hope you're okay . . .

Lottie shook her head and opened up Ollie's number. It rang six times before he answered.

"She lives!" came the sarcastic voice on the other end.

"Ollie!" She almost choked on his name as she uttered it. So much had happened since she had last seen him, and here he was, innocent Ollie, her best friend from a simpler time in her life, and she was going to have to let him down again.

"I assume you're calling to ask us to meet you at the station tomorrow? Which we'd obviously be happy to do."

Lottie's heart sank. She hated having to keep things from him.

"Actually, Ollie, I need to tell you something."

The other end of the phone went silent and she could feel the disappointment and anger radiating through the speaker.

"Okay," he said at last.

Lottie took a deep breath. "I can't come home for the summer, or at all . . . I've written to Beady about it. I don't know when or if I can come back . . ." Her voice trailed off and she was met with silence again.

"Lottie, what aren't you telling me?"

Lottie almost gasped at how serious he sounded. It was so unlike him. He made everything into a joke.

"Are you in trouble?"

"No, Ollie, I'm fine. I can't tell you right now, but I promise I'm fine and I promise I'll come and see you as soon as I can."

She heard a groan on the end of the phone. "Fine!" He sounded hurt. "If you're not going to explain to me what's going on, then . . ." His voice petered off and she heard him make an annoyed noise. "Whatever. Just have a good life."

The phone went silent in Lottie's hand and she looked down, tears trickling onto the screen. She'd done it. She just had to hope it was the right thing to do.

42

LOTTIE HAD GROWN UP HEARING the name Madame Marie's, dreaming that one day she might be lucky enough to see the white-pillared shopfront where the world's most glamorous gowns were sold. And now Lottie found herself not just marveling at the outside, but actually *inside* the shop, trying on dresses as if she herself were someone special. It was a sunny Tuesday morning and the girls had been shuttled to Paris to collect their dresses for the ball. From the window in the consulting room, Lottie could see the Eiffel Tower glittering away—floating specks of dust caught in the sunlight, making it look like a statue within a snow globe.

"Welcome, Princess," six sweet assistants trilled as they walked through the door, curtsying in their puffy powder-blue uniforms and white aprons. It was like stepping into a cloud kingdom; the white marble floor melted into the white walls, giving the impression that they were floating. They'd been shown to the bright consultation room by the notorious grandson of Madame Loulou Marie, Léon Marie. He had a pouf of white hair and a flamboyant grace that

reminded Lottie of a peacock. He proceeded to bring out a bespoke selection of dresses, carefully chosen for the two of them. As planned, the staff of Madame Marie's believed that Ellie was Lottie's "guest of honor" at the ball and required a dress of equal elegance.

"Princess Wolfson," he'd declared with an elaborate bow, "it has been my most aching desire to one day be privileged to dress you. I've heard such"—he lingered to raise his eyes at her theatrically—"mysterious stories about you." He blinked and stood straight as if fully registering Lottie for the first time. "Hmm," he mused, a hand on his chin. He bent down low, his face coming awkwardly close to her own, and his icy-blue eyes in darkly lined sockets staring into hers.

"Yes?" Lottie asked tentatively.

Léon's eyes shifted over to Ellie, then back to Lottie. "You're not quite what I was expecting, Your Highness."

Lottie gulped nervously. What exactly were people expecting? She hoped it wasn't someone less ordinary.

"I never like to be predictable," she said with as much indifference as she could muster. This seemed to do the job, and a glint appeared in his eyes.

"Day and night!" he called out abruptly, making both girls jump in surprise. "Day and night . . . night and day. You two scream opposition and unity, day and night. It's perfect."

Lottie sat perplexed as Léon continued to bring out dress after dress. He glided around them with so much drama she felt as if she were watching an Olympic figure-skating performance.

"Is this a stupid Cole Porter production?" Ellie hissed. She was less than thrilled about the whole excursion, finding little joy in luxury dress shopping. She'd been a bit off all day, worried about going back home, so Lottie was trying her best to be as happy and positive as possible. The only thing that seemed to be softening Ellie's mood was seeing how much joy Lottie was getting out of it.

"Yes, and I love it!" Lottie squealed, beaming back at her, eyes sparkling.

Ellie rolled her eyes, but her smile gave her away. "Let's just be quick, okay? We only have about forty-five minutes before Jamie comes bursting through the door all paranoid that we're in danger."

Ellie spoke with a hint of exasperation, and Lottie had to admit there was a truth behind her words. Jamie had become both distant and almost oppressively protective since school had ended, and Lottie couldn't blame him. Which made her feel even guiltier for not telling either of them about the Valentine's Day message. She figured that because nothing had happened since, and as long as she was there to take Ellie's place, then it would be okay. All things considered, being allowed a little frivolity after all

she'd been through lately seemed fair.

Once Léon was completely satisfied with the dresses he'd chosen for them, he clapped his hands twice and two blue-clad girls appeared on either side of him, holding gem-covered boxes.

"There's one final item to add to the equation," he said. He picked up the box to his left and tossed the lid over his shoulder dramatically, revealing a pair of exquisite black heeled shoes with delicate twinkling embroidery along the sides. "These will be for our little goddess of night." He thrust the box into the hands of the girl who stood in front of Ellie and grabbed the other box. "And these," he said, eyes widening like a mad scientist revealing his mysterious experiment, "these are for our ray of sunshine."

He lifted the lid slowly and Lottie gasped when she saw the treasure contained within. Lottie did not consider herself much of a shoe person, but inside the box were the most beautiful pumps she'd ever seen, white with veins of rosy gold that twisted and twirled amid hundreds of individual tiny glimmering crystals. The shoes quite literally glowed; the light seemed to emanate from the material itself. Lottie's mind instantly recognized this same sensation from the first time she saw her family's tiara, as if the two items were fashioned from the same magical substance.

"They're for me?" Lottie couldn't hide the wonderment in her voice, and yet even as she asked the question she felt as

if the shoes were calling to her, like they were meant for her.

A broad smile appeared across Léon's face. "They are *only* for you," he replied. "Custom-made to your measurements. They won't fit anyone else."

Lottie took the box ceremoniously. She felt the moment—and the shoes—deserved a sense of ritual. She was sure she could hear the box twinkling as it moved.

"Thank you so much! I love them!" She beamed at him and he returned the look with a soft nod, before clapping his hands again, turning off the spell.

"Right, my little birds, see to it that these delightful young ladies are taken care of." And with that he turned dramatically to exit the room. The two "little birds" immediately began undressing Lottie and Ellie with speedy efficiency. It lasted about ten seconds before Ellie nearly elbowed one of them in the face and promptly booted them from the room.

"We are perfectly capable of dressing ourselves!" Ellie shouted before slamming the door.

When she turned back she faced a frowning Lottie, arms firmly crossed over her chest disapprovingly. Something was definitely bothering Ellie, but Lottie had no way of figuring out what it was unless she opened up.

"Don't give me that look," Ellie said, mirroring Lottie's stance. "I'll play along with the dress-up game, but I'm not gonna be someone's doll."

Lottie rolled her eyes and began flicking through the dresses on the "day" hanger. They all had gorgeous heroic-sounding names like "Celestial" and "Solar." One stood out from the others, glowing in a similar way to her shoes. It had a small blue tag with the name "Summer Calm." She gently pulled it out from the rack and watched in awe as the fabric swished gently like liquid silk.

"Ellie, look at this dress—it's perfect!" She turned excitedly to Ellie but froze as she caught a glimpse of her friend's face. She was staring straight into the air between them, fingers lightly tracing the tip of her locket. There was no hint of sarcasm; her bravado had cracked and behind it was a very lost girl.

"Ellie . . . what's wrong?"

There was no point in asking if she was okay; Ellie would just lie. Lottie needed to be blunt or she'd risk losing her.

Upon hearing Lottie's voice, Ellie returned to herself. She hesitated for a moment and Lottie was sure she'd shrug it off.

"It's just . . ." she began slowly, clearly uncomfortable, "Jamie and I had an argument before we left the hotel." She relaxed her shoulders as she spoke, as though she were releasing the plug on her emotional bathtub. "He wanted to escort us—he's so convinced something bad is going to happen—and I ended up losing my temper and saying something really stupid, and it came out all wrong. I'm just

so sick of it, of him having to always . . ." It was rare for Ellie to trip over her words, an indicator of how upset she was. "I said if he found me so difficult, why didn't he just leave?" She turned away abruptly. Lottie tried to respond with some comforting words until Ellie added dismissively, "Whatever. You wouldn't understand."

Lottie's heart sank. Not because she was offended, but because Ellie was right. For all the good it did having Ellie confide in her, Lottie couldn't really help because she didn't understand Ellie and Jamie's relationship. If she was going to be of use to her or Jamie, she needed to be part of the inner circle; she needed to know what they knew.

"Ellie," she said firmly, "you have to tell me how Jamie became your Partizan."

43

ELLIE CRINGED AT THE QUESTION, pushing her hair back as she turned to inspect the dresses laid out for her. She coughed, clearly trying to regain her composure.

"I don't know if we should get into this," she said, flicking through the dresses.

Lottie ignored her attempts to avoid the topic. "It's just, well, you two get so—and he's so young!" She was tripping over her words, but she didn't know how to phrase it. Ellie and Jamie got so moody and serious around each other, and they were so close in age. She knew Partizans were trained from birth, but she didn't know where Jamie had come from. It just didn't make sense in her head.

"Most Partizans are young," Ellie said calmly, but Lottie detected a hint of regret in her tone. "They need to be unassuming and blend in, so it's preferable that they're the same age or similar to their master." Lottie thought she might end the conversation there, but she stopped flicking through the dresses and continued. "They usually finish their base training at about twelve and will be picked based on suitability; they get to know their family and master

over their last few years, and then they become fully registered. It's a very rigorous procedure. It's a bit mad really."

Lottie took a deep breath, preparing to ask the obvious question, but Ellie's face became distant and sad, and she couldn't locate her voice.

"Jamie . . ." Ellie's voice trailed off and she shook her head and turned to Lottie, a determined look on her face. "Jamie is different because he's been with us since he was born."

Lottie had guessed as much from the pictures she'd seen of them as children in the palace.

"I've seen photos of her, his mom," Ellie said. "She was a Pakistani immigrant living in the city." Ellie rubbed her eyes with one hand in thought before continuing. "I don't actually know how, and I don't know why, but she got into the palace. She was heavily pregnant and sick and apparently she begged my parents to take her child and, well . . . they did."

Although Ellie was not the most elegant storyteller, Lottie found herself enthralled: the fancy setting around them melting into images of a desperate woman determined to save her unborn child.

"What happened to her?" Lottie asked without thinking, but the answer was obvious. She braced herself for the terrible response.

"She died after giving birth," Ellie replied bluntly.

"And his dad?"

"No one knows and no one cares; he's probably dead too." There was a hint of irritation in her tone and Lottie couldn't place what it was aimed at.

So that was it, she thought. *Their response to an orphan baby was to turn him into a personal assassin?*

Something didn't fit right with that story.

"So . . . you made him a Partizan?"

Ellie turned to her, looking furious at the world, a storm raging inside her that was ready to strike anything that moved. "*I* didn't make him ANYTHING. My parents did!"

The silence that followed was stifling, filling the air with a static energy. Lottie looked away, ashamed for asking something so stupid.

Slowly Ellie released a long breath and turned to the dresses once again.

"I hate them," she said bitterly, a coldness in her voice that Lottie had never heard before. "No one should have their life decided for them when they're born. Everyone should get to choose." Her fists balled at her sides as she spoke. This was not just venting anger; this was an agenda. Lottie watched her and realized she was witnessing a private side of Ellie. This was a secret that she trusted Lottie with, and yet Lottie was still hiding something big from her. She wasn't helping anyone by keeping secrets.

"Ellie . . ." she said, thinking about the Valentine's poem.

"I've been keeping something from you. I don't think it's fair to hide things from you. We need to trust each other." Ellie looked up, her cold expression replaced with inquisitiveness. "On Valentine's Day, in my cupcake of all things, there was another message."

"What?" Ellie asked in alarm, her anger replaced with concern. "What did it say?"

Reluctantly, Lottie recited the cruel rhyme to Ellie, shuddering at those final lines: "*Watch your back, Princess. I'm coming for you.*"

"Why didn't you tell us?" Ellie's voice rose slightly as she spoke and Lottie flinched.

"Because," Lottie whispered, "I don't want your family to take you away."

The tension seemed to melt from Ellie, and a sad smile appeared on her face.

"Lottie, I won't ever let anyone separate us. But I don't like the idea that you're in danger. I can't be responsible for that. I—"

"I'm not scared, Ellie, and you shouldn't be either," Lottie lied. "I would have told you guys if I was worried, but I'm not, and that's why I don't want anyone to make a big deal out of it." She forced out a determined smile, scaring herself with how good she'd become at lying. "I'm fine, so we don't need to tell anyone."

Ellie hesitated. "You promise you're okay?" she asked, a

pained look on her face.

"I promise." Lottie felt the dread in her stomach flex as she said this, but she kept smiling.

The sound of singing cut off their moment, music chiming from Lottie's phone in her bag. She rushed to pull it out, wondering in the back of her mind if it might be Ollie. But, as if he knew he was being talked about, Jamie's name flashed up on Lottie's phone with a message reading:

You have ten minutes.

"Come on," she said, grabbing both pairs of shoes from the table. "Let's try on these clothes before we get *rescued*."

Lottie happily pulled on her dress, then watched in confusion as Ellie kneeled down on the floor in front of her, reaching out to put Lottie's slipper on her foot.

"What are you doing?" Lottie asked, pulling her leg away instinctively.

"I'm being your Prince Charming!" she said, winking as she grabbed her ankle. Lottie felt her cheeks go hot as Ellie slid the shoes on before hurriedly pulling on the first dress she'd picked from the hanger. The two girls stood in front of the mirror side by side: storm and calm, night and day.

A feeling of rightness slowly began to return as Lottie took in the sight of them together. She had to admit they both looked silly—neither one done up properly to be in

clothes of this sort—but somehow, standing next to Ellie, it didn't matter.

Ellie picked at a nonexistent mark on the hip of her dress. "I suppose this outfit will do, though I'd rather be wearing a suit. Are you happy with yours?"

Lottie turned to look at Ellie directly. "Very happy," she said, grinning. "In fact, I'd quite like to never take it off."

Ellie smiled back and wrapped an arm around her shoulders, their bodies and clothes merging in a pattern of black and white. They held on to each other until Lottie said what they'd both been thinking.

"I shouldn't have kept the poem from you and Jamie."

Ellie was silent for a moment and Lottie could feel her hands fidgeting.

"I know," she whispered, her gaze falling on Lottie's reflection in the mirror without meeting her eyes. "There're a lot of things I shouldn't have done too."

44

THEY ARRIVED AT THE PALACE in the afternoon, the day before the ball. There was something painfully familiar about Lottie's flight to Maradova. Although the circumstances were different, she was once again avoiding Jamie and sitting next to Ellie on the other side of the plane. She just couldn't look at him in the same way since learning about his past. A terrible guilt filled her—she hated keeping secrets from him when she now knew so much about him. Her life now appeared to have become built around secrets and lies: the lie that she was a princess, the secret of Edmund's message, the lies to Ollie, and now this new lie that the poem meant nothing.

The air was even colder than on her first visit, and the sky looked as if it were threatening to snow. She suddenly understood Ellie's mockery of the term "summer ball."

She expected to be met at the palace by girls who looked like they were in costumes, and to be deposited in an untouched and extravagant room all alone.

It was nothing like last time.

Lottie was greeted at the door by the queen, whose

billowing embroidered gown danced around her as she came rushing down the corridor so fast she nearly knocked them over. Lottie was amazed that she managed not to yelp in surprise when Queen Matilde pulled her into a tight embrace; instead, she found that the scent of lavender that surrounded the queen soothed her, and she relaxed into her arms as if being greeted by her own mother.

"Our little pumpkin princess, we're delighted to have you back!" She held Lottie by her shoulders, taking in the full length of her.

"Thank you for having me," said Lottie.

It was the only reply she could think of that would be appropriate, but she felt silly saying it. The queen smiled at her. They really could have been mother and daughter, her cascading golden locks and blue eyes matching Lottie's appearance far more than they did Ellie's. Anyone who didn't know better would easily mistake her for the real princess.

"I hope our Eleanor has been behaving herself."

Ellie rolled her eyes and pulled Lottie out of her mother's grasp. "Mom, would you please stop harassing my Portman?" she teased, dragging Lottie down the corridor as she stuck her tongue out petulantly.

Jamie took a step to follow them but was stopped by the queen. Lottie lost sight of him as Ellie took her on a long, winding journey through the sea of portraits of previous

rulers to her room, a brisk reminder of how otherworldly the palace was.

Although Lottie had been in Ellie's room before, last time she'd been too overwhelmed to take it in. The lavish four-poster bed that seemed far too large for one teenage girl was on the left-hand side of the room as they entered. Ellie paid no mind to the Persian rug on the floor, happily traipsing over it in her shoes. There was an obvious disconnect between Ellie and the room—though it was decorated in dark colors to match her moody appearance, the room didn't have any of her personality.

"Why did you choose such different decorations for your dorm room?" Lottie asked, skirting around the fact that the room was so bare.

Ellie snickered, understanding the unspoken message. "This is just where I sleep; I'll show you my *real* room some other time."

Ellie made her way over to two mahogany doors opposite the bed and flung them open to reveal the most extensive walk-in closet Lottie had ever seen. "You'll probably appreciate this more than I ever did. Help yourself to anything in there."

Lottie almost choked. The closet was filled with gorgeous dresses and accessories, all neatly stored and displayed, glittering jewels and expensive fabrics lining every shelf. In the center, on two crystal mannequins, lit from

underneath, were their dresses and shoes from Madame Marie's. Lottie was about to reach out to them when her phone vibrated in her cardigan pocket. She frantically grabbed it, hoping it might be Ollie.

It was not. A number she didn't recognize appeared, and she turned around to see if Ellie was watching her before she opened it.

I look forward to getting to know you properly tomorrow evening.
Xx

Lottie instantly blushed.

How did Edmund get my number?

She involuntarily held her phone against her chest and covered her mouth. She felt silly for feeling so smitten over a message, but she couldn't contain herself.

"What are you looking so swoony about?"

Lottie almost jumped out of her skin at Ellie's voice behind her.

"N-nothing!" She rushed to put her phone away, realizing too late that it made her look even more suspicious.

Ellie cocked an eyebrow playfully. "Who are you messaging that's got you so flustered?"

"No one. It's nothing. I love these rings by the way!" She could have punched herself for how painfully bad her

attempt at changing the topic was.

Ellie squinted at her suspiciously and Lottie tried to pretend she didn't notice as she turned around to the closet. "I need to pick some accessories for the— HEY!"

Ellie grabbed her arm, twisting her back around and pinning her to the closet doors, making them clatter.

"Ellie, what are you doing?" she spluttered.

Ellie loomed over her menacingly, her mouth in its little side smile and looking far more dangerous than usual.

"You are going to tell me your secret or I'll bite you," Ellie growled teasingly.

Lottie felt her face going hot. "*Ellie!*" she exclaimed, laughing nervously.

Ellie responded by pulling her arm and giving it a little toothless nibble that tickled so much Lottie nearly kicked her.

"I can't!" Lottie blurted out through fits of laughter. "You'll be mad at me."

Ellie instantly stopped and Lottie was able to compose herself again. Ellie's face turned sweet and she slowly let go of her arm. "Lottie, I thought we weren't doing secrets anymore."

Lottie looked away, hoping it might remedy some of the guilt. "You promise not to be mad at me?"

Ellie let out a long sigh. "If I promise, will you tell me?"

Lottie began biting her cheek in worry; she was so sick

of keeping secrets and lying. It had to stop. It wasn't right. It was simply too unprincessy.

She looked into Ellie's eyes, her Ivy House roommate. For some reason, their house motto sprung to mind: *Righteous!* An idea occurred to her suddenly. It was so simple.

"I'll only tell you if you'll let me tell Ollie about Portmans."

Ellie hesitated, her face falling. She chewed her lip as she weighed the pros and cons.

"Okay," she said at last. "But . . . we have to tell Jamie about the poem."

Lottie felt her heart skip a beat, but nodded slowly. Even though she was terrified of Ellie leaving Rosewood, she knew it was the right thing to do. Satisfied, Lottie squeezed her eyes shut, unable to look Ellie in the face as she confessed.

"Edmund Ashwick left a letter for me at Rosewood saying he'd see me at the ball and I really want to dance with him again tomorrow." Lottie blurted the words out as fast as possible, afraid she might chicken out if she spoke at a normal pace. She opened her eyes, expecting to see Ellie looking enraged but instead she just seemed shocked.

"And this has been going on how long?" she asked, her face still blank with shock.

"Since New Year's," Lottie replied guiltily.

"And you managed to keep it from me *and* Jamie this whole time?"

"Umm . . . yes?"

Ellie's face unexpectedly lit up again. "Well, I'm impressed!"

Lottie couldn't stop her jaw dropping; she'd expected Ellie to be as furious as when she'd spoken about the prince before. Impressed was definitely not the reaction she'd imagined.

"I mean, even I struggle to hide things from Jamie and I've been doing it since I was born. He has this way of just—"

"Knowing things," Lottie offered in agreement.

Ellie nodded.

"Ahem." Lottie and Ellie both jumped at the sound of the not-so-subtle cough coming from the other side of the room. They peeked out of the closet to see Jamie leaning against the doorframe looking less than pleased.

"What sort of things do I just *know* exactly?"

They were well and truly busted.

45

"*JAMIE!*" ELLIE EXCLAIMED FURIOUSLY. "DIDN'T anyone ever teach you to knock?"

He strolled casually into the room, ignoring her, and sat on the bed.

He looked up at them sternly in a way that told Lottie a serious conversation was about to be had.

"If you two are keeping something from me, you have to tell me. Now."

The two girls exchanged a glance, trying to wordlessly decide what to do. Lottie gulped. She was sick of the secrets eating away at her, and if she didn't come forward soon it might be too late. She turned back to Jamie, preparing to spill it all, but as she opened her mouth Ellie interrupted her.

"Jamie, you have to promise not to be mad."

Lottie was overcome with déjà vu. It was an echo of the moment between her and Ellie just minutes ago. To her amazement Jamie's face softened in the exact same way Ellie's had; it was almost creepily similar.

"I can't promise not to be mad, but I'll hear you out."

That's more like Jamie, Lottie thought to herself.

Ellie reached over and squeezed Lottie's hand before continuing. "We found another . . . um . . . message."

There was a brief silence in which Lottie could see Jamie's top lip twitching in a desperate attempt to stay composed. Ellie quickly filled him in on the details before he could ask any questions. She spun the story as if they'd found the message together. The entire time Jamie remained deadly calm.

"So we don't even know if it was really from the same person," Ellie concluded. "It could have been a terrible secret admirer for all we know."

Lottie felt a shiver go up her spine at how good Ellie was at manipulating the truth. When she'd finally finished explaining, the room went cold—the only sound was their breathing. Lottie was sure Jamie was about to start shouting at them, telling them how irresponsible they were and how Lottie was putting Ellie at risk. But there was no shouting. There was an expression on his face that didn't seem quite right. He looked pained.

"You know what the queen just asked me?"

Both girls shook their heads at his question, racked with anxiety.

Jamie took a long breath before continuing. "She asked me if I had anything worrying to report, and you know what I told her? I told her that everything was fine—*better*

than fine. I told her you were both doing exceptionally well in school and there was absolutely nothing for them to be concerned about."

Lottie could feel Ellie relaxing, but the information only made Lottie feel even worse.

Jamie looked directly at Lottie, forcing her to hold his gaze. "I lied to my queen." His face twisted in anguish. It was awful to see him like this.

"No, you didn't. Everything *is* fine. You didn't lie," Lottie said firmly.

Jamie's features regained some of their usual disapproval and she found she was actually relieved by it. "I find it hard to see how death marks and ominous rhymes are *fine*."

Lottie realized the answer he needed. "Okay, listen. Both of you," said Lottie decisively. She could feel resolve building up inside her. If she wanted Jamie to see her as helpful, she needed to stop doubting herself. "I am Ellie's Portman, and I know you think I'm not cut out for it, but so far everyone believes I'm the real princess." Something flashed across Jamie's face but she continued. "You're clearly used to being her sole protector, but you need to start trusting my judgment. I can handle whatever danger there is."

Again the room filled with silence. Slowly a wry smile crept onto Jamie's face. Ellie watched it unfold and responded with a furious expression. Jamie had been

acting, and they'd both fallen for it.

"You little—"

Jamie quickly cut Ellie off by standing up. "Good job, Lottie," he said calmly, all hints of his earlier anguish entirely untraceable. "I knew things would be fine so long as you were able to stick up for yourself." Lottie stared at him dumbfounded as he sauntered over to them and patted her on the head condescendingly.

The poem was a test.

"I doubt we have anything to worry about from the sounds of your story."

A test from Jamie to see if I was serious.

"But, just in case, I had to be sure you understood your role."

A test to see if I'd be willing to put myself in danger for Ellie.

Lottie knew it was stupid after everything she'd just said, but she'd never considered that for Jamie to be happy with her as a Portman he'd have to also be okay with the idea that she might get hurt. That she might die. She suddenly felt like an absolute idiot. Ellie looked as if she were about to bark at him, but Lottie held up her hand to stop her.

"Of course," Lottie said, feigning as much composure as she could. "I'm glad you understand me."

Jamie nodded at her. "I'll see you both tomorrow then."

And with that he walked out of the door, leaving them alone again.

Jamie walked calmly to his quarters. He walked past Hanna and smiled warmly at her. He walked past one of the cooks on a break and nodded in recognition, being absolutely sure to give nothing away. After all, it's what he'd been trained to do from birth. He finally reached his room and pushed the door open, entering just as he would normally. He waited until the door was firmly shut behind him before he allowed himself to be consumed by his dread, and then he broke down.

⚜ 46 ⚜

LOTTIE'S HANDS FIDGETED NERVOUSLY IN her lap as her mother's tiara was carefully lowered and clipped onto her head. She had requested permission to wear it with her gown and no one had protested. She was convinced it was the only way she'd power through her nerves.

Any moment now she would be joining the ball; she could hear the guests on the other side of the white doors. Ellie had failed to inform her that as this was the first time the princess was attending a royal function, she would be getting a grand entrance and official announcement. Lottie thought back to when she'd been in the Ivy dorm all those months ago with Ellie and Jamie, before any death marks had appeared in her room, before the pool, before all the secrets. She'd been so excited to attend a real ball with real royalty, and she was determined to find that part of herself again. She couldn't let the dreadful feeling in her stomach win.

Lottie looked over to her left and saw Ellie, wringing her hands, wearing a dress she resented, to please people she didn't like. She reached over and grabbed her hand like

Ellie had done for her during their trial.

"It's going to be fun," Lottie said, offering her best reassuring smile.

Ellie turned to her with a look of surprise that melted into a genuine smile. "I'm so glad you're here," she replied, furrowing her brows.

The two girls paused as the hall beyond the doors went quiet.

It was time.

"Good luck."

Lottie was genuinely startled at Jamie's voice behind her, not just because he was so committed to rules and logic that she didn't imagine "luck" was in his vocabulary, but because there was no hint of irony at all. She turned to him and gave him a little wink, like she'd seen Ellie do a million times.

"I don't need luck," she teased, before turning in preparation for her grand entrance.

A short fanfare played out, and then she heard the words she'd been waiting for. The words that weren't really meant for her.

"We are delighted to introduce Her Royal Highness, the princess of Maradova."

Then the doors to the ballroom opened and light flooded over her, illuminating her dress and shoes like glowing liquid over her body. She stepped out gracefully and stood at the

top of the marble stairs, looking out over the assembly below her. Lavish golden streamers hung from the ceiling, dangling elegantly between cherubic paintings. It was as if the heavenly scenes on the walls were extending out into reality.

The congregation below her was like something out of a fairy tale, a massive display of opulent and over-the-top gowns and suits. Dresses flared out in colorful puffs across the shimmering white floor. Many heads were topped with different types of ornamentation. It was a room filled with royalty. The magnificent flowers around the room bowed and curtsied as Lottie began her descent. The crowd parted for her as she made her way over to her "parents," and once she was safely at their side the festivities continued, and Lottie became fair game for conversation.

Ellie's mother happily embraced the role of Lottie's mother, whereas the king continued to keep himself apart from her, which to most people probably just looked like a stern father-daughter relationship.

"A wonderful entrance," the queen praised, tenderly brushing Lottie's cheek with her hand. "Don't you agree, Alexander?"

The king nodded briskly. "Yes," he said, giving Lottie a sideways glance, "quite the natural it would seem." It didn't feel like the words were intended as a compliment.

The queen leaned over to Lottie and whispered in her ear softly. "Go and find Ellie and Jamie and they will take

you on the rounds." She gave Lottie a gentle push into the crowd.

Lottie had taken no more than three steps before the person she'd been hoping for appeared before her.

"Edmund," she breathed.

The prince was wearing white again, but this time he wore an elegant crown as well as his pristine regal outfit. He bowed low in response, but before he straightened up a hand grabbed Lottie from the side and yanked her away, leaving Edmund looking around in confusion.

"Let go of—"

Lottie looked up to see Jamie's face looming over her. They stood close together as if they were about to dance. He looked incredible. In the short time she'd been in the hall he'd changed into his black suit, the shoulder pads and ruffles making him look like a valiant knight.

"Wow!" The word came out a whisper.

Music began to swell and she looked around to see various couples pairing up to dance.

"You are *not* dancing with Edmund," Jamie said sternly.

Lottie pouted indignantly. "Well, who can I dance with then?" she asked, fully aware that she sounded like a petulant child. She wanted to have a perfect night and that included at least one royal dance.

"I don't know. Ellie will be here soon; you can dance with her."

Lottie had every intention of doing that, but it seemed that was not a choice right now. The dance floor filled up and Lottie found herself and Jamie in the middle of the crowd. She looked at his grumbling face and it became blindingly obvious what needed to be done.

"As your princess, I order you to dance with me."

Jamie gazed down at her, completely bewildered. He had no choice. Couples around them began to get into position. He couldn't leave now without causing a scene. Lottie smirked at him, and to her amazement he effortlessly moved her into position just as the music started.

"As you wish," he muttered, as he placed his hand on the small of her back.

He was far too rigid to be a good dancer, yet there was something comforting in the way they moved and stepped together. It probably looked very awkward to anyone watching, and it definitely was, but somehow Lottie didn't mind. She was happy he was allowing her to be close to him again and figured this might be the first opportunity to talk with him candidly since the pool.

No more secrets.

"Ellie told me how you came to be her Partizan," she said gently into his chest. If it was possible, he went more rigid. "I know you have a complicated relationship with Ellie and her family, and I know you think I'm just some naive girl, but"—the music swelled again and she had to tiptoe to

reach his ear—"I want to help you, if you'll let me."

Jamie abruptly spun her out and pulled her back in under his arm so she was facing forward with his arm wrapped round her waist. He leaned his head down over her shoulder and murmured in her ear. "I don't think there's anything that can help me since you showed up."

Before she could react, he spun her again and when he twirled her back he dipped her, leaning in again. "But thank you," he added, before returning to a standing position.

Not such a bad dancer after all.

They came to a stop as the music faded, the two of them slightly breathless and still holding one another.

"Jamie . . ." She said his name delicately, as if she worried it might break in her mouth if she spoke too loud.

"Ladies and gentlemen, if you would please gather with a partner in the center for the royal waltz."

Lottie looked up at Jamie hopefully, but his gaze was behind her. He leaned down to her again. "Our princess is here."

Lottie turned abruptly, all at once forgetting Jamie as she turned to see Ellie. Jamie slunk away while he had the chance, leaving the two of them alone.

They stood opposite each other: Ellie in her deep black gown twinkling with crystals, looking as if she were wearing the night sky itself, and Lottie, a vision in white and peach, the gold lining of the fabric shining like a gilded

dawn. With her dress flowing behind her, Ellie took a confident step toward Lottie so they were face-to-face, their breath in sync.

"May I have this dance?" she asked with only a hint of irony in her voice.

"It would be my pleasure."

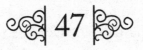

ELLIE TOOK LOTTIE'S HAND AND kissed the back of it dramatically, making that familiar static shoot up her arm. She spun her into an embrace, Lottie giggling as she landed comfortably in her arms.

"Hi," she said, their faces mere inches from one another.

"Hi," Ellie breathed in response, the air from their words mingling together.

When the music started the two girls began moving together so fluidly it was as if they were a single being, effortlessly floating across the hall. As they spun around the marble floor, the liquid fabric of their dresses melted into each other, the black and white forming a yin and yang effect. Ellie led naturally, a strength and determination in each step that seamlessly matched Lottie's delicate movements. Lottie leaned into Ellie, resting her head against her shoulder as they slowed down.

"I forgot to tell you how amazing you look," Ellie said gently.

Lottie smiled, a warm feeling spreading through her body. "Thank you . . . I'm sorry you had to wear one too,

though you look lovely in it . . . if that helps."

Ellie chuckled, its low rumble vibrating against Lottie's cheek. Lottie let herself completely relax into her as they swayed together. But as they turned, she was abruptly taken aback by three familiar faces. Anastacia, Raphael, and Saskia were standing by the wall near a massive spread of fruit on a gilded table.

Anastacia was dressed in a deep-red dress that puffed out at the sides like one of the flowers from the overhanging bouquets, her chestnut brown hair partly up, the rest cascading down her shoulders. Lottie felt as though she were looking at a character from an old French film. Raphael was dressed in a deep burgundy suit, matching Anastacia, though it was unlikely she'd agreed to that. Lottie was surprised that Saskia had chosen a dark suit instead of a dress, and yet it was so natural on her that she could have been born in it.

But it wasn't their effortless beauty that caught her eye. Anastacia seemed on edge, fidgeting in a way that was out of character. Saskia slowly looked up and her gaze fell instantly on Ellie and her. She smiled and Lottie returned the gesture, relieved she was there to calm Anastacia.

"I can distract Jamie if you *really* want to dance with Edmund, but *just* a dance, okay?"

Lottie looked at Ellie in surprise. She had entirely forgotten about him while dancing with Ellie. She tensed up suddenly.

"Lottie?" Ellie asked questioningly. "Are you okay?"

Lottie buried her face back in Ellie's chest. "I'm nervous." The words came out muted against Ellie's skin. "What if he kisses me?"

Ellie laughed outright and Lottie immediately felt embarrassed.

"Bite him," Ellie said frankly.

"Ellie, I'm serious. I've never kissed anyone before!" Lottie looked at her pleadingly.

"Good." She chuckled again and Lottie grumbled at her lack of sympathy.

"Haven't you ever been with a boy?" Lottie asked.

Ellie raised an eyebrow. "Lottie, the only thing I've ever been *with a boy* is annoyed."

Lottie almost laughed, but she was too nervous. She sighed wistfully. "I just want it to be perfect."

Ellie looked at her seriously, slowing them down so she could be as clear as possible. "Listen, Lottie"—she lowered her hand to pull her even closer, so their foreheads gently touched—"if anything isn't exactly how you want or expect it to be, then I will be there for you to break his pompous nose."

"Ellie!" Lottie tried to groan, but it came out more as a giggle. "Thank you."

The music came to an end and Ellie spun Lottie one last

time. "I do not condone this, but"—she gave Lottie a gentle push, not dissimilar to her mother's actions earlier—"go dance with the prince."

Lottie felt a strange physical loss as she moved away from Ellie, but she didn't have time to think about it as she practically fell into Edmund's arms. He caught her as she tripped forward ungracefully to where he had been standing patiently at the edge of the dancers.

"I was starting to think I'd never get my turn," he said with a cunning smile.

Lottie felt her heart skip a beat as he escorted her back to the dance floor. They assumed the same positions they had at the etiquette class, and Lottie smiled up at his icy-blue eyes. Now that he was there in front of her she instantly remembered how he made her feel.

"I thought it would be good to make you wait," she said, amazing herself with how casual she was being.

He purred a low laugh as the next waltz began. It wasn't the same thrill as it had been with Ellie, and the movements were far more predictable than when she'd danced with Jamie. Instead they were the poster children for a classic waltz, just as someone would expect of a prince and princess.

"I'll be honest, I was hoping a girl like you would have found a way to contact me," he said, spinning her out and bringing her back in, closer than before. Lottie found her

cheeks going hot, confused by the undertone to his words.

"Too many watchful eyes," she replied honestly, missing the thrilled look in the prince's gaze.

He tutted. "Ah, I understand that very well." The smile on his face turned wry, and he gave a sharp look in the direction of where Lottie assumed his parents were. When he glanced back he gave Lottie a knowing look, which she didn't quite understand.

"But . . ." Lottie said as they glided through another step, "I'm sure I can make it up to you." *By you giving me my first kiss*, she added in her head.

He looked down at her again, the smile on his face replaced with a considering look. The waltz wasn't even halfway through when he leaned closer and whispered gently in her ear, "Let's go somewhere quieter, away from all these *watching eyes*. I have something I want to share with you."

Lottie's breath caught in her throat. *This is it!* she thought. *I'm going to have my first kiss . . . at a ball . . . with a prince . . . and I'm not dreaming!*

She beamed at him, forgetting she'd promised Ellie that she'd only *dance* with the prince. "I know just the place!"

He smiled back, mirroring her excitement. "Of course you do," he purred softly, and grinned at her.

Lottie took his white gloved hand and guided him

through the pairs of dancing figures, the two of them gliding across the floor almost unnoticed as they pivoted among the other guests. She led him out of the ballroom, deeper into the palace, already knowing exactly in which room she wanted their first kiss to take place. It would be in the creamy, floral room with the huge arched window overlooking the fountain that Ellie had shown her on the tour of the palace.

He laughed as they approached, giving her a sideways glance as they came to a stop. "Such a hurry," he panted, leaning against the wall to catch his breath.

"Sorry," she replied breathlessly. "I'm just excited."

She felt her familiar blush creeping onto her cheeks and didn't mind that it wasn't just from the running and dancing. She opened the door, anticipation building in her stomach as a million butterflies danced around inside her.

"Follow me."

Edmund complied, stepping behind her, a grin splitting his face. He gently closed the door, a sharp click echoing through the room as it shut. Then he turned to her, a strange manic smile on his lips that Lottie had never seen before.

A chill ran through her and a voice in her head whispered: *Lottie, you're a fool.*

48

"FINALLY WE'RE AWAY FROM ALL those boring pests," said Edmund. A malicious tone crept into his voice, making Lottie feel uncomfortable.

Then, before she could register what was happening, he grabbed her head with both hands and crushed his lips against hers. Her eyes widened in shock; things were happening too fast and forcefully for her to comprehend. He pulled away, leaving an odd dryness on her lips. She froze. She didn't feel wonder, as she would have expected after her first kiss, but confusion at how unpleasant the experience had been.

This isn't right. The kiss lingered on her lips with a sickly taste that she wanted to wipe away. He didn't even look at her as he proceeded to walk over to the window, staring out at the grounds.

I have something I want to share with you.

Lottie gulped. Confused by what she was seeing and feeling, she sat down hard on the chaise longue in the center of the room, her fingers still hovering over her lips, her

mind telling her that something was wrong. This was not the kind of behavior she'd expected of Edmund. This is not how she'd wanted this to go.

"What do you mean?" she asked, suddenly afraid that she may have completely misunderstood him horribly.

"You *know* what I mean."

He shrugged off his jacket and unbuttoned the top three notches of his shirt before running his hands through his hair. When he took his hand away from his face Lottie almost gasped at how different he looked. The transformation was terrifying. He'd entered the room as a bright and elegant Prince Charming and was now a messy, feral animal.

It was all backward: she'd kissed the prince and he'd turned into a frog.

"All these tedious airs and graces," he continued. "Everyone so pathetically easy to fool."

Lottie felt her hands start to tremble and quickly stood up, moving to the other side of the room, away from this stranger. They'd both gotten each other completely wrong.

Does he really *believe I'm like him? How on earth am I going to explain this misunderstanding?*

"I think—"

He cut her off before she could explain. "I can't tell you how thrilling it was when I saw you at Lady Priscilla's." A

sarcastic snicker escaped before he carried on. "I'd heard so much about you, and then to see you were just like me, pretending to be a good little royal." He smirked as if laughing at his own joke. "Unfortunately your reputation precedes you, but we can remedy that if you do what I say. I've been tricking people for years. I'm an expert." His eyes narrowed.

Then there was that inner voice again: *Lottie, you are a fool!*

She'd fallen for Edmund's charming persona and conjured up naive ideas about her first kiss, her fantasies running away with her. Ellie and Jamie had warned her and she hadn't listened and now she was trapped in a room with a boy who thought she was someone completely different. And the worst part was he didn't even think he'd tricked her. He thought she was like him. Lottie's mind raced, trying to figure out how she could get out of this situation without causing any more trouble.

"On second thought," she said carefully, "I think I should get back to the party. I have royal duties to attend to and I can't have people getting suspicious." Her heart was racing and she slowly edged toward the door.

"You can cut the act now," he said. "Though I have to say, even I'm impressed by your commitment to this role." He casually sat down on the chaise longue, looking up at her. "We all know what you're really like, Princess Wolfson."

He gave her a look as if he expected her to agree.

Lottie froze, her mind going completely blank. "I think maybe there's been a misunderstanding." She could hardly get the words out with her shaky voice.

He leaned his head back and gave a brutal bellowing laugh that made her flinch.

This is not Edmund. This has got to be an evil twin.

Her brain was trying to come up with a million explanations other than just *"You're an idiot."*

He stopped laughing and gave her a terrifying sharp look, like an animal about to attack. "Okay, I'm getting bored of this now." He stood and moved toward Lottie. "Let's see that notorious girl I've heard so much about."

She slowly stepped backward as he edged toward her, feeling for the door handle behind her.

How could I have been so stupid? she thought desperately.

"I'm such a fool!" she breathed.

"What was that?" He took a step forward. "I can't hear you." He was grinning maniacally, and Lottie wanted to slap him for thinking that Ellie would ever waste her time with a slug like him.

"I said, *you're boring me.*"

She turned to the door, forcing herself to sound as calm and dismissive as possible. She placed her hand on the door handle.

Edmund slammed his arm against the door, banging it

shut and trapping her. She jumped at his sudden forceful-ness and turned to find him looking confused.

"Let me go," she said assertively, glaring furiously at him.

He faltered for a moment, caught by the intensity of her expression. In her anger she could now see all the cracks in his persona. He wasn't a Prince Charming of any sort; he was just a spoiled little rich boy.

"What did I do wrong?" he said playfully, making her even more annoyed.

"I said," she repeated firmly, "let me GO."

She thrust her palms into his chest as hard as she could and he toppled backward in surprise before catching his balance.

She held her breath, expecting him to be angry, but he laughed again.

"Now *that's* more like the girl I heard about." He held his hand out for her again and she grunted in exasperation. There was just no getting through to this idiot.

She lifted her hand and smacked his hand away so quickly that he spun, stumbling on the embroidered car-pet. Taking advantage of Edmund's surprise, Lottie rushed to the door. But before she could reach the handle, she felt a hand grab her dress.

A harsh tearing sound ripped through the air and Edmund succeeded in pulling her away from the door. Her

tiara flew off her head and clattered onto the floor.

"My dress!" she cried as she landed roughly on the chaise longue. In a mirror on the wall she could see that there was a huge rip up the back that had caused one of the sleeves to fall down. Uncontrollable tears pricked her eyes and she wailed, "No, no, no! You ruined my dress, that was a gift from—" She quickly covered her mouth with her hands, but it was too late—she'd given herself away.

Edmund stood very still in front of her, looking blank. Slowly, like blood seeping from a wound, a dark smile wormed its way onto his face.

"You . . ." he began, taking a step forward so he towered over her again. "It wasn't an act, was it? You really thought I was—" He laughed again, a nasty mocking cackle, and he grabbed his stomach as if his sides would burst. "You fell for my charming routine, didn't you?"

Lottie cast her eyes to the floor and hiccuped back a sob.

"Stop that, I'm the real victim," he chided unsympathetically. "Here I was thinking I'd finally found a wild royal girl, someone just like me who—"

"I'm nothing like you," she said fiercely, outraged that he would ever think he and Ellie had anything in common.

"Apparently so," he said vacantly, as he leaned down, propping her chin up with his hand. "You're just as boring as everyone else."

His words rekindled every insecurity Lottie had about her place in the world of royals. She felt the tears building again when the door burst open with a crash.

"YOU COMPLETE—"

Everything suddenly moved very fast yet very slowly, all at once. Ellie and Jamie surged through the door furiously. Edmund turned in surprise to see Jamie trying to hold Ellie back, but she evaded him and came storming toward them. Lottie didn't have time to explain the situation; it was too late. Ellie balled one hand into a fist and with the other grabbed Edmund by his collar.

And then Princess Eleanor Wolfson punched Prince Edmund Ashwick, hard, in the face.

☙ 49 ❧

EDMUND FELL BACK AGAINST THE wall, clutching his nose as a bright stream of blood gushed out between his fingers, running down his lips and neck, and leaving a crimson crescent mark on his shirt. It was a violent display—Lottie had to cover her mouth to stop from screaming—but the fact that Edmund was still conscious, and yelling loudly, indicated that he wasn't *that* badly injured.

Lottie hiccuped back another sob as Ellie rushed to her side and squeezed her. "I'm so stupid. I'm sorry. This is all a stupid misunderst—"

Lottie was cut off by a furious growl from Edmund. He looked down at his blood-covered hands and cringed. "You filthy little commoner!"

Oh no, thought Lottie.

"How dare you interfere—" He stopped as Ellie turned and gave him what could only be described as a death glare, her eyes like daggers. It was as if there were tendrils of electric air surrounding her, threatening to awaken a storm. Edmund hesitated for only a moment before continuing. "You broke my nose . . . you . . . you *animal*!"

"I'll break more than just your nose if you don't keep your dirty mouth shut," she barked, her face contorting into a furious snarl.

What is it with these people calling each other "dirty" and "filthy"? Lottie couldn't help but think.

"That's enough." Jamie's voice came out clear and sensible, his pragmatic manner welcome under the circumstances. "Ellie, see if you can fix Lottie's dress, and, Prince Edmund"—he turned sharply to the bloody mess that was the prince, his voice becoming icy—"I will fix your nose."

Edmund froze as Jamie approached him, his whole body going rigid as the dark shadow of an uncompromising Partizan stepped closer, hands outstretched.

"Don't touch me!" Edmund cried dramatically, covering his face with his other arm.

Jamie let out a terse growl and pushed the prince's arm out of the way, holding it firmly so Edmund couldn't move. "Don't be melodramatic; I just need to look at it."

Edmund remained cowering, backed against the wall like a scared little mouse, while Jamie turned to Lottie and Ellie, still holding Edmund's arm to stop him from making a run for it.

Ellie looked at Lottie, who gently reached out for her hand and gripped it tightly. Choking back another sob, she took a deep breath and spoke as clearly as she could. "He's not going to hurt you, Edmund."

Edmund stared at the two girls, eyes wide as if seeing them properly for the first time, then slowly he relaxed. He'd managed to leave a bloody handprint on the soft floral wall behind him. Carefully Jamie let go of his arm and silently began working his fingers over his nose. Edmund watched as Ellie, who was simply the dark-haired girl to him, assisted the princess in trying to salvage the dress. His vision blurred, the two fading to a white-and-black glittering haze. An unpleasant feeling in his stomach began to build, as if his own blood were telling him to be ashamed of himself.

"Keep your eyes forward."

Edmund jumped as Jamie's voice yanked him back to reality, pulling his eyes to his so he was face-to-face with the burning hazel of Jamie's irises.

"She was . . . I didn't . . . I mean . . . I thought she was like me!" Edmund spewed out the words quietly, tripping over his tongue as he said them. Jamie remained silent as he continued to delicately feel the bridge of Edmund's nose. "The dress was an accident."

Jamie's fingers carried on with their methodical work, the lack of response making Edmund tense.

"I know," Jamie said finally, his face remaining blank.

Edmund regained a semblance of his previous posture, thinking that Jamie was on his side. "Good, because I'm really completely innocent. I was just—" Edmund yelped

as Jamie pushed his nose back into place.

Jamie leaned forward slowly, so his lips were in line with Edmund's ear. His words came out cold and ominous, leaving no room for misinterpretation. "If I thought for even one second that you'd intentionally hurt her, you'd be leaving this room with more than just a broken nose."

Edmund gulped. He managed to muster an indignant pout, but his silence made it clear he'd gotten the message.

Lottie watched Jamie as he expertly dealt with Edmund; somehow he'd managed to keep him keep silent for a while. She turned her attention back to Ellie as she attempted to pull the back of the dress up with no luck. It was well and truly ruined and yet . . . Lottie found she didn't care anymore. She was still upset, mostly with herself, but she'd realized something when Ellie and Jamie had gallantly appeared. She'd been wrong. She'd spent all this time dreaming of her wonderful Prince Charming who would sweep her off her feet, but the truth was she didn't need a valiant prince: she already had two. She'd had them all along. Their names were Jamie Volk and Ellie Wolf and they were more courageous than any prince from any fairy tale she'd ever read. But she couldn't always rely on them; she needed to be strong herself. She needed to show she could be tough in her own princess way.

"It's okay, Ellie. The dress is a lost cause." Lottie carefully

sat up and rescued her tiara from the floor. She slowly lowered it onto her head, feeling it rejuvenate her.

Kind, brave, unstoppable.

Righteous, resolute, resourceful.

"As long as my shoes are okay!" She allowed herself a little laugh at that. "I think what we all need now is to—"

"What on earth is going on in here?"

Lottie faltered as an unexpected voice came from the door and the group looked over in surprise to see a mop of thick blond curly hair. Saskia.

Even Jamie appeared caught off guard. Lottie assumed he had been too preoccupied with Edmund's nose to be aware of his surroundings.

"Lottie, your *dress*!" Saskia gasped. "Are you okay?"

Lottie was amazed it was her dress and not Edmund's bloody nose that caught her attention.

"Saskia, what are you doing here?" Lottie asked. The last thing she needed right now was another person getting involved in this mess.

"I saw you come up here and then I heard some commotion and, well, here I am." She smiled at her and Lottie found that even Saskia's brazen personality felt comforting under the circumstances.

Ellie sat up, taking in the situation. "It's fine—we're fine. Lottie's just upset because she ripped her dress."

"Oh! I can help," Saskia chirped. "I brought loads of spare dresses. We'll get you cleaned up no problem." She winked at Lottie, who had to admit the idea of getting out of that unpleasant room was very welcome. The three looked at each other in silent deliberation.

Jamie gave Saskia a once-over before reluctantly nodding his head. "We'll meet you downstairs in the hall by the ballroom in twenty minutes," he announced, leaving no room for discussion.

"Perfect," Saskia replied with a reassuring smile. "I've seen dress disasters a million times." She held the door open for Lottie, a matter-of-fact look on her face. It made sense that Anastacia would be drawn to someone so straightforward.

Lottie paused, decidedly ignoring Edmund. She gave her best *I'm okay, really* smile to Jamie and Ellie before leaving with Saskia.

Saskia escorted Lottie quickly to a room at the end of the wing they were in, which overlooked the back of the manor through a large white-paneled sash window that was cracked open slightly. Lottie thought it a little strange to have the window open on such a cold day but found the coolness in the room soothing.

Saskia poured Lottie a cup of hot tea from an ornate tea service on a side table before going to the wardrobe. "Anastacia requested space to keep some extra outfits in

here. I'm sure she'd be more than happy to lend you a dress." The grin on Saskia's face suggested she knew very well how Anastacia would really feel about it.

A thought crossed Lottie's mind. *Maybe this is a good time to ask Saskia about Anastacia.* She couldn't pass up any opportunity to get more information.

Lottie took a small sip of tea, letting the warmth calm her. "That's really kind of you, both of you. I'll take anything that fits really. I'm not fussy. Actually . . . I wanted to ask you about Anastacia," Lottie said, smiling awkwardly at her. Saskia didn't respond. "If that's okay . . ." she added, feeling a chill creep up her spine.

Saskia returned the smile, but there was something not quite right about it. The chill worked its way through Lottie's body and she suddenly found her vision blurring. She coughed a few times but found she was struggling to catch her breath. The cold chill gripped Lottie's stomach; a thought crystallized in her mind.

I've been poisoned.

She gasped, trying to muster the breath to scream. Saskia kept smiling, a nasty tranquility settling on her features, and then it hit Lottie.

"It was you . . . the note . . ."

Her thoughts became hazy and she lost control of her senses. She dropped the teacup and could barely register it smashing on the wood floor.

"You could ask me about Anastacia, I suppose"—Saskia's tone changed dramatically, her voice dripping with an icy humor—"but she's not the one you should have been watching."

The room began to spin around Lottie and she desperately tried to make sense of her words. She frantically reached a hand out to the bed as her knees gave way.

"Five, four, three . . ." said Saskia.

Lottie gripped the bedding, trying to pull herself toward the door, but her limbs weren't cooperating. *I have to do something.* In a moment of clarity, she kicked her left shoe off and shoved it under the bed.

"Two . . . one . . ."

Saskia's voice slowly faded away and everything turned to black.

50

ONLY NINE MINUTES HAD PASSED since Lottie had left with Saskia to find another dress, and Jamie was already getting agitated. He put a last bit of tape gently over the bridge of the prince's nose. He saw no point in causing more commotion by hurting him unnecessarily; the broken nose Ellie had gifted him was harm enough.

Ten minutes.

"Finished," Jamie said matter-of-factly, pocketing his emergency mini first-aid kit.

The prince let out an exasperated groan, which was very clearly a desperate attempt to save face. "Finally. I need to get away from this"—he turned to scowl at Ellie—"unsavory company."

Eleven minutes.

Jamie rolled his eyes discreetly. He knew he could easily put this spoiled boy in his place, but felt no need to lower himself to his level. Ellie let out a cackle and ground her knuckles into a fist. This was exactly the behavior that worried Jamie the most. Ellie was tough, and the truth was she could probably handle most situations on her own, but

she was undisciplined and irrational, and he worried that one day she might take on someone out of her depth. And that's exactly why he needed to be by her side.

Twelve minutes.

"I thought you liked *wild* girls, Ashwick?" she said mockingly, cracking her knuckles again in a particularly menacing display.

The prince glared at her, his face twisting into a snarl. "Only pure breeds like myself," he spat furiously, "not some common rabid mutt like you who's somehow wormed her way into our society."

Jamie couldn't stop a chuckle from escaping his lips at the irony.

Ellie let out a sardonic howl. "This is too much!"

She laughed, clutching her stomach. Jamie gave her a sharp look and she held up her hands to reassure him she wouldn't say anything stupid.

Edmund stared at them in irate confusion, frustrated at being the butt of a joke he didn't understand.

Thirteen minutes.

"This is ridiculous," he declared. "It's your princess's own fault that she created something sentimental between us."

Ellie instantly stopped laughing and Jamie tensed, prepping himself in case he should have to intervene.

Fourteen minutes.

They needed to get out of there and back to the ball-room before people started getting suspicious.

"Sentimental?" Ellie questioned, a furious calm in her voice. "How can you expect her *not* to be sentimental when you sneak love letters into her dorm?" It took Jamie all of three seconds to realize what this meant. Ellie and Lottie had been keeping *another* thing from him.

Fifteen minutes.

"*Love letters?*" Edmund almost spat the words as if they left a bad taste in his mouth. "What on earth are you talking about?"

Jamie turned to face Ellie, his hands crossed over his chest in a questioning stance.

She glanced at him with guilt before quickly turning back to the prince. "You know," she demanded, though he continued to stare at her as if the very idea were outrageous. "Like the one you left in her mailbox on New Year's?"

Sixteen minutes.

Edmund's face turned from disgusted to genuinely per-plexed, and acid began to creep through Jamie's body.

"I've never sent a love letter in my life." Edmund's con-fusion was turning into mockery. "Why would I waste the energy on such an easy conquest?"

They both ignored the childish jab, but Jamie could feel the acid in his veins bubbling away as his mind began to clear.

Seventeen minutes.

"I mean, it wasn't a love letter," Ellie began. "It was more like a *see-you-soon* kind of thing." She was rambling, so Jamie knew she was getting nervous. "The one in the golden envelope? That said you'd see her at the ball?" She continued staring at him as if this would jog his memory, a hint of desperation creeping onto her features.

Jamie turned to Edmund, his face serious as he looked him in the eyes.

Eighteen minutes.

The prince exhaled sharply through his nose and raised his hands. "Listen, I know you both despise me," he said slowly, "but I've never sent a card like that."

"Well, then who—" Ellie blinked, but Jamie had already arrived at the terrible truth.

Nineteen minutes.

Whoever had left the death mark had also left the "love letter." Ellie's eyes were electrified as she locked her gaze with Jamie's.

"Lottie's in trouble!"

51

Biting cold nipped at Lottie's nose. She imagined droplets of ice surrounding her in a quiet floating pool.

Where am I?

She was awake, but her eyelids were leaden, too heavy to open. Her fingers felt stiff and numb as the cold wriggled over her skin.

You have to open your eyes, said a distant voice inside her head.

Who is that? A metallic thumping noise made its way through the fog in her mind. *I'm in trouble.*

Unstoppable. Resourceful.

Lottie willed her eyes to open and made out the shape of a van, and it was getting closer. Tiny dust like snow was falling around her.

I'm tired. Her eyes became heavy again.

The voice chimed in: *The prince and princess need to be able to find you.*

What prince? Her body was numb, but she could feel herself being picked up and tumbled into the van.

Ellie . . . Jamie. Tendrils of the memories of the night

flittered in her mind but she struggled to grasp them.

She blinked and looked about groggily. The van door was open.

Resourceful.

One foot felt lighter than the other. She remembered— her shoe had come off; she'd hidden it. She frantically kicked off the other one before sinking back into sleep.

"She's not here."

They had run back to the ballroom as fast as they possibly could, leaving Edmund alone and confused.

They'd checked the buffet, the stage, and every inch of the marble floor.

"She's not here," Jamie repeated. His face was inscrutable, but Ellie knew he was worried. She'd never seen him this concerned about anyone except . . . well, except her. Lottie should have been there ten minutes ago, according to their arrangement, but she was nowhere in sight.

"I can't believe you two kept something so important from me. I can't believe you would do something so stupid."

Ellie looked away in shame, her fingers curled into fists at her sides, nails biting into the skin of her palms so hard she thought they might draw blood. It took all her self-control not to start trashing the buffet. She so badly wanted to break something; she had half a mind to storm back upstairs and pick a fight with Edmund, but she knew it was

nobody's fault except her own. Jamie was right, how could she be so stupid? STUPID! STUPID! STUPID!

She inhaled sharply and squeezed her eyes shut, preparing to say the most difficult thing she'd ever had to say. They would have to tell her parents that Lottie was missing. She opened her eyes and turned to Jamie. "Jamie, we have to—"

"Is something the matter?"

Ellie shut her mouth suddenly at the sound of the cool voice behind them.

The two turned to find Anastacia, poised elegantly in her lavish red dress, her calm demeanor the total opposite of theirs. "You both seem awfully disturbed."

Jamie tensed, and Ellie took this as a sign not to say anything.

"Everything's fine," she lied, her teeth gritted.

Anastacia seemed unaffected by Ellie's mood. "Are you sure there's nothing at all that I can help with?" She spoke so steadily that Ellie didn't catch the edge in her voice.

Jamie instantly picked up on what Ellie missed, his eyes narrowing before he discreetly, but very firmly, took Anastacia by the arm and moved to the edge of the room. Ellie flinched—not at the sudden movement, but at the deadly look on Jamie's face, one she recognized well.

"What do you know?" he whispered sharply.

Anastacia laughed, patting Jamie condescendingly on

his chest with her free hand.

"A true Partizan," she said, the humor not quite reaching her eyes. "Nothing gets by you, does it?"

"Don't play coy, Anastacia," Jamie growled. "If you know so much about Partizans, you should know that they'll do anything to protect their masters."

Anastacia held her ground, not allowing herself to be intimidated, and Ellie was impressed. Then Anastacia said something neither of them could have prepared for.

"If you need to protect your master, surely you should be focusing on Ellie and not . . . whoever Lottie is." They looked at her, confused for a moment, and she gave an exasperated sigh. "I know she's your Portman, Eleanor Wolfson."

Ellie's mind whirred. So Anastacia knew *everything*. But how? Had she told anyone? And more importantly—where was Lottie?!

Before Ellie could speak, Jamie broke the tense silence. "What on earth are you talking about?"

Anastacia let out a humorless laugh. "*Quels imbéciles!*" she hissed. "Ellie Wolf, Eleanor Wolfson, the rebel princess from Maradova . . . How anyone who knows anything could have mistaken such a ludicrous attempt at a cover-up! I mean, Pumpkin alone is a completely ridiculous—"

"Enough!" Ellie commanded. "How long have you known?"

A blush had crept up Anastacia's neck, and her brow had furrowed slightly, a light sheen of moisture upon it. Ellie realized this was the most perturbed she'd ever seen Anastacia. Ellie so badly wanted to tell her they'd have to kill her now, but not even her dark humor could distract her.

"Since breakfast . . . the first time I saw you. Lottie introduced you as her roommate and I just knew."

"But how? There's no way—"

"You can't escape who you are, Ellie. It's in our blood. We'll never be like them and they'll never be like us. It's etched into us the second we're born, and I could spot it on you from a mile away."

Ellie stared at her. In what way was she anything like Anastacia?

"What could you possibly—"

"Privilege," Jamie interrupted, slowly releasing Anastacia's arm. "She's talking about privilege. But we don't have time for character growth right now; Lottie might be in danger."

"Danger?"

Ellie felt annoyed at what seemed to be genuine concern on Anastacia's face.

"Yes, she's missing, and the last person she was with was your good friend—"

"Saskia!" Anastacia spat the words out, cutting Jamie

off and surprising both of them with the hurt on her face as she spoke. "She's been obsessed with the Wolfson princess ever since she found out she was attending Rosewood. She wanted to know everything about her. She demanded I introduce her and get close to her. It was . . . not like her at all."

Jamie and Ellie glanced at each other, both coming to the same conclusion.

"Anastacia, do you know if she left anything under Lottie's bed?" Jamie asked hurriedly.

Anastacia looked down sheepishly. "No . . . All the messages . . . that was me . . ."

"*What?*"

"You don't understand. I was doing it to protect her . . . I—"

"By putting a *death threat* under her bed!" Ellie exclaimed.

"No. Shut up! Listen!" Anastacia took a deep breath. "I was trying to scare her away—both of you . . . Saskia, she's not just a friend. She's my—"

Jamie grabbed her by both shoulders. "Anastacia, spit it out—we might be running out of time."

She bit her lip and turned to Ellie, staring intensely as though she were trying to communicate something to her that only Ellie could understand.

She's not just a friend. She's my . . .

"She's your Partizan."

It wasn't a question; Ellie knew it was true.

Anastacia nodded and Jamie slowly released his grip. It felt as though light had exploded over the situation, and Ellie all at once understood why Anastacia had done what she'd done. For some reason Saskia had been dangerously obsessed with the princess, who she believed was Lottie. Anastacia couldn't turn her in. Ellie tried to imagine turning Jamie in. It just wouldn't be possible; she could never do it. So Anastacia had done the next best thing, and tried to get her and Lottie as far away from Rosewood as possible.

"I understand," Ellie said gently. She'd never imagined she'd feel any kind of connection with Anastacia, but in that moment she felt she understood her better than anyone else.

"Okay," Jamie said, trying to remain calm, though his teeth were clearly gritted in frustration. "We have to overlook this for the moment because it's now been well over thirty minutes and Lottie is still missing and presumably abducted by a rogue Partizan, which—"

He stopped, horrified, as he took in the severity of the situation. Then he shook his head, a determined and furious look resting on his features, before he said decisively, "We have to find her—*now.*"

Ellie pushed her hands through her hair. It would take

days to search the grounds. "Where do we even begin?" Her voice came out strangled and desperate, and she resented not being able to keep steady like Jamie.

Anastacia's voice pulled her out of her despair. "Have you tried calling her?"

They both blinked at her for a moment.

No, they had not.

"Yes, I have the princess. No, she's unharmed. I think she's waking up. Okay. We'll be there. *Svobadash!*"

Lottie tried to make sense of what she was hearing. She felt a gradual tightness around her wrists, the squeezing sensation snaking her back into full consciousness.

"You're awake."

She opened her eyes to see Saskia kneeling in front of her, meticulously binding her wrists. This time there was no murky feeling; the world and her thoughts were fully lucid.

She'd been kidnapped.

She pulled her knees together, willing the nausea not to win as she sat up straight. Feigning as much confusion as possible, she looked around the van, discreetly taking in everything she could.

Saskia had tricked them all. Saskia had been planning to kidnap her since the moment she had met her. Lottie couldn't feel movement from the van, so that meant that

they might still be within the palace grounds. She was missing her shoes.

But the main mystery was . . .

"Why are you doing this?"

Lottie was relieved by how groggy and choked her voice was, hoping it would lower Saskia's guard.

Saskia turned to her. There was an eerie soft smile on her lips that made Lottie shiver. Yet Saskia didn't betray any hint of instability. If she was unstable, Lottie was sure she could distract her, but she was too alert, too primed. It made her think of . . . Jamie.

"Well . . . the short answer is"—she made a sign with her fingers, rubbing them together—"money."

Lottie jumped on this, saying the first thing that popped into her head.

"Okay then, why don't you take me back? I'll tell my parents you rescued me and we'll give you a big reward."

Saskia laughed, reminding Lottie of all their time together over the past year. "Nice try, Princess, but there's a bounty on your head bigger than you could imagine. You're top of the list."

Lottie shook her head; the words didn't make sense.

"Whose list . . . ? Who were you talking to on the phone?"

Saskia's "friendly" smile melted away and she looked off into the distance. "*Them.*"

She spoke with a reverence as if she were talking about a god, and a chill ran up Lottie's spine. "They're called Leviathan. They're here to change things, and you're my ticket to being fully initiated. I have no idea why, but they want the Maravish princess—you, more than anyone." Saskia pulled a package from her suit jacket and began fiddling with it. Lottie saw two small knives and gulped, wondering how many other weapons Saskia was concealing.

"These Leviathan," Lottie began, trying to keep up her groggy and confused tone, "do they have bounties on lots of people?"

"Not just any people—the children of royalty and important, wealthy families. They want to—" Before Saskia could finish, a pleasant melody floated out from under Lottie, accompanied by a harsh vibrating noise.

Her phone.

Saskia knelt down by Lottie and gently tilted her to retrieve the phone from her evening bag, still on its delicate silver chain over her shoulder. The action could have been mistaken for an embrace.

"Answer it." She shoved the phone in front of her face. "Convince them you're safe or I won't be so nice."

Lottie looked at the phone, watching it vibrate in Saskia's hand. Ellie's name flashed on the screen and Lottie's heart began to race frantically. This could be her chance. She

racked her brain for every ridiculous espionage trick and code she'd absorbed from the stories she'd read.

"Well, hurry up, Princess," threatened Saskia.

Princess . . .

Lottie knew exactly what to do.

"Hello."

"Lottie, oh my God, are you okay?" It was Ellie's voice.

"Yes, I'm fine. Sorry I missed our meeting time. I'm just a little frazzled. I think I'm gonna crash."

"Are you sure? We could come and see you?"

Jamie. She was on loudspeaker. They must be away from the ballroom.

"No, no, it's really fine. I just wanted to get out of that stupid dress—and those uncomfortable shoes too . . ."

There was a brief silence on the other end and Lottie felt as though she were about to burst.

"Okay." Ellie's voice came out so steady that Lottie worried she may have missed the hint. "Is there anything we can do for you at all?"

"Actually"—at that, Saskia gave her a sharp look and gestured to hurry up—"you could save me one of those apple tarts I saw in the buffet?"

"Of course. I'll make sure they know to save you one."

"Thank you." Lottie squeezed her eyes shut and on instinct she added, "I love you guys."

She opened her eyes to see Saskia's finger on the hang-up button, her lips twisted into a satisfied grin.

Now Lottie just had to pray they'd figure out her message.

❧ 52 ❧

JAMIE WATCHED AS THE PHONE went dead.

"I love you guys."

His heart was pounding; he knew something was not right, but he had to remain calm and rational.

"So she's fine?" Anastacia said hopefully.

"No," Ellie replied bluntly. "I think she's left us a secret code."

Anastacia's face melted into despair. "Oh, Saskia," she sighed. "What have you done?"

Jamie pointedly ignored her. Anastacia's worries about her dishonorable Partizan were not their top priority.

"What are our clues?" he asked, already preparing to make a move.

"Well," said Ellie, "she's allergic to apples—that's how we know she can't say she's in trouble, and then the shoes . . ." Ellie rubbed her forehead in thought, looking desperate. "I know she's trying to tell me something by mentioning they were uncomfortable. They were tailor-made for her; she loves them. I just—"

"It's Cinderella, you idiot!" Anastacia barked. Tears

were pouring down her cheeks now and she sniffed loudly, but continued talking as if she weren't crying at all. "She's probably put her shoes somewhere as a way to find her."

Jamie nodded. "We can't alert the guard yet. If the palace goes under lockdown, Saskia will have a separate escape plan and Lottie will be in more danger."

"How do you know?" Ellie asked, not sure of his reasoning.

"Because that's what I would do," he said simply. "So, we have to find the shoes."

It took them all of ten minutes to find the first shoe. Jamie rationalized that it had to be on the west side, as that's where Saskia had found Lottie, and it had to be in one of the rooms with a gate-facing window for quick escape.

Ellie saw the broken teacup first, and from there she spotted the missing shoe. There it was, shoved under the bed, almost completely hidden but for the light glittering off it, just enough to catch her eye.

"She went out the window?" Ellie asked in disbelief.

"Yes," Jamie said. Saskia's plan was obvious to him now, and she had clearly underestimated both Lottie and the situation. It was a classic polite parting, a cute name for a procedure they were taught as Partizans in case an event arose in which they needed to escape a high-profile event unnoticed.

He'd never considered a Partizan might use the same technique to kidnap someone.

"This means they'll probably be leaving any moment."

"So why don't we just tell the guard not to let anyone leave the grounds?" Anastacia suggested. She'd calmed down and was determined to help, feeling somewhat responsible.

"Because then she might start killing people," he said frankly.

Anastacia scoffed. "Saskia would never—"

"I'm sure you thought she'd never kidnap anyone either."

Anastacia instantly bit her tongue. It was insensitive, he knew it was, but the stress of the situation was getting to him. Lottie was being held by another Partizan, she was in imminent danger, and he needed to save her without prioritizing her safety over Ellie's.

"Guys," Ellie called over. "I think I've found them."

Jamie dived over the bed in a rush to join Ellie at the window. He followed her gaze but it was hard to see anything in the frosty dark. He was about to tell her off for imagining things when he saw it.

A van, not far from the building, seemed to be glowing from underneath. It was subtle enough that you might assume your mind was playing tricks on you. The three of them ran downstairs to the veranda by the entrance, the cold wind slapping them in the face as they crept outside.

Anastacia kept her hand on the door to stop it from shutting. "Are you sure that's the one?" There was a pained look in her eye, knowing that she was about to condemn her Partizan forever.

"Positive," Ellie replied. She didn't bother trying to reassure her; there was nothing to be said.

Anastacia bowed her head, flinching from her feelings. "I'll alert the guard. You guys keep watch." She turned to run back the way they'd come, but paused and grabbed Jamie's sleeve. "Don't hurt her," she whispered.

He wondered if he should spare her feelings, but knew there was no point in lying.

"I might not have a choice."

❧ 53 ❧

"Anastacia has informed the guard. We'll wait here until they arrive."

Jamie was trying to persuade a shivering Ellie to go back indoors, but she was refusing. Instead she stubbornly rubbed her arms to stay warm. They hid in the shadows of the veranda, keeping out of sight of the van but peering out occasionally to check it wasn't moving. She'd acquired a golf club from somewhere and propped it by her side, apparently hoping to use it as a weapon.

"But what if it's too late by then?" she cried.

Jamie shook his head, knowing what she was thinking but trying to stay as logical as possible.

There was no way he could put Lottie's safety before Ellie's. He wasn't allowed to do so, even though it was killing him to leave her. He had to protect Ellie, no matter what.

"I have to keep you safe, Ellie," he said sternly, even though every fiber of his being was telling him to run to the van. Then, just as he finished talking, he heard the soft low rumble of an engine starting up.

There was a sound of tearing and Jamie turned to see Ellie ripping the cumbersome bottom of her dress.

"I'm sorry, Jamie, but I'm not risking it," she said. And then she grabbed the golf club.

Jamie reached out to stop her, but it was too late: Ellie had flung her shoes away and dived over the veranda's edge, racing toward the van.

She was running to do what Jamie wished he had the freedom to do. Running to save Lottie.

Lottie had been moved to the front seat of the van, wrapped in a shawl so her tied wrists were covered. She was shivering; she didn't know if it was from the cold or fear. The instructions were simple: she had to act upset, so upset that she wanted to temporarily leave the palace, and Saskia, a registered Partizan, had kindly offered to drive her. If Lottie failed to convince them, Saskia would start hurting people.

Saskia had assured her that if anyone looked at the CCTV footage, it would appear as though Saskia was simply helping the distraught princess. An easy-to-believe story considering Ellie's run-in with Edmund. It was smart and it matched the story she'd given Jamie and Ellie, that she didn't want to return to the ball.

Please—I hope they've figured out my code.

Saskia looked down at her watch, waited a few more

moments, then put the key in the ignition.

"Okay, Princess, are you ready for your performance?"

Lottie could have laughed if she wasn't so terrified. *I've been performing the whole time.*

Instead Lottie nodded mutely; it wasn't going to be hard to pretend to be upset. Then the van rumbled underneath them and they were moving.

I guess this is it then, Lottie thought to herself hopelessly.

Saskia pulled them out of the spot and pushed her foot down on the accelerator, taking them onto the path to the gate.

They had moved no more than a few feet when everything went completely mad.

A figure dived in front of the van, arms outstretched, a feral shriek roaring out of its mouth.

"What the—" Saskia cried out as she rammed her foot on the brake.

The van halted suddenly and Lottie jerked forward. The figure shone in the headlights, a wild mass of black hair flying around her head, teeth bared in a furious snarl.

Ellie!

Her dress was torn and she was standing barefoot and furious in the snow with a golf club that she swung violently, smashing one of the headlights as she screamed a vicious war cry into the air.

She was terrifying.

"WHAT DID YOU DO?" Saskia screeched.

Lottie jumped as Saskia grabbed her. She faltered, unable to answer.

What the hell is Ellie doing?

"I didn't—"

Her words were cut off as the driver's-side window was smashed, shards of glass falling around them. She shrieked at the impact, and the biting whirlwind of cold that accompanied it.

"Saskia, get out of the car NOW!" Ellie barked, the words a ferocious growl as she prepped her club to swing again.

Saskia's face turned cold in front of Lottie and a chill that had nothing to do with the wind ran up Lottie's spine. Saskia grabbed Lottie by her hair and threw her into the back of the van. Lottie screamed as she landed. Unable to cushion her fall with her hands tied, she smacked her head on the floor, her tiara flying off. She heard the driver's-side door open and called out for Ellie to run as she tried to pull herself up.

The van doors opened. Saskia stood there restraining Ellie, from whom she'd wrestled the club. Ellie threw her head back and spat on her. Saskia let go of her abruptly, and smacked her before shoving her in the van next to Lottie.

Ellie looked up at Saskia and grinned. "You're in trouble," she cackled, her freshly bleeding lip making her look

as if she'd just feasted on a live animal.

Saskia raised an eyebrow, then Lottie saw what Ellie meant.

Jamie was hurtling down the snowy track so fast he was almost a blur in the frost. Alarm registered on Saskia's face, and Lottie watched as she spun gracefully, pulling something from the inside of her jacket and pointing it at the figure thundering toward her.

"JAMIE, LOOK OUT!"

Lottie screamed the words hopelessly into the air. Before Lottie could comprehend what was happening, Jamie was in front of them, ducking out of the way then surging upward.

He swung his left hand, pushing away the handle of the pocketknife, followed by his right hand, which struck Saskia's wrist hard. He deftly manipulated her hand so that the knife was now pointed at her. It happened so fast that Lottie could barely process what she was witnessing. Saskia reacted by stepping on Jamie's foot and twisting around, causing both of them to drop the knife. She kicked it a few feet away. If she couldn't hold the knife, it was better to have it out of reach than risk it being turned on her.

Jamie grabbed Saskia and flung her as far away from the two girls as possible before storming toward her.

And then the dance began.

They moved fluidly, sophistication and precision in every step that made for a terrifying but beautiful display.

Lottie watched in horror as they laid into each other, amazed by the intricate accuracy of their dance.

This was a Partizan fight, and it was deadly.

They seemed to be a perfectly even match until Jamie thrust his elbow to block Saskia's arm and was able to land a blow to her stomach. Saskia doubled over and he used the opportunity to knee her in the nose. Lottie covered her face at the impact, disturbed by how effortlessly dangerous Jamie could be. Then, before Saskia could right herself, Jamie dived into the air as though he were weightless. Lifting his knee up, he easily spun his body to deliver a bludgeoning kick to Saskia's head before landing and picking up her pocketknife.

It was clear that the move could have been lethal if Saskia hadn't managed to hold her arm up in a last-ditch attempt at defense.

She fell to her knees and slowly raised her head to see the knife, all her previous composure beaten out of her. She looked at him, manic and bloody. She laughed, but it came out more as a wail. The sound made Lottie flinch.

"You are such a perfect little pet of a Partizan, aren't you?" Blood spilled out of her mouth as she spoke, and she spat on the floor as though she were a snake shooting venom.

"You've lost, Saskia," he said coldly, his face calm as the frosty wind howled around them.

She laughed again, the sound becoming a wheezing cough. Lottie recoiled, but Jamie remained steady, pointing the weapon at her with no hesitation.

"I haven't lost anything," she cackled. "I found myself years ago. You're the one who's lost."

Jamie didn't say anything, and there was no sign that the biting cold was having any effect on him.

"You could be free of them," Saskia went on. "You could use your training to fight for a righteous cause instead of being wasted on these fools." In the clouded moonlight Lottie was sure she could see tears forming in Saskia's eyes. "They don't care about us. We're just tools to them; everyone is a tool to them. They'll never let us live how we want." She reached a hand out desperately. "Join us."

Lottie held her breath, the wind billowing between them as she sat helpless in the van, not knowing what Jamie was thinking. Her heart lurched as he opened his mouth to speak and she thought she saw his hand quiver for just a second.

Before he could respond a voice blared out. "Put your hands in the air where we can see them."

Lights flared around them so brightly that they almost blinded Lottie as twenty or so figures in black swarmed them. They grabbed Saskia and instantly cuffed her, pushing her up against the side of the van. Jamie carefully deposited his weapon on the ground and sat in the van

beside Lottie, completely unaffected by the sudden siege, as if he knew they were coming all along.

They were all escorted to the palace entrance and Lottie saw one of the masked figures pull off his headgear to reveal a weathered face with a severe scar. He nodded at Jamie, who responded with a salute.

Someone untied Lottie's hands and wrapped a silver blanket around her. Everything melted into a warm and confusing blur of questions and anxious voices. Jamie and Ellie both shrugged off their questioners and bolted to Lottie.

"Are you okay? Are you hurt at all? Either of you—Ellie, your lip!" Jamie frantically fussed around them in a way that seemed very unlike him.

Ellie shook her head, not really paying attention, and pushed past to grab Lottie and pull her into a tight embrace.

"Lottie! Oh, I'm so sorry. I'm so, so sorry." Ellie kept repeating the words as she held her, but Lottie was distracted by what she could see over her shoulder.

By the door to the palace, standing tall and unflinching, was Anastacia. She didn't look at Lottie, Ellie, or Jamie. Her eyes were on Saskia, a trail of moisture on her cheek, and her dress flapped around her in a blaze of deep red. Saskia was escorted to where Anastacia stood. Her guards paused by Anastacia and one of the figures bowed.

"We'll be taking her in for questioning, ma'am. Your father will also be informed."

Anastacia didn't respond; she simply stared at Saskia, a fire burning in her eyes.

The Partizan's face turned from anger to something akin to determination. They began pulling her away again and Saskia cried out, "Ani, I was going to come back for you. *Ani!*"

But Anastacia didn't even turn around as her Partizan was dragged away. She clenched her fists so hard her knuckles turned white. Tears spilled in an uncontrollable wave of woe. These were not the tears of a shocked young girl; this was something more.

Lottie's mind conjured up the photograph of them in Paris. And suddenly it hit her, and she couldn't believe she'd missed it before.

They were in love.

❧ 54 ❧

LOTTIE, JAMIE, AND ELLIE ONCE again found themselves standing outside the main hall in a perfect line, waiting to be allowed into their trial. Fewer than twenty-four hours had passed since the ball. The festivities had ended early and the guests had been asked to vacate the premises. What had followed was a sleepless night of blurry questions and raw emotions, and Lottie was desperate to throw on some pajamas and sleep for a hundred years. Her world had altered, and she knew that things were going to be drastically different now.

They had all agreed to stick with their story—that they hadn't had any clue that the attack was being planned, and that Anastacia knew nothing about it. Except, it wasn't a story. It was the truth.

Ellie and Lottie had both sustained mild injuries: Ellie had cut her lip, but not badly enough to leave a scar, and Lottie had a bruise on her cheek and a sore bump from where she'd hit her head. Jamie remained unscathed, outwardly at least.

Lottie held her breath as the doors opened. The light hit

her again in that same flooding bright stream, but this time she did not flinch from it. Instead she marched forward confidently to embrace her fate.

In the hall sat the king on his throne, his wife and his mother by his side, with Simien Smirnov, the glass-eyed man, standing behind him. To Lottie's surprise, a fifth person was seated with a permanent scowl on his face—it was the gruff man who Jamie had saluted the night before.

"It is clear, after the events last night, that there is a serious and present danger among us." The king spoke intensely, leaving no room for questions.

Lottie stood firm, eyes straight and emotionless as she'd seen Jamie do so often. She understood now the importance of presenting yourself as unflappable. It was like a suit of armor, not just to protect yourself but to protect those who might worry about you. Lottie could not have Ellie worrying about her if she was going to remain her Portman: she needed Ellie and her family to think the traumatic events at the ball were easy for her to brush off and that she'd readily put herself at risk again for Ellie's sake.

It wasn't true. Lottie had never been so terrified in her life, but that was exactly why she needed to be there, to make sure it never happened to Ellie.

"Sir Olav"—the king gestured his hand to the scarred man—"we understand that we have the rogue Partizan in confinement, but she will not speak."

Lottie thought of Saskia, a girl she'd been jealous of and trusted as a mentor, and her heart lurched. She couldn't imagine what Anastacia must be feeling right now.

Sir Olav rubbed his hands together in thought and Lottie could see a strange dagger-shaped tattoo just above his wrist.

"So far the only information we have is from your Portman."

Lottie mentally stored the fact that he knew she was a Portman; it was important to know who was high-ranking and trustworthy.

"The Alcroft parents knew nothing," continued Sir Olav. "Their daughter, Anastacia, claims her Partizan had an unusual but not worrying interest in the princess."

Lottie knew that was a lie. Jamie and Ellie had filled her in on how most of the notes had been left by Anastacia as a way to scare them out of the school.

The king turned to Lottie and gave her a sharp look. "I see. And what exactly have you learned, Miss Pumpkin?"

Lottie took a deep breath, trying to remember the information without slipping back into the memories of the van, of Saskia's bloody face, of Anastacia weeping. She shook her head, clearing the thoughts away. "We know they're called Leviathan, Your Majesty," she began. "We know they're targeting the children of important

families, particularly royalty and"—she prepared herself before she said the next words, worrying about the reaction they might provoke—"we know there's special interest in the capture of the Maravish princess, but we don't know why."

The king simply nodded his head. "Good work."

It took everything in Lottie's power not to start smiling in excitement. *Did I just get praise from the king?*

She had to quickly remind herself of the circumstances. The queen smiled at her, as if she could read her thoughts, and Lottie returned the look with one of the respectful nods she'd so often seen Jamie and the king exchange.

"Well then."

All Lottie's good feelings evaporated at the raspy voice of the king's mother.

She tapped her fingers on her cane irritably as she looked at them with her scathing gaze. Her hair was down this time, a flowing wave of silver cascading over her waist, which made her look as if she could at any moment cast an evil spell on whoever crossed her. "Let us move on to the more pressing matter."

The three of them held their breath, knowing what was coming.

"Why on earth was the real princess, our Eleanor, allowed to be put in harm's way for this girl?"

Lottie felt her body go hot and her hands twitched nervously at her side. She was amazed at Jamie's ability to stay completely calm.

"It is unacceptable that the princess should put herself in danger for her *Portman*." She said it like it was a dirty word. "The idea is simply atrocious." She looked at each of them, as she tapped her cane. "Well, do you have anything to say for yourself?"

Lottie gulped, feeling all at once furious and ashamed. She'd believed there was nothing she could have done to stop Ellie running out to the van, but that was not the truth. She could have prevented it by truly pretending everything was fine when they'd called—but she hadn't even considered that. She had to remember that she was expendable. "I'm sorry, Your Majesty, I—"

"Not you!" the king's mother screeched. "Her Partizan!" She gave Jamie a fierce look before turning back to Lottie. "*You* behaved exactly as a Portman should in that situation. Portmans are very difficult to come by; it would be most inconvenient if we lost ours."

Inconvenient.

Lottie's mind went blank. They didn't know. They didn't know that she hadn't even remembered she was a Portman in the van. She hadn't been thinking about how *inconvenient* it would be if they lost her. She hadn't thought about surviving for her princess. She'd only been thinking about

herself. She wasn't what they thought she was, and part of her resented them for it, but a larger part resented herself for it. She didn't want to react like a regular kid would in that situation. She wanted to be strong; she wanted to have a place in this extraordinary world no matter how dangerous it became.

She turned to Jamie. He continued to stand tall, accepting the scolding words without flinching.

"Quite," the king said, though his posture and tone suggested he disliked having to agree. "Sir Olav, would you please prepare an appropriate punishment for your student?"

Lottie felt a sense of injustice building in her. *Jamie had saved them. He'd done everything he could to . . .*

Jamie gave her a look of warning. She bit her cheek hard to stop herself from saying anything. Before he could give the same look to Ellie, she stepped forward to speak. To Lottie's amazement, she didn't protest. She didn't even raise her voice.

"May we leave now?" Her fists were clenched as she spoke, but that was the only indication of how she felt.

The king rubbed his forehead as if he had a terrible headache, and then sighed. "You may leave."

They all turned to the door, and as they did the king spoke again.

"I'm glad you are all safe, and I'm impressed with how

you handled yourselves—but these are our rules."

Ellie paused at the door without looking back, then they made their way out, leaving an uncomfortable silence behind them.

◆§ 55 §◆

BEFORE THE THREE OF THEM headed back to Ellie's room, Ellie asked Jamie to give her a moment alone with Lottie. He nodded somewhat reluctantly and went on by himself.

"Come with me," she said softly, grabbing Lottie's wrist. Her words were slightly muffled through her swollen lip.

She walked Lottie through the corridor, up a winding staircase to a tower room with a huge balcony overlooking an endless garden covered in thick snow. Ellie leaned against the stone balcony, her face inscrutable, looking more like Jamie than herself. Lottie followed her gaze out over the garden, wondering what it would be like once the snow cleared.

"Lottie," she began, not looking at her, "I have something important I need to ask you, but I need you to promise me something first." She turned to her then, holding eye contact in a way that Lottie couldn't pull away from.

"Of course," she replied, ignoring the hesitation in her gut.

Ellie shook her head. "No, Lottie—that's the point," she

said with a sigh, the lack of sleep suddenly showing on her face. "I want you to promise that before you answer my questions you're not going to think about me. You're only going to think about yourself and how you feel."

Lottie froze, thinking of her mother and the promises she'd asked of Lottie on her deathbed. There was that strange and awful crawling on her skin, the knowledge that this was not a promise she could possibly keep. She couldn't explain it to Ellie; it was something only Jamie would understand. She couldn't answer only for herself, because this was her life now, being there for Ellie. But she didn't vocalize this; instead she held her breath and nodded.

"I promise," she said reluctantly, knowing it wasn't quite true.

"Okay." Ellie looked shaky, her hand fidgeting. "And I want you to really think about this before you answer." Lottie nodded again. Ellie let out a short breath before continuing, looking as if it hurt her deeply to ask. "Would you be happier if you'd never become my Portman?"

"No," Lottie replied, almost before Ellie had even finished the question.

She didn't need to think about it, and it had nothing to do with devoting herself to Ellie. She knew deep down that it was true. She didn't care how scary things became, or what she had to sacrifice. The last year she'd spent with

Ellie had been the happiest she'd been since losing her mother. This was the closest she'd ever been to fulfilling her promise to be happy. She felt like she'd found a part of herself that she didn't even know was missing.

"This is where I belong," she said earnestly, grabbing Ellie's hand and squeezing it. Tears trickled down her cheeks, but she didn't care. "Being with you is the happiest I've ever been; you make me a better person."

Ellie's face scrunched up in a desperate attempt to hold her emotions in, and she sniffed loudly to try to maintain her composure. She pulled Lottie into a tight embrace, squeezing her so hard she almost couldn't breathe.

"Me too," Ellie whispered in her ear.

56

JAMIE, ELLIE, AND LOTTIE SAT in silence on Ellie's black satin bed.

Jamie had propped himself on the edge, head in his hands, looking remarkably like Rodin's *The Thinker*. Ellie lay sprawled in the middle, staring up at the patterned wood ceiling, her head resting on Lottie's lap while Lottie absentmindedly stroked her hair.

"This is my fault!" she exclaimed.

Lottie paused between strokes, but she didn't know what to say.

"We all know it's my fault," Ellie continued. "They know it's my fault—and they're doing this as a punishment for me."

Jamie made a strange noise that sounded a little like a laugh. Talk of Jamie's punishment had given Ellie back some of her usual fire.

"Sir Olav will just make me take some extra training classes"—he pushed his hair back so he could look at them properly—"and I like training, so it's not really a punishment."

Ellie grumbled. "But it's the *principle* of it!" she said, punching the air as she pouted with her swollen lip.

Lottie smiled to herself, remembering how fierce Ellie could be. "I think it was worth it, though," Lottie said with a giggle.

Ellie stopped punching the air and Jamie turned around questioningly.

"Not just the punishment," said Lottie. "The whole kidnapping ordeal—it was definitely worth it."

Ellie shot upright suddenly, forcing Lottie to move back to stop their heads from colliding. Jamie and Ellie both stared at her in confusion, sharing a look as if she'd gone mad.

"In what way is any of this worth it?" Ellie asked, raising an eyebrow.

"It was worth it because"—she sat up straighter as if she were about to tell a story—"I got to see that wild show of you smashing up a van, barefoot in the snow like some kind of feral, murderous animal." Lottie burst out laughing as she spoke. The more she'd thought about it, the more she'd decided it was funny. If she had to choose between traumatic and hilarious, she'd go with hilarious. "When the headlights first shone on you I thought you were"—she had to pause to catch her breath through her hysteria—"I thought you were an angel." She wiped a tear from her eye as she continued to laugh.

A wry smile appeared on Jamie's face, and Lottie knew

he understood that her way of combating the situation was to keep positive. He understood because he had his methods too.

"An angel?" he said mockingly. "More like a demon. I mean, really, who goes after a Partizan with a golf club?"

Lottie burst into a fresh set of giggles, falling back on the bed.

"Hey!" Ellie exclaimed, trying to look angry. "I was going for full-on banshee, thank you very much."

"That explains all the irate screaming," Lottie teased.

Ellie gave her a look of mock indignation before jumping on her. "We'll see who's irately screaming," she said menacingly as she held her hands up preparing to attack.

"No, no, no, I surrender!" Lottie pleaded playfully, holding her arms up. "You make a wonderful banshee." She snorted the words out, fully prepared for the repercussions.

"That's it!" Ellie howled, an evil grin on her face. "You're gonna regret that!"

The three of them spent the whole day in Ellie's room, watching films and playing video games. Lottie was determined that they should have some fun and forget about the previous night before they had to go back to reality and face their problems.

At some point in the early hours Ellie passed out in the blanket fort they'd made. Lottie wanted to join her, but

she knew that sleep wasn't an option for her right now; her mind was too chaotic.

"Lottie." Jamie's voice sounded uncharacteristically vulnerable and it brought back memories of the pool. "Lottie, I have to know something." His face was serious, but there was a soft edge to it.

"Go on," she replied apprehensively.

"You didn't think about Ellie when you were in danger— your only thoughts were on how to survive the situation. Am I right?"

Lottie stared into his eyes for a moment, not giving in to the sick feeling of shame.

"Yes." She forced herself to say it even though it hurt. It was true—she hadn't thought once about her responsibility to Ellie while in the van, only about escape. Before the ball Jamie had tested her to see if she placed her safety lower than Ellie's, but when it had counted she forgot completely. Even if Ellie's family hadn't realized, part of her already knew that Jamie had.

"Good," he said briskly.

"*What?*" Lottie almost choked. "I failed. I'm every bit as disappointing as you expected me to be."

Jamie shook his head, a sweet smile appearing on his lips. "Lottie." He grabbed her shoulders and held her gaze, squeezing her slightly to hold her attention. "The only

thing I could ever be truly disappointed in is myself, if I lost you." The intensity in his eyes was enough to leave most people breathless. "I don't mean you losing your life. I mean I'd be disappointed if I lost *you*—your character, your unwavering positivity. You must never let anything in this world take that away from you."

There was genuine concern on his face and Lottie felt a happy warmth, but that was instantly quashed by anger. She'd spent this whole time trying to impress him so he'd trust her to be a Portman, and *now* he's telling her he's worried about her! There was only one solution to all this.

"Well," she said, the irritation in her voice catching him off guard, "if you're so worried about losing me, teach me to fight."

"I— What?" This was not the reply he'd been expecting and he faltered, tripping over his words.

Lottie quite liked seeing him flustered. "You heard me. I want you to teach me to fight, so I can protect myself and Ellie and you. I was so terrified in that van. I had no idea what was coming. I never, ever want Ellie to be in that position. Also, my life choices aren't allowed to be your source of weakness, is that clear?"

His face went blank for a moment as if he were questioning his entire life, and then he laughed. He laughed genuinely and openly, and Lottie realized it was the first

time she'd seen him do that. He finally composed himself and smiled at her.

"You are the most unpredictable person I've ever met, and I've lived with Ellie for thirteen years," he said affectionately.

"Is that a yes? Will you teach me?"

He rolled his eyes, but the smile remained. "Yes, I'll teach you."